Blood Origins

Blood Origins

Book One of the Bloodlines Series

T. Isilwath

Writer's Showcase presented by *Writer's Digest*
San Jose New York Lincoln Shanghai

Blood Origins
Book One of the Bloodlines Series

Published by Writer's Showcase presented by *Writer's Digest* an imprint of iUniverse.com, Inc.

For information address:
iUniverse.com, Inc.
620 North 48th Street
Suite 201
Lincoln, NE 68504-3467
www.iuniverse.com

Cover art by Cynthia Carey

ISBN: 0-595-00503-9

Printed in the United States of America

Dedication

For Rain and Sky.
For Skywise and everyone who believed in me.
For everyone who weeps for Mother Earth and the destruction of the Balance.

Preface

This book graphically depicts both heterosexual and homosexual relationships in a loving, respectful manner. Much of the work contains elements of pagan and goddess religions. One or both of these elements may offend some readers.

Prologue

Aerth was there when Aiya opened the cocoon. She was standing at the edge of the circle, some yards from the altar. She wasn't the only one present as the goddess revealed Her newest creation, but she was the one who most understood what it had taken for Aiya to make the child, and the reasons why.

The air inside the stone temple was tense, in spite of the spring breezes that blew through the open archways. The eerie silence was broken only by the low hum of the goddess, and the squirming of the infant wrapped inside the glowing cocoon. The bundle was small, the body within struggling against its confines as Aiya held it in both hands. Aerth thought She looked tired, almost sad; as if She had taken no joy in forging this one; nor should She have, for he was made out of necessity and not desire. It did not mean, however, that the goddess loved this child any less. If anything, She loved him more, because he would need that love in the hard times ahead. He was Her hope for the future of Earth.

The glowing light strands of the cocoon crackled and hissed as Aiya peeled away the layers, bringing the infant into the world. The sheath fell away to reveal the boy-child, pale of skin and fair. The child drew a breath, his thin voice echoing in the silent chamber, and reached with his tiny hands for the goddess who made him. She smiled, Her eyes sparkling in the dimness, for a moment outshining even Her own natural glow, and kissed his forehead.

Welcome to the world, my son, She said in Her broadcasting mental voice.

The baby let out a plaintive mew, gurgling, and the goddess slid the material from Her shoulder, bringing him to Her breast. His mouth opened and closed upon the offered flesh, making Aiya gasp as he bit down. He began to nurse as She drew him close, coveting him next to Her body.

No one spoke as the child fed, and Aerth knew it was not milk that the infant drew from the goddess' breast, but something else entirely. He drank the life essence of the goddess Herself as he was made to do: hunter, killer, and drinker of blood. He was the first. He would be many. He was their hope.

When the child had taken his fill, Aiya took him from Her breast and presented him to the witnesses in the temple.

I give you Aurek, my son. Hunter of the humans, my sword against the swarms of Ja'oi's folly.

One by one they came to see him, Aerth going first and touching Aurek with her hands. He was warm beneath her fingers, and he looked at her with wide, brown eyes. His lips were stained red from the goddess' blood, and when he opened his mouth she could see his tiny fangs.

"I am Aerth. I stand for the avatars. I welcome Aurek into the Circle as my brother," she announced as she was expected.

Aiya smiled at her, a private smile that spoke of what had happened here and why.

Thank you, my daughter, Aiya answered. *Stand by me.*

Aerth obeyed and took her place beside the goddess, watching as the others came forward to pay their respects.

She was the oldest of the avatars, chosen by Aiya Herself from the humans, and forged into an immortal. She was small in stature, about five feet tall, and her skin, which had once been a dark olive, now was merely tan. Her hair was a muted brown, thick and long, and she held it back from her face with a golden clip. Her face was kind and her eyes were brown, the gentle brown eyes of a deer. She looked as ordinary and plain as any human, but if one looked closely the remnants of her ancient heritage could be seen.

Aiya had reshaped her to be more modern, to emulate a more evolved human, but she was still just slightly off, her jaw just a little too prominent, her forehead just a little too broad. At first glance such subtle differences went completely unnoticed, but more careful inspection easily revealed that not all was as it seemed. Aerth was clearly one of the oldest beings in the room.

Cryus and Khirsha approached, their claws clicking loudly on the marble, and Aurek stared up at them in delighted wonder as they lowered their massive heads close to catch his scent. The infant laughed and reached for them, showing no Dragonfear at all.

"I am Khirsha. I speak for the Silvers. I welcome Aurek as my kin," the ancient silver dragon spoke.

Cryus, a gold dragon, repeated almost the same incantation, then they both withdrew to allow the others to come forward. There was a representative for each of Aiya's children, all the elders of their kind, come to see Aiya's hunter, the first child She had ever made whose chief purpose was to kill. The ritual was necessary in order to bond the new child, and all his subsequent progeny, to the other children the goddess had made. This bond was called the Circle and it connected them all to each other. Through the Circle, they would recognize each other as kin, despite their considerable differences in appearance and powers.

As the last of the witnesses greeted the child and filed out, Aiya turned to Her avatar and handed her the infant.

You will be his guardian, She said.

Aerth nodded. "He will be safe with me."

He will grow fast and learn quickly. Watch him and teach him. He must be ready when the time comes.

"I will not fail you."

Aiya smiled. *I know.*

With that, Aerth took the baby with her, cradling him in her arms, and carried him out of the temple.

True to Her word, Aurek grew fast. Within two months he was at his full height and filling out beautifully. He was tall, with wavy, chestnut brown hair, and long, graceful limbs. He had an open, flawless face, with large, almost lupine brown eyes. When he smiled he could outshine everyone short of the goddess Herself. He was a quick study as well, learning at a rate that almost equaled his growth.

Aerth taught him what he needed to know about humans, about the Circle and the Webs of Life. She took him to see Aiya's Webs in the Heart of All Things, showed him how a change in one affected changes in all the others, and helped him to understand his purpose for being made.

Ja'oi's humans were disrupting the Balance with nothing to hold them in check. They were destroying the land and the animals, and would continue to do so. Their creator Ja'oi had laid claim to the planet, and was doing nothing to teach them the ways of Balance. More and more were turning from the paths of harmony and symbiosis with the land, and travelling along the paths of destruction.

Aiya saw what was happening, and had tried to persuade Ja'oi to guide the humans back to the ways of Balance, but to no avail. Instead He railed against Her, treating Her with contempt, until She felt She had no choice but to introduce a new hunter to the Web. She created Aurek in the humans' own image so he would blend with them, live among them, and hide within their numbers while he hunted them down.

Aerth helped him discover and use his mental powers. He was a strong telepath, and could affect things with his mind. He could use some of the High Magic and cast certain spells. His senses were sharp and keen; he could hear heartbeats, smell faint scents, and see in almost total darkness. He was many times faster and stronger than a mortal human, and he could move with stealth and silence.

Water taught him knifework and the art of the hunt. At these things, Aurek was a natural. He took to learning tracking from the dragons, who were amazed at his talent and skill, and he sought instruction from the elves in archery and lance. He was brilliant and innocent, wise and naive. His emotions covered an entire spectrum from ecstasy to despair, with wild fluctuations in-between. After his body came of age, Aerth and Water taught him the art of sensual pleasures, showing him the method of lovemaking required of his kind in order for his body to perform.

He was a paradox, able to kill with a ruthless lust for blood, which he feasted upon voraciously, and then return to the quiet of the cloister to dance and play the flute with his mentors. He was highly intelligent, his thirst for knowledge almost equaling his thirst for blood. He hounded his mentors and the goddess Herself for answers to his questions, even seeking out the old dragons who knew the ancient histories and interrogating them. He was annoying, but they adored him. They all adored him. Even Aerth, who was fairly certain he was the son she would never have.

His childhood was short. Within two years of his birth, it was decided that he would be sent to Earth to take his place in the order of things. Aerth would go with him and teach him the ways of survival among Man until he was able to live on his own. He wept, for he did not want to leave the safety of home and the security of his friends, but he knew he had no choice. He and Aerth would go to Earth, and he would kill humans as well as procreate his species, and eventually, when his duties were fulfilled, he would come home.

The night before they left, Aerth and Water made love to him slowly, drawing out each intimate caress in an attempt to prolong the experience and perhaps keep the dawn at bay. But the morning came, and the Gate was opened. He looked upon his home for the last time and kissed his goddess farewell. He and Aerth then passed through the portal to the mortal world.

Their destination was Sumeria, but they were not there three days when Ja'oi attempted to destroy Aiya's newest creation by making sunlight lethal to him. Aurek was badly burned, but Aerth was able to heal him before any permanent damage was done. She was not, however, able to counteract Ja'oi's spell and Aurek was condemned to darkness, as presumably would be all his children. In answer to Ja'oi's attempt on Aurek's life, Aiya cast a spell of shielding over the vampire, hiding him, and subsequently all of his kind, from the questing eye of the god. The spell had a negative side effect, however. Aiya could not render Aurek invisible to just Ja'oi, only to all the gods, so when She cast the spell, She knew that She would also not be able to sense or easily find Her son.

After the shielding was cast, Aerth took Aurek east into ancient India where the lush forests would help to protect him from the sunlight. Out of necessity, he became a nocturnal hunter, keeping to the deepest shadows of the forest by day, and venturing out only at night. They were to live in the forests for sixty years before Aerth was called away. She left Aurek with his companion, Roshan, and returned to the Sanctuary.

No one had ever seen or heard from Aurek or Roshan since.

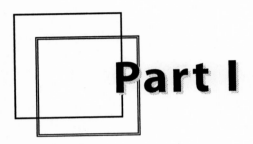

Part I

One

Rain removed her hands from the memory stone, clearing her head of the disorientation she always felt after she touched one of them. Sighing, she brushed back her long, black hair from her face before turning her head to see her companion. Song was seated on a mat near the stone, his legs crossed, watching her.

Song had once been Water; the same Water who had mentored and cared for Aurek. But a tragedy had befallen the first avatars of the goddess, a tragedy so horrible that the only way Water survived it was to destroy himself and take on a new persona. He killed Water and rose again as Song. Now he was the keeper of the histories, the one who Remembered.

She gave him a small smile. He smiled back, the sharp angles of his Nordic face softening for a moment.

"Do you understand?" he asked her in his deep voice.

"Yes, I think so. You want me to find him," she answered.

Song nodded, his blue eyes losing focus for a moment. "Yes. The events you witnessed happened five thousand years ago. Aerth and Aurek crossed into India in 3100 BC, Gregorian time, and all knowledge of Aurek faded from memory within a thousand years from that. We know he fulfilled his duty by procreating his species, but of what became of him, we have no idea."

"Yes, I know. The vampires have always been elusive to us and Aiya cannot track them because of Her shield spell," Rain commented.

"Aiya has searched for Aurek but has never found him, and Aerth has also been unsuccessful. That is why you have been chosen for this task. You have an affinity for vampires because you were bitten. You can find them. It is hoped you will succeed where they have failed," the historian answered.

"I can find Tobias, no other, and it is a hard task for me. It took me weeks to track him the last time."

"I know, but Aiya wants to know what has become of Her vampire child. As you know, She is considering abandoning Earth to Ja'oi, but She does not want to do so without first knowing what happened to Aurek. We suspect that Ja'oi has done something to him. She wants to find him. She feels guilty for having neglected him for so long."

"One cannot question the motives of the goddess, nor should She question Herself," Rain replied.

Song looked at her for a moment. She had been Hindu Indian in life, before her rebirth into an ecomancer, an avatar of the goddess, and she still held the tenants of her religion. He hoped she would lose such ideals as she grew older; if not, she would suffer a crisis of faith when she realized the truth. But there was time for her. She was young, barely five hundred, and an infant compared to his twelve thousand years or Aerth's many more years above that. She would learn in her own time. For now, there were other, more pressing matters.

"No, She should not, but She still worries. She knows Aurek is still alive for She has not felt his Passing, but yet he has not returned or tried to contact us in any way. It has Her concerned."

"And you want me to find Tobias to see if he knows where Aurek is."

"Tobias can lead you to others. We want to know what happened to the vampires. We want to find Aurek. We have reason to believe that the Circle has been broken."

She thought for a moment, remembering. "Yes. I think you may be right. When I found Tobias in Germany, he did not recognize me as kin. I had to assume the form of a vampire in order to catch his attention.

When we were together, he had no concept of what he was or why his kind was created."

"Exactly. If the Circle has truly been broken, we need to know when and where. If Ja'oi has tampered with the sacred bonds, there will be…consequences. We need to find out what happened to Aurek."

"I understand," she answered.

Song gave her a look that said he doubted that she really did understand, but he remained silent.

"It is very important that you find out what happened. The success of your mission may influence Aiya's decision to abandon Earth. I do not have to tell you what could happen if Earth's Balance continues to deteriorate. The repercussions could be widespread," Song added.

"I understand," she answered, a coldness seeping into her. If Aiya abandoned Earth, what would become of the vampires?

Slowly, Rain stood, smoothing the silk of her black sari with her long, delicate hands, trying to quell her fear and worry. "I will do my best, Song. I will find Tobias and reveal myself to him."

Song regarded her calmly. "It is something you have wanted for a long time."

She nodded. "Yes. I welcome this opportunity."

"Be careful, Rain. To love a vampire is to love danger, and do not forget Sky."

She blanched at the sound of her partner's name and looked away. "I will not forget him," she assured and quietly walked out of the Library.

She had not traveled twenty feet into the forest when a heavy weight struck her from behind. She gasped as she landed face down on the moist earth; her mouth full of grass, her hands digging into the moss as the weight finally eased. She looked up at the creature that had pounced on her: a panther, all muscle and ebony, feline grace. She scowled as it flopped down beside her, amusement sparkling in its green eyes.

"Sky," she growled, not pleased.

The big cat's mouth opened, its tongue lolling out as if laughing at her, then its entire head began to shrink back upon itself, and the sleek, feline body shifted until the form of her erstwhile partner was left in its stead. Deep, masculine laughter echoed off the trees, and it seemed that the wind laughed with him as Rain sat up and brushed the torn grass from her sari.

"Got you again," Sky enthused, his sapphire blue eyes dancing with mirth.

"So it would seem," she answered, casting an impatient glance at the naked male figure seated next to her.

"Want to play?" he asked hopefully.

"I can't. I'm going to Earth."

Sky sat up straighter, his face suddenly serious, and swiped a stray tendril of his long, white hair from his face.

"Why?"

"Aiya wishes me to find someone."

His brow furrowed in concentration. "A wounded sparrow?"

Rain smiled, chuckling softly. Decades ago she had used a wounded bird to teach him a lesson, and he had used the symbol as a metaphor for healing ever since.

"In a manner of speaking, yes. I have to find Tobias, and have him help me find the one I seek."

"Am I going too?"

She shook her head. "No, little bird," she replied, using one of her pet names for him. "You will stay here unless I need you."

"Will you be gone long?"

"As long as it takes."

Sky bowed his head, then reached to touch her. She embraced him, forgetting all her earlier anger and indignation.

"Come back safely," he whispered into her hair.

She smiled at him and kissed his nose. "Always, my dearest friend. Always."

She felt his arms come around her and they hugged for a moment. Then he pulled away, his concentration on something in the forest that had caught his interest. She waited a moment or two to see if he would acknowledge her again, and when he did not, she resolved to leave.

Rising to her feet, she moved to continue on her way. Looking back, she saw Sky still sitting on the grass. He was tracing intricate patterns in the air with his hands, smiling as he made little puffs of light that swirled around him and landed on his hair. He seemed to have forgotten she was there, and she would not have been surprised if he had. Sky's attention span was often limited. Since she had told him that he would not be going with her on the mission, and was therefore not required, he had put all thoughts of it out of his mind. He could do that; it was a side effect of animal thought- the ability to focus only on the here and now to the exclusion of all else. She knew that he would soon go off on his own, morphing into one animal form or another, and she would probably not see him again until she returned from Earth.

As if he had read her mind, she watched him stand and shake himself off, bits of glowing light cascading all around him like tiny fireflies. He sniffed the air, pulling back his upper lip as if to taste the scents on the wind, then folded his body in half, shape-shifting as he did until a spotted jaguar stood where the man had once been. Without so much as a backward glance, the jaguar gave a rumbling growl and stalked into the trees.

Rain was not distressed at Sky's disregard of her. Animals had little use for farewells since they had no real sense of time, and there were times when Sky was more animal than anything else. Oftentimes that was a blessing. While Sky could be completely coherent and sentient when needed, often displaying an intelligent and calm exterior, she knew better than to expect it of him on a long-term basis. Sky spent nearly all of his time in animal form, shifting from one creature to another, and she had learned that it was better that way. However, she knew that if she needed him all she had to do was call his name, pull on the bond between them and he would return to her. There was a time when such a call would not have worked, but Sky had been steadily improving over the last hundred and fifty years. In fact, Rain could honestly say that he was growing more stable with each passing decade. She doubted that he would ever be fully healed, but he was a far sight better than he had been over 350 years ago when he had first been given into her care.

Originally, she had thought to go home, but her mind was reeling from the implications of what Song had told her. After centuries of wanting, she would finally be able to reveal herself to her vampire savior. It was more than she had ever wished for, but her wish came with a price. She was only being allowed to contact Tobias because of her affinity for vampires, because Aiya wanted to find Her vampire child, and while the thought of showing herself to her forbidden love filled her with joy, she was worried as well. Song had hinted that finding Aurek could influence Aiya's decision about Earth, but would She take Her son and abandon the failing planet or would She choose to stay and try to restore the Balance? If the choice were the former, would she be allowed to return to Earth if she wished? Would she ever see Tobias again? The thought of leaving Earth forever did not sit well with her, nor did it sit well with many of her ecomancer brethren. They had all originally been human, born of the Earth and mortal parents. For them Earth was *home*, and they did not want to leave it.

As always when her mind was in turmoil and she needed guidance, her feet took her to the cloister and to her mentor, Aerth. She found Aerth sitting on a stone bench in the garden, watching the sun set, and knew the ancient one had been waiting for her. She sat down next to Aerth and folded her hands into her lap. Aerth did not speak.

"I am being sent to find Aurek," Rain whispered finally, not looking up from her hands.

"I know," Aerth replied, still focusing on the dying light.

"Song says I am to reveal myself to Tobias and ask for his help."

"That would be a wise course of action."

"But I am worried. What will happen if I find Aurek? Will we abandon Earth?" she ventured, turning her head to see Aerth.

Aerth looked at Rain, her brown eyes revealing nothing of her inner feelings, and Rain was concerned to see her mentor so closed off.

"I do not know," Aerth answered.

"But if Earth is abandoned, its Balance will continue to fail."

"Yes, it will."

Rain shook her head. "But…how can such a thing be allowed?"

Aerth was silent for a moment. "It has happened before, when a world is too out of Balance and its ruler too hostile to change. There are ways to minimize the damage benign neglect causes, although the result will still leave holes in the Web. They are not the preferred ways, but they can be employed in the absence of another choice."

"But…what of the vampires? Will they be left behind?"

"I am not certain. If you are able to find Aurek and repair the Circle, it is possible that the vampires will be given the same choice as the dragons, elves, and other children of Aiya who once walked on Earth."

"And if I cannot mend the Circle?" Rain prompted, afraid of the answer.

Aerth's expression turned sad and sympathetic. "Then they will not know what they are."

Rain lowered her gaze and wrung her hands. She knew what Aerth meant. If the Circle stayed broken, then the vampires would be abandoned as well as Earth. The thought made her heart ache and she wanted to cry, wanted to rage against the wrongness of it all, perhaps even refuse to do Aiya's bidding. But no, that was unthinkable. She could not refuse to do as Aiya had commanded. She had no choice but to obey, even if she dreaded the outcome.

"Of course, it does not mean that I will not do my best to fulfill my mission. I would never deliberately refuse to do as I was asked…" she stammered.

Aerth's hand covered one of hers and squeezed, commanding her attention and she looked up.

"I know. And you will find him. I know that you will. You will succeed where I have failed."

"How can you be so sure?"

"Because if you do not, then Aurek will be lost forever."

Rain swallowed and turned her eyes away as Aerth withdrew her hand. They were silent for several moments, but the air was heavy with unspoken words. Rain realized that Aerth knew Aurek would be abandoned with the rest of the vampires if Rain failed. The knowledge could not be sitting well with her. Aurek was the closest thing to a child Aerth had ever had.

"You never speak of him," Rain said, purposefully not saying Aurek's name.

"He was my foster-son."

Rain ventured a glance at Aerth. The other ecomancer was tense, her body stiff.

"You loved him very much."

Aerth nodded slightly. "I did."

"It must have been…very hard to leave him."

Aerth drew a deep breath. "I had no choice."

"I know, but it cannot have been easy. I know you've looked for him…"

"Yes. I never found any trace of him or Roshan." Aerth sighed heavily. "I never should have left them. I knew they would be vulnerable without my protection. Ja'oi found him once, He could do it again, but there was nothing I could do."

"So you do suspect that Ja'oi had a hand in Aurek's disappearance."

Aerth looked at Rain. "Was there ever any doubt? He was my son. If he were anywhere I could find him, I would have. If he were anywhere where he could hear my calls, he would have answered. No. This reeks of Ja'oi and His minions," she said with conviction.

"But if Ja'oi is responsible for Aurek's disappearance…"

"Then He has tampered with the Circle and broken the Law."

"Would He take that risk?" Rain asked, concerned.

"Only if He knew He would not be caught. Aurek is not an avatar or part of the High Magic. His loss would not be significantly felt. The Others would consider it a petty dispute, unless Aiya could prove He deliberately harmed Aurek and broke the Circle," Aerth argued, then she sighed. "His timing was perfect. He did it when Aiya was too grieved from the loss of Fire and Air, when we were all in shock from their Passing. He has waged silent war upon Her ever since."

Rain seized upon an idea. "But if we could prove Ja'oi broke the Circle, then Aiya would be able to make a case against Him."

Aerth nodded. "Yes. If She could prove that He broke the Law, then She could seek retribution." She looked full at Rain and held her gaze. "Now you see the importance of your task. It is not merely righting a wrong, or finding a lost one who should have been found long ago. If you can find evidence that Ja'oi is behind Aurek's disappearance…"

"Then Aiya could seek co-rulership and She would not abandon Earth!"

For the first time since she was given the mission, Rain felt hopeful and she filled with joy. Perhaps things would not end as she feared, perhaps her success would yield her more than she could ever hope to obtain.

Aerth's expression remained neutral, however. "Depending upon what you discover, that is one way the Wheel might turn."

Rain smiled, then she recalled part of what Aerth had just said and mentioned it. "You said 'finding a lost one that should have been found long ago.' Does that mean you think Aurek should have been found before this?"

Aerth lowered her gaze. "I think his disappearance should have been given more scrutiny, especially after I failed to find him. Aiya has neglected Earth far too much in Her grief over the death Fire and Air. While Her back has been turned, the Balance has suffered. The situation there is near critical."

Rain agreed. "I know."

"But I have hope. Aiya is recovering from Her grief and She has returned her gaze to Earth. I think we will see change there soon. Else, She will goad Ja'oi into doing something unwise."

Aerth gave Rain a small, wry smile and Rain smiled back, understanding. Then she sobered and made a vow to her mentor.

"I will find him for you, Aerth. I promise."

Aerth took Rain's hand and squeezed. "I know. Thank you."

Rain stood and pressed her lips to Aerth's forehead, then rested her brow against Aerth's, her hands cradling Aerth's face.

"I will succeed for you, and for Tobias; for all of the vampires. If I can repair the Circle and teach them what they are, what they are meant to do, perhaps I can begin to repay some of the debt I owe to them."

Aerth covered Rain's hands with her own and drew them from her head, holding them gently. "I wish you good fortune and safe travels."

"Thank you."

"And now, you should get some rest. Daylight will come all too soon."

Rain nodded. "Yes. I will see you when I return. You'll look after Sky?"

"As best as I can, I will."

Rain smiled. "Thank you."

She stepped away and gave a little bow.

"Goddess go with you," Aerth blessed.

"And with you," she answered, turning and heading for home.

Home for Rain was a single room carved into the massive trunk of an ancient willow tree. Older than her by many centuries, the tree had grown to a height and size never seen on Earth. In the Sanctuary there were no violent storms to tear down branches and rip out roots, no droughts to slowly starve a tree to death. The trees grew tall and wide, lived long lifetimes, and because only the outermost layer of a tree's trunk contained the precious sap, her hollow in the tree did no harm to it. Placing her hand upon the trunk, she reached into herself for the power to part the wood, and felt the rough bark soften and give, pulling back to reveal a narrow doorway. Smiling, she crossed over and closed the door behind her.

The room was small, but larger than the hut she had lived in as a mortal child. No more than double and half again the length of her body in any direction, it was well furnished but not cluttered. Her mattress pallet covered in pillows and woven blankets occupied the rounded wall to the East, furthest from the doorway, while her table and two chairs took up the center. Along the wall to the North was her dresser plus a small desk, and the South wall was covered from floor to ceiling with bookcases full of books. Reading was one of her passions, and she prided herself in her tiny library. Some of the books that lived upon her shelves were rare treasures.

There were fourteen avatars of the goddess. Each of them, with the exception of Aerth and Sky, had been chosen while still mortal by another avatar and mentored. Rain had been chosen by Aerth in 1512. Once the pupil was deemed ready, he was reborn as an immortal, an ecomancer capable of shapechanging, and controlling nature and all the elements of weather. There were ecomancers representing some of humanity's greatest civilizations, some of which had long since vanished from the Earth. Of the fourteen, however, only she, Song and Stars loved to read.

Stars, having originally been from Egypt, had given Rain some books rescued from the Great Library in Alexandria before it was burned in 391 AD. The Greek poetess Sappho had written volumes of poetry from her island home of Lesbos. Her talent was heralded throughout the ancient world, but the unchecked burning of ancient "heretical" texts by orthodox Christians had reduced her legacy to a scant handful of poems and frag-mented quotations. Three of the prized, lost volumes occupied space on her crowded shelves, their goat-hide covers well worn and well loved.

Her entire room was well loved. The space was her safe haven from the busy, often demanding work she was given to perform for the goddess. She had once lived in the Cloister with some of the other ecomancers, but she found this small room more suited to her needs. It lacked facilities like a kitchen and washroom because she did not need them. She bathed and took most of her meals in the Cloister with the others, and returned to the willow in the evenings to read and sleep. Sky would join her there sometimes, or sleep in the den he had dug underneath the South side of the tree. When lit by the flickering light of tallow lanterns, the room was a cozy hollow, safe and warm and comfortable.

She lit two of the lanterns with a small pulse from her mind, and slid out of her sari, folding it neatly and placing it on one of her chairs. She then retrieved a volume of poetry from one of the shelves and curled up on her bed to read. A long time later, when exhaustion finally caught up with her, she blew out the lanterns and went to sleep.

She wasn't sure how long she had been asleep when something awakened her. Focusing in the darkness of the willow room, she heightened her hearing and sight to identify the disturbance. Most of the other ecomancers left her alone when she retired to her room, with the exception of Aerth and, of course, Sky. Her ears picked up the sound of another heartbeat and she caught the familiar scent just before Sky's hand touched her shoulder.

Sky? she queried.

He did not answer her either mentally or verbally. Instead she heard and felt him sniff her, and then felt his weight shift onto the bed. He was touching her lightly, mapping her body through the bed covers with his fingertips. She rolled to her back, giving him more access to her, and stifled a giggle when he pressed his nose into the hollow of her throat. Wiggling his lithe form, he squirmed his way under the covers and pressed himself against her, curling up and draping his arm across her chest.

Rain waited until she was certain he had surrendered to sleep before making sure he was covered and warm. He shifted a little under her touch, but stilled when she wrapped an arm around him. He gave a little mumbled mutter and settled in, his long hair brushing against her cheek. His need to be with her this night told her more about his feelings than any words of his ever could, and she felt a rush of tenderness mixed with her usual love for him.

I'll miss you too, priye, she told him, using an old Hindi endearment, knowing some part of his subconscious would hear.

A tiny whimper was her answer, and she soothed him with her hands. Drawing him close, she pressed her lips to his forehead and tried to return to sleep. In the morning she would leave for Earth.

Two

Tobias walked down the streets of Seattle. It was raining. It was usually raining in Seattle. The city averaged three months of sunshine a year; perfect for someone who was fatally allergic to sunlight. Now if it were only warmer. He turned up the collar of his coat and hunched down into its downy softness, pointedly ignoring the water dripping off his brown curls. What did he care if his hair got wet? It wasn't like he was going to catch pneumonia. The thought made him laugh. There had been a kindly old woman who had admonished him as he left the airport.

"You'll catch your death out there, young man," she scolded, no doubt seeing his pale skin, flushed cheeks and lack of hat and gloves.

He'd only smiled and dipped his head. He hadn't the heart to feed on her, even though he was hungry from the long flight. His sentimentality had always been his greatest weakness. At least his younger brother, Dorian thought so. Etienne hadn't, though. Etienne loved the fact that he wouldn't feed on just anybody. He sighed. He didn't want to think about Etienne. He knew he was obsessing about his estranged lover, but the young man he had brought into this life to be his companion in eternity was never far from his thoughts. And it was Etienne who brought him to Dorian's door on this cold September night.

For the first time since his lover left him, Tobias knew where to find him, but Etienne had been seen with another vampire, a powerful vampire named Barias. Dorian knew Barias, and Tobias hoped his brother would accompany him to see Etienne in order to ease tensions and prevent hostility. Tense-at least that was how he wished it to happen. Dream and reality were often two very different things when dealing with vampires, but if Dorian were with him he would not be alone, and that would make him feel more secure.

The streets were empty; an unfortunate side effect of traveling after dark. Still, lack of prey was a small price to pay for not smoldering in an airplane. Planes, after all, did fly above the clouds; they gave new meaning to the words 'spontaneous combustion.' He giggled at his own wit and realized that he was getting punchy. He needed to find a victim before he saw Dorian. It would put him in a better mood in which to face the younger vampire.

Extending his sharp hearing, he honed in on a lone heartbeat somewhere just north of him. Following the sound as he would a Siren's song, he tracked it to a dark house at the end of a cul de sac. Inside he could hear five distinct heartbeats, all slow in sleep, but three slightly faster than the others: children. His quarry was outside the house, navigating the shrubbery beneath a rear window. He smiled ferally: a burglar. How convenient. Silently, as only his kind could do, he approached the man skulking in the shadows until he was nearly upon him. Then he allowed his feet to make a sound. The would-be robber jerked and peered owlishly into the darkness.

"Pete? Is that you?" the man hissed.

He stepped out of the shadows, letting the diffused beam from a motion sensor light activated on a house two lots down illuminate him. He knew what the burglar would see: a slender but robust young man with long curly brown hair that fell over his shoulders, dressed casually in corduroy trousers and a heavy, down coat. He watched the man take him in, shamelessly reading his mind, sifting through his thoughts like so much garbage. Too short to be considered a threat, his youthful, round face and big blue eyes fooling his prey into a false sense of security.

"Who the hell are you?" the man demanded.

He shrugged. "No one," he answered in a sibilant whisper, letting his nostrils flare at the scent of the blood thrumming just under the man's skin.

"What are you doing out here?"

"I've come to see my brother."

The burglar gave a short laugh. "He live here?"

"No."

He saw the confusion cross the man's face as he closed the distance between them. Under ordinary circumstances he would have prolonged the game, playing with his victim as a cat would a mouse, but he was hungry and it was late. Within heartbeats he had the man pressed firmly up against the side of the house.

"What the hell do you want?" his prey choked.

"You," he replied simply, just before he sank his small fangs into the hot flesh beneath his lips.

He drank swiftly, with little finesse, easily holding his quarry both silent and immobile. When savored, the act of feeding could be the ultimate pleasure for his kind. Tonight, however, he swallowed the pulse of blood greedily, sucking his victim dry until the heart stopped. He pulled away, taking in gulps of air and shaking off the feeling of euphoric vertigo he always experienced after making a kill. Oftentimes he wondered if this was what doing whiskey shots felt like to mortals; that sweet burning, followed by a sense of weightlessness, then the heavy fall back to earth. Carefully, he used his sharp nails to slit the dead man's throat, effectively obliterating the puncture wounds from his fangs, then dropped the body into a dumpster at a nearby construction site.

Less than an hour later he was standing outside Dorian's house. Dorian did not live in Seattle proper, but some distance northwest of it on a large tract of undeveloped land. His high, wooded property had spectacular views of the Sound. He had a double prow home with huge windows facing the Sound and the view to the east as well. The home was built on a slope, with the lower level set into the hillside. A large wrap-around deck on the main level encircled three quarters of the house. The landscaped property gave way to a row of pine trees and redwoods about fifty yards from the house, then progressed into heavy forest another twenty yards beyond that. He had a painstakingly cared for garden on terraces carved into the hill, and a rock garden centerpiece set with large slabs of blue slate and a cherub fountain at the center. To get to the house one had to go up a long, wooded driveway and pass through a security gate. Tobias had taken a cab to the beginning of the drive and walked up the roadway in the rain. Getting through the security gate had never been a problem. The gate was meant to keep out mortals, not vampires, and it was easily jumped over.

The lights were on so he knew the younger vampire was home, but he wasn't certain how well he would be received. Although he and Dorian had come to a reluctant truce, and perhaps even a tenuous friendship in the last fifty years, there were still unhealed wounds left behind from decades of fighting and sibling rivalry. Many of the fresh scars came from Tobias' knowledge that Dorian had been created because he failed to live up to their maker Ian's expectations of him. Even though he was some two centuries older than Dorian, he still felt like a recalcitrant child in his presence.

Living in Dorian's shadow had never been easy; resentment and jealousy ran high between them. It seemed Tobias could never forgive Dorian for being everything he wasn't, and for some reason Dorian could never forgive Tobias for being Ian's firstborn. It wasn't fair. It had never been fair, but after nearly six human lifetimes' worth of existence, he knew that life wasn't fair. In fact, life often...how did they put it in this day and age? Royally sucked. Which, considering that was exactly what he did in order to survive those six human lifetimes, was a stroke of irony that nearly threw him into hysterics.

As he stood staring at the entrance to the house, the wind caught his wet and now riotous brown curls. He swept them back with one hand and secured them in a club at the base of his neck. With a bitter smile he remembered that Dorian had always accused him of looking rather like a poodle when he had his hair pulled back. Scowling at the memory, he pulled the club free and let his hair fall loose once again, the ever-strengthening wind lashing the tendrils against his face and neck. Steeling himself, he quieted the butterfly tremors in his stomach and approached the closed door, comforting himself with the fact that, regardless of whatever arguments were between them, Dorian had never refused him help.

The door opened before he could ring the bell, and Dorian stood there in the entry looking rather unkempt, or so he thought.

"Oh, it's you. What do you want?" his brother demanded.

After a heavy pause he replied in his softest voice, "May I come in?"

Dorian regarded him for a moment then shrugged, opening the door wide to admit him and walking away, his back to his brother. As Tobias stepped into the house, he took a moment to wipe his feet and look at Ian's second son.

Dorian's hair was still long, still jet-black except for a single shock of silver that came from the right side of his forehead all the way down to his chin. He always suspected that Dorian was intensely proud of that single band of gray, it made him look older and somewhat more distinguished. Considering that Dorian was almost three hundred years old, the thought of anything making his brother look older seemed preposterous to him. He was tall, thin, but well muscled, and he dressed in clothing that flattered his svelte body. Tonight he was wearing a pair of snugly fitting black trousers and a loose white shirt with wide sleeves.

Dorian led him down a flight of stairs to the lower level of the house and into the den. Tastefully appointed with bookshelves and comfortable furniture, and warmly lit from a fire in the large hearth, it seemed that Dorian had been there for quite some time. Briefly he wondered where Aaron, Dorian's on-again/off-again lover was, but he didn't ask. Aaron came and went in Dorian's life; it was a simple reality and probably the only thing that kept the two of them from killing each other. Tobias knew first-hand how difficult Dorian could be to live with.

"I'd offer you a drink, but I killed the last one this morning," Dorian told him, a telltale smirk on his face, his green eyes flashing.

Tobias always thought the slightly slanted green eyes spoke of an Asian influence somewhere in Dorian's bloodline, but he doubted that Dorian's English aristocrat father would ever have admitted to it. While Dorian wasn't finely made like a China doll-he was robust and had a strong English jaw, his eyes and delicate hands bespoke of Asian genes. Tobias had no doubt that the blood of the Orient once ran in Dorian's veins, but he politely resolved to keep his mouth shut on the subject.

"Good," Dorian snapped, proving once again that Tobias' mental shields were no more effective in protecting his thoughts as tissues were against plague. "Now if you'd only keep your brain shut on it, and tell me why you're here."

With a flourish, his younger sibling turned and lowered himself into a plush wingback chair set close to the fire. His long legs crossed while the rest of his body flowed over the arms of the chair as if it belonged there. No one could sprawl like Dorian. The very fact that the English vampire could make his thin body take up so much room seemed to defy the laws of physics. He had no time to dwell on the science of his brother's body, however, because said sibling was glaring at him in irritation. He sighed and lowered his gaze, suddenly feeling very sad and small. It always began this way, the old rivalry and anger creating walls between them.

"Please," he said, his voice cracking slightly. "Can we not…"

He sighed again and took a deep breath, clenching and unclenching his fists. As always, Dorian waited patiently for him to calm down. He knew Dorian had learned from experience that if Tobias did not rise to take his bait, it meant his elder brother had come to him on some matter of importance. Dorian remained silent as he let the wave of anger crest then die, allowing the red haze and all the old pain it brought with it to fade.

When he spoke again, it was with the voice of reason, or so he hoped. "Please…Ian is thousands of miles away. We are not in his house any longer. I am not the Firstborn and you are not the Prodigal Son. Can't we simply be brothers?"

His request was met with a silence that went on too long, and his hopes fell flat on the carpet. Defeated, he turned for the door.

"I am sorry. I should not have come."

No. Wait. There is no need to go, came the mental plea, followed by Dorian's soft voice. "I'm sorry. You're right. We are a long way from the castle, both in time and distance." He shrugged, a sheepish smile on his thin lips. "Old habits die hard."

Tobias agreed with a nod of his head, water dripping from his damp curls onto the Oriental rug. Dorian snorted in disgust.

"Oh Hell. You're getting my rugs all wet. For Crissakes go get a towel from the bathroom and dry your hair. You never did have any sense Toby. It's pouring out there. You could have at least carried an umbrella."

He smiled at the false anger. "Umbrellas are for English wimps like yourself, Ri-Ri. And don't call me Toby," he jibed.

A book that had been sitting on a table next to Dorian's chair thumped loudly against the doorjamb as he skittered out of the room.

Ten minutes later he sat in a second wingback chair next to the hearth sans his coat and sodden shoes with a towel wrapped around his neck. The fire warmed his damp feet while a ceramic mug of hot water pleasantly warmed his hands. Warmth was comfort to a vampire. It was one of the reasons mortal lovers were so pleasant. Snuggling up to a hot, human body was wonderful even if certain types of mortal sex were not an option. Tobias had always attempted to avoid certain situations by favoring male lovers. Most of them had been more than pleased at his performance. In fact, only Etienne ever seemed to mind his impotence. A flash of memory struck him, of Etienne while still a mortal man, flushed and sweaty from sex, the scent of his blood and arousal heavy in the dark room, his dark blond hair stuck to his wet skin...

"So what brings you to my doorstep on this dark and stormy night?" Dorian asked slowly, breaking him out of his erotic memory.

Dorian's voice was oddly calm and Tobias suddenly realized that he must have broadcast the image to his brother. Flushing as much as his kind could, he placed his cooled mug on a table next to the chair and looked at his hands.

"I met Khristopher last week," he began, dropping the name of their vampire cousin.

"Ah. Is he still riding around Miami on the back of a '57 Harley?" Dorian quipped with a wry smile. "Y'know, there is something fundamentally wrong with a vampire who voluntarily chooses to live in a place called the Sunshine State."

The last comment made Tobias laugh, and it felt good. It warmed him from the inside out like wine did when he was mortal and young. He heard Dorian laughing with him.

"So, what did Khristopher have to say about Etienne?" the younger vampire finally asked.

The mention of his lover's name stilled his laughing. "How did you…?" he began, then stopped. Of course Dorian could read his mind.

"No. Not this time. I didn't have to. I know that lost look on your face usually means something has happened with Etienne."

"He left me."

"He's left you before."

"Four years ago." 'Four years since he walked out of my life and took my heart and soul with him.'

"He'll be back. What's four years when you have forever? Look at Aaron and I. He's left me for decades at a time."

"Khristopher said he saw him in Ecuador."

"Nice country. A little too remote for my tastes, though."

Tobias cast a glance at his brother. "He was with Barias."

The name made Dorian straighten up a little. "Barias? Was Khristi sure?"

Tobias nodded. "He said he was certain. Etienne and Barias were together in Ecuador."

Dorian sat back again, his face thoughtful. "Hmm. That is interesting."

Tobias waited to see if Dorian would be more forthcoming with his thoughts, but the younger vampire kept his counsel to himself. After a few moments of silence, he unveiled his meager plan.

"I am going to Ecuador. I mean to go and find them. There were so many things left unsaid…"

Dorian's pale hand covered his own. "No, Toby. Leave him be. When he is ready, he'll come back to you."

"But…"

Dorian cut him off. "No. I know what you are trying to do Toby and it's not right. Etienne needs to grow on his own. He needs to breathe and feel the vampire blood you gave him pound in his veins. You know it is not unusual for a fledgling to leave its maker. You love him enough to give him his freedom. Don't make the same mistakes with him as Ian did with us, like I did with Elizabeth."

He saw a shadow fall across Dorian's face as he remembered his first and only fledgling: a spirited Commoner the younger vampire had made at the turn of the twentieth century. She had lasted barely a decade before going mad. Ian had killed her out of necessity, but in doing so had destroyed the close bond he shared with his younger son. Dorian knew there was nothing else that could have been done, but he truly had never forgiven his maker for killing her. He and Ian did not speak to each other for eighty years, and in those eighty years Ian's two sons found reconciliation with each other. It was one of many good things that had come from the disaster that was Elizabeth.

"But I miss him so much…"

"You miss the familiarity of him," Dorian corrected. "You hate to be alone. You need someone to tell you what to do and who to be. Do you forget the reasons why you put up with all the rivalry and fighting after Ian brought me? You stayed because you didn't want to leave home, because you had no idea how to live on your own. And when you tried to go out your own, you just found someone else to cling to until Ian dragged you back. I blame Ian for that. He kept you needy, dependent."

"He was my savior," he argued, bristling. "Without him I would have died on the streets or been caught and executed for stealing."

"All you did was trade one master for another," Dorian shot back. "I swear Toby, if you wanted to be a mindless minion, you should have entered the clergy! Tell me, do you still believe in all of that? That crap about God and Satan and the sanctity of the Holy Catholic Church? You used to. You ate it up like blood."

Anger simmered just under the surface of Tobias' skin. It was an old argument that would see no end. Dorian, born in 1682 and made in 1703, had been raised in the Anglican Church while his older sibling had been brought up in the shadow of Rome.

It was 1490, people believed that midwives were Satan-spawn and that the Church was the only source of Truth in the civilized world. Pope Innocent VIII ruled the Vatican, sending his Inquisition out to bring down the heretics and roust the witches that plagued Europe. Priests taught that the devil had come back to earth in the form of an old hag, and only the Inquisitor stood between you and the minions of Hell. To break ties with Rome was the ultimate sin, and Excommunication was a fate worse than death. God and Satan were real, and the agents of both walked the earth, vying for human souls. That had been his world for the twenty years of his mortal life and the first two hundred of his immortal one. God was wrathful and those who murdered belonged to the devil. It was a good thing vampires lived forever because if he ever died, he knew he was going straight to Hell.

"Thou shalt not kill. Those are the words. That is the law. I am damned, as we all are, and always have been," he replied tightly.

Dorian laughed. "Oh, Toby, you always did make me laugh. Those laws, those tenants, we lost them when we lost our mortal flesh. We aren't part of them any longer. Why do you still cling to the old faith when you know it's only a bunch of fairy tales and forged documents?"

"Sometimes faith is all we have. If I don't have faith how can I justify our existence? I find evil mortals and send them to Hell. It's what I do. It's what I have done for five centuries," he answered, gripping the arms of the chair tightly.

Dorian gave him a small smile, one that struck at the very heart of his anger. Dorian was the scholar, the one who always knew everything, who could out-think, out-talk and out-class his elder sibling who was, for all intents and purposes still stuck in the Renaissance. Dorian's smile turned bitter.

"Yes. I was smarter, and stronger, and more independent. I fought every day to be perfect, to be exactly Ian's image of me. Every day I had to earn his love, but he gave it to you freely. I would consider that a fair trade."

Now it was his turn to smile bitterly. "Nothing in life is fair. We should not have had to earn his love. He was our maker, our father; he should have loved us in spite of our weaknesses."

"But you see Toby, that's the whole thing. Ian did love us. He loved us the only way he knew how. There are many things I would accuse the old man of doing, but not loving us isn't one of them. It took me almost seventy years to realize that, but once I did, it helped me…be at peace with some things."

Tobias nodded. He knew what Dorian meant. After Ian killed Elizabeth, both of his children left him. Dorian had disappeared into the wilds of the New World while he had made a pilgrimage to the Holy Lands. The time away from his maker had allowed him the necessary distance needed to look more kindly and objectively upon Ian's motivations.

It had been his first successful foray into the world of his own independence; the first time he had run away and Ian had not tracked him down to drag him back home. While he had not liked it, and often found others to be with because he hated being on his own, he never became lonely or desperate enough to return to his maker. But he did come to realize that Ian had done many things out of love for his children, including kill Elizabeth. In retrospect, with ninety years gone by, he could even sympathize with Ian's hopeless situation. He had no choice but to kill the mad vampire woman. It was that or risk the lives of his sons. He often wondered if Ian knew killing her would break up his family, and surmised that was why Ian did not hunt his two errant sons down after they left. Whatever his reasoning, he had never told either Tobias or Dorian why he waited for his sons to come back rather than chasing after them. Maybe Ian had realized it was time to let his fledglings fly. He doubted he would ever really know the answer. Ian was notoriously closed lipped on many issues, especially ones regarding the heart. There were times when Tobias had not been certain that Ian loved him, and he did not want Etienne to ever have those same doubts, and he told Dorian as much.

"That is why I want to find Etienne and talk with him. I do not want him to question my love for him."

"In his heart he knows you love him, just as we know Ian loves us. What you need to do is find out why he left you," Dorian corrected.

"He told me he could get more attention from a doll than he could from me," he admitted softly.

Dorian regarded him calmly. "From what I saw of the two of you eight years ago, I would agree. You were distant and cool towards him. He desperately wanted your attention Toby. He needed you. He was newly made and still reeling from the change. I was surprised that you were so cavalier towards him. I always expected any child of yours would be smothered with affection."

He fought back tears, remembering his confusion and desperation. "I wanted to. Every time he came to me, I wanted to wrap him in my arms and comfort him."

"Why didn't you?"

"I didn't know if it was what he wanted. Things…changed after I brought him to me. *We* changed. We could no longer enjoy some pleasures. It was very awkward."

Dorian smiled knowingly. "He wanted you to be the leader and you lost the vampire-mortal lover dynamic which allowed you to feel comfortable dominating him."

"Perhaps," he hedgingly agreed, looking at his hands. "But you know how it is with maker and fledgling. The child usually leaves the parent after a while. Ian held us with him through our weaknesses: my fear of abandonment and your need for love, but I refused to do that with Etienne. I fully expected him to leave me. He no longer had a reason to stay."

The slap that struck him was fast even for his vampire reflexes. He barely had time to tense before the blow knocked him out of the chair, and he found himself sprawled on the floor, looking up at a furious Dorian.

"Fatalistic idiot! No reason to stay? He *loved* you! Isn't that a decent enough reason to stay? If this is how you treated him, it's no wonder he left!" Dorian spat, his eyes blazing.

Tobias bared his teeth, his cheek still feeling the sting of the blow.

"What do I know of love, Dorian? All those I have loved abandoned me," he countered, not bothering to get up. "My mortal family sold me to the duke as a bed servant. My vampire father gave me love only when I was dependent upon him, and he took the only true vampire lover I ever had away from me. My brother in immortality was my hated enemy. My mortal lovers used me until I learned to use them."

He paused, looking away, his anger fading to be replaced with despair. "Only Etienne was different. I had hoped he could teach me how to love."

He heard Dorian sigh heavily then saw him offer a hand to pull him up off the floor. He took the peace offering and allowed Dorian to yank him to his feet. No one was more surprised than he when the younger vampire did not halt the pull once he was upright, but continued until he was crushed into a tight embrace.

Ri-Ri? he ventured mentally.

No one can teach you how to love. It's either something you intrinsically know, or something you learn on your own- usually the hard way.

The iron grip eased and he found himself looking into Dorian's tear-rimmed eyes. The sight was shocking to him. Dorian rarely cried. It was something that just wasn't done. To see him so close to weeping unnerved him greatly.

"Don't be so surprised. I can cry, you know, and I do. Just ask Aaron. I cry over him all the time. Love hurts, Toby. It's all the best and worst things about mortality brought into this vampire life. It means doing things that go against your very nature, things you hate doing, but you do them anyway out of love. Sometimes it means letting go when the only thing you want to do is hold on tight."

Dorian stopped, a strange, almost mortified look upon his face, as if he realized that he had just revealed something intensely personal to a potential enemy. Tobias hurried to reassure him.

"It's all right. All past now."

The younger vampire shook off the look and let his arms drop to his sides. Then he turned to stare at the fire.

"I'm sorry. I'm rather maudlin tonight."

Tobias raised a hand and gently placed it on his brother's shoulder. "I am the one who is sorry. I came here bemoaning my absent lover and gave no thought to your pain."

He felt Dorian stiffen and raise his chin. "I'm fine. Never better. You know me, stiff upper lip and all that. My father was very big on how boys should behave. I'm used to it."

He ignored the statement. He had not known Dorian's father personally, hearing only secondhand stories from his son and Ian. What he had heard of the Earl had left a bitter taste in his mouth. The man had been a tyrant by English standards and by German ones. He doubted any love was lost between father and son when the Earl, an officer in the Royal Navy, was killed in one of England's many Naval battles.

"Will you come with me to find Etienne?" he asked gently, changing the subject. "You know Barias. You could speak to him for me…"

Dorian shook his head, still focusing on the fire. "I can't. I have a painting arriving this week. I thought it would look nice in Aaron's room. It's a Monet, one of his more cheerful ones. It will brighten up the walls a bit I think," he answered, then looked at Tobias with a wry smile on his face. "But if you need money…there's always plenty of that, you know."

"No. I don't need money. I think finance was the one thing you and I both excelled in," Tobias replied warmly.

"Well, one must have money. Money buys tolerance for one's eccentricities, and fixes damn near everything. It's amazing what one can buy when one has enough money."

"Or who," Tobias added without humor. They both knew too well what he was talking about.

Dorian looked away again. "Or who."

He let his hand slide from his brother's shoulder. "I have to go."

"Will you not stay until tomorrow?"

"No. I can't. I must strike while the iron is hot, so to speak."

"Then I wish you safe travels."

He smiled. "But not luck?" he asked fondly.

Green eyes met blue ones. "Always that."

Dorian turned to face him and he offered a tentative embrace that was accepted. The hug lasted barely a moment, but they parted smiling.

"I'll see you soon," he promised.

"I'll be here."

With a final smile and a pat on the arm, he retrieved his now dry shoes and coat, and donned them, preparing to once again face the storm outside.

"I took the liberty of calling you a cab since I know you won't take my car. It will meet you at the end of the drive," Dorian informed a few minutes later.

"Thank you."

"Here," he said, offering him a wide-brimmed hat.

Tobias grinned and took the gift, fitting it over his curls. "Now all I need is a trench coat and I could be Humphrey Bogart. Here's lookin' at you, kid."

Dorian rolled his eyes as he opened the door. "Don't quit your day job. Oh wait, you don't have a day job."

"No, I just lounge around all day feeding on Playmates and critiquing art films, like someone else I know."

"Out! I shall not have my honor insulted in my own house!" the younger vampire ordered with mock anger.

"Too late for that, Ri-Ri," he teased and slipped out the door before Dorian could swat him.

"Good riddance to bad rubbish!" he heard his brother yell over the wind and he smiled.

He was still smiling as he walked towards the road where the cab would meet him. Although he had not secured Dorian's company on the trip, their meeting had gone a long way to raise his spirits. His step was lighter and his mood more optimistic. Even the storm seemed to have eased some of its fury. Happy, he raised his face to the falling water, and listened to the steady patter on the drive and treetops as he quickened his pace. He'd always loved the sound of rain.

Three

Ecuador was a beautiful country. It was a smorgasbord of ecological treasures stretching from the Galapagos Islands to the Andes to the Amazon, and depending on where you traveled, you could end up in a coastal town, a high mountain sierra or an untouched tropical jungle. Unlike some of her neighboring countries, Ecuador saw her natural beauty not as a resource to be exploited, but as a treasure to be preserved, and the little country was leading the way in eco-tourism and environmental preservation. The tropical rainforest, a forest so thick and deep that sunlight never touched the ground in places, was one of the main reasons why Barias had brought Etienne to the tiny South American country.

It was a clear, moonlit night when Tobias emerged from Mariscal Airport near the capital city of Quito. High in the Andes, it took him a moment to acclimate to the altitude, but his vampire body adapted quickly. It had taken him longer than he'd wanted to get to Ecuador, not only because of the distance, but because he had to travel at night. He was thankful for his money, for it was able to secure him a chartered jet in Houston. The same jet he would take to Coca just as soon as he had fed. Coca was a small city in western Ecuador, and the city near which Khristopher had said he had seen Etienne. According to Khristopher, Barias had brought Etienne to the Amazon because of some artifacts recently unearthed in the jungle, artifacts that the old vampire wanted to examine. Khristopher had no idea exactly where Etienne and Barias were going, but Tobias hoped that they were still there. It was the first time in the four years since Etienne left him that he had a fair idea where his fledgling was located. He wasn't about to let the opportunity to see and talk to Eti pass him by.

Quickly, he walked the darkened streets of Quito. The population, mostly Hispanic or Quichua Indian, was predominantly Catholic and superstitious, therefore tended to stay indoors after dark. In the city, there were always those who ventured out to prey on unsuspecting tourists, but once he left the metropolitan areas, finding victims might prove to be difficult. As much as he hated the prospect, he knew that he might be forced to feed on animals or the innocent. Feeding well now would help him in the scarce time he knew lay ahead.

He had thought to find a cutthroat or a robber to slack his thirst, but he was fortunate in that a robber found him. He heard the young man stalking him, but pretended not to hear. He kept his hands deep in his pockets, his pace relaxed, and even offered the mortal the opportunity to jump him when he paused along a darkened street to look at the stars. Hands came around him from behind and a knife was pressed to his throat.

"Money! Now!" the man hissed in thickly accented English.

The young man thought he was being smart by choosing an easy target. His utter surprise was evident on his face when his 'easy target' whirled in his grasp and disarmed him faster than he could blink.

The man's terror was like an aphrodisiac to him, the scent of fear assaulting his nostrils as he dragged his struggling victim into an alley. He pressed them both to the wall of a crumbling building, ignoring the man's pleas in English and in Spanish, and smiled at his victim when the young man dug fingers into his neck, trying to break his iron grip.

"Struggling will do you no good," he told the man in Spanish.

"Let me go!" the man cried, also in Spanish.

"Would you have let me go? I think not, amigo," he answered, pulling back his lips to reveal the tiny fangs.

His victim struggled and he had to cut off a scream. "Shhhh, if you struggle and scream I will only make this worse for you. If you are quiet, it will go quickly and without pain."

"Devil! Demon! I curse you in the name of God! Go back to Satan where you belong!"

"Give him my regards when you meet him."

With that, he wasted no more time. Holding the man against the building, using his knees pressed into his victim's legs to quell his kicking, he exposed the man's throat and bit down into the tender flesh.

The man's mind offered little resistance to his probes, but also had little to offer him by way of mental visions. The man, little more than a boy really, had lived a short, brutal life of violence and poverty. Living on the streets since he was twelve, he had taken to mugging tourists in order to survive. Hunger and destitution had turned an otherwise good and innocent child into a murdering cutthroat, and he felt the old rage at the people in power that allowed such travesties to occur.

Once the pleasure of the bite overtook his victim, he ceased his struggles and surrendered, dying quietly. After a while, the boy let out a slow sigh and his body gave a final shudder as his life ended. Tobias released him, letting the corpse slide to the ground, and used the very knife that the boy had threatened him with to obliterate the puncture wounds on his neck. Looking at his watch, he saw that he had less than an hour to return to the airport to meet his chartered jet. He used his mind to draw a taxi to him, a very handy talent to have, and soon a battered old Ford was sputtering its way towards him.

"Mariscal Airport, por favor," he said in clipped tones.

The taxi driver nodded and drove off in the direction of the airport. The jet was waiting for him when he arrived, the pilot slightly annoyed at his tardiness. He didn't care. The short flight to Coca was uneventful, and he released the chartered jet from his service upon landing. He explained to the pilot that he would be going into the jungle and he did not know when he would be returning. He told the man that he would call from Quito if he were in need of his services for a flight back to the States. Giving the young

Texan a wan smile, he shouldered the backpack he carried for appearances' sake, and hiked into the Amazon.

Two nights later, in a nameless, ramshackle town three hours southeast of Coca, his world shattered.

He'd come to the region looking for Etienne, following a vague lead on the artifacts Khristopher mentioned, but found a territorial coven instead. Under normal circumstances, such a belligerent coven would be easy to handle, which was why he had not been overly concerned when he came to South America. He was not, however, anticipating one of the coven members being strong enough to shield against his considerable mental powers. He'd assumed an old one strong enough to fight him would not be living in these isolated villages, feeding on farmers. He'd been wrong.

Now Tobias was afraid. He wasn't often frightened; very little scared him anymore. He'd lived too long to still have a fledgling's fear of shadows. However, tonight the things that hunted him were not shadows, and the reason to fear was very real. He cursed his stupidity, for he'd let love make him blind and lead him right into danger. He rounded a corner and hid behind a run-down shack. Maybe he could conceal himself long enough to get out of the town. In this instance, he felt it was better to flee than to fight. If he left the coven's hunting grounds, they probably wouldn't follow. Besides, he still needed to find Etienne, and Etienne certainly was not here.

Hearing someone approaching, he slipped into the shack, veiling his thoughts and keeping himself very low, but it was too late. There was a crash as a burning bottle came flying into the hut to land on the dirt floor. He looked at it, realizing that he had run right into their trap. How could he have been so stupid! Another bottle came in through the broken window, followed by two more. Then he felt the presence of the old one and knew there was no way out. He panicked, reaching for the door just as the entire hut exploded…

• • •

Pain. All around him was pain and darkness. He was drowning in it, a horrible, ceaseless burning. Slowly, he was becoming aware. He remembered the exploding light, the heat, the searing of his flesh, his screams...

He is coming around, a male mind-voice spoke in the darkness.

Tobias. Tobias, wake up. Wake up, Tobias, you have had a bad dream, a female mind urged. He fought it.

'Bad dream? No. I am dead, aren't I? I am in Hell,' he thought to himself.

Wake up. Show us your beautiful eyes, the female implored.

'And see what? The spirits of the countless mortals I have killed?'

"You aren't dead, Tobias," came a soft voice.

A breath of sweet scented air and a cool touch on his damaged skin followed the soothing voice.

'But Hell should smell like death and decay...' he questioned, confused.

"You aren't in Hell. You aren't dead. Open your eyes, Tobias."

The voice was quietly pleading and he sighed, feeling the breath escape his lips, flowing over his sharp fangs. His senses were slowly returning to him, and he could distinctly hear two steady heartbeats, smell two separate individuals, but the scent was like no other he had ever smelled on a mortal. It was the scent he caught but briefly on occasion, fading on the wind, the scent of spring that would caress him lightly on the cheek, then disappear. He breathed deeply to take in the smell, and felt the tightness as his chest expanded, and the sharp, wrenching pain. With a cry, his eyes flared open, and, blind with agony, his hands flailed out, searching for the owner of the soft voice. Fingers touched his burning skin and his body was flooded with cool relief. He moaned lowly.

"There. You won't be in pain much longer."

His blindness was fading, and slowly things began to take shape as his vision cleared. There was someone leaning over him, looking down at him. Gradually the fuzzy outline came into focus. It was a woman. A beautiful woman with straight, black hair that fell far past her shoulders, and eyes the color of storm clouds. Her face was delicate, with high cheekbones, her lips full and soft. She had soot on her cheeks and neck, stark black against her pale complexion. As he looked at her, her gray eyes filled with tears and she smiled softly. She then took his blackened hand in her thin, delicate one and pressed his palm to her cheek, tears rolling down her face.

"We very nearly lost you," she said, her voice trembling with emotion.

"Wh…" he choked, trying to speak, but found himself unable to move his charred lips. He felt the skin crack and smelled his own blood. 'Oh what a hideous sight I must be.' The woman shook her head.

"No. You are beautiful," she whispered, reading his thoughts.

Where am I? he demanded.

Safe.

Am I dead? 'I should be dead. The hut exploded…'

No.

Who are you?

I am called Rain, she answered as if it would explain everything.

Rain? What happened to me, Rain? Why isn't this Hell? Why aren't I dead?

All will be explained once you have been healed. You will go before the Mother and She will tell you anything you wish to know.

Healed? 'Healed? How bad is it? Oh, I hurt. Everything hurts…'

Yes. I will heal you. I could have healed you before this, but I wanted you to be conscious for it.

Why?

Because I wanted you to believe in me.

Rain stroked his forehead with her free hand, her eyes full of affection, and it was now that he searched his surroundings for the second person he had heard. He was in a cave that had no visible exit, and the only light came from a cluster of dimly glowing crystals in the far wall. His eyes scanned the rock and fell upon a startling figure.

The second person in the cave was a man. A man like no other man Tobias had ever seen. He was a vision of masculine beauty: thin, well muscled, and perfectly formed. His face was a divinely carved visage of sharp angles and fine bones, and his naked body gleamed in the soft light. Like his female counterpart, he looked fragile and delicate, but Tobias could feel the strength emanating from him.

The most startling aspect about him was his coloring. His skin was alabaster white, almost luminescent in sheen, his long hair was silver white- the color of ice on newly frozen snow, and his eyes, his eyes were perhaps the most striking of all. His eyes were deep sapphire blue. Not the color of the daytime sky, but the color of twilight, when the sun has just set and the last red and yellow hues are giving way to a midnight blue, star-speckled sky. The two sapphires sparkled, and Tobias could almost imagine stars twinkling in them as the man looked at him and smiled...even his teeth were perfectly white.

'Oh my...' *Who?...*

He is called Sky.

'Sky. What an...appropriate name.' He was abruptly brought out of his thoughts as Rain placed both hands on either side of his face and lifted him into a sitting position.

I must heal you now. The Mother is waiting.

She took him into her arms, resting his head against her shoulder, his lips just millimeters from her throat, and held him close. He could smell the seductive aroma of her blood, and his injured body cried out for it.

"Now," she spoke gently. "Drink from me. Let my blood heal you on the inside while I heal your body."

But... Could he feed on the one who had saved his life?

"You cannot harm me. Drink. It will restore you. Believe in me."

The strong scent of her blood filled his nostrils as she pressed his lips to her jugular. The vein throbbed beneath his blackened mouth, and he could feel the heat coming from her. Unbidden, his lips parted, his tongue slid out to lick her soft skin, and his fangs found their mark.

Yes! he heard in his mind, but he wasn't certain if it was Rain or himself, and in moments it didn't matter as the hot fount of her blood hit the roof of his mouth, spreading over his waiting tongue and down his throat. Sweet, sweeter than anything he had ever tasted; her blood filled him as he drank in great draughts.

Good. Drink. Now the healing can begin, she commanded him telepathically.

Tobias felt pure power arc from her and course into him. She drew him closer, his charred and naked skin pressed against the smooth silk of her garment. Cool tingling flooded him and he could almost feel his skin softening, sealing the seeping cracks and absorbing the blisters. His pain disappeared, replaced by the pleasure of the bite, the delicious warmth that was making its way down to his limbs, and he delved into her soul. Almost by habit, he pushed his way into her thoughts, using the intimacy of the bite to overcome whatever defenses she may have had, and joined with her consciousness. He was an expert in exploring the minds of his victims while he drank, but he was not prepared for what he found.

Love. Deep, unadulterated love. Love for him and for all vampires. It washed over him like a great tide. Her thoughts were a myriad of faded memories, memories of an Indian servant girl in Early-Sixteenth Century Rome, and the fledgling vampire who came out of the blackness of the night to descend upon her. The fledgling fed upon the girl with cruel relish, sucking her life into himself, and she swooned in the vampire's embrace, welcoming the death.

Tobias saw the fledgling leave the dying body of the girl in the gutter and a woman come for her after the vampire had gone: a woman in a brown toga, with brown hair and a loving face. She touched the girl, lifted her into her arms and carried her away.

You made me what I am. You gave me this life. I will always, always love you.

The thought gave him pause, and he delved back into her memory, pulled up the face of the fledgling vampire...and saw himself.

Shock jolted through him, breaking him out of his meld with her, nearly losing his grip on her neck, and his eyes opened wide. *You! You were my victim!*

I... The thought broke off as she came out of the swoon, suddenly realizing what had just happened between them. Her mental defenses went up, thrusting him out of her mind with force, and simultaneously severing the flow of healing energy she had been sending to him. *No! NO!*

Tobias screamed as the mind bolt hit him, and he fell back from her, sprawling on the cave floor. She collapsed too, landing in a heap at his feet, her hands clutching her head. Tobias saw a blur of white as Sky ran to her and laid hands upon her. He raised himself up as Sky tended Rain, and looked at himself. To his amazement, his skin was smooth and unblemished with no trace of the earlier burns. As he turned his hands over in the light, he saw the last of the cracks fade to soft, supple skin. Dumbfounded, he stared at the two figures in front of him, his mind a jumble of confusion. Then he saw Sky helping Rain sit up.

"Forgive me," he whispered, full comprehension finally coming to him. "Forgive me, I did not mean to hurt you."

Rain put a hand to her forehead, wincing in mild pain.

"You didn't hurt me," she replied, her voice soft. "I just didn't want you to know. Not right away. In time, it would have been revealed, but I didn't want it to be now."

He did not answer, but merely looked into her gray eyes. Rain. Her name was appropriate too. Her fingers brushed his long, brown hair away from his face tenderly, and her touch was electric, sending shivers all through his body.

"I really did it, didn't I?" she spoke absently, a hint of surprised awe in her voice as she traced his jaw and ran her fingertips over his lips. "You are here. You are alive. I saved you."

He knew she wasn't looking for an answer, but he gave one anyway. "I guess you did."

"I've never done it before. Brought back someone who was so far gone. There was very little left of you after the explosion. I didn't know if I could do it, but I had to try. Better to have tried and failed, than to live the rest of eternity knowing I had lost you to the Void without a fight."

"But why? Why did you save me?"

She blanched and a spasm of pain crossed her face. "Because…because you weren't meant to die. You are needed… You…" She broke off abruptly, visibly shaken, and stood. "We should go…The Mother will be expecting us soon…"

Tobias grabbed her arm. "Wait! Answer me. Why did you save me? Who are you? What are you?"

Rain did not answer. She shook her head and stepped back. He persisted, wanting to know.

"You said I wasn't meant to die. How do you know this? You are immortal and have great power, that is obvious, but what are you? Are you an angel?"

"No," she answered, becoming more upset by the moment.

"Who is the Mother?" he questioned urgently. Was she the Blessed Virgin? The Mother of God?

Rain extended her hand. "Come with us and you will see who She is for yourself. She is waiting for you to come to Her."

Tobias took her hand, feeling the electric energy pulsing into him when he touched her skin, and stood. His legs were still shaky and uncertain, but he soon gained his balance. Rain released him and turned to the wall. Then to Tobias' surprise, the rock swirled as if it were made of liquid and parted into a tunnel. He could see a bright light at the end of the passage and he caught the strong scent of grass.

"How did you…" he began, amazed and not a little frightened.

Rain did not answer. Instead she instructed Sky, "Go ahead and tell the others what has happened. I will take him to the steam pools so we can wash before we go to the Temple. Send someone back with garments for him."

Sky looked confused and cocked his head. "Why not stand before Her as he is? She certainly would not mind."

Tobias looked down at his naked flesh, at Sky's equally naked body, and shook his head. Normally nakedness did not bother him, but in this instance, it did. "I think not."

"No Sky. Tobias wants clothes. Go on now. We will meet you back at the pools."

Sky nodded in acknowledgment. "Okay."

Giving Rain a swift kiss on the cheek, he turned and jogged through the tunnel, his white hair streaming behind him. Then as Tobias watched, the man's body morphed its shape, his feet leaving the ground and his arms spreading into wings, until a bird of prey flew where the human had just been. His jaw dropped in amazement, and he looked at Rain to see if she, too, would turn into an animal. But she did not, she merely met his frightened gaze calmly.

"What are you? What is this place?" he demanded.

He saw her sigh, but it did little to calm his fears.

"We are shapechangers. We can assume any form we desire," she explained gently. "You will find that Sky is especially fond of animal form. In all the years I have known him, I can count on both hands the number of times I have seen him wear clothes."

He blinked at her, eyeing her warily, and she continued.

"I mean you no harm. You have no need to be afraid. I am what I am. I cannot change that any more than you can change what you are."

"What else can you do? You can heal and change shape…" he pressed. She could do all of these things, and yet she said she was not an angel.

"I can control the weather and all the agents of nature," she replied, becoming uncomfortable again.

"The weather? Can you bring rain? Do you control your namesake?"

She nodded. "Yes. I can call the storm, but my power is not limited to rain. Any weather, be it sun or wind, or snow and ice, is at my command. I am what is modernly known as an ecomancer. But we are wasting time. All this will be revealed and explained to you when you go before the Mother. We should go now."

She did not wait for him to answer. With a gesture, she motioned for him to go with her. He paused for a moment, looking behind him at the dark cavern, then followed somewhat uncertainly.

"There are things you must know about the place we are going to," she told him, speaking over her shoulder. "Firstly, here in the Sanctuary, the sun cannot harm you."

"The Sanctuary? Is that the name of this place?" he questioned. 'Not Heaven?'

"It has many names. The Sanctuary is one of them," she replied, then stopped and faced him, an earnest look upon her face. "Secondly, you will see things fantastical and wondrous, things you never believed really existed or could exist. Know that, though they may look frightening and beyond reality, nothing here will harm you. No matter what you see, no matter how unbelievable it is, it will not hurt you. Do you understand?"

"I understand." He really didn't, but at the moment he did not care.

They reached the end of the tunnel and Tobias hesitated, peering worriedly out of the passage at the golden light.

"It's all right. It cannot hurt you," Rain assured.

She walked ahead of him, into the sunlight, then held out her hand.

He stared at her for several moments, still well in the shadows. His heart was pounding in his chest.

What if she was right and the sun could not burn him here? What if she was wrong?

If I am wrong, you would still not be harmed because I have the power to heal you. You know this. But I am not wrong, came her gentle answer.

He weighed her words. He wanted desperately to feel the sunlight on his skin, but...

"Trust me, Tobias. I would not lie to you," she soothed.

He focused on her hand, still outstretched and waiting for him to take it. Gritting his teeth, he squeezed his eyes shut and reached for it, moving his hand into the light. He half expected to feel the searing of his flesh, but all he felt was solid warmth as Rain's hand closed over his.

Opening his eyes he could hardly believe that his unprotected skin was not smoldering in the sunlight, but his hand was whole and undamaged. He looked at Rain, his eyes wide with shock and disbelief. She merely smiled at him.

"See?" she said, then tugged very gently on his hand. "Come into the light, Tobias."

Slowly he scraped his foot along the sandy ground and stepped gingerly into the sunlight. It was too bright at first, blinding him until his eyes adjusted, but when his vision cleared he beheld the sight before him, and he gasped.

They were on a cliff, part of a rocky mountain range that loomed behind them, and stretching out below them for endless miles was a valley. Everywhere green grass and trees blanketed the ground. He could see a large river banked by huge willow trees, with water as blue as the cloudless sky, lazing its way down the length of it. In the distance more mountains reached up to touch the horizon. Below he could make out moving shapes of animals half hidden by the tall grass, and the sweet scent of spring filled his nostrils.

It was so beautiful that he fell to his knees and began to weep.

"Oh, oh God. Oh Holy Mother…" he sobbed.

He opened up his arms and raised his face to the sun, drinking up its warmth like a man dying of thirst. The light bathed his nude body, heating it as only the sun could, and he was warm all over. Giddy with joy, he laughed drunkenly, his face to the sky, tears running down his cheeks. Rain waited patiently, an understanding smile on her lips.

"I have not seen the sun…" he began, looking at his hands, turning them over in the light.

"I know," Rain answered, kneeling next to him and taking his hand. "Ja'oi did that."

"Ja'oi?" he questioned, not familiar with the name.

"The god who rules Earth. But you will learn of Him from the Mother."

"Learn of Him?" he repeated, his brow furrowed in confusion.

Rain recognized the signs of truth meeting dogma and hastened to cut it off. She knew Tobias was raised in a time when religion was powerful and all knowing. The lessons Aiya was going to teach him would not be easy ones for him to swallow, but she did not want him to be concerned with that while he was still so weak and disoriented.

"Everything will be explained in time," she assured, urging him to his feet. "For now, let us go to the pools and get you cleaned up."

He blinked at her, still feeling rather shell-shocked, and spared another glance at his surroundings before rising and allowing her to lead him away.

Four

The trail led down towards the valley floor then veered off into the rocky crags. He tried to take in his surroundings, but it was like a dream to him, a surreal and amazing dream. The only thing that was at all real was the feel of Rain's hand holding his own, everything else was hazy and out of focus. When they cleared several large boulders, he saw wisps of steam rising above the rocks, and a series of large natural hot springs came into view. The heat wafted around him from the hot water, and he paused as Rain released his hand and walked to the edge of one of the smaller pools. Deftly, she unwrapped the gray silk Sari she wore, and folded it neatly away from harm on a nearby rock.

"Come," she said as she stepped into the water and sat down.

Without hesitation, Tobias obeyed and joined her in the pool, coming to rest in the shallows beside her. He did not want to make decisions right now, and she had proven to be trustworthy so far. He was happy letting her tell him what to do; it was easier than trying to think for himself. He was, in theory, capable of free thought, but it would have required more effort than he was willing to put forth at the moment. Ian had known he was independent only when he was secure in his place, and often used that against him. He knew Rain was not trying to control him, or dominate him, but he obeyed her anyway, simply because it was easier.

He looked down into the reflective surface of the water to see himself looking back. His features were the same as they had always been: a soft, oval shaped face with a small nose and large, blue eyes, and a mop of chestnut brown curls that fell haphazardly over his shoulders. He saw his reflection smile back at him, his full lips curling up softly, and sighed. The heat of the water was deliciously soothing, and he relaxed, smiling with pleasure. Amazing the effect that heat and light had on his cold skin. He looked over at Rain, and saw her washing the soot and ashes from her face and neck.

My ashes... he thought, shuddering. *They were my ashes. I was ashes.*

The pain came back briefly, then faded when Rain looked at him and smiled. He smiled back.

"I know. It's so nice here," she commented.

"Yes, it's wonderful," he agreed.

"I knew you would like it. The heat is good for you, and the water has some small healing properties of its own."

"Ah, I understand." The water did have a strange tingle and scent to it.

She offered her hand. "Here, I'll help you. There's still some burned skin on you."

Nodding, he placed his hand in her palm, and she guided him deeper into the pool. When they were both standing waist deep, she stopped and began scooping the hot water over his back and shoulders, rubbing his muscles. He allowed it, this gentle washing, enjoying the feel of her hands on his preternatural flesh. She pressed down lightly on his shoulders, and he crouched down, bending back to immerse his hair in the water as her fingers brushed through his curls, rinsing out the dirt and ashes. Her touch was comforting and pleasurable, and he smiled, closing his eyes. Relaxing, loving the warmth, he knelt down in the water until it came up to his neck, and let his whole body be warmed by the heat.

"Ahhhhhh," he sighed as the water lapped at his chin.

Nearby, he was aware that Rain was splashing, probably washing her hair. As he relaxed, the events of the past week drifted into his mind. Flashes of Khristopher telling him that Etienne had been in Ecuador, and the inside of the plane that landed him in the tiny country, the thick, dense forest and the simple people living in it. Then the sight of the old one and his followers. His powers being wrested from him, useless against the ancient vampire. Being hunted, chased into a falling-down shack, the fiery bottles crashing through the glass, his whole world rupturing and being engulfed in flames. The pain came back with a fury. The smell of his roasting flesh, the agony as his body burned. He screamed and thrashed at the phantom flames licking at his skin.

Hush! Rain's voice cut into his mind. *It's a dream! It's all a dream!*

What is happening? Etienne! Where are you? Etienne! What happened to you? How long have I been away? he thought wildly, reaching out with his mind.

Rain's hands were upon him, holding him firmly. *You have been unconscious for two Earth days. You needed the time to recover, but you are all right now. I am here. Nothing can harm you.*

A flood of cool healing power washed over him and he calmed, clinging to her in desperation as the last waves of terror faded, his face pressed to her chest. Then he heard a loud cracking noise, like the breaking of rock, and suddenly became aware that they were no longer alone. He opened his eyes and froze.

On the opposite side of the small spring, dwarfing the rocks that it rested upon, was a huge, light gray lizard. He could only see the front half of its body, its massive chest and large reptilian arms...that it had crossed in front of it in an almost human way. The large, elongated head sat atop a tall, skinny neck that was angled down at him in a curious, questioning manner, and the two black eyes regarded him with intelligence and amusement.

Fear raced through him. What was this thing? Its head was almost raptor-like in shape, a hooked upper lip that curved beak-like over its lower jaw, and two razor sharp canines peeked out. There was a ridge of spines connected by translucent gray flesh running in a single line down its neck. Frantically he tried to identify the species. His mind flipped through hundreds of genus names, trying to fit one to the creature now before him. Finally he heard it snort, and an old, wise woman's voice pierced his brain.

I think not, Child.

The beast shifted and two huge leathery wings rose above the rocks, blocking the sunlight. He gasped. It was a dragon. An honest-to-goodness, bonafide dragon. It was magnificent, awe inspiring, breathtakingly beautiful…and he was terrified. He was about to scream when Rain smiled at the dragon.

"Hello, Khirsha."

The dragon grinned, showing her rows upon rows of sharp teeth, and bowed her head. "Hello, Child," it spoke in the same old woman's voice Tobias had heard in his head. It was almost…grandmotherly.

"What brings you here?"

"Your friend. Mind screams carry, you know."

Rain blushed. "Yes, they do. I'm sorry. He is unstable. I'll try to shield him from now on. I brought him here to bathe. The warm water is good for him."

She glanced at him to see his frightened face and her brow furrowed. *She will not hurt you. She is Khirsha, a silver dragon. She means you no harm. I told you that nothing here would harm you. She came because she heard you screaming.*

Tobias looked at the dragon again and saw that it *was* silver. It had only looked gray because the sunlight was behind it, but now that she had her wings outstretched; he could see the metallic sheen of her scales reflecting the light.

"And I am old, my scales have lost the bright sheen of youth," Khirsha said, reading his thoughts, then stretched her neck out to see him better. "So this is Tobias, Child? Come, come closer, Tobias, so I can see you better. My eyes are not what they used to be."

When he did not move, Rain gave him a little nudge and a commanding look that said: Go on now. When a dragon tells you to do something, you do it! His legs shaking, he waded deeper into the pool, moving closer to Khirsha as the water came up to his chest. Khirsha curved her head down to be level with his, although it was the length of his whole body from his hips to his chin. As she looked at him, he tried to still his quaking and push the memories of an old fairy tale from his mind. What was it? Red Riding Hood? All the better to see you with, my dear. All the better to eat you…

"I think not, Child. You are hardly a meal for me. Too scrawny and not much good meat. I much prefer raw deer."

Tobias trembled and swallowed hard. Khirsha laughed softly.

"There is no need to fear me, Child. I will not harm you."

"Forgive me my fear. I have never seen a dragon before," he replied, trying to still his quaking.

"And I haven't seen one of your kind in nearly five thousand years."

Khirsha's massive head came within touching distance, and he could feel the heat of her breath.

"You may touch me, Child."

Tobias lifted up his hand and gingerly placed it upon the dragon's muzzle. Her skin was smooth and warm, not at all what he thought it would feel like. Charmed, he smiled and ran his fingers over her nose. Then, playfully, Khirsha butted her head against his chest and knocked him off his feet, dunking him under the water. He came up sputtering and she laughed. Behind him, he could hear Rain giggling.

"That wasn't very nice, Khirsha," Rain admonished with mock anger.

"Why not? You said you brought him here to bathe. Besides, it's retribution for disturbing my nap," the old dragon retorted with a wry grin.

"Oh really?"

"What devilment are you up to now? Frightening our new guest already?" came an impish, female voice.

Tobias looked behind him and saw a strange woman sitting on the rocks above the opposite side of the pool. She had a long mop of flaming red hair and bronzed skin, and a big toothy smile.

"Fire!" Rain said jubilantly, rushing towards the newcomer and opening her arms.

Fire grinned and hopped down from her perch with feline grace, a bundle tucked under her arm. She was dressed in skin-tight deerskin leggings with matching boots and a halter-top. She came to the edge of the pool as Rain reached her and they embraced.

"You're back! What took you so long?" Fire said to Rain.

"It took me two weeks just to find him. Even with the bond we share through the bite, I still had difficulty tracking him," Rain explained.

"Well, it is good to see you, sister!" she enthused, then looked up at Khirsha. "And you too, you old trickster!"

"Trickster am I? You should have seen me in my youth!" the dragon retorted.

"Ah, you should have been turned into a coat and several pairs of boots a long time ago, you old bat," Fire quipped, her large, amber eyes dancing with mirth.

Khirsha snapped back her head and laughed. "Same Fire. You haven't changed a bit."

"Neither have you, old bat. Old dragons don't die, they just become part of the landscaping."

While Fire and Khirsha were joking, Tobias waded back to the shallows and moved to stand behind Rain. As he exited the pool, Rain turned to him and smiled.

"These are for you," Fire said to him, offering him the bundle. "Sky was going to bring them, but I wanted to bring them here myself."

"Where is Sky?" Rain asked after a moment.

Fire gave her a knowing look. "He was with Aiya at the Temple the last I saw him."

Rain gave an understanding nod. "Ah, you just wanted to be the first of the others to see him," she joked.

Fire snickered. "You know me too well."

Tobias took the bundle, and quickly realized it contained fresh clothes.

"Thank you," Tobias said, unfolding the black trousers and loose, billowy shirt.

There were towels in the bundle too. Rain took one and began rubbing him down with it, drying him off and removing any remaining burned skin that hadn't been washed away by the water. He allowed her to dry him, enjoying the feel of the soft towel against his flesh.

"Ahhhh," he sighed, flexing his arms and stretching.

"Mmmm, impressive," Fire commented, looking him over with an appraising eye.

Tobias jolted and blinked at her. She chuckled and gave him a slow wink. Rain had finished drying him and was now drying herself, so he sifted through the clothes and pulled out the undergarments. Donning them, he brushed back his curls and slipped into the shirt and pants, ever aware that he was very much on display. Then he knelt on one knee and put on the black leather shoes that had come with the clothes. When he was finished dressing, he turned to Rain and saw that she had re-wrapped the sari around her. She was absently combing through her hair with her fingers when he moved next to her and silently commanded her attention. She looked at him and he could see her brow furrowing at his dark, sunken eyes and haggard expression. Her features softened with affection again; the same look she had given him in the cave, a look of quiet love and empathy.

"Things are happening too fast for you, aren't they," she whispered, stroking his hair.

He sighed. His head was spinning now that he thought about it, splitting actually, bordering on migraine. Did vampires get migraines? It certainly felt like he had one now. Closing his eyes, he nodded.

"Come here, sit down and rest," Rain said gently, taking his hand and guiding him to sit on the rocks as Khirsha settled back down on her perch and Fire made herself comfortable beside Rain.

Suddenly very weary and feeling very old, Tobias rested his head against Rain's shoulder. He wanted to be out of the sun; its heat was making him sleepy. He wanted to be back in the cave he had awakened in, safe in the cool darkness, alone with Rain, and he wanted to feed on Rain again, to join with her mind and let her teach him more about this place. He felt Rain's fingers caress his face and he opened his eyes.

"This is Fire, Tobias. She is like me, one of the ecomancers," Rain told him, then turned to Fire. "Fire, this is Tobias."

"The infamous Tobias," Fire teased. "Hi."

"Hello," he answered, not lifting his head from Rain's shoulder.

"You're having a bad day, aren't you? First you're turned into a torch, then Rain brings you back, then if that wasn't enough, you get dunked by a dragon. You must be going into emotional overload by now," Fire commented.

"Yes," he agreed, trying to ignore the pain in his head. Too much, too fast. Fire *was* right. He was going into overload.

Fire cast a knowing glance at Rain. "I think Aiya will understand if you take him to the willow and let him sleep for a while."

Rain nodded. "I was thinking that myself."

"I think you ought to. You know She will want to teach him, and I'm not sure he's ready for that."

"Yes. I think you are right."

Rain patted him affectionately and rose to her feet. "Come. I will take you to a cool, shady place where you can lie down and rest your poor weary mind."

In that moment nothing sounded more appealing. Smiling softly, his eyes misty, he stood and waited for Rain to lead the way. Her hand clasped his, firm and comforting, and he pressed his face to her hair, closing his eyes. He was expecting her to move at any moment, and when she did not, he opened his eyes, confused. Rain and Fire were transfixed, staring at the sky; even Khirsha had raised her head in concern. They were motionless, listening to something he could not hear. Then he felt it, a great stirring and a massive movement of power.

"What is it?" he asked, suddenly very afraid.

Rain turned to him, her eyes sad. "It's Aiya. She has called a council. We must go. I am sorry our rest will have to wait."

Fire snapped out of her trance, clearly agitated. "We should fly. Can you carry him or do you need my help?"

"I...I am tired, but I can carry him," Rain stammered, torn and bothered.

"I will carry him," Khirsha broke in, standing and moving towards them.

For the first time, Tobias saw how big the dragon really was. She was enormous, at least a hundred feet long from her head to the tip of her tail. She towered over him, and he was struck by another spasm of irrational fear. But for all her size and age, she moved with amazing grace. She came to him and lowered one wing.

"Climb on, Child. There is no time to waste."

Tobias didn't have time to think or even to make the conscious decision to lift himself up onto the huge, leathery wing and slide behind her neck; he was just suddenly there, holding on tightly to her ridge of spines. He saw Fire leap into the air and soar upwards.

I will be right here beside you. Don't be afraid, came Rain's troubled voice as she spread her arms and rose from the ground.

Once she was out of the way, he felt Khirsha gather her muscles and prepare to fly.

"Hold on, Child, we're going up."

The silver dragon bobbed down then, in an incredible burst of brute strength, thrust herself into the sky. Her mighty wings caught the wind and pushed her upwards until she was clear of the ground, and Tobias found himself too amazed to be afraid. He clutched Khirsha's ridge in both hands and stared at the ever-shrinking ground below. A blur of black and gray caught his eye and he saw Rain flying nearby, just off to Khirsha's left, but out of the way of the dragon's wings.

There was a great rush of wind as they rose into a jet stream. Khirsha stretched out her wings to let it propel her forward, and they soared over the mountains. The air was cold up in the clouds and it whipped through his hair. Tears stung his eyes from the pressure of their flight and the brightness of the sun. He couldn't gauge how fast they were going, he only knew that the ground beneath them was speeding by almost too fast to see. They were crossing over a large forest that then gave way to an open grassy plain.

Look! Off to your left! See them? Rain's voice told him.

Tobias obeyed and turned his gaze to his left to see two other dragons, both burnished gold, coming to join them. Suddenly they were catching up to others, merging into a great flight of dragons, a dozen at least, some gold, some silver and some bronze. There was a flurry of leathery wings as the flight gave way to the two ecomancers and the ancient silver. They sped by, taking the lead, heading the legion of dragons across the sky. Ahead, dark specks on the horizon marked an area where the dragons were convening and landing, and he could see a great crowd gathering. Below, on the ground, swarms of creatures, only a few he could identify, were heading to the same place. Finally, he saw a circle of huge stones seated on a rise. Most of the crowd was gathered outside the ring of stones, but Khirsha, Rain and Fire sailed over them, and prepared to land. The two ecomancers went straight down, but the dragon circled first, entering a downward spiral. As they neared the ground, Tobias could see creatures he never dreamed could ever exist. Gathering in small groups were unicorns, winged horses, griffons…almost every creature ever written about in mythology, and some he had never seen or heard of, were clustered within the circle and on its fringes.

And why does that surprise you, Child? If I exist, then so must they, Khirsha's voice said with amusement, responding to his surprise and disbelief.

They are the creatures from dreams, the subjects of fairytales and fantasies!

So they are. Does that mean this is a dream? came the wry answer.

Is it? he asked, wondering if this was all just his imagination.

He heard the dragon's wry chuckle in his head. *There are those who believe that everything is a dream, Child.*

If this is a dream, how do I wake up?

Do you want to?

He thought a moment, trying to grasp the idea. 'If I wake up, I will still be in Ecuador…'

Maybe you are still there. Maybe you never left.

The idea made his head spin even more. *Stop, please. You're confusing me.*

As you wish, Child.

Khirsha fell silent as she landed lightly, her sides heaving, and walked towards where Rain and Fire were waiting.

"Glad to know these old wings can still carry me as fast as the young mumps," she said, catching her breath.

Rain hurried to the dragon's side and raised up her arms to catch Tobias as he slid down from her back. He was shaking, both from fear and exhilaration.

"It's all right. Come, we must join the others," she assured.

Without waiting for his answer, she took his hand and led him towards a group of waiting humans. He soon realized that these were not humans at all, but other ecomancers. He saw Sky almost immediately. He was on the fringe of the group, and the only one who wore no clothes.

"Welcome, Tobias," one of the men said.

The vampire looked askance at Rain.

"He is Song, the Historian," she told him.

Song was of obvious Nordic lineage. He had long blond hair, strong bones, an angular face, and striking fierce blue eyes. As Tobias looked him over, Song smiled at him and nodded his head in greeting.

"Thank you," he murmured, his anxiety rising.

"You will see Her soon," Song whispered reassuringly.

"See who?"

"Aiya. You will see the Mother. You will drink Her blood."

"I will do what?…"

Tobias meant to continue, to demand of Song why he would do such a thing, when he felt the great power again, the same power he had felt earlier when the council had been called, and a voice rang in his head, sweet and seductive.

Tobias, my son. Come to me, Tobias.

Tobias froze and slowly turned to face the center of the stone circle. There, resplendent in emerald green robes, was what could only be a goddess. But not the Blessed Virgin, at least not in any guise he had ever seen Her portrayed. This goddess glowed with power, a warm light eclipsing Her body. Her face was angelic, more perfect than any painting of any goddess ever created, more beautiful than could be described. Her hair was alternately brown, black, and blonde, depending on how the light was reflected off it, and Her eyes were like an endless field of stars. She opened Her arms and beckoned him.

Rain meant to ask Aiya to give Tobias time, to say that Her son was tired and confused, to beg off this lesson so that Tobias could rest, but before she could open her mouth to speak, Tobias began the walk towards Her. Rain watched with baited breath as he entered Aiya's arms.

The moment Tobias touched Her, he knew who She was. This was the Earth Mother: Rhiannon, Estarte, Hecate, Inanna, Queen of the Heavens. In ancient history, before the dawn of recorded time, God was a woman. Stone artifacts of Her had been found in the oldest archeological digs. The first humans worshipped Her as the mother of all things. She was older than the Almighty God, as old as time itself. He looked into Her eyes, eyes that seemed to go on forever, that seemed to hold the entire galaxy in them, and tried to speak, but no sound emerged. She smiled at him, and Her voice sang in his head.

Tobias, my brave son, my wayward son, will you come home to me? Will you now drink of me? Would you accept the blood of the Goddess, your Mother?

Tobias stared at Her in shock, tears streaming down his face. "How can I?…"

Drink from me, Tobias. Learn the truth about the Rogue God, Ja'oi.

It was no longer a request, it was a command; Tobias could do nothing but obey.

He took the goddess into his arms and sunk his teeth into Her neck.

Five

From the moment Her blood touched his lips, the lessons began, sweeping him into a place where time and space had no meaning. He was adrift in the cold darkness, alone, until he felt an overwhelming sense of consciousness all around him. He was in the Earth Mother's mind.

Aiya. Peacekeeper. Mother of the Universe. Goddess of the Web, and Keeper of the Balance. She was heart of all things, and She took him to places he had never dreamed of. There in that space inside Her mind, he saw the truth. He saw how all things, including the vampires, were connected in an intricate lattice, meshing and overlapping, each securing a special place in the natural order of things. As Her blood filled him with light, he saw it all, and it confused him utterly. It was She who had created the first vampire, and in becoming a vampire, Tobias had ceased to be a child of Ja'oi, and became a child of Aiya. A child of the Earth Mother.

It was beyond his comprehension and went against all he had been taught, but there were no lies in the vampire bite and there was nothing he could do to shut it out. He fought, trying to pull away, feeling the power of the goddess keeping him close, almost forcing him to continue drinking. He heard himself sob, felt his body struggle in the embrace as he tried to stop the deluge of information. He felt something akin to pure panic and he started to shake. The visions slowed then, faltering, as if She realized what was happening, but it was too late. He was losing consciousness, his mind reeling, roiling from the revealed truth, and he groaned, silently begging to be set free.

She released him and he sunk to the ground, his eyes rolling back into his head, Her blood stained his lips and trickled in a thin line from one corner of his mouth.

I have cut short the lesson because you are weary. When you have rested, we will begin again.

Tobias didn't answer Her. He lay on the grass, panting, dazed, on the brink of Oblivion. Everything was catching up to him now, and his mind was shutting down. Too much to process all at once. He felt Her power receding as She moved away from him, and he shuddered. Then Rain's hands were upon him and her mind touched his gently, soothing, comforting. No words, only a steady stream of reassurance and affection. He sighed as he felt himself being lifted up. He smelled the scent of Sky. Yes, Sky was there; he was helping Rain carry him to safety.

Sleep now. Sleep. We will watch over you. Sleep, he heard Rain tell him.

He tried to laugh, but only a thin croak came from his lips. Rain was holding him now; he heard the rustle of feathers and smelled horses. Darkness was rising up to claim him as he felt himself being lifted once again. Rain pressed his head to her shoulder and held him close as he slipped into blackness.

He didn't know how long he had slept. When his eyes opened, he found himself in a small, roundish shaped room, and he was on a mattress pallet lavishly draped with pillows and woven blankets. Rain was asleep behind him, her body curled around his own, her arm encircling his chest protectively. The room seemed carved out of solid wood, a hollow almost. There were softly glowing lanterns hanging on the walls, and some sparse furniture: a desk, a table, a couple of chairs, a small dresser, bookcases. There was no discernible door, but one section of the wall was left completely bare so Tobias guessed that was where the exit must be.

He was still disoriented from his lesson with the Earth Mother. Her blood still danced in his veins, sparking like white-fire inside him, but he remembered the lesson with vivid, heartbreaking clarity. She was Aiya, a goddess; one of many. She had created the world in which he now was, the Sanctuary, to be a safe place for Her children, and She ruled supreme here. In his mind he heard Her voice telling him that Ja'oi was an outsider, a rogue god who had placed Himself above the Others, and that He was upsetting the natural order of things. But the natural order of things changed constantly, evolving and morphing into a host of new realities and existences that he never dreamed could possibly be created. He saw worlds upon worlds, and worlds within worlds, each existing within the fabric of the universe, ever-changing, always growing.

The whole picture made his head spin, and he tried desperately to shut out Her voice and stop the endless stream of visions She thrust into his brain, but he could not. She was like Pandora's Box, beautiful and alluring, but releasing a whole Hell full of demons when opened. Only this time, no one was there to slam the lid closed before the last one could slip out. This time, even hope was gone, and he was utterly, and completely, alone and lost.

Aiya's first lesson had taught him that everything he had believed in was a lie, that there was no One True God or way to salvation. There were thousands of gods, each with their own idea of goodness, each with their own way to redemption. It went against everything he had ever been taught. God and Satan were not the beginning and ending of all things, they were but two of multitudes. He saw the stars and an endless, twisting web stretching out before him all over again. Everything in the universe connected with fine strands of thread, weaving into each other in an infinite labyrinth. It confused him completely. He became lost in the maze, desperately trying to find his way out. All his illusions were shattered, all his beliefs broken. There was no meaning to anything anymore, no understanding, and no peace.

Weeping, he clutched the blankets in his hands and held tight to them, curling into a ball and sobbing, his misery complete. Rain heard him and tightened her grip around his chest. Still crying, he rolled to face her, burying his face in her shoulder, and gave in to his grief while she stroked his hair comfortingly.

Why? Why didn't you just let me die? Why did you save me? he pleaded.

He looked at her, his face streaked with tears, pleading silently for an answer, and her expression was one of tortured pain.

Because I love you.

I am a killer! How can you love me?

Because I do.

She was crying now, silent tears rolling down her cheeks. It made him weep even harder.

I'm sorry. Forgive me. He did not want to hurt her.

She rested her forehead against his, her hand in his curls. *No, forgive me. If you truly wish for death I will…I will return you to the Void.*

I want to die. I am damned. I belong in Hell.

"You aren't damned and if I were to kill you, you would not go to Heaven or Hell," she said aloud, her voice eerily soft in the dimly lit room.

"Why not?" he questioned, fear fluttering in his stomach.

"Because you are not a child of Ja'oi. You are a child of Aiya. Aiya does not hold Her souls like Ja'oi. She sets them free. You would return to the Void from which all Wells of Souls are filled."

"But I thought…" No. This could not be possible. Would he even be denied the eternal damnation he deserved?

"You would go to Hell? No. Everything you have learned and heard, does not apply to you. There is no heaven or hell for you."

Tobias stared at her in shock and disbelief, his mouth open. Then he ripped himself from her arms and left the bed. It was too much. Everything was too much. He was dangerously close to breaking.

"No! You do not speak the truth!" he cried, rebelling against these new chains as they chafed him.

She looked at him with sadness. *Yes. And you know I would not lie to you. Priye, if I could spare you these revelations, I would. I love you…*

"No!" He gripped his head in his hands, covering his ears, but he could not block out the voice in his mind. His world was spinning. His mind cracked and everything shattered all around him in a rain of broken beliefs.

"No! Lies! Lies! I do not believe any of it!" he screamed, rejecting all he had learned, and bolted for the empty wall, clawing at the wood and making deep gouges in it with his nails.

LET ME OUT!!

The wall swirled and parted, revealing an opening that grew until it was large enough for him to pass through. He pushed his way out before the door was even fully opened and ran out into the night.

Rain moved to follow him. She exited the willow tree that housed her room and called after him.

"Tobias! Tobias, come back!"

She reached into herself to affect a shape change, but felt a restraining hand on her shoulder. Swiftly she whirled around to see Sky standing there, his eyes oddly calm and sentient.

"Let him go," he said solemnly, casting a glance at the line of trees Tobias had fled into. "Aiya will take care of him."

• • •

Tobias ran blindly through the forest, his tears streaking down his cheeks, until he had no more strength to run. He fell to his knees in a small clearing and wept bitterly, his sobs echoing eerily off the trees, and the night suddenly getting very still and quiet. Using his hands, he began to dig a grave in the moss-covered earth, wanting only the peace of death and the end of this nightmare. The soil was moist and soft in his palms, and smelled of damp and decay. It was just what he wanted: to lie down in the cold earth and pray for Oblivion. He was halfway finished the hole when he felt a great movement of power.

"No..." he choked to himself and dug faster, but it was too late. She was already there.

Tobias looked up at Her, his face stained with his tears, his arms and knees covered in dirt. She was standing there, Her glow cutting through the night like a beacon, staring down at him, motionless. He opened his mouth to speak when She outstretched Her arms and stepped towards him. He recoiled, sobbing.

"No…no please…" he begged. The edge of Her light touched him and he felt Her power and nearness. He closed his eyes to shut out the sight of Her. "No! No! Nooooo!"

His mouth was pressed to Her throat, and Her blood flowing over his tongue cut off his cries. Darkness rose up around him and he was back on the field of stars, seeing forever. Aiya's voice spoke to him, clear and soothing, and he was no longer afraid. The second lesson had begun.

Rain and Sky arrived as Aiya was finishing Her lesson, just as the dawn was beginning to show its light over the trees. They found Her and Tobias kneeling on the ground, locked in an embrace. Tobias was eclipsed by Her light, his thin body enclosed in Her arms. He wasn't moving, and there was no sound at all, save for the distinct hum of power emanating from the goddess. They waited patiently on the edge of the circle of light until Aiya's eyes opened and She called them to Her. Silently they approached as She tenderly released Tobias, offering his limp body to Rain. Rain knelt down on the moss and took Tobias into her arms, resting his head against her chest and stroking his hair gently. He did not respond or acknowledge her presence.

"Will he…?" Rain began.

He will be all right.

"If what you have done hasn't killed him inside again. Must you be so hard with him? He cannot comprehend what you are trying to teach him," she argued.

I know. Do you think I would do this if I had the choice? He must believe. He must be ready when the time comes.

"And does he believe now? Does he have the faith?"

No. The Circle was broken, but now it is mended. I have taught him all I can. The rest must come from within him.

Aiya rose and moved to leave. Sky regarded Her with silent respect and bowed his head in acknowledgment. She bowed Her head to him in return, a soft smile on Her lips.

"How was the Circle broken?" Sky asked.

The goddess looked disturbed, then angry. *Ja'oi broke the Circle. He has done something to Aurek. It is His way of telling me He wants me off His planet.*

"What are we going to do?" Rain questioned, shocked.

Aiya turned Her head to see Her daughter. *I don't know. Much has yet to be decided.*

"Will we abandon Earth altogether and leave its Web as it is?"

Perhaps. It depends on what happens next. I do not have these answers for you, my child.

"What can we do?"

Wait until the Wheel turns again. For now, take care of my son. Then try to find my Aurek. Find out what Ja'oi did to him, and bring him home. I will not abandon Earth before I know what has become of him.

With that, She was gone, leaving Rain and Sky with Tobias. Sky went to Rain and placed his hand on her shoulder comfortingly. Looking at him briefly, she knew that he was all *there*. His eyes were clear and held none of the helter-skelter gleam they so often did. They were her window into his soul and a testament to the bond they shared. Sky had great hidden reserves of strength inside him, strength he rarely employed, but he could pull the pieces of himself together when he needed to, or more specifically, when she needed him to. He could be the strong one of their pairing if she could not, holding it together, making decisions, and doing what needed to be done in order to get them through. She knew it hurt him to do it, and he would pay for it with months, even years, of instability because of it, but he would do it for her. He did it for no one else.

"I don't know what to do. He wants to die," she murmured, her voice flat.

"Does he still wish for death now?" his baritone voice asked, making her shiver. He sounded so rational, so…sane.

"I don't know. He did when he left me."

"Perhaps now he does not. Aiya has finished teaching him, and repaired the Circle."

Rain shook her head. "But Her first lesson left him suicidal. What will he be when he wakes up from this?"

Sky's warmth pressed against her, and he sighed as he wrapped his arms around her shoulders. "Don't worry. Aiya had to cut short his first lesson, remember? She broke his faith in Ja'oi and was not able to replace it with an understanding of the new order. Now he has all She has to teach. When he wakes, he may not have the faith, but he will have the knowledge."

She looked at him, her eyes wet. "Your faith never wavers, does it? You never doubt that the Wheel will turn for the best."

"Faith? What is faith except a certainty that, no matter what I do, what is meant to be will be?" he answered with a little shrug.

She nodded. "Yes. I wish I could have learned that from you as you were learning from me. I have never understood it, but then you care very little for the children of Ja'oi."

Sky shrugged again, his white hair brushing against her cheek. "That is true. I hate them..."

"And I love them too much," Rain broke in, her hand reaching up to hold his. "Together we balance each other."

Sky smiled. It was a secret smile, one only she had ever seen. It was a smile that was just for them, one that spoke volumes about their relationship and the bond between them.

"Yes," he whispered, squeezing her hand lightly.

They spent a brief moment in comfortable silence before Sky shifted impatiently.

"Come, let's take him to the hot springs and get him cleaned up," he said, patting her shoulder.

Rain gazed down at Tobias' angelic face and stroked the white cheek sadly. "I suppose that would be a good thing. He is covered in dirt."

"Mmm-hmm," Sky replied, kneeling on all fours. "Hop on, I'll carry you there. Save you the walk."

Rain shook her head. "That isn't necessary, Sky. I..."

It was too late. Where Sky had been now waited a griffon, its feathers and lion-like body a perfect replica of the real thing. Sighing in defeat, she lifted Tobias up and climbed up on the griffon's back. Once she was settled, the griffon spread its wings and took to the air, carrying them to the mountains and the hot springs.

Sky the griffon landed lightly on the edge of the smallest of the natural baths as the sun lifted off the horizon and began its upward climb. The little pools were too small for the dragons that frequented the area, and were usually left empty. Rain slipped off his back and set Tobias down on the ground as Sky shape changed back into a man. The power surged through him, morphing his feathers back into skin, condensing his lion body to a human one, and turning his talons into fingernails. His face was the last to transform, the eagle-like beak and bird head folding in upon itself to recreate his nose, mouth and brilliant blue eyes, and the feathered crest elongating and lightening into his mop of silver-white hair.

Sky stood motionless, slightly dazed from the shape change, getting his bearings, and then he helped Rain undress Tobias and slip him into the water. He held the unconscious vampire steady in the warmth, while Rain undressed and stepped into the pool. She always wore dark colored saris, so unbefitting of her beauty, and they made her look so serious. He liked it best when she did away with them. He smiled at her and let her take Tobias from him, watching her face as she began to bathe him tenderly.

How she loved this little vampire. For as long as he could remember, Rain's life had included looking out for Tobias. The one who made her. That always confused him, because it was Aiya who had made her, not Tobias. But he didn't argue with her belief. Sky accepted the fact that she loved this creature more than anything, and he knew that he had no choice but to help her when that same little creature got turned into a torch. He was bound to Rain, and always had been, by ties stronger than anything he had ever known. He loved her dearly, but it was not the love of mates, it was the love of partners. He was her balance, yin to her yang, darkness to her light, and he knew that they would always be thus, no matter what happened now between her and Tobias. He shuddered at the memory of what was left of Tobias after his accident. The smell of charred flesh and the sight of the burned body struck a very sensitive chord in him. Sky had wanted to go off after that, to stay a long time in animal guise until he could erase the stench and vision from his mind, but he could not. Rain needed him, so he was forced to stay in human form, and now he was helping Rain clean the soil from Tobias' body. The irony of the whole situation brought a small smile to his lips.

Tobias moaned and moved his head, his eyes fluttering open. He looked up, focusing, and saw Rain and Sky gazing down at him. He blinked, trying to remember what had happened, and lifted his hand to touch Rain's face. He stopped when he saw the hand was wet. Pausing, he analyzed his situation: warmth and wetness surrounded him, Rain's arms were under his back, supporting him. He then realized that he was in a hot spring and they were bathing him. At least that made sense. He made motions that he wanted to be set down and Rain slipped her arms out from underneath him obligingly. His body touched bottom and he sat up in the shallows, running his hand through his hair absently. His head hurt.

"Tobias? Are you all right?" Rain asked.

He looked at her, his eyes still glazed and nodded slowly. "Yes."

She sighed, clearly relieved that he wasn't the raging lunatic he had been before, and he almost smiled. They let him be as he finished what they had started, watching him warily as he rinsed the last of the soil from his skin and cleaned the dirt out from under his fingernails. Their silence bothered him greatly, and he wanted to be left alone.

"Why do you stare at me like that?" he asked, his voice low and tired.

"Because we are concerned about you," Sky answered calmly.

"If you are thinking that I am going to run off again, you are mistaken."

"That is good to hear," Rain said.

"I have no intention of killing myself. As I have learned, there would be absolutely no point to it."

"I am glad that you no longer wish for death," Rain replied.

"Death? No. I do not wish for death. I wish for peace…and solitude."

The two ecomancers looked at each other, then nodded to Tobias. Without a word, they rose from the pool and left him alone. When they were gone, he felt a mixture of relief and remorse. He knew he was not being very charitable, but at the moment he really didn't care. He stayed in the pool for a long while, enjoying the warmth and thinking about his situation, until he finally tired of the water and left the spring, climbing onto the rocks to look out over the forest. A few moments later, he heard the sound of breaking rock, and saw the head of Khirsha rise up beside him.

"Hello, Child," the old dragon greeted.

"Hello, Khirsha," he said, not feeling the rush of fear that hit him when he saw the dragon before.

"It's called Dragonfear, Child. It's a natural warding. Everyone reacts to us that way unless they were forged from the same High Magic as we. You no longer feel it because you are part of the Circle again."

Tobias nodded. "Ahhh."

Khirsha settled down next to him, her massive chest dwarfing him, and tried to look down at him, but she was too big and the angle was odd.

"Oh, this will never do," she snorted, shifting uncomfortably.

Tobias heard her utter a few guttural words. There was a flash and a sense of disorientation, then the dragon vanished, to be replaced by an old woman with long, silver gray hair. The woman sat down beside him as he stared at her in amazement.

"It's an old trick. Sometimes being huge has its disadvantages, so we have the High Magic to cast shape spells," she explained.

"Like the ecomancers do when they shift their shape," he commented absently.

"Oh no, Child. Theirs is an entirely different kind of magic. This guise is merely an illusion of sorts. When any one of them changes, they become that thing, not merely look like it. It isn't High Magic, but it's something akin to it."

"Oh. I didn't know that there were different kinds of magic, aside from the usual white and black magic," he remarked, grasping at the ideas.

"There are many different forms of magic. Each is special in its own way. For instance, I may be able to cast a Gate spell, but I cannot bring a dead tree back to life. I was made before such magic was needed, before the sentients began damaging the Balance," she replied in an off-hand manner. "I was old when Aiya made my brothers and sisters, the ecomancers."

Tobias' brow creased. "Brethren, yes. We're all brethren. But how can that be? We're all so different. But I feel you, I know you. I know all of you. It's like you're part of me and it sets off this tingling in my body. I feel like my head has been turned inside out, and I cannot make any sense of any of it!" he bemoaned, digging his fingernails into the rocky earth. The earth was solid. The earth was *real*, unlike so many other things in this strange world.

"It is the Circle, Child. All of Aiya's children are connected to each other through the Circle, and through the Circle we are all connected to the Web. Now that you have been brought back into the Circle, you will always know and recognize one of Aiya's children as kin."

"It's so confusing," Tobias sighed, shaking his head. "I do not understand."

"I know, Child." Khirsha paused then laid a hand upon his shoulder. "Want to talk about it?"

He looked down at his feet. "I don't know anything anymore. Everything I believed in has been turned upside down. All my certainties are now doubts, and all my faith is gone."

"Pretty scary place to be, isn't it?"

"Yes."

"You know, I've been around a long, long time. I've been old for eons. I've seen whole civilizations destroyed in a single day. I have seen the rise and fall of despots and would-be gods. But I will tell you this…" The dragon-woman paused ever so briefly before continuing. "Everything is nothing without the Web. The Web and the Great Wheel turn the universe. There is nothing outside of the Web. We are all a part of it and surrounded by it."

Tobias eyes turned haunted and full of pain. "No. I am not part of it. I am trapped in it. Lost in it. It ensnares me. I wait, helpless, for the black widow to come and devour me."

He was on the brink of tears, trembling, and he suddenly wanted to run to Rain and beg her to hide him.

"Then go to her, Child. She will not refuse you."

"I cannot. You do not understand. I wanted to die. She stole that from me."

Khirsha snorted derisively. "So you punish her for loving you? For wanting you to live? You are a fool."

"Why would anyone want me to live? I am a loathsome killer of my brothers."

"No. You are not. You do what you were made to do. You are not Cain. They are not your brothers. Ja'oi is not your Maker."

Rage surged through him and he clenched his fists, unable to hold back the emotions any longer. "Everything I have ever believed in is a lie! A lie! Do you know how that makes me feel?"

Khirsha looked at him, her eyes showing thinly veiled anger. "So you want pity? I will not give you pity. I am too old for that. I am too old to mourn the broken dreams of the young."

"I do not want your pity!" the vampire snapped, then wilted like a tender shoot under first snow, his body quivering. "I want to understand. I don't understand."

Khirsha's face softened as Tobias buried his face in his arms. She ran her finger through his brown curls, then lifted his chin, and pointed out towards the forest, towards a tree that grew higher than all the rest. "See the mother tree?"

He nodded that he did.

"Go there. There you will find Song, the Nord. Go to him, he keeps all the histories. Learn from him what he knows. Perhaps he can give you the understanding that you crave."

Tobias roughly wiped his moist eyes. "You must think me a blubbering child."

"No, Child. I do not. I am not so old as to forget what it was like to be young, alone and frightened."

"Yes."

Khirsha patted his shoulder. "Go on now, Child."

Tobias smiled softly at her. "Thank you, Khirsha."

"Anytime, Child."

He stood and walked down to the hot spring for his clothes. There he found new ones, neatly folded where his old ones had been. Rain must have brought them while he was up on the hill with Khirsha. He felt a pang of sorrow. He knew he was being mean to her; he only hoped she would understand. Vowing to remember to thank her for the clothes, he dressed and headed towards the forest.

Six

The sun was high by the time he was nearing the mother tree, and he was glad to be in the cool shade of the woods. Though the sun could not harm him in the Sanctuary, his eyes and skin were still very sensitive to its heat and light. He found Song sitting under the boughs of the great oak. He watched him for a moment before entering the space. Song was dressed in the ancestral clothes of the Nords, a deerskin jerkin adorned with intricate leatherwork and metal beading, and he had his long blond hair pulled back into a neat braid. Finally, he stepped into the small clearing made by the shadow of the tree, and his presence was immediately acknowledged.

"I was wondering if you were going to stay hiding behind that maple tree all day," Song mused.

"I did not want to disturb you," Tobias replied, bowing his head in respect.

"You are welcome here," the ecomancer greeted, his voice soft and soothing, like a melody.

"I thank you," Tobias said as he sat down, cross-legged on the grass beside him.

"What brings you to me?"

Tobias looked at the ground, humbled and afraid. "I am in need of guidance."

"I see," Song answered simply.

"Will you help me?"

"I will do my best."

Tobias raised his eyes, gathering his courage. "Why me? Why was I chosen for this?"

"Because you are the vampire Rain could find."

"Because I bit her, and because the Circle was broken."

Song nodded. "And because of Aiya's shield spell that hides your kind from Ja'oi. Rain can find you because of the bond you share through the bite. All others of your kind are hidden from us."

Tobias grew thoughtful, recalling the Lessons of Aiya. "She cast it because Ja'oi tried to kill Aurek."

"Yes."

"And you want me to find Aurek."

"Yes."

The simple answer made him angry and he bristled. "I have never heard of Aurek. I have no idea where I could even begin to search for him."

"You can find others and ask them."

"Do you have any idea how difficult that will be? How dangerous? Vampires are territorial and easily provoked. I was nearly destroyed because I wandered into the wrong coven's territory!" Tobias snapped.

Song seemed unruffled by the vampire's outburst. "I think you will find that habit slowly begin to fade as more and more vampires are returned to the Circle. You are the ambassador now. Every vampire you meet will be brought back into the fold, and they will in turn bring every vampire they meet back. As more and more vampires return to the Circle, you will find that a feeling of…kinship will prevail."

Tobias snorted and crossed his arms. "I'm not sure how true that will be."

Song shrugged.

"Why now? If I have learned correctly, Aurek has been missing for four thousand years," Tobias demanded.

A flash of pain crossed Song's face. It was brief, but Tobias saw it.

"It is true that Aurek has been missing for quite some time. There have been attempts to find him, but they have failed. It is only because Aiya is considering abandoning Earth, that She has employed Rain's help now."

The revelation came as a shock. "She's what?"

"Aiya has expressed the possibility that She will remove Her influence from Earth and allow Ja'oi to rule it without Her intervention."

"But that would hurt the Balance, wouldn't it?" he blurted.

Song regarded him with mild shock, then smiled slightly. "It would."

"Then why would Aiya do such a thing?"

The sadness returned to Song's eyes and he looked down. "There are reasons. Ja'oi is aggressive. He wages silent war upon Aiya at every turn. Already She has withdrawn many of Her children from Earth. Of the creatures She created to keep the Balance, only a few still walk the mortal plane, and they do so by their own choosing. Only the vampires remain in any significant number."

"What would happen to the vampires if Aiya abandoned Earth?" Tobias asked.

Song looked thoughtful. "Now that the Circle has been repaired, any vampire that has returned to it would probably be offered the opportunity to come to the Sanctuary."

"But I could refuse? I could stay on Earth?" Tobias pressed.

"Of course."

"And Rain?"

"Rain is an avatar of the goddess. She goes where Aiya bids her."

"I would never see her again."

"It would be unlikely," Song admitted.

Tobias felt a twinge of pain at the thought. Rain had been kind to him, and professed to love him deeply, and while he could not say that he returned her feelings, it did not mean that he had no desire to see her again. He bowed his head and looked at his hands.

"If I help Rain find Aurek, will Aiya abandon Earth?"

"That is one of the things She could do. The results would be far-reaching; the loss of Earth would leave a hole in the Web, but there are things that can be done to protect some of the affected areas, and there are other choices at Aiya's disposal. She may choose not to abandon Earth. It depends on what you find. We already know Ja'oi severed the vampires from the Circle. Now we need to know how He did that, and what has become of Aurek," Song replied honestly.

"And if we don't find Aurek?"

"I do not know."

Tobias sighed, his mind heavy with uncertainty. "Why was Aurek left unprotected in the first place?" he said aloud.

He heard a gasp and looked up. Song's face was a mask of white, his blue eyes dilated with shock and grief.

"What is it?" Tobias asked immediately, wondering what he could possibly have said that would have upset the ecomancer so much.

Song shook his head and the look disappeared, leaving only a haunted ghost of it in his eyes.

"What is it?" Tobias asked again.

Song looked away and put a hand to his forehead. "Things I do not care to speak of."

Tobias did not question him again, respecting Song's wishes, and sought to change the subject. He had come to Song for understanding, and understanding continued to elude him. Perhaps he had not been asking the right questions.

"You...you believe in all of this? The Circle and the Web?" he whispered, breaking the awkward silence.

Song appeared to relax a bit and returned his gaze to Tobias.

"Yes. It has been my existence for millennia."

Tobias then had an idea and voiced it without reservation.

"Then share your blood with me, please. Give me your faith."

"I cannot."

Tobias winced. "Why?"

"Because what I have to teach will not help you find the faith that you need."

He looked at Song, pleading. "If you let me drink from you, I would be able to understand..."

"No. Even if you were to drain every drop of blood from my body, you would still not have my faith. You would have my knowledge, but not my belief. It would be like learning all the words of a new language, but none of its grammar or diction."

Tobias looked away. "You are refusing me then?"

"Not by choice," Song insisted, moving closer to him. "Tobias, I was born a pagan. I was a shaman in my mortal life. I have always served Her."

Tobias started to shake his head in dissent, but Song continued, trying to explain. "You have always been a Christian. Even when you professed that you did not believe, you still had faith in the God Almighty. You still believed in Him."

The brown-haired vampire began to tremble. "And now God Almighty is no longer. He is Ja'oi, one of thousands..."

He hid his face in his hands. It was all coming back now, the lessons, the visions, the things Rain had told him. It was too much.

"Oh! I am so lost! Help me please."

Song put his arm around him. "I want to, but I cannot give you what you need, my friend. You must find it for yourself, within you."

"How?"

"Look into your heart. The faith is there, as is the strength to face what lies ahead."

Tobias looked at Song, his face a mask of anguish. "All my faith is gone! What is left for me now?"

"Love," he replied, his voice comforting. "Love is all we have."

"Love? What is love, but that which withers and fades away?" Tobias retorted. "No. You are wrong. Love is everything. Love is the only thing that lasts forever."

Tobias' face cracked, his eyes opening wide.

"Love is the only thing that lasts forever..."

The words echoed in his head like a ghost from the past, crashing over him like a tidal wave. They were Andrea's last words: Andrea, his ill-fated and beloved friend. Andrea who died in his arms in 1989 after being hideously stabbed. He had killed her, at her behest, when it was realized that the stab wound had severed her spine. She had been a musician and dancer in life, and the injury had left her paralyzed: a fate worse than death. She begged him to kill her, opening her soul to him, and he had obeyed. He still heard her music in his mind, the part of her that would live forever, and her voice, whispering in his mind like a forgotten dream. "*Tobias, love is the only thing that lasts forever…*"

With a strangled cry, he wrenched himself from Song's arms and stood, his face a mask of shock, and backed away.

"Tobias? Tobias are you all right?" Song asked, concerned.

Tobias' mouth moved, but no sound came out. He continued to retreat, a horrified look in his wide, blue eyes. Song rose to his feet and stepped towards him.

"Tobias?"

The Nord tried to probe the brown-haired vampire's mind, but was met violently with a shield Tobias threw up to prevent him.

"No!" Tobias choked. "No!" Then he whirled and ran into the forest.

"Tobias!" the ecomancer called and moved to follow.

Let him go, the voice of the goddess ordered gently.

Song turned to see Her standing beside the tree.

"Will he be all right?"

I will take care of him.

• • •

Tobias wandered for days, aimless, avoiding all contact with sentient beings, his mind and heart in turmoil. What does one do when his entire belief system is yanked out from underneath him? How does one cope with that? He had no idea and he didn't want to think about it. He didn't know what they wanted from him, or even if he could give it if he knew. All he wanted now was to get away, to lick his wounds and regroup. He blocked off his mind, making himself deaf to anyone who would try to call him.

Crossing the mountains, he entered the valley he had first seen when Rain brought him to the Sanctuary. He stayed there, burying himself into the earth by day and roaming by night. His thoughts were consumed by memories of those he had loved and lost. He dreamed of Ian, the vampire who made him; of Andrea, humming her music to himself to assuage the pain. And Etienne.

Etienne had been his mortal lover for nine years, before Tobias made him a vampire in 1991. He had loved Etienne desperately, giving him everything he could ever desire. Their affair had been like being inside a tempest, Etienne at once ecstatically happy, and viciously angry at the same time. Etienne wanted immortality, and Tobias had refused him for almost a decade. Finally, when a freak car accident nearly killed him, Tobias gave him the full draught of his blood.

They had less than five years together before the tension between them drove them apart. Etienne left to be with Barias, one of the oldest vampires in the world, leaving a huge hole in Tobias where his love had once been, and taking his security and independence with him. Tobias had been heartbroken, but not surprised. He had known for centuries that maker and child often separated, and he knew that Etienne would eventually leave him. Better to have worked the magic and know that Etienne was alive, than to let him die. He did not regret his choice. Etienne made a fine vampire. Tobias only hoped Barias would be able to give his beloved fledgling the guidance he required.

The memories of his loved ones gave him both comfort and pain. Ian, Etienne and Andrea had been great loves in his life, but there had been another. Another whose memory he had suppressed for three hundred years, and had buried completely for the last ten. Another who had been Tobias' greatest joy, and greatest sorrow. Another whose face now haunted both his dreams and his waking thoughts. Silaene.

Silaene had come to him in the early 1700's. Tobias was barely over two hundred years old, and in his period of greatest despair. Ian had just brought home a new heir, Dorian, a young Englishman with black hair and green eyes. Tobias was heartbroken at what he interpreted as punishment for all his shortcomings. The new object of his maker's affections was beautiful, intelligent and independent: all the things Tobias knew he was not. In a sudden surge of defiance, he had run away from the castle he had lived in for nearly a century and fled to his homeland of Germany. He had no idea what he would do when he got there, he had never been alone in his life, but he knew that he had to get away. The pain had been unbearable.

Silaene had found him in Bonn. She was beautiful and full of life. He could still see her standing on the riverbank, her long brown hair flying behind her, and her teasing smile meant just for him. She had come and turned his whole world upside down. For days they had shadowed each other through the nighttime streets until finally he managed to catch her and demand to know her identity. To this day, he was certain she had let him sneak up on her. She had told him she was a lone vampire, abandoned by her maker and left to fend for herself. She had seen him, another loner, and had hoped to become his companion. She was lonely and wished for company and someone to hunt with. He was lonely as well. Their brief relationship would become one of the greatest loves of his life.

Silaene bonded to him, giving him direction. She guided him without dominating him, and tried to make him stand on his own. Her belief in him fed him, renewed him with life again. He began to see the world through a different pair of eyes, and it was not so dark and hopeless as it had once seemed. Her love was his greatest source of comfort, her arms the safest place he had ever known, and he was deliriously happy. They had a few short weeks together before Ian found them. He should have known that, in spite of Dorian, Ian would never let him go. His maker confronted him outside a tavern and demanded that he return home at once.

Panic-stricken, Tobias had rushed to rendezvous with Silaene whom he had left in their quarters, grabbed her and fled the city. It was a feeble attempt to escape; he knew Ian would find them no matter where they ran, so he made a choice. If Ian saw Silaene as a rival for his love, then Ian would surely kill her. Tobias knew he had to return to his maker, and that his lover could not go with him. They argued on the banks of the Rhine until finally, he had broken down. He had emptied his soul to her, telling her everything: of Ian, of the new Prodigal Son, of the danger to her should they stay together. He did not want her to die. He could suffer anything if he knew she was alive and safe. She took him into her arms and let him cry, rocking him like a lost babe, crooning to him under her breath and stroking his back. Afterwards, she swore no one would ever know, that she would keep his secrets. She had kept her word.

Before they returned to Bonn, Silaene took him into a Summerhouse left vacant while the owners traveled abroad, and bathed him in the sumptuous, opulent marble bath. It was an Oriental ritual of massage and washing that she shared with him, and it was one of the most erotic and pleasurable experiences he had ever had. With tears in her eyes, she had left him the following evening, but she gave him a final promise that he still held close to his heart.

"You will see me again. This world will not swallow me because I can change with it. I will always love you, and when you are ready, I will come for you."

It was the last he had ever heard from her. He returned to Ian, going back to the castle in Scotland, once again resigning himself to the pattern of submission and dependence. Ian had kept tight controls on him afterwards, watching him carefully. He had had no other opportunity to escape his domineering father, so he stayed, all the while raging inside as the new Prodigal Son was flaunted before him, mocking him and all his weaknesses.

Almost three hundred years had passed since Silaene had disappeared from his life, and he had never seen or received any message from her. There had been times, however, when he thought he felt her or caught a stray thought from her traveling across the vampire mind links, but he was never to see her face in the mind of another vampire or to hear anyone speak her name. It was as if she had never existed.

Over the centuries, he had learned to live with his grief and even to love again, but it was never the intense passion he had felt for Silaene. The only regret he had was that he had never given her a taste of his blood. She had let him take small drinks from her in their lovemaking, a sign that she trusted and loved him. To share blood with another vampire, or human for that matter, was to lay claim to that person, to say 'You are my lover. You belong to me.' He had never had the courage to share his with her, perhaps because he knew they would not be together for very long, or perhaps because he feared she would not take it. She was always a free spirit, and she may not have wanted to be tied to him with the sharing of blood.

Tobias still loved Silaene. There were times when he missed her with a desperation that bordered on insanity. He even had some small hope that she would be true to her word and come for him, appearing out of the dark like a muse to sweep him off his feet once again. Thinking of her often brought him great sorrow, so he buried her memory deep within him, vowing never to think of her laughter or her love again. And he had not, until he came to this place and his world was once again in turmoil, and he was drowning in change. Her memory then returned to him with vivid force, and now he could not forget.

On his fifth night in the valley he rose, the thirst eating away at him like a raging beast. He had been ignoring it, neglecting it for two days, but now it would not be denied. He had been at a loss, uncertain as to where he could find blood to satisfy his hunger, and too distracted by other concerns to make it a priority. Now he was feeling the weakness, the thirst bringing him out of his stupor, and he was in terrible pain. Trembling with need, he mustered the energy to cross over the mountains again, to go back to the forest on the other side, back to the one person he knew would help him.

Seven

Rain was beside herself with worry. Tobias had been gone for almost six days and no one knew where he was. For some reason Aiya was blocking their efforts to find him, and preventing their mindcalls from reaching him. She knew that Aiya would not allow anything to happen to him, but she did not know what sort of mental state he would be in when he returned; if he returned. The others had kept her from trying to track him, telling her to have faith and be patient; that Aiya's plans were not always revealed or clear to Her children. She had obeyed, burying herself in the preparations for what was to come in an attempt to keep herself from going mad.

Aiya was deeply concerned. Her Teaching of Tobias had confirmed Her suspicions that Ja'oi had broken the Circle. It was a profound violation of the Code and the Law. It was Her duty to keep the Balance, to preserve the Web. Her children could be found in some form on every world where maintenance of Balance was needed. She was respected and revered by all the other Supreme Forces, even the most despotic ones, and all knew the importance of Her duties. Aiya kept the Balance and the Balance kept the universe. They all knew this, They all accepted it. All but one.

Ja'oi was the rebel. He defied Balance and sought to make His own, outside of the Web. He waged war upon Aiya's children to remove them from His world. He kept His angels ignorant of the existence of other gods and told them all non-believers were heretics. None of Aiya's children had ever been able to make useful contact with any of Ja'oi's avatars. Ja'oi was shrewd,

He hid His offensives behind religious principle, using His children's faith as the drive against Aiya, and therefore had never declared official war against Her. He was not so conceited as to not know that to do such a thing would mean immediate retribution from the Others. Not that war among them was uncommon, but that none would ever be so foolish as to attack the one who held the entire Balance together. No, He had not waged war upon Her, rather He had systematically harried Her children in an attempt to remove Her influence from what He believed to be His planet. He thought He could create His own Web and Balance, using His plan.

So far it was a colossal failure, all the Others knew that, but it seemed that Ja'oi was the only one oblivious to His situation. In doing so, He was jeopardizing the stability of the Web, and there were signs that the Others were becoming concerned. Avatars for some of Aiya's closest allies had been seen, but none had openly questioned Her or any of the ecomancers. It was as if they were observing, waiting to see what Aiya would do, how She would respond to this newest revelation, and if She would ask for Their help. They were showing Their presence, letting Her know that They were there, and that They knew what was going on, and were ready to help.

The truth was that Aiya did not know what Her next move would be. There was dissension among Her children as to how She should respond. Many sided with Her suggestion that they abandon Earth and deal with the ruptured Balance later when it reached a critical point, but others, mostly the ecomancers, wanted to respond to Ja'oi's religious fervor with a renewal of the Earth Mother religions. They wanted to return to Earth, to counteract the damage humankind had done and do it openly, so that all would see the power they wielded. It was as direct a front as they could offer without interfering too blatantly. They would not counter Ja'oi's religion, but merely let their actions speak for themselves. Followers of the ancient goddess clans would flock to them. Word would spread, more and more would learn the ways of Balance, and the Earth would begin to heal. It was a good plan, except for one thing: Ja'oi was sure to retaliate.

Aiya was uncertain. She did not want to lose any more of Her children, but She also did not want to abandon Earth. She was at a loss. She decided to give Her avatars a chance, offering them time to try their plan until Aurek could be found, but leaving the option of abandonment open in the event that Ja'oi declared war. Now the ecomancers were meeting, trying to decide on a feasible plan of action and to prepare for the worst. They gathered after sunset, on the fringe of the flat plain that stretched out across the land until it reached the sea some five hundred miles away. The plain was littered with large outcroppings of rocks, jutting out like great spires and tables above the grass. They met among one cluster of rocks, just on the edge of the plain, less than fifteen feet from the forest. There was a temple nearby, with a cloister and walled-in garden; its white pillars could be seen peeking above the lower trees. It used to be home to many of the ecomancers, but they had since out grown it. Two or three still stayed in its marble halls and neatly appointed rooms, and its formal baths were often frequented, but it was mostly left empty.

Almost all of the ecomancers were there. In fact, the only ones missing were Song and an ecomancer called Leaves. Song not being there was not unusual. Song was the historian, he recorded all the events, and therefore had to remain unbiased. He tended to avoid these heated debates between his brethren, opting instead to let the facts tell him the story. As a historian, he was not truly concerned with what could have been, only with what actually happened. Leaves, Rain was certain, would arrive soon, as Leaves was almost always late.

Aerth was seated furthest from the forest, her brown hair reflecting the soft glow of the fire they surrounded. None of them knew exactly how old Aerth was, and it was possible she did not even know herself. It was fabled among them that she was made the day after Eve.

Standing near the center of the circle was Stars. Stars was Aerth's eternal consort, an Egyptian born in the time of the pharaohs, and his angular face and long, black hair were a contrast to Aerth's softness. Where Aerth's eyes were brown, Stars' were black; his lean body was clothed in dark, form-fitting trousers and a loose shirt, a marked difference to Aerth's Greek-like robes.

To the left of Aerth sat Moon, a male ecomancer whose heritage had originally been Mayan out of the Yucatan Peninsula, but now his gray hair and eyes gave him an other-worldly look. As the fire danced in the center of the circle, its shadows played on Moon's face, making dark patches on his skin, much like the moon itself had its craters and dark places. Beside Moon was Sun, a former Amazon with blazing blonde hair and deep, golden bronze skin. Where Moon was dressed in somber robes, Sun was wearing a white toga that showed off her young, female body.

Several paces from Sun was Seed. She was of African descent, her dark hair and skin accentuating the woven, multi-colored cloth she wore. She came from a tribe long dead, whose ancestors fathered the Masai. She had the tall, thin body and long, sensitive hands of her people, and a pair of dark, liquid brown eyes. To her left was Stone. Stone had been the son of Mongol traders, and in his rebirth into an ecomancer, he had retained his characteristic features, but his black hair had been turned slate gray and his black eyes lightened to brown. He sat cross-legged, his stocky, strong body draped in a silk tunic and loose leggings.

To Aerth's right was Wind, a male ecomancer of Native American heritage. He was dressed in shaman's leathers, with his long, black hair braided, and his dark eyes serious. Next to him was Sea. Sea was graced with pale blonde, luminescent hair, vivid green eyes, and shimmering white skin. It was believed that Sea had originally come from the continent of Atlantis, but she had never confirmed those rumors; and those who knew the truth were either silent or dead: the deceased Air had been Sea's mentor and mate. Her fingers and toes were webbed, and she sported a set of small gills in her back. She was scantily clad in little more than a bikini adorned with pearls and coral beading. To Sea's right were Fire and Ice. Ice was Fire's teacher and best friend. His hair was silver-white like Sky's, but it did not have the shimmer that Sky's hair did, and it was shorter. He also had violet eyes that were almost multi-colored and they retained the slant of his Japanese ancestry. He was dressed in blue and silver.

Fire had been a Celt in her mortal life and she still possessed the heated temper of her people. With her blazing red hair and amber eyes, she could make quite an impression when she was angry. She was unique, however, in that she was the only ecomancer ever to be reincarnated. The first Fire had been one of the original four ecomancers Aiya had created, but she had been killed along with Air during a civil war on another planet. Some 4000 years later, a new Fire was born, forged from the same soul that had once lived in her predecessor. The new Fire had only the vaguest memories of the first Fire, and in truth was very little like her, but most of the ecomancers never knew the original Fire so they had no means of comparing the two.

Rain and Sky completed the circle. She was sitting on the perimeter of the forest, at the base of a boulder Sky had chosen for his perch, and all of them were listening to Stars address some of their concerns about the plan. It seemed simple enough to her. Some of them would go to undo what humans had done, while others would go to teach whomever of Ja'oi's children were willing to listen. Once Tobias was ready, and the timing was right, they would go to find Aurek and teach the vampires about their heritage. She was hoping for aid from Tobias in that matter, but there was no telling when and if he would ever have the faith.

"I will go and begin to heal the northwestern forests of America," Stars said.

"And I will begin to purify the oceans," Sea added.

"I will help you," Wind told her, offering his hand in pledge.

"I cannot help," Seed informed in her quiet voice. "I have Placide to care for, but I can do some things and use it as part of his training."

Seed was referring to a young man who might become the newest ecomancer. A Tutsi who escaped the genocide in his home country of Rwanda, he had been under Seed's protection and care for nearly four years. She had left him in Uganda in order to come to this meeting, but she was anxious to return to him. The time was coming for him to make the choice to join the ranks of the goddess' avatars or to reject the teachings and forget all he learned. According to Seed, he was showing much promise and she had high hopes for him. If he were to cross over and become one of them, he would be the second ecomancer made in a century.

Rain was about to speak when Sky touched her mind with urgency. She looked up at him and he motioned to something behind her, his face grave. She turned her head to see what he was so concerned with, and her heart caught in her throat.

It was Tobias. He was standing at the edge of the trees, filthy, his clothes in tatters. Even in the darkness, she could see how horrible he looked. Tears brimming her eyes, she stood and hurried to him. His skin was sunken, pulled taught over his bones. Two dilated eyes peered out from a face that was little more than a thinly covered skull, and his hair had lost all its preternatural luster. He looked like something out of the old photographs of Nazi concentration camp victims: the epitome of pain and suffering. He was starving, and when she touched him, he was ice cold.

"Tobias," she breathed, taking his hand. It was limp. "Oh Goddess, what have you done to yourself?"

He did not answer, he merely stared at her with a glazed look in his blue eyes. She became aware that the others were watching with concern. Ice had stood and was making no attempt to hide his shock. It looked as if at any moment they were all going to converge upon them, and she knew that they had to get out of there immediately. She mindtouched Sky and received his acknowledgment. He would prevent the others from following if need be.

"Come, priye," she soothed, while tugging on his hand to lead him away from the gathering.

He followed obediently, his mind a perfect blank when she tried to probe it. He was in shock from lack of blood, and she knew if he didn't feed soon, he would go into a killing frenzy.

She led him to a private place in the forest, guiding him as gently as she could, then she sat down with her back against a tree and opened her arms. He blinked at her, uncomprehending until she reached up to her neck and tore open her jugular with her fingernail. At the sight of her blood, Tobias moaned and dropped to his knees. Crawling to her, he licked it away eagerly, closing his mouth over the wound, and Rain wrapped her arms around him, bringing him to rest between her legs, pressing him close to her warmth. When the tear she had made for him healed, she heard him whimper with frustration, then felt him shudder with blood lust as he drove his teeth into her neck.

He took her so fiercely it hurt, his arms seizing her and nearly crushing her against his chest, but she bore it without complaint, knowing the pain would not last long. She clutched him to her as he fed desperately, and listened to his small mews of relief. His body began to warm almost immediately as the heat of her blood reached his limbs, and he relaxed, feeding more gently and loosening his vice grip. A moment later, Rain felt something warm and wet splash onto her skin, and she touched her fingers to it to see what it was. It was Tobias' tears. Tobias was crying silent tears as he drank, rolling down his face until they dropped onto her neck. She sighed and tangled her hand in his filthy, matted curls, pressing her face to the side of his head, rocking him soothingly and crooning under her breath.

At first he just drank, wanting only to quench his burning thirst, but after a few moments, when the first swallows began to satisfy his need, she felt the gentle tap of his mind against hers. She opened to him immediately, letting him feel the extent of her relief and happiness that he was safe in her arms, and he wasted no time in joining with her. The essence that was Tobias melded with her consciousness, and there was no separation between their thoughts.

Thank you. Thank you, she heard him sigh.

I am so glad you are safe, priye. I was so worried about you. There are no words to express my joy.

Forgive… he begged.

There is nothing to forgive. I understand. Don't you know how much I love you?

Why? Why do you love me? Why are you so grateful to me for having nearly killed you?

Rain smiled to herself. *Oh, my dear one, this is why I love you…*

She opened the floodgates of her memory and let her past wash over them. Tobias quickly lost himself in the kaleidoscope of her thoughts, a slave to the perfection of their union and the taste of her blood. Together they swooned as she took him back five hundred years, back to the gutter he had left her in.

Her name hadn't been Rain then, she had had an Indian name, one given to her by her long dead parents. A name she had until the fall of the Sultan Ghiyās-ud-Din in Delhi into whose harem she had been sold. Sold again by the new Sultan, a man of cruelty and sadistic wiles, because she was Hindu; this time to traders who took her from Delhi to the trade port of Surat, and from there by ship and overland again to the Black Sea. She was bought by Florentine slavers in Constantinople where a Roman nobleman took a liking to her, bought her under the pretense of placing her in indentured servitude, and took her to Rome.

Her Roman master named her Pythias, a common name for a slave girl in a Comedy, and set her to tending his every whim. Pythias, the servant girl to a Roman nobleman, had always had a talent for gardens. It was her gift that she could make any plant grow, even under the harshest of conditions; it was nothing short of magic. Her only solace was her garden, the garden of her master, which soon became the talk of Rome for all its splendor, and she was happy, until the accusations of witchcraft came and the Almighty Church burned her beautiful garden to the ground. Breaking the contract, her master sold her to a brothel and paid handsomely to the coffers of the Church to avoid a taint on his good name. Pythias, the servant, her garden in ashes, was led away from her home once again.

The brothel was a dark and dismal place full of disease and evil people, but in spite of the dark, Pythias still made her flowers grow. They grew almost unbidden, and when her new masters discovered that her unusual talent had not been quelled by the burning of her garden, they beat her terribly for fear that the Church would rise against them. Still the flowers grew, no matter how hard they beat her, no matter how dark her tiny cell, the flowers always grew. Then one night, when Pythias had lost all hope, after her masters had beaten her once again, and she lay weeping with despair on the floor of her tiny cell, the door to her prison opened. Her masters had forgotten to lock it, or so she had thought. Blindly she stole her chance and ran for the open door, slamming solidly into a figure standing just inside the hallway and falling to the stone. She looked up from her knees and saw two luminescent blue eyes gazing down at her. Moonlight from the window filtered in and fell softly on a young man with brown curls.

Oh God! I remember! I remember this! she heard him gasp.

His hands had descended and taken her by the arms, lifting her up effortlessly, as she stared transfixed into his huge eyes.

You were the most beautiful thing I had ever seen, priye! she told him.

When he smiled, she didn't even notice the sharp fangs; all she saw was his beauty. The man took her into his embrace, and she gave herself over to him willingly as he sunk his teeth into her throat.

Once again, Tobias saw himself feeding upon the girl, draining her almost to the point of death, then, in an odd moment of tenderness, lay her in the gutter with her hands upon her chest in quiet repose. Only now, did he remember the flowers that grew in the gutter. He had laid her body upon the flowers. Then he saw himself slip off into the night, heading back to Ian after his kill. His mind's eye looked down upon the body of the girl, and saw in amazement that the flowers had begun to grow around her. He watched the green tendrils encircle her limbs and wind into her hair. Moments later, a shadow fell across the body of Pythias, and a plain woman in a brown toga knelt beside the silent form. Aerth…that was the woman's name…stroked Pythias' cold cheek, gently lifted the limp body into her arms and carried her away.

When Pythias opened her eyes again, she was in a different place and Aerth was with her.

"I am Aerth. I will be your teacher. You are to be one of Aiya's Chosen."

From that day forward, Pythias began to learn the true nature of her powers. Together with her consort, Stars, Aerth taught Pythias the ways of the Web and the gifts of the Chosen. Years went by until the time came for Pythias to make the choice to become a true Child of the Mother or to forever lose her powers to the Void. Aerth took Pythias to an ancient willow tree. There in the shadow of the great willow, the very earth parted and took Pythias into itself. When she rose from the earth three days later, she was Pythias the servant girl no longer. She was Rain, Child of the Earth Mother. Her black eyes had turned gray and her dark skin had turned a milky white. An immortal daughter with all the powers of nature and the Web at her command. Shapechanger and weather worker, she could assume any form she so desired and call a storm from a cloudless sky on a whim. In later centuries they would name her kind "ecomancers," but for now she was merely Daughter Rain.

Daughter Rain thought herself blessed with this new and wonderful life. She thanked the vampire who set her free, and vowed to protect and serve his kind as best as she could. The fledgling vampire was never to know that he had a shadow, a shadow that protected him from harm.

For five hundred years she had looked after him, nurturing the love that she had for him, letting it grow and blossom inside her as she followed him through his long life. She had been his unknown benefactor, never letting him see her in her true form, keeping the truth from him. Until now. Until the day he had gone to Ecuador in search of his lover. Until the day he had been trapped in a dilapidated shack and burned alive. He saw and felt her anguish, heard her scream when the hut exploded. He watched his body erupt in flames and a single panicked woman, with all the demons of Hell in her eyes, thrust her hands through the fire, grab his burning form and pull it into the ground.

I was so afraid I was too late. You were so burned. There was so little left of you. I was certain I had lost you, but Sky was there. He caught your spirit and held you while I healed your vital organs...

Rain, her face stained with tears and soot from his ashes, poured every ounce of power she had into his blackened remains, while Sky weaved a net to hold his soul. She was trembling from the effort, crying uncontrollably as she worked. 'Don't die, please, don't die.' Then finally, like a Phoenix rising from its own funeral pyre, his body began to take shape. As soon as his vitals were whole once more, his own spirit slipped back into his body without persuasion, and he drew breath. Rain, exhausted and drained, wept happy tears and collapsed in Sky's arms. The male ecomancer stroked Rain's hair and comforted her as she slipped into unconsciousness. Then, in an amazing transformation, he shape-changed into a huge white wolf, and wrapped himself around her sleeping form.

Now, priye. Do you understand? she asked him as the visions faded.

Yes. I understand, he answered, and began to reciprocate.

She had shared her story with him, allowing him into her private memories, and now he felt the need to share some of his own. Opening his mind, he began to tell her his tale. He took her back to the beginning, to the late 1400's in Germany. He had been a beautiful young boy and the duke who controlled the lands his family lived on took a liking to him. His father sold him to the duke as a bed servant, and he lived in the man's household until he grew too old to please his lord. He was turned out, but could not return home. He lived on the streets as a beggar and thief until he tried to steal a purse from a well-dressed man in a tavern. The man turned out to be a vampire, the one who would become his maker, Ian. The vampire took the young Tobias under his wing and kept him close. In 1490, Ian gave him the blood, sealing the bond between them. He went with Ian from Germany through France and Italy to Rome where they stayed for half a century, and then north to the British Isles and Ian's castle in Scotland.

Oh the years of bliss he had spent with Ian, happy to serve and be needed, wanted, loved. Then he showed her the night two centuries later when Ian brought Dorian home to their castle in Scotland, destroying the happiness he had found, and the bitter rivalry that developed between them. Three centuries were spent in emptiness and despair, broken only by Silaene, until Ian killed Elizabeth and both his children left him.

For as long as he could remember, even before Ian had made him a vampire, his life had been a series of upheavals. A pattern of brief moments of peace followed by years of turmoil and pain. It had begun in the 1400's and had continued through to the present. A weaker spirit would have perished long before now, but Tobias was strong, a stark contrast to his needful soul. He held on to life no matter how tenuous his grasp or how shaky his footing. Somehow, he always found a way to survive.

Telling her everything, he spared no detail, and when he was finished, he felt as if he had just laid himself bare before a pack of hungry wolves. He released her neck, having long before taken all the blood that he needed, and gently rested his head upon her chest. Her arms were around him, her hand stroking his hair comfortingly, and a strange sense of peace came over him. She would hold the wolves at bay. They had shared a level of intimacy that he had experienced with only two others in his long life, Etienne and Silaene, and now he felt bonded to her. They had opened themselves to each other, shared their deepest memories with each other, even become one in mind and body for a short time, and he knew now, the depth of her love. He also knew that he could love her, love her as much as he had loved Etienne. The taste of her was still on his lips, her blood pulsing inside his veins, warming him, sustaining him, and he snuggled closer to her, nuzzling her with his nose as he felt her kiss the top of his head.

Do you love me now? she asked.

Yes. Yes, I love you, he answered, feeling it with his whole being.

He moved to pull away, to get up so she could go back to her meeting, but she held on to him tightly.

No. Stay? Let me hold you? Just for a little while. I've waited 500 years for this. Just let me hold you.

He obliged her, settling down again, warm and comfortable, with his head pressed to her chest and his hand tangled in her long hair. In her arms he felt completely safe, as if a tempest could come and she would protect him from it. She would not allow anything to happen to him. He could lay his soul at her feet and she would not harm him, she would never betray him, she would always love him. The only other time he had ever felt so utterly safe and accepted was when he was with Silaene.

Where? Where have you been all my life?

Rain chuckled softly. *I have been here.*

But why did you never come to me? Why did you never reveal yourself to me?

She didn't answer, merely kissed his head again and wrinkled her nose at his filthy hair.

"We should get you cleaned up. There are baths in the temple cloister," she said aloud, patting him on the shoulder.

He chuckled softly, and moved to get up. "Lead the way."

She stood and took his hand, and they walked side by side to the marble cloister. Rain opened the garden gate and led him to the living quarters. At the end of a long, white hallway was a large bathroom with a huge tub and padded tables for massages. Someone had been there before them, firing up the boiler, laying out a set of clean towels and placing several vials of colored liquids on the edge of the tub and on one of the massage tables. Tobias thought he caught the scent of Sky on the towels, and listened to see if anyone was nearby, but he heard only one heartbeat and that one was getting farther and farther away. They were being left alone, their privacy being respected. Behind him, Rain was turning on the water to fill the tub. She poured a few drops of jasmine scented oil into the running water, and the sweet scent wafted through the room with the steam.

Tobias felt the electricity of Rain's touch as she laid hands upon him, her fingers caressing his breasts as she removed the remains of his shirt. He sighed and closed his eyes, enjoying the feel of her skin smoothing over his, sensuous and erotic. Deftly she unfastened his trousers and lowered them until they fell to the floor, letting her hands trace the curve of his buttocks and thighs as she pushed the material down. He moaned. It was all so familiar, the smell of jasmine, the steam from the bath, the knowing, expert hands gliding over his flesh. Pure pleasure. Just like it had been with Silaene…

"You really miss her, don't you?" Rain spoke pensively, breaking the stillness.

"Hmm?" he asked, leaning into her as she began to loosen the tight muscles on his arms from behind.

"Silaene. You really miss her."

"Sometimes. That reminds me…you never answered my question."

Her hands were on his back now, rubbing, caressing, sweet tingles of pleasure running through him as she worked his shoulders.

She paused as if waiting for him to continue. "What question?"

Tobias smiled and turned to face her, taking her arms in his hands. "Why you never came to me before."

She looked at him with the most peculiar expression on her face, as if some long forgotten memory had resurfaced. She pulled out of his embrace and turned away.

"Do you ever wish she had come back for you?" she asked over her shoulder.

"Who?" he questioned, placing his hands on her shoulders.

"Silaene," she whispered.

"Yes, sometimes. I do not understand. Why do you wish to speak of Silaene? She is dead. What does her memory have to do with you and I now…"

He stopped in mid-sentence, then he slowly turned her around to face him. She met his shocked gaze with waiting sadness, and he knew. He knew before she spoke a word, before her hair shortened in length and turned chestnut, before her eyes darkened to brown and her face elongated, her skin turning preternatural white and her lips curling into that familiar teasing smile.

"Silaene…" he whispered, touching her face with his fingertips. Same arch of her brow, same delicate chin. A doll made of fine bone china, until the doll moved and two tears rolled down her cheeks. Rain was a vampire now. 'When one of them changes they become that thing, not merely look like it…'

"No. No, don't cry…" he choked.

As he wiped away her tears, he understood. She had come to him. She had come to him during one of the darkest times of his life to guide him and feed new life into his dying soul. She had begged him to come with her, but he had refused. Now he knew why he was never to see or hear from her again, why no other vampire had ever heard her name or seen her face. She had become a vampire just for him.

"You are so beautiful," he breathed, all his composure stripped away.

"Do you still love me now?"

His answer was a swift, passionate kiss. "Yes. Yes, I love you."

She stared at him for long moments, her expression a mixture of torment and joy, until she turned her attention to the tub. It was nearly full. Quickly, she reached down and turned off the water before it could overflow. As she straightened up, Tobias' mouth found hers again, and they kissed as Rain shapechanged back into an ecomancer. Tobias released her lips and smiled, his eyes warm with love.

"I wondered why there were things about you that seemed so familiar, how you knew me so well, why you loved me so much," he said, fingering her long hair, feeling the soft black mane between his fingertips.

"I have always loved you. I loved you the day you took me from the brothel. You made me love you with your beauty and your savage need. But I did not know the depth of my love, or the strength of it, until I came to you as Silaene. I likened myself to a young woman-child, worshipping an idol from afar, a dream lover, and then…the dream became flesh," she told him, kissing his palms.

"I feared that I had been deluding myself, that my love was just a fancy, a brief and fleeting thing. For this is how it is with us, you see. Permanent bondings among us are rare indeed," she continued, looking into his blue eyes with unadulterated love. "But when I came to you as Silaene, I fell in love with Tobias the vampire, not Tobias the ghost savior appearing out of the dark, and the longer I was with you, the more I loved you. It did not fade or weaken; it grew. It grew until it encompassed all of me. I would have been content to stay there in Bonn forever with you…"

She bowed her head, her expression sad and wistful, holding his hands loosely as she sighed, "But it was not to be. I had to leave you. I was forced to leave you. Leaving you was the hardest thing I have ever done. I lost part of myself that night; I left it with you, and every day since I have prayed that you will forgive me for hurting you, for abandoning you, that somehow you will understand that I had no choice."

"But why? Why did you never come back?" he implored.

"I could not. There were other concerns. I was no longer free. Sky was still unstable and Aerth told me he would respond to no one but myself. I had to take care of him. By the time I was free to return, you no longer needed me," she replied.

"I always needed you!" he insisted, taking her face in his hands. How could she have thought such a thing? Didn't she know how much he craved the kind of love Silaene had given him?

"No. You always wanted me, but after the first time I came to you, you didn't need me anymore. And Sky did."

Tobias lowered his gaze. "Is Sky...is he your lover?" He was afraid to hear the answer.

"Sky? No. No no, my dear one. Sky is not my lover. Rather he is my partner, sometimes, and, in many ways, my child. He is the other part of me. We are bound to each other...I cannot explain."

"Do you love him?"

"Yes. But not as a lover. We are, however, more than friends," she paused, as if unsure how to continue, then brushed away her pensive expression and changed the subject. "You should get into the tub before the water gets cold. We can continue this while you bathe."

Her words comforted him and gave him hope. His hands moved to unwrap her sari.

"Join me?" he asked.

Rain nodded and he unwound the sari, letting it fall to the tile floor. Bending his head down, he kissed her breast gently, then took her by the arms and led her as he stepped backwards into the tub. The water splashed and licked at the edge of the tub as he lowered himself into a sitting position, holding Rain's hands and looking into her eyes as she joined him. The tub was more than big enough for both of them; Rain didn't say that they had gotten three and even sometimes four into it on previous occasions, and the temperature was still deliciously warm. Tobias leaned back into the water and doused his matted hair as she poured some shampoo into the small of her palm. When he sat up, she rubbed the shampoo into his wet curls and worked it into a lather. He allowed it, but his eyes showed mock exasperation and resignation, like an unappreciative little tough guy, or a teenager who felt that he was old enough to wash himself. His expression, compiled with his hair in bubbles and his youthful face was so funny, Rain had to laugh. She giggled, trying to hold back, but failed miserably.

"What are you laughing at?" he sniffed.

"You look so cute."

He pouted with indignation, which only served to make her laugh harder. It was infectious. His pout melted into a smile, and they snickered for a few moments. Then, as suddenly as he had begun to laugh, his smile faded and he seized her in his arms, clinging to her in desperate fear, his face pressed to her chest.

"I love you," he managed, the confession wrenched from him. Every one he had ever loved left him…

"I love you, too, priye," she answered.

She held him close, letting him draw comfort from her embrace, until he pulled away and rinsed his hair. When he finished, she took him by the shoulder and whispered into his ear words he had not heard in three centuries.

"You are to do nothing. I am your slave until this ritual is finished. I will bathe you, dry you and massage every inch of your body. Your only duty is to feel pleasure."

His breath escaped him and he closed his eyes, trembling with anticipation. "Yes…do that to me. Make me feel it again. It's been so long. So very, very long."

Her hands glided over his flesh, caressing him with the soap she had spread on them. He leaned into her, letting her wash his back, and rested his chin on her shoulder. The smell of her blood mixed with the scent of jasmine and other aromas from the shampoo and soap, filled his nostrils in humid wafts, teasing him, exciting him. He wasn't hungry, her blood had satisfied his need completely, but the fragrance of her so close to his mouth was more than irresistible.

As she continued to bathe him, he began to kiss her throat, licking and nipping at the flesh. His lips, soft as moths' wings, brushed over her skin, making the small hairs rise in their wake, and he heard her moan.

I thought I told you to do nothing, she admonished gently.

Forgive me. I cannot help myself.

Soft mental laughter, then a tiny cry as his teeth punctured the surface of her skin and he licked at the seeping blood.

Just a few droplets, my darling, with the promise of more later.

You are breaking the rules, she teased.

I know. Forgive me. It is too much. Silaene. My Silaene is reborn and come back to love me. I am overwhelmed.

Sense of disappointment and concern.

Do you love me or Silaene?

Both. Since you are both, I love both.

Rain pushed him away very gently. *Let me finish.*

He slipped back into the water, gazing into her eyes with unadulterated adoration.

Yes, anything. I am your slave. Command me. I am yours to do with as you will.

Her brow furrowed. *I will only that you love me and be my equal.*

Whatever you wish, liebchen. I will be whatever you wish, he replied using the German word for beloved.

She did not reply. His words bothered her, but she did not want to spoil their tender moment with doubts. She knew he had a tendency to become dependent, particularly when he was in need of guidance, but she was hoping this would just be a temporary phase until he was more secure. If it continued, she would have to do something about it, but for now, it didn't matter. All that mattered was Tobias. That he was there, that he loved her, and that he needed her. Everything else would fall into place later.

She met his loving eyes with a sweet smile. *Now, shall we begin again? You are to do nothing...*

Eight

Rain awakened in the early hours of morning, as sunlight filtered through the window of the cloister bedroom, with Tobias wrapped around her. His naked body was spooned against her back, his face in her hair, his arm draped across her chest. He smelled of sandalwood and musk. He was cold, but not nearly as cold as he had been when he first came out of the forest, and sound asleep.

Sky had been there not long before, the room was laced with his energy patterns. He had left her breakfast on the dresser: fruit and fresh baked muffins, and the smell of the muffins piqued her appetite. Gingerly, she lifted Tobias' arm from around her and slid carefully out of bed. He settled onto his side in a semi-fetal position, his hand just under his chin, not rising from his slumber as she reached for a muffin and consumed it. He slept peacefully while she ate her breakfast and studied his sleeping form in minute detail.

He was perfect. Everything about him was perfect, from the rich brown of his curls to the neat row of toes on his feet. His white skin reflected the light streaming in through the lace curtains, his hair sparked rainbow colors. With his eyes closed in sleep and his thin mouth turned into a secret smile, he was a vision of beauty and flawlessness. An angel with a youthful face and perfect, male body. She could still feel the smoothness of his skin sliding under her hands when she massaged him last night, exploring very curve and crevice of his prone form, and hear his sounds of pleasure as she rubbed him.

Vampires were such sensuous creatures. Everything about them exuded sexuality, from the brush of their fingers to their kiss. They were the physical embodiment of eroticism. Their entire bodies were erogenous zones, ultra-sensitive to all types of feelings, but responsive to pleasure most of all. You could bring pleasure to a vampire no matter where you touched him. Face or foot, back or stomach, it was all the same, seamless pleasure. Not even their genitals were more sensitive than any other part of their bodies. Still, Rain had spent long moments caressing and fondling him there, knowing that it brought no more pleasure to him than a caress to his chest or neck, and, if anything, the promise of blood sharing was the most pleasurable of all. But she enjoyed the feel of him in her hands and he had not protested. On the contrary, he had lifted his leg to allow her better access to his groin and crooned with pleasure as she stroked him. The only protest he made was a silent one, when she moved to fondle his anal ring, and he had gently pushed her hand away.

Rain was familiar with the lovemaking Tobias and Etienne had engaged in while Etienne was still mortal. She knew that Tobias had played bottom to Etienne's top, allowing his lover to penetrate his body during passionate evenings of blood sharing and sex. She was aware that the act both excited and frightened Tobias, but that the experience was extremely pleasurable for him. Even more so, she knew the feelings surrounding their lovemaking, both then and now. There had been a time when Tobias had craved Etienne with mortal need, but it had been years since Etienne had been able to satisfy that need because neither of them knew how to make the vampire body perform. Neither knew such a thing was even possible, and the transition back to sexual celibacy had been difficult for Tobias. As a result, he now resisted any attempt to reawaken those feelings. When Rain had sought to caress his opening, she came very close to triggering a sexual response in him, so he had tenderly, but firmly, guided her hand to other places.

At the time, she had respected his wishes and moved on to other parts of his body, kissing and massaging him until no part of him had been left untouched, but now he was asleep and she could do anything she wished to him. She wanted something that had no connection to Silaene, some-thing that would be uniquely their own to share. She wished to impress upon him that she was not his old vampire lover, but rather that Silaene had simply been another version of herself.

Finishing her breakfast, she took a moment to light a wand of incense; a scent she knew Tobias associated with love and intimacy. Then she returned to the bed, bringing one of the bottles of massage oil with her, and knelt next to him. Tentatively, she began to caress his buttocks and upper thighs, testing the depth of his sleep and when he did not awaken, she carefully pulled his upper leg forward, separating his thighs slightly, and brushed her finger across his anal ring. She paused, waiting to see if he would rise, and when he did not, she proceeded with care...

• • •

Etienne was waking him up again, doing that exquisitely pleasurable fingering he so loved. How long had it been? Too long. 'Yes, do that to me. Soon you will be inside me.' Mouths on each other's necks as they shared blood, joining together mind, body and soul. 'Oh yes, take me! Make me mortal again! Let me be your mortal lover. Never make me have to forget how wonderful this feels ever again!' Etienne was back. Back to stay. No longer would he pine with mortal need for his lover to return. No longer would he pace and scratch at the white walls of the house in frustration, or submerse himself in cold water to forget that his lover had gone away again. No. Etienne was back, and he was being loved, loved as only Etienne could love him. 'Oh, Etienne. I love you, Etienne. Never stop doing this to me. Never stop making me feel this ecstasy. I thought I would never have you again after I brought you to me'.

Consciousness pierced his dream. Etienne was a vampire now. There would be no more nights of mortal passion and lovemaking. Those times were irrevocably and permanently broken. But if that was so, then why was Etienne doing this to him now? Why was he being expertly prepared for that which would not come to pass? Why was his need and passion being awakened when there would be no fulfillment? Confused, he shook away his dream, angry to have dreamt it, for now he would be aroused with no male lover to satisfy him. But the sweet, pleasurable sensations did not stop when he opened his eyes. Quickly, he assessed his situation, trying to remember where he was and who would be cruel enough to torture him like this. His whole body screamed for satisfaction; his need, now fully awakened, was howling like a beast in pain, gnawing at him like a starved animal, and he was ready, very ready, but there was no one there to satisfy him. The only other person in the room was Rain...

"No!" Tobias cried, coming fully awake and twisting around to grab her wrist, snatching her hand away. "No!"

She stared at him in mute shock, and he fumed at her, his teeth gritted in frustration and stymied passion.

"Why? Why are you doing this to me?" he demanded, his voice cracking.

"I want to share this pleasure with you," came her even reply.

"Share it? Do not tease me!" he snapped, then grew sympathetic at her bruised expression. "Please, if you have any love for me at all, please do not do this to me. Do not awaken this need which you cannot possibly satisfy."

Carefully, she slipped her hand from his grasp and patted his rump tenderly, a wry and knowing smile on her lips. "But my love, I can satisfy you."

"How...?" he began, but stopped as she leaned into him, bringing her face very close to his.

"You can make love. There is a way...to make your body perform. I know how. We did not have the opportunity when I was Silaene, but I will teach you now, if you let me."

Tobias trembled as the meaning of her words settled upon him, and he met her steady gaze with a pleading in his eyes that was unmatched by anything she had ever seen. He opened his mouth to receive her kiss, his lips quivering as they touched, and surrendered himself up to her. His hand tangled into her hair as they kissed passionately, bodies pressed against each other and Rain moved atop him.

Tell me what I must do, he asked.

He heard and felt her chuckle. *You are to do nothing...*

He smiled against her lips. *This again?*

Yes and no.

Hm?

Yes, in that I mean you are to do nothing. No, in that this is not what we have done before, she explained, nibbling at his ear.

Pleasure surged through him and he breathed deep, smelling the scent of her blood just beneath the surface of her skin. So close. He lifted his lip.

NO! Rain warned and drew back suddenly.

"What is wrong?" he questioned, confused.

"You must not bite me. It will ruin everything."

"But I am a vampire. The blood..."

She placed her fingers on his lips to quiet him. "I know, but you must trust me. You do trust me, don't you?"

He blinked at her, then nodded. She smiled. "Good. Then listen to me. You must not bite me, no matter how strong the blood lust becomes. You must fight it. There will come a time when it is safe for you to bite and drink from me, but not until I tell you it is all right to do so. Understand?"

Again he nodded, unable to speak, lost in the heat of her gray eyes and the fluttering in his belly. Opening his mouth, he received her as she bent down to kiss him. Their lips melded, and he relaxed into her embrace as she stroked and caressed his arms and chest. Her touch was light, yet sensuous, sending ripples of delight rolling through his body. He sighed and bit his lip, closing his eyes only to have them fly open again as her mouth closed on one nipple. He gasped, then let out a long, low moan and carded his fingers into her hair.

Torture... he sent.

Patience...

"Vampires are not known for their patience," he managed as she moved to explore the other nipple.

That's why none of you have ever discovered how to do this. There is some value in tantric practices, you know.

Is that what this is? Tantric sex? I'll have you know, I was never very good at... He paused and groaned as Rain nipped lightly at his breast. *Controlling myself.*

You'll just have to learn.

I am...your devoted and apt pupil.

You are? she answered with amusement.

Yes...as long as you keep doing what you're doing.

Just what I'm doing? I had plans to do much more.

He moaned again. *Please.*

Please what?

Mercy.

But we've only begun.

She was licking him now, just under his breasts and across his chest. His breath increased, his heart rate accelerating, and the blood lust rose along with the tingles in his head.

I shall not survive.

*Yes, you will. *

Her teeth nipped at the soft place underneath his arm. He shuddered, breaking out into a sweat.

The French call this the little death, he told her, trying to remain coherent. The bloodlust was causing a red haze to slip over his vision.

I know.

He would have answered her, continued the conversation, but she lifted her head and began to suck at the sensitive spot where his neck met his shoulder, right along the pulsing vein. Then he felt her teeth bite him, not hard enough to break the skin, but enough to send him reeling. Rational thought left him completely and he cried out, his neck arching and his hands flying from her hair to grip the mattress. He heard the bedclothes rip under his nails. It was his last lucid moment before her hot mouth plunged him into a sea of ecstasy.

An eternity later Rain had reduced him to a sweating, quivering mass of nerve-endings and heated flesh. Sounds were coming from his throat but he did not recognize them as words, or even that he was the one making them. The moment had long since past when he would have bitten and ravaged a mortal lover from the sheer need and power of his lust, but she had displayed her remarkable strength and ability to keep him from giving in. Now he lay on the bed, sobbing, beyond begging, lost in a maze of rapture the likes of which he had never experienced.

Some time ago he had noticed an unfamiliar scent permeating the air around him. He had wanted to ask Rain about it, to tell her that it was making his whole body thrum and tingle, but he could not form a single sentence, even in his mind. The scent was stronger now, not pungent or even definitive; it was more a feeling that was somehow *inside* him, under his skin. It was like bloodlust but more, so much more. It settled over him like a heavy weight, holding him down, pressing him into the mattress.

Under normal circumstances to be so confined would have sent him into a panic, but he was not afraid. In fact, fear was not even present in the room. Whatever it was, it was **wonderful** and he knew he had no reason to be concerned. Rain was there and she loved him. She would never allow him to come to any harm. Dimly he was aware that her mouth had moved considerably lower on his body, and that her tongue was now licking his inner thighs. Almost by habit, he spread his legs, giving her easier access and it seemed that she took it as an invitation.

Warm, wet heat surrounded his flaccid organ. That in and of itself was a shock. Then she sucked and the tingling in his body rushed downward. The pleasure was so sharp and unexpected that he arched up, curving his back like a bow. He felt something snap inside of him, followed by a great surge of power that flooded into his loins. He screamed hoarsely as his body roared to life, his organ filling for the first time in five hundred years.

Tobias collapsed back to the bed, panting, his mind swimming, the heavy weight of his erection as alien to him as the memory of food. He babbled something, but even he knew it was completely incoherent. He forced his eyes to focus, to see Rain. She was smiling at him, her hand wrapped loosely around his organ, stroking lightly. He gasped, his eyes rolling back into his head, his vision seeing spots and bright flashes of color. Then he felt her lift up and straddle him.

He screamed again as Rain impaled herself on him, the burning heat of her body surrounding his own inflamed flesh. His body writhed of its own volition and she grabbed his hands, leaning forward to push him down as she rose up, sliding along his organ slowly, then sitting back down again. He froze, shell-shocked and choking as she repeated the motion until he was raising his hips to meet her as she moved.

That's it. Now you are remembering, he heard her encourage.

Gritting his teeth, he forced himself to concentrate. He raised up his arms, still holding both her hands, balancing his elbows on the mattress. It gave them both better leverage as she quickened the pace. She leaned onto his arms, bending his wrists back, as she goaded him to go faster. He was picking up the rhythm quickly now, meeting her steadily, and antici-pating her next move. She was moaning with pleasure as she rode him, her face registering every thrust, and he was encouraged.

Focusing intensely on what he was doing, Tobias lifted his hips in time with her motion, matching her pace, and triggering the memories of his mortal lovemaking. Yes, he was remembering now; Isa, in the pantry behind her master's kitchen, he and her, struggling together in the throes of passion. He was remembering the patterns, growing more confident with every thrust, picking up Rain's silent signals, a shift in her weight, a tightening of her thighs, that gave him direction. Still moving his hips, he sat up, taking his hands from hers and wrapping his arms around her. His lips found her mouth and he kissed her deeply as they kept the pace going, but now he was taking the lead. She moaned, and embraced his shoulders, letting her tongue enter his mouth, as he began to lift them both up.

In as smooth a motion as he could manage, Tobias turned them both over so that he lay atop Rain. The switch had caused him to almost pull out, but he rectified that immediately. He spread her legs with his thighs, balancing on his knees for leverage, and resumed the rhythm. He was being extremely gentle, by vampire standards, not even using a tenth of his strength, but it was perfect. Rain was beneath him, her face glowing with ecstasy, her eyes closed, and he was filled with delight. Her body tensed around him, giving him a signal to go faster and he obliged, reading her face to find her approval there. Her eyes opened, and she smiled at him, draping her arms around his neck and kissing him passionately.

Rain moved with him, rocking in time to his rhythm, matching him stroke for stroke, and it seemed as if they were one being, seamlessly connected to each other. Her passion fed him as she began to build towards climax, gripping him tightly and moaning his name.

Now! Now! Bite me now! she ordered.

With a keening wail, he released his blood lust and buried his face in her neck, sinking his fangs deep. She cried out as he bit her, the muscles of her passageway pulsing around his organ, the pleasure of his vampire kiss sending her spiraling higher with ecstasy. He drank from her, riding her hard and fast, letting her sounds of pleasure guide him. He felt his own pleasure rising, not only from the sweet blood pouring down his throat, but from the pressure building in his loins as well.

"Oh Goddess, Tobias!" she gasped, her nails digging into his skin as his hips pumped furiously.

Rain...my beautiful Rain. I am yours. I am yours forever! he cried, driving them both towards orgasm.

Tobias, my beloved...

Her thoughts cut off as her body strained with his, the waves of pleasure increasing as she neared her pinnacle. She was moaning and sobbing with delight, raising her legs to force him deeper, moving her hips to meet his. Tobias could feel her nearing climax, her passage constricting tighter and tighter around him until finally, it clamped down. She let out a strangled cry, her whole body going rigid as she came. The burning heat seized him in a vice grip, and he felt his body answer with its own powerful release. The energy burst from him, wracking him, flooding from him with five hundred years' of pent-up force behind it. He screamed for the third time that night as the pleasure exploded, sending shockwaves through his loins, up his spine and into his brain.

In the aftermath, he found himself unable to continue moving, as if his body had cried mutiny and refused to obey his mind's commands. He collapsed atop her, trembling, sweating. Finally, when the last of the strong aftershocks subsided, he was able to remove his mouth from her neck and lift his head so he could look down at her. Her eyes were closed, her mouth slightly agape, and a thin layer of sweat beaded on her forehead. Grinning, he pushed once more into her and kissed her tenderly. She kissed him back with equal passion, her tongue licking his reddened lips and exploring his mouth.

"I love you," she whispered breathlessly when they broke the kiss.

He smiled. "And I love you."

She was drying up, he could feel the wetness dissipating, and he gently removed himself from her body, coming to rest beside her and taking her into his arms. She snuggled close, sighing with contentment, and placed a hand upon his chest.

"Did I please you?" he asked, kissing her forehead.

"More than I ever dreamed was possible. Did I please you?"

He closed his eyes with relief, full of satisfaction and pride. "Yes. I...I love you."

"And I love you," she echoed, then murmured, "Thank you for trusting me."

Tobias nuzzled her hair. "Thank you, for everything. I cannot believe...I am...I have no words..."

"You don't need them, priye. I already know."

He nodded in agreement, drawing the blankets around their naked bodies, and held her dear to him. She was precious, the most wonderful thing that had ever happened to him, and he was full of love and joy. Pressing his body close to hers he let her rest in his arms, watching over her as sunlight flickered patterns over the floor and walls of the bedroom and the incense turned to ashes.

Sometime later, he lay quietly, listening to Rain's breathing as she slept beside him. He was content, his body pressed snugly against hers, and satisfied, full of love. Their lovemaking had satiated his need completely, but even more so, it helped to heal old wounds. Sighing with contentment, he nuzzled her hair and kissed her temple. He did not expect her to wake up, the lovemaking had exhausted her, and to be honest, he liked watching her sleep. He used to watch Etienne sleep, guarding his mortal lover's slumber. He had sweet memories of Etienne's peaceful face, his lover's lips turned into a soft smile as they cuddled together. Rain's expression was much the same. Her features were relaxed, her black tresses clinging slightly to her forehead. She was a picture of mortal beauty. But Rain was not mortal, and the thought filled Tobias with hope.

Here was a lover who was as immortal as himself. She would love him forever, never asking of him more than he could give, never wanting his blood, except in the sharing of mutual pleasures. She was capable of satisfying his needs and would never make him suffer with those needs. She knew him, understood him, and loved him with every fiber of her being. He had found his eternal consort, the one who would weather the centuries with him, and share his life with him, its joys and sorrows. Side by side they would stand by each other, loving, learning and growing together. He would no longer be the abandoned one, alone and in despair. He had found the other half of himself in Rain.

It was the fulfillment of all his dreams, and he wanted so desperately for it to be a reality, but he was afraid. He didn't know if Rain loved him for himself, or if she loved him for what he was to her, loved him for being the vampire who had given her this life. Maybe the fear came from his own doubts, maybe it was because he was such a fatalist, or maybe it was just because nothing in his life had ever worked out the way he had wanted it to. No matter the reason, he needed to know the truth. He needed to know before he committed himself too completely, before he surrendered his heart and soul to her, if she truly loved him. If she did, he would belong to her for all time, and he would do anything, even prostrate himself at her feet, to keep her with him.

Gently, he shook her awake, calling her name softly, afraid to mind-touch her because he feared what he might find there. She mumbled in protest, rolling to her back, then opened her eyes.

"What is it?" she asked sleepily.

Choking on his apprehension, he replied urgently. "Do you love me?"

Her brow furrowed in confusion. "Of course I love you."

"No. You love what I am, and what I did for you, but do you love me? Do you love Tobias?"

She regarded him calmly for long moments, and he held his breath, nearly quivering with anticipation. Then her hand reached up and stroked his cheek tenderly as she nodded, her eyes filling with love. "Yes, I love you. I love Tobias."

Tears brimming his blue eyes, he raised his wrist to his mouth and bit into his flesh. Then with the innocence and nervousness of a child, he offered her his bleeding arm. Did she know the significance of what he was offering? Could she possibly understand what it meant? Love me! Accept me! Be mine forever! All in one simple gesture, all in the sharing of his blood, the one thing he had never had the courage to give Silaene.

Rain looked at his hand, at the blood running over his white skin, and reached up to take his wrist. Bringing it to her mouth, she closed her lips upon the open wound and drank. Tobias moaned and sobbed, the floodgates of his emotions bursting open. Gasping, he took her into his arms, and buried his face in her hair. She released his wrist and searched for his mouth, finding his cool lips and kissing him passionately. She tasted of his blood, driving him insane, and he pressed himself to her, seeking to cleave to her forever. Wild with desire, he forced his tongue into her mouth, nearly crushing her in his embrace. After a few moments of kissing, Rain gently pushed him away and gave him a single, knowing look. Tobias stared into her gray eyes and obediently lowered himself to the mattress, lying on his back and reaching up to accept her. Her lips closed on his, her hands caressed his chest, and the loving began again.

Nine

The room was warm and cozy, not like the large opulence of the bedroom in the cloister. Rain's little place inside the trunk of a huge willow tree was her own piece of paradise, and now Tobias shared that paradise with her. They were snuggled together on the mattress pallet, sequestered under the blankets, and Tobias was watching her sleep. Around him he could hear the sounds of the tree breathing, feel its life emanating from the walls, and he felt protected.

Looking down at her sleeping face, he traced the curve of her jaw until it was lost in the black sea of her hair. Like the night time waters of the ocean, her hair reflected the light from the lanterns, coloring it with rainbow swatches of yellows, reds, oranges and even a few hints of blue. He smiled, letting his eyes wander over her features, lingering on her closed eyes with their soft black lashes, her full mouth, and finally coming to rest upon the warm skin of her neck, just below her ear. Bending his mouth down, he kissed the tender spot, letting his tongue lick the salt. The blood underneath rushed to the surface, flushing the skin a sweet blush, and he shuddered as the smell wafted into his nostrils.

Feeding his own desire, stoking his lust from ember to flame, he trailed a line of kisses down her neck, and over her collarbone, allowing his hands to wander across her naked body. She moaned softly, still asleep, but her lips curled into a soft smile. He kissed the tip of her breast, flicking his tongue over the nipple, then made his way back up to her throat, searching out the jugular, and very gently sunk his teeth in. He heard her gasp, felt her mind rise to consciousness, as the droplets of blood slid over his tongue, and groaned lowly as she tangled her hand in his hair. He released her and brought his lips to her mouth. She responded eagerly, stroking his lust even more, letting her taste herself in his mouth, such exquisite pleasure. He moaned and wrapped his arms around her as she rolled towards him.

The kiss lasted forever, ending finally, when Rain pulled her lips away.

"I don't care how many times you do that. It is still such a wonderful way to wake up," she said with a contented sigh.

"Watching you sleep incites my...more passionate side," he murmured, kissing her neck again.

Sharp teeth pricked the skin a second time, flooding her with warmth. "Ah. I love that."

As do I, he said, feeding lightly, taking the blood in little sips.

And I love how you love me. In five centuries, I never dreamed that I would be holding you like this. That you would love me as I am and I would be with you.

And I. To be loved for myself.

I'll love you always, my beloved, just as you are.

"I know," he answered verbally, lifting his mouth from her throat.

She smiled at him. "Good breakfast?"

He grinned, showing his reddened teeth. "Yes. And you? Are you wanting breakfast?"

"Yes, I am a bit hungry."

Tobias released her, and she rose from the bed. He watched her move, entranced by her gracefulness and beauty. Just as he was perfect to her, she was perfect to him. He roused himself and began their little morning ritual. She went to the small cupboard and pulled out several pieces of fruit, while he arranged the pillows and covers and selected a sari from her sparse collection. He chose a black and gray one with a delicate filigree pattern dyed around the edges, and brought it to her as she bit into an apple. She let him wrap it around her and secure it, then allowed him to brush her hair.

He loved attending to her, dressing her, doing her hair, and she allowed it, simply enjoying his loving touch. As he ran the brush through her hair, she could feel him caressing it, running it over his hands, and she closed her eyes. Such a simple pleasure. In a little while their roles would be reversed, she would dress him and comb his brown curls. It was their special routine, a tender moment of give and take, shared by no one else.

"So what would you like to do today?" she asked, looking up at him.

"Anything you wish," he answered. This was love, to do anything your lover wished of you.

"I know, but isn't there anything you'd like to do?"

"What is there, except but to do as you desire? I only want to do what you desire, my beloved," he answered without reservation.

She frowned. "Tobias…my love. I want you to express your own desires. I want you to have a say in the things that we do," she said carefully.

He brushed through her hair with loving gentleness. "I am happy to be with you. To be by your side is all that I want." What more could he ask? To ask anything more would be asking too much.

Rain turned herself around on the chair and stood to face him, taking the hand that held the brush, and meeting his surprised eyes.

"Tobias, beloved. We cannot continue this way."

He was shocked and a nameless terror crept into his eyes. Quickly, she moved to stave the tide of his fears.

"I love you, but I want a lover not a servant. I do not want you to be submissive to me. I want you to express your mind, to tell me what you want. I want us to be equals, not dominated and dominator," she explained gently, trying to soothe him.

Dealing with him in this way was a delicate matter. She knew Ian's love had been contingent upon his submission, and that all of his other lovers had been some variation of the same dynamic. The only time she had known him to be different was when he was with Etienne. There she had seen his potential.

But Etienne had controlled Tobias in his own way by insisting upon his lover's domination. Tobias assumed the role that Etienne created for him and played the part. But after Etienne became a vampire, the entire framework of their relationship changed and Tobias fell back upon his old habits. Tobias had not been able to handle the change. Recognizing that he was no longer fitting the mold Etienne wished him to fill, he pulled away, all but abandoning his new fledgling. He did not realize this, of course, but Rain saw it easily. Etienne's departure had crushed his maker, destroying the fragile self-esteem and self-assurance Tobias had found. Now he was the needful soul once again, desperate for love and the thought of losing it drove him to panic. His recovery would be a long time in coming.

Trying to impress upon him that she wasn't going to leave him if he didn't yield to her constantly was difficult at best, but she had to try. His submissiveness was driving her insane.

"Now tell me, my beloved. What do you want to do? Speak your mind."

He had the look of a trapped animal in his eyes. "I don't want you to leave me!" he blurted, the brush falling from his numb fingers.

Firmly, she took his arms and held his gaze. *I am not going to leave you.*

I...I do not please you. I do not...

You do please me, Tobias. You do. I just want you to be my partner, my companion, she assured emphatically.

I'll be anything you want. Please love me, don't ever leave me, he begged silently, clutching her, trembling.

I love you. I love you. I've always loved you. I'm not going to leave you. You must believe me, she answered, holding him.

"Tell me what to do. Tell me. I'll do anything..."

She met his eyes steadily. "I want love of equals. Neither of us will dominate the other. Equals. Partners. Best friends. Do you understand?"

"Love of equals," he repeated slowly, nodding, swallowing hard.

"Yes. Love of equals," she intoned, stroking his hair.

He relaxed, nuzzling against her, and she sighed with relief. Another panic attack avoided.

"Now. Tell me what you would like to do."

"I would like..." he whispered softly, flicking his tongue across her ear. "...to make love with you."

Her heart sank. He always did this, he always brought it back to sex, to seduction: the one thing he undoubtedly knew how to do. He was irresistible in his seeming innocence, undeniable in his need. She found herself kissing him with as much passion as he, her hands running covetously over his shoulders as he picked her up and carried her to the mattress pallet. Dimly, she was aware that they had resolved nothing, but the urgency of the situation faded under the persistent tugging of his lips upon her flesh.

"Tell me about Andrea," she asked afterwards, when they were lying in bed together, and Tobias was calm and agreeable from their lovemaking.

He blinked at her, his mouth drawn. "Why?"

"I keep seeing her in your mind. She must have been very special to you."

Tobias looked away. "She was."

She placed her palm over his. "Then tell me about her. Share with me these memories that are so dear to you."

He sighed. "We met her in 1989, when Etienne and I were living in Pennsylvania. I was going by the alias of Adam Chandler. Eti was bored so we took some classes at Penn State University. She was a student there. She was a good friend. She meant almost as much to me as Etienne. I still hear her music."

She gave him a loving, tender look and smiled. "You loved her very much."

"Yes, I did. She knew what I was, and she still loved me."

"Show her to me. I would know her as well."

He nodded and reached for her, drawing her close so their heads were touching, then he opened his mind and let the images flow into her. The world tilted and swirled, and she was inside his memories, but not only his, but Etienne's and Andrea's as well.

It is best to tell this story from all points of view, my love. How better to know Andrea, than to see through her eyes? This is her legacy, all that is left of her, but she lives on in me, she heard Tobias tell her.

She agreed, understanding what he was about to do, and preparing for the shifts in point of view. The world dimmed, and when it cleared she found herself standing outside a classroom building at Penn State University in the winter of 1989…

• • •

Andrea watched with amusement as the two figures bustled into the classroom and found seats. They were trying not to draw undue attention to their late arrival, but she saw a few people turn their heads and smile knowingly at the well-known pair. Everyone knew Adam and Etienne. Well, everyone knew Adam, he seemed to make it a point to know everyone, or maybe it was the other way around, that everyone made it a point to know him, she wasn't sure. He certainly had a strange magnetism to him, it emanated from his youthful face and vibrant eyes, and it drew people to him like the Pied Piper. Everyone liked him, everyone wanted to be with him, but his only steady companion was the tall, dark blond-haired Etienne. Where there was Adam, there was almost certainly Etienne. The two men seemed attached to each other, almost physically, as if neither could exist without the other nearby. She had never seen the brown-haired man without the taller blond tagging along. 'Young lovers,' she thought to herself. 'Still marveling in the mystery of each other and afraid to miss a moment of each other's lives.' It brought a small smile to her lips.

Her attention was drawn back to the slow, monotone of the professor by the shuffling of papers on the desk. The elderly man was sifting through a stack of assignments, muttering to himself as he was wont to do.

"Now you all know from your syllabus that there will be a group project as part of your final grade…" The class let out a groan. "Oh, now don't groan, group skills are important in the real world…" The class let out another groan and the professor cut short his diatribe. "Now, since I know it would have taken you at least half the time allotted to you for the project just to choose who you will be working with, I have taken the liberty of doing it for you. I have also given you your topics to save time as well. So now there will be no excuses about not being able to find partners or suitable topics. There will be no extensions, and I expect these projects to be complete and written according to my instructions to the letter. You will have to the end of the semester to turn them in, but you may turn them in early if you wish. HA!" the professor snorted.

"He really is a miserable old bat, isn't he?" the young man sitting next to Andrea whispered hoarsely.

Andrea giggled softly and murmured in answer, "That's what happens to old political science majors, they live long and phosphor."

The young man chuckled and flashed her a brilliant smile. She smiled back.

"Now the group lists are here at the front of the room. Come up and find out who your partners in crime are and congregate in your groups. I will then hand out your assignments and you will have the rest of the class to grumble over them."

Andrea waited until most of the class had already inspected the assignment sheet before going up herself. She saw Etienne go up and return to Adam with a smile on his face. They were now sitting next to each other as usual and she smiled wryly; the professor had been smart enough not to separate them. So he wasn't as dull witted and slow as he seemed to be. He had noticed how close the two were, but then how could anyone not have noticed? Finally she raised herself from her seat and walked to the front of the room. There were sixty students in the class and they had been split up into twenty groups of three. She scanned the paper for her name and was surprised to find it listed in the same group as the aforementioned pair. She shook her head slightly and laughed to herself. Then she turned around and looked at them. Her gaze was met by both sets of eyes: Adam's wide blue and Etienne's glittering hazel. Adam smiled secretly and whispered something in Etienne's ear as she approached. The blond immediately reached for the nearest desk and chair, and pulled it close to theirs, preparing her seat.

"Hi," she said shyly, smiling and sweeping back her long, copper hair from her forehead.

"Hello," Adam answered, his voice soft.

"I guess I'm your partner in crime," she noted, mimicking the professor's words.

"I guess you are," Etienne replied, smiling as Adam made a small chuckle and cast him a private glance.

"I'm Andrea." She extended her hand. Etienne reached forward and shook her hand warmly.

"Etienne Turac."

"Etienne, that's Steven in French, isn't it?"

The dark blond-haired man nodded. "Yeah. My dad's American, but my mom is French."

"Can I call you Stevie instead?"

Etienne grinned. "Sure."

"And I am Adam. Please, join us," Adam offered smoothly, motioning to the chair next to Etienne.

"Thanks, I will, but I have to go get my back pack. I'll be right back."

He nodded almost imperceptibly as she went to retrieve her things and returned. While they waited for the professor to hand them their assignment, Andrea took the time to study the two men. She had never been this close to the infamous Adam or his consort, and she tried to stare without really staring, making idle chit chat while she let her eyes take in the sight of both of them. Adam was something to look at, his face was young and smooth, a young man with a generous head of shimmering brown curls that gave off sparks of rainbow colors when the light hit it at certain angles. His skin was pale, his facial bones well defined and there was a warm ruddiness to his cheeks. His eyes seemed too large for his face, wide and innocent, and a vivid blue that reflected light and shadow. He had clothed his slender body in a navy blue, loose cable knit sweater, a pair of crisp blue denim jeans, and black leather docksides. He had his long, delicate hands neatly folded on the desk, the fingers were thin and beautifully sculpted and his nails gave off a faint iridescence. Everything about him was neat and clean, a perfectionist down to the smooth, precise sweep of his hand along his arm to brush off a stray piece of lint.

'Damn, he's handsome. It's almost a shame he's gay. What was it Tricia always told me? All the good ones are either married or gay.'

She almost sighed, but then she saw him looking at her with his gentle, knowing eyes, and she suddenly got the distinct impression that he had just read her mind.

She could feel the heat rushing to her cheeks and she quickly looked away to study Etienne. He was taller and older looking. She guessed that maybe he was twenty-five or thirty. He had sharp angles to his face and high cheekbones. His hair was an unruly brush of dark blond atop a thin, lanky body, and his eyes were a bright hazel that sparkled with fire. He was more rough and unkempt than his immaculate counterpart; there was a shadow of stubble on his cheeks and his clothes were well worn. He was dressed very much like his companion, a loose sweater in tones of green and blue, and a pair of faded jeans. He seemed almost out of place next to the perfect figure seated so closely to him, the arms of their sweaters touching comfortably. Out of place, that is, until Adam looked at him, then it was obvious that he was exactly where he belonged. He was a balance to Adam, the imperfect reality next to unreal perfection, and Andrea suddenly realized that Adam needed him, Etienne was the one who kept him sane.

'Almost a shame this one is gay too, but they suit each other well.'

Again, she felt Adam's eyes on her and she thought she heard him laugh softly, and she looked up to see him gazing intently at her, a sweet smile on his lips. She blushed and his expression softened to one of almost sheepishness, somewhat apologetic, as if he couldn't help himself. She was about to say something when the shadow of the professor cast over them. The old man was looking at Adam with a wry smile and a twinkle of amusement in his eyes as he handed the assignment sheet to him.

"I wouldn't have dreamed of splitting up you two lovebirds. Just make sure you get this project done and don't spend all your time just looking stupidly at each other."

Andrea laughed. "Don't worry, Dr. Lenley, I won't let them stare at each other for more than a few hours at a time."

"I'm counting on it. That's why I put you with these two. You're the most levelheaded student in the class. You'll keep their minds on their work and not...on other things."

She laughed again. "You don't know me very well, Dr. Lenley, but I'll try."

The old man nodded and toddled off to the next group.

"So what subject did he decide to torture us with?" she asked as Adam showed the assignment sheet to Etienne.

Etienne leaned back so she could read it as well and her eyes darkened. "Sixteenth Century Germany? That's a direct slight at you, Adam."

Andrea was referring to a previous class period when Adam had vehemently argued with Dr. Lenley about the political strategy and policies in Renaissance Europe, particularly in Germany. The professor had gotten quite upset at Adam's point of argument and obviously he remembered his earlier displeasure. By giving Adam this particular subject to research, he was essentially throwing all Adam had said back into his face. He was telling Adam to prove his points in writing and research or to shut up. This angered Andrea. University was supposed to be an open discussion of all theories and a free exchange of ideas; the broadening of the mind, not the soapbox for one bitter old man to push his viewpoints unchallenged on all his students. She looked at Adam, expecting to see a similar anger reflected in him, but his face was calm and serene.

"I know what he is trying to do. It does not concern me," Adam answered nonchalantly. "I know what I say to be true and I will prove it to him. He will be the one..." He thought for a moment, trying to remember the phrase. "...eating crow."

Andrea had to smile. She was starting to understand why so many people were enamored with this young man. She was starting to like him very much already.

"Well, I know we have quite a bit of time to do this…project, but I'm one of those people that doesn't like to let things slide, so I'd like to get started on it right away. If you'd like, I'll do the preliminary research tomorrow or Friday after class," she offered.

"No no. This is our project, we will do it together. We will help you with the preliminary research," Adam insisted.

"I'm afraid I can only work at night. I work in the afternoon and I sleep most of the morning."

"That's okay. We are on much the same schedule," Etienne told her. "How about we agree to meet somewhere tomorrow night to start on this?"

"Sure, sounds great. I have chem. lab tomorrow until ten, how about you meet me in Whitmore? I'm in lab 215."

"That would be acceptable," the brown-haired gentleman replied.

"Great, it's settled then." She looked around for the professor. "I wonder if he'd let us leave early, or if we need to waste the remaining fifteen minutes of class grumbling about this project."

"I think it would be all right to leave. Rather, I don't think he will stop you from leaving," Adam answered.

"Well, if you think he won't have a conniption, I'll take my leave."

"We will stay and make sure he does not have a…conniption. I'm sure we can find something to do with ourselves for the remaining class time," Adam assured.

"We'll just sit here and stare stupidly at each other," Etienne quipped with a grin.

Andrea laughed. "Okay then. I'm outta here. I think I can miss seeing you two stare stupidly at each other, besides I'm hungry. I'm gonna go nab some food then go home and get warm. I hate East Coast winters, they get so damn cold so fast. It's not even Halloween yet and it's already freezing. We'll have snow soon, I'm sure of it."

Adam smiled. "Yes, but I like the snow."

"Yeah, me too, from inside a nice warm house. Not when I have to go trudging off to class in it. Take care, I'll see you tomorrow at ten. 215 Whitmore."

"We'll be there. Have a good night," Etienne said as she stood to gather her coat.

"Yep, I will. See you tomorrow," she replied, putting on her coat and scarf. "Nite."

"Good night," Adam spoke softly, smiling one last time at her.

She smiled back, slung her book bag over one shoulder and headed out the door.

The following evening they met her after her class and headed to the library to begin their research.

Ten

So you met her by chance, Rain commented.

Yes. If the professor had not preassigned the groups for the project, we would never have had cause to spend any time with her, Tobias replied. *I never thanked the old man for that. I think I probably should have.*

Please. Go on. Tell me more.

We met in the library on the following night. Andrea was doing research on the computer system, looking for reference materials...

• • •

Etienne watched his lover with awe as they worked in Pattee Library the following night. It always amazed him how easily Tobias could pass himself off as human; maybe it really was true that people were blind. Andrea smiled at him and touched him easily. He knew Tobias loved it: Tobias, his vampire lover. Andrea had no idea that the man she knew as Adam wasn't human at all. She was just as enamored with him as all the other mortals Tobias smiled at, completely oblivious to her own danger. He cocked his head and examined Andrea more carefully. She had long, lustrous copper hair and flashing blue eyes. Her face was delicate and fine boned, in fact everything about her was fine boned. Fragile, much like a butterfly, and she moved with grace and balance. He saw her laugh at something Tobias had said and rub him between his shoulders. Ah! Tobias loved it when mortals touched him, he must be in heaven right now.

'Don't you know what you are touching?' he wanted to shout at Andrea. 'He is dead and has been dead for five hundred years. He walks and talks and charms the pants of anyone he meets, but he isn't human.

He is standing right in front of you and you still cannot see that he is not one of us.'

No, she can't. Mortals are so easy to fool, Tobias' soft voice pierced his mind, sweet and seductive as always.

Tobias walked towards him, that same sinewy grace and fluid motion.

Why so melancholy, Eti? Tobias asked, smiling gently and kissing Etienne on the cheek.

Etienne shrugged and rested his forehead on Tobias' shoulder, nuzzling the white neck affectionately. He felt Tobias' arms enclose around him and the cool lips search for his. Tobias kissed him with passion, making Etienne swoon, then the same cool lips moved to his neck, resting against the throbbing vein, teasing him with the promise of the bite but not fulfilling it.

Etienne groaned. *Yes.*

Not yet. Later.

No, now. Spirit me to a dark corner of this dusty library and take me.

Later, Eti. There is work to do.

Etienne whimpered in frustration as Tobias pulled his lips away, slowly, agonizingly. *God! You have complete power over me.*

Hush. Calm yourself. Now is not the time for these things.

"You two are so cute," Andrea's voice broke in. "You're so much in love. How long have you been together? Two months? Three?"

"Seven years," Tobias replied, gently releasing Etienne and moving to stand beside him, his arm still around his lover's slender shoulders.

Andrea looked shocked. "Seven years? Adam, you don't look older than twenty!"

"I am much older than I look. I am cursed with such a youthful appearance. In fact, I am older than Etienne."

It seemed that she would press the subject, but Tobias gave her a steady stare, impressing his will upon her.

Perfectly normal, all that you see and all that I say.

She seemed confused for a moment, then shook her head slightly and smiled. He smiled back. Yes, so easy to fool them.

"Seven years. I don't believe it. You act like star-struck teenagers. What's your secret?"

"Love, Andrea. Just love and patience. Etienne takes a lot of patience."

Andrea laughed as Etienne rolled his eyes. Tobias nuzzled his cheek and kissed his temple lovingly.

"Have you found something?" he asked Andrea.

"Yes, come see. I think I've found several useful articles."

Tobias' eyes lit up with curiosity and he followed Andrea to the computer screen she had been working on. Etienne lagged behind, choosing to watch Tobias rather than participate.

Seven years. Seven years of his life spent with this vampire who said he loved him. And Tobias did love him, he knew that, and he knew that he loved Tobias. But Tobias' love was the agape love only a god could have. No matter how Etienne strayed, no matter what he said or did, Tobias forgave him, Tobias still loved him. Tobias would do anything for him, even fit himself into the mold Etienne had created for him, being whatever Etienne wanted him to be. He had seen Tobias change so much over the years, becoming more independent and sure of himself.

He knew that, in many ways, Tobias was just imitating the examples his lover set before him, altering his behavior to suit what he thought was expected of him. He was an actor, playing a part, and doing it well. Anyone who did not know the vampire would not realize that his strong, self-sufficient demeanor was merely a façade. Etienne had seen that façade crumble on many occasions, seen Tobias' self-assurance fade into dependant uncertainty the moment he stepped out of his comfort zone. Etienne prided himself in pushing Tobias to his limits, in forcing him out of that comfort zone time and time again, but there was nothing Etienne could do to shake his lover's unwavering devotion. Well, nothing that Etienne was willing to do, that is. He was certain he could lose favor with his lover if he were to break all the rules that so tightly bound him. If he were to reveal Tobias' true name. Tobias would probably kill him then. Maybe he would be better off.

No, liebchen. I would be displeased and I would probably punish you if you did such a thing, but I could never ever hurt you. I would explain your error away if anyone heard. Mortals will believe anything I say if I want them to.

Etienne jolted. He still wasn't used to the fact that Tobias could easily read his thoughts. Even after seven years, the sweet, seductive voice whispering in his head still shocked him.

What would you do to punish me? Take me over your knee and spank me? he replied mischievously, one eyebrow arched.

Tobias' eyes met his and he smiled wryly.

Perhaps. But I guarantee, if I were to spank you, you would not like it.

Sticks and stones may break my bones, but whips and chains excite me.

The blue eyes opened wide, registering the shock, then he grinned, not enough to show his fang teeth, but enough to express his humor.

Shall I shackle you to the bed now, liebchen, when we make love?

Ooo, sounds interesting. Will you use feathered handcuffs?

This time Tobias did laugh and it caught Andrea's attention.

"Hey, we're supposed to be working here. Will you two quit staring stupidly at each other. I've got articles we could be reviewing!"

"You do spend an inordinate amount of time staring at me," Etienne agreed, smiling.

"I can't help it. You are indescribably beautiful to me. I love looking at you," came Tobias' love-filled reply.

'God, he's shameless. What did I ever do to be worthy of such unconditional love?'

You are my beloved. My dear one. Without you by my side, I would die from loneliness.

"Hey, hey! You're doing it again! I hereby declare no staring at each other for twenty minutes. Okay guys? Or we'll be here all damn night," Andrea complained indignantly.

"Okay, okay," Etienne conceded, coming to sit beside them in front of the computer. Tobias happily put his arm around his shoulder.

"Good, that's better. Now pay attention. We're going to have to write down all these articles and go look them up. Some will be in the stacks and others will be on microfilm. We'll print it all out for now and do the searching another night, okay?" Andrea informed.

"Okay," Tobias agreed.

"That way you two can go and stare stupidly at each other in the privacy of your own home."

"Of course," Tobias quipped.

Andrea grinned and sent her search list to the printer. A few minutes later, papers in hand, they left Pattee Library and went their separate ways.

Over the next few weeks, the three became good friends. They were known in class as Andrea and the terrible twosome, and now Dr. Lenley had three openly dissenting students instead of one. He was not amused. They began spending most of their nights together, sitting in the living room of Andrea's fourth floor apartment, talking, laughing, playing games, and every now and then they would work on their project. They would get into long discussions about politics. Andrea hated politicians. It often made them wonder why she was a political science major when she hated politics so much. Often Etienne would opt for an opposing viewpoint, just to antagonize her. They had heated arguments about President Reagan and Bush. One night while they were headed to Andrea's apartment, Etienne commented that he thought Reagan's Presidency was on par with FDR's term. He did it to get her hackles up. It worked.

"You're joking, right?" she asked, falling into step beside him.

"No. Look at the amount of Bills Reagan passed through Congress. He was one busy man."

"Busy ruining this country. Did you see all that he did? He dismantled our entire regulation system on manufacturers and companies, and Bush is following in his footsteps," she snorted.

"Who needs regulations anyway?"

"We do! We need them to keep down pollution and waste and the loss of our natural resources. If Teddy Roosevelt hadn't started the National Parks program, the timber companies would have cut down almost all the forests in the West by now," Andrea argued. "Isn't that right, Adam?"

Adam raised an eyebrow and shrugged slowly. "I am not certain. I have not been a student of politics for very long."

"Thanks for the back up, Adam," she grumbled.

"You're welcome. I think."

"Reagan was interested in conservation and the environment. Look at what he did with the EPA," Etienne offered.

"Oh come on, Etienne! Reagan was a patsy for big business and Bush is just like him! Reagan didn't give a shit about the environment! He's an actor. They told him what to say and he said it!"

"Maybe so, but he sure knew how to play the part. And ever notice how much he looks like Bob's Big Boy?"

Andrea fumed, her face turning almost the same shade as her hair, and she clenched her fists.

"Ooohhhh! Go play in traffic, Stevie!"

She knew her comment would make them laugh but she hadn't expected Adam to be so taken with it. He erupted suddenly into peals of laughter, stopping in mid-stride and grabbing his sides as he shook with mirth. Andrea and Etienne turned to watch him, surprised.

"Go play in traffic, Stevie!" he repeated through his giggles, and went reeling off into hysterics again. He grabbed a lamppost for support and laughed heartily, his glee infecting the others and soon they were all laughing.

"Oh, come on, Adam. It was funny, but it wasn't that funny!" Andrea chided.

The brown-haired young man looked at her, his eyes dancing with joy. "Go play in traffic, Andie!"

"Oooohhhh! You go play in traffic!" she shot back.

Adam laughed again, released the lamppost and came towards her, his arms open. He embraced her lovingly, still giggling.

"I love you, Andrea. You always make me laugh. What would Etienne and I do without you?"

"Spend all our time staring stupidly at each other, instead of working on our project," Etienne quipped with a smile, coming close.

Adam looked at him happily, taking one arm from around Andrea and putting it around Etienne, and then kissing him sweetly on the cheek.

"Go play in traffic, Stevie," he chortled, snickering again.

They laughed again and continued down the street to Andrea's apartment. Go play in traffic, Stevie. It became their mantra.

The following Wednesday only Etienne came to class and Adam's absence was highly conspicuous. Even Professor Lenley raised an eyebrow at the empty seat next to the blond man. Etienne's face was drawn and sullen throughout class, and he periodically cast furtive glances at the door. After the lecture, Andrea went to him and put a hand on his shoulder.

"Where is he?" she asked gently.

"Dunno. We fought, he ran off, or I ran off, or something like that."

"C'mon, let's go to Zeno's. We'll get some food, have a few drinks and maybe you'll feel better. No sense in stewing, it will only make it worse."

"Yeah, you're right."

Etienne stood and Andrea put an arm around his shoulder. They walked down to Zeno's and sat talking over sandwiches and drinks. Andrea was a little alarmed at how heavily and quickly Etienne drank. She watched him down three Screwdrivers in less than an hour.

"You're drinking pretty heavily," she commented as he guzzled a fourth.

"I'm in a Vodka mood. This isn't Stoli though, Stoli is the best."

"What happened between you two? Monday night you were all lovey-dovey, tonight you're Hatfield and McCoy?"

Etienne sighed. "It's complicated."

"It always is, isn't it? Relationships aren't easy."

"Tell me about it." He fingered the empty glass and hailed the waitress for another. The young blond cast a worried glance at Andrea.

"It's okay. I'll take care of him. He can drink himself into a stupor if he wants to," she told the waitress. The girl nodded and went off to fetch another Screwdriver. Andrea returned her attention to the young man sitting across from her. "So? Want to talk about it?"

"Not really."

"Okay, so sit there and pickle your brain. See if I care."

Etienne sighed. "I'm sorry. He's just got me so upset. You don't know what he does to me. He gets me wound up tighter than Bo Derek's corn rows."

Andrea laughed. "What a metaphor!"

"Yeah. But it's true."

"What did he do?"

Etienne shook his head. "I can't talk about it."

"It's okay. I won't tell him anything."

"You don't have to. He gets into my head. I can't lie to him and I can't keep anything from him. Best if I just keep my mouth shut."

"Okay. Do what you think is best."

The waitress placed the Screwdriver on the table. Etienne reached for it, his eyes misty and contemplative.

"Andie, do you believe in the supernatural?"

"What do you mean?"

"I mean, do you believe in ghosts and spirits and demons and stuff like that?"

"I believe in the possibility of their being."

"Do you believe in vampires?"

Andrea chuckled. "You mean the blood sucking kind?"

"Yes."

"Absolutely. They're everywhere. They're called lawyers nowadays, and politicians, but most politicians are lawyers anyway."

At least it got a small laugh out of him, but the reprieve was brief.

"No, I mean real vampires. Vampires that live forever and kill people."

She thought for a moment. "I dunno. Never really thought about it. I guess anything is possible. There are a lot of things on this Earth that we don't know about or understand. Vampires have been the object of legend for centuries, I suppose there could be some truth to the old tales. Do you think they exist?"

He paused, his eyes crossing, and downed his drink. The waitress came to see if he wanted a sixth.

"Just bring a pitcher. Relationship problems," Andrea explained.

"Oh, I know all about that, honey. I'll bring a big pitcher," she replied, patting Etienne on the shoulder. "Poor baby. And you're cute too. Girl doesn't know what she's missing."

They said nothing as she walked away.

"Thanks," Etienne muttered.

"No problem. So, do you think vampires exist?"

He didn't answer until the waitress returned with the pitcher. "Yes."

"Really?"

"Yeah. I do. Do you think they're evil?"

"I dunno. Do you?"

"I used to, but I don't anymore."

"Why is that?"

He took a big gulp from his glass and cleared his throat. "Wow. Bartender made this batch strong."

"Seeing pink elephants yet?"

"Nope, but there's a whole herd of you now, and you refuse to sit still."

"I think you are fast reaching your vodka limit."

Etienne snorted. "I haven't even begun to drink. It is my goal in life to drink so much alcohol that when I die and they cremate me, the fire will last six days."

Andrea couldn't help herself, she burst out laughing. "Go play in traffic, Stevie."

He grinned drunkenly. "I would, but I don't think I can stand anymore."

"You'll have to crawl up to your apartment."

"Nah, I'll just find a bench somewhere and sleep it off."

"Adam won't be happy about that."

"Screw him. I don't care."

Andrea frowned. "Yes, you do," she scolded gently.

Etienne sighed and stared sadly into his drink. "You're right. I do. I love him. He drives me crazy, but I still love him."

She reached out her hand and placed it over his, feeling the tremors that raced through his fingers. 'He is really gone. I'm surprised he's even coherent with all the alcohol in him. His brain must be drowning.'

"Adam has a lot of needs. He's a very complex person. I can see that in him. He needs you desperately. You're his anchor to reality."

"Adam doesn't need me. He keeps me around because he hates to be alone."

"That's not true. He loves you. He loves you so much."

He shook his head, drinking again. "No. He doesn't love me. He doesn't need me. That's why he tortures me like he does."

"You're torturing yourself. Look how drunk you are! That is torture! Adam lavishes affection on you. He buys you everything you could ever need or want. He fawns over you like a lovesick puppy. How can you say he does not love you?"

"All a charade, Andie. All a charade."

"I don't believe that. You're drunk out of your mind. He loves you. He'd go to Hell and back if it meant you'd smile at him. Which is something you haven't been doing lately. If there is anyone whose love should be questioned here, it's yours."

Etienne hid his face in his free hand. "No, no. I love him. I love him though he hurts me so. I can't live without him. He's my life."

"Then why do you do this to each other? Why do you do this to yourself? If you love each other so much, why do you fight like this? It's silly. Go home, tell him how much you love him, lay him down, fuck his brains out and stop hurting each other."

"I can't. I can't. There is so much you don't know, Andie. So much I can't tell you. He isn't normal. I'm not normal. Our whole relationship is like something you have never seen before nor will again."

He was raving but at least he stopped drinking. Andrea just hoped he wouldn't start throwing up before she could get him back to her apartment. She wanted to keep him talking, what he was saying was intriguing. She wondered what he meant by saying Adam wasn't normal. She had always thought the brown-haired man was a little otherworldly.

"It doesn't matter. I know love when I see it, no matter what form it comes in. Come on, let's go back to my place. You can sleep this off on my couch and that way you'll be safe. I'll call Adam and he'll be there when you wake up."

"No! Don't call him! Just let me be. I'll go home when I can," he cried, suddenly afraid.

"Yes. This may not be a big city but you aren't safe on the streets here. I'd never forgive myself if something happened to you after I let you leave here. Adam will be beside himself with worry. He isn't going to be mad at you. He loves you. Now stop being a blithering drunk and come with me," she insisted, tugging on his hand.

Without warning, Etienne started to sob. He pulled his hand from beneath Andrea's and cupped it over his face. "No! No! I can't! You mustn't tell him! He'll be so angry that I've told you as much as I have! You don't know. You don't know what he does to me. He's got me so messed up inside I don't know what to do. But I love him. I love him, and that's the worst of it!" he insisted.

"Etienne, stop this. Adam would cut off his own head before he hurt you. You aren't being rational anymore. Come on, stop your sobbing and come home with me."

"I can't."

"You can and you will. Now come on, before I have someone carry you."

"Oh, Andie, you don't know what you are getting into, being with me. You have no idea the position you are putting yourself in! You don't know what I am, Andie," he blurted, weeping. "If you knew, you'd run screaming out of this place and never want to see me or Adam again."

Stunned, Andrea was quiet for a moment, watching him cry. She ached to reach out to him, to get him to open up to her, so she would know what this was all about.

"No, I wouldn't. I know what you are. You're gay, and I don't care."

"No, you don't. You don't," he insisted, and dropped his head to the table, sobbing loudly, attracting attention. Andrea decided to humor him.

"Then tell me. What are you?"

"I am...I am..."

"Etienne!" came Adam's sharp voice, laced with anger and concern.

Andrea jerked her head to see him. He was standing by the table; she hadn't seen or heard him approach. He was just...there. Etienne lifted up to look at him, his cheeks streaked with tears. The sharp movement made him dizzy and his eyes crossed. When he focused back on his lover, his pupils were dilated with terror.

Andrea looked at Etienne and then at Adam. Something was very wrong with what she was seeing. Adam was dressed entirely in black, only excentuating the pallor of his white skin, and there was an otherworldly light in his eyes. He moved almost too fast as he grabbed Etienne's arm and steadied him as Etienne nearly fell over. Etienne recoiled, obviously petrified and with good reason. Adam was angry. Andrea had never seen Adam angry. Nothing he did overtly showed his anger, but she could feel it emanating from him. Etienne shook violently with fear, the tears still streaming from his eyes. He locked gazes with Adam for long moments and it seemed some silent communication was passing between them, something Andrea was not privy to. Whatever it was, Etienne stopped shaking and his fear subsided. Suddenly, he reached out with his arms and tried to stand, his legs barely holding him up. He fell against Adam's chest with a sob, hugging him tightly. Adam's face softened with love and he held Etienne close. Andrea saw him nuzzle Etienne's blond hair, his eyes closed, his face suffused with relief, and kiss Etienne's temple. Then his mouth traveled down to Etienne's neck, half his face being hidden by Etienne's hair, and let his lips settle against the pulsing skin. Andrea saw

Etienne stiffen and all the hair on her neck rose. Something very important was going on. After a moment, Etienne let out a deep sigh and Adam lifted his head, pressing his cheek to Etienne's hair. His eyes opened and he gazed calmly at Andrea.

"Thank you for watching over him," he whispered, yet she heard him perfectly.

"It's okay. He's had a lot to drink."

"I know."

He released Etienne gently, letting the tall man lean against him for support and fished out his wallet. He drew out several twenties and gave them to Andrea.

"For the bill."

She stared at the money. "Oh, no Adam, this is way too much."

"Keep it. I must get him home."

Before she could object, Adam took hold of Etienne, lovingly but firmly, and led him from the table. "I thank you again. We will see you Friday for class, and we will work on our project then as well."

"Okay, call me if you need anything," she murmured, meeting his steady gaze. His eyes drew her out of herself, and she was disoriented for a moment just looking at him.

Adam smiled. "Thank you, Andrea. You are such a good friend. Thank you. We will see you Friday. Good night."

"Good night."

She watched them leave, then stood and met the eyes of the stunned waitress. She had to stop herself from laughing as the blond saw Etienne clinging tightly to Adam; the crushed look on her face was almost too funny. She smiled sheepishly and shrugged.

"You know what they say. All the good ones are either married...or gay," she said almost apologetically.

The waitress glanced forlornly at her, then shook her head and went into the kitchen. Andrea laughed softly, placed two twenties on table for the check and tip and left Zeno's herself.

Eleven

What happened after the night at Zeno's? Did she ever question you or Etienne about it? Rain asked, interrupting the visions.

No. She never did.

And your project?

She heard Tobias' mental laughter clearly.

We finished the project on time and even handed it in a few days early. The whole paper was nearly 80 pages long. It looked like a thesis. Professor Lenley was so surprised. Most of my points had been confirmed and supported with our research and Lenley had to concede that I had been at least partially right. He gave us an excellent grade, but I was happy knowing that Lenley was the one…eating crow.

Now she chuckled. *What happened then?*

The class ended in mid-December, but we remained close friends. We still met almost every night. Andrea became our partner at any shows or movies we attended. She also became a mediator between us when we were fighting. Usually one of us would go to her, unhappy and upset, and she would listen patiently. Then she would bring us together again, get us talking to each other, and finally, get us to make up. She had a talent for smoothing the waters and promoting communication between us. I forget how many times she stood between us, talking in her gentle, even voice. She could get us to agree on anything. By the end of the night we would be cuddling contentedly in each other's arms again.

That must have been a full time job for her, she teased.

She felt his chagrin and smiled to herself.

It wasn't until after Christmas that we really learned anything about her. Although she admitted that she had family in California, she did not fly home for Christmas. Instead she spent her Christmas with us, exchanging gifts and whiling away the evening at our apartment. We were on our best behavior to please her. No fighting for the entire holiday season. Then she didn't go home for New Year's and that made us wonder. We spent New Years Eve with her, keeping her company and playing Trivial Pursuit until it was time to watch Dick Clark announce the New Year...

• • •

"Have you ever gone to Time's Square for New Year's, Andie?" Etienne asked as they turned on the TV.

"Once or twice. I didn't like it. Too many drunk people."

"We went last year. It was entertaining, but you are right, too many people who have had far too much to drink," Adam commented.

"Yeah. This is much better. A quiet New Year with my two best friends, safe and warm and dry. Can't beat it. Except maybe if we were in Florida where it's hot. My thin California blood hates the cold here."

"How come you never go back to California to visit your folks? You always talk about them, but you never go," Etienne inquired innocently.

Andrea paused from cleaning up the coffee cups. Once again, Adam had left his cup for Etienne to drink, the dark brown liquid left untouched. A shadow fell over her pretty face; his question disturbed her more than she thought it would. She glanced wistfully at her keyboards, her guitar.

"I'm in exile."

"Oh, I see. Don't get along, huh? I know how that feels," Etienne commented.

"Oh, no. It's not like that. They would love to see me and I'd love to go home. It's that I can't, at least not yet."

"Why not?"

She bowed her head and sighed. "You see. I'm in hiding. I'm not what I appear to be. I'm not a political science major, in fact I hate the whole subject…"

Etienne snickered. "I'm not surprised to hear you say that, with the way you carry on about politicians."

"Why are you in hiding, Andrea?" Adam asked, his curiosity piqued.

Andrea took a deep breath, settling herself for the memories and pain, and began telling her story quickly, to get it over with.

"Four years ago, I was in a band. We were pretty popular, actually. Then I started dating this guy named Louis. I didn't know he was a homicidal psychopath when I met him, but I soon found out. One night he beat me senseless and left me for dead. I lived and testified against him in court. He was found guilty and sentenced to five years in prison for aggravated assault. He swore on the day that they convicted him, that he would hunt me down and kill me when he got out. The police didn't take him seriously, but I did. So last year when Louis came up for parole, I did a disappearing act. I dropped the band, which was my life, and came here to Penn State to hide. I took up political science because it is as far away from music and dance as I can get, and he is less likely to find me."

The two men were stunned and silent for a few moments.

"Wow," Etienne breathed, breaking the eerie quiet.

"So your family doesn't know where you are?" Adam asked, concerned.

"My dad knows and a couple of my closest friends know, but no one else. I thought it best that only a very few people know my whereabouts. Louis is up for parole; they could let him out any day. I'm laying very low for now, until he does something stupid and gets himself thrown back into jail."

"Smart choice," Etienne commented.

"Yeah, well, I've already had my brains rearranged once in my lifetime, I think I can do without a second."

They laughed nervously.

"Hey, don't sweat it, guys. I guess you never would have thought I wasn't a natural redhead."

"Oh?" Adam asked, smiling.

"Yeah, I'm a natural blonde," she answered with a laugh. "But at least as a redhead people don't treat me like I'm stupid."

She grinned at them then turned her attention to the television. It was almost midnight. Quickly, she popped open a bottle of champagne and poured three glasses just as the apple was about to fall.

"Okay, here it comes! Five! Four! Three! Two! One! Happy New Year!"

They toasted and Andrea and Etienne downed their glasses.

"Here, can't let good champagne go to waste," Etienne said as he took Adam's glass and drank it.

"Don't drink alcohol, either, eh, Adam?" Andrea asked, smiling.

"Unfortunately, no," came the smooth reply.

"That's okay. I still love you," she answered, kissing him on the cheek.

Then she kissed Etienne. "You two are the best friends a girl could ever have. I'm so happy to be with you tonight. I wish for 1990 to be as wonderful as 1989 has been."

They put their arms around her, a happy huddle of three, hugging, kissing, laughing. Later Etienne would look back on that night and remember it as one of the happiest nights of his life.

Andrea's classes started again in January. This time, Adam and Etienne were not taking any, but they still met her at least three nights out of the week, usually arriving just as her Chemistry lab was ending. The terrible twosome, come to escort her home. Andrea felt like she was the safest woman in State College, not because her escorts were so formidable, but because being with them made her feel protected. Adam truly wasn't afraid of anything, except losing Etienne that is, and it made her fearless too. She often wondered why he was so nocturnal and so pale. Sometimes watching him made her dizzy, but then he'd smile at her and everything would be all right again.

One night in late January, they arrived a few minutes early, just as Andrea was completing an experiment. They hovered around her workstation, watching her intently.

"Okay, guys, just let me finish this and then we'll be free to go," Andrea said, reading the thermometer in the water bath again.

Adam curiously inspected the complex arrangement of flasks and glass tubes interconnected with rubber joints. "You look like an alchemist," he mused.

"Yep, I'm turning benzene into gold," she quipped with a smile.

Just then a small, slight figure came up behind Andrea and tapped her on the shoulder. Andrea turned around and was speechless for a moment before she let out a whoop of glee, and hugged the woman.

"Tricia!"

"Hey, Andie!"

"Ohmigod! Tricia, I can't believe it's really you!"

"In the flesh!"

Andrea laughed happily. "Oh! It's so good to see you! You must meet my friends!" She faced her friends, her eyes bright with joy. "Adam, Etienne, this is Tricia, one of my best friends from back home! Trish, this is Adam and Etienne, my partners in crime."

"Hi there," Tricia greeted.

"Hello, pleased to meet you," Adam replied as Etienne moved to shake her hand.

Tricia was small and thin with wavy, shoulder length brown hair and brown eyes. She had a broad, toothy smile and a mischievous glint in her eyes. Her clothes were casual and comfortable: a big knit sweater, jeans and boots.

"So, Andie, if I light a match to this contraption will the whole building blow up?" Tricia asked, eyeing the apparatus.

"No," Andrea answered with a giggle.

"Damn."

"Trish!"

Tricia laughed again, a warm hearty laugh that was contagious. Etienne laughed along, but then he noticed that his lover was gazing at this new person very intently.

What is it? he asked, concerned.

I don't know, liebchen. Something is wrong with her heart. I can hear it. It beats irregularly. I am not sure of the cause.

Etienne frowned, but neither woman seemed to notice. Andrea had finished her experiment and was hastily dismantling her apparatus.

"As soon as I clean up, we're out of here. God! I can't believe it's really you! How did you find me?"

"Your dad gave me your address and class schedule."

"God bless Daddy! How long will you be staying?"

"Just for tonight. Then I'm off to Florida."

"Oh! Take me with you! It's so awfully cold here! I miss the California sunshine!" Andrea begged, putting her things swiftly away.

"Here Andie, I'll wash your glassware for you, help you out," Etienne offered.

"Oh, Stevie, thank you! God, I'm so excited! You must tell me all about what's going on with the band and all the old gang," Andrea blurted. "We'll go to Zeno's from here and get some dinner, and then we'll go back to my place and catch up on everything."

"Sounds great to me. I just got here an hour ago, so I haven't had time to eat. Just checked into my hotel."

"Where are you staying?"

"The Sheraton on Pugh."

"Oh yes! I know that hotel. Very nice."

"Yeah."

"So, Tricia, are you from California like Andie?" Adam asked.

"Yeah. Andie and I grew up together. We went to the same school, played in the same band."

"Oh! I can't wait to get back to my apartment. Adam, you'll finally get to hear a real musician play on my keyboards! Trish is a real wiz!"

"Oh, don't put yourself down, Andie, you're an accomplished musician too."

"Yeah, but no one can play the synth like you can. And you always had better synths than I did."

"Yeah, Michael bought me a Roland for Christmas."

"Wow! Nice!"

"Yeah, it is. Pretty advanced too. I like it a lot, it's rad," Tricia replied.

"Rad?" Adam repeated, leaping on a new word as he always did.

"Yeah, rad. Cool. Like, totally radical," Tricia explained. "Jeez, I sound like a Valley Girl."

"Ahh, I understand."

"Trish, Adam is one of the strangest people you will ever meet, but he's a great guy. You'll love him. He's a blast. So's Stevie-boy."

"Stevie-boy?" Etienne reiterated, feigning offense. "Want me to shatter all your glassware all over this nice, little sink?"

"Go play in traffic, Stevie," Andrea drawled.

Adam snickered and helped Etienne dry the glassware. In minutes the task was completed, and they were headed out to Zeno's. They got a table for four off in a secluded corner of the restaurant and perused the menus. Soon a waitress came to take their orders.

"What can I get for you folks tonight?"

"I'll have a mushroom and Swiss burger, no lettuce, no tomato, with fries and a coke," Andrea started.

"Okay, and you sir?" the waitress asked Etienne.

"Erm, give me the grilled chicken sandwich with mayo, fries and a coke. And a Screwdriver."

"You and your Screwdrivers, Etienne!" Andrea chided.

"And for you, miss?"

"Um, I'd like a baked potato with butter and sour cream, a bowl of your beef vegetable soup, a tall glass of orange juice…and water," Tricia answered.

"Okay. And you sir?"

"Nothing for me, thank you," Adam demurred.

"Really, Adam? Aren't you hungry?" Trish asked, concerned.

"He never gets anything. I swear he lives on love and air," Andrea mused.

"Well, the air part I can see. This is Happy Valley. You get all your minerals in one breath," Tricia joked.

They giggled.

"We shouldn't dally here. I want to get back to the apartment so you can play for us, Trish. You guys have got to hear this woman play. She could play circles around Elton John."

"Impressive," Adam commented.

Is her heart still bothering you? Etienne's mind voice asked.

Yes. It bothers me. Her heart is weak, it flutters like a bird trapped in a cage. Very strange. I do not know what is wrong, but I do know something, Tobias replied, his brow furrowed.

What is that?

She is dying.

Etienne paled and took a better look at Tricia. She did seem rather off. Her skin was pale, but her cheeks were flushed a deep rose. It could be the cold, but they had been inside for a while, they should have warmed by now. He looked at her fingernails and saw that the flesh underneath was bone white, which was also not a good sign. Also she was very thin, almost fragile looking, and her eyes were slightly sunken. He hadn't noticed it at first because of her warm, friendly manner. It caught him off guard. He observed her carefully as she talked animatedly with Andrea. Her personality was vibrant, her face very malleable and expressive, but he knew his lover wasn't lying and he wondered what it was that he sensed. He watched them talking until the food was delivered and they ate quickly. Afterwards they walked happily to Andrea's apartment where Tricia played the keyboards for them for almost two hours. It was after midnight when she stopped.

"Oh, that's enough for now. My fingers are getting cramped," she said, stepping out from behind the racks of synthesizers.

"Trish that was wonderful. You're still the best keyboard player I know," Andrea complemented.

"Excellent. You are truly talented," Adam added, genuinely entertained, but then Adam loved music of all kinds.

"I told you she could play circles around Elton John!"

"That she can," Adam agreed.

"Well, I dunno about anyone else, but I'm thirsty. Anyone for a soda?" Andrea asked, getting up from the couch.

"I'll take one," Etienne answered.

"Water for me," Tricia said.

"Okay, two sodas and one water. Don't worry Adam, I know you don't want anything. I know the routine," she smoothed, disappearing into the kitchen.

Tricia sat down on the leather recliner with a sigh.

"You really do play rather well," Adam told her after a few moments of comfortable silence.

"Thanks. I try to. I'm a bit out of practice."

"So am I, but I try to keep up with it. I want to be as good as you, someday," Andrea piped, slipping out of the kitchen carrying two cokes and a glass of ice water. She handed Tricia the glass, gave one of the sodas to Etienne and sat down next to Adam on the couch. Tricia drank deeply and then burped.

"Oh! Excuse me! It must have been that soup I had at Zeno's. It had peppers in it," she apologized.

"Yeah, must be," Andrea concurred. "Zeno's food is okay. I don't go there often. In fact, I think the last time I was in there was with Stevie. He was packing away Screwdrivers and asking me if I believed in vampires."

"Vampires?" Adam and Tricia said in unison.

Etienne shrugged sheepishly as Adam cast him a concerned glance.

"Yeah, he wanted to know if I thought vampires really existed."

"Did he?" Adam asked.

"Yeah."

"And what did you tell him?" Tricia inquired.

"I told him I'd never really thought about it, but I guess that they could. Oh! And he also wanted to know if I thought they were evil. What do you think, Trish?"

Tricia smiled. "Now you know better than to ask me that kind of question, Andie."

"I know, but I never learn," Andrea said with a knowing wink.

"Why is it bad to ask her that kind of question?" Etienne asked.

"Because Etienne, I have a rather different outlook on life and chances are you'll never get an answer quite like the answers you get from me, out of anybody else," Tricia replied.

"Yep, that's why I ask. I love to hear your interesting answers."

"So, enlighten us. Do vampires exist and are they evil?" Adam questioned, trying to hide his discomfort, but profoundly interested in what she had to say.

Tricia grew thoughtful for a moment then answered in a scholarly voice. "Yes, vampires exist and they are not evil. In fact, vampires play a very important part in the web of life."

"What do you mean?" Adam pressed.

"I mean, that vampires, and other creatures that prey on humans serve a necessary purpose."

"I do not understand. Please explain."

"Well, look at the human race. We're running rampant over the earth, polluting and destroying and otherwise doing a wonderful job of disrupting Nature's balance. We're very good at getting rid of the things that are supposed to kill us: war, famine, disease, and pestilence. So now we have an empty niche in the web of life. This is where the vampire comes in. A predator of human beings. A creature that feeds on humans but that humans can't easily get rid of. A creature that most people don't even believe in, but that is its greatest defense. Since people don't believe in them, they aren't actively hunted. They go about their business unaccosted, serving their purpose without any hindrance from us."

"And this is not evil?" Adam asked.

"No. It's necessary," Tricia argued, carefully making her point. "There must be a predator of humans. We no longer control our numbers, so now Nature must provide one. It's not evil. It's balance. Vampires are neither good nor evil. They simply are what they are. If they didn't kill and drink blood, they would starve. Besides, I can think of a lot of things more wor-thy of being called evil than vampires, and all of them are human."

"Such as?" Etienne questioned.

"Such as people like Charles Manson and Hitler, or serial killers. People who kill because they enjoy it, or get others to kill for them. People who murder others in horrible, sadistic ways. When did you ever hear about a vampire hanging its victim from a ceiling with piano wire and then quartering it with a butter knife? For the most part, the vampire doesn't hurt his victim. Yes, he kills his victim, but it isn't a ghastly death. They don't maim or torture their victims. Not because of any moral code, but because to do so would be a) a waste of time and b) a waste of the food. The easiest way to get what they need is to lock onto the biggest source of blood they can find, i.e. the jugular, and drink directly from that source. Sort of eating directly from the proverbial pot so to speak. It's a quick and painless death, and compared to what some murderers do to their victims, it's positively humane."

Etienne sat back against the cushions of the couch. "You're right, Tricia. I have never heard an answer quite like that."

"I tried to warn you."

"And you insist that even though the vampire kills, it is not evil," Adam noted.

"No, it's not. Granted, it does kill, and dead is forever, but I could think of a lot worse ways to die than at the hands of a vampire," Tricia replied.

"Like what?" Etienne asked.

Tricia met his gaze with a calm coldness. "Like being eaten alive from the inside out by your own body."

The two men were quiet as they considered her words. However, Andrea suddenly sat up straight and stared at her friend with wide eyes.

"I know why you're here," she said, a tremor of fear in her voice.

Tricia looked at her expectantly.

"You're sick again."

The brunette lowered her eyes and nodded. "Yes."

Andrea seemed crushed, but then she rallied. "It mustn't be that bad though, since you're not in a hospital."

"No, it's bad," Tricia corrected softly.

"But it can't be if they are treating you as an outpatient," Andrea insisted.

"They aren't treating me as an outpatient."

Andrea was confused, her brow creased.

"But…how then?"

"They aren't treating me at all."

"Why not?"

"Because I refused treatment. I'm over 21 and in full control of my faculties. If I don't sign a release, they can't force me to receive treatment," she answered evenly, carefully.

Andrea was quiet as she let the words sink in, then realization filled her face and she gasped. "No!"

"Yes," Tricia replied calmly.

"But you can't refuse treatment! You just can't!" Andrea insisted, a note of desperation in her voice.

"I can and I have."

Andrea could not believe what she was hearing. She started to shake, refusing to accept what she knew to be true. "No." she breathed, shaking her head. "No! No! No!"

"Yes, Andie."

"No! What's happened to you, Trish? This isn't like you! You're giving up! The Tricia I knew would never give up! Never!" She started to cry.

Tricia sighed. "I'm not giving up, Andie. I'm just accepting the inevitable."

"It's not inevitable! Now you go back to California and get treatment!"

A look of infinite sadness came over Tricia's face and she stood slowly. With her eyes still on Andrea, she carefully rolled up the sleeves of her sweater to reveal her thin, almost skeletal arms. She showed them to the three figures seated motionless on the couch, turning her wrists so the undersides could be seen. They saw the deep pock marks on the inside of her elbows, left behind by countless IV needles, the pocks were sunken and badly discolored. For a moment, no one spoke, then Tricia's calm, even voice broke the silence.

"I'm twenty-five years old. I've spent eleven of those years in and out of the hospital. I've seen enough of the inside of hospitals."

Andrea said nothing. She only stared at the marks and at her friend, a crushed expression on her face. Tricia bowed her head.

"Andie, I'm tired of it. It isn't worth it to me anymore. I've had enough. I've been through chemo six times, I've endured over forty spinal taps, I've had more tubes and wires connected to me than Carter's got pills, I've been pumped up with enough radioactive garbage that I'm now considered a national security risk. If the Russians get a hold of me, I could waste the entire Eastern seaboard," she explained gently. "I'm riddled with scars. Look, see I've got them everywhere."

She pulled back the collar of her sweater to reveal two circular scars the size of quarters on either side of her chest, just at the base of her neck. Then she lifted it to show her sides. Numerous incision scars laced her abdomen. But the worst was her back. Her lower spine was covered with tiny round scars about a 1/4-inch in diameter. There were dozens of them, dotting her lumbar region like freckles. Chills went up Etienne's body, all the hair rising on his neck. This woman had cancer; she had had it for a long time, and it was killing her now, slowly. She turned to face them again, smoothing her sweater back into place and rolling down the sleeves, covering the ghastly mutilation of her body. Her eyes had a certain pleading in them, begging Andrea to understand.

"It has to end sometime, Andie. And it's over now. I'm not going through it again."

"But…" Andrea started but Tricia cut her off.

"No buts. I've thought about this carefully and I've made my decision. Maybe if my mom was still alive, maybe if there had been some advances in the treatment of this monster that I have. Maybe if they could show me some small hope that in a year, or two years or five years, they could lick this thing. Maybe then it would be worth all the pain and the sickness and my hair falling out and my body wasting away to skin and bones in a bed. But there haven't been any advances, and there isn't anything promising in research. The medical field is no closer to curing lymphatic cancer than it was eleven years ago, when they diagnosed me with it."

Tears rolled down Andrea's cheeks and she spoke in a small, trembling voice. "But…you'll die."

"Yes, I will die," Tricia answered simply. "But nothing can stop that now. I always knew this thing was a death sentence, it was just a matter of when."

"Then there's no hope at all?"

Tricia shook her head slowly. "No. It's in my head, Andie. It's in my kidneys and my liver and my chest. It's everywhere. Even now I can feel it strangling my heart and lungs, suffocating me from the inside out."

Andrea let out an anguished moan and hid her face in her hands. Tricia knelt at her feet and took her shoulders, forcing Andrea to look at her.

"It's okay, Andie. It's okay. I'm not afraid. I've seen the face of Death more than once, it doesn't scare me anymore. Besides, my greatest fear was that I would die without ever having lived. I've done that now. I have enough good memories to last me a dozen lifetimes. I've been places and done things and I've made the best friends in the whole world. I'm ready to go now."

Andrea stilled and stopped crying. She licked her lips and swallowed hard. "How much time do you have?"

"Not long. A month at most, probably less. I don't think about it."

Etienne cast Adam a questioning look, his eyes full of fear.

She is right. Less than a month. Two weeks, no more, came the grim answer.

"What will you do?" Andrea asked softly.

"What I'm doing now: going to see my friends, living. I'm living as much as I can now. I hardly sleep. I don't want to miss a single moment of it. I've been to see Melissa and Karen. I'm here tonight to see you. Tomorrow I'm going to Miami to see Stephen. Then I go to Brian and Jason. I want to see all my friends. I want you to remember me alive, not dead."

They were quiet for a few moments, then Tricia patted Andrea's shoulder and stood. "But enough of this gloom and doom. I'm weary of it, besides we are ignoring your friends."

"It's all right," Adam insisted gently, casting a worried glance at his eerily silent lover.

"No it isn't. It's rude," Tricia countered and looked at the clock. "Hey, it's only one. The night is still young. Let's go out. I'm sure we can find a hopping place to jam tonight. C'mon, let's go. Before I give my blood back to the earth, I want to feel it pound in my veins!"

"Go out? You're dying and you want to go bar hopping?" Andrea gasped.

"Yeah, why not? Would you rather have me be depressed and sullen?" Tricia dropped her head and cocked a slumped pose. She drooped her shoulders and sighed wistfully. "Oooooh, I'm gonna die. I'm gonna die. Soon I'll be pushing up the daisies. I'm gonna die die die. Ohhhh, it's awful, I'm so depressed. I'm gonna die," she moaned in a whiny voice. Then she perked up, stood up straight and grinned. "Okay, 'nuff of that. I'm tired of it. Let's go!"

Andrea's jaw dropped. "I don't believe you. How can you be so happy? You're dying of lymphatic cancer and you can laugh?"

"Sure I can laugh, Andie. I'm alive. I'm out in the world. For the first time in three years I have a full head of hair. It's wonderful. I'm not wasting a minute of my time being unhappy. I'm living, not strapped to a bed in some sterile hospital while nurses take bets on when I'm gonna croak."

"But, aren't you in pain? You said it was in your chest, how can you..." Andrea pressed.

"Sure I'm in pain. Every breath I take is painful. Every step hurts. Getting up in the morning is agony," she admitted. "But, Andie, I'd rather feel the pain, than be drugged up shell on a hospital bed. Besides, if I die of a heart attack tonight, that would be a good thing, yes?"

"Oh God, don't say that!" Andrea blurted.

Tricia laughed then grew serious. "C'mon Andie. Stop this. I didn't come here for you to be sad. I won't die tonight. I may not be able to tell you exactly when I will, but I know it won't be today. Come, be happy with me. Live with me. Feel the life pulsing in you because it's too brief and too precious to miss." She extended her hand. "Come."

Andrea stood and brushed her jeans off nervously. "All right. Let me go brush my hair and put on some make-up."

"Oh yeah, I was meaning to mention that. I love the new color. It really suits you."

Andrea fluffed her hair. "Thanks. It'll make it harder for Louis to find me."

"Yeah, and speaking of him…Melissa wanted me to tell you that he's out now. Be careful, lay very low, Andie."

Andrea paled and nodded. "I will."

Adam and Etienne stood. "We should go," the brown-haired man said as Andrea went to the bathroom.

"Oh no no no! Come with us. It'll be great fun! Besides, it'll be great to have two wonderful, good-looking men to protect us," Tricia insisted.

"Yes, we fragile females need protection!" Andrea agreed, poking her head out of the bathroom.

Adam smiled. "As you wish. I couldn't live with myself if I didn't protect my 'fragile females'. Should I carry you down the stairs so you don't trip?"

"Don't push it," Tricia warned in mock anger.

Adam laughed softly but Etienne remained quiet.

Come on. Let us do as she asks. She is right. Life is too precious to waste, Adam pleaded.

Easy for you to say, you'll never die, came the sullen retort.

Adam frowned. *Please, Eti, let us be happy tonight. I know you are upset. So am I, but Andrea needs us to be happy right now. Please?*

All right. For Andie.

The smile returned to Adam's lips and he kissed his lover tenderly.

I love you.

Love you too, Etienne replied dutifully.

"Okay, I'm ready," Andrea announced, coming out of the bathroom.

"Let's go then!" Tricia enthused. "C'mon Adam, stop cuddling with your boyfriend, and move that gorgeous ass of yours, before I do something obscene to it."

How shocked Adam looked; it made the rest of them laugh as they headed out the door to walk to a nearby bar.

"Yikes! It's cold! I can't wait to get to Florida!" Tricia said, shivering. "Miami, now that is a place where I'd expect to find vampires."

"Oh? Why is that?" Andrea asked.

"Coz it's the perfect place. Always warm, plenty of prey. Think about it, all the drug trade and immigrants? There are hundreds of people that a vampire could kill and no one would miss them."

"Oh, that's morbid, Trish."

"I know, but it's true."

"I'll get us a table," Adam offered uncomfortably, walking ahead of them to enter the bar.

"Thanks, handsome," Tricia teased and watched him as he disappeared through the door.

Twelve

And what happened after you and Etienne got home that night? Rain questioned.

Etienne was badly shaken in spite of all the laughter and fun, he answered, sorrow tingeing his mindvoice.

I can imagine. Was he all right?

No. As soon as we left Andrea and Tricia back at Andrea's apartment, a gloom settled over him and he grew sullen and silent... he explained, continuing the story.

• • •

Tobias glanced over at Etienne worriedly as they rode back to their own flat. There was a blank look in his lover's eyes, a look he hadn't seen before. Yes, Eti was very badly shaken by Tricia, by her fate and her calm acceptance of it, and if he would allow himself to admit it, so was he. He had never met a mortal quite like Tricia, never seen peace and serenity in the face of such a ghastly and agonizing death. Yet she accepted her destiny. She chose to die rather than live in pain any longer. The very memory of her face when she said, 'Yes, I will die' made him shudder with fear. He was as unsettled as Etienne, but he was not concerned about himself. Etienne was his concern now, his mortal lover whose beautiful hazel eyes were impassive and cold. What had tonight done to his delicate love? He had essentially looked into the face of Death herself. What had it done to his already frightened soul? He

157

moved closer across the back seat of the cab, seeking the warmth and comfort that Etienne's human body offered. His own heat was fading, the warm blood of his kill cooling over the hours. But there was another chill coming over him, a chill he felt deep in his soul, as he snuggled close to Etienne and received no comfort in return. Etienne ignored him, did not even look at him. He merely continued staring blankly out the windshield, past the driver's head, to the falling snow. Tobias sighed and dropped his head to Etienne's shoulder, letting the soft knit of the sweater fold around his face, the familiar smell of his lover filling his nostrils. He did not know what to do.

The cab stopped outside their building, the driver announcing their arrival. Etienne said nothing as he exited the taxi and stood waiting for Tobias. Tobias paid the driver and thanked him, then got out of the cab himself and moved to Etienne's side. Gently he kissed the impassive cheek and pushed Etienne towards the door.

"Go on up. I will join you in a little while," he spoke softly.

Etienne looked at him suddenly, confused, then his eyes registered his understanding and he nodded. Tobias watched him as he unlocked the door to their building and disappeared inside. When he heard the click of the bolt in the latch, he went off to hunt. He wasn't really hungry, but he was cold and he wanted to be warm, warm for Etienne. There was another reason too, one he didn't quite understand, the need to kill; kill because he was hurting and the blood brought a reprieve from the pain. He wasted no time stalking a victim, he knew exactly where to find one to send to Hell, and in minutes he was feeding. When it was over, he dumped the body in the woods. His task completed, he hurried home to Etienne.

Etienne was waiting for him when he returned, sitting sullenly on a chair in the living room, his long legs curled up to his chest, his arms wrapped around them. He didn't look at Tobias when he came in, but Tobias knew he had been waiting. Emotions boiled in Etienne like lava. His lover could feel them before he even entered the room. He envisioned Etienne as a smoldering volcano, a volcano that was about to erupt. The image was not a pleasant one. If they had the argument that was brewing in Etienne, they would waste the rest of the night.

'Do you think you are the only one who is hurting here?' Tobias wanted to shout. 'Do you think I am not as shaken as you? Shaken to my core by a mortal who is not afraid of death?'

He let the words and the thoughts die inside him, to yell at Etienne now would only cause the eruption, and he didn't want that. He wanted to lie beside his lover, let his new heat warm him, and hold him as they kissed, as the blood passed between them, strange healer that it was. But even as he approached his now trembling love, he knew that Etienne would have this fight, the emotions had been brewing in him for too long. The best hope he had was to keep it contained, while ever ushering Etienne to the bedroom, to the soft bed and the embrace. He knew he could control Etienne with sex. It had always worked before, there was no reason to think it would not work again. He stood silently before his Etienne, waiting, steeling himself against the words that were about to be thrown at him, preparing himself for the immanent fight.

'I will not get angry with you, liebchen, I will hear what you have to say. I will listen to you and let you scream at me. Then I will take you gently and lay you down and make you forget this night ever happened,' he vowed to himself.

"You would let me die that way, wouldn't you," came Etienne's strained voice.

Tobias was stunned. This he had not expected! "What?" He had to hear it again, to be sure he had heard Etienne correctly.

"You would let me die that way. That horrible, terrible way. You would let me die," his mortal repeated, looking at him for the first time since he returned, his hazel eyes bloodshot and anguished.

"Never," he blurted, aghast.

Tears welled in Etienne's eyes. "You would let me die. You would watch me in agony and you would still let me die."

"I could never watch you suffer, Etienne. I'd rather die myself than see you in pain."

"Don't give me that! You know it as well as I do. You'd let me die. You'd enjoy it, watching me die," Etienne snarled back.

"Never!"

"Yes, you would!" Etienne screamed, slamming his hands against the chair cushion, tears streaming from his eyes. "You would find it all so interesting! My hair falling out, the endless maze of tubes and wires connected to my body, the very path of the monster that was eating me alive! You'd watch it, track its progress, have stimulating conversations with the doctor: 'Where do you think it will strike next?' You would find it all so entertaining! A new experience, watching your mortal *slave* die of cancer!"

Etienne's terror hit Tobias like a physical blow and he recoiled. He was not prepared for this type of onslaught. How could Etienne even think that such a thing was possible of him?

"I know that you are upset, but believe me, you are wrong. I could never watch you die." Where was this coming from and how could he contain it? He scrambled frantically for answers, feeling the situation quickly slipping out of his control.

"I don't believe you. You'd watch my face as I died and find it amusing!"

"No, you are wrong! How can you think me capable of such things? I love you!"

"Oh, no. I am not wrong! You taunt me with immortality! You know how I want it!"

"You don't understand…"

"I do understand! I know what happened with Dorian's fledgling. I know Elizabeth went crazy. But that will not happen to me!"

"How can you know that? Ian said it happens all the time. How can you be sure that I will not have to kill you? I could not bear that!" he argued, trying to make Etienne see reason, but his lover would have none of it.

Etienne sneered. "Ian would have told you anything to get you to stay with him, to keep you from making another and leaving him. He wanted you weak and dependent on him!"

"No…"

"You know it's true!"

"No." It was true, but he did not have to admit it.

Etienne stepped up his attack, growing more vicious in his rage. "You don't love me. You've never loved me. You use me, use me to keep you company because you're too weak to be alone. You would give me cancer if you could, just to watch me die from it."

Tobias was shocked speechless and he stepped back, horrified.

"Admit it! You would! You would!" he seethed, slamming his fists into the arms of the chair for emphasis as Tobias stared mutely at him. "You, the eternal student. It would be a grand experiment for you. Watching, wanting to know everything! So brilliant, so talented! Such a genius! It would amuse you for years, watching me waste away to nothing. Until I was nothing but a dried up husk connected to countless IVs!"

Tobias' eyes opened wide as he saw Etienne's face twist into a grotesque mask of fury and loathing. Instinctively, he flinched from the waves of anger buffeting him from all sides, trying desperately to shield himself from this relentless emotional onslaught, but Etienne was merciless, driving his bitter words further into Tobias' heart with every accusation.

"What kind would you give me, my dear lover? Lung? So you could watch me suffocate slowly. Liver? For a slow, agonizing death. How about brain? Brain is a good one, lots of seizures and fits of madness. You'd enjoy brain."

"Stop it," Tobias pleaded, his heart breaking. He could feel his tenuous hold on his masks slipping. The old fear was rising in him and threatening to take him over.

Unyielding, Etienne attacked again. "What about bone? No, that is too fast. You'd choose one they could treat for a while, just to see what would happen to me. Leukemia is one that takes a few years, and there's always lymphatic, but you've already seen what that does. You'd choose a differ-ent one."

"I said, stop it!" Tobias shouted, his voice cracking under the strain.

"Why should I? Give me a reason why I should stop! You never do!"

"No! You are wrong! I am not capable of these things you accuse me of!" he asserted desperately.

"Yes you are! And you would give me cancer if you could! You'd enjoy it!"

"No, liebchen, I swear it! No!"

"How dare you call me beloved! I'm not your beloved! I'm your toy! You play with me because I amuse you! When I cease to amuse you, you'll toss me aside like an old doll! Until then you'll torture me, drive me mad! Tease me with your immortality until you weary of it!"

Tobias fought for control, his fists clenched, his whole body shaking. "Beloved, you're upset. You don't know what you say. I don't tease you. I would never take pleasure in seeing you suffer. I would never give you cancer. You are my beloved. You saved me from loneliness. I could never, never hurt you. You must believe me." He stopped and held out his arms, beseeching.

Etienne scowled with rage, ignoring Tobias' silent plea for peace. He saw his lover's outstretched arms but refused to go into them. Bitter bile rose in his throat.

"I hate you for what you do to me! I hate you! You can give me what I want! You can make me live forever! But you won't! You'd rather watch me die than make me one of you!"

"You are not rational, liebchen..."

"The Hell I'm not! You torture me! Your very presence tortures me! You'll torture me until my last breath, and when I'm dead and gone, you'll be the one to throw the first shovel of dirt on my rotting corpse. 'Alas, poor Etienne, I knew him well. He amused me for many years, but then he grew old and died. Now I must find a new mortal to play with!' Then you'll go off and find another hapless soul to drive mad!"

"Eti, please..."

"Don't call me Eti! I hate that nickname! I HATE YOU!"

Tobias covered his face with his hands. He was losing control. All his defenses were being stripped away.

"Please…I love you! How could you think such things of me?" he cried.

"Then give it to me, damnit! Prove you love me! Give me immortality!" Etienne ordered, rising from the chair and grabbing Tobias' arms.

Tobias let Etienne pull his hands away from his face, revealing the tears that rolled down his cheeks.

No, he answered silently, sending the word directly into Etienne's crazed mind.

Etienne's face twisted again in rage and grief. "You'd let me suffer! You would let me die of cancer!"

No. I would kill you before I let that happen. But you aren't suffering and you don't have cancer.

"But you wouldn't save me either. You wouldn't bring me to you. Not even to save me from that awful death."

A strange calm settled over Tobias as he let the tears fall. *No.*

Etienne pushed away from him angrily and turned his back. "You don't love me."

I do love you!

Etienne looked at his vampire lover sadly, most of the anger fading from his earlier outbursts. "No, you don't. You won't give it to me and you won't set me free. The worst of it is, I can't live with you and I can't live without you."

Etienne hid his face in his hands, sobbing quietly and Tobias saw his chance. With vampire speed he closed the distance between them and took Etienne into his arms.

This is how I love you! he said and sunk his teeth deep into Etienne's neck.

At first Etienne actually fought him, something he had never done before, but as the rapture filled him, he grew limp and surrendered, languishing in Tobias' embrace. After a moment, Tobias drew back and looked at Etienne's flushed visage. He saw the hazel eyes flutter open, misty with passion, then watched as they hardened with anger, as the smooth mouth grimaced with rage. Furious, Etienne spit in his face.

YOU DON'T LOVE ME! came his enraged thought, slicing into Tobias' mind like a hot knife.

Tobias did nothing. He stood perfectly still, holding Etienne loosely, not bothering to wipe the spit from his cheek. Etienne's wide, terrified eyes met his calm gaze, then started to tear up again.

"You don't love me," he whispered, weeping.

I do love you.

"No…"

Yes. Yes, Etienne. I love you. I love you.

Gently Tobias drew Etienne close, pressing the beloved face to his chest and holding him, his lips pressed to the sweaty forehead. He felt the thin shoulders heaving as Etienne wept, and he closed his eyes.

I love you. I would die without you. I love you.

Etienne sobbed and buried his face in Tobias' neck, wrapping his arms tightly around the slender body, crying uncontrollably. Tobias held him, listening to him cry, letting the last traces of anger fade from the both of them. This is what he wanted, his love in his arms, the familiar body pressed deliciously against his own. 'Yes, this. My love, my Etienne. I would do anything for you. Anything but that.'

I'm sorry. I don't mean to hurt you, Etienne sobbed.

It is all right. I love you.

You are my all-loving god.

And you are my life.

Etienne raised his head and kissed the spittle from Tobias' cheek, then sought the pale lips. Tobias was burning hot from his recent kill, his lips soft and supple as Etienne kissed him. He felt himself being lifted as Tobias carried him to their bedroom and laid him tenderly on the bed. Now he would join him and they would embrace, the kiss would come and the blood, the stinging vampire blood would burn his lips. Surprisingly though, Tobias drew away as soon as he placed Etienne on the bed, and

stood quietly beside it, looking down at him. Etienne was confused. Then
Tobias began to undress, dropping his clothes on the floor like used rags
until he was naked, his gleaming white skin glowing in the darkness. The
white hands descended and began removing Etienne's clothes, stripping
him lovingly until he, too, was naked. Etienne closed his eyes as the cool
skin of Tobias' hands glided over his bare flesh. He felt the mattress sink
and knew that Tobias had joined him on the bed, and soon the lean, lithe
body was pressed against his own. It was a wonderful sensation, so much
flesh against flesh, his own human skin rubbing against Tobias' unnatural,
silk smooth skin. The arms came around him, one leg wrapped around his
own, the chest cleaved to his side. Their nakedness would serve to further
the bond and the pleasure. Etienne's hair tickled his sensitive skin as he let
their bodies slide against each other. Ah, yes. Delicious. Now for the kiss.

Etienne felt Tobias' lips kiss his neck, felt the tongue slide across his skin,
making all the hair rise on his body, then the prick of the sharp teeth, the
mouth covering the wounds. He sighed, pleasure filling him, his whole
body on fire. He ran his hands over Tobias' skin, exploring the curves and
crevices of this being that he loved so desperately. His passion grew as he
caressed the body next to his and he moaned with desire. Tobias gripped
his right arm and pulled him to his side, his mouth never leaving Etienne's
neck. Etienne rolled with him as Tobias lifted his leg and slid it around
Etienne's hip, letting their pelvises touch. The movement continued until
Tobias was on his back and Etienne was half atop him, his groin pressed to
the inside Tobias' hip. Then Tobias' hand cupped Etienne's buttocks,
encouraging him to work his passion out against his body. Etienne's organ
was hard, straining with need as he began to thrust against his lover's form.
Tobias tore his own throat slightly with his fingernail and guided Etienne's
mouth to the wound. Etienne's lips locked on it, his tongue lapping at the
blood that seeped from the scratch.

It was ecstasy. He bucked against Tobias as the blood stung him, gripping
his body tightly, crushing his chest to Tobias' chest. He could feel Tobias'
hand on his rump, the silken fingers digging into the soft cheek of his

buttocks. He felt Tobias shift positions, lifting one leg to curl around his, forcing their pelvises more firmly together, and then the fingers caressing his back and finally finding his sensitive breast. Etienne moaned. Ahh, this lover, he knew Etienne's body so well.

The blood passed between them, heightening all of Etienne's senses. His desire and need were building; he wanted release, but it wasn't enough. He strained, sucking and thrusting hard, but still release did not come. He needed more.

Want you! Want you! Need you! he thought desperately.

Always, my love, all you have to do is ask.

Immediately, Tobias stilled and gently drew his mouth away from Etienne's neck. Etienne whimpered and clung to him as he felt Tobias' hands take hold of his arms. Effortlessly, in spite of his lover's protests, Tobias lifted Etienne up and smiled at him for what seemed like moments unending. Etienne watched the scratch on the white neck heal, and he groaned as if in pain. Without a word, Tobias pushed Etienne back to rest on his knees. Then while his lover watched, he carefully positioned himself on his back, resting his head squarely on the pillows, and parted his legs.

If this is what you need, liebchen. Gladly I will give it to you. Come, take me.

Tobias raised his hands in welcome, ushering Etienne to climb atop him. It took a few moments for Etienne to come his senses, but soon he was fumbling in the bedside table drawer where they kept the tube of lubricant. His hand was trembling violently as he placed the tube on the mattress within easy reach. Every time they did this, it always shook him to his very center.

Come, take me. I am yours, liebchen.

Still reeling, he knelt between Tobias' legs and took in the waiting body. 'Mine. All mine.'

Tobias smiled lovingly at him. He bent down and kissed Tobias' breast, sucking gently on the pale nipple. Then he moved to the other breast, kissing, licking, and sucking gently. Soon he was exploring Tobias' whole body with his mouth and tongue, feeling the pleasure and the need rise within him.

Tobias was quiet, patient, and accepting of Etienne's attentions. His lover needed this and it was something he could give so he was willing to allow Etienne to mount him. It was always strange, but had never hurt him, and right now he was willing to give Etienne anything he could to reconcile their argument. He hated to see Etienne so upset, so angry, so hurt. It broke his heart. If doing this would help to heal Etienne's wounds, then Tobias would give it and give it willingly.

Etienne's tongue was making little wet circles around his breast, his teeth nipping playfully at the white skin. Smiling, he tangled his hand in Etienne's blond hair and pressed Etienne's mouth to his nipple, making it linger there for long moments. Then he released Etienne's head and looked at him, his face calm and peaceful. It was all very pleasurable, everything Etienne was doing to him. He could smell the rising blood in Etienne's skin as his need grew, and he saw Etienne's face flush with it. The scent filled him with desire: that was where his satisfaction lay, in the throbbing warmth of Etienne's neck. Lust was rising in him as well, blood lust. He wanted to have Etienne again, to feel Etienne's sweet blood flowing into his mouth, to feel the pleasure in him. Love filled him; right now, he wanted nothing more than to take his lover and send him reeling with rapture.

Finally, Etienne pulled back, breathed nervously and reached for the tube of lubricant. Tobias' eyes followed the path of the tube as Etienne brought it to his other hand and opened the top. His hands involuntarily gripped the sheets in anticipation of what was to come. Soon his lover would be inside of him. He watched as Etienne squeezed a small amount of clear jelly onto his fingers and lowered his hand between Tobias' legs. Tobias took a deep breath, preparing himself mentally, resigning himself to do this thing. Then he felt a coolness and a gentle probing, and he realized that Etienne had not been about to mount him. He had put the lubricant on his fingers and was now carefully exploring Tobias' body, thrusting into him gently, testing the tightness and resiliency of his lover's opening. Tobias almost laughed. 'He is preparing me, like any mortal lover. Making me ready for him so he will not hurt me.'

The thought seemed absurd, but he did not object. He lay quietly, focusing on the new sensations as Etienne probed him, first with one finger then with two, stretching him, opening him. The feeling was pleasurable, rather like an expert massage. He closed his eyes and enjoyed Etienne's attentions.

His eyes were still closed when Etienne removed his fingers. He cracked them open, questioning. Etienne was sweating, his blond hair clinging to his forehead, his eyes filled with passion. He saw Etienne open the tube of lubricant a second time and squeeze some onto his erect organ. Again Tobias felt himself breathing deeply, readying himself for the invasion. Then Etienne's hand gripped his hip as he slid forward and covered Tobias with his body. He felt the hips come down between his legs and the brush of Etienne's pubic hair against his skin. The pressure followed, easy at first as Etienne positioned himself, then more insistent as he pushed forward, into him. Tobias' eyes flew open wide and he gasped, arching his back as Etienne mounted him carefully. He felt himself opening as his lover entered slowly, oh so slowly, until finally Etienne was completely buried within him.

"Does it hurt?" Etienne's raw voice asked.

"No," he answered, his voice ragged and breathless.

He shifted a little, bending his knees and pulling Etienne further atop him, settling himself into a comfortable position. He was acutely aware of the member inside him: he could feel its full length and its pulsing in time with his lover's heart beat. To think, all that blood pooled in one place…The thought made him lick his teeth and bare his small fangs. He could hear the fast thrumming of Etienne's heart, pounding like a drum in his lover's chest. Etienne's excitement was rising and he felt the organ inside him swell with more blood, growing even longer and harder as it filled. His lover's lips came down upon his, the warm, mortal tongue probing his mouth as he pressed their bodies together. Reflexively, he placed his hands on the small of Etienne's back as his lover began to thrust cautiously, his eyes opened wide as the organ slid against his sensitive skin. Yes, he could feel it, its entire length moving slowly, first pulling back then filling him again and pulling back once more. He was now the singular object of Etienne's desire and pleasure, soon Etienne would bring everything to a pinnacle and climax. The thought excited him more than he thought it would, and he was swept away by his lover's moans and need.

Love you! Love you, you wonderful thing!

I love you, Etienne.

Wholeheartedly, Etienne gave in to his need, burying his face in Tobias' neck, fancying that he could smell the blood pulsing in the blue vein, thrusting into him desperately. He licked the white throat, gasping with pleasure as Tobias' hands began to stroke his back and buttocks, sensuously, ardently, sending tingles all through his body. The sensitive fingers found his breasts and teased his tender nipples expertly, like a seasoned lover. Etienne moaned and sighed, his mind reeling. Then he felt Tobias' hand travel delicately up his back, between his shoulder blades, to his neck, and the long fingers curl on the skin beneath his hair, pulling his throat back slightly. Soft lips touched his jugular like a moth's wings and he tensed, waiting, quickly becoming insane with want and need.

Yes! Yes, take me! Yes!

The tiny fang teeth drove into his skin and he shuddered, his whole body shaking. The heat of the bite flooded him, feeding his passion, and he moaned aloud. His moan was answered by Tobias' low growl. After a few tortuous moments, Tobias' hand left his neck and moved to his own. Dimly Etienne saw the gleaming fingernail tear at the flesh and the blood rise to the surface. He needed no coaxing or instruction. Hungrily, mad with passion and love, he locked his mouth on the seeping wound and drew the blood into himself. Rapture! The blood was hot, sending sparks like electricity through his body; the bed sighed and groaned under their weight, the walls rattled. Overwhelmed, Etienne rode harder and faster, plunging into Tobias over and over with uninhibited passion. Vaguely he was aware that Tobias was moving with him, rocking with him, matching his break-neck pace. Arms wrapped around him, holding him close; he felt the pull of the mouth on his neck, the sweet moaning that came from his lover's throat over the rush of the spilling blood. He heard the headboard of the bed slamming heavily against the wall in time with his rhythm. They might wake up the neighbors…I don't care! I don't care! Tobias raised his legs, balancing his feet on Etienne's hips. The new position forced Etienne deeper, increasing his penetration and feeling. He slid his arms under Tobias' back and crushed their bodies together as he thrust wildly into him, drawing with all his strength on the tear Tobias had made for him.

They were one, joined in two places. It was perfection, beyond perfection. It was the fulfillment of everything. There was no separation between them anymore. It seemed that even their souls had joined. They were moving, rocking, moaning in unison. It was heaven. Then Etienne felt Tobias tense and his hands grip a little tighter so that the fingers dug almost painfully into the muscles of his back. Tobias was reaching a pinnacle, something that had never happened before even during their most intense lovemaking. His sucking increased in his abandon, his delight expressed in the long, low groans escaping him. Etienne struggled to hold back from his own release until Tobias reached his, listening with his entire being for that wondrous moment.

Yes! Come on, Toby, come! Let me experience every moment of it and let me know it is because of me that you have reached it!

Etienne…

Yes, my beloved. I am Etienne.

Mouths sealed against each other's necks, blood flowing between them, powerful, all consuming liquid life. Etienne's organ pounding into his lover, sweat pouring off his mortal body, his cries filling the room.

Etienne!

Bodies pressed to each other, rocking together in a primal rhythm, heartbeats throbbing in each other's ears. The very fabric of the universe folding around them, the moon and the stars coming down from the sky to swim in their eyes.

Etienne!

Hips raised to meet Etienne's thrusts, fingernails tearing into the flesh of his back and the deep growl building in the back of his throat.

Etienne!

Yes, come! Come, Toby!

Tobias' sudden violent shaking, the half scream from the lips against his lover's neck, the feeling of the blood spilling from his open mouth. Etienne's answering shudder and scream, a world of tiny explosions going off in his head as he climaxed, semen rushing out of him in a great wave. Then the tremendous moment as they both lay trembling, bathed in sweat, when their souls entwined and embraced as if to say: 'We are one and nothing can separate us now! Perfection, this is perfection. This is everything. I never want it to end.' The quiet sighs escaping both of them, the receding passion and coolness, the fading of the roar to silence. Nothing but him and his love nestled in each other's arms. Perfection.

Etienne lay heavily atop Tobias, unable to move, his mouth still covering the now closing wound on Tobias' neck. He felt Tobias release him and press his fingers to the seeping wounds in his own neck, then the tongue lick away the spilled blood on his skin. It sent little tremors of pleasure through him. He was drowsy, full of love and satisfied pleasure. He had never been so completely and totally satiated, his need utterly fulfilled. Tobias' feet slid down his thighs and landed with dull thuds on the mattress, then they continued down the sheets until his legs lay limp against the bedclothes. Etienne raised his head and drew a deep breath before looking down at his lover. Tobias was staring dazedly at the ceiling, his eyes blank as they so often were when he was thinking. A thin film of sweat clung to his face which Etienne licked away, kissing him all over his flushed cheeks and lips. Happily, Etienne nuzzled him and smiled.

"Penny for your thoughts," he whispered lovingly, giddy with joy.

The life came back to Tobias' face suddenly, the blue eyes blinking and dilating.

"Oh Etienne. What have you done to me? And what have I done to you?" the vampire murmured, his voice flat.

"Oh, don't tell me that I have to tell you what we just did to each other."

Tobias' eyes searched his frantically. "You are whole?"

"Yeah, why shouldn't I be? Actually, I'm better than whole."

His lover let out a visible sigh of relief. "I was afraid that I...I lost myself in it, I was afraid that I had taken too much."

Etienne kissed him. "Calm yourself. I'm fine and so are you."

Tobias' eyes met his. "You should try to stand. You should make certain that you are all right."

"I'm fine."

Etienne moved to prove it to him. He lifted himself from Tobias, gently disengaging himself and slid off the bed. His feet hit the floor and he rose to stand. No sooner had he done so when a terrible lightheadedness overcame him and he nearly fell. Within an instant Tobias had caught him, cradling him as he sank to the carpet.

"What's wrong with me?" Etienne asked, confused.

"I took too much from you. Now you will be weak for days. I lost myself and now you will pay the price. Forgive me," Tobias answered guiltily.

Etienne rested his head against Tobias' smooth, white chest and sighed, loving the closeness, the comfort.

"Forgive you for what? For liking it? For enjoying yourself? For climaxing? Go play in traffic."

Lips pressed to his forehead. 'Yes. Love you.'

"Oh, Eti..."

"Don't you want to go clean yourself a little? I did..."

"Later, love. It can wait. I am more concerned with you."

Gently, as if he was the most precious thing in the world, Tobias lifted Etienne to the bed and laid him down. Then he pulled aside the blankets and draped them over Etienne's naked body, tucking the sheets around his shoulders lovingly. Etienne felt the weakness, his limbs were heavy and sluggish. He thought it had just been his exhaustion from lovemaking, but now he realized it was not. He felt a little shudder of fear. Soft fingers brushed through his hair tenderly and caressed his face.

"I'll be back in a few minutes," Tobias' voice floated down to him from somewhere above.

All right, he wanted to answer, but he was suddenly so tired. His eyes were leaden. Tired. So tired.

Sleep, Eti.

'Yes, sleep.' Etienne's eyes closed and he slipped quickly into oblivion.

Thirteen

While Etienne and I were arguing and making up, Andrea was with Tricia back at her apartment. It was Tricia who knew what I was, and it was she who told Andrea the truth, Tobias explained. *I did not learn of this until much later, however.*

She managed to keep her knowledge from you? Rain asked, surprised.

Yes, and to this day, I do not know how she did it. But this is the record of that night as seen through Andie's eyes.

• • •

"So, what did you think of the terrible twosome?" Andrea asked, flopping down on the sofa.

"Adam is very intriguing," Tricia answered, taking a sip from her large glass of water.

"I know. He puzzles me sometimes. He is the only truly nocturnal person I know. I never see him before sundown. Stevie I see sometimes, but Adam, never."

"Ever think about why that is?"

"I used to think it was because he worked during the day, but I'm not so sure any more. He stays up so late, if he works during the day, when does he sleep?"

"Unless he sleeps on the job," Tricia offered.

"True, but he doesn't strike me as the type."

"No, he doesn't strike me that way either. He strikes me as something else entirely."

Andrea cocked her head in confusion. "What do you mean?"

Tricia placed her glass on the cocktail table slowly, pensive. "Did you see the look he gave Etienne when you mentioned vampires?"

Andrea shook her head. "No. I didn't."

Tricia was quiet, unsure of how to proceed. "Let's just say, he wasn't too happy. He had the look of someone who has been betrayed. Etienne saw it too. Etienne is terrified of Adam."

Andrea laughed. "You're kidding. Stevie adores Adam. You should see them. They can't keep their hands off each other. He isn't afraid of Adam at all."

As soon as she said it, she paused, remembering. She recalled Etienne's abject terror when Adam interrupted them in the bar that night. She saw the horror and fear all over again. She had chalked it up to his drunkenness and surprise, but now she was not so sure.

"Ahh, now you see what I mean," Tricia said, noticing the expression on her friend's face.

"You always were more observant than me. Why is he frightened of Adam? Adam is his lover, Adam fawns over him. You saw them tonight, they are positively, hopelessly in love."

"Because Adam is different from us. Adam is a vampire."

Andrea laughed out loud. "Are you sure you didn't have anything to drink? You must be drunk! Adam? A vampire?"

"I am serious, Andie. It all makes sense. The pale skin, the nocturnal habits, Etienne's fear of him, the fact that you've never seen him eat or drink. I am telling you. Adam is a vampire."

Andrea stopped laughing and grew pensive. "You're serious, aren't you?"

"Absolutely."

"How can you be so sure?"

Tricia shrugged. "I'm close to death. It makes me see things I normally wouldn't see. It's like a great door has been opened in my mind. Now I see all the world's mysteries and treasures."

Andrea didn't answer.

"You aren't in any danger, and really neither is Etienne," Tricia went on to explain. "Etienne just knows what Adam is and it frightens him. The truth is Adam loves both of you. He would never harm a hair on your head, and he will protect you from your enemies. But you must never let him know that you know what he is. Whenever he is around you must hide your thoughts from him because he can read them."

Andrea agreed, her eyes wide. "Yes. I have experienced this, and sometimes I swear he and Etienne are talking but they aren't saying anything."

Tricia nodded. "Yes. You must think of unimportant things when you are near him. You must veil your mind. Force yourself not to think about what he is or else he will know that you know."

Andrea felt a twinge of fear. "What will he do if he finds out I know?"

"I don't know. I don't think he'll harm you. He loves you far too much for that, but I'll bet he has ways of making you forget. Telepaths that strong can do mind sweeps."

Andrea grimaced at the thought of her mind being 'swept.'

"There is no reason to be afraid," Tricia assured.

"I still am not certain if I believe you. Adam not being human, that I could believe, but a vampire? That is a little too much of a stretch for my poor mind to make right now."

"Of course. But remember, don't dwell on it while he is around you. Watch him, store little things you notice away and examine them later after he has gone. Examine them during the daytime when he is asleep and cannot hear you thinking about him."

They were silent, then Tricia sighed and put her hand to her chest.

"Are you in pain?" Andrea asked, concerned.

"Not badly. There is always pain nowadays, but it's a good pain, one I don't mind feeling."

"Are you tired?"

"Yes, but I don't want to sleep. Why don't you play for me, Andie? Certainly you have written something since you left California. Would you play it for me?"

"Okay," Andrea agreed, going to her keyboards.

Tricia sat down on the couch and propped up her feet as Andrea began to play.

• • •

When Etienne opened his eyes the room was dark, but outside the town was awake and alive. It was evening. He'd slept through the entire day. His body was lead, not wanting to move as he tried to lift his head to see the clock. Six-thirty, past sunset. Tobias wasn't there. He probably went out to hunt, but he would be back soon, urging him to get up. He didn't want to get up. He wanted to sleep again, but his body was protesting. He had to go to the bathroom, and he was parched with thirst. Gingerly, he moved an arm, then a leg and slowly crept out of bed. He knew he couldn't stand, so he let himself slide to his knees and crawled towards the bathroom. The room was chilly to his naked skin and the tile of the bathroom floor was positively freezing! Using all his strength, he pulled himself up to the toilet seat and slumped down on it. He didn't like having to urinate sitting down, but he would manage. Exhausted, he leaned his head against the sink as he commenced his business. When he was finished he fumbled for the handle and flushed, but he could not muster the strength to lift himself from the seat.

"Damn, this is worse than being drunk," he moaned mournfully.

He moved his head to look at the sink and saw the glimmering drop of water clinging to the spigot. His thirst returned to him with a fury and he groaned. With heavy hands he reached for the knob and turned on the faucet, cupping his hand under the cold stream and slurping the water from his palm. It wasn't enough to quench his thirst. He tried to rise, to put his mouth into the flowing water, but his legs gave out under him and he went crashing to the floor, knocking his chin on the rim of the sink as he went down. His teeth bit into his lip and he could taste the blood seeping into his mouth from the wound. He had also hit his head on the tile floor; the resulting headache was already commencing to split open his skull. Miserable and weak, he laid dejectedly on the cold ceramic, not bothering to try to get up.

'Let him find someone else to drag to the movies tonight. Let him take Andrea, she'd be thrilled for a night out. I'm out to lunch tonight.'

A shadow fell across him, blocking the bathroom light. He cracked his eyes open to see a figure standing over him. He squinted, trying to focus, and the image cleared to reveal Tobias gazing worriedly down at him. He smiled stupidly.

"Hi, honey. You're home."

The angelic face came close, the lips brushing his forehead as the strong arms gathered him up like a child and carried him to the bed. The blankets reached up to accept him. Clean sheets. Tobias had changed the bed, bless him. So warm, so soft, fluffy clean blankets being tucked around his chilled body. The only thing that would have made them better would be if they had still been warm from the dryer. Yes, warm and cozy. Heaven was a warm, cozy bed and a vampire lover with the face of an angel.

Etienne sighed and the thirst caught in his throat. Thirsty, so thirsty.

"I know. I will get you something to drink," Tobias said gently.

Etienne watched dimly, struggling to make his eyes stay focused on the figure clad in a loose beige sweater and jeans as it glided from the bedroom to their kitchen. Such a light, delicate step, his feet barely touching the floor; his hair a long, flowing angel's mane of rich brown curls. How could anyone think this beautiful, ethereal thing was human? Tobias returned with a pitcher of cold water, a plastic tumbler, a wash cloth and an ice pack. Solicitously, he poured water into the tumbler and sat on the bed next to Etienne, helping him to sit up and holding the tumbler steady as his lover drank deeply. Etienne drank three glasses in quick succession.

"Steady, liebchen. Do not drink so fast. Your stomach is empty, you could get sick," Tobias warned

"Thirsty," he gasped, reaching for the glass as Tobias pulled it away.

"I know. Here, drink again, but slowly this time."

Etienne obeyed as Tobias held the glass for him. After the fifth tumbler-full, his thirst ebbed and he sunk down to the blankets with a sigh. Tobias dipped the wash cloth into the pitcher of water and tenderly wiped Etienne's face and neck. Then he lifted the ice pack and pressed it against Etienne's temple, the temple that had hit the floor when he fell.

"What did you do to yourself?"

"My face had an abrupt and unplanned rendezvous with the bathroom floor," he quipped sarcastically.

Tobias laughed softly. "I gathered that. You should have waited for me. I would have helped you."

"Didn't know when you'd be back. Thought we were doing the movies tonight."

"We were."

"Take Andrea."

"No. I'm not going."

"No need for you to ruin your night because I'm not up to it."

Tobias laughed again, softly, and bent down to kiss Etienne's cheek, removing the ice pack and setting it on the nightstand. His lips were hot, he had already fed, that was why he was so late in arriving.

"No, I must take care of you," his lover insisted gently.

"I'm not helpless, I'm just a little weak, that's all."

"Weak because of me. No, I must stay and make sure you are all right, if only for my own benefit."

"Fine, suit yourself."

"You should eat. I have brought you soup and bread."

Tobias left the bed and went back into the kitchen, taking the ice pack and washcloth with him. He returned carrying a bed tray upon which was a bowl of Wonton soup, some bread, a small carton of orange juice, a spoon

and a cloth napkin. As Etienne watched, he placed the tray on the table and
retrieved the backrest from beside the bed. Struggling, he sat up as Tobias
placed the backrest behind him, his eyes crossing from sudden vertigo.

"Steady," Tobias whispered, holding Etienne's arm lightly to keep him
from falling over.

When he was certain that Etienne was settled, Tobias turned his attention
to the tray of food. Deftly, he opened the carton of juice and poured it into
the empty tumbler, slipping the tumbler into the space meant for it on the
tray. Then he moved the tray to span Etienne's thighs and sat on the bed.
He saw Etienne lift a hand for a slice of bread, his fingers trembling, and he
lovingly steadied the hand and placed the bread in its palm. Etienne smiled
slightly, embarrassed at his weakness, and brought the bread to his mouth.

"Thanks," he sighed, taking a bite.

Tobias smiled at him, his eyes full of love as Etienne slowly consumed
the bread. Then he lifted the spoon and used it to slice the Wonton in the
soup into small pieces, scooping up some broth with some noodle and
bringing it to Etienne's lips. He fed Etienne with expert care, dabbing at
his mouth with the napkin when a bit of broth was spilled.

The smell of the broth beneath his nose made Etienne realize how
ravenously hungry he was and he allowed Tobias to feed him. As always, his
lover's patience and tenderness amazed him. Such a paradox, this beautiful
creature that could kill in an instant, yet be so gentle, so caring in the next.
The very thought of it confused Etienne utterly. Yet it suited Tobias, the
gentleness, suited his youthful face and wide, innocent eyes. Etienne often
wondered what Tobias' kill was like; Tobias had never allowed him to watch
when he took a victim. If it was anything like the feeling Etienne
experienced when Tobias took him, they must die very happy people.
Tobias' bite was the ultimate pleasure. Combine that with the hot, searing
pleasure of physical climax, and he had the mind-blowing release he
experienced last night. Yes, they must die very, very happy people.

"They accept death willingly enough," Tobias murmured, wiping
Etienne's mouth again to catch a droplet of broth clinging to his bottom lip.

"Yes," he conceded, feeling Tobias' discomfort. Tobias disliked any talk at all of killing.

Tobias nodded and fed him another spoonful of soup, his eyes misty and far away.

"Thank you," Etienne said, changing the subject.

The blue eyes cleared, the pupils dilating again as the pale lips broadened to a smile. So loving, so beautiful.

"I love you," Etienne blurted suddenly, as if he needed to say it quickly, lest he stop.

"I love you, too, Etienne," came the sweet, soft voice, so full of love and gratitude.

Etienne felt strong enough to reach for another slice of bread and Tobias paused in his feeding to wait until he wanted more.

"Do you forgive me?" his lover asked.

"Forgive you for what?" he answered, chewing and swallowing.

"For what I did to you."

"There's nothing to forgive, Tobias."

"But I…"

"Shut up and kiss me," he ordered sternly.

Tobias was surprised at the command. Etienne rarely gave commands and Tobias rarely obeyed them, but this time he smiled and leaned forward, avoiding the tray. Their lips joined in a sweet kiss then Tobias pressed his mouth to Etienne's neck, but did not bite. Etienne sighed with pleasure, weaving his hand into Tobias' long hair.

"I love you," he whispered, pulling back to look into Tobias' face and kiss him. "I forgive you."

Tobias' eyes were rimmed with tears, his lips trembling as Etienne kissed him a third time.

"Here," he said, motioning to the tray. "Get rid of this. I'm not hungry anymore. Come get into bed with me. Come cuddle."

His lover shook his head. "No, you must finish. You must eat or you will not regain your strength."

"You're acting like a mother hen," he scolded gently.

Tobias picked up the spoon and fed Etienne another mouthful of soup. "I know. Humor me."

"All right," he sighed, letting Tobias feed him the last of the Wonton.

"Here, drink," Tobias said, holding the tumbler of orange juice out for him.

He sipped the orange juice slowly while Tobias held the glass and finished it after a few moments. When the glass was empty, Tobias took it away, placed the tray on the floor, and gently lifted Etienne so he could push the backrest off the bed. Lying back down, Etienne snuggled under the blankets and closed his eyes, settling in a semi-fetal position, the weariness catching up with him again. There was a rustling of cloth and the sound of things being dropped on the floor, then the mattress sunk behind him as the weight of another body came on to it. Etienne felt the unnatural heat emanating from his lover's body as Tobias slid behind him, spooning his own form against Etienne's. Flesh against flesh. Delicious. So comforting. Tobias' arm came around him, snuggling close, his face in Etienne's hair, both heads sharing the same pillow. Etienne smiled to himself. He felt safe and protected. Tobias was here. Tobias would take care of him.

"I love you," he whispered, feeling sleep coming to claim him once again.

I love you. Sleep, my love. I am here. I will watch over you.

Etienne relaxed, sending his lover a rush of unabashed love, and sighed happily. Sleep settled over him like another warm blanket, and he let it wrap him in its sweet softness as Tobias held him close.

Tobias lay quietly, listening to Etienne's slow breathing. Warm, so warm, his mortal lover. Perhaps a little feverish. He felt guilty all over again. He should never have let it go so far, he should never have let himself lose control. Etienne was ill now because of it. He had hurt his love. He could have killed him. He didn't want to think about what could have happened. He had lost control in those last dizzying moments before Etienne's climax. He had even…felt something. That had never happened before, and it frightened him. In those seconds there had been nothing but the blood flowing between them and the pleasure of Etienne's organ thrusting inside of him. Everything else had miraculously ceased to exist. He forgot what he was, monster that he was, horrible, murdering creature, and became totally human once again. It was nothing short of a miracle. He was still reeling from it.

He still wasn't sure what had happened between them. That something had happened, he was certain, but exactly what it was, he did not know. There were no answers to his questions, questions that swarmed like locusts in his brain. What had caused his unrequited abandon in those last moments? What was it that he felt as climax hit him? He had never experienced such a climax before. Had he achieved a physical climax for the first time in five hundred years? If he had, it was dry; nothing had come from his flaccid organ. Tobias didn't know. He knew that in the joining they were truly one: one seamless being connected mind, body and soul. It was glorious. It also terrified him. He was shaken to his very core by the intimacy they had achieved, by the repercussions it could have had and the feelings it left behind in its wake. Suddenly he was aware of holes he never knew he had; painfully they let themselves be known to him. Etienne and their joining had filled the emptiness, only to leave him reft and bereft again when it was over. Now they throbbed dully, begging to be filled again, filled by the love and closeness. He shuddered and cuddled closer to his lover, suddenly feeling very alone and afraid.

Tobias wished there was someone he could talk to, someone he could trust to answer his questions, but there was no one. Dorian would only laugh at him, and he knew too well what Ian thought of his taking mortal lovers. The one time his maker had discovered him and a man together in a sexual embrace, Ian had ripped the man from atop him, killed him, and thrashed his fledgling raw. No. He was alone, alone with this mystery and the knowledge that his enjoyment of the sex had led him to hurt his lover. It was something he could not abide. The realization settled upon him uncomfortably and he sighed, nuzzling Etienne's neck just for the sake of feeling the warm skin and smelling the familiar scent. Etienne stirred and lifted his head.

"Mmm? What?" he murmured drowsily.

Tobias kissed him gently on the cheek. "It is nothing, my love. Go back to sleep. I didn't mean to wake you."

"Mmmm. S'kay. Love you."

"I love you too. Rest now. You are weak. You need your rest."

"Rather take you again. Loved it. Love you. Tomorrow maybe. Take you again," his lover whispered sleepily, kissing his nose.

Tobias remained silent as Etienne settled down again.

'No, love. Not tomorrow, or the next night, or the next. Not until I figure this out. It's too dangerous. I could hurt you again. I could kill you. I know you don't care, but I do. We must never ever take it that far again. I have too many questions and no answers for them. And in truth, I liked it far more than I ever thought I would.'

Fourteen

So you felt guilty about hurting him, Rain commented.

Yes. It frightened me badly. You must remember I knew nothing of what I know now, about our bodies and how to make them respond.

You do realize how close you came though, don't you? What you are showing me tells me that you and Etienne were reaching the higher levels of arousal on your own. If you hadn't bitten him when you did, you would have made it all the way, she told him.

How very ironic...

Yes. But tell me what happened next.

By Friday, Etienne was strong enough to go out and we went to meet Andrea after her psychology class. Etienne was quiet and sullen. Earlier he had tried to persuade me to make love again, but I gently refused. He was sulking badly when we met Andrea and escorted her to her apartment...

• • •

"Is he being Mr. Pouty-face again?" Andrea asked Tobias quietly as they entered her living room. She was a little quiet herself. Tricia's visit still weighed heavy on them all, and she was still rather distracted.

Tobias cast Etienne a sad glance as his lover slumped into Andrea's leather recliner, and nodded. "Yes, but it's my fault."

"Want to talk about it?" she offered.

He shook his head. "No. Not now. Give it time."

"Okay. I'm here when you need me. Just remember that, and don't let it get out of hand, okay?"

Tobias nodded, gratitude filling his blue eyes. "Thank you."

"Hey what are friends for?" she asked with a smile, patting his arm.

He smiled back and watched as she moved to sit on her couch, near to Etienne.

"So, what's new with you, Etienne?"

"Nothing much."

"You seem kinda upset."

"Talk to my demon familiar."

Andrea snorted. "He's not your demon familiar."

"You don't know him like I do," the man answered angrily, ignoring Tobias' warning stare. "He giveth and he taketh away."

"Relationships involve a lot of give and take, Etienne."

"Yeah, well ask him what he gives then takes away."

Andrea looked at Tobias, silently asking for guidance, but the young man shook his head sadly, lowering his gaze. She sighed heavily, closing her eyes.

"I've never met two people more in love who fight as much as you two do. You're always fighting, and somehow I always manage to be the one who patches things up for you," she said forlornly, her lower lip trembling. When she looked up again, she was on the verge of tears.

"Well, right now I don't need you to be fighting. One of my best friends in the whole world is dying, and there is nothing I can do to help her. This knowledge is driving me crazy. I never know if today will be the day I get the black letter, or tomorrow or next week. So I don't need you to fight, or to put me in the middle. I need you to be strong for me, because I'm the one falling to pieces right now."

Two tears slid out of her eyes as she looked at them, begging for peace. Within moments Tobias was seated next to her, his arms outstretched and she was in them, crying softly, hugging him. Etienne moved from the recliner and sat on her other side, his hand on her shoulder. He met Tobias' pleading gaze, trying to muster up his earlier anger, but he couldn't make it last, not against those wide, innocent blue eyes so full of love and grief. Sighing he wrapped his arms around Andrea, pressing his cheek to the back of her head and felt Tobias' hands closing on his shoulders. He held Andrea, Tobias held them both. She was nestled between them, drawing comfort from their presence and love.

"We're sorry, Andie. We're very very sorry," Tobias whispered.

"It's okay. I love you. I love both of you. Please love each other for me, at least for a little while."

"Of course. We love you too," Tobias answered.

"Good, because I need that right now."

Two weeks later Andrea received a telegram. She got it after class one night, Adam and Etienne were with her. It was pushed under her door and waiting for her when she opened her apartment. For a long time she sat on the couch, sequestered between Adam and Etienne, staring at the unopened yellow envelope. Finally, she sighed and ripped open the casing to draw out the message; it informed her of Tricia's death. Her friends held her as she started to cry.

"She died last night. The funeral is Saturday...I can't go," she sobbed.

"Why not?" Adam asked.

"Because I don't have the money for a plane ticket, if I could even get one on such short notice."

"Never mind about that. I'll take care of it. You pack your things, you're going to that funeral."

He kept his promise, hand delivering a first class airline ticket to her the very next night. Andrea was shocked and overwhelmed by his generosity. She accepted his gift gratefully and flew to California for the funeral. Tobias and Etienne were there to meet her at University Park Airport when she returned the following Wednesday.

Etienne strained to see as the passengers exited the plane, watching the steady stream of people come through the doorway.

"I still don't see her."

"She is on the plane still, liebchen. She will come out in a moment," Tobias assured.

"Are you sure? Maybe she decided to stay in California."

Tobias cast him a dour look. "Yes, liebchen, I am sure."

"But…"

"Patience, liebchen, she is coming up the ramp now."

Etienne watched the doorway as the last few passengers deplaned. He still did not see any sign of Andrea, then a figure emerged from the plane that looked like her except that she had brilliant, golden blonde hair. He watched her stop for a moment, adjust the large, rectangular carry-on she had slung across her shoulder and look around. Her head turned to see him and he saw her face. His jaw dropped. Even Tobias was speechless as she grinned and came towards them. She stopped a few paces away, submitting herself for their approval, a sheepish smile on her face.

"Hi," she said, blushing under their stunned gazes.

"Wow," Etienne breathed.

Andrea fingered her blonde hair. "Told you I was a blonde."

"Yes, but…"

"It really is true what they say about California girls," Tobias commented, cutting Etienne off.

"Oh? Are you thinking about leaving Stevie and running off with me, then? Have I converted you?" she teased.

Tobias smiled. "I think not. However, if Etienne is willing to share…"

She laughed. "Go play in traffic, Adam."

They smiled and giggled, then Andrea came forward and wrapped her arms around them both.

"It's so good to see you. I'm so glad to be back. I missed you both terribly."

"We missed you too," Tobias conceded as they pulled away.

"What's in the big bag?" Etienne asked curiously.

Andrea's expression turned to one of sadness and she caressed the black leather case absently.

"It's Tricia's Roland. She wanted me to have it."

Etienne's face fell. "Oh, I'm sorry."

She brightened again. "No, it's okay. Hey, I'm hungry. You know how airplane food is. Let's go pick up my other bag and go get something to eat."

"Yes, I'm starving too," Etienne agreed.

"Let me carry that for you, Andie," Tobias said, offering to take the synthesizer. She paused, uncertain at first, her hand reflexively gripping the strap, then she nodded and let him take it from her.

"I promise, I will keep it safe," he told her.

"I know," she whispered sadly as they left the gate and walked down to baggage claim.

"So, are you okay now, Andie?" Etienne inquired.

"Yeah. I'm okay. I'm sad, but I'm all right. It was a beautiful ceremony, and it was good to see everyone again, even if the occasion was so sad. Funerals are like that; bring people who haven't seen each other in a long time back together again. I saw people I haven't seen since I graduated from high school. It was good. We talked, we found our own peace."

"I'm glad."

They arrived at the bag claim and waited for Andrea's bag to arrive.

"Where do you want to go for dinner?" Etienne asked as she moved to grab her suitcase from the conveyor belt.

"Some place quick. How about we just get some Chinese take-out and go back to my place?"

"Sounds great."

"Cool. Let's go."

Andrea hooked the strap onto her suitcase and pulled it along behind her as they followed Tobias outside.

"Um, where are we going? The taxi stand is over there," she asked, confused, as Tobias walked towards an idling limousine.

"We hired a car for the evening," Etienne explained as a well-dressed chauffeur gently took the synthesizer from Tobias and carefully placed it in the trunk of a large, silver, stretch limousine.

"A limo? You guys are too much!"

"Hey, blame him. It was his idea."

"May I take your bag, miss?" the driver asked politely.

"Oh, um, sure. Thanks."

After the luggage was put into the trunk, the chauffeur held the door open while they got in, and they headed off.

"Wow, this is nice," Andrea mused, caressing the velvet seats and checking out the bar. "Gee it isn't every day my two best friends pick me up in a limo."

Tobias sat easily, his legs crossed, his eyes bright and dancing with humor. "Anything for you, Andie."

"Thanks, Adam."

"So, where do you wanna go for takeout?" Etienne asked, his stomach growling loudly.

"Ummm, I dunno…Oh! I have a marvelous idea!"

"Oh? What's you're idea?" Etienne questioned.

"I'll tell you later," she answered, turning to the driver. "Would you head for the Nittany Mall McDonalds drive-thru, please?"

"Drive-thru? You want to take a limousine through a McDonalds drive-thru?" Etienne inquired, a huge grin on his face.

Andrea smiled. "Yes, it's perfectly camp, don't you think?"

Tobias laughed, his face becoming absolutely ecstatic. "Yes, Andie, it's perfect."

The limo pulled up to the ordering stand at the McDonalds drive thru and they slowly lowered the back window. Andrea looked like a movie star with her golden hair, and the terrible twosome, with black sunglasses on, looked like formidable 'minders.'

"Hi, I'd like two Big Macs, two large fries, two cokes and three packets of Grey Poupon. You do have Grey Poupon, don't you?"

"Um, no ma'am, we don't," came the voice.

She sighed petulantly. "Well, I suppose regular mustard will *have* to do."

They pulled around to the pick-up window, and Andrea handed the young man the money, bitching at him about their lack of Grey Poupon while he glanced nervously at Tobias and Etienne.

"I don't understand. All the LA McDonalds have Grey Poupon. I don't understand why you don't have it. I don't know how I am possibly going to manage to choke down these burgers with ordinary mustard on them. It's positively heinous, really it is. My agent swore to me that Pennsylvania was the same as LA. Well, it isn't…"

Etienne decided to have some fun as the edgy young man handed Andrea her change.

"Don't touch the lady," he said in a serious, dour voice. "I wouldn't want to have to rip your hand off."

The teenager jumped back immediately, frightened, his eyes wide.

"Oh, Brutus! Relax. He's only giving me my change, sweetie. There's no need to get defensive," Andrea poo-pooed.

Shaking, the cashier shoved the bag of food towards the window. Tobias intercepted it swiftly, ripping it from the boy's hands and opening it with ferocity.

"Checking it for poisons," he informed menacingly, lifting out the burgers and inspecting them.

"Y- your drinks, Ma'am," the boy stuttered.

Etienne grabbed the sodas and drank from each one.

"Don't mind them, sweetie darling. They're big pushovers, really," Andrea smoothed.

"They're safe," Etienne said, giving Andrea her sodas.

"Oh, thank you sweetie, but I don't know why anyone would want to poison me at a McDonalds."

"Can't be too careful," Tobias deadpanned.

"Hey, what are you looking at?" Etienne barked at the staring boy.

"N.. nothing, sir!"

"Good, keep it that way," the blond man snarled.

"Bye, sweetie darling," Andrea cooed, as she waved her fingers and raised the darkened window.

As soon as it was closed and they were leaving the drive-thru, they burst into laughter.

"Did you see his face when Adam snatched the bag from him?" she snickered.

"You would have thought we were gonna shoot him!" Etienne added, chortling.

"And Adam, looking like the Terminator in those sunglasses!"

"I'll be back," Tobias said in his best Schwartzenegger impression.

It sent Andrea reeling and she laughed heartily.

"That was so much fun! I should come back from California more often!"

They laughed all the way to Andrea's apartment where the chauffeur carried her bags up to her door, then left for the evening. They gave him a big tip. Tobias and Etienne watched as Andrea reverently unzipped the Roland case and carefully removed the synthesizer. It seemed that they were watching a religious ritual as she dismantled one of her own keyboards and replaced it with the new one. When she was done, she stared at the synthesizer for a long time.

"What is it?" Tobias asked.

"Oh nothing, just that Stephen told me that Tricia had recorded a song for me on this thing before she died. She left a note with her will, indicating the memory number, saying I should play it when I got back here."

"Well, play it," Etienne said. "Or, would you rather be alone when you do?"

She shook her head. "No, I don't mind if you're here. I'm just afraid. I miss her…"

It looked as if she was going to cry and they came up beside her, their hands on her shoulders, comforting.

"It's all right, Andie," Tobias whispered.

"I know," she replied, wiping her eyes roughly. "Well, here goes nothing."

She pressed the proper sequence of buttons to replay the song stored inside it and soon a sweet melody was finding its way through the speakers. It was a lovely piece, both melancholy and joyful at the same time, a skillful duet performed by synthesized strings and woodwinds, each answering the other in turn, the strings lamenting in their richness and the woodwinds calling to joy with their high, clear notes. It was the song of Andrea and Tricia, two friends learning to say good-bye. By the end, the strings and woodwinds had come together, singing one melody, a mixture of both harmonies, a resolution being reached in music. As it reached its coda, Andrea was weeping softly in Tobias' arms.

Tobias stroked her hair. "It will be all right, Andie."

She sniffled and pulled away. "Yes, it will be. I just need a little time."

"Look, Andie, why don't you skip class tonight. Adam and I are going to the movies. Come with us," Etienne offered.

"I'm not going back to class. I'm dropping out of Penn State."

"Oh? Why?" Tobias asked.

"I'm giving up this charade. I'm dropping political science. I hate it. I'm going to be a musician and a dancer. It's what I want; it's what I've always wanted. Trish was right. Life is too short to miss a moment of it."

"What about Louis?" Etienne asked.

"He's a risk I'll have to take. I can't let fear rule my life. If he comes for me, I'll deal with him then. I'm still going to keep my name listed under a false identity, but I'm not going to hide anymore."

"Whatever you do, Andie, you know we will be there for you," Etienne told her.

"I know, Stevie," she replied, kissing them both on the cheek. "Believe me, I know. That makes my choice a lot easier. I know that no matter what, I have the two of you to help and protect me."

She hugged Tobias one last time, giving him a fond, loving look, then went to get ready for the film.

Fifteen

*How long before things fell apart?** Rain questioned.

*Less than a year,** he answered, his thoughts tinged with sadness. *Andrea had dropped out of Penn State and had taken up dance at Centre Dance. She applied to New York's Academy of the Arts and was waiting to find out if she'd been accepted. She was much happier. Etienne and I were still having problems, but that was nothing new. It seemed that every other week, she was patching us up again after another fight. Even then, I knew I was losing him. I could not keep him with me. All of my efforts were for naught. Still, I held on, trying to make it last, trying to be what he wanted me to be. Andrea helped us so much. I owe so much to her kindness. Then one night in late April I met her as she was leaving dance class...*

• • •

Adam was waiting for her when she emerged from the dance studio, still clothed in her leotard and leg warmers. He materialized silently into the light of a street lamp, alone and forlorn. His sudden, soundless appearance didn't surprise her. She had long ago ceased to believe he was human, but he didn't know that. Somehow she had managed to keep that little secret from him.

She had come to her conclusion not long after her conversation with Tricia; she began to notice all the things her friend had mentioned and had to agree. Adam wasn't human, he was something else, and all the fights he had with Etienne stemmed from that basic difference. Poor Etienne. Andrea pitied him sometimes, the sullen, brooding young man who loved Adam, was terrified of him, yet needed him desperately. She also began to notice a pattern and a common theme. The arguments were always about something Adam wouldn't do, but they would never say exactly what it was he wouldn't do.

What was it that had kept these two very different beings together for so long? She remembered Adam's answer to that question: love and patience. How much patience could an immortal have? There seemed no end. Yet he wasn't all that different from her. He still felt love and pain, he still needed affection and acceptance…

'Ah, you are starting to let your mind think about it, time to think of something else!'

"Where's Etienne?" she asked, already knowing the answer.

Adam lowered his gaze. She patted his shoulder and took his arm, guiding him as she headed home.

"He's been Mr. Pouty-face a lot lately," she remarked.

"Yes," he admitted, walking slowly alongside her, his hands deep in his pockets.

They remained silent until they arrived at her apartment. She tossed her keys on the cocktail table and draped her jacket over the back of the couch.

"I'll be right back, I'm gonna go change."

"Okay," Adam replied, moving to sit in his usual place on the sofa.

She went into her bedroom and donned a pair of sweat pants and a T-shirt, all very casual and comfortable. She had an inkling that she was going to be up late tonight. Adam would not have come if he was not deeply upset. She glanced over at her answering machine on the bedside table. The message light was blinking. Curious, she pressed the play button.

"Andiiieeee. You know who this is, don't you Andiiiee? Thought you could hide from me, didn't you? I've found you, Andiiieee. I know where you live. I've been watching you. I'm coming for you. When I get through with you, they'll have to identify your body through dental records, if they ever find your teeth."

The familiar, sadistic voice terrified her. Her first impulse was to pack her bags and run, but then she remembered Adam in the living room. Adam was upset, he was hurting and he needed her. He had come to her for comfort, the immortal with the broken heart, come to her for help. Taking a deep breath, she calmed herself and made her choice. She tried not to let on that anything was amiss as she sat beside him on the couch and waited for him to start speaking.

"Is everything all right?" he asked suddenly.

"Huh? Oh yes. Everything is fine," she lied. "I'm more concerned with you. Wanna talk about it?'

Adam dropped his head in despair. "Etienne and I had a terrible fight."

"You seem to be having a lot of those lately. Any particular reason?"

He shook his head, his face a mask of agony. Quietly, without hesitation, she put her arms around his shoulders and drew him close. Then she kissed his forehead, eyes and cheeks tenderly, and let him go. He looked shocked.

"Why did you do that?" he asked, amazed.

"Because it seemed to be what you needed most."

The youthful face fell and he slumped against her shoulder, his white, perfect hands in her lap. She put an arm around him and patted his back, offering what comfort she could.

"Tell me what is wrong," she urged gently.

"I'm losing him, Andie. I'm losing him and I cannot bear to live without him."

"Don't think that way, Adam. Etienne loves you. He's stayed with you for seven years. He isn't about to leave you now."

Adam disagreed vehemently, pulling away from her and wiping his bloodshot eyes with the sleeve of his black sweater. His curly, brown hair was ruffled and mussed, and he compulsively smoothed it back into place.

"No. He is leaving me because I cannot submit, I will not submit."

Andrea curled her legs up on the cushions of the couch. It always came back to this, this deed Adam would not do.

"What is it that he wants so badly that you will not give him? For as long as I've known you two, you are always fighting about this. You've probably been fighting about it since the day you met," she offered boldly.

"We have."

"Then what is it? Why, in seven years, have you not reached a reconciliation? My God, you love each other desperately, but you tear each other apart over this. Is it that important?"

"Yes! I made a vow. I cannot break it."

"Vow? What? Are you married? Do you have a wife somewhere and that's why you are here in State College? Did you vow never to tell your family that you're gay?"

Adam sighed. "I wish it was that simple! No, I am not married and I have no family to speak of. Etienne and you are my family."

"Then what is it?"

He looked at her, his eyes wide and full of grief. "No, I cannot tell you. There are dark secrets I hold, Andrea. Believe me when I tell you I am not what I seem to be."

'Of that I have no doubt, my friend, but I can't let you know that, can I,' she thought to herself, then quickly pushed it aside.

"And does Etienne know these secrets?"

"Yes. They are what is driving him away. There is nothing I can do to stop it, nothing I can give..." He paused, as if uncertain then, continued. "He will leave me and I cannot bear to live without him."

Andrea was thoughtful for a moment. "You seemed uncertain that there was nothing you could give to make it better. Why is that?"

"No, I am certain. He has gotten so much worse in the last few weeks. I cannot console him."

"Why has he gotten worse?"

Adam hung his head in shame. "Because of something I did. Something I never should have done, and now it has made things much, much worse."

Andrea's curiosity was piqued. "Oh? What did you do?"

Adam seemed to wrestle with himself. "My relationship with Etienne is not normal, in ways you cannot even begin to comprehend…"

"Okay…so just give me the short version."

"I hurt him when we made love. I hurt him badly and I cannot abide myself because of it."

Andrea shrugged. He wasn't making any sense, or rather he was, but she couldn't let on to that. "You'll just have to be more careful next time."

Adam's head snapped up in alarm. "No! There must never be a next time. Not until I know why it happened. It is far too dangerous."

It seemed that his misery balled around him and he hid his face in his hands.

"So you got carried away during anal sex and were a little too rough. Next time you'll be more careful, use more lube. Does he blame you for hurting him?"

"No and that is the torment of it. He doesn't. He liked it. I pleased him far more than I ever thought I would, and now…"

"And now he wants more, but you're afraid."

He nodded. "Yes."

She was quiet for a few seconds. "Did you like it?"

Adam paused, then nodded again. "Yes, I enjoyed it," he admitted guiltily.

"Then what is the problem? He liked it, you liked it. Do it! Use a lubricated condom and lots of KY if you have to, but do it. There's nothing wrong with it. You have needs the same as other men."

"No, no. I can't. You don't understand."

Andrea was getting frustrated. "I understand that you can't give him something like that with one hand and then take it away with the other. No wonder he is upset."

Adam stared at her, dumbfounded. Andrea never took sides, but tonight she was and she was siding with Etienne.

"You need to decide what is more important: Etienne's needs or your own fear. When you decide, you needn't tell me what the answer is. Tell Etienne."

"Andrea, I…"

"Don't give me any excuses. I understand completely why Etienne is so distraught. What bothers me is why you don't understand why he is so unhappy," she said, cutting him off.

He didn't have an answer for her. She waited a long time before speaking again.

"Etienne loves you. You love him. You gave him the fullest, most complete expression of that love. Of course he is going to want more. He's even going to want to reciprocate. Is that what you are so afraid of?"

'I'm afraid of killing him,' he thought angrily but did not say it. Andrea was right.

"No, that it is not what I fear. I fear causing him pain. He couldn't stand for two days afterwards. I do not want that to happen again."

"Wow. You must have really pounded him into the mattress. I guess it got pretty wild."

Adam blushed at her candid manner and had to smile. "It did," he conceded.

"Stevie is a big boy. He can take care of himself. Don't worry about him. He'll tell you when he has had too much. For now, just let yourself enjoy it. Give in to the love and the pleasure. You don't know how lucky you are to have someone who loves you as much as he does."

"Yes. I am lucky. I need him. I am nothing without him."

Andrea patted his hand. "Then show him. Love him. Give him the very best of yourself. Give it freely, without restraint or conditions. God knows what I would do to be loved like that. What you have, in spite of all the ups and downs, is the closest you will ever get to perfection."

He regarded her intently and was silent for a long time. "You are right, as always, Andrea," he sighed finally.

"So, have you figured out what's more important?"

He nodded. "Yes."

"Good. Want to tell Etienne?"

"Yes."

"Okay, I'll call and see if he's at your flat."

Andrea picked up the phone and dialed their number. After six rings, she shook her head and hung up.

"He's not there. He's probably at a bar somewhere, drinking himself into oblivion," she commented.

No sooner had she put the receiver down when it rang. Terror coursed through her as she watched it vibrate with the sound. She wasn't sure if she should answer it. What if it was Louis? What if it was Etienne? Biting her lip, she picked it up.

"Hello?" she asked timidly, trying not to sound frightened. "Etienne?" She breathed a sigh of relief. "Yes, Adam is here. We were just talking about you. He wants to talk to you. Where are you now? Zeno's? Are you sober enough to walk? Oh, only two Screwdrivers, eh? You're slagging, Stevie. Okay then, we'll wait for you here. See you soon. Bye." She hung up the phone. "He's on his way now. He'll be here soon."

Adam smiled at her then grew serious. "Andrea, you are such a good friend. I do not know what Etienne and I would do without you. We are in your debt. But now I have a confession to make." He placed his hands on her shoulders, looking deeply into her eyes.

"I have very good hearing, Andrea. I heard the message on your machine and it frightens me. Louis has found you and you are in danger. I do not want anything to happen to you. I want you to come and stay with us, if only for a few days until you can find a safe place. It will be odd, our lifestyle is very odd, but we will be with you and Louis will not know where you are."

"Adam, I'm flattered, but I can't. Especially not tonight, not after what we discussed. You are going to want your privacy," she demurred, looking away.

He shook her gently to command her attention.

"No, I insist and I am sure Etienne will agree with me. Your life is more important than our...nocturnal activities. I know he will understand. When he gets here, pack a bag while we talk and you will come with us."

"That sounds kinky, Adam," she joked with a weak smile.

He smiled. "You don't know the meaning of the word, Andie."

She raised an eyebrow. "Oh? And you do? Oh! that's right. You're the one who rode his lover so hard he couldn't stand for two days. Of course you know what kinky means."

He laughed heartily. "I love you, Andie."

"I'm pretty fond of you myself."

"Will you come? If only to ease my troubled mind?" he asked.

She thought a moment and he pressed on, trying to convince her.

"He's threatened you, Andie. If we leave here tonight and something happens to you, I will never forgive myself."

Andrea sighed. "All right. I'll stay over, but only for tonight. I'll move into a hotel tomorrow until I find a new place. Deal?"

Adam smiled. "Deal."

"Okay, when Etienne gets here, I'll pack while you two kiss and make out...er...up."

He laughed again, clearly comforted, and was about to speak when there was a knock on the door. Andrea eyed it furtively.

"I'll answer it, if you'd like," Adam offered.

"No. It's Stevie. I'll get it."

She opened the door and Etienne stood there, dressed in rumpled clothes. He reeked of alcohol, but his eyes were clear and alert. He was at least partially sober.

"Come on in, Stevie."

He entered, casting a sullen and guilty glance at his lover. Andrea whispered softly to him, her hand on his arm.

"Go to him. Things will be better now, I promise. He has something to tell you."

Etienne looked at Adam then reluctantly went to him. He didn't move or speak when Adam wrapped his arms around him and kissed his cheek.

"I love you," Adam said tenderly.

Etienne sighed and gave in to the hug, putting his arms around his lover in a gesture of peace. Andrea watched for a few moments, making sure they were all right, before going into her bedroom to pack. She closed the door to give the two men in the living room some privacy while they talked. Pulling a suitcase out from underneath her bed, she began to gather up some clothes she would need to take along. With her back to the closet, she did not see the figure emerge from in back of the folding doors and come up behind her.

"I must beg for your forgiveness, liebchen," Tobias sighed, smoothing back Etienne's tousled hair.

Etienne shrugged and refused to meet Tobias' eyes.

"I love you, Etienne. With everything I am."

He cupped Etienne's face in both hands and kissed him passionately. Etienne responded with an answering hunger, his lips searching and begging for more.

"I promise we will talk, and I will try to give you more of what you need."

Now Etienne looked up at him, his hazel eyes full of hope. "You will? Tonight?"

Tobias shook his head and Etienne's face fell.

"No liebchen, but let me explain. We will not be alone tonight. Andrea will be staying with us."

Etienne cocked his head in confusion. "Why?"

"Louis has found her. He left a threatening message on her answering machine tonight. I have asked her to stay with us until she can find a safe place, and until I can find this man and kill him, of course."

Etienne regarded his lover grimly. "I understand. I agree with you. The sooner you get rid of him, the better."

"I know. I will hunt him down tomorrow. But come, we must make haste. I want to get her out of here now. Let us go help her pack and be off."

"Okay. I am a little disappointed, though," he said with a mock-pout and a teasing smile.

"I'll make it up to you, liebchen."

"I'll hold you to that, you know," he replied wryly, coming close for a kiss.

"I don't doubt that," Tobias whispered as his lips touched Etienne's.

Their kiss was interrupted by Andrea's scream and a loud crashing. Immediately they turned to face the closed bedroom door, terror seizing them. Tobias moved too fast for Etienne to see. He heard a rush of wind and the tearing of metal, then saw that his lover had literally ripped the bedroom door from its hinges. Etienne rushed to the bedroom and arrived in the doorway in time to see Tobias lift a strange man: Louis, away from Andrea's fallen body and throw him through the picture window. The man screamed and there was a tremendous breaking of glass as the pane shattered, sending Louis falling down four stories in a shower of broken shards. He landed with a sickening thud on the sidewalk. A passerby screamed and a crowd started to form around the body as Etienne peered down from the splintered frame. People looked up at him, pointing accusingly, and he drew back quickly, afraid.

Horrified, he looked around to find Tobias and Andrea. They were a few paces away, on the floor at the foot of the bed. Andrea lay on her side. Tobias was beside her on his knees, his head bowed. Etienne could see blood on the carpet and a soiled knife nearby. Disbelieving, he crept closer, afraid of what awaited him. There was blood all around her, seeping from wounds in her sides and on her arms. Apparently she had fought Louis when he grabbed her, but he must have been slashing at her with the knife before she fell. She had been stabbed several times, but she was still alive. He could hear her ragged breathing, but he knew instinctively that something was very wrong. She was unnervingly still, her eyes closed.

He has broken her spine, Tobias told him, reading his thoughts as usual.

"I'll call an ambulance," he offered nervously

"One is undoubtedly already on its way."

Will she live? he had to ask.

She has lost much blood, but if she gets help very soon, yes, she will live.

Andrea's eyes opened and locked on Tobias. She was looking intently at him, taking in his whole face, and there was grim determination in her eyes, as if she knew what had happened and had made a choice. Her lips moved and Tobias dipped his head low to hear.

"Adam..." she whispered, almost inaudibly.

"I am here. Etienne is here too. Help is on the way. You must remain still. Louis has stabbed you in the back," he told her gently, trying to sound reassuring.

"I know. I can't feel anything below my shoulders. I can't move..."

Tobias stroked her hair comfortingly. "Help will be here soon. They will make everything all right."

"No...Too late. Bastard did it on purpose."

She was right. Louis had stabbed her there first, right between her shoulder blades. He had aimed to do the most damage should he fail to kill her. He knew dance and music were her life, and sought to end her ability to dance and play forever. It was an act of pure, unrestrained cruelty, and it made Etienne want to scream and go pound the crushed body on the pavement right into the concrete, but he didn't, he just started to cry.

Sirens, still far away, but coming, could be heard wailing through the broken window. Andrea heard them and gasped, her eyes widening with fear. Again, she looked at Tobias, this time beseechingly, as if she knew he could save her.

"Adam..."

"Yes?"

"I know what you are."

With the admission, her soul broke open, flooding him with a torrent of images. She knew what he was, she had known for a long time and had managed to keep it from him. But now, she revealed her knowledge because she wanted something from him, wanted something desperately.

"Adam…there is not much time. The ambulance will be here soon…I do not want to be alive when it gets here."

His eyes registered his shock. Etienne sobbed loudly.

"No, Andie…" Etienne gasped.

She ignored him and continued to look directly at Tobias, her gaze unwavering, her eyes showing no fear.

"Tricia was right. Life is too precious to waste. If I am alive when they come, I will live out the rest of my days confined to a bed, unable to get up, or walk, or even move. I'll never dance or play my instruments again. That is worse than death. I ask you now, please, kill me. End my life. I know you can."

"Andrea, I…" Tobias began, recoiling from the idea.

She cut him off with an angry glare and clenched her teeth.

"Do it, Adam! Spare me this death in life. Please. If you do not, I could waste away for decades! Don't let me go that way. Please! I'm begging you. Kill me. Take my blood and my soul into yourself. Do it in memory of our friendship, and the love I have for both of you."

Her eyes were pleading with him. It was more than he could bear. The sirens were getting closer, only a few moments at most were left. Weeping, letting her see the tears streaming down his face, he gathered her into his arms and held her close. She heard Etienne's agonized sobbing and felt his hands stroking her blond hair.

"Oh, Andie…" he choked.

"I will always love you," she murmured as Tobias sunk his teeth into her neck.

For a second time, her soul opened, pouring into him with her blood, and music, sweet, wonderful music rang in his soul. All the music she had ever written and had yet to write came gushing out of her in a steady stream of melodies. Beautiful, so beautiful.

Yes, listen. Remember it. Remember me.

Always, he answered.

She was fading quickly, giving herself up completely to the swoon. He lost himself in it, delving into the heart of her.

I am Tobias, he told her, giving her his real name.

Yes. Tobias. I knew Adam was not your true name.

I love you.

I know. I have always known, but now I must leave you and Etienne. Love him. Love each other. I can't be with you any more.

She was almost gone. Another moment and her heart would let go. The sirens were right outside the building now. People were running up the stairs.

Tobias, she sent faintly.

Yes.

Love is the only thing that lasts forever.

Yes.

I have to go now, Trish is waiting for me.

I know, liebchen.

Thank you.

Her life was ending. He could feel the death coming over her like a great shroud. He felt her body relax and let out a deep sigh as he released her.

I love you.

It was the last thing she said. Then she was gone, her body limp in his arms, her music silenced forever. Etienne was crying uncontrollably beside him, even as he tried to curb his own tears. Quickly, he used his sharp fingernails to erase the puncture wounds on her neck, just as the police began pounding on the door. He wiped the tears from his face and stopped his weeping as Etienne went to let them in. When they entered the bedroom, guns drawn, all they saw was a grief stricken man holding his dead friend.

Sixteen

Oh Goddess. Priye, I'm so sorry, Rain consoled.

Thank you. Losing her was...difficult, Tobias admitted. *After the police came in and secured the crime scene, Etienne and I were taken down to the police station and held for questioning.*

Were you suspected of killing Louis?

No. I glamoured them. They believed Louis fell out the window. Etienne had a harder time of it because they kept us in separate interrogation rooms.

• • •

Questions. Endless questions. Tobias had told his story a dozen times to seven different police officers and detectives. It was late, he was weary of being kept at the police station and he wanted to go home. He was numb with grief and all he wanted to do was see Etienne. But they wouldn't let him see Etienne; Etienne was being questioned in another room. Poor Etienne who could not stop crying, who told his story in-between sobs. They had been grilling both of them for hours, refusing to let them take comfort in each other, and now Tobias was out of patience.

Finally, they let them go, telling them not to leave town, that there would be more questions later. Etienne ran into his arms and clung to him as a police officer called them a taxi to take them home. He clung to him in the back of the taxi, sniffling, inconsolable. Tobias held him close,

letting him cry. It was all he could do. It was a mere two hours before
dawn and he was exhausted. His body was cooling, the heat Andrea had
given him wearing off over the hours. She had not had much blood left
for him to take. He hated the chill, even more so now that he had Etienne,
acutely aware that cuddling with a cold body would not be a pleasant
experience for his mortal lover, and he did want to cuddle. They were both
still in shock, and Etienne had not spoken a word since they had gotten
into the cab. Gently, Tobias reached for Etienne's hand and sighed when
he felt the warm fingers curl around his cold ones. He smiled and kissed
Etienne's cheek.

"I'll warm up before I come in," he whispered.

"Okay."

The cab pulled up in front of their building and they got out. He gave
Etienne a swift kiss and watched as he went up to their apartment, then
he went off to hunt.

Etienne was crying bitterly when Tobias returned, a ball of misery
curled on the bed, his arms wrapped around a pillow, sobbing into the
sheets. Tobias undressed and settled next to him. Etienne rolled over and
pressed his face into Tobias' chest as his lover wrapped arms around him.

"If we hadn't been fighting…If we had left with her as soon as I got
there…" Etienne choked.

"She knew the danger, liebchen. She made the choice. Don't you think
I feel badly about it? I was there when she got the message. If only I had
grabbed her and taken her out of there instead of talking. She'd still be
alive. If only I hadn't been so upset about you, I would have distinguished
the closer heart beat from the others in the building, and found him
hiding before he had the chance to reveal himself."

"And the police! The endless questions! And them calling me a blubbering faggot!"

Tobias stroked his hair. "Hush, liebchen. It's all right." "No it's not all
right! Andie is dead! As dead as I'll be one day, if you don't take pity on me."

Tobias didn't answer. He didn't want to think about Etienne dying. It was bad enough thinking about Andrea being dead and the hole her absence left behind. If Etienne begged for immortality tonight, he might just give it to him. He couldn't bear to be without his Etienne. Not even if it meant breaking his vow. To never be without you, my Eti. But he knew it wouldn't be that way. He could attempt bring Etienne to him, and lose him when he left his maker, or let him remain mortal where he would grow old and die. Either way, Tobias would lose him. The thought was almost unbearable, but it didn't matter now, Etienne was kissing him, pulling him away from his thoughts. The warm lips were on his throat and licking his breasts. It seemed horribly morbid, to make love on the same night Andrea died, but Etienne needed the comfort. He did not refuse.

This time, Tobias actively tried to please his lover. He did all the things he knew Etienne loved, purposefully trying to drive him wild. He kissed Etienne's breasts, licked his soft skin, and explored all his soft places. The urge to bite was unbearable, but he fought back his need until Etienne mounted him, until they had locked into the primal rhythm. It was as it was before. Less frenzied but no less glorious. They were one again, rocking in unison, sharing the blood. He was careful, refusing to allow himself to get lost in the pleasure, no matter how wonderful the whole experience felt. Once again, he achieved the strange, powerful climax, followed by Etienne's frantic release and the feeling of their souls intertwining. It was perfection all over again.

When it was over, they rested in each other's arms for long moments. Etienne dozed contentedly, his head nestled in the crook of Tobias' shoulder until Tobias gently removed himself from the bed.

"Mmm?" Etienne asked wearily.

"It is nearly dawn."

"Okay."

"I'll be back in a moment."

Etienne heard the sound of material rustling and looked up to see Tobias lowering the blinds, closing up the curtains. Then he left the bedroom to close up the rest of the apartment and seal it from the coming sunlight. True to his word, he was back less then five minutes later and climbing under the covers. Etienne kissed him and snuggled close, letting sleep take him.

When Etienne awakened it was not yet sunset. Tobias' body was next to his, cold and still. The arms were wrapped around him and he turned his head carefully to see Tobias' face. The youthful visage was peaceful, the eyes closed, the breath deep And even. He sighed and glanced at the clock: only another hour before sundown. He could doze for that long without any problem. The electric blanket they kept on the bed was doing an admirable job of keeping him warm, in spite of Tobias' coldness. Content, he settled down again and closed his eyes. He didn't really sleep, just dozed lightly, dreaming, thinking. He was aware of the darkening room as the sun went down, and he was daydreaming when the body next to his began to stir. Etienne watched Tobias' face as he awakened; the vampire's internal body clock telling him it was sunset. He saw the large eyes open and focus on his smiling face. At first, Tobias seemed profoundly confused then he relaxed and smiled.

"Hi there," Etienne greeted.

"Hello, lover. Did you sleep well?"

"Yes. Hungry?"

"Starving."

"Me too. Better get up then."

Tobias rose from the bed and Etienne followed suit. Yawning, Etienne sauntered into the bathroom and turned on the spigot in the tub. When the water temperature was right, he climbed in and flipped on the shower. Tobias came into the bathroom while he was showering, pulled aside the curtain and joined him. Etienne sighed with pleasure and allowed Tobias to wash him, until he bent his lips to Etienne's neck and nipped. Etienne swooned and gasped.

Don't tease me, he chided.

I'm not teasing you. I'm whetting your appetite.

Etienne moaned as Tobias released him, giving him a quick kiss on the lips before finishing his task. They finished in the bath and moved to the bedroom to dress. Tobias seemed to be in a hurry, but Etienne did not know why. Where were they going tonight?

At first, Etienne thought that they would have to go meet Andrea at her chemistry class, the way they had done for weeks. They would meet her, then go somewhere for dinner, and then out some place Tobias would drag them to, and finish the evening at her apartment. But Andrea was dead. The memory of her death hit him suddenly and the grief threatened to take him again. Tobias held tight to his arm, forcing him to look into his blue eyes.

Stay with me, Eti.

Tobias, Andie is dead, he replied, starting to cry all over again.

"I know. I know. Come, lover. I am hungry. Let us both satisfy our need to feed, then we will come back here and pack our things. We are leaving here tonight. This place has lost its luster for me."

"Where will we go?"

"Florida, I think. I would like to see if it really is a vampire's state."

"But what about the police telling us to stay put?"

"What do I care for your mortal police? No, I am not staying in this town any longer. I wanted to go a long time ago, but Andrea held me here. Now that she is gone, there is no reason for us to stay."

Etienne did not argue. Andrea's death weighed heavy on him. As they went out, every place they passed reminded him of her. He would be glad to leave, to go to a new city that had no sad memories. Tobias left him at The Corner Room then went hunting. He returned almost an hour later with first class tickets for the ten o'clock flight out of State College, with an interchange in Pittsburgh, to Orlando, Florida. They had only two hours to pack and get to the airport.

Etienne watched the twinkling lights of State College get smaller and smaller as they rose into the sky, the world below seemed so cold and sterile next to the blazing lights, and a great sadness came over him.

Good-bye, Andie.

Tobias' hand touched his shoulder gently and he turned to face him, looking into the endless blue eyes. There was sadness there too.

"I miss her."

"I know. So do I, liebchen."

"Think she's gone to a better place?"

"I don't know."

No, Tobias didn't know. No one knew unless they were truly dead and then they couldn't tell anybody. Etienne hung his head, fighting tears again. Tobias' arms came around him and he rested his cheek against the hard chest.

It's all right to cry.

*I still don't know why she had to die. * He began to sob softly.

*It was what she wanted, my love. She did not want to live confined to a bed. To insist that she live just because we wished it so, would have been a terrible selfishness, * he answered tenderly.

It's not fair!

*No, it's not. But then life rarely is. *

Don't ever leave me.

*Never, my love. Never. I will be with you always. *

*Thank you. *

Etienne snuggled close, letting the tears trickle slowly down his face while his lover held him.

Tobias coddled Etienne in his arms, trying to comfort as best he could. He closed his eyes and listened to something deep inside of him. If he was quiet, he could still hear Andrea's music. The songs played in his head like a record, melodies that had never seen the light of day. Andrea's music lived forever in him; she had wanted it that way, now it would never die. He would have to have someone write it down for him when they got to Florida. He would find someone who would be able to listen to him play the songs on the guitar and know what the notes were, preserve the songs on paper and maybe have someone record them. He smiled, listening to the concert only he could hear. Beautiful, delightful music.

'Oh, if only I could share this with you, liebchen. If only you could hear this music, then you would understand why she made the choice that she did.'

But Etienne couldn't hear it and he couldn't understand. Tobias knew that, so he just held his mortal lover, knowing the holding would comfort him more than any words ever could.

The lights of State College were gone, replaced by the twinkling lights of the countless stars one could see when flying above the clouds. Tobias gazed out the tiny porthole of a window, unable to fathom their number. The enormity of it all overwhelmed him and he suddenly felt very small. What had Andrea tried to tell him that he only understood in her last moments? That in all the world, love was the only thing that truly lasted forever. Yes, now he understood.

Quietly he dipped his face into Etienne's hair, smelling the musky odor that rose from his scalp. Such a sweet perfume, belonging only to his Etienne, his lover's unique, singular scent. He had loved this mortal from the moment he had laid eyes on him, sitting in the tavern in Paris. His beauty had astounded him; how the life radiated around him like an incandescent glow. 'Yes, beautiful Etienne. My Etienne.'

His lover stirred and Tobias let him go, watching with kind and patient eyes as Etienne lifted the armrest that separated them and snuggled against him again, his whole body pressed next to Tobias'. He wrapped an arm around his immortal beloved's chest and rested his head in the crook of his arm, his forehead nestled under the delicately molded chin. Tobias smiled to himself and pulled Etienne closer.

*I love you, liebchen. * He kissed the precious forehead tenderly.

I love you too.

Etienne let out a deep sigh and relaxed, then his eyes closed as Tobias gently lulled him to sleep. He dozed there, safe in his lover's arms, until they landed in Pittsburgh.

• • •

The tale was told and the memories ceased, leaving only the faint sound of Andrea's music echoing in their shared thoughts. When they

separated both of them were crying, and Rain tenderly brushed away
Tobias' tears while he did the same for her.

"Thank you," she whispered, humbled.

"Anything for you, my love," he replied.

She smiled and kissed him, tangling her hands in his curls. He laughed
softly, understanding her invitation and settled back under the bedcovers
with her.

An hour later they left the cozy solitude of the willow room and
ventured outside. Walking hand in hand, they lazily strolled along a
gurgling stream, enjoying the warmth of the sunlight and each other's
pleasant company. They came upon a small pond, its waters so smooth that
it could have been mistaken for glass, and Rain smiled fondly.

"What is it?" Tobias asked, seeing her thoughtful expression.

"That is the pond where I used to scry for you."

"Scry?"

"Yes, whenever I would try to find you. I would try to scry for you, to
see if I could feel you or sense you. It was hard."

"Because of the shield spell you told me about," he noted. He didn't
really grasp the concept, but he understood enough to know that this
'shield spell' prevented Aiya and other gods from finding the vampires.

"Yes. And because Ja'oi broke the Circle."

The Circle was another thing he was having difficulty with, and why it
was so awful that it was 'broken,' but he was trying to understand it all. It
felt that he ought to, seeing as he was now the 'ambassador,' as Song called
it for all the vampires. He knew the Circle tied all of Aiya's children to
each other, but he wasn't certain how it worked. He guessed that it had
something to do with the Web and how that worked as well, but the Web
was another concept entirely.

"You can't find any others of my kind, can you?" he questioned.

"No. Which is why we need your help to find Aurek. Both Aiya and
Aerth have looked for him and Roshan, but they've never found them."

Tobias shook his head sadly. "I have never heard of Aurek, nor has anyone I have ever met ever mentioned him."

"I know, and that is the mystery. It is obvious that he made children because your kind has survived, but why were none of the histories passed on, and when was the Circle broken? And where is Aurek?"

"I don't know, but I think I want to find out as much as you do. I want to find out what he was like," he admitted, folding his hands in front of him.

"Aerth is the one to talk to about that. She was his guardian and the one who went with him to Earth. She knew him best. He was practically her son."

"Then we will have to find him for her," he said with finality. He knew too well what it was like to miss someone he loved.

"Do you have any ideas as to where we can begin?"

The vampire nodded. "I have given it some thought. I will take you to my brother Dorian. He lives near Seattle. We can go there first."

"Do you think he will help us?"

"Dorian and I have had our differences, but we have always helped each other. If he cannot, there is always my maker, Ian," he admitted with some trepidation. "He is one of the older vampires; he can help us find others, and hopefully one will lead us to Aurek."

Tobias returned his attention to the pond, seemingly to gather his thoughts.

"Rain, what will happen if..."

His question was cut off as the water in the pond suddenly scattered and dispersed in a great splash. He reeled back, lifting his eyes to see what had caused the spray of water, and saw Sky, naked and dripping wet, standing knee deep in the pond.

"I was wondering when you were going to show up," Rain mused, wiping the water from her face.

Sky giggled and hopped onto the shore.

"I was just waiting for the right moment to pounce on you," he quipped, shaking himself like an animal.

Rain and Tobias shielded themselves from the spray as best they could, but received a good dousing anyway.

"Ha! Now you have to change," Sky teased. "Maybe you will wear something other than black!"

Rain gave him a dour look. "I'll make you a bargain, Sky. I'll stop wearing black when you start wearing anything at all," she answered dryly.

Sky grinned. "You look nice in black."

Rain smiled. "Now how did I know you were going to say something like that?"

"I dunno," the male ecomancer jibed, flopping down on the grass. "What were you doing?"

"You mean when you so rudely interrupted us?" Rain asked innocently, but she was smiling. "We were talking."

"Oh? Talking about what?"

"Aurek."

"Ah, I see. I guess you can't play with me then."

"Not right now."

Sky shook himself again and stood. "Okay. I'll pounce on you again later."

"I have no doubts about that," Rain said as Sky shifted into a stag and bounded off.

Tobias blinked at the figure as the stag body disappeared into the trees, feeling as if he had just been visited by a whirlwind.

"Why does he do that?" the vampire questioned.

"Do what?"

"Appear like that. Why does he never wear any clothes?"

Rain looked in the direction Sky had gone. "You've seen how much he shapeshifts. He does that all the time. Clothing would be inconvenient at best. And he really doesn't like them. If he gets cold or needs more protection from the elements, he merely shapeshifts into a creature more suited to the conditions."

Tobias nodded and followed Rain as they continued on their walk.

"You were going to ask me a question," she stated as he fell into step beside her.

"What?"

"Before Sky interrupted us, you were going to ask me a question."

"Yes," he answered uncomfortably. He remembered the question he had been about to ask her when Sky arrived.

"So?"

"So what?"

She stopped and looked at him, her brow furrowed in concern. "So what was your question?"

He shook his head. "It was not important," he insisted, and moved to continue walking.

A hand on his arm stopped him, and he raised his eyes slowly to meet hers.

"I know when you're lying, priye. Please talk to me," she whispered. "You will never know the answer if you do not ask me."

He looked away again. "I do not know if I want an answer."

"I see." Her hand released his arm, but he did not move. "You know that you can ask me anything. I will not lie to you."

"I know, and that is what frightens me," he replied.

There was no answer to that, so she remained silent. The wind rustled softly through the trees and she heard the calls of the birds in the canopy. She made no comment and waited beside him. Finally, his hand sought out hers and closed around it, bringing her palm to his chest. Then he drew a deep breath and began to speak.

"Beloved. What will happen if we fail? What will happen if we do not find Aurek?"

She drew a shuddering breath. "I don't know."

"Song said Aiya may abandon Earth."

"That is a distinct possibility."

Tobias frowned. He no longer thought of Aiya's abandoning Earth as an acceptable solution. At first he thought it would solve all of his problems; She would go and take Her teachings with Her, and he could pretend nothing had ever happened. But now he was in love with Rain, and he knew the thought of abandoning Earth hurt her deeply.

"I do not want Aiya to abandon Earth."

"Nor do I," she agreed. "Aerth has told me that there are ways to limit the damage to the Balance, but the thought of just letting Ja'oi do as He pleases regardless of the consequences...It frightens me. It goes against everything I was taught."

"Song said much the same thing."

"The results could be catastrophic," she said.

"Why?"

His simple question brought her up short. The concept was ridiculously simple to her, but then she remembered that the universe's interconnectedness was one of the lessons he was having difficulty understanding.

"Because what happens to one part of the Web affects the entire Web."

"Why? How? How can a butterfly flapping its wings in Africa cause a thunderstorm in New York?"

"What?" she asked, confused.

He shook his head. "Nothing. It doesn't matter. You say abandoning Earth would be a bad thing. I do not understand how one world can dictate the fate of so many others, but I accept the fact that it is so."

"It is a beginning."

He smiled gently at her and kissed her hand. "And I understand that the thought of abandoning Earth brings you pain. For that reason alone, I would not wish for it to happen."

She returned his smile. "Thank you."

"Aiya would let me come with you if She did abandon Earth, yes? She would not make you leave me behind," he said, trying to keep the fear from his voice.

"I would never leave you behind," she answered vehemently.

"But if we could prove how Ja'oi broke the Circle, and find out what was done to Aurek, then Aiya may choose to stay and fight."

"Yes, She might. It would depend on what we found."

He met her gaze, his hand squeezing hers almost painfully. "But it would put us in a much better position to argue our case."

Rain nodded. "Yes."

"Then we must not fail. We must find Aurek and get the proof we need."

She looked at him and spoke with conviction. "We will not fail."

"I believe you."

"Good." She slipped her hand from his grasp and wrapped her arm in his, urging him to move. "Come on now. I'm hungry. Let's go see what food there is at the Cloister."

"Your wish is my command," he answered, matching her pace as they headed for the Cloister.

Seventeen

You missed a spot.

The unicorn tossed his head and snorted at a patch of uncurried hair. Tobias sighed and ran his brush over the offending spot. He had been brushing the same flank for nearly twenty minutes, and still the unicorn was not satisfied. Who had talked him into this anyway?

No one did. You volunteered remember?

The voice was wry, but full of humor, and the sparkle in the unicorn's eye gave away his friendly intentions.

"So I did. I have not forgotten," the vampire replied, making doubly sure the patch was taken care of.

Rain was currying another unicorn a few paces away from him, and there were several others loitering in the little meadow, waiting their turn. The fact that unicorns actually existed was still surreal to him, but he was getting used to seeing them. He was getting used to a lot of things. The slow, easy days in the Sanctuary gave him a great deal of time to learn and reflect upon things. But sometimes, that was more curse than blessing, and Tobias was impatient for something to do. As a diversion, the two of them had volunteered to groom the unicorns as a way of passing the time. That was when Rain had given him the currycomb. It had been downhill ever since.

"Is Jeren complaining again?" she asked over her shoulder.

"Yes, he is."

"He always does. He's Mr. Picky."

Jeren whickered and stamped a forefoot, shaking his mane. He sent a private thought to Rain, but Tobias was not to know exactly what he said to her. He only knew that she laughed and tossed her brush at him. Jeren snorted and pranced, picking up the currycomb in his mouth and flinging it back at her, then he lipped Tobias playfully in thanks and trotted off. No sooner had the unicorn slipped off into the trees, when another came sidling up to Tobias, this one a female. She met his blue eyes and touched his mind gently in greeting.

*I am Idra. *

"Hello, Idra," he answered, and set to currying her flank.

Thank you.

"You are very welcome."

Just then there was a loud rustling in the underbrush, and a large white wolf came bounding out of the trees to pounce happily on Rain. Rain yelped and fell to the ground, pinned to the grass by the wolf as the unicorn she had been brushing skittered out of the way. Laughing, she wrestled with the wolf until it morphed into the naked body of Sky.

"You!" she blurted through her giggles as he laughed and scrambled on all fours.

"Play with me!" he said, grinning from ear to ear.

For a moment, Rain's entire face lit up with joy and she moved to go with him, but then she stopped, sobering, and cast a guilty glance back at Tobias. He met her gaze with sorrow as Sky tugged at her sari.

"Come on! The wind is high and the thermals run low! It's a perfect day!"

"I…I can't."

Sky snorted. "Why not?"

"I…I should stay here with Tobias."

Tell her she can go, came Idra's voice in his head. It was a command, not a request, and he obeyed, not really knowing why.

"No no, liebchen. Go. I'll be fine here," he interrupted.

Rain's eyes filled with hope. "Do you really mean it? You won't be mad?"

"No. I won't be mad; now go. Go and play."

"See, he said it was okay. You've gotten permission! Let's go!" Sky insisted, grabbing her arm and pulling her away.

"I'll be back soon!" she called, as she ran off, her silk sari fluttering like a lost handkerchief as she tossed it aside.

A moment later he saw a gray wolf trotting away where the woman had just been, following in the path of the white one, and he sighed with envy and sadness.

You must let her go. She will be just an empty cage if you kill the bird, the unicorn told him.

"What do you mean by that?" he demanded, glaring at Idra angrily.

*You must allow her to be what she is. She loves you very much, but she cannot be everything to you all of the time. You must let her live; you must let her go. It is the only way you will be able to keep her. *

"I don't understand," he said, but it was a lie. He knew exactly what Idra was talking about.

In spite of their talks, and his efforts to improve, Rain still had been constantly by his side, telling him what to do. From the moment they woke, to the moment they went to sleep, she was with him. She fed him, kept him company, and yielded to his every wish and desire. In turn, he continued to depend upon her completely for guidance and support. As long as she was with him, he did not feel so confused and lost. Things made sense when she was around, and he was starting to understand the meaning of Aiya's lessons. He had been clinging to Rain, keeping her from doing other things, but she had borne it. Only now was he beginning to realize that she was suffering under his dependency, sacrificing her own desires and needs to keep him content.

He was content, for the most part. Rain's love and lovemaking kept him very happy and satisfied. It was no small feat. One of the reasons he had buried his need, once he lost Etienne as a mortal lover, was because he had been made so young. Twenty he had been when Ian gave him the blood, a young man with an over active sex drive. While he was still alive, he had found himself bedding men and women daily, releasing his need in whatever way he could. A sensuous creature immersed in sensuous pleasures, with the wealth of Sixteenth Century Rome at his fingertips, its opulent baths and secluded trysting places. Yes, trysts. Dozens of them, mostly with men and women he had just met. Slaves, servants, others like himself, anyone who would care to share pleasures with him. Now, more than five hundred years later, his twenty-year-old body was once again clamoring for satisfaction.

When Etienne had started it, neither of them had any idea as to what it would become. But once Tobias' body grew used to being loved, it began demanding loving. Every night, sometimes twice a night, he and Etienne would struggle in the throes of passion. Poor Etienne was very hard pressed to keep up with his vampire lover on the nights when Tobias' libido exceeded his own. Tobias was often left behind when Etienne went away, alone with his newly rediscovered need, raw and wanting, pacing like a caged animal until Etienne returned. Tobias would wait, impatiently, but resolutely, for the first night, letting Etienne get settled in and reacquainted. But God help Etienne if he was not willing to perform the second night.

Once when Etienne had been away for several weeks, Tobias was desperate and nothing he did eased his suffering. He went out and lured a strange man into his bed. The union was a disaster, leaving Tobias doubly frustrated and the young man dead. The young man had not wished to take his time with Tobias, as Tobias was used to; he took Tobias roughly, not properly preparing him, and rode him furiously for his own pleasure. He had climaxed and pulled out long before Tobias was even ready, and Tobias, in a fit of stymied need and rage, took the pleasure of swallowing death in place of the pleasure he had initially sought.

Only Etienne, because he knew Tobias' needs and was willing to take the time, had ever been able to bring him pleasure. It was a careful, measured event that required a great deal of control, but it was perfection and penultimate bliss for both of them. Now Rain was bringing him to ecstasy as well, but their joining was more intense and unrestrained; especially now that he could reciprocate. No longer worried about killing or harming his lover, Tobias let himself go, and gave himself over completely to the joining. So far, the intensity was controlling his sex drive, keeping it within manageable levels, and he was satisfied.

Tobias loved Rain even more now as their bond grew stronger, replacing the initial infatuation with a deeper, more permanent love, and he did not want to do anything that would jeopardize their relationship. He watched with a heavy heart as she and Sky frolicked together in the grass. They were changing shape often, morphing into a myriad of different creatures in a merry game. He could feel the joy emanating from them. How often in the past month had she denied herself this pleasure because she was afraid of leaving him alone? How often had she stayed with him when she would rather have been elsewhere? He didn't know, but he suspected that it was often. Rain was used to being free; she was not accustomed to having someone to whom she must hold herself accountable, and he was certain it grated against her. If he continued to cling to her, he would only lose her.

Tobias saw Rain and Sky shape change into birds of prey and sail upward into the thermals. He followed their flight until he could not see them any longer, then sighed heavily as Idra nudged him.

You have much to learn, but now you realize your mistakes and are willing to correct them.

He looked at her and nodded, but then frowned. *Does it....does it all make sense to you, Idra?*

Yes. And it will make sense to you as well, soon. You are ready to learn now. Ready to see what you would not have seen before.

Yes. Yes, I am. When Rain returns, we will talk. I must think about what I want to say to her.

Idra smiled at him, as much as a unicorn can smile, and bumped the brush with her nose. *You can brush and think at the same time, can't you?*

Tobias laughed softly and resumed his currying. "Yes. Yes, I can."

• • •

Rain landed on the rocky crags high above the steam pools, her falcon body shifting until she was a woman again, naked and crouched on the stone, and full of inexpressible joy. She had forgotten what it was like to be a bird, the sheer wonder of having wings and sailing effortlessly on the currents of the wind. She was laughing with pleasure as Sky landed beside her and morphed back into a man. He was so beautiful, even with his hair blown in disarray by the strong gusts of wind, and his eyes sparkled with joy as he smiled at her.

"You were right," she said, sweeping back her long, black hair as the wind sought to play with it. "It is a perfect day."

Sky nodded, grinning from ear to ear. "Yes."

Above them they heard the shrill cry of griffons and looked up to see a mated pair circling over the mountains. Rain mind called to them in greeting and received a welcome in return. The griffons swept low over them, then drifted down to the steam pools below. Rain watched them, smiling and waving as they passed. Her arms caught the wind and she opened to it, standing and letting it swirl around her like an invisible sari.

"Gods, how I have missed this!" she sighed, reveling in the feelings of freedom.

"And I have missed you," Sky spoke softly, his voice barely audible above the rush of the wind.

She looked at him, her brow furrowed.

Bina, he mindspoke, a tremor of sorrow in his thoughts.

It was her name. Her ancient name. The name only Aerth and Sky knew, and it was used only to express great need or to command her attention. The moment he sent it, she moved to sit once again on the rock as he came into her arms and rested his head on her shoulder. He was trembling, but not from cold. No. She knew what this was.

"You are remembering again," she stated quietly, stroking his hair.

She felt his head nod.

Yes.

She sighed. "Sky, my dear friend, these past few weeks have not been easy for you."

"I can't stop remembering!" he blurted, his voice laced with pain.

"I know. That always happens when you stay too long out of the now."

*Make me forget? Please, I do not want to remember! *

"Of course, little bird."

Sky laid his head in Rain's lap as she placed both hands on his skull. Pulling the power from within her, she weaved a wall inside his consciousness, blocking off the memories of his past.

It was the only way. Sky's birth into an ecomancer had been one of extreme pain and suffering, and his life as a mortal had been an exercise in torture. He had never fully come to terms with what had happened to him; never reconciled himself with his past. Instead he recoiled from it, using the now of animal thought to keep himself from remembering. But sometimes, like now, he was unable to keep the memories from coming back, and bouts of insanity would result. Raving, crazed with pain, Sky would disappear for years at a time until he had suppressed his memory once again. After the first few times it happened, Rain, with the help of a young and gifted dragon, devised a way of inhibiting Sky's memories by creating a barrier in his mind that effectively blocked them. So far it had worked rather well, as long as he shifted to animal form frequently, but these past few weeks had been taxing the barrier.

Sky had been forgoing his usual time in animal form because he was needed, and now memories were starting to leak through. Rain went into his mind and began to seal the cracks in the wall, cutting off his long-term memory once again. She did it because she did not know what else to do. It was the only way to keep him sane. Not that anyone would call Sky sane. They all knew he was severely flawed, but Aiya Herself had chosen him, and they were not about to question Her motives. Rain did what she could to keep him balanced. The rest was up to him.

Sky sighed with relief as she finished, his whole body relaxing visibly.

*Thank you. *

Anytime, priye.

"You've always understood me."

"No, I wouldn't say that. I have always accepted the fact that I do not understand you. I accept that you are different from me."

Sky smiled and raised himself up, but he did not stand. Instead he positioned himself so that he was facing her, with his legs curled the opposite direction to hers. His long hair blew silver, like cirrus clouds, in the wind. 'They say he is one of the strongest,' Rain thought to herself. 'If he ever heals, he will be Ja'oi's worst enemy. He is a formidable foe now.' She only hoped nothing would ever provoke Sky enough to make him challenge the Rogue.

"Shall we fly again?" he asked, his voice calm and even.

He was always like this after she had just rebuilt the walls. Free from the memories that leaked through the cracks, Sky could be rational and present for days. She treasured those times because it was the only time she saw his true potential.

Rain looked at the setting sun and shook her head. "No, I should be getting back to Tobias. He will be worried about me."

"He knows you can take care of yourself. Besides, he has been clinging to you an awful lot lately."

"As if you have room to talk, you who clung to me for more than a century," she teased gently.

Sky snorted. "At least I let you breathe. He doesn't. He is not one of us. He cannot share with you the way your own kind can."

Rain lowered her gaze. "I know, but that does not mean we cannot share in other ways."

He sighed heavily and placed his hand on her shoulder. "I'm sorry. I didn't mean that. But it scares me, how you spend all of your time with him. Bina…I fear to lose you."

Rain kissed his forehead tenderly. "My dear friend, you will never lose me."

"In a way, I already have. How long has it been since we have run together? Hunted together? But that's not Tobias' fault. It was happening before. I fear to lose you even more."

She put her arms around him and hugged him tight. "I promise you, I give you my word, that we will run and hunt together again. We will join the pack and howl at the rising moon, and feast on the fresh meat of the kill. I promise you, we will do this. Just as soon as this business with the Rogue is over."

"But it will never be over, Bina," he moaned.

"Yes it will. And who knows, perhaps Tobias will be running beside us."

Sky pulled back and gave her an incredulous look. "Tobias? Hunting with us? Now that is an interesting thought."

"He is a predator. Like any other predator, he revels in the hunt," she answered, then grew sad. "But he must find the faith first. He must make whatever connection he needs to make, to be able to grasp the concepts Aiya is trying to teach him. Right now he depends upon me completely to show him the way, and I cannot give him the understanding that he needs. If he does not make it for himself, he will not survive without me."

Sky regarded her with regret and nodded. "Yes, you are right. He will not be able to adjust, and the world will swallow him whole."

"But I have high hopes. He is starting to make the associations. He has the beginnings of understanding. I think that soon I will take him to see the Webs. If I do it when he is ready, they should be all he needs."

He ran his fingers through her hair lovingly. "You excel at giving people what they need. Look at all you have done for me."

She smiled, her eyes warm, and nuzzled his cheek with her nose. They embraced again and held each other close.

Never forget how much I love you Rain.
Never, my dearest friend. Never.

Eighteen

It was past dark when Rain finally returned to her room in the willow tree, and Tobias was waiting for her. He was not in bed, as she half expected; rather he was seated cross-legged on the floor, deep in thought. She went to him, and sat down beside him, waiting for him to speak.

"I am no good at this," he finally said.

"No good at what?"

"This love of equals. It is new to me, and I am not very good at it."

"You just said yourself that it was new to you. Why not give yourself more time to get used to it."

He looked at her, his eyes sad. "And what in the meantime? Do I chain you to me? Clip your wings? No. I saw you today. I saw how happy you were with Sky. You are not that happy with me."

Rain glared at him. "That is an awfully big assumption to make. I am very happy with you. Gods, Tobias, don't you know how much I love you?"

Opening her arms, she embraced him, and he nestled his face in her neck.

"I know that you love me, but it is not enough. I must begin to stand on my own. To walk beside you, instead of in your shadow," he admitted.

She nodded. "Yes. You must begin to exist for yourself, not just for me."

"I must find the faith I need. I must do it for myself. You cannot give it to me," he sighed, parroting back his own realizations.

Rain smiled to herself, although Tobias could not see, and her heart warmed with hope. "I know. I have known all along."

"But I do not know how to do this."

"I'll help you as much as I can."

He snuggled closer, seeking to cleave himself to her body. "I know. But I am afraid. I am so afraid. If I do not do this, I will lose you forever, and I cannot bear to lose you."

"That will not happen. You will not lose me," she assured strongly.

"If I continue to hold you to me, I will. Idra said it today. You will be just an empty cage if I kill the bird," he answered.

"Idra said that?" she asked, her voice pensive.

"Yes. But she also said that I was ready to learn," he answered.

"You are. I have felt it in you. You are starting to let go of your old beliefs. I know it is a long and hard process. It took me many years to become comfortable with my faith."

"But this is not just about faith. This is about me. Ian kept me dependent. I have so little experience in standing on my own."

She looked into his eyes and took his hands. "Does the infant learn to walk all in a day? Does a child learn to speak all at once?"

"No," he replied. "But…"

"I know you are not a child, but the analogy remains the same. You will not walk in a day, nor will you speak all at once. I will hold your hand until you get your balance as long as you try to take the steps. I will teach you the new words as long as you try to speak," she promised.

He rested his forehead on her shoulder. "Thank you. I know…I know it hasn't been easy for you. Thank you for your patience with me."

"Always, my love."

They fell silent for long moments until he laughed softly. "It's funny. I spent most of the afternoon thinking about what I was going to say to you when you got home, but now I can't remember a single thing!"

Rain stroked his hair lovingly. "Maybe that proves that there is nothing more that needs to be said."

"If there is, it is that I love you. I love you desperately and completely. I would do anything for you. I would die for you…" he breathed.

"No," she broke in. "No. Do not say that you would die for me. Say that you will live for me. Love me enough to live for me and share my life with me."

"Yes! Yes, I love you enough to live for you. I never want to lose you. If it is all that I have, let it be enough."

She kissed his temple. "It is. It always was."

Tobias tightened his arms around her and punctured her throat lightly with his teeth, sucking gently on the trickle of blood that flowed from the tiny holes.

I love you, he mindspoke, joining with her.

And I love you.

Tell me again about the Web and the Circle. I want to understand it. I am ready to understand it.

As you wish, she replied, and opened her mind fully to him, letting him delve into the heart of her, allowing him access to the place where she kept her faith and her truths.

Two hours later Tobias found himself walking beside her, going to a place where he had never been. She led him deep into the forest, deeper than he had ever ventured, until the trees blocked out all the stars, and only his preternatural eyes saved him from being completely blind. The forest had a strange feel here, as if the trees were watching, listening to them pass. Rain moved with unearthly silence, her feet making no sound as she stepped through the undergrowth, and it was the first time he truly realized that she was not, in any way, human. Her movements reminded him of Silaene, seeing now in Rain many of the quirks and singularities he had come to treasure. Rain did not speak as they traveled, as if she was afraid to break the stillness with sound.

They came to a large opening in the side of a small hill and paused at its entrance. Tobias could see nothing when he looked into the hole, only a tunnel that led down into blackness, and he felt an eerie coldness coming from deep within.

"What is this place, liebchen?" he asked, all the small hairs on his neck rising as a cool breath of air blew out of the passage.

"It is the Heart of All Things," she answered, and crossed over the entranceway.

Down they went, and through, Tobias holding firmly to Rain's arm as they walked. He could see nothing, but he knew there were things in the darkness, things that could see them and followed at their heels.

Pay them no mind. They are the young ones, the ones yet to be born.

Finally the darkness was broken by a faint blue-green glow. A mortal would not have been able to detect it, but Tobias' vampire eyes adjusted immediately, allowing him to see. It was some kind of plant growing on the walls of the tunnel, a plant that made its own soft light. He could see the tunnel widening, emptying into a large room from which emanated a warm glow, and they passed into a cavern.

Stopping at the edge of the cavern, he gasped at what he saw. Webs. Thousands of them. They were made of tangible light, like thin strands of fiberglass, spun into every crag of the cavern, and into each other. Everywhere he looked, there were webs. Some large.

*Those are the old worlds, * Rain's mind voice told him.

Some small.

Those are the ones just beginning.

Some were just balls of tightly woven strands held in place by a few anchoring threads.

*Those are the worlds yet to be. *

Some glowed brightly, their light bursting in brief flashes.

They are the young ones, still full of untamed energy.

Some glowed warm and steady.

Those are the ones in balance.

Others glowed dim, with sections fluttering periodically into darkness.

Those are the ones that are dying.

Tobias stared at the webs, awestruck, turning around and around, slowly, to take in all of them.

"Amazing," he whispered. "So many!"

"Yes, but there is one in particular that I want you to see."

He came out of his reverie as she took his arm and led him deeper into the chamber. They passed by dozens of webs until she brought him to a cul de sac off to one side. There she pointed to a beautiful web, large and perfectly formed, glowing brightly, but steadily. Tobias took a moment to study its intricate latticework, noticing that soft pulses of light ran down the individual strands, sometimes running into each other and bursting in tiny flashes.

"This is Indio. A world co-ruled by Aiya and her ally Inhotek," Rain explained. "See how the web is complete. This world is in its prime. The creatures there live in balance and harmony."

"Yes, I see. I understand."

Then Rain turned and pointed to another web. This one was smaller than Indio's, and it glowed dimly, with parts of it completely dark. The lattice was in shambles, and broken in places, the lifeless strands hanging like forgotten cobwebs. Brightly lit strands from other webs were running to it, as if to feed it new life, but their energy pulsed into the broken web briefly, then fizzled out.

"This," Rain said with a heavy heart. "Is Earth."

Tobias nodded, his face grave.

"This is what Ja'oi has wrought. See how the web refuses the life from the others? He has cut it off. It is dying slowly. But see how it is connected to so many other worlds? If Earth dies before its time, it will take many others with it."

He looked and followed the threads to the other webs, two of which were embryos waiting to be born. If Earth died before they reached fruition…

"They will die too. Yes."

Now Tobias saw that every single web was intrinsically and irrevocably linked with the others, and he was suddenly reminded of the genealogy maps Etienne had once shown him. The map of his family with the bloodline traced through over twenty generations. The family had spread over the globe, its lines reaching into every sect of the world, unifying it, connecting it. Connected. Yes. Everything connected.

Khirsha's words came back to him, 'Everything is nothing without the Web. The Web and the Great Wheel turn the universe. There is nothing outside of the Web. We are all a part of it and surrounded by it.'

Tobias' eyes opened wide and he drew breath as everything suddenly made perfect sense. "Yes! Yes, I understand."

This was the Web. The Web of Life. Thousands of individual worlds intimately tied to each other. He followed the lines, taking in the entire picture, as he had with the map of Etienne's family tree.

'Yes, there they are,' he thought. "Ties that bind. Touch one thread and the whole thing feels it. Break one strand and the whole thing is compromised. Action and reaction, choices and consequences, everything is part of the greater whole and the decisions of one affect many. Everything is balance and to upset the balance is to risk disaster.'

His immortal heart was racing, and the cavern seemed to be reacting to his rising excitement. Pulses of light flashed across the webs nearest him, and he could feel the energy in the room building. He looked up, and saw all the strands and webs converging into one unified whole. It was as if a great light had just been turned on in the darkness of his cognitive mind, and he now had the knowledge he needed.

Yes! This! I understand! I am part of this! he cried to himself, feeling the new power filling the holes within himself.

As he thought it, a great flash of blue light rushed at him from several webs, and the threads from those webs lashed out and attached to him, sending their energy directly into him. He gasped, tears streaming from his eyes, as he was filled with light, channeling the power through him, until it left his body and joined the collective.

He glanced over at Rain and saw that she was connected to the webs too, the strands running into her thin form. Her face was a mask of ecstasy as she transmuted the life energy and transformed it into pure power. He heard her speak a word in a language he did not know, and a new thread lashed out from herself and connected to him, linking them. The power surged through the new bond, flowing into him, and he cried out with joy.

Raising his arms up, he saw a line materialize out of his chest and dash out, flashing until it joined with the largest web there. The web for the Sanctuary. Through his tears, he saw the new thread meld with the web, the power flooding into it, making it pulse with blue light, and watched in amazement as two new lattices were added right before his eyes.

That is me! That is me and my kind. I have taken my place in the Web of Life.

Yes, came a familiar soft voice inside his head, and he turned to see the goddess standing before him, Her hair the strands that made the webs, Her life the light that fed them.

I am the hunter. The predator of Ja'oi's creations. I am the one made to bring the humans to heel, he sent to Her, telling Her his own revelations. *I am the one who was made to fight the tide of Ja'oi's folly. I am the one meant to feed on the death of the His souls!*

My son, at long last, you have come home.

Aiya opened Her arms and he went into them willingly. There were no fears, no hesitations anymore, and he joined with Her mind without pause. He knew who he was, he knew what he was, and who he was meant to be. There were no more questions or doubts. There was only Aiya, the Web, and the sense of complete peace that now filled him where his emptiness had once been. Her light surrounded him, flooded him, and he felt himself meld into Her. He laughed, ecstasy firing along every nerve in his body as he danced on the field of stars.

I am yours, my mother. I am yours for all time, he told Her.

You always were, my son. You just didn't know it. The deceiver kept you from me.

Ask what you will of me!

Find my son. Find my Aurek and bring him home.

If it takes a thousand years, I will find him, he pledged, feeling the cool darkness in his hands and flowing over his body.

I believe you, my son.

Suddenly the field shifted and he saw himself looking outward into space, pulled further into the cosmos as galaxies and solar systems whirled by him. The further back he was pulled, the more he saw the threads of light that criss-crossed the universe, equalizing and joining everything that touched them. He flew higher, deeper into that cold, velvety darkness until he could go no farther. Then he felt gravity take him and pull him back, but he was not afraid. He embraced it with his entire being and let go. He let himself fall

He awakened several hours later to find himself back in the willow-room. He had been undressed and Rain was snuggled next to him in bed. For a moment, he wasn't sure if the cavern of Webs and his meeting with Aiya had been real, or if he had dreamt it, but then he closed his eyes, and felt inside himself to find that his sense of serenity and wholeness was indeed still there. He smiled to himself and kissed Rain's forehead lovingly. She stirred in her sleep and opened her eyes, looking at his beaming face, her expression turning from questioning to simply happy.

"Hi," he whispered.

"Hi."

He grinned, showing his fang teeth and snuggled closer, turning to his side so he could kiss her lips.

"How are you feeling?" she asked when he pulled his mouth away.

"Wonderful. I feel wonderful."

Gently, she pushed on his shoulder, and he obligingly rolled to his back as she moved to her side, propping her head up on her elbow.

"I'm glad," she said, placing a hand on his white chest.

Although her skin was very pale, it was still several shades darker than his unless he had just fed, then his skin had a ruddy color to it that almost matched her own. Caressing him was like sliding her hand over satin, only satin didn't sigh and croon with every well-placed touch.

"How tired are you?" he questioned, a knowing twinkle in his blue eyes.

She cocked her head in thought for a few seconds, and he raised his eyebrows and gave her a little sound. It was a query-like sound, a high pitched 'hmmm?,' and she knew what it meant. Giggling, she smiled and caressed his cheek.

"I'm not too tired to give you some attention."

"Good, because I'll be asking you for a great deal of attention, for a very long time," he smoothed, returning the smile.

She kissed him tenderly, and murmured in his ear, "I think I can live with that."

"So can I."

Sometime later they lay contentedly in each other's arms, Rain with her head resting on Tobias' shoulder as he stroked her hair.

"How much longer do you think we have here?" he asked.

"I am not sure. The last time Fire talked to me she said it was nearly spring."

"We will go in the spring?"

"Yes."

"Has there been any response from Ja'oi yet to the earth healing?"

"The last I heard, no. We are being very discrete and trying not to attract too much attention. Although Aerth told me Stars' work in the Pacific Northwest forests was being noticed. It seems that his patches of new trees are showing up on satellite pictures. And Sun tells me that several American Indian tribes are reviving the Earth Mother religion."

Tobias worked a snag out of her hair with his fingers. "Are you concerned that Ja'oi is so silent?"

Rain thought a moment before answering. "Yes, I am. It bodes ill. He must know what is going on. I suspect that He is planning something."

"What do you think He will do?"

"That is what I am worried about. I don't know."

"I guess then we will deal with it when it happens, and for now not worry about it."

She raised her head and kissed him. "Yes, you're right. I don't want to worry about it. I am far too happy right now to worry about what will happen later."

"I could not agree more," he told her, then nuzzled her throat and whispered softly, "I'm hungry, liebchen."

Rain arched her throat in offering. "Then drink."

Silently his arm enfolded around her, and he raised his mouth to her jugular, breaking the skin with his tiny fangs and feeding gently.

Soon I will not have to do this. Soon your blood will be only for my pleasure and not my nourishment.

*Yes, but it will also mean that we will have left the Sanctuary. You will once again need to hide from the sun by day and only venture out at night. *

Will we ever come back here?

Yes, I am sure we will, but it will not be until all this is over.

Then I will let you be my sun until we return. You will be my sun, my moon and my stars.

Ach! You will drown me in sugar and syrup.

Forgive me, I am a hopeless romantic at heart.

I love you, anyway.

Forever and always?

Forever and always.

Nineteen

Tobias walked into the cool shadows of the main temple. Khirsha had told him he would find Aerth here and she had flown him there. He decided to talk with the ancient ecomancer while Rain was out spending time with Sky. It seemed the perfect opportunity, so he leaped at the chance, and now he was wandering along the quiet hallways of the large building.

The main temple was much larger than the cloister where he and Rain had roomed the night he returned to her. It was also much further away from the willow tree, over the far mountains and past what Khirsha called the Nursery. But like the cloister, it was made of white stone, and set in the same, half circle pattern.

He meandered down one wing, searching for Aerth, and wondering why no one seemed to be around. He thought there would be handmaidens or someone to tend the altar and the rooms, but all was quiet and still. He did not even hear heartbeats. Finally, after he had gone completely around in a circle, or so it seemed, he heard hearts and faint voices, and moved towards them. He found Aerth and Stars sitting on an exterior stone patio, over-looking the gardens. They were talking quietly, then Stars began to play a small flute as Aerth mended what looked to be a broken doll.

"Excuse me," he said softly, stepping onto the patio.

Stars ceased his playing, and they both looked at him as he approached.

"I'm sorry. I didn't mean to interrupt."

Stars smiled, his dark eyes sparkling. "You didn't."

"You are welcome here, Tobias. How may we serve you?" Aerth said, placing the doll in her lap.

He looked down at his hands, suddenly shy. "I came to talk to you…about Aurek."

"I see," she replied softly and stood. "I am the one to talk to," she added, her voice sad.

"What is that?" the vampire questioned, indicating the toy in her hands, trying to diffuse the air of uneasiness that had settled around them.

"Oh, this. It is a doll. One of the elven children brought it to me," she answered fondly, referring to the temple. "This is a house of healing after all. Dolls included."

She gave him a small smile, and set the doll down on the stone bench. "Come, walk with me and we will talk."

Stars stayed on the patio while she led the way down into the garden, and Tobias followed, falling into step beside her.

"If you don't mind my asking, how old are you?" he inquired respectfully, when they had passed onto the grass and were walking among the carefully tended flowers.

Aerth paused and reached out her hand to a flowering vine, and Tobias watched in amazement as the plant extended its tendrils towards her to wrap around her wrist and palm.

"I am the oldest," she answered after a long pause. "Exactly how old I am, I don't know. Time is alien to me, I have been out of it for so long. Ask the dragons, they know when I was made. They kept the records before Song. Time has meaning for them."

Gently, she pulled her hand from the vine and they continued on their way. When they came to a grotto with three statues of dancing figures, a fountain and two stone benches, Aerth stopped and sat down on one of the seats, folding her hands in her lap. Tobias sat down next to her and waited for her to speak.

"What do you want to know about Aurek?" she asked.

"Everything," he replied, then continued. "What was he like?"

She thought a moment, and Tobias saw the play of emotions run across her face: sadness, joy, love. When she finally spoke, her voice was full of fondness and affection.

"He was smart, and fast, and strong. He loved to laugh. He loved to play. He loved to hunt. He was a creature of extremes. There was no middle ground with Aurek."

"What happened after you took him into India?" he asked next, leaning a little closer to her.

"We settled in the forest only a few leagues from a little village. We made ourselves known to them by trading meat and skins for textiles and vegetables. Aurek was a great hunter and his talents were respected. But we were also feared because we were different. They knew us as the witch and her white son," Aerth replied, a small, sad smile on her lips.

He smiled with her, then said, "Rain told me Aurek had a companion, a young man."

Aerth's smile broadened, and she nodded. "Yes. Roshan. Roshan was from the village. He sought us out after Aurek killed a tiger that had been preying on the village's children. He wanted Aurek to teach him to hunt. They became very good friends."

"I'm surprised he didn't kill the boy," he mused thoughtfully, knowing that he would most likely have killed a mortal who had sought him out.

She chuckled. "He almost did. He mistook Roshan for his usual prey: raiders coming over the mountains. It was only at the last moment that he realized the boy was a native."

"What did he do?"

"The boy was an outcast from the village. Apparently they were willing to take our meat and furs in trade, but to actually seek us out was anathema. Roshan's father disowned him when the boy announced his intentions to find us. Aurek brought him home and taught him to hunt."

Tobias smiled, seeing the image of Aurek with his new friend in her mind. "And did he learn?"

Aerth echoed his chuckle. "Oh yes, he learned, and learned well. He possessed none of Aurek's superior strength and speed, but he had patience and skill. He was a good hunter."

"You said Aurek and he became good friends," he prodded, sensing there was more to it than she was saying.

"They were lovers. It took them five turns of seasons to finally admit that they loved and wanted each other, but once they did, they were completely devoted to one another."

"Aurek taught him how to make love?"

That brought an enigmatic smile to her lips. "Oh yes, Aurek taught him. That was another thing he learned well."

Now that they were on the subject, Tobias felt more comfortable asking Aerth more questions. "Aerth, do you know why Aiya made lovemaking so complex for us?"

"It was for your own protection. She knew that intimacy between two vampires would be dangerous because of your predatory natures, so She created safestops to make sure none of you could be taken advantage of," she explained gently.

Tobias thought about what she had just told him, digesting its meaning and repercussions in his mind.

"She made it such that none of us would be able to be forced or to force another," he noted with sudden awe.

"Exactly. Vampires are dominating enough without being able to use forced sex as a weapon. Besides, rape is a violation to the goddess. The union of two beings in mind, heart and body is sacred to Her, and should never be abused."

Tobias placed his hand over Aerth's. "No, it should not. Aiya is wise."

Aerth gave him a small smile. "Most of the time," she answered cryptically.

"Why did you have to leave Aurek?"

She looked away, her eyes closing for a moment. "A civil war broke out between two gods on a world far away from Earth. Aiya was asked to intervene because the world held a pivotal place in the Webs, and many other worlds were threatened. This has happened before. Usually, the Others will try to handle it themselves, but sometimes when things get too bad, Aiya is asked to help. There were only five of us then, myself, Fire, Water, Air, and Sea. Aiya sent Fire and Air to Kvist to help deal with the situation."

"What happened?" Tobias asked, suddenly feeling a strong sense of dread.

He felt Aerth tremble and saw tears well into her eyes.

"A terrible battle broke out. Fire and Air were trapped in the crossfire. Both were killed."

Tobias gasped. Yes, now he remembered Rain telling him that two ecomancers had been killed long before she was made. One had been Sea's lover.

"Air. Sea was bonded to Air," Aerth answered, reading his thoughts. "She took it very hard. She has never bonded since. Water himself was so traumatized by what happened, that he chose to destroy himself rather than live with the pain. He killed the persona known as Water and rose again as Song. He chose to keep the histories, to be the one who remembers so that no one would ever forget what happened. As for myself, I was called back after the fact, to help deal with the aftermath."

"That was a terrible tragedy. What happened to the gods and to Kvist?"

"They were all destroyed and the planet given to another goddess."

"Both of them?"

"Both gods, all their avatars and all their children. Such is the price for killing the avatar of another deity. It is the highest crime."

Tobias was shocked. "But it was an accident, wasn't it?"

"Not really. Both sides knew Air and Fire were there. Both sides saw them. Neither would let them escape. They let their hate for each other destroy two innocent lives."

"I see. Then perhaps they deserved what they got."

"Yes," Aerth agreed.

"And where was Aurek when you returned to Earth?" he questioned, returning to their original topic of discussion.

"They were gone. And I could find no trace of them."

"Them?"

"Aurek and Roshan."

"Roshan? Roshan was a vampire?" he blurted, surprised.

"Yes. Aurek made him eight years after they met."

"Did Roshan ask him?"

"No. Aurek did it to save him."

"Why? What happened?"

Aerth sighed. "Roshan was always trying to prove himself to Aurek. One day he went off to hunt a tiger. The tiger mauled him horribly and mortally wounded him. Aurek found him, but I was too far away to get to him in time. Aurek had a choice: lose his lover or bring Roshan to him. He offered Roshan the choice and Roshan chose vampirism."

She paused, remembering that day. There was blood all over the tall grass, and a thick trail of it where Roshan had dragged himself out of the sun in order to reach Aurek. The tiger had gutted him, his entrails hanging out, the muscles of his legs ripped and bleeding. Aurek's screams were heard for leagues. She had gotten there as soon as she could, but it was already too late. Roshan's mouth was sealed to Aurek's throat, drinking greedily as the vampire held his ravaged body close, and when it was done, she saw his great wounds heal and his body take on the vampire eyes, teeth and nails.

Roshan had been happy, now he was as strong and fast as Aurek. He rejoiced in his new powers and his new life, and Aurek, even though he was drained from making his first child, had seemed pleased. She had called a cloud cover and helped Aurek carry his new fledgling back to their hut and put them both to bed. They had slept, curled around each other, for nearly a full day.

"Roshan was as fine a vampire as he was a hunter, and he was completely and totally in love with Aurek," she told him.

"He and Aurek didn't fight?"

"Never. I never saw them raise a hand to each other or say an angry word. They didn't vie for power, but shared everything instead."

"How can that be? Most maker and child relationships are full of power struggles and arguments," he said, confused.

"I think Aurek was unique. He had the goddess' love inside him, and his upbringing was different from any of his children. He had no need for power, and never did. I think the dominance struggles rise from your predatory natures, and the further you are from the goddess, the more you struggle."

Tobias nodded. It could make sense. Maybe all the struggling came from the broken Circle, maybe that was an effect of the severed tie. He didn't feel so contrary and in need of power now; maybe the others were just fighting in an attempt to regain what they had lost. If that was the case, how would resealing the Circle affect other vampires? Would they all treat each other as kin? Would the territorial fighting stop? It was too much to think about now, especially with the time he and Rain would be returning to Earth approaching swiftly.

"Have I told you all you wished to know?" Aerth asked him quietly.

He looked at her, for a moment not realizing what she meant. "About Aurek and Roshan?"

"Yes."

"Yes, I think so. I want to find him. I want to find out what happened to him."

She gave him a sad glance. "I want you to find him too. By the time I returned from Kvist, over two thousand years had passed on Earth. Ever since we discovered he was missing, not a day has gone by that I haven't thought of him and wished for his safe return."

"We'll find him and bring him home. I promise."

She smiled. "Thank you. And now, you should go. Rain is looking for you."

"She is? Where?"

"Actually, she's coming here. I just told her you were here with me, so she'll be here soon."

Sure enough, a moment later Rain appeared in the garden, all smiles and happiness.

"There you are. You had me worried. I thought you had run off without me," she joked.

"Never," he assured, standing and hugging her.

"So, what brings you here?"

"I was talking to Aerth about Aurek."

"Oh? And did you find the answers you sought?"

He grinned and kissed her. "Yes, and then some."

"I'm so glad."

"Me too. And where have you been? Are you finished playing with Sky?"

"Yes, but we've been invited to a concert in the cloister garden."

"That sounds lovely. Let's go."

"Aerth, Sun asked me to tell you that you and Stars are invited too," Rain said to her.

Aerth stood and smiled. "We will be there."

Rain gave Aerth one more brilliant smile, then took Tobias out of the garden.

• • •

The sun was warm on Tobias' back as he sat on a small ridge overlooking the valley. Down below, he could see two juvenile unicorns frolicking in the grass, and it brought a small smile to his pale lips. Rain was off with Sky, he had seen them flying overhead earlier, their hawk bodies reflecting gold in the afternoon light, so he was left to his own devices for a while, and he had come to sit upon the ridge in order to do some thinking. Ever since his experience in the cavern of Webs, he had never known such peace or joy in his entire vampiric existence. His contentment rivaled his days with Ian before Dorian, except that now he and Rain were not master and son. They were partners, consorts, and best friends, as well as lovers. He could not imagine a happier time. Every day was bliss, every night a new discovery of paradise, and he was ecstatically, deliriously happy. But the fatalist in him was still waiting for it all to fall apart. Soon, he and Rain would leave the comfort and safety of the

Sanctuary, and brave the uncertainty of Earth. He was afraid, deathly afraid, of what Ja'oi was planning. There had still been no retaliation from the god, and it was making all the ecomancers nervous. It made him nervous as well, feeding the seeds of foreboding and concern taking root in his gut, and he fingered the ring on his left hand absently. As usual, the feel of the ornament calmed him, and he looked down at it fondly.

Rain had given it to him. It was a ring made from a narrow braid of her hair encircled in thin helixes of gold. It was unique and beautiful, and he loved it. She had given it to him three days earlier, in the shadow of the mother tree. Sky, Stars, Aerth and Song had been present, and he had been confused as to why they were all watching him with expectant faces, until Rain outstretched her hand and Sky placed the ring in her upturned palm. Then she had taken his left hand, slid the ring on his third finger and said "I give you this ring as a sign of my eternal love. Made from my hair, it is part of me. With it, you will never be without me, even when we are apart. Take it now, and wear it proudly, and know how much I love you."

He had accepted it with tears in his eyes, lifting it to the small pools of sunlight that filtered in through the boughs of the great oak, and letting the light flash brightly over it. Without a word, he had taken her face in his hands and kissed her, his lips trembling with emotion, while the others let out a soft cheer. It had been a simple ritual, without fanfare or pomp and circumstance, but it was probably the most beautiful he had ever witnessed.

He had wanted to reciprocate, to give her something as a troth of his love, but Sky told him that a ring would only get lost in a shapechange. Unhappy, he asked Sky for assistance with something he could give to her, and Sky made for him an ornament for Rain's hair. It was a dangle of rose quartz, amethyst, and silver with a lock of his brown hair weaved into it. Rain now wore it hanging from a thin braid that ran from the nape of her left ear, falling over her shoulder and laying neatly above her breast. She had cut her hair there so the braid would end just over her shoulder, letting the dangle come to rest just beneath her collar bone, and when she shapechanged, it stayed attached, regardless of what her hair became. He still remembered her look of wide-eyed joy and amazement when he presented it to her, and it made him feel warm all over.

He was lost in his own thoughts until he suddenly realized that he was no longer alone. Turning his head, he beheld the goddess seated next to him and he started with surprise. He didn't know how long She had been there, but She was just sitting quietly, looking very much like a mortal woman dressed in green Grecian robes, gazing down at the playing unicorns. His brow furrowed in confusion, but he did not speak to Her. Rather, he let Her be and returned his attention to the antics below. They spent long moments in comfortable silence, then Aiya leaned over unexpectedly and kissed Tobias on his cheek. The touch of Her lips sent electric shocks through his body as She let Her mouth linger against his skin, and when She finally pulled away, he was trembling.

I love you, my son.

With that, She stood and walked purposefully down the hillside, the wind catching the folds of Her green robes and billowing them about Her as She moved.

Tobias watched Her in mute shock, staring as She joined the two unicorns, running Her hands over their white coats as they rubbed against Her. He blinked a few times, utterly confused, then felt Rain's gentle mindtouch.

Come home.

Immediately, eager to tell her what had happened, he obeyed and returned to the willow tree. He found the door open and Rain sitting on the bed, her head bowed pensively and her hands in her lap. He stopped for a moment in the doorway, just to look at her, before she realized he was there. Could it possibly be that she was getting more beautiful with every passing day? 'Tobias, you are pathetic, snap out of it.'

"I am here, liebchen," he whispered softly.

"I know," came her equally soft reply.

Her voice was sad. Concerned, he went to her and took her hands in his own.

"What is wrong?"

"It is time. Aiya told me a little while ago. We are to leave for Earth after night falls in Washington."

"Oh."

Quietly, he moved to sit beside her and took her into his arms. She rested her head against his chest, holding him close as he nestled his chin into the top of her hair, taking in her scent and simply loving her. After a few moments, he loosened his hold and tenderly lifted her chin with his hand. Her gray eyes met his brown ones as he caressed her cheek, and her lips parted to receive him as they kissed lovingly. They had a few hours, didn't they?

Fingers lightly brushed across her shoulders as his lips trailed tiny kisses on her face and neck, and she tipped her head back when they came to rest on her throat. She felt the little prick of the fangs as they sunk into her skin, filling her with throbbing warmth and pleasure, and the smooth silk of his hands as they slid her sari down to her waist. His lips left her neck, pulling back and bending his head to her chest as his palms cupped her breasts. Silently, he worshipped them, gliding his tongue over their soft mounds, as enthralled and taken by them as any mortal twenty-year-old. Rain moaned as his mouth closed on one nipple, sucking gently, then moved to do the same to the other. She tangled her hands in his hair as he wrapped his arms around her, pressing his face to her breast and opening his mouth.

Tobias smiled to himself when he heard her cry of surprise and ecstasy as he bit down on her breast. He swirled his tongue around her nipple, lapping up the thin trickle of blood that seeped from the wounds his teeth made, and then moved to pay homage to the other. He ran his tongue across her skin, using it as a feeler until he found the other breast. Licking and nipping teasingly, he worked the nipple until it was erect and flushed a lovely pink. His mouth closed on it, his tongue pressing it to the roof of his palette as his fangs found their mark. She cried out again and it was music to his ears. He could spend hours doing this, just listening to her sounds of pleasure, and letting his desire build. For now he was content to let her be his woman, reveling in her softness, her smooth curves, her female scent and taste. Later she would be something else to him, but now, in the present, she was his lady, and he was happy with that.

Part II

One

Dorian walked slowly down the dark path. It was a typical early spring night in the Pacific Northwest; damp, cool and humid, where the mist clung to the trees like forgotten ghosts or lost souls. The thought brought a twinge of unbidden pain to him, and he glanced furtively to his side to see the slight figure just slightly out of his peripheral vision.

Aaron was beside him for the first time in five years, and he was glad. It was always so good to see his lover, even if Aaron had told him that he was there only as a long time friend. Such statements from the young vampire never bothered him. Aaron had broken off their relationship more times than he could count, and each time, Dorian had bided his time and waited until Aaron returned to him.

Ever since Aaron had learned of Tobias' death, he had been by Dorian's side, never straying far from him. He knew that Aaron was afraid, afraid he would try to exact revenge upon the coven that killed his brother, but that fear kept them together so he was pleased. He looked at Aaron again, walking by his side, calmly taking in the night. Dressed in jeans and green sweater, his pale hands and face gleaming in the darkness, he was perfect in Dorian's eyes and always had been.

The bastard son of a wealthy banker and a poor Chinese immigrant, Aaron Lian-Chen Spencer was barely twenty-two when he was made into a vampire in 1890. His maker, a vibrant French vampire named Victoria, had preserved him in all his youthful glory. Where Dorian had barely a hint of the Asian blood in his genes (As if he'd ever admit it!), Aaron had inherited the full cup. His hair was black like Dorian's, but thicker, silkier and glossier, lacking the shock of gray Dorian had. When they first met, Aaron's hair had fallen past his waist and he'd kept it in the traditional single braid. He was shaped like a true China Doll: lithe, delicate, and fine-boned with a set of slanted, jade green eyes that could see right into the soul. Dorian had met him twenty years after Victoria brought him over, only two years after the death of his beloved Elizabeth, and from the moment they had laid eyes on each other, it had been lust at first sight.

The lust had given way to a growing affection, and finally, to love. Together they had made a devastating pair of green-eyed, black-haired killers, hunting the streets of San Francisco and Sacramento with surgical precision. But Aaron had suffered from growing pains as all young vampires did, and the early years of their relationship had been tumultuous and fraught with arguments. Part of their problem was that they were far too much alike. Both were intelligent, cultured, and independent, yet desperately needy for acceptance and love. Aaron also had self-esteem problems, and suffered from a fear of attachment. Dorian suspected that Aaron's frequent departures were the younger vampire's way of 'leaving before he was left,' of dulling the pain of termination by ending the relationship himself. Victoria had played love games with him, some of which were anything but loving, and as a result Aaron was very timid when it came to love and commitment. What Aaron didn't realize was that Dorian did not place any timeframe on when and where Aaron would come back to him, he simply waited until he did. Dorian knew he had forever; a few years apart meant nothing to him, but Aaron, barely over a century old, was just coming to terms with his immortality.

Their last fight had been five years ago, and had ended with Aaron once again severing the relationship and walking out. Dorian found it amusing, however, that it was Aaron who rushed to his side when the word of Tobias' death got around. Dorian barely had time to recover from the shock of the news before Aaron was letting himself in the back door. He didn't remember much of those first few days. He remembered Aaron comforting him, caring for him, even hunting for him, but the details were a blur. He knew that Toby had come to see him regarding Etienne on September 28th, and that he'd gotten the call on October 6th, at 11:42 PM exactly. It had been raining. Now it was early spring. And it was still raining. There was a time when he liked it that way, but now it only made him depressed. It had been raining the night Toby came. He'd given Toby his old Fedora to help keep his hair dry. Toby cracked some joke about Humphrey Bogart. He had told him not to quit his day job...

'If only I'd gone with him. He asked me. He asked me to go with him...'

He gasped at the pain of the memory and Aaron's hand closed around his arm immediately. He covered the long fingers with his own, and looked into the jade eyes that gazed worriedly at him. He mustered a little smile, silently telling his lover that all was well, or as well as it could be. Aaron reluctantly let go and they continued on their way home, but Aaron remained even closer than before, protecting him, guarding him from any unforeseen enemies, including ones he made up himself.

Halfway home, taking their time and walking with mortal slowness, the rain stopped and patches of starry-night sky peeked through holes in the clouds. Dorian smiled up at them; it was good to see the stars. Rain reminded him of his loss and the memories would return in full force. Even though he and Tobias had not always seen eye to eye, they were brothers and he had loved him. His grief was strong and unpredictable.

He looked at Aaron again, close to his side and Aaron looked back, then curled his arm around his. He patted Aaron's hand pleasantly, and yawned, looking forward to curling up in bed and letting Aaron lull him to dreamless sleep. He still had nightmares; horrible, hideous nightmares that threatened his very sanity. It was one of the reasons Aaron kept so close. His presence was enough to guide him through these difficult and strange times.

Strange times indeed. Huge sections of clear-cut forest in Washington and Oregon had grown back in the course of a single night. The fish population of the oceans was increasing dramatically. The radiation level around

Chernobyl had decreased. The holes in the ozone were closing. The rain forests were reclaiming thousands of acres of abandoned farmland. Rain was falling in the deserts. Global temperatures were normalizing. All around the world environmental miracles were happening. Many were attributing them to the coming of the second Messiah, but there were others who believed that another force was behind them. Word was passing through the vampire mind net of the revival of the goddess religions, and of strange angels who claimed to be servants of a goddess not a god. So far, no vampire had truly laid eyes on one of these new avatars, but rumors about them abounded. Dorian himself wondered about what was going on. It seemed as if the environmental happenings were almost a challenge to conventional, organized religion. He didn't know if that was the case, and if he hadn't been so emotionally distraught from Tobias' death, he would have probably gone to track down one of these new angels. But as it was, he couldn't bring himself to really care.

It had been six months since Tobias had been destroyed in Ecuador, and Dorian lived with the guilt. Even though Aaron insisted that he was not to blame for Toby's death, he still felt responsible. If he had gone to Ecuador with Tobias, perhaps the coven that killed him would have left them alone or merely issued a warning for them to get out of their territory. Tobias on his own was powerful, but the two of them together were a considerable force. Maybe the coven would have thought twice about attacking both of them. There was no way of knowing because he had refused to go with Toby, and now Toby was dead. And no one could convince him that he wasn't at least partially to blame. Aaron had tried, running him through the course of events, proving over and over that there was no way he could have foreseen the danger or the outcome. But the mind and the heart are often at odds, and even though his head knew Tobias' death was not his fault, his heart still felt as if a part of him had been ripped to shreds.

'It's my fault. If I hadn't stayed to wait for that damn painting…'

He'd destroyed the painting. Aaron had never seen it. He had taken great pleasure is setting the thing on fire with his mind. The cheerful colors had turned black, melting and peeling into a charred, twisted mass. Charred like Toby. Blackened like his heart…He felt the wetness of tears on his cheeks and quickened his step. Beside him, he heard a concerned murmur from Aaron, but he didn't care; they were almost to the house.

Aaron did not question Dorian as they turned from the main trail and took a back way home, nor did he ask what was wrong as Dorian navigated the small game paths. He watched and waited, staying next to his ex-lover as they headed home, wondering what was going on inside Dorian's head, but too polite to pry. He had learned in the eighty-odd years he'd known Dorian, never to try reading Dorian's thoughts when the older vampire wanted to keep them to himself. It was hard enough for him to read thoughts even without mental barriers, and it was a battle not worth fighting. Dorian would talk when he was ready. In the meantime, he looked out over the dark, rain-misted trails, and remained silent, lost in his own thoughts.

Being here brought back a lot of memories for Aaron. It had been five years since he'd last left Dorian's company, and he hadn't realized how much they had missed each other. Perhaps it was true that absence made the heart grow fonder, and Dorian was actually being very accommodating and kind- nothing like his usual argumentative self. Maybe he would stay a while and see how long this change of heart lasted. Maybe they would actually stay together for longer than two years this time. Maybe he would be a lover and not a possession. He smiled to himself when he explored the possibilities, and looked fondly at Dorian as they turned the last corner towards home. As they said in these modern times, fat chance.

The moment Dorian spied the house, he knew there was something amiss. The doors of the deck overlooking the Sound were open and candles had been lit inside, the light streaming out into the darkness. Then as he narrowed his eyes to get a better look, he saw a strange woman with long, black hair come to stand on the deck. Rage surged through him at having his house and lair violated, and he gritted his teeth as he raced to the house with all his vampire speed and leapt onto the deck with one jump. With a vicious growl, he grabbed the woman by the throat and pinned her to the side of the building.

"What are you doing in my house?" he demanded.

He didn't want to hurt her, just scare her a little bit. He was not in the habit of killing so close to his home. Behind him, he heard Aaron rushing to catch up, coming in the back door and up the stairs. He was probably concerned that more intruders were inside the house. Satisfied that, between the two of them, they had the situation under control, he returned his attention to the woman he still had pressed against the wall.

She was completely calm and still, and did not speak a word. Her eyes were a deep gray, and she met his gaze unwaveringly, her expression giving away nothing of what she was feeling. Her hair was a straight mane of ebony black that fell over her shoulders and down her back. In it, hanging from a braid on the left side, was a string of rose quartz and amethyst beads bound together with silver and strands of brown hair. Brown hair…where had he seen that shade of luminescent brown before…?

A hand came down on his shoulder, gripping firmly and strongly, and a voice spoke from behind him in a commanding tone.

"You will release her."

Dorian froze, his whole body going numb. He knew the voice. It was a voice from the dead. It was the voice of Tobias. Swiftly, he let the woman go and spun around see his dead brother standing there. At the sight of the familiar boyish face, the brown curls, the blue eyes, he began to shake. Then Aaron came bursting onto the deck. The young vampire's expression was like his, one of abject shock.

"Tobias?" he heard Aaron choke.

The vampire who looked like Tobias turned to face Aaron, and fear spurred him into action. He thrust past the stranger and put himself between him and Aaron.

"Don't touch him! Get away! Who the Hell are you?!" he demanded.

Who was this intruder who wore Tobias' face? What did he want? Tobias was dead! Ian had told him so. This had to be someone's idea of a colossal joke. Well, it wasn't funny, and he was not amused! He would be twice damned if he was going to let this Tobias-impostor anywhere near Aaron.

The apparition took a step towards them. He concentrated his energy and tried to thrust it away. The bolt struck an invisible shield, leaving the doppelganger, and the woman behind him, untouched. Dorian recentered and tried again, this time with more force behind his thoughts. He sent the burst of power, and felt it be ripped from his control and redirected. A tree across the lawn exploded. He stared in horror at the shattered redwood, and then back at the impostor who still stood motionless and silent. What force was this that could wrench his power from him? A chill crept up his spine.

"Dorian," the thing said.

"Get away from me! How dare you! What the Hell are you?" he spat.

"Dorian please. Calm down," the apparition implored.

"I'll kill you if you come any closer!" he warned, baring his teeth and preparing to fight.

"Ri-Ri, it's me…"

"Tobias is dead!"

"Dorian, please…"

"My brother is dead! You are not my brother!" he cried.

Tobias looked past him, at Aaron.

"Aaron? Don't you know me?"

Aaron shook his head, his green eyes wide with fear. It looked like Tobias, down to the stray tendril of hair that fell over his eyes, but they both knew that Tobias had been dead for six months.

"No," the figure spoke, reading their minds. "No. I am not dead. Nor was I ever dead. I am alive."

"How can this be?" Aaron asked, his voice full of awe.

"Don't be afraid. I'm not here to hurt you," Tobias replied, then lifted his arm towards the woman who now stood adjacent to them. She moved silently to his side. "This is Rain, Daughter of the Mother. She is the one who saved me."

"Who is the Mother?" Aaron questioned.

"That is what we have come here to teach you about."

Dorian stiffened. "This has to be a trick. Tobias is dead. Ian told me so."

"Dorian, I am alive. I am not a ghost or a demon or an imposter. It's really me."

Aaron felt Dorian bristle with anger.

"How do we know you are telling the truth? Why should we believe you?"

Tobias' face softened. "Tell me what I can do to convince you that I speak the truth. Name it, my brother, and it is yours."

Both of them met his gaze, and he knew what they wanted without them having to answer.

"Give me your blood," Dorian responded lowly.

After a moment of eerie silence, Tobias nodded gravely and looked to his female companion, who also nodded. Without a word, they moved into the house. Dorian kept himself between Aaron and Tobias, remaining protective as they stopped in the living room. With a gesture, he urged Aaron to stay behind him, gladdened when the young vampire obeyed.

They watched Tobias unbutton his collared shirt, baring his neck and part of his chest, and face them, his arms open. Cautiously, Dorian moved close to Tobias, taking the older vampire into his embrace and nuzzling the white, offered throat. Aaron saw Tobias close his eyes and shiver as Dorian's teeth bit into his skin.

Dorian did not have to swallow the blood to know that Tobias spoke the truth. All that was necessary was for his teeth to break the surface. It was the bite, after all, that was the crux of the meld. The elixir that was vampire blood bathed his tongue, a taste unique and singular, and he groaned. He had never tasted Tobias' blood, but he knew immediately that it was Tobias in his arms. You couldn't lie in the swoon; it was the ultimate honesty, no walls, no barriers, no masks. The bite stripped away everything, revealing the victim's very soul. There was no deception here. Tobias even let him explore his mind, opening to him completely, letting him take whatever he needed to be convinced of Tobias' sincerity. In moments, he had released

Tobias and was weeping in his arms, holding him so tightly that he would have crushed him if he were a mortal man.

"Tobias!" he sobbed.

Tobias tangled hands in his black hair. *Yes.*

Love washed over him and Dorian wept even harder. He couldn't help himself, he wanted to, but he could not cease his tears of joy. His legs went weak and they collapsed to the floor, but he did not care. He began to babble, talking very fast and laughing as Aaron joined them in the embrace, his lips brushing his face and his arms closing around them.

Aaron reached down to kiss Tobias and whispered his name as Tobias arched his throat. Tiny teeth pierced his jugular as Aaron took a little drink. Tobias sighed, his fingers searching and finding Aaron's shoulder. He nuzzled Aaron's neck and reciprocated with his own bite. Aaron shuddered and he tasted the sweet taste as the liquid filled his mouth. Then Dorian bent near again, his cool lips coming to rest on Tobias' cheek and then moving lower. They drank from him as he drank from them, switching between them, hugging, kissing, murmuring endearments, until they all tasted of each other, the blood mingling and melding.

Rain watched silently as the two vampires bathed Tobias in hugs and kisses. They were alternately drinking from her lover, taking small mouthfuls of his blood to affirm his identity, and showering him with mortal kisses on his face and neck. He was kissing back, reaching for them, holding them, accepting them. Dorian was still wrapped around him, practically in his lap, but Tobias didn't seem to care. She saw Aaron bend his mouth to Tobias' throat as Tobias bent his to Aaron's for a small exchange of blood and pleasures, and she sat down on the sofa and waited for the display of affection to end.

She took the time to study the two new vampires. Dorian had glossy, shoulder-length, black hair streaked with one tinge of gray, and vivid green eyes. He was thin and tall, with a narrow face, and powerfully built body. Aaron was smaller with very long, waist-length black hair and slanted green eyes. His face was sweet, almost heart-shaped, and he wore an open, innocent expression on it.

Several minutes later, the three vampires separated, their lips red with the blood they had just shared, and Tobias turned to face her, his shirt ripped open by immortal fingers, the puncture wounds on his neck still seeping blood. They had taken quite a bit from him, his pallor revealing that fact, and he stood to approach her. Sitting beside her on the sofa, he took her gently into his arms and buried his face in her neck. Her hands held his shoulders as he began to feed lightly, keeping him close and holding him dear, while the others watched with horrified looks on their faces. They did not know what she was. They had no idea that Tobias could not harm her.

"Tobias…" Dorian breathed. Not that he cared if Tobias killed her, but not in the house.

It is all right. I cannot harm her. She is immortal, same as we. Just a different kind, he assured.

A moment later, Tobias lifted his mouth from her skin, and she turned her head so that the others could watch the wounds heal. He had not taken all that he could have, nor all that he needed. He had only taken enough to curb the rising blood lust.

"I want to hunt," he whispered, his voice thick with the blood he had just consumed.

"Of course you do. The predator does not want to be hand fed," she replied.

He turned to the others. "I will be back shortly."

Dorian threw something at Tobias, which Tobias easily caught. It was a set of keys.

"Take the Jaguar."

"Thank you," Tobias grinned and stood.

Without another word, he walked out of the living room, leaving Rain alone with Aaron and Dorian. They stared at her, their glittering preternatural eyes catching the glow of the candles, and she shifted nervously in her seat.

"Who are you?" Aaron asked, a tinge of awe in his voice.

"I am Rain."

Dorian moved to his feet and drew close, his eyes boring right into her as he looked her over. His gaze fell on the dangle in her hair and he touched it gingerly.

"What are you?" he asked finally.

"I am what is modernly known as an ecomancer."

Now Aaron had joined Dorian in scrutinizing her, but his eyes were kinder and less fierce. "What's an ecomancer?"

Rain blinked in surprise. "You've never heard the term?"

"No," Aaron replied innocently, reaching to brush her face with his fingertips. She smiled.

"Then I will show you."

She turned to Dorian. "You broke your shoulder some years ago, and it never healed right. It gives you pain every now and then."

Dorian jolted, his eyes opening wide. "Yes. It does that sometimes."

She lifted a thin hand and placed it gently upon his shoulder. A small pulse of power flowed through her fingers and into his muscle, diffusing, finding the source of the pain, and nullifying it. She heard Dorian's small gasp.

"Ecomancers are empathic healers," she said, removing her hand.

Dorian touched his shoulder lightly, his expression thoughtful. "What did you do?"

"There was a minor aberration in the nerve, probably damaged when you broke the bone, and it didn't realign when your body healed. It wasn't enough to cripple you, but it was off just enough to cause discomfort. I've fixed it now. It won't trouble you again."

He nodded that he understood. "Thank you," then he asked suddenly, "Is this how you saved Tobias?"

Rain nodded, her face clouding with the memory of Tobias' blackened body. "Yes. It was the greatest healing I have ever performed, and I had help. Another of my own kind was there to assist me. Without that aid, I would have lost him. As it was, Tobias was unconscious for two days after the first round of healing, and I was drained completely."

Aaron seemed intrigued. "What was left of him?"

She looked at him sadly. "Very little. A charred corpse. Without someone else there to hold his soul while I healed his vitals, I would have lost him. He was very nearly gone. You burn very quickly."

Aaron nodded uncomfortably. "Yes, we do."

"How was he, afterwards?" Dorian questioned.

"In body, he was fine. In mind and spirit, he was broken. He took much healing, but he is whole now."

"But he is Tobias? The Tobias we knew?" Aaron pressed, needing confirmation that the vampire who had returned to them was indeed Tobias.

"He is and he is not. You will have to decide for yourself what has changed and what has stayed the same."

"What else can an…ecomancer do?" Dorian broke in.

Rain stood and seemed to shimmer, flickering out of sight for a moment, then reappeared behind them, standing closer to the deck doors.

"What the…?" Aaron began.

"You can teleport," Dorian breathed.

"Yes, but what I just did was not teleportation. It is something we call 'out-of-phase.' I can alter my temporal resonance and shift temporal phases. It allows me to walk through things. Like I just walked through the two of you."

"How…?" Aaron started.

"Because in another phase just milliseconds from this one, you are not where you are, but this house is. Time isn't linear; it layers upon itself in temporal levels. By altering where I am in those layers at any given time, things in one phase may or may not be in another. Like you and Dorian kneeling in front of the couch. When I shifted phases, the house I walked through looked much different," she explained.

"You saw the house as it was before I had it redecorated!" Dorian noted, grinning.

She smiled in acknowledgment. "Exactly."

"But you can teleport too, right?"

In answer, she vanished. They waited a few seconds to see if she would reappear, then heard the tap of a pebble being tossed against the deck doors. They quickly moved outside to the deck and looked down into the backyard. Rain was several yards away, in the landscaped garden.

"I guess that's our answer," Dorian mused, then hopped over the rail.

Aaron hesitated. "I can't..."

"Oh, come on, Aaron," Dorian sighed, exasperated, then grabbed his lover and took him down to the yard himself.

He set Aaron down on the blue slate. Aaron, his pride ruffled, jerked angrily away, giving him a sullen glare as he fixed his clothes defiantly. Dorian almost burst out laughing, but that only would have made Aaron angrier. Instead he moved to Rain, who was standing beside the rose garden.

It was still just slightly too cold for the roses to be coming out of their winter hibernation, but there, before his very eyes, shoots were forming, elongating and growing on one of the bushes. As he watched in amazement, the bush began to move, its stems stretching and its leaves fanning as it increased in height. Buds began to form on the new stems, unfolding and blooming into magnificent peach flowers. Then, as if nothing at all was out of the ordinary, Rain reached over, plucked a rose from the bush and brought it to her nose.

"Mmmmm...I love roses," she commented.

Aaron and Dorian were still staring at her, their jaws open. Then, as if to tease them even more, the other rose bushes began to grow and bloom. They heard her giggle at their shocked expressions. Dorian bristled and snapped his jaw shut.

"What other surprises do you have for us?"

She grinned. "Well, I could make it snow, but I think that would attract too much undue attention."

"You're probably correct. So you can control the weather," Dorian stated flatly.

"Yes."

"Anything else?"

Rain looked at him coyly, a wry smile on her lips. "There is one other small thing I can do…"

Dorian crossed his arms. "And what might that be?"

"I can change my shape."

"How do you mean?" Aaron asked, curious.

She looked past Dorian to Aaron.

"It means I can be anything. I can assume any form I so desire. I can even be you."

Studying him carefully, she shifted herself to look just like him, inwardly laughing to herself as she watched the expression on his face. She only held it for a moment, then shifted back to her normal form. She had scared them enough for one night, she was certain. They were giving her a very wide berth now, eyeing her warily.

"You were also the one who took the power from me and blew up that tree," Dorian said evenly.

"Yes, and I will take time to heal the tree once things have settled here," then mindspoke to him. *I'm also a rather strong telepath, but since Aaron is somewhat lacking in that ability and I want to be polite…*

Acknowledged, he sent back.

"How? How did you come to be this way?" Aaron inquired, profoundly intrigued and frightened at the same time.

"I was human once. Same as you. Then I was reborn. I became a child of Aiya, the Mother."

Realization hit Dorian and he nodded. "Avatar of a Goddess. Yes. We have heard about your kind recently, and seen the effects of your power."

Rain regarded him with surprise, and he smiled smugly to himself.

"You are correct. My brethren have spread out over the globe. We are undoing what humans have wrought," she answered carefully.

"And reviving the Earth Mother religions," he added.

"That is only partially our doing. The religions were always there, but now with proof of Her existence, the followers are returning."

"Is it a challenge?" Dorian questioned, a fierce light in his eyes.

"No. It is not. If there is one, it has not come from us."

"If it is not a challenge, then what is it?"

Rain absently fingered the leaves of the rose bush, pensive. "We have our reasons for why we are doing what we are doing. Mostly it is because the balance has been so badly disrupted, and now it is tipped out of synch even more. It is reaching critical and dangerous levels."

"So you are here to restore balance," Aaron said thoughtfully.

"In a way, yes. I am also here to find someone. Which is why Tobias and I came to see you."

"Who do you need to find?" Dorian asked.

"Aurek. The first vampire."

"Who?"

"Aurek. He was the first of your kind. Aiya made him. No one has seen or heard from him in four thousand years, and we want to find him."

Dorian was dumbfounded, uncomprehending. He was about to ask her what she meant when Tobias entered the courtyard. Tobias, his face warm and ruddy from the blood he had just drank, went immediately to Rain, seized her in his arms and kissed her.

Rain gripped Tobias' strong arms in her hands as he kissed her deeply. He had a new shirt, probably taken from his victim, and it smelled of salt and a strange human's sweat. His lips were burning hot, hotter than they had ever been when he had fed only upon her, and his skin was soft and pliant. Then she felt his tongue push against her teeth, and she opened her jaw obligingly.

I saved some for you, he mindspoke to her as a gush of warm liquid flowed into her mouth right after his tongue.

It was only a little bit, but she knew what it was immediately. She recognized the taste from her days as Silaene. It was mortal blood. He had saved a small amount of his victim's blood and had now given it to her, sharing the feast of his first kill. She opened her throat and swallowed his gift, letting her tongue wrap around his as it explored her mouth.

I love you, he sent, sighing happily and holding her close.

I love you too.

Dorian didn't know what was going on. Something was very seriously up, that was obvious, but the nature of it was a mystery to him. Tobias had his tongue in Rain's mouth, and was cleaved so close to her, they could have been mistaken for Siamese twins joined at the mouth, chest, stomach, hips…This was clearly much more than a case of rescuee and rescuer affection. He saw Aaron give him an "I'm-as-clueless-as-you-are" look and shrug.

Shrugging back, he looked at his watch. That was when he noticed a big difference about Tobias. In all the years Dorian had known Tobias, he had never seen the brown-haired vampire without adornments. He had always worn a host of necklaces, rings, and most recently, a hooped earring in his left ear. Now Tobias wore none of those things. In fact, his only decoration was a black and gold ring on the ring finger of his left hand. Dorian could see the ring clearly on the hand that gripped Rain's shoulder. It was a thin band of gold spiraled around some kind of dull black stone in desperate need of smoothing and polishing. No, it wasn't stone at all, it was curved and swirled in places. He focused to examine it more closely, and soon realized that the gold metal was wrapped around a braid of black hair, Rain's black hair. His eyes moved up to see the dangle of stones in Rain's hair, confirming that a lock of Tobias' hair was indeed intertwined among the rose quartz, amethyst and silver. What did it mean? Each was wearing something made with the other's hair. Was it a kind of troth? He was profoundly intrigued. He would have to ask them when they came up for air.

Tobias prolonged the tender moment for as long as he could, reveling in the softness and heat of his beautiful lover, until he realized that the others were staring at them, then he reluctantly pulled away. He kept an arm around her, however, holding her close and pressing her to his side.

"Let's go inside. We can sit in the parlor and talk," Aaron said, offering his hand to Tobias.

Dorian noticed with bemusement that Aaron was using the same patient, comforting tone of voice that his lover used when trying to calm him down during his fits of temper. He watched as Aaron led Tobias with that voice, like a Pied Piper, into the house. There they talked until the small hours of the morning, seated in a makeshift circle on the floor. Rain and Tobias shared stories of the Sanctuary and Aurek. Aaron seemed intrigued by the whole idea of the Circle and the Webs, and asked many questions. Rain and Tobias did their best to answer and hoped that they were able to help him understand.

Dorian offered the use of his library as a starting point for the search for Aurek. He had many old texts that had been written by vampires, and Aaron had occasionally added to the collection. While he could not say that he had ever seen a reference to a vampire named Aurek, now that he knew what he was looking for, there was a possibility that one might be found. It might, however, take a few days to go through all of the volumes. Aaron feared that any books that could have been helpful might have been burned during the Dark and Middle Ages when many old books were destroyed. The subject of searching Ian's library in Scotland was brought up, but neither sibling wanted to contact Ian unless it was absolutely necessary.

Dawn was coming and Dorian stopped the conversation so he could secure the house against sunlight, closing the heavy drapes and obscuring the view of the Sound from the ground floor. The second floor, the floor with the prows, was off limits on all but the cloudiest of days. Still Dorian loved the views and often braved the sunset to watch the stars come out. The first floor, the floor built into the hill, had two forward gathering rooms with picture windows that faced the Sound, a fire-lit den, a fire-lit library, and four windowless bedrooms.

Aaron gave a heavy yawn and rubbed his tired eyes. Looking after Dorian these last few months had been hard on him, and the conversation, while intellectually stimulating, was also very tiring.

"I'm to bed," he announced when Dorian returned.

"Want company?" Dorian asked with a gleam in his eye.

Aaron gave him a slow smile. "No, but thank you."

Dorian made it a point to look disappointed until Aaron sighed heavily and placed a gentle kiss on the older vampire's cheek.

We've discussed this, Ri-Ri... Aaron chided mentally.

I know. I know. But I don't have to like it.

After Aaron went to his room and it was decided that Tobias and Rain would sleep in the larger guest bedroom, Tobias climbed onto the couch with Rain, stretching out in a reclining position and rested his head on her chest. She was on her back, her head cushioned by the arm of the couch while he, with his slender body, was wedged between her and the back of the sofa.

"Will you come to bed with me?" Tobias asked, absently twirling a strand of her hair in his fingers.

"Hmm, I'm not really tired, love. I think I'll explore the area. It's been a while since I've been here. There have been many chemical spills and intentional dumps into the Sound and streams. I may go to see what clean-up I can do there."

"That's sounds good," he agreed, inwardly disappointed that she would not be sleeping with him.

"I'll probably nap and find food as well."

"Will you be back before sundown?" Tobias asked hopefully.

She smiled and kissed his nose. "Yes, priye."

"I'm so glad. I'm used to seeing your face when I wake up." He paused, then added sadly, "I'm used to spending the day with you, too."

"We will have the nights together."

"Yes, that is true. I'll still miss you," he admitted, trying not to sound too childish.

"I'll miss you too."

"I still love you."

"And I still love you."

Watching them made Dorian ill. They were so horribly sweet and loving to each other that if he were human, he would have puked a long time
ago. They were like two newlyweds getting ready say good-bye to each
other while "Jim-dear" went to work. Honeymoon's over kids. But they
were just like newlyweds, weren't they, and now the honeymoon really was
over, and he felt a little sad for them. Until now, the fact that Tobias was
a vampire and she wasn't hadn't made that much of a difference, but now
that they were back on Earth, it really threw a monkey wrench into their
housekeeping plans.

He observed them silently, noting how they constantly touched and
kissed each other. Tobias' face was such a picture of perfect love that it
made his heart ache. Had anyone ever looked at him that way? The way
that Tobias now looked at Rain? Tobias' whole soul was right there on his
face, his eyes holding nothing but affection and sweet adoration. Never
had anyone ever looked at him like that. Not Aaron, not Elizabeth, not
any of his other lovers. Never had he experienced such complete and utter
devotion. But oh how he wanted it! Wasn't it what every vampire wanted?
Isn't that why they craved companionship? Was it not a desperate attempt
to find this love? To find the partner who would spend the centuries with
them? After all wasn't it love that, aside from blood, was the only thing
that sustained them? Love fed vampires like the blood they drank. It suffused them with new emotion. Love was what every vampire he had ever
known, truly wanted.

They were sitting up now, side by side, holding hands, their heads
bowed. It was almost dawn. The room had been getting increasingly
lighter as daylight neared. Kissing her, Tobias stood, allowing his hand to
linger in hers for as long as it could, sliding it from her loose grasp until
just the fingers brushed, and slowly backed away. She stayed on the couch,
reaching with her hand as their fingertips touched then drew apart. No
words, only sorrow on their faces as he left.

Dorian rose to his feet and silently led the way to the bedrooms, where he and Tobias could sleep safely away from the sun. He saw Tobias look back to see Rain still sitting on the sofa, watching them leave, and then heard his sad sigh as he fell into step behind him.

"Sunset isn't that far away," Dorian consoled as he stopped outside Tobias' room.

"I know. I also know you must think me a love-sick fool," he whispered, painfully aware that Dorian had never viewed his dependence in a positive light.

"No. You have what I have always wanted, my brother. Enjoy it. May it last forever."

Tobias smiled softly and kissed Dorian sweetly on the lips. "Thank you."

Dorian moved to walk away, then he paused and turned back. "It's good to see you again, Toby."

"It's good to see you."

"I am so glad…" He stopped, unable to continue, but Tobias seemed to understand and opened his arms.

They embraced, letting their hug say all the things pride would not let them say, and then reluctantly pulled away.

"Sleep well," Tobias whispered.

"And you, sleep well."

Two

Rain watched the sunrise from the deck. It was going to be a beautiful day. There were some pretty cloud formations that were reflecting pink and yellow from the rising sun, and she saw them swirl and disperse. When it was full daylight, she reentered the house and moved silently to the guest bedroom. It was furnished with dark wood furniture, and a huge bed. Her lover was sound asleep under the covers. Gingerly, she pulled back the blanket and looked down at the still form. He was on his side, curled into a semi-fetal position, his face preserved in quiet repose. His brown curls fell haphazardly over his forehead, partially hiding his eyes, and blending with the soft wisps of his eyelashes. He was so beautiful. He had always been beautiful to her, even from the very beginning. Bending down, she kissed his cold cheek. His body stirred, rising from sleep. She waited. Slowly she watched as his hand raised up, moving towards her warmth, and touched it with her own hand, opening her palm and spreading her fingers as it pushed against her. The hand stopped, frozen for a few moments, then closed upon hers, the cold fingers curling between her own. She smiled, her eyes going misty, and bent down to kiss him again. He opened his eyes and smiled at her, tugging on her, seeking to pull her closer, and she obliged, until she was halfway in the bed with her arm around him. Cold lips pressed against her forehead.

"I love you," he whispered.

"I love you too."

Gently she pulled away, sending tender thoughts of regret and promises to come back later. He let her go, his arm folding back to where it had been, his hand tucked neatly under his jaw.

"I'll be back soon, I promise," she whispered, kissing him one last time.

He gave her a tender smile and closed his eyes. She covered him back up and silently left the room.

Her first order of business was to heal the tree she had destroyed with Dorian's redirected mind bolt the night before. She had known that she did not have time to diffuse the power, so she had thrown it at the nearest safe target. Now the tree was severely damaged, its trunk splintered and half its crown scattered on the lawn. She laid her hands upon it, easing its pain, and pulled the power to her. It took her some time, but she was able to restore the tree to health and vitality. Afterwards she moved to wander the coastal forests, avoiding people as much as possible. Her clothes and coloring always made her uncomfortable among humans. Besides, the Sound and forest were so full of teeming life, she felt more at home. The animals and plant life there knew her kind and welcomed her. She could speak with them, but the communication was very basic and minimal. There were times when she had used animals and plants to find out information. Animals had no real memory or sense of time, but they could retain certain things, and since they were mobile, chances were she could get more information out of them. Plants had much longer memories, but their scope was limited by their stationary lives. Trees were veritable libraries of time, but only for their immediate surroundings. If you found the right one, you could learn the entire history of an area, but it was a matter of finding it.

Trees remembered best of all the plants. They were the gossips of all flora. They could recite whole conversations, recreate scenes. Somewhere, she was certain there was a tree who had heard and seen Lincoln composing and practicing his Gettysburg Address. She was looking for a tree, a tree in just the right spot, one that would have seen and heard things that would help her undo the pollution in the water. She spied one that she thought might be of some help, growing on the edge of a causeway, and went to it, touching it with her hand and mind.

'*Who?*' the tree responded.

She identified herself as best she could.

'*Ahhhh…yes.*'

Amazing to join minds with a tree. They were an entirely different form of sentience. Memory passed through them, recorded in their many growth rings, each level revealing new things and events. She spiraled down, through the tree's long lifetime, learning the history of the area, and seeing the passage of time through the tree's 'eyes.' Many people had come over the life span of the tree. Chemicals and pollutants from boats had leaked into the water. Then there were strange flavors in the water, coming from further up stream, flavors that made it hard for the tree to breathe and turned its leaves yellow.

Rain took what she needed from the tree then disconnected her mind from it, thanking it as she did so and promising that soon it would be easier to breathe. Stripping down and putting her long hair up in a twisted braid, she stepped into the water. Opening her mind she channeled the earth power through her. She turned within herself, giving herself new eyes, eyes that could see the unnatural substances in the water, and began to systematically destroy them. The power was pleasure coursing through her veins, and she became part of the water, a pillar of pure energy radiating outward, sending healing throughout the channels all the way to Pacific.

She first became aware of the 'watcher' when she went to find something to eat. She was sitting outside a little bistro in a suburb community enjoying a small lunch, when she felt the indisputable sense that she had been singled out of the crowd, and later, while she was combing the area north of the Sound, she felt it again. It unnerved her, because whenever she moved to see who was there, no one was visible. At first she thought it was merely Sky playing a little joke upon her, but Sky had never left such a sinister impression. She mind called to see if any of her brethren were within the vicinity, but received no answer. There was, however, a faint energy trail in the Pacific that suggested Sea had been there recently. Aside from that, there was nothing to indicate that any of the ecomancers were nearby. Shrugging it off as her overactive nerves, she set to the business of identifying the pollutants that were dumped into the water. Then she felt it again: eyes boring into the back of her head from an unseen entity. She whirled around and searched the trees with her eyes, invoking Othersight in case it was a spirit. Nothing. But the air was unnervingly still.

"Hello? Who is there?"

The wind rustled through the leaves.

"Show yourself. I can feel you. I know you are here."

Tentatively she mindtouched the area trees.

'Who is it?' she asked them.

'Don't know,' came the overwhelming response. 'Cannot see.'

She was getting angry, the static electricity building around her as her anger grew.

"If you aren't going to show yourself, go away," she ordered, backing up her command with a warding pulse that would have frightened off any spirits or unwitting entities.

The feeling dissipated and, satisfied that she had dealt with the problem, she went back to her work. It was back, however, in less than an hour, this time stronger than before, and it soon became so distracting that she could no longer work. It was getting late anyway, in another two hours it would be sunset, and she was tired. She stopped working, climbed out of the water and began to dress. As she wrapped her sari around her, she felt the eyes grow closer, and the animosity oozing from it could not to be denied. It frightened her badly, and she quickly headed for the house. She could feel it following close at her heels, and she found herself running. She invoked out-of-phase and passed through buildings and cars in an attempt to get away, but it was still right behind her when she arrived at the house. Holding back her panic, she teleported herself into the living room. It did not follow, but it was there, in the yard, waiting.

Rain shuddered with fear and exhaustion. Out-of-phase and teleportation took a great deal of energy out of her, and she was nearly depleted. Mustering up the last of her energy, she weaved a protection spell that encompassed the entire house, creating an invisible shield in an attempt to prevent the watcher from gaining entrance. The presence in the yard shimmered for a moment, then receded to just outside the perimeter of the shield. Rain waited to see what it would do, but it just stayed there, still unseen, on the edge of the perimeter pines. When she was relatively confident that it could not enter the house, she went to Tobias' bedroom and collapsed on the bed.

• • •

Tobias' eyes snapped open suddenly, and for a moment he was disoriented. He had become so used to waking up in the willow-room, with Rain at his side, that this new place momentarily confused him. He took in his surroundings, and soon remembered where he was. Rolling over, he bumped into the sleeping form of Rain and smiled. He looked down upon her peaceful face and kissed her tenderly on the cheek. She did not stir at the touch of his cold lips, and he guessed that she was exhausted from her day's work. Reluctant to wake her, he slipped from the bed and went to feed. He knew Dorian would be rising very soon, but he decided not to wait for him, and he was back within half an hour, coming in through the deck doors. No one was there to greet him. Aaron had yet to rise, and Dorian had already left to go on his nightly prowl. With no one to detain him, he went immediately to the bedroom and curled up next to Rain on the bed. A short while later the door opened, and a crack of light streamed in from the hall as Dorian peeked in. He raised his head from the pillow and looked at the black-haired vampire.

Yes? he asked, mildly surprised to see Dorian there.

Just wondering where you were, Dorian replied.

Ahh. Have you need of me? he said, moving to sit up.

No.

Okay.

Is she all right?

Yes, just sleeping, he replied, looking fondly at his lover.

When she wakes, tell her I want to talk to her. Aaron says the house feels strange.

How so? he questioned, concerned.

I'm not sure. He doesn't have my powers and I don't have his. He is so much more earth bound than I…but he says that there is something surrounding the house. I can't feel it, but I don't think he has any reason to lie.

Tobias furrowed his brow. *I did not feel anything out of the ordinary when I went out.*

Neither did I, but as I said…he feels things I don't. I was hoping she could tell us what it is. It has Aaron rattled.

I will tell her when she rises, he assured.

Thank you.

Tobias nodded as Dorian slipped his head out and closed the door. He nuzzled Rain with his nose, taking in the scent of her hair, and settled down again, holding her close.

Two hours later, while he was dozing peacefully, the body next to him stirred. He opened his eyes to see Rain staring back at him, her gray eyes dark and brooding. He raised up happily and kissed her, letting her feel his hot lips, heated with the blood of his earlier kill. She responded favorably, kissing him back, a small sigh escaping her lips, and he began to caress her body. His fingers unclasped her sari and slid under the silk to find her breasts. Carefully, as if he were opening a precious gift, he revealed her chest to his hungry gaze, and he lowered his mouth to kiss them. She was limp and pliant in his arms, allowing him to do anything he desired. He kissed her nipples, nibbled and teased them until they were erect and flushed pink, then he covered one of them with his mouth, biting down. A tiny cry came from his lover and her hands gripped his hair, combined with the soft sucking sounds of his mouth on her breast. Oh how he loved this silent worship, although he knew it would not go anywhere. Dorian and Aaron were just a wall away, and there would be no lovemaking without complete privacy.

Releasing her breast, his mouth found hers again, and they kissed, her hands parting his shirt and bringing their naked chests together. He held her, pressed to him, as his tongue flicked across her teeth and probed her mouth. The sweet taste of her on his lips made him sigh with contentment, then he tenderly pulled away.

"Did you sleep well, liebchen?" he asked.

"Yes, and you?"

"Cold and lonely, but not anymore," he replied with a smile.

She was about to reply when someone knocked softly on the door.

"Come in," Tobias said.

The door opened and Aaron entered, highly agitated.

"Oh, you are awake," he blurted, looking at Rain, but when he saw that she was half naked, he bowed his head in shame and moved to back out. "I'm sorry. I did not mean to intrude…"

"It's all right, Aaron," she assured, pulling up her sari and rewrapping it as they both sat up on the bed. "Stay. There is something upsetting you. I can feel it. What is wrong?"

"There is something surrounding the house. It wasn't there last night. It's all around. Dorian can't feel it, but it's driving me crazy."

"It is all right, Aaron. What you are feeling is a protection shield I put around the house today. It is a spell used to keep out unwanted things," she explained gently.

'He can feel the shield, but can he feel the watcher? Is the watcher even there?' she wondered.

Aaron scratched his head in a most human manner, and she had to suppress a smile.

"Keep out unwanted things? What kind of unwanted things?"

"Oh, any number of things, Aaron. It's just a precaution. I put it up so you would have protection during the day if I am not around," she glibly answered.

"Do you expect some kind of trouble?" Tobias questioned, a suspicious glint in his eye. "Did you have trouble today?"

She met his gaze, dreading what she was about to do. "Oh no, my love. Like I said, it's just a precaution. You know that we have no idea what Ja'oi is up to. I thought it best to be safe," she lied.

She didn't want to lie to him or keep the truth from him, but she was still uncertain as to what the watcher was, and she knew Tobias would probably panic if he knew that she was being followed while he was unable to protect her.

Turning her face quickly away from his scrutinizing eyes, she addressed Aaron.

"I can make you not feel it so keenly, if you like. Had I known you would be sensitive to it, I would have told you beforehand."

"No, that will not be necessary. It was not knowing what it was that was bothering me. Now that I know what it is, it is all right."

"Very well. I am sorry that it has caused you such distress."

He bowed gentlemanly. "Oh, no. I am just glad that it is nothing we need to worry about."

"No no, not at all. I am sure in a couple of days, you won't even notice it is there anymore."

Aaron nodded and put his hand on the door. "I'm sure. Well, I will leave you two alone. I am sorry to have…interrupted you."

Silently, he retreated from the room, closing the door as quietly as possible.

"Odd that he can feel it, but Dorian cannot," she commented.

"I cannot feel it either."

"Hmm, I wonder why that is."

Tobias thought for a moment, trying to think of a way to explain. "Aaron is not very strong and he still holds many ties to his former life. He has a lot of what I now recognize as Earth Sense. He has almost no telepathy to speak of…"

Rain agreed. "I know. I have attempted mindspeech with him. It is very difficult. He does not receive very well."

"Yes. But he has powers we do not. He can feel the spirits, and sometimes hear them. Those of us who are stronger cannot. That is why he feels your shield, but the rest of us don't."

"I understand. I wonder if he is closer to the Circle than most of you. I wonder where his bloodline goes."

"Victoria made him."

"Yes, but who made Victoria?"

"The one who made Ian, a vampire named Orion. But he is dead."

"And the one who made Orion?"

Tobias shook his head. "I don't know. I never knew him. He is dead as well."

"How did he die?"

"He was killed by another coven master."

"I see..." she mused and looked thoughtful.

"In all honesty, I think it was Aaron's upbringing much more than his bloodline. He was raised in the Chinese way. They have always been closer to nature and the supernatural than Europeans," he explained thoughtfully.

"That was not always so."

"No, but in contemporary times, it is."

"True."

Tobias smiled and looked as if he were going to lie down again. However, Rain was still feeling guilty about lying to him, and she was afraid that she would be unable to keep it from him if they stayed in bed.

"I'm hungry," she told him. "I see that you have already fed, but my work today has left me famished. I would like to go find something to eat. Do you have any suggestions?"

"But of course. Seattle has many wonderful restaurants," he answered, smiling warmly. He rose from the bed, buttoning his shirt and offering his hand. "I used to take Etienne all the time when we visited here while he was still mortal. There was this one small place in Tacoma that he just loved..."

Tobias paused, his eyes growing sad with the memory of his Etienne. Rain came close and kissed him on the cheek lovingly.

"You still love him, don't you?"

He nodded. "Yes. And miss him too. Our years together were glorious. He had such passion and fire, even after I brought him to me. It was wonderful and terrible at the same time. He was my beloved…"

"I know. You've told me."

He stopped and looked at her, his blue eyes filling with warmth. "Yes. And now you are my beloved."

"You're getting sappy again."

"I know," he snickered, kissing her. "I don't care either. I love you."

She nudged him playfully. "Ahhh, you're just rammy."

He laughed softly and played with her hair. "That too."

She patted his rump and he shivered. "C'mon, love. Your beloved is hungry."

"My beloved's wish is my command," he smoothed, putting his arm around her, and gently guiding her from the room.

The watcher was still there when she peered out the deck doors. She had already discerned that Aaron could not feel it, nor could any of the others. She alone could feel it staring through the glass doors, waiting for her. It followed her and Tobias as they went to a nearby restaurant, and hovered outside while she ate. It seemed to avoid heavily crowded places and well-lit areas, and it was afraid of Tobias. She could feel its fear of her vampire lover, noting that it constantly kept a good distance away when he was near her, so she stayed close to him. If he noticed her unusual closeness, he did not say, but then he was too happy to be with her. They walked arm in arm, two young lovers strolling along the city streets.

Like a teenager with his newfound girlfriend, Tobias was all smiles and bubbling joy. She looked at his beaming face and her heart sank. How could she trouble him with something that she herself was not sure of? No. She would wait. Wait and try to find out for herself what was going on, and then, if it was dangerous, she would tell him, but not until she knew for sure. In the meantime, when he looked at her, she smiled, counting her blessings for being so loved, and not worrying about the shadow that followed behind.

Three

Two nights later there came a knock at the door. The four of them were on the upper floor, sitting in the large living room with its massive prow windows looking out to the Sound, and enjoying a fire in the huge stone hearth that took up a good section of the North wall. Piles of books littered the cocktail table and floor as they each pored through a tome. When they heard the knock they looked at each other, wondering who could be coming to the house. The fact that there had been no alarm from the security system suggested that the unplanned visitor was a vampire. Both Tobias and Dorian sent out mental queries, trying to identify the visitor, but were met with a mental shield. Dorian frowned and one could almost see him bristle, preparing for an attack. Aaron's eyes widened a little, and Tobias moved to place himself in a position to better protect both Aaron and Rain. Rain, sensing her lover and Dorian's growing anxiety, and Aaron's rising fear, sent out her own query to touch the visitor/intruder with Empathy.

"I sense no malevolence or evil," she said softly, trying to diffuse the rising tension. "Only nervousness overlaying reined-in hope."

She thought her statement would help ease their fears, but Tobias' face only darkened and Dorian deepened his frown. She looked to Aaron who blinked at her and shrugged. At least he was no longer so afraid.

"I'll go see who it is," Dorian said after a moment.

He rose from his seat on one of the couches and walked through the large open area to where the front entrance to the house was marked by a

set of large wooden doors and a tiled foyer. Aaron watched him go, the
entry being in his line of sight, and saw him open one of the doors. The
young vampire fully expected Dorian to announce the arrival of whoever
it was, but the English vampire was eerily silent, making all of them sit up
a little straighter. Rain put a hand on Tobias' arm as she felt him tense
again. She reached out to Dorian to Touch him and was nearly floored by
the torrent of emotions roiling inside the vampire: love, hate, rage, pain,
joy and desperate sadness all balling and twisting in a tangled mass. She
was wondering who could incite such a reaction from the normally so
controlled vampire when Dorian stepped aside to allow the newcomer in.

The dark-haired vampire that entered made Aaron gasp and Tobias
flinch. Aaron stood and immediately went past the newcomer to stand
beside Dorian who had stayed in the foyer. He solicitously closed the front
door since Dorian seemed incapable of doing so at that moment, and
placed a comforting hand upon Dorian's shoulder. Meanwhile, Tobias had
also stood, motioning a hand for Rain to stay seated, and faced the visitor
with his shoulders rolled back and his head high. Empathy, however,
revealed his true feelings as Rain discovered when she Touched him. He
was nearly as upset as Dorian, his emotions swinging wildly between joy
and sorrow, anger and elation. She took a moment to study this new
vampire, taking in his short-cropped dark hair and deep brown eyes. He
was dressed in a pair of casual trousers and a cable sweater with a raincoat,
even though it was not raining. Nothing about him seemed overtly
threatening or evil, yet the way Tobias was standing so protectively in front
of her told her that her lover considered him dangerous. Then Tobias said
a name in short, clipped tones, and all was made clear.

"Ian."

"Tobias," Ian answered calmly, his voice low.

"What brings you here?"

"You."

"Why?"

"I heard you were dead, and then I heard you were alive. I came to see which was true," the elder vampire stated.

"The reports of my death have been greatly exaggerated," Tobias replied, quoting Samuel Clemens.

"So it would seem."

"You should have called," Aaron scolded, calling attention to himself and Dorian. He was guiding Dorian back into the living room, but keeping himself in the position of protector; an interesting turn for the usually submissive vampire. "Then we would have known you were coming."

Ian looked from Dorian, who had a dazed and wounded look upon his face, to Tobias, who was practically vibrating with tension.

"Am I not welcome in my son's house?"

Aaron sighed. "You are always welcome here, Ian. It's just that…"

"I did not come here to cause trouble."

"No, Elder, we know you would not come to cause unrest," Aaron assured, falling into his Oriental habit of treating older vampires with extreme respect- particularly this older vampire.

"He just knows I need fair warning before you show up on my doorstep," Dorian said, coming out of his shock. "Why did you come here?"

"I thought that this would be the most likely place to start if I were looking for Toby. You and he have remained…close over the years."

"No thanks to you," Dorian snapped.

"Dorian…" Aaron cautioned, placing a hand upon Dorian's arm.

Ian let out a soft laugh. "It is all right Aaron. My youngest son and I have had this argument often. I doubt it will ever be resolved."

Dorian retorted, "Not in this millennium at least."

Ian ignored the last comment and turned to Tobias, reaching out a hand to cup his eldest son's cheek. Tobias stiffened but allowed it.

"I have no words to express my joy in seeing you alive. I…suffered greatly when I thought you were dead. No matter what has happened between us, Toby, I have always loved you." He looked back at Dorian. "Both of you."

"I would never wish you to suffer, Vater," Tobias answered, using the German word for father, and pressing Ian's palm to his face. The feel of the old vampire's hand upon his skin brought back many old memories. Ian had always been able to control him with a single word or touch.

Dorian snorted and turned away, shrugging off Aaron's comforting hand, and stalked out of the room. Aaron, knowing better than to follow Dorian when he was in one of his moods, returned to his seat on the second couch in the living room. They heard the downstairs, outside door slam before Ian returned his attention to his first born.

"My grief knew no bounds. I am so glad to know that the rumors were untrue."

"They were not untrue, Vater. I did nearly die."

Ian stiffened. "Then it is true? You were almost killed in Ecuador?"

"Yes," he replied without emotion.

The ancient vampire trembled. "Why? Why did you go there?"

"I heard that Etienne was there with Barias, and so I went looking for him. I wanted to talk with him, to ask him to come back. But I did not find him," Tobias replied, looking into the fire, his eyes misty.

"He was not there," he added after a moment of silence.

"I am so sorry."

"So am I, but I am glad of it now."

Ian stared at Tobias in disbelief. "What? You are glad that you were almost burned to a cinder?"

"If I had not, then I would not know what I know now, and I would not have Rain."

"Rain?"

Tobias smiled and stepped back, showing Rain. Shyly, like a son bringing his new fiancée home to meet his father and hoping they will get along, he brought his maker to meet his lover.

"I give you Rain, Daughter of the Mother."

Ian bowed to the woman seated on the couch, and she nodded to him in acknowledgment.

"Rain is the one who saved me. She is an avatar of Aiya, the Earth Mother," he said with an air of quiet awe.

"The Earth Mother?"

"Yes. There is much I have to tell you. Come, sit down, and I will begin."

Ian obeyed immediately, too happy and amazed to do otherwise.

"Perhaps it would be best if I began at the beginning..." Tobias said, taking his maker's hands in his own. "When I went into Ecuador, I encountered a hostile coven with a powerful leader. I am sure you have heard of what happened."

Ian nodded. "Yes. You ran into Leith. If you had told me you were going, I could have warned you about him. But what happened next? How did you survive?"

"Rain saved me. She has loved me for a long time, and she was looking for me. When she saw me burning in the fire, she could not let me die. She took me and healed me. I have been with her in Aiya's Sanctuary," Tobias answered. "But there is more. I have learned of our origins, of the first vampire. His name is Aurek, and Aiya created him. He is missing and we have been sent to find him. We need your help, your knowledge."

"Tell me everything and I will do my best to help you in any way that I can."

Rain watched them, remaining silent, as they settled down on the couch. As they began their talk, she stood and walked out onto the deck, looking out over the well-tended property to the line of small trees several yards away. The watcher was still there. It had not left, not even for a moment, since it had arrived. It hounded her whenever she went out alone, and now she had voluntarily confined herself to the house. Tobias did not know this; she kept it carefully from him, and he was oblivious to her rising apprehension.

The watcher was getting bolder, periodically testing the integrity of her shield. She had expended much energy repairing and reinforcing weak spots in an attempt to keep it out. So far it had not been able to breach her protections. It wanted to though, and it was getting stronger, probably feeding on her rising fear. She knew things would reach a breaking point soon, and she had no idea what to do. Tobias would panic. How long could she hold it off? She didn't even know what it was, although she had a pretty good idea that it had been sent by Ja'oi. She had sent out queries to her brethren to see if any of them had experienced similar phenomenon, but so far, no one had answered. In the meantime, she waited, fear knotting in her stomach like a cold supper. She glanced furtively back at Tobias and sighed sadly. He looked so happy, so full of life. She did not want to trouble him, besides, she doubted that there was anything he could do.

"How do you know?" came a quiet voice behind her.

She nearly jumped out of her skin, and whirled to see Dorian standing behind her. She hadn't even realized he had come back. She blushed furiously aware that he had both come up on her unawares and invaded her mind.

"Oh. You are back."

"I did not wish to leave Toby alone with Ian for long," he explained. "And I didn't invade your mind, my dear. You were leaking."

She put a hand to her head to push away her forming headache and sighed. "I suppose I am…" She was so tired. Had she ever been this tired?

Dorian came very close, his green eyes seeing right into her soul, and his voice pierced her mind in a lock-send that she knew Tobias could not hear.

What is it? You are frightened and becoming more frightened every day. He gestured dismissively at Tobias, who was still obliviously talking to Ian, though Ian had already cast several concerned glances Rain's way. *Lover boy may have his head too far in the clouds to see what is going on, but I don't. Something is bothering you. It's scaring you.*

He looked past her, to the line of pines. *It's something out there, isn't it? Something I can't feel, but you can.*

She wilted, her defenses wavering. Should she tell him the truth? Or should she try to lie as she had lied to Tobias? Tobias was easy to deceive because he was blind with love, but Dorian…Dorian had no such blinders. Her shoulders slumped as she nodded.

"Yes," she breathed, and it felt as if a great weight had been lifted from her. *There is something out there. I don't know what it is. I have never laid eyes on it, but I can feel it. It follows me wherever I go.*

You're being stalked.

She nodded again. *Yes.*

And you don't know what it is?

No, but I've stopped it for now. It can't get past the shield.

So that is why you put the barrier up. I had a suspicion that it wasn't just a precaution like you told Aaron. How long do you think it will hold?

I don't know. It's getting stronger. For now I have it at bay, but I am so tired and it's always there. It tests the shield, trying to find a weak spot. It wants in, and I have no idea how long I can keep it out.

She bowed her head and hugged herself, shivering. She was tired and hungry and afraid. Goddess how she wished Sky was there. She had been unable to reach him since they arrived on Earth. It did not bode well. Usually that meant he had gone deep into the now. Dorian put a hand on her shoulder.

Is it dangerous? he asked carefully.

I don't know. My guess would be, yes, it's dangerous. Not to you, I don't think. It's me it wants.

Can it harm you?

It depends on what it is. I am not invincible. I do have my weaknesses. Another ecomancer or entity with equal power to one could harm or even destroy me.

Dorian's eyes grew dark. *You think this thing is that strong?*

I don't know, but I don't think I want to find out.

Why have you waited so long to tell us about this?

Rain turned away. *Because I didn't want to trouble anyone with it...*

Dorian snorted derisively. *Trouble us with it? Rain, you are being hunted! Don't you think we have a right to know these things?*

Well what would you have had me do? she sent angrily, facing him again, her eyes flashing with rage and pain. *Tell Tobias that I'm being followed? That something is out there that stalks my every move? That it is there during the day, when he cannot protect me? That it might hurt or even kill me? He'll panic, you know he will!*

Dorian sighed and shrugged. *You're right. He will. But you cannot keep this from him. You are in danger. Perhaps all of us are in danger. We must find out what this thing is, and how to destroy or get rid of it.*

She glanced at the trees, growing silent and still, as if she could hear something he could not.

Yes. Yes, I cannot do this alone anymore. I need help. I have called for my brethren and received no answer, she admitted.

Why is that?

I do not know. It could simply mean that they are too busy to answer me.

Or it could mean that they have been attacked like you have. Maybe some of them have already been defeated.

Don't say that! She looked at him, her eyes wide with her own nightmares.

Would you know if they had been killed?

I...I don't know. I think so. The only ecomancers ever to die were killed many years before I was made, but it is said that all the others felt their passing.

How did they die?

There was a war...in a place far away from here, out of this galaxy. The planet was very badly scarred. Fire and Air were sent to help, but got caught in the battle between the avatars of the two warring gods. Their deaths were an accident, she replied, turning her face to the glass door once again.

And what did Aiya do? Dorian asked respectfully.

Rain did not answer at first, her eyes were locked on the presence outside, her heart turning cold with fear.

It is said that She did not have to do anything. An avatar of the Earth Mother was killed, this is a great offense for we are always neutral...peacekeepers, healers...

Like the Red Cross, Dorian quipped dryly.

She ignored his jibe. *The Others rose against the two warring gods and crushed them. It is said that they, their Avatars and all their worlds, are gone.*

Dorian winced. *Ouch. So, what are you afraid of? If Ja'oi tries to kill you, He'll be destroyed by these Others, right?*

I do not want to be the next ecomancer to die.

Good point.

I must think of Tobias. If this thing does pose a threat to you and your kind, I must protect him. I can't…I can't lose him. I almost lost him before, when he was so burned… she thought desperately, growing more distressed by the moment.

It's all right, Dorian consoled, becoming sensitive to her growing agitation.

No! It is not all right. I cannot lose him. I will not lose him. I brought him back. When he was nothing but a pile of ash and charred bones, I poured every bit of my heart and soul into saving him. I gave him everything I had, and was drained so completely, I was exhausted for two days. Now, after waiting for him for five centuries, I have him. He loves me…and I will not let anyone or anything take him away from me, she answered, her distress turning to hard anger. *No one, not Ja'oi, not His minions, not even all the powers of the Others, is going to harm a hair on his head. I will kill and eat anyone who tries.*

Dorian was shocked by the power of her rage, feeling it crackle in the air around him.

Do you hear me? she mindscreamed to the presence outside. *I will not yield! I will not let you harm him! I will not let you take him from me! I will fight you until I have no more strength to fight, and if I must die, I will take you with me! Do you understand, servant of the Deceiver?*

There was no answer from the watcher, if anything there was an eerie silence, but Rain's outburst had cost her dearly and her legs trembled. She hadn't realized how weak she was until now. Gripping the wooden railing, she tried to steady herself, but to no avail. Dizziness swept over her, vertigo caused by hunger and exhaustion, and she lost her balance. Dorian caught her and she started to cry softly, slumping down to the deck.

I can't lose him. I love him…Oh Goddess, what am I going to do?

Dorian knelt beside her and took her into his arms, trying to comfort her as best he could. Her sobs caught Tobias' attention immediately, and he was there in less than a heartbeat, his face pained and worried.

"Liebchen?" he cried and moved to take her from Dorian, growing angry. "What have you done?" he accused, snarling.

Dorian refused to let her go, getting angry himself. "I haven't done anything."

Tobias' eyes showed his anguish as she stayed in Dorian's arms, leaning against him, her hand gripping his collar. "Liebchen…what have I done?" he begged, automatically assuming her tears were his fault.

"Nothing. You've done nothing," she whispered, her voice barely audible.

"Then why are you crying? What is wrong?" he asked, once again reaching for her.

Dorian clamped down on Rain again, refusing to release her, glaring and baring his teeth. "What is wrong? Only a fool wouldn't see that she's exhausted, half-starved and nearly frightened to death!"

Tobias was stunned, his jaw dropped in amazement, then snapped shut. "What do you mean?"

By now they had gotten everyone's attention, and they gathered around Dorian and Rain.

"What is it? What is going on?" Aaron asked, concerned.

"Look at her, you idiot! Can't you see how worn out she is? How gaunt and pale?" Dorian seethed at Tobias.

"I thought it was because she has been working so hard during the day…" Tobias stammered in reply.

"Dorian…please…don't…" Rain murmured pleadingly, but it was too late, the words were already on his lips.

"She's being stalked! Can't you see how scared she is? Haven't you noticed how closely she clings to you when you go outside?"

Tobias dropped his gaze. "I…I thought she was just doing that out of love…"

"I was!" Rain insisted, then abruptly left Dorian's arms and moved to Tobias, her face buried in his chest. "Forgive me!"

Tobias wrapped his arms around her, pressing the side of his face to the top of her head, his expression pained. "Who? Who is stalking you?"

"I don't know, but it's out there in the trees, waiting."

"Out there?" Aaron said, his voice frightened. "Then it knows where we lie!"

"Calm down," Dorian commanded. "It cannot harm us, or rather, it does not want us. It's Rain it wants." 'We think...'

"Rain?" Aaron repeated. "Why would it want Rain? Unless..."

"Unless it was sent by Ja'oi, yes," Dorian finished for him.

"Ja'oi!" Tobias blurted, afraid. "Liebchen, can this thing harm you?"

"I don't know. It is possible."

"Then we must return to the Sanctuary immediately, where it cannot hurt you."

Rain shook her head. "No. I cannot abandon my assignment. Besides I have no proof that it is dangerous, only that it follows me wherever I go, night or day."

"Night or day? Then this thing is around while I must hide from the sun?"

"Yes."

Panic seized Tobias the way she knew it would, his face becoming a mask of terror. "Then you must ask Aiya to release me from the enchantment cast upon my kind, so that I will be able to protect you."

"No. Aiya has chosen to let the spell stay. She must have Her reasons for doing so. Maybe it is for your own protection. Whatever the case, I cannot ask Her to lift it."

"But you are unprotected in the light!"

"Tobias, I am not helpless. It is my shield that has kept the thing at bay since it got here. The problem is that I am tiring and that makes my powers less effective."

"But..."

"What you need, then, is to rest and pool your energy at night when we are certain we can keep it from harming you," Dorian broke in.

"Yes. It is afraid of you, the vampires. It will not come close when I am with one of you," Rain concurred.

"Then you regain your strength and let us be your guardians. You can even take the shield down, if you like. It won't come in while we are around."

"No," Aaron disagreed. "What if it can hurt us?"

"It will not challenge me…" He paused, looking at his maker. "Or Ian. Don't worry, Aaron. I won't let anything harm you," Dorian assured.

"What do you need, liebchen, so that you will be able to fight this thing?" Tobias asked her.

"I need to eat and sleep. Sleep will rejuvenate me, and recharge my power. Food will help me gain my strength."

"Then that is what you will get," her lover told her. "What would you like to eat?"

Food was brought to her courtesy of Aaron. She ate under Tobias' doting gaze, while Dorian stood at the deck doors, glaring at the neat row of pines, willing himself to see the watcher that Rain said was down there. Focusing his energy, he left his body and cast himself out into the spirit realm. Floating as spirits float and seeing with spirit eyes, he circled the house and grounds trying to find the intruder, until he saw it standing just within the row of trees.

It was a Seraphim, a lesser angel. Many would be surprised by this; angels were often seen as friendly benefactors doing God's will. What most people forgot was that Ja'oi's angels were also his soldiers, and they could, would and did fight for their creator. Ja'oi made them loyal by design and only a handful had ever dared to question him. The others had seen what happened to Lu'fahr, and after the Archangel's Fall, none had challenged Ja'oi's authority. The remaining angels were unwaveringly loyal and would do anything their god asked of them. The Seraphim was doing as it was told, but it was angry to have been sent to watch this heretic.

In his current form, Dorian could hear its thoughts perfectly. He came up behind the angel, and gave it a mental 'tap' on the shoulder. It turned around to see his spirit.

You! it cried.

Yes, me! he answered with a wicked grin, as he jerked himself back into his body, and let loose a bolt of power that was sure to send the little creature running back to his god.

After the wave of weakness faded, he went to Rain. "Now, my dear, is it still there? Can you still feel it?"

Rain swallowed the bit of chicken she had been eating, and went to the deck doors. After a moment, she shook her head.

"No. It's gone."

Dorian smiled with self-satisfaction. "Good. It's gone for now, but I have no doubt it will be back, or another will be sent to take its place."

"What was it?" Ian asked.

"A lesser angel. I scared the liver out of it. It went running off."

"Let's just hope that it isn't running to get its big brother," Aaron cautioned.

"So? I can handle anything Ja'oi throws at me."

"Be careful, Dorian. We aren't certain what we are dealing with," Ian cautioned.

"Why should it matter? You made me strong and independent, right? Powerful and self-assured. I'm not afraid," Dorian answered haughtily.

"Self confidence is not the same as arrogance. Arrogance can kill," his maker warned.

"If I am arrogant, it is because you made me so."

"I did not raise you to be arrogant, Dorian," Ian corrected.

"No, you just raised me to depend on no one but myself."

Ian sighed. "That was never the lesson I meant to teach you."

"Maybe not, but it was the one I learned," Dorian spit back.

"Then I am asking you to learn a new lesson. Act with caution, my son. Use wisdom and discretion when dealing with these things. I have but two living children and I cannot spare either of you. The news of Toby's death nearly drove me to my own. Do not give me cause to grieve that way again."

Dorian had no answer for his maker. Instead he stared at Ian in silence for several moments, then changed the subject.

"I assume you'll be staying here."

"If I am welcome."

"I'll go make sure the other guest bedroom is ready."

Before anyone could answer him, he turned and walked towards the stairs to the lower level.

"Well at least we didn't end up screaming at each other," Ian noted.

"The night isn't over yet," Aaron reminded.

"True. What's our record?"

"In my presence?"

"Yes."

"Eighteen hours."

"I'll try to make it twenty-four this time."

Aaron shrugged. "Good luck."

"Vater, Rain is finished eating," Tobias said. "She and I are going to retire. She needs her sleep. May we continue our conversation tomorrow night?"

"There is no need to do that. The two of you can talk while I sleep," Rain offered.

"I don't want to leave you alone."

"Then come in and mindspeak to each other. You won't disturb me."

Tobias looked at Ian who gave a little nod of agreement.

"All right, liebchen, if you're sure we won't keep you from your rest."

"I'm sure."

With a good night nod to Aaron, Tobias put his arm around Rain and escorted her to their bedroom. Ian followed closely behind.

Four

When Rain awakened it was past daybreak and Tobias was wrapped protectively around her. Gently, so she would not wake him, she slipped herself out of his embrace and rose from the bed. The first thing she did was check the integrity of the shield. It was holding, but weak in places, and she immediately set to repairing it. Once that was done, she checked for the watcher. Thankfully, it was nowhere to be found. Dorian's little stunt had effectively chased it away for the time being. She ate the breakfast that had been supplied for her and read the morning paper. Then she ventured out, always carefully watching her back and listening for any signs of trouble.

Trouble did not come for several hours, but when it did, it hit with the force of a hurricane. There were at least two, probably more, this time, stronger than the one Dorian had frightened away. She fought them off as they attacked her with wind and tearing, invisible claws. They ripped her sari to shreds, but she was unconcerned with the clothing. If her shield around the house did not hold, these creatures could harm the vampires as they slept, invading their lairs and dragging them out into the sun. She raced back to the house with all the speed she could manage, invoking both out-of-phase and teleportation at once to cover greater distances. She arrived to find them attacking the shield, and she willed herself inside, shoring up the protections and settling in for a battle of minds.

The vampires were still asleep. In any event they wouldn't be able to help her because the sun shone straight into the house through the large prow windows, and she could not devote any of her energy to calling cloud-cover to protect them. Her attackers would probably burn away any cloud-cover she could create anyway. No, she could not wake them. Tobias would surely panic. He would be confined to the lower level, unable to get to her without facing the sunlight. He would act rashly, perhaps even running up the stairs and exposing himself to the deadly rays. She could not take that risk. She would have to do it alone. It was only an hour before sunset, if she could hold them off for a little longer it would be safe to awaken the vampires for help.

With everything she had, she held the shield together, drawing upon every ounce of strength she could muster. Again and again they buffeted the shield, seeking to find its breaking point and shatter it. Again and again she made it hold. They took turns, striking the barrier in different places, trying to determine its weak spots. Half naked, her silk in tatters, Rain stood in the center of the living room, and linked her very essence to the strength of the shield. It was a horribly risky thing to do, for if the attackers managed to crack the barrier, she would be in danger of losing herself. Sweat pouring down her face, she pulled one more time as another wave of attacks came, calling upon the powers of nature and the Earth Mother.

"Aiya, help meeeeeeee!" she cried.

Light flooded the outsides of her closed eyes, and pure power surged through her as she tapped the largest energy node she could find. She became a channel of energy, giving her body over to it completely. She saw nothing, she felt nothing, and then, she was nothing.

Rain's scream made Tobias nearly bolt from the bed. He threw back the covers and raced out of the bedroom. He ran into Dorian in the hallway.

"What is it! What has happened?" Dorian demanded.

"I don't know. I heard Rain scream!"

Tobias headed for the stairs, but Dorian grabbed him.

"Toby, wait! It's not safe!" he warned, knowing that sunlight was still coming in from the prow windows on the first floor. He could see the patches of light shining on the stone tiles of the front foyer and the main doors at the top of the stairs.

"But she's not answering my mind calls," the older vampire argued, struggling.

"You can't go up there! You'll burn!"

Dorian took Tobias by the shoulders and forced him back, holding him against the hallway wall.

"Let me go! Rain!"

"What is going on?" Ian commanded, seeing his youngest son pinning his firstborn to the wall.

"Rain! Rain is in trouble!" Tobias wailed.

"It would appear that we have more unwanted visitors," Dorian explained.

Ian scanned the house and grounds, nodding. "Yes. Many more."

"No! Rain!"

Dorian snarled with rage. Tobias was nearly incoherent with fear. His brother's terror brought out the protectiveness in him, and Dorian sent out the largest mind bolt that he had ever thrown, blasting the attackers with the sheer force of his vampire mind. It was backed up by another from Ian. They felt the offense scatter, scurrying away like frightened rabbits, leaving the house unnervingly still.

"What is happening?" Aaron asked, coming out of his room.

Dorian glanced at the large watch on Ian's wrist, displaying the time as almost exactly a half-hour to sunset. Although night would not have fallen completely, in fifteen minutes the sun would no longer be coming in the prow windows. Technically it would safe to go upstairs.

"We have to wait another fifteen minutes. Then we can go up," Dorian said.

"Then it might be too late!" Tobias cried.

Dorian wrapped his arms around his brother and stilled him.

"Breathe Toby, just breathe," he whispered, trying to calm Tobias down.

"I…"

"Shhh, listen with your vampire ears. Can you hear her?" he soothed almost hypnotically.

Tobias drew a shuddering breath and shook his head.

"Shhh, just listen. Reach out with your ears and your mind. Can you hear her? Can you feel her?"

Tobias let out a deep, hissing breath, and they waited in heavy silence.

"Yes. I can hear her," he said finally, his eyes closed.

"Where is she?" Dorian coaxed.

"Above us, and towards the front of the house. Her breath is shallow and faint. I can hear her heart beat. It's weak, but there."

"And can you feel her?"

"When I reach out I touch nothing but blackness. She is…"

"Probably in shock," Dorian finished. "But she is alive?"

"Yes."

"Only another ten minutes, then we can go to her and see how bad it is. Keep listening to her. Hold her with you by the force of your own will. Make her heart match yours," he instructed gently.

Tobias nodded, concentrating. The minutes passed slowly by and none of them uttered a sound until the sunlight no longer shone on the doors. The time seemed to crawl by with nothing but the steady tick of the grandfather clock in the den and the beat of the vampires' hearts to break the silence.

"Stay here," Dorian ordered Aaron, and released Tobias.

Tobias thrust past his brother and raced up the stairs, followed closely by Ian and Dorian.

Rain's unconscious body was collapsed on the living room floor, her blood staining the rug from the numerous lacerations on her limbs, and her sari had been reduced to shreds of ripped silk. They looked down upon the landscaped terraces and saw that the planted trees and flowers had been ripped asunder, and were strewn like so much debris all over the yard. Tobias was desperately trying to wake Rain, calling to her with voice and mind, until she stirred and let out a thin, hollow moan. They gathered worriedly around her, wincing at her bruised and battered face, as her gray eyes fluttered open.

"Liebchen?" Tobias choked.

"The shield..." came her faint voice.

"It is intact," Ian assured. "They could not gain entrance."

"Ian and I have once again gotten rid of them," Dorian added.

She smiled slightly. "Good. Were going to kill you...take you out into the sun..."

A cold chill passed through all of them. If Rain had not succeeded in protecting them, they would most likely be dead.

"You did it, my darling. You protected us," Tobias praised as she lay limp in his arms, her eyes rolling back into her head.

"Why didn't she wake us? We could have helped," Dorian questioned.

Tobias shook his head. "I don't know."

"She may have been afraid to wake Tobias, given his habit of overre-acting," Ian offered. "She may have thought he would run up the stairs and into the sunlight."

Neither Dorian nor Tobias answered, but Dorian thought that his maker was probably right. Rain probably did not realize that he and Ian did not need to see their attackers in order to fight them.

"My God, what happened here?" Aaron exclaimed, disobeying orders and coming upstairs anyway.

"I decided I didn't like the décor and thought I'd try a new style," Dorian snarled sarcastically. "You know, something like Contemporary Neo-neuveau Deconstructionism or Romantic **Demolition**! Something that would go well with Grunge."

"It would appear that we had more visitors while we were asleep," Ian replied, ignoring his youngest son's peevishness.

"Are they gone? Are they gone now?" Aaron questioned, clearly highly agitated.

"Yes, for now, they are gone, but they will be back come dawn, I can assure you," Ian replied.

"We must scatter, abandon this place," Aaron said, his green eyes wide with fear.

"They will just find us again," Tobias countered.

The brown-haired vampire felt a touch on his hand, and he looked down to see Rain staring at him. She opened her mouth to speak; a small, croaking sound coming out.

Mindspeak to me, liebchen. Don't try to talk.

Weak…too weak…No strength left, not even to heal.

What can I do? How can I help you?

Must take me to a wild place, where nature is undisturbed…must draw strength from the earth…

"She says we must take her to a wild place, where nature is undisturbed, so she can heal," Tobias relayed.

"The mountains to the east of us. Old growth forest. That's as undisturbed as you get these days," Dorian answered.

"Let's go," Ian said, standing.

"Agreed," Tobias spoke, lifting Rain into his arms as if she were a feather.

They took the car, with Dorian driving quickly. Aaron had to feed, and the others stood guard while he chose and took a victim, afraid that if they split up the attackers would come while they were separated. Then they made their way to the mountains and went deep into the forest until they found an overgrown thicket, surrounded by old trees.

"This looks like as good a place as any," Dorian said, stopping in the thicket.

Tobias nodded in agreement and gently set Rain's body on the moss covered ground. Then they sat in a semi-circle around her and waited. They did not have to wait long.

The earth around Rain's still form moved, letting out a noise that sounded like a soft sigh, and buckled as the roots from the trees lifted up from the ground to touch her. Thin tendrils from the plants snaked out and made their way to her, and soon there was a thin latticework of plant roots connecting to her body. They watched in amazement as the plant roots found her lacerations, delving into the open wounds and sealing them. More roots covered her until they could no longer see her, but they knew that something was happening because the power throbbed like a great heartbeat, inciting all of their hearts to beat in time with it.

A long time passed, the night crawling on, until the thicket grew still and quiet, and the plant roots began to recede. When they could see her again, her body was completely healed, and she seemed to be sleeping peacefully. What was left of her sari was gone, but there was a new sari, this one a deep midnight blue, hanging on a branch nearby.

Tobias went to her, taking the new sari as he passed, and took her into his arms, wrapping her naked body in the new silk as he examined her carefully. She was unblemished, with no sign of her earlier wounds and bruises. She was warm, her heartbeat strong and steady, and the smell of her so close to him reminded him that he had not yet fed, but he would not yield to his blood lust. Instead, he drew her head to his chest and held her, whispering her name like a soft caress. Then her mind touched his, and he knew she was coming around.

"Liebchen?"

"Is…is everyone safe?" she asked, her voice weak but steady.

"Yes. Everyone is safe," Tobias answered.

She sighed. "Good. I was worried."

"We are all here. Alive and well, thanks to you," Aaron said.

Her gray eyes cracked open, and she looked at the young vampire, smiling slightly. "You're welcome."

Taking a deep breath, she moved to sit up. Tobias released her and she knelt on the moss, combing through her long hair with her fingers.

"How do you feel?" Aaron questioned.

"Like I've been hit with something very hard and very heavy, but I'm all right."

On shaky legs, she rose to her feet, adjusting the new sari, and inspecting the color and quality of the silk.

"Why didn't you wake us? We could have helped you," Ian asked.

Confusion crossed her face before she answered. "I did not think…"

"We don't need to see them to throw mind bolts. Next time, wake us," Dorian informed.

"Oh."

"Could you hold them off again if they were to come back?" Ian inquired after an anxious pause.

"I don't know. It would depend upon how many there were."

"What are we to do, liebchen?" Tobias broke-in. "You are alone, and we cannot protect you during the day unless you do not leave the house and we do not sleep."

Rain's eyes grew sad and pensive. "I need help. I cannot do this alone. The shield nearly ruptured today. The only way I could keep it from breaking was to link it to my own life essence. I am going to send a message once I get my strength up and tell Aiya that things here are critical."

"Doesn't She already know?" Ian asked.

"She probably does, but it might be a matter of Her having to deal with a lot of things at once. I have not been able to contact any of the others. Something is definitely very wrong."

There was a heavy silence in the thicket as they all looked up at Rain. The gravity of their situation weighed heavily upon them, and they were at a loss.

"We are defenseless. We cannot run and we cannot hide," Aaron whispered.

"Will Aiya release us from the enchantment now?" Tobias questioned.

Rain hugged herself. "I don't know."

There was a movement of something in the heavy brush on the edge of the thicket, and they heard a deep, throaty growl. Rain looked at the trees while the others tried to ascertain the seriousness of this newest threat. A moment later, a white tiger came bursting out of the bushes. The vampires cried out in alarm and Dorian stood, prepared to blast the big cat into tiny furballs.

"Peace!" Rain commanded, her hand raised.

Dorian felt a restraining field around his power, preventing him from throwing any bolts. Even in her weakened state, she could still control him, and he did not know if he liked that. He watched as the tiger circled, rumbling bunga-bunga sounds as it walked, its huge paws padding noiselessly on the overgrown grass. It sniffed each of them briefly, then returned to Rain as she knelt down in front of it, and butted its head into her chest. Her arms wrapped around its massive neck, her fingers scratched behind its ears, and when she looked up, she was smiling.

"Always have to make a grand entrance," she murmured fondly.

The tiger snorted and flopped on its side with its head in Rain's lap. As she scratched its underbelly and sides, it rolled slightly and lifted a foreleg, placing a paw on her shoulder. Then, as all the others, except Tobias for he already knew who it was, watched in amazement, the foreleg thinned and condensed into an arm, the paw elongating into a hand with long, slender fingers, the claws becoming the fingernails. Now, lying on the grass where the tiger had just been, was a nude man. The man sat up and looked at the vampires.

Aaron's heart caught in his throat as the tiger shapechanged into the most beautiful man he had ever seen. Skin a pearlescent, alabaster white, hair the color of mother of pearl, and eyes as blue as cobalt. Who was this perfect creature that now looked at him with those brilliant blue eyes, laughter reflected in his warm gaze? The man's vision settled on Tobias and he smiled. Tobias went to him and hugged him tight, relief written all over the vampire's face.

"Sky," Tobias breathed.

"Hi," the man said, pulling back and putting an arm around Rain. "I'm sorry. I wanted to come earlier, but Aiya sent me away."

"Who?" Ian whispered to Dorian.

"I don't know," Dorian replied, then mindtouched Tobias. *Who?*

He is Sky. Another avatar. It would seem that our reinforcements have arrived.

"Are you another ecomancer, like Rain?" Aaron questioned.

Blue eyes searched and settled upon the owner of the voice, taking in Aaron's long hair and vivid green eyes, and a small smile came to his lips. "Yes. They call me Sky. I help Rain."

"We need it. We have been under attack."

Sky swept back his long, white hair and nodded. "I know. You're not the only ones."

Rain gasped. "Oh, no...have the other vampires been threatened too?"

"Not vampires. Us. You were the only one alone. Ja'oi won't go after a pair of us. I am here. The attacks should stop now," Sky replied in a rush.

Rain gave him an odd look, as if she knew he was holding himself together for a reason, but she said nothing.

Aaron breathed a sigh of relief. "I am glad to hear that."

"Ja'oi knows better than to challenge the two of us."

Rain put her hand on Sky's arm. "I have been unable to contact anyone. Sky, what is going on?"

Sky shook his head. "It is bad. Aiya sent me to Indio. Inhotek sent Aiya an offer of refuge. She is sending the weaker ones there."

Rain's face showed her horror. "Oh no...it can't be that bad..."

"It isn't. Aiya is just being cautious. Ja'oi has been silent, except for these little bits He has been throwing at us," Sky answered.

"Will it be war?"

"If it is, it will be Ja'oi's biggest mistake. He can't fight all of Aiya's allies, and they'll side with Her," the male ecomancer said with a shrug.

"I should hope that it will not come to that," Rain demurred as Sky stood up and stretched.

She noticed with amusement how Ian, Dorian, and Aaron could not keep their eyes off Sky as he worked the kinks out of his muscles.

"Cats have such wonderful spines," Sky bemoaned, releasing tension in his lower back. "Human spines are very poorly designed." They heard the cracks from the vertebrae snapping back into place. "Ahhh, that's better. I also have a message from Song."

"What does he have to say?" she asked.

She watched him close his eyes and recall the memorized message. He sent it directly into her mind, giving it to her as one would deliver a parcel. It passed from his mind to hers completely intact.

"He wants us to gather as many vampires as we can in one place. He thinks that we will be able to find Aurek, and repair the broken Circle faster if we can reach a number of them at once," she announced to the others. "Time may be of the essence."

"I have a large keep in Scotland. The castle has many rooms and can hold a number of us. I volunteer that as our gathering place," Ian offered. "It also has an extensive library that, as I mentioned to Tobias last night, has several tomes that may be of some help to you."

Rain looked at him and smiled. "Thank you." She turned to Sky. "Sky? Is that all right with you?"

Sky nodded. "Yes. I go where you go. I am with you."

"Tomorrow night I will go and try to find as many vampires as I can, and bring them to Scotland with me by the time we meet."

"How much time do you need?" Rain inquired.

"Not long. Give me three weeks," Ian answered.

"Then I will tell Song we will meet at your house in three weeks, Ian. Thank you," Rain said quietly.

"You saved my life today, my lady. I owe you a debt. If I can repay it by finding more of my dark brothers and sisters, then I will do my best."

Sky offered his hand to Rain and pulled her to her feet.

"Are you all right?" he asked, eyeing her warily.

"Yes, but I need your help in protecting the house. We should call a heartstone."

Sky smiled. "Okay. You up to it?"

"Not really. I should eat. I took quite a beating today. Although I am healed, I am still not fully recovered."

Sky's face grew serious and grim. "I know. I should have been here. They would not have dared."

She squeezed his hand. "I am glad you are here now."

He smiled fondly. "So am I. So? Shall we go? Where to?"

"I should eat," she repeated.

"I should feed as well; I have yet to this evening," Tobias added.

"All right then. You go find food, then go back to the house. Sky and I will meet you there," Rain decided.

"Agreed," Tobias concurred.

"Wait! Is it wise to split up? What if those things come back?" Aaron asked, worried.

"They will not challenge Dorian or Ian. They are cowards, attacking only when they know you are at a disadvantage," Rain replied bitterly. "We'll meet you at the house."

With that both ecomancers vanished from sight, leaving them alone in the thicket.

"Come on. They will be there when we get back," Tobias said, leading them back to the car.

They arrived home an hour later to find that Rain and Sky had been very busy. The garden trees and plants had been replanted and the slate cleaned up. They had also removed the cherub fountain and cleared a space in the center of the blue slate about two feet square, where slabs had been removed to reveal the earth beneath.

"What are you going to do?" Dorian asked curiously.

"We are going to call a heartstone," Rain replied, as if he should know exactly what she was talking about.

"What's a heartstone?" Aaron inquired.

"It's a pillar of bedrock, supposedly linked directly to a node of earth energy," Ian answered, looking to Rain for confirmation.

"That is correct. Once the stone is in place, we will link the protection shield to it. The Earth itself will then power the shield. Nothing, not even Ja'oi Himself, will be able to break it then," Rain affirmed.

"Unless the stone is cracked or its power supply is interrupted," Ian cautioned.

"That is true. However, stones called by us are no mere heartstones. They are not like the ones made by humans. Our stones are completely connected to the Earth's crust, and their power comes from the core itself. They are extremely hard to break. In fact, none have ever been broken, and believe me, Ja'oi has tried," she assured.

"How do you know so much about heartstones, Ian?" Aaron questioned.

"I have studied many types of magic and paranorma. I've even touched a heartstone." He looked at Rain. "The one in Minos, under the ancient palace. Amazing piece of work."

"That is one of ours. It was put there to stabilize the land after the tectonic shifts underneath that city disrupted a major energy flow," Rain informed.

"Okay," Sky's voice announced as he joined their little group. "Are we ready to begin?"

"May we watch? Or do you want us out of the way?" Aaron asked.

"You are welcome to watch, just don't get too close to us, and don't be alarmed if it seems like the ground is buckling and rising. It will be to some extent, but most of it is an illusion, spawned by the building power," Rain answered.

"We'll sit on the deck," Dorian said, pointing to the deck surrounding the house. "Will that be far enough out of the way?"

Sky glanced upwards and nodded. "It will be fine."

Tobias came forward and gave Rain a kiss, his eyes saying all that his mouth would not say. Then he caressed her face tenderly and went to join the others on the deck. Sky stood on one side of the cleared square and Rain took the side opposite to him, linking their hands and preparing themselves for the task at hand.

Are you up to this, Bina? he questioned.

Yes. I don't have much of a choice. I'll be all right if you do the pulling while I do the calling.

Okay. Ready?

Yes.

Rain closed her eyes, reaching into herself, finding the thin stream of energy that delved down into the earth, and following it deeper and deeper, through miles of ancient rock until she touched the molten core. The earth roiled and responded to her touch; a ball of energy pooling where the power stream emptied into the center. Using all her strength she called the energy to her, willing it to rise up and come to her. She felt the power lurch upward, hitting the crust and cracking the bedrock, and then felt Sky's energy join her own, this time pulling the power, and drawing it towards the surface. The earth beneath their feet began to vibrate as the energy obeyed, pushing its way through the miles of compressed rock, a stream of molten core rising behind it.

The vampires watched, transfixed, as the two ecomancers called their stone. The electricity and tension in the air was building to almost unbearable levels. Dorian felt Aaron's hand grip his arm, and his slender body come close, as they felt the ground start to shake. He looked briefly away from Rain and Sky to see that Tobias was gripping the rail tightly, pressed very close to Ian. Could it be that Ian was the only one who wasn't feeling any fear? Ian's eyes held only wonder and awe, his attention completely locked on what was happening in the garden.

The bare earth in the square collapsed in upon itself as the power neared the surface. Rain let go of Sky's hands and stepped back as the first wave of energy broke out, sending a shower of soil and pebbles spurting into the air. A moment later, the second wave hit, and it felt like the ground was buckling under her feet, rising up and down like a wave. She could sense the molten rock getting closer, hear the hissing of it as it broke through the bedrock, and feel the increasing heat. Then she saw the first glimmer of bright red breaking the surface as Sky pulled it up out of the ground. He wrapped the lava in a containment field, forcing it to rise vertically, until it was a pillar of searing hot, orange-red light about seven feet high and two feet in diameter. It took up almost all of the exposed space in the stone, and caused the edges of the slate to melt. The heat from it pulsed off the stone, bathing the entire area with warmth, and it began to cool almost immediately, sealing to the ground. Sky reached out with his hands and began to smooth the sides, molding it before it could harden, and Rain followed suit, sculpting and shaping the rock as if it were clay.

Dorian gasped as he watched Sky and Rain place their bare hands upon the molten rock, seemingly immune to the extreme heat. They were working the pillar, forming it, smoothing it, arcing swirls and ornamental designs in it. Sky then made the top of it bubble outward and he molded an eagle, with its huge wings outstretched in flight, to decorate the crown. When they were finished, it was a work of art, cooling slowly in the night air: a work of art that all but pulsed with power. Dorian looked over at his companions to find the same look of utter surprise and amazement upon all their faces. Playfully he slipped his fingers under Aaron's dropped jaw and flicked it closed. Aaron jerked and gave him an indignant glare, snorting and rubbing his chin, but Dorian merely grinned. He then watched as Rain slowly sunk to the ground, a small sigh escaping her lips, and Sky moved to catch her as she fell, breaking her landing and kneeling with her on the slate. Less than a second later, Tobias was beside her, his lips on her temple as she rolled to lie against his shoulder. The rest of them followed, gathering around the heartstone, staring at it and inspecting it with their eyes, afraid to touch the still very hot stone.

It was quiet and eerily still until Ian broke the silence with his voice. "Thank you, for letting us witness this. It was…incredible."

"Yes," Aaron seconded. "Truly incredible."

"We aren't done quite yet, but the stone needs to settle for a little while," Sky told them.

"What is left to do?" Aaron asked.

"We have to link the shield to it and make sure it's properly anchored. Won't take very long or much energy, but right now, all we can do is wait for the stone to cool and stabilize," the male ecomancer replied, wiping a bit of sweat from his brow.

"This thing goes all the way down, doesn't it? It's miles deep," Ian commented.

"Yes, all the way down to the center of the earth, and fused to the crust. Let Ja'oi try to break it," Sky confirmed, preening his hair.

"Amazing."

"Now you must promise to protect this stone. No matter what happens to this house, you must keep this stone safe from humans," Rain warned.

"Why? You said that not even Ja'oi could harm it. Why worry about mortals?" Dorian questioned.

"Because it will hurt them, and that will bring more. They will seek to understand it, to analyze it. And, in the fashion of mortals, ignore what is right in front of them," she replied wearily.

Dorian nodded. "I understand."

"If there comes a time when it becomes too much of a center of attention, you can be assured that we will deal with it. You have but to contact us, if we haven't already responded to the problem," she added.

"Acknowledged," Aaron agreed.

"Shall we go inside?" Dorian said.

"Yes," Tobias said, helping Rain to her feet.

They walked inside and Tobias took Rain into the bedroom almost immediately. Ian went with him while Dorian went onto the deck to look down at the heartstone. Sky stayed in the living room, kneeling in front of the hearth. There was a fire crackling in the stone fireplace, and the eco-mancer stared at the flames as Aaron watched him curiously.

"Do you, ummm…want some clothes?" Aaron asked him. "We're about the same size, you and I…"

Sky looked at him, his blue eyes dilated and soft. "No, thank you. I'm fine. Don't really wear clothes…" He paused, as if a memory flashed back for a moment, then shook it away. "Haven't worn them for almost a century."

Aaron sat down on the rug, highly intrigued. "How old are you?"

Sky thought for a moment. "Two hundred? No, older than that. 1633 right? Three hundred."

"You were made in 1633?"

Sky yawned and curled up on the rug, balling himself up like Aaron had seen animals do when they were preparing for sleep. "Something like that. Don't really remember. Was a long time ago."

Aaron stared off into space. "I remember the day I was made. I could tell you the exact date, and time, and even what stars were out that night. You don't remember the day you became what you are?"

When there was no answer, Aaron looked at Sky and started in surprise. A black panther, its shiny coat reflecting the light from the fire, showing its all-but-invisible spots, now lay sleeping on the carpet. He blinked, then reached out a shaky hand to touch the soft fur, pulling it back quickly when the panther raised its head and snuffled at him. The big cat made a rumbling sound, and sniffed the back of his hand, the pink tongue flicking out and licking it gently. It was wet and warm and raspy like a domestic cat's tongue, and Aaron was utterly charmed. The panther butted his head against Aaron's hand then lowered it back down to the rug, letting out a deep cat-sigh and closing its yellow-green eyes. The vampire waited to see if the cat would do anything else, until he heard what sounded like a snore, then he stood and went to join Dorian on the balcony.

"How is our new friend Sky?" Dorian asked as Aaron stepped on to the terrace.

The black-haired vampire thought for a moment, then answered dryly. "He's...taking a cat nap."

The older vampire glanced through the glass doors to see the panther and laughed at Aaron's subtle joke. "Literally."

"So, you think that thing will do the trick?" Aaron asked as they looked down at the heartstone, noting that it was growing darker and darker in color as it cooled.

"I hope so," he answered.

Dorian put his arms around his lover, his heart catching in his throat. "If it doesn't..." He broke off suddenly, and simply kissed Aaron as tenderly and as sweetly as he could, doing it before his pride made him stop. "I love you."

Aaron moved closer, putting his arms around him. "I love you too."

Dorian sighed, feeling the tears well in his eyes, but holding them back, and tightened his grip on his love. He pressed nearer, his face in Aaron's soft hair, and his body saying all that he could not say.

Shortly before dawn, Rain and Sky linked the shields to the new stone. It accepted the tie without a glitch and powered the spell with a steady stream of energy. The vampires took to their beds satisfied that they would be safe and protected while they slept, and rose the following night to find that everything had moderately returned to normal. Ian left with the promise to meet them in Scotland in three weeks, and Tobias and Rain went off together, stealing away to a deserted and aging home, finally having the time and energy for a proper loving. Tobias had been waiting patiently for days, holding his desire in check, but now he let it go. He and Rain tumbled playfully among the creaking, old walls of the abandoned house, kissing, caressing, building their passion until they released it in the old master bedroom, Tobias tearing the deteriorating mattress to shreds with his nails and cracking the plaster with his cries of pleasure. They returned to Dorian's house three hours later, Tobias sporting a happy grin, and Sky looked at them and smiled, winking slowly.

The other vampires still did not know the realities of Rain and Tobias' sex life. It was something they kept private, thinking that their companions weren't quite ready to know about the possibilities. Aaron was becoming curious though. Everyone brushed Aaron off, at least in part because he liked it that way, and they did not give him credit for what he was best at: watching.

Aaron would have made an excellent spy. He easily faded into the background, but not much slipped by him. He was intelligent and quick-witted, and he knew how to glean information from things just by observing. And he had been observing Tobias and Rain, noting how they touched each other secretively when they thought no one was looking, seeing how Tobias seemed to react sexually to some of the things she did to him. It raised many questions in his mind, but he was unwilling to give away his cover and ask Tobias. Instead he decided to bide his time, and wait until a better opportunity to discover the truth presented itself. After all, he was one of the most patient of vampires.

Five

Etienne gritted his teeth and pushed through the milling crowd of mortals in the airport, careful not to crush them in his hurry to get past. Once he was clear, he took off again, moving so quickly that his feet barely touched the ground. He had left Greece two nights after he had heard the news that Tobias was alive and in Seattle, and now he was arriving in the northern city, having followed the night across the Western Hemisphere. Barias had given him his blessing before he left, wishing him luck and fortune. The ancient vampire knew better than to try to keep Etienne from going to Tobias. Besides, after four years together, they had both pretty much decided that it was time to go their separate ways, and Etienne had only stayed with Barias for another few weeks because Barias offered him comfort when Tobias was killed. The message that Barias received had been passed down from many so there was no telling how long Tobias had been back. A week at least, probably more.

'And why didn't the little bastard come looking for me?' Etienne thought furiously, letting his anger build again.

He snagged a cab outside of Sea-Tac airport and barked out his destination to the driver. He was headed for Dorian's house; Tobias was with Dorian. The knowledge boiled inside him and he barely contained his rage as the taxi entered the expressway and headed north. He stewed the entire trip, telling the cabby to stop at the beginning of Dorian's driveway and practically threw the fare at him. When the cab pulled away, he turned and glared at the wooded drive.

'No, he wouldn't come to me. He went to Dorian. He'd go to the one who hated him for centuries before coming to me. Son of a bitch,' he fumed to himself, pacing along the road at the base of the driveway. 'Get a hold of yourself, Eti-boy. Calm your anger, you'll broadcast that you are here and they'll fry you to a cinder before you even get one punch in.'

We already know you are here, came his answer, and he stopped dead in his tracks.

I felt you a long time ago, Etienne, Dorian's mindvoice continued. *Come, join us.*

And what of Tobias? Does the little prick know I'm here too?

No, I have told him nothing. Come. You know where we are. We will be waiting for you.

Etienne shrugged. So much for his surprise entrance. Would they prevent him from going to Tobias? He didn't know, but he was about to find out. Using his superior speed and strength, he ran up the drive, hopped over the security fence and landed on the deck outside Dorian's house. Throwing open the doors, he stepped into the living room and locked eyes on Tobias.

"You!" he snarled.

Tobias looked up from the couch as the deck doors burst open to reveal his fledgling and former lover, Etienne. His dark blond hair was unkempt and ragged, and his hazel eyes were flashing with his emotions.

'How did he get here? Why did he come? Where is Barias?'

There was no time for answers to these questions as Etienne screamed his name and rushed towards him. He was then grabbed by the collar, swung around and thrown out the deck doors. Tobias hit the side rail heavily, feeling the wood creak and nearly give way under the force of his body landing against it. Stunned, he was trying to get up when Etienne was upon him again, his fists pummeling his chest and abdomen, all the while screaming obscenities. Pain ripped through him from the blows, and he clawed at Etienne, trying to get away.

"Bastard! You fucking bastard!" Etienne screamed, as the railing gave way, sending them both crashing to the ground below.

The others watched the fight from the deck, looking down on the two struggling vampires. Aaron was in a titter, pacing and gasping.

"Isn't anyone going to stop this?"

Rain and Dorian looked at him calmly, though Rain's face betrayed her pain.

"No," Dorian replied.

"I won't...I won't let them hurt each other," Rain said quietly, her eyes turning once again to the brawl below.

"But how can you watch this!" Aaron demanded.

Tears fell down Rain's face. "This is its own kind of healing."

"How could you do it? How could you do that to me?" Etienne roared, pounding Tobias' chest, slamming him to the blue slate.

Tobias was bleeding from every orifice on his face; his nose and jaw had been broken, his skull cracked. Etienne showed no sign of relenting and Tobias' only choice was to try to kill him. He pooled the power, looked into Etienne's enraged face...and let it die within him. He went limp, refusing to fight anymore because he could not bring himself to kill his child, the child he desperately loved. Etienne lessened his punches, over and over demanding how Tobias could do it to him, until he finally stopped altogether, and knelt, sobbing uncontrollably next to Tobias' battered, broken body.

"That is enough," Dorian's stern voice said as he took Etienne firmly by the shoulder.

Etienne looked at Tobias, dazed and exhausted, as a black-haired woman swept past him and laid her hands upon his maker. She took Tobias into her arms, and he sunk his teeth into her neck, drinking from her as she held him. Etienne expected her to die at any moment, payment from the devil in her arms for her kindness, but the time wore on, and she still did not weaken or die. Finally, Tobias lifted his mouth from her throat and rested the back of his head against her shoulder, looking at Etienne with his wide, blue eyes. His broken bones and lacerations had been completely healed, and his skin was flushed with the blood he had just consumed. Etienne was dumbfounded, and he got angry all over again.

"You bastard!" he cried again, moving towards Tobias.

Dorian's hands on both his shoulders stopped him. "I said, that's enough."

"How could you do it? How could you let me think you were dead?"

Now it was Tobias' turn to be angry. "What should you care what happens to me? You left me, remember?"

Etienne's face showed his shock. "I left you? You left me long before I walked out the door! You left me the day you made me!"

"How can you speak such lies? I made you because I loved you and could not bear to live without you!"

"We should take this inside, just as long as the two of you promise not to break any furniture," Aaron said.

Etienne ripped his shoulders abruptly away from Dorian's hands. "I won't break anything."

"And I didn't start this," Tobias retorted. "I wasn't the one who threw you off a deck before you even had the chance to get a word out."

"Yeah? Well I wasn't the one who was stupid enough to get blown up!"

"That's enough," Dorian interrupted. "Let's go inside."

Etienne rose to his feet, eyeing Tobias warily as the other vampire did the same, watching him as he brushed the dirt from his ripped and soiled clothes.

"It's all right, priye. We'll get you new clothes," the black-haired woman consoled. "I think those are ruined."

"I would tend to agree," Tobias said faintly.

"Priye?" Etienne repeated, looking at Tobias, then at the woman.

Tobias appeared as if he were going to say something, but he stopped, his mouth closing and merely gave Etienne a sad, wistful glance, before turning his back and moving to enter the house. The woman, the strange immortal woman, went with him, her arm around the small of his back, as they walked into the den. Etienne followed, Dorian directly behind him, with Aaron bringing up the rear.

"Just tell me. Why did you do it? Why the hell did you go to that god-forsaken place? Why did you put yourself in danger like that?" Etienne demanded, once they were in the den. He was standing with his back to the fireplace, while Tobias and the woman sat side by side on the couch.

"Come on," Aaron whispered in Dorian's ear, gently tugging on his sleeve. "Let's go. Give them some privacy. I think Rain can handle Etienne if he tries anything."

Dorian looked at Aaron and nodded, then they wordlessly exited the room and closed the heavy wooden doors behind them.

Tobias watched them leave, thankful that they were kind enough to give him and Etienne privacy. Rain was there, but he knew she would not interfere unless she had to. He returned his gaze to his child, his eyes sad.

"I could give you lots of reasons, Etienne."

"Just give me one."

"I had nothing to lose and nothing more to live for," came his simple answer.

The words hit Etienne like a physical blow and he winced. "Oh. So I'm nothing then? Did you stage the whole thing for my benefit? To get my attention? Well, you've got it now."

"I didn't stage anything, Etienne."

Etienne's eyes flashed his anger, and fire leapt out of the smoldering logs in the hearth. "Well it certainly looked that way!"

"For all intents and purposes, Etienne, I should have died. I would have died..." He took Rain's hand gently. "... if Rain had not been there."

"Rain?" Etienne said, his eyes locking on her. Who was this woman? *What* was this woman? He would find out... later. "You saved him?"

"Yes," she answered, meeting his gaze calmly.

Etienne looked away, his eyes downcast, his hands shoved deep into the pockets of his blue jeans. He turned to face the fire.

"Thank you," he murmured almost inaudibly.

The admission spoke volumes about what he didn't say, and Tobias suddenly realized why Etienne had come. Etienne still cared about him!

Seeing him again was almost physically painful for Tobias, his heart spasming and pounding in his chest. Memories of their tumultuous love affair came back with vivid clarity, making his eyes sting with tears. It all made sense now. Etienne's rage, his attack, his bitter words… all veils to hide the real reason. Etienne still loved him! He saw Etienne put his hands on the stone mantelpiece, his shoulders slumped, and his forehead resting against the crossbar. Taking a chance that he was right, Tobias stood and went to him, reaching out a hand.

"Etienne," he said softly, touching his shoulder.

Etienne jerked away, turning his head so Tobias could not see his face. Tobias stepped closer and placed the hand upon him again.

"Etienne."

Etienne stiffened, but did not move, and Tobias gently moved his arm to encircle his fledgling's shoulders, whispering his name a third time. Etienne trembled, then sobbed and broke away.

"Don't touch me!" he cried, staggering two steps back, then sunk to his knees beside the fireplace, his face in his hands.

Tobias remained standing, his arms limp at his sides. "I'm sorry. Forgive me."

Etienne didn't answer. He stared at the fire, hugging himself, tear tracks staining his smooth, pale face.

"I was alone, in despair, with no one to love me. For years I waited for you to return, for you to come back to me. But you never came back. I abandoned the home we made because I could not stand to stay there any longer without you," Tobias explained tenderly.

"I wandered, lonely and sad, looking for something to fill the empty spaces in my heart. Nothing helped. Nothing filled me. I bore it until it had eaten away part of my soul. Still I hoped, still I prayed, that someday you would come back, that you would love me again."

"And I hoped and prayed that one day you would show up in Greece, and tell me you still loved me. That we would be together again, like old times," Etienne admitted.

"Eti, I had no idea you were in Greece. I went to Ecuador to try to find you. It was the first time I had any concrete knowledge of your where-abouts," Tobias argued.

"Barias and I were only in Ecuador for a week. We've been living in Greece for two years."

"I did not know that." He paused, drawing breath, then asked the one question he desperately needed to ask, "But Eti, why did you leave in the first place?"

"Because I thought you didn't love me anymore."

Tobias was shocked, then his face grew sad. "How could you think such a thing? You know I love you. I made you because I loved you too much to let you go."

"But you did let me go. After you made me, you went cold and unreachable on me. We didn't kiss anymore, or hug, or touch or even really talk. At first I just thought it was because we had company, but after they left, and you still didn't warm up..." Etienne answered, miserable.

"I thought you were going to leave me any day, that you now had what you wanted and no longer needed me. I expected you to grow tired of me and leave."

"Tobias' fatalist streak again," Rain piped in. "You should have stomped on his foot and knocked some sense into him."

Etienne managed a small smile at her, and Tobias shuffled his feet, blushing. She grew quiet again, watching, knowing already where this was leading. It was obvious that Tobias still loved Etienne very much, and now that he knew Etienne felt the same way, he would feel torn between her and his old love. She was torn herself, wondering how to solve this situation. Etienne obviously wanted Tobias back, and she knew that Tobias would feel that he had to choose between them. Who would he choose? Who did he love more, as if you could measure love as something tangible. Now that she had him, she did not want to lose him, or even take the chance of losing him. But she also did not want to make him feel as if he must have one or the other.

Rain looked at Etienne, taking him in, studying his face and well-made body. She liked him. She had always liked him. He had fire and passion, and soft hazel eyes that sparkled with his emotions. She had grown very fond of him when he was mortal and with Tobias, in spite of his shortcomings and temper and somewhat selfish streak. She had grown to care about him for the same reasons Tobias had, for his love of life, his wildness, his fearlessness. But could she love him? Could she hold the same passion for him in her heart as she did for Tobias? Could she love and please them both? Rain looked to Tobias, then back to Etienne, her resolve firming as she watched the tortured expression on Tobias' face grow deeper and darker.

Etienne shifted, hugging himself even closer, as if he was feeling very exposed and vulnerable. Tobias had no doubt that he was. Vampires were very proud, self-assured creatures; they did not like to admit weakness or need. For Etienne to be making the admissions he was making must have been very hard. It was difficult to swallow one's pride, especially in matters of the heart; Tobias knew that himself. There was a time when he would have thought nothing of proclaiming his love for Etienne, of lavishing him with gifts and affection, but then Etienne had hurt him, left him alone, and now he had Rain to consider. Rain, whom he loved as he loved no other, or so he thought… but as he looked at Etienne sitting there on the floor, holding himself, his heart ached with longing. Tobias raised his eyes and met Rain's, searching her smooth, calm face for any sign of what to do. She was motionless, staring at him with her storm colored eyes, revealing nothing of what was going on behind them.

"Toby, you put me through Hell," Etienne whispered, to himself more than to them. "At first I couldn't believe that you would do such a…a *stupid* thing, but then Barias said it was true and I knew he wouldn't lie to me. I was…inconsolable."

"For me, it wasn't stupid at the time…" Tobias began but was cut-off.

"But how? How could you do that to yourself? How could you do that to me? Don't you know? Don't you know how much I love you?"

Tobias' heart wrenched at the words, at Etienne's pleading tear-filled eyes, and he nearly lost all resolve. He ached to take Etienne into his arms, to hold him and comfort him, but he dared not. He had pledged a troth to Rain. He loved her, he worshipped her, and he would be faithful to her. Even if it meant letting Etienne go. His hands raised up, briefly, then fell to his sides again. Tobias was on the verge of tears himself, when he saw movement in his peripheral vision. Rain had stood and was moving towards them, but not to him. No, she was going to Etienne.

The woman, Rain, knelt before him, pulling her hair away from her neck, and opened her arms to him.

"I will share him with you," she said gently.

For a moment, Etienne was utterly stunned. She was offering herself to him, and proposing a ménage à trois; doing it so Tobias would not have to choose between them. He was speechless.

"Are you serious?" he tremored when he found his voice.

"Yes."

His hazel eyes searched her gray ones for any sign of deception, but found none. They held only love and quiet acceptance. He reached up to touch her face, letting her feel the coldness of his vampire skin, and waited to see if she would flinch or change her mind. She remained still, unafraid. Casting a glance to Tobias, and noting that the brown-haired vampire appeared as shocked as he was, he lowered his mouth to her throat.

Tobias' heart nearly stopped when he heard Rain speak. She was accepting Etienne, offering to share him with his fledgling. This was the depth of her love, and he was completely humbled by its power and strength. He trembled as he watched Etienne bend his head to drink from his lover.

"No…" he choked, his voice faint.

Etienne heard and paused, pulling his head back as they both looked at him.

"No," he repeated, this time with more force as he knelt beside Rain and put his arm around her. "Do not do this. You do not have to do this.

I love you. I have pledged my eternal faithfulness to you. I will not break my vow."

Rain shook her head, letting her hands come to rest in her lap. "I do this of my own free will. Each of you has holes in yourselves that only the other can fill."

"Tobias," Etienne spoke, his voice hopeful, but restrained. "Can't we try?"

Tobias looked to Rain again. "You are willing to do this? You are willing to do this for me?"

"I am," she replied without hesitation.

Why, liebchen?

Because then you will never wonder 'what if?' You will never feel as if I made you choose. You will not be torn or hurting and truth be told, I can love him.

Do you love him now?

I am very fond of him, though I am not terribly pleased with him for attacking you the way that he did. But if you are asking me if I love him as I love you, the answer is no. I am, however, willing to try.

There was a long pause as they waited to see who would make the next move, then Tobias reached out and put his free arm around Etienne, kissing his cheek. Etienne responded, leaning forward and hugging his maker. No words, only small sounds of acceptance and comfort as they touched and caressed each other tenderly. Then they both bent their mouths to Rain's throat and drank from her in unison, and when they had taken a small bit of her blood, they pulled back and bit their wrists, offering her the cup of their blood together. She tasted from each in turn, taking a tiny drought from each seeping wound. The pact was sealed.

Six

Aaron was reading comfortably in the lower sitting room, the picture window open to the warm night breezes, when he heard the rustle of wings, and a hawk came gracefully sailing in to land lightly on the carpet. He immediately marked his page and closed the novel as Sky looked up at him from his cross-legged position on the floor.

"Hello," Aaron greeted, his heart fluttering as Sky's blue eyes locked on him.

This one was stirring something deep inside him, something old and long forgotten. He had loved with passion once, a very long time ago. He had loved a French beauty with flaxen hair and ruby red lips. That same French beauty had made him into a vampire under the pretense of being eternal lovers. But eternity for Victoria was only until someone or something else took her interest. In his case, eternity had lasted twenty years. He still carried the old wounds from Victoria, even after almost eight decades. He knew that he sabotaged and doomed his relationships because of it.

Dorian was a prime example. He loved Dorian, but they had met in the heat of passion, when both of them were in great pain and in need of comfort. Their love was like fire; it burned and consumed everything. Dorian wanted all of him, something he swore he would never do again, and he made no attempt to disguise his feelings. The strength and depth of Dorian's love frightened him. The elder vampire could be very possessive and moody as well, which was another reason to be cautious. Aaron hoped

Sky was different. Sky captured something deep inside of him and held it in thrall. He loved to watch Sky covertly, watch how the light played on his gossamer hair, how it danced in his sapphire eyes, and flashed in his warm smile. He could spend an entire night just stealing glances, enjoying the rush of emotion that hit him every time he would, the quickening of his heart, the sudden anxiety… all things long buried, but now climbing their way back to the surface. The sensation was not unlike how he had felt about Dorian after their first meeting: this magnificent being, so unearthly and so beautiful. Aaron was utterly taken with him.

"Hello. Rain told me to come in this way. Things going on in the living room," Sky said, cocking his head at an odd angle as Aaron stared at him.

"Ah, yes. Etienne, a vampire Tobias made, arrived tonight. Since I no longer hear any smashing, screaming or banging, I would guess that things are faring better than earlier," Aaron explained.

"So that is why Rain is so tired, and the heartstone so agitated. It must have been a big fight."

"Nothing with us is ever small, Sky. We do everything in a big way or we don't do it at all."

Sky smiled at the insight, although he knew it was meant to be a slight at the vampires. Aaron's dry sense of humor pleased him, and he had been spending quite a bit of time with him these last few days, but tonight was the first night since he had arrived that he and Aaron were alone.

"So where did you go off to tonight?" Aaron asked him.

"Hmm? Hunting."

"Hunting?"

"Yes. Have to eat you know. Well, actually, I don't have to eat. Not really. I could get all I need by tapping the Earth, or I could become a plant and let the sun feed me."

"Photosynthesis."

"Yeah, that. Humans always have such strange, long names for such simple things," the ecomancer commented, scratching an itch.

Aaron sat forward in his chair, curious as always, and eager to learn.

"So why don't you?"

"Why don't I what?"

"Become a plant or take energy from the Earth."

Sky gave him an incredulous look. "What fun would there be in that? Boring."

"So you enjoy the hunt then."

"I enjoy the meat and the hunt. I'm not like Rain; I don't usually eat processed, human-cooked food unless I have no choice... except chocolate. I like chocolate."

Aaron laughed softly. "Chocolate was one of my favorite foods when I was still mortal."

Sky grinned. "Yes, chocolate is pretty tasty stuff."

"So what did you catch tonight?"

"Hawk caught a gopher. Swift, clean kill. A good kill. And you? Did you have a good kill tonight?"

Aaron grew solemn and disturbed. "None of my kills are 'good' kills."

Sky's eyes lit up with a strange fire. "But you hunt the greatest prey of all. You hunt humans."

"The Most Dangerous Game they are not. Mortals are no match for me. I kill them quickly. Most of them don't even know what hit them until they are dead."

"The Most Dangerous Game?" Sky repeated.

"Yes. It's a story about a man who has gotten tired of hunting animals, and gone to hunting his own kind."

The ecomancer snorted. "Humans are not your kind."

"I used to be one."

"Used to be. I used to be a human too. I also used to be a vampire. Was a fun experience. Was also the last time I wore clothes."

"You shapechanged to a vampire?"

"Yes," he admitted, shifting to a more comfortable position. "It was a long time ago... I tried it for a little while. I thought I would make a good vampire, but I didn't like having to wear clothes or live among humans. And I missed the sun."

The vampire looked wistfully out the window. "I miss the sun too, sometimes."

"If you ever go to the Sanctuary, you'll see it. Sunlight can't hurt you there."

"I know. Tobias has told me."

"I'm sure Tobias has told you a lot about us."

Aaron's eyes glowed with warm light as he smiled softly. "Only enough to make me more curious."

"Oh? About what?"

"Can you really be anything you want?" he asked in a conspiratory whisper, leaning close.

"Anything that I can imagine, if I know how it's made and how it lives or exists. I have limitations. I have to know it," Sky answered with a shrug.

"What is it like to be able to change your shape? To be a bird, for instance. What's it like to be a bird?"

Sky thought for a moment, trying to put the intangible into words. Aaron's questions were forcing him to think. Thinking wasn't always such a good thing, but he'd do it for Aaron. He liked Aaron.

"It's like... It's like losing yourself. When I shape shift, I become that thing. I became the hawk tonight. I saw as a hawk, I thought as a hawk, I was a hawk. All the instincts of that bird were my instincts, all its fears became my fears, and all its wants became my wants. To be a thing, is to know a thing, and to be intimately connected with the essence of that thing," he replied, trying to be eloquent.

Aaron was intelligent and cultured, and Sky had noticed that the young vampire shied away from him when he was too feral; so Sky had made more of an effort to be what could be called as marginally civilized.

Aaron edged even closer, drawn as always by Sky's beauty and quiet grace. "What is it like to have wings? To fly under your own power?"

Again Sky pondered Aaron's question. "I can't tell you in words. I have no words to describe it."

Aaron looked disappointed, but Sky continued. "I could try to share it with you. Share my memory of tonight, and you would see as I saw and feel as I felt."

The vampire shook his head. "My mental capacities are very limited."

"I know, but you should still be able to meld with me. Come, sit beside me and I'll try to show you."

Aaron obeyed, highly intrigued, and joined Sky on the floor, sitting close as Sky reached out to touch him. He shuddered at the pulses of electric energy flowing from Sky's pale fingers, and closed his eyes.

"You're so soft..." Sky whispered, touching his face lightly.

Aaron opened his eyes to find Sky very close to him, their noses almost touching, his sapphire eyes wide with wonder. Sky smiled secretly at him and stroked his cheek. Aaron's hand came up slightly, but paused in mid-air.

"May I... may I touch you?" he asked shakily.

"Yes," the ecomancer answered, his voice barely louder than a breath.

The vampire placed his fingertips upon Sky's bare shoulder, feeling the soft, warm skin of the ecomancer for the first time. The skin responded to his gentle touch, rising in little goosebumps that spread all over Sky's chest, and the veins on his throat pulsed out. Aaron felt Sky run his fingers through his soft hair, while he in turn felt Sky's silver-white mane, marveling in the fine texture of the hair, the soft, cobweb-like feel. Silently, they discovered each other, touching gingerly, tentatively, letting their curiosity about each other feed their explorations.

Dorian had heard Sky come in and felt his presence when the ecomancer entered the house. A quick mental scan of the house revealed that Sky was in the lower sitting room with Aaron, and he frowned. He'd been unobtrusively trying to keep the two of them from being alone together, and so far he had managed to succeed. It would seem, however, that tonight was the exception.

Aaron was becoming rather preoccupied with Sky, and Dorian was not at all certain if he liked that. His feelings of possessiveness towards Aaron had not diminished, but he knew that if he were to react jealously towards the obviously budding relationship, he would only succeed in driving Aaron away, not to mention angering an avatar. No, he had no intention of tangling with avatars, even if they were gorgeous and irresistible…

He scowled, pushing aside the visions of Sky's lovely face and perfect body; rousing his anger and jealousy again. Sky was alone with *his* Aaron, and there was no telling what mischief they were getting into. He stood and immediately went to find out.

There was a small sound in the doorway, and they looked up in unison to see Dorian staring down at them, an odd expression of surprise and hurt on his face. Sky stood up, and touched him fearlessly, putting a hand upon Dorian's cheek, as Aaron rose to his feet.

"Hello," the ecomancer greeted.

"Hello," Dorian repeated.

"Dorian," Aaron said carefully.

"Aaron," the black-haired vampire answered just as carefully.

Sky smiled and brushed Dorian's hair with his fingers.

"What were the two of you doing when I came in?" the older vampire queried, trying not to be too obvious but failing miserably.

"Just touching. I was going to share some memories with him when we got side-tracked," Sky explained.

"Really? What kind of memories?"

"Bird memories. He wanted to know what it was like to be a bird, so I was going to share my memories of tonight with him."

"Oh. Interesting."

Sky turned to Aaron. "Do you still want to do that?"

"Yes."

"Okay then, sit on the couch… Dorian, would you like to join us?"

"Ah no, I'll just watch," Dorian answered.

"As you wish," the ecomancer said, ushering Aaron to sit on the edge of the sofa, and sitting beside him. "Now. I want you to clear your mind of all thoughts. I am going to put my hands on your head and create the link. Soon, you will be experiencing my memories. If you start to get afraid I will stop. Okay?"

Aaron nodded. "Okay."

"Okay, let's begin."

Dorian watched with mixed feelings as Sky put both of his hands on Aaron's head, and they closed their eyes. Sky was so beautiful. He could not deny that his heart would start beating wildly whenever he saw him, and his insides would wrench. Seeing him there on the couch, his eyes closed, his forehead creased in concentration, made him hold his breath. This was Adonis revealed in all his splendor; the godlet come down to Earth, and he wanted desperately to worship him. Sky was an enigma and a paradox, and Dorian was utterly smitten. He knew it was probably hopeless, Sky was such a free spirit, but it was good to feel the passion again, to feel the longing and desire after feeling numb for so long. Bitterly, he recognized that, while he was falling hopelessly in love, the ecomancer seemed to be favoring Aaron. What a fine mettle that would be, but it brought a devilish smile to his lips.

He saw Aaron's face fill with wonder, even with his green eyes still closed. His mouth opened and he gave a tiny gasp, his eyes moving furiously under the shut lids. Dorian watched him touch Sky's arm gently, then grasp it, as he tipped his chin back, allowing Sky to cradle his head in both hands. Aaron's expression of joy almost made Dorian go to them and try to join them, but he stopped himself. He wanted to be part of them. He loved both of them. He wanted both of them. It was an impossible situation.

• • •

"So you are basically an Avatar," Etienne said thoughtfully.

"Yes, you could say that," Rain answered, positioning herself on the bed and resting her chin on one knee.

They were in Tobias' bedroom, and it was getting very late, almost five, not much time left before sunrise. They had retired there after more discussion and some explaining of Rain's origins and powers. Tobias sat down next to her and put his arm around her lovingly. She was getting tired and he knew it, kissing her temple tenderly and nuzzling her with his nose. Leaning against him, she tucked her head under his chin and snuggled close.

"You are tired, liebchen," he whispered. "You should sleep."

She nodded wearily and watched as he pulled aside the bedclothes, preparing her resting place. Slipping off his shoes, he brought her with him as he lay down on the mattress, and they cuddled, Tobias covering her with the blankets while she rested her head on his shoulder. Etienne paused, uncertain as to what to do, until Tobias beckoned to him and bade him to lie on the bed next to him.

"Come, Etienne. Come lie beside me. I am tired, liebchen. I want to sleep."

Etienne did as he was asked and crawled into bed next to Tobias. He lay on his side, facing Tobias, watching as Tobias and Rain kissed lovingly, not knowing what to do, or what was expected of him. Then Tobias turned his head to face him and kissed him, his hand reaching up to stroke his dark blond hair.

"I love you," his maker whispered.

"I love you too," he answered.

Tobias looked at Rain, who was now leaning up on her elbow, and pulled her down for a kiss. "I love you."

Rain smiled. "I love you."

Etienne raised his gaze to meet Rain's and stared at her for long moments. What was his place with her? What would she accept from him? Tobias was their common passion, but would she let him love her too? Tentatively he leaned across Tobias' chest to kiss her and she did not back away. Their lips met in a chaste kiss, with none of the passion with which they had kissed Tobias, and parted. Rain looked down at Tobias, who was gazing up at her in quiet adoration, and smiled softly. Tobias opened his arms and welcomed them to come lay in his embrace. Obligingly, they both lay down and rested their heads in the crux of his shoulders as he held them close. He kissed each of their foreheads tenderly and murmured endearments in German. Rain placed her hand on Tobias' chest and closed her eyes. Etienne did the same, placing his hand delicately over Rain's and settling in for sleep. The last thing each of them heard was Tobias' steady heartbeat thrumming in their ears.

Rain was awakened by a gentle mindtouch, and she opened her eyes to see Sky, sitting on the chair next to the bed with his knees up to his chest.

What have you gotten yourself into, Bina?

He was referring to the two vampires who shared the bed with her; Tobias, who was wrapped around her as usual, his arm holding her protectively, and Etienne, who was spooned behind Tobias, one hand on the brown-haired vampire's shoulder.

To be honest, I don't know. And you? What are you getting yourself into? You spent a long time in Aaron's room this morning.

Sky's brow furrowed. *I like him. He makes me laugh. And Dorian isn't bad company either.*

I never thought I would see the day when you admitted to enjoying someone's company.

Sky smiled softly. *I've always enjoyed yours.*

Yes. Yes.

Rain carefully slipped herself from Tobias' grip and rose from the bed, going to Sky and ruffling his vagabond hair. He seemed confused and bewildered about something, and she patted his shoulder. In all honesty, she was growing concerned for him. He'd been entirely too calm and rational lately. She knew he still spent a good deal of time in animal form, but he was interacting and actually holding conversations with Aaron and Dorian. It had to be wearing on him.

"What is it? What is on your mind?"

His expression turned dark and pensive. "I don't know. He makes me feel...he makes me feel good. But...but he looks at me like I am a god sometimes."

"Who? Aaron?"

"Yes...And he is so soft. When I touched him, he was so soft."

Rain creased her brow with concern. This was the first time she had ever heard him speak of anyone but herself in terms of affection. Not even his lover Waylan: the lover who was killed in front of Sky's very eyes when he was still mortal.

"Do you like him?" she asked cautiously.

"Yes. There are times when he is so sad...so sad. I just want to hold him. Do you know what he said to me today?"

"What did he say?"

"He said he wishes he were like me. That he could make things grow and change his shape. That he was sad because all he could do was kill."

Rain shimmied her way onto the chair, sitting on the arm and resting her chin on her hands. "And what did you tell him?"

"That he had a special purpose, and he didn't just kill. He didn't believe me."

"I see."

"And Dorian was there too. He came in before Aaron and I shared memories. He is beautiful, vibrant. And he likes to stare at me."

She chuckled. "He finds you very attractive."

"I know. And I find him attractive too, but Aaron is so...I like them both."

"What a merry triangle that would be."

Sky smiled. "He's getting curious, you know."

"Who is getting curious about what?"

"Aaron. About you and Tobias and what you do when you go off together."

Rain sat up straight. "Oh really?"

"Mmm-hmm. He's been watching the two of you very closely. If you don't want him to find out, then you had better be very careful."

"I'll keep that in mind."

"Yes. Aaron is rather interested in knowing why Tobias is so happy, and why he is reacting to you in sexual ways."

"Aaron sees and knows things the others don't..." she spoke to herself. "Yes, I should have foreseen this. I will talk to Tobias, and see what we want to do about it."

"Sounds good to me."

He stood and stretched, shaking his long mane of white hair. "Shall we go?"

"Where to?" she asked, moving to stand beside him.

"West. Back to the Sound."

"Okay."

Rain gave Tobias one last kiss and a ruffle of his hair before following Sky out of the room. As they spent their day healing and preventing further damage to the environment, Rain wondered and watched Sky. He was being drawn to Aaron and Dorian like a moth to a flame. They were intriguing him, enchanting him, and it boded both ill and well at the same time. If he was falling in love with either, or both of them, the effects could be beneficial. Sky might finally start to heal, and to accept his past. But if it went poorly, it could push him even further into his madness. She was both worried and hopeful. It was the first time since Sky regained some semblance of sanity that he was showing interest in anyone, and she was wishing for it to go well, for Sky to feel love again and to be loved by a lover or lovers. It would help him, she was sure of it. In the meantime, she would watch where the relationships were going, and see if there were things she could do to foster or nurture them.

Seven

Rain was sitting by herself in the library. It was a small room, but cozy with its own small fireplace and rows upon rows of books. Almost all of Aaron and Dorian's collection was there, and she sometimes would pick up an old tome to see what it contained in its yellowed pages. She and Tobias had gone off together earlier in the evening to make love, and now he was giving her some private time to herself, while he engaged Aaron in a game of chess in the living room. She was reading an old biography of Chaucer when Etienne slipped silently into the room.

"Hi," he spoke quietly.

"Hello."

He shifted nervously and sat down in the chair opposite hers, fidgeting, and Rain watched him curiously for a few moments.

"How is the third of our terrible trio doing tonight?" he asked.

"He is doing very well."

Etienne nodded, growing more and more nervous with every second. Something was obviously bothering him and he was highly agitated.

"What's on your mind, Etienne?"

He met her steady gaze, then flushed and lowered his eyes, staring at the fire burning low in the hearth. She put her book down and folded her hands in her lap, waiting.

"Tell me what is bothering you."

Etienne swallowed hard and answered, his voice small and meek. "You're making love with him, aren't you."

Rain was silent for a minute, measuring her answer, trying to read Etienne's emotional state. Finally, she replied evenly.

"Yes."

Etienne sighed, as if all his suspicions had been confirmed.

"I knew. I recognized the look on his face. The look of contentment and sublime joy…I saw it nearly every night of my life for nine years."

They fell quiet as Etienne returned his gaze to the flames, letting the soft yellow light dance in his hazel eyes, and Rain waited patiently for him to continue.

"Do you please him? Do you keep him satisfied?" he questioned timidly.

"Yes. I please him and keep him satisfied."

He glanced at her, a knowing twinkle of humor in his eyes. "Not easy, is it."

She smiled. "No, it's not."

Etienne grinned. "Never thought he'd be such a little slut, did you?" He waved his hand before she could reply. "Ahhh, don't answer that. I didn't know he would be either."

Rain giggled. "He's not that bad."

"Speak for yourself," Etienne quipped. "For years, every night we were together, he was on me to take him, sometimes more than once. There were nights when that was all we did from sunset to sunrise. He would go out, feed, come back, and we would stay in bed the whole night, just making love."

"Must have been difficult to keep up with him," Rain commented.

"It was. But…" He paused, trying to find the words. "But…he made me want to. It wasn't like he exerted his will on me or anything. No nothing like that. He never forced me. He didn't have to. All I had to do was look at him, see him there, all sultry and sensuous on the bed, or wherever, and I'd want to."

Rain nodded in understanding. "He does have a great deal of sex appeal."

Etienne agreed. "He's perfect. Always was. But horribly insatiable."

She cocked her head. "Not so insatiable anymore. He is learning to control it."

"That's good. When I was alive, he was. Nothing I did satisfied him for very long. We could make love for hours and twenty minutes after, he'd be ready again. There were times when I just couldn't...couldn't..."

"Perform?" she offered, ignoring his discomfort.

"Yeah. Perform. He'd get so upset. I could see he was trying to be understanding, to realize that I was mortal and had limitations, but I could tell he was disappointed," Etienne sighed, a note of dejection in his voice.

"His need was very great, almost out of his control."

"Yeah."

Rain laughed softly and he smiled, losing his nervousness.

"I tried everything I could get my hands on, but nothing would make him happy except me. It was so draining and frustrating..."

"Yet you loved it as much as he did," she broke in.

Etienne sighed heavily and nodded. "Yes. I did. I loved it. He'd give me his blood while we fucked, we'd be locked to each other's necks while I did him. He wouldn't climax without the bloodsharing, blood always had to be involved. That's why he always wanted me face-to-face. Doggie style was okay for getting him ready, but he wanted to be looking into my eyes when he reached a certain point. He'd rip his throat and bite mine, and after that...It'd blow my mind. I would've done anything for the blood. I'd have screwed him in the middle of the mall if he'd wanted me to."

He fell silent, feeling very vulnerable, and shifted uncomfortably in his chair.

"I'm not being too blunt for you, am I?"

Rain shook her head. "Not at all. I want you to be honest. This has a lot to do with how you feel about him now, because at one time you were so very close."

"Close? We were practically joined at the hips. When we weren't fucking, we were fighting, and the fights would end with us fucking again. He'd give me a little bit of his blood, a pittance for what I really wanted, but enough to keep me stringing along."

He hung his head, remembering. "Even before we started having sex, there were times when I had to get away from him. I'd go off on my own for a couple of weeks, visit friends, family, whatever, just to keep my own sanity. I tried to leave for good once. I missed him terribly." He looked at the fire.

"He loved you very much," she said, carefully. "He still does."

Etienne's face twisted with pain, and he clenched his fists. "I know. But he also hasn't forgiven me."

"Forgiven you?"

"For making him do it. For putting myself in danger time and time again until he finally had no choice. I was driving that night, too fast on wet roads. I was reckless, careless. Sometimes I think he should have let me die just to punish me for being stupid, but I always knew, deep down inside, that he wouldn't let me die," he admitted, his voice low and strained.

She stood and went to him, placing her hand upon his thigh and sitting on the rug in front of the chair. "He has forgiven you. It's himself he has never forgiven."

Etienne's eyes squeezed shut to hold back the tears. "I know...I thought that after he did it, things would be perfect, that we would be together forever. I loved him so much. But after..."

"But after he made you he turned fatalist, and assumed that you'd leave him, because you now had what you'd wanted all along," she finished for him.

"Exactly. We didn't talk or kiss or share blood. I waited four and a half years for him to come around. I knew he still loved me, but I was at my wits end."

"So you left to be with Barias."

Etienne sighed. "I didn't love him. He knew I didn't, but he didn't care."

Rain's brow furrowed with confusion. "Why did you go with him then?"

"Barias and I had always gotten along. After I left Tobias, Barias was there to dry my tears."

"I understand."

Etienne flushed again and stumbled on the words. "And things...changed so much after I was a vampire. We couldn't make love anymore." Etienne blushed even more and looked down at his hands. "I knew that it was hard for him. He'd gotten so used my...loving him. I knew that before, when I was still mortal, when I'd come back to the house and find that he'd gouged big scratches in the woodwork with his nails, and when he'd be practically stripping me down and making me hard the night after I got back. He tried going down on me once. His blood lust took over while he had my cock in his mouth and he bit me. I climaxed and fainted in about three seconds. He was gagging for the rest of the night."

"Your absences were very difficult for him," Rain agreed, trying to keep from bursting out laughing, the corners of her mouth twitching with restrained mirth.

"The night after I'd get back, we'd have to go someplace deserted to make love because he'd break the windows of the house and rip the bed to shreds if we stayed there. When we lived in Florida we had a little spot on a tiny island about two miles off shore. He could be as loud as he wanted there. And he was. He'd cry my name, beg me to fuck him forever, yell things in Old German and Latin...Never knew what he was saying..."

Rain smiled sheepishly. "I speak Latin and Old German."

"Oh, so you know what he is saying then? I can gander a pretty good guess."

They shared a small laugh and a look of complete understanding, then Etienne grew serious again.

"I knew...that part of our problem after he made me, was that I couldn't do that anymore. I'd see him struggling with it, raking his nails on the furniture, forgoing blood to make himself too hungry to think about sex..."

"Picking up strange male mortals and bringing them home in hopes that they would be able to satisfy him," she added.

Etienne's face registered his shock. "He did? When did he do that?"

"The time when you were gone for six months."

He lowered his gaze sadly. "Oh. I didn't know that. What happened?"

"He killed him. The man was only interested in his own pleasure. He did not treat Tobias well, so Tobias got angry and killed him."

Etienne winced and played with his thumbs nervously. "I should have known he would get that desperate. After he made me, he sorta took a fatalist approach to it. He figured I was dead now and couldn't anymore, so there wasn't any sense in wishing for what he couldn't have. I was the only one who could trigger the orgasm…until you, of course. I am assuming you bring him to climax."

Now it was Rain's turn to lower her gaze. "I do…And so can you."

"What?"

"You can be sexually potent. There is a way…"

Etienne shook his head. "No. Believe me, I've tried. It doesn't work."

She raised her hand in a gesture that he listen. "It is possible. It is not easy and it can take a long time, but you are capable of achieving sexual arousal."

"You're joking."

"No. I'm not. There is a way. I have taught Tobias how and I can teach you."

"I don't believe what I am hearing. I tried for four years to find a way to be able to do it again. I was willing to try anything, to attempt the impossible just so I would be able to give him what he needed."

"Because you loved him and wanted to make him happy again," she said quietly.

"Yes. I loved him so much I would have done anything for him. Have you ever loved someone that much? Loved so much that you would do anything for that person?"

Rain motioned that she had, her gray eyes turning soft and misty. "Yes. I have loved that much. I have loved enough to break the rules that bind me, to risk being found out before my time. I have risked disrupting the Balance for this love. I have risked my very life and soul."

Etienne stared at her, his face grim and serious. "For Tobias."

She closed her eyes. "Yes. For Tobias."

"That was why you accepted me, because you could not stand to lose him. That is why we are both in this triangle. He is the one who holds us together, and our love for him is strong enough to make us share, rather than not have him at all."

She opened her eyes again and looked at him. "Yes."

"Tell me, is there any place in your heart for me? Do you feel anything for me at all? I have to tell you…I have grown quite fond of you these past six nights."

Rain smiled and placed her hand in his. "Yes. I have always been fond of you. You hold a place in my heart, and I cannot love Tobias without feeling some love for you as well. In time we may find that our passion for each other equals our passion for Tobias."

Etienne's face warmed. "Then we will leave it at that."

"Yes."

She stood and thought for a moment, looking at the almost extinguished fire. "Do you want to come with us the next time Tobias and I go off together? Do you want to me to teach you?"

Etienne gripped the arms of the chair anxiously. "Yes. If you will permit me."

"I will."

"Then I will try, and we will see what comes of it."

"Yes."

She moved to leave, suddenly lost in her own thoughts of the ramifications of what they had just decided.

"Thank you," Etienne whispered. "For everything."

She turned her head slightly, not enough to see him, but to look over her shoulder. "You're welcome," she answered softly, then quietly walked out of the room.

Etienne's chance came two nights later when he followed Tobias and
Rain to the old house and slipped into the master bedroom as they were
settling onto the bed. Rain knew he was there, she had known that he
followed them. What neither of them knew was that Etienne had been
followed himself, by a black haired figure in dark clothes.

Tobias lay on his back with his eyes closed as Rain planted soft kisses
on his face and throat. He moaned and gripped the sheets in clenched
hands, his body aching with passion. Then another set of lips, these ones
cool and firm, kissed his cheek. Surprised, Tobias opened his eyes to see
Etienne standing next to the bed, half-naked and smiling.

"Etienne? What are...?"

Rain placed a silencing finger on his lips. "Shhh. He is your lover, is
he not?"

"Yes, as are you, liebchen," he replied.

"Then he has every right to be here, and tonight we both will bring
you pleasure."

Tobias had no answer. He watched as Etienne climbed onto the bed,
keeping his blue jeans on, and lay still while both Etienne and Rain began
to peel off his clothes. Their hands slid over his skin, finding all his soft
places, caressing his white skin. He reached up and slid Rain's sari from
her shoulders, baring her breasts to his hungry mouth, and took one of
her nipples as she and Etienne fondled and kissed him. He kept her breast
in his mouth as he encircled one arm behind her back, acutely aware that
Etienne was now releasing him from his pants and pulling them off. Cool
hands slid up his bare thighs...'Oh Goddess yes, he remembers. He
remembers everything.' Then Etienne's tongue was playing with one of his
breasts, nipping at the small tip and sucking gently. Tobias groaned.

"You like it when I do that, don't you," came Etienne's husky voice.

Tobias moaned an answer, releasing Rain's breast and searching for
Etienne's lips. "Yes..."

He was naked now, and Rain was divesting herself of her sari, but
Etienne was making no motions to remove his jeans. Tobias thought it

odd, but he didn't really care. Perhaps Etienne was a bit modest about baring his entire body in front of Rain. It seemed strange to him, but he knew it wouldn't matter once things got started. He knew from experience that Etienne was very uninhibited in his passion. He returned his attentions to Rain, lifting up to once again worship her chest and throat.

"Shall we teach him?" she asked softly, her voice low and inviting.

"Yes," he breathed.

They separated and Rain moved to stroke Etienne's bare back.

"The first lesson is not to bite. Biting will destroy the process. You must not bite until it's time," she whispered, licking Etienne's ear.

"How will I know when it's time?" the young vampire asked, closing his eyes as Tobias' hands ran over his breasts.

"You'll know," his maker breathed.

Allow me, liebchen, please? Tobias asked.

Of course, she replied, and pulled back from them as Tobias rose up to his knees, situating himself between Etienne's bent thighs.

Both vampires were now kneeling on the bed, facing each other, hands exploring and stroking.

"Do you trust me?" Tobias asked tenderly.

Etienne drew a shuddering breath. "I've always trusted you."

"Good," he answered, nuzzling Etienne's neck and licking at the flushed skin.

Etienne moaned and arched closer. There was something...something about Tobias' smell that was drawing him in, but he couldn't place it. His vision was going a little out of focus and he couldn't concentrate.

"Shhhh. Patience. You must relax. In a moment you will begin to feel a warmth seeping into you and a tingling."

He managed a small nod, gripping Tobias' arms loosely as his maker's hungry mouth began to suck and nip at his ears. He shuddered, feeling the warmth stirring in him, and his nostrils flared. His fingers tightened reflexively, kneading the flesh of his maker's biceps. The bloodlust was rising. He could smell the vampire and ecomancer blood, and hear the pounding heartbeats.

"Easy," Tobias soothed, lips still against his neck. "Relax. You're starting to feel it, I know. It begins as a tingle and works its way up your body. That's the first stage. We've gotten there before. We've even gotten to stage two. Do you remember our lovemaking in State College?"

The words came through the red haze. "Yes."

"Do you know that if I had held off biting you that night; if I hadn't taken your blood, we would have made it to stage three? What a surprise that would have been, hmm?"

He managed a small chuckle.

"Relax, Eti. You must be completely at ease and without fear. Fear negates this. You must give yourself completely to me without compunction."

He didn't answer as Tobias wrapped arms around him and very gently laid him down on the bed. The beautiful face hovered over his for a moment, then sank down, the soft curls tickling his chin as a mouth claimed his breast. He groaned and threaded his fingers into his maker's hair.

"Please," he whispered, pressing his nipple into the sucking mouth.

Not yet...

Tobias teased his breast, licking all around the sensitive bud then nipping quickly, briefly, but not hard enough to draw blood. His body jerked from the sensation and he tensed as his blood lust rose, the warmth increasing. Then he felt lips on his neck, just behind his ear, and teeth very gently nibbling at the lobe. Hot air passed over his ear and he was nearly drowning in the sounds of the heartbeats. He tried to take a deep breath but found he could not. Tobias' mouth moved to the other nipple and both he and Rain timed the next nip simultaneously, so that his breast and his ear were bitten in unison, again not hard enough to break the skin. His eyes flared open as the warmth flooded into heat and a tingling overtook his body. The blood lust was screaming at him and he pulled back his upper lip.

No, liebchen, you must not bite. Not yet, came Tobias' warning.

But...

Not yet. Soon, Eti, soon, but not now.

Tobias' curls slid out of his fingers as his maker moved further down his body. The cool lips were now kissing his belly and sides, licking and sucking, as Rain's mouth moved down as well, to take his breast. Her mouth was much hotter and wetter than Tobias' and she breathed over the wet nipple, making him shudder. Tobias' nimble fingers undid his jeans and he felt the coarse material slide from his body as the cool air hit his naked skin. He had no time to worry about his nudity as Tobias' tongue licked its way up his legs, over his hip to his navel.

For long moments his entire world was condensed into the sensation of the two mouths on his body. He was shaking with blood lust now, barely containing it. At one point, Tobias actually placed an arm across his chest to prevent him from lifting up to bite Rain. He groaned in disappointment, only to be sent into raptures again when both his nipples were bitten lightly at the same time. After the shock passed, he felt a heavy heat pooling in his lower belly and a strange scent filled the air.

Ah, there it is. Do you smell it, Eti?

He couldn't bring himself to answer verbally. *What is it?*

The scent of your arousal building. Do you smell mine?

He breathed in, catching the scent he had smelled earlier on Tobias only this time his body reacted to it, the tingles spreading into his limbs and the heat in his abdomen growing. There was a word for this type of chemical reaction, a term he had heard just recently to describe the chemoreceptors produced by the body.

"Pheromones," he choked out loud.

"Hmm?" Tobias, asked, nibbling at his side.

"Pheromones," he repeated.

What is that, liebchen?

"Pheromones. That's the smell. Pheromones. Chemicals produced by the body that..."

He was cut off as Tobias' teeth bit into his hip, the tiny fangs scraping across his skin, promising to bite but not following through.

Tease! he accused.

Stop analyzing it and just enjoy it.

I was enjoying…Oh God!

He gasped and cried out as a hand cupped and gently squeezed his testicles.

Are you ready, Eti? I think he's ready.

I think he's ready too, Rain's mind voice agreed.

Are you ready, my love?

Yes, he answered, fighting for breath.

Do you want this? Do you want to be loved?

Yes!

Do you give yourself to me? Do you come to me of your own free will?

Yes! Damnit! Yes!

Good, because I can't wait any longer.

He was thinking of a suitable retort to the last comment when Tobias' mouth engulfed his organ. The first sensation was warmth, then wetness, then Tobias' fangs scraped against the underside of his cock and his world exploded. The heat that had been pooling in his belly flared into an inferno that rushed into his groin. He screamed as the phantom fire seared him, feeling the blood flooding into his cock, feeling it rise and come to life for the first time in seven years. He arched off the bed, curling up and grabbing Tobias' head as he thrust his hips up.

"Toby!" he wailed.

The mouth wrenched from his cock and he heard Tobias draw a deep breath. Then a body hit him hard as his maker threw himself on top of him, slamming him back to the mattress. They kissed roughly, fingers digging into the flesh of their backs, this time hard enough to draw blood and the scent made them even crazier with passion.

We must… We must… Tobias was trying.

What? What! he cried, seeking to shove his tongue as far down Tobias' throat as he could.

Tobias pulled away, ignoring his protests and gasping. He moaned and reached up to grab him again, but the older vampire was just out of reach.

He sat up, looking down at his erect organ with awe. His eyes traveled to Tobias' groin and saw that he, too, was erect and ready. Both of them were panting and slick with sweat.

"We must, slow down. We are forgetting Rain," Tobias managed.

"You could have continued, my love. I don't mind. It would have been nice to watch," she assured.

"No, this is for you as much as it is for us. Besides, Eti knows what I want now."

Tobias took Rain into his arms, pushing her down to the mattress and kneeling over her, offering his rump to Etienne in silent invitation. While he was placing soft kisses on her breasts and shoulders, he felt a hard finger press cautiously against the muscles of his anal ring, and he sighed with pleasure. Etienne was going to finger him, just like old times. He mewled with pleasure as the finger probed him, taking Rain's breast back into his mouth and biting down. He heard Rain gasp and felt her covet his head in her arms as Etienne continued his explorations. Sweet, delicious pleasure, both from the bite and the finger inside him. Then he felt a second finger, this one smaller, enter his rectum to slide beside Etienne's, and he bucked as they both began to work him gently.

Together they rolled him to his back, making him release Rain's breast, and concentrated on loosening his anal muscles, getting him ready for the moment when Etienne would mount him. He raised his legs and made soft cries of pleasure as they stretched him open. Both of their mouths were on his breasts as they increased the pace of their probing and added more fingers, then he felt Etienne bite down, driving him nearly mad with need.

Take me. Take me please. Want you...need you. Don't torture me any longer...Please..., he sent desperately.

The reply was a nip on his breast and Rain's lips raising up to find his as Etienne inserted another finger into him. Pleasure, searing and hot, coursed through his body, and he sobbed as he kissed Rain. His whole body was thrumming with pleasure, his organ hot and heavy and demanding. Then Rain's wrist was pressed to his mouth, his teeth were biting through her soft skin, and her sweet blood was flowing over his tongue. Ecstasy. The bite filled him with throbbing warmth as his lovers worked him steadily. He was insane with it, clawing at the mattress, moaning and crying.

Please! I cannot bear it any longer!

There was a pause in their lovemaking as Etienne and Rain stopped what they were doing. Her wrist was still pressed to his mouth, but the fingers were slowly leaving his body, leaving it empty and cold. Moments passed and still nothing replaced the fingers that had been inside him. He whimpered with frustration, sucking hard on Rain's wrist, tears rising in his eyes as he wrestled with his need. What was taking so long? Did Eti lose the erection? He whined pleadingly, letting go of Rain's wrist.

Suddenly, cool hands were on his thighs, lifting them, spreading them open, and a third hand, this one warm, grasped his leg just under his knee and pulled it forward, bringing it nearer to his chest. His pelvis was tipped up, exposed, and he felt something hard press against his anal ring.

He opened his eyes and beheld Etienne, kneeling between his spread legs. One hand was gripping Tobias' left thigh, pushing it back, while the other was positioning his organ carefully. Again, Tobias felt the pressure against his anus. Etienne moved his hand away, and Tobias saw Etienne's cock, glistening in the moonlight from the lubricant that had been spread on it. Tobias held his breath, his eyes opening wide and they met Etienne's hazel ones, held enthralled as Etienne rose up on his knees, grinning.

"Remember this?" his fledgling said, and plunged the organ fully into him in one hard thrust.

Tobias arched his back as the organ invaded his body, convulsing as Etienne's pelvis came slamming into his own, and screamed. His scream was muffled by Rain's mouth covering his own, but he continued to scream as Etienne began to ride him, pumping into him with even, hard strokes. This was not the tender lovemaking he and Rain shared, the sweet joining of bodies in a tender embrace. No, this was hard fucking, the kind of fucking only Etienne had ever given him. Rough, fast, furious and burning hot. He loved it. Forcing his tongue into Rain's mouth, he thrust it into her throat, grabbing onto her arms to steady himself against Etienne's pounding hips.

Faster! Harder!

A moment later, Etienne increased his pace and Tobias screamed into Rain's mouth again, tears streaming down his cheeks. Then Etienne's mindvoice pierced his mind.

You like it? You like it when I fuck you? You like getting fucked by me?

Yes! Yes! Oh, Goddess! Yes! Fuck me!

Etienne laughed and thrust harder, as Rain pulled back to watch them, curling her body near Tobias' shoulders. Etienne's hips were moving so fast, she could hardly see them, they were just a blur of white furiously moving in and out between Tobias' spread-eagled thighs, and Tobias' mouth was open in a silent scream, his face a mask of pleasure. His hand reached up and grabbed her hand, squeezing tightly, and gasped as the first contraction of muscle closed around Etienne's organ.

"Oh! Oh, Goddess…"

"Starting to name deities now, eh?" Etienne quipped between thrusts.

Tobias shuddered as another wave swept through him, stronger than the one before: his climax was building.

"Etienne…"

Etienne rocked forward on his knees, catching Tobias' legs in his arms and bearing down, folding Tobias' body in half until he could reach Tobias' throat. He licked Tobias' white skin and then bit down, ignoring the cry that escaped his maker's lips.

Tobias bucked and clawed at Etienne as the ecstasy of the bite filled him, consuming and compiling the pleasure he was already feeling from Etienne's thrusting organ.

"Etienne!"

Shut up and bite me.

Tobias obeyed, sinking his teeth into Etienne's neck, completing the circuit of bloodsharing. The rush of the blood pounded in his ears as they rocked together, the sweet taste of Etienne's blood filling his mouth.

Etienne plunged into him over and over, riding him furiously until finally he felt the last wave hit him and physical climax, with its heavy force, crashed through his body as the blood brought him to vampiric orgasm. He cried out, the sound being muffled by his lips against Etienne's neck and gripped Rain's hand as he shook uncontrollably, Etienne giving him a few more hard thrusts, just to tease him.

His trembling stopped several minutes later, as Etienne pulled away from his neck and disengaged his organ. Rain bent down to kiss his reddened lips and he opened his mouth to receive her, still panting from the lovemaking. The shudders subsided as they caressed and cuddled each other, murmuring, making small sounds of love and tenderness, until Tobias rolled to his side…and saw Aaron standing in the doorway, staring at them in wide-eyed shock.

"Aaron!" Tobias gasped, sitting up.

Etienne and Rain looked worriedly at Aaron as he stood motionless, speechless in the entranceway.

"Aaron!" Tobias spoke again, rising from the bed.

Aaron made a choking sound and backed away as Tobias approached him. "Aaron, please…"

"NO!!" Aaron cried and whirled around, bolting for the stairs and running out of the house.

Rain gathered her wits about her and called for Sky.

Eight

Aaron ran blindly. He had never been so utterly shocked and mortified in his entire life. He was embarrassed and humiliated and profoundly intrigued all at the same time. He refused to accept what he had just witnessed; yet he knew he had seen it with his own eyes. He also knew he had violated Tobias and his lovers' privacy, and he was horribly ashamed of himself. He had watched the whole dizzying scene, knowing what he was doing was wrong, but still transfixed, unable to tear his eyes away as he saw Etienne mount Tobias, and perform an act that was not supposed to be possible for any of them. His mind still a jumble of confusion and shame, he ran into the woods, and saw a blur of white appear in front of him just before he slammed into Sky.

"Oh!" he blurted in surprise, and tried to go around the ecomancer who was now in his way.

Sky's hands gripped his arms and held him steady.

"What is it?" he asked, concerned.

"I…" Aaron stammered, breathless, distracted. "I don't want to talk about it."

"What happened? Rain said I should find you as soon as I could. What is going on?"

Aaron lowered his eyes, refusing to meet Sky's gaze. "I…saw something I wasn't supposed to see."

Sky paused, thinking, and realization suddenly came to him. "Oh. I understand."

"You do?"

"Yes, and it's all right."

"No, it isn't! I...I followed Etienne. I only wanted to see where they were going. I walked in on them while they were...while they were...and I couldn't stop staring! I knew it was wrong, but I just couldn't move!"

Gently, Sky encircled his arms around Aaron and held him. "Hush. It's okay. We all knew you were going to find out sooner or later, it was just a matter of when and where. But it's all right. I am sure no one is angry with you except yourself."

"Oh, I'm so ashamed."

Sky's arms around him were warm and comforting, and he sighed, letting his panic and nerves calm. He rested his head against Sky's bare shoulder as the ecomancer stroked his black hair tenderly, soothing and consoling him, and for a moment, he felt completely safe. Then he heard Sky's soft crooning break into a small gasp, and felt him stiffen, as he dropped his arms suddenly.

"What's wrong?" Aaron asked, upset that his comfort had been disturbed.

Sky's face was a mask of confusion and surprise. "I..." Then the look vanished, but he still seemed a bit out of sorts. "We should take you back to the house. I am sure Tobias and Rain will want to talk to you."

Before Aaron could answer, Sky placed arms around him again, but in a hold, not an embrace, and they rose from the ground. Startled, Aaron grabbed Sky around the shoulders and waist, and looked down.

"You can fly?"

"Sort of," Sky replied.

Aaron held close to Sky as they traveled over the trees and rooftops until they landed on the deck. Sky opened the doors to reveal that all the other members of the household were already there, waiting for him. All four faces turned to look at him and Sky as they entered the living room.

"Tobias tells me you have had quite a shock," Dorian said carefully.

Aaron nodded but did not speak, and as Tobias stood and walked to him calmly, he found it very difficult to meet Tobias' questioning eyes.

"Aaron. Do you want to talk about what you saw tonight?" the brown-haired vampire asked gently.

Aaron recoiled, flushing with shame, and Tobias continued. "I am not angry, Aaron. Do you want to talk about it with me?"

Aaron reluctantly nodded his head. "Yes. I do. I...I think we should."

"Very well. Let us go to your room and we will talk."

Aaron met Tobias' blue eyes. "But what of the others?"

"Rain and Etienne will explain things to them."

Tobias offered his hand and Aaron gingerly took it.

"All right," he said, and allowed Tobias to lead the way to the bedroom. Once they were in Aaron's room, Tobias shut the door and quietly sat down on the plush chair, waiting. Aaron paced nervously, fidgeting and playing with the ends of his long, black hair.

"Speak your mind, Aaron," Tobias said softly.

Aaron made a grunting sound and paced harder. Tobias waited in silence, letting Aaron's agitation build until it broke, and Aaron spoke.

"Did I really see what I think I saw?"

"You did."

"You and Etienne were really...?"

"We were. And Rain and I have made love as well."

"You've made love to Rain?"

"Yes," Tobias answered calmly.

Aaron settled and looked introspectively at Tobias. "But how can it be possible? We are dead things. Physical intercourse is no longer an option."

"Obviously not," Tobias deadpanned, then looked at Aaron sympathetically. "Aaron, it is possible for us to make love. Rain taught me how in the Sanctuary, and tonight Etienne learned."

"Is it as pleasurable as drinking blood?"

"Yes, it can be as intense as drinking blood, and sometimes better."

Aaron cocked his head. "Better than drinking blood?"

"Yes. Because afterwards, your lover can hold you and keep you warm and tell you sweet things, and you can feel safe and loved. You can't get that with blood. Once the victim is dead, it's over. With a lover, it doesn't ever have to end."

Aaron sat on the bed and looked questioningly at Tobias. "When did you first do it? What's it like?"

"I first made mortal love with Etienne…to end an argument. I was expecting to get nothing from it, to merely be a vessel in which Etienne could vent his mortal passion. But instead we discovered that, when combined with the sharing of blood, I could get pleasure from it. We began making love regularly, and made love regularly until I brought Etienne across to me," he replied, crossing one leg over the other and sitting back in the chair. "After that I was celibate until Rain and I made love in the Sanctuary, and she showed me how we could make love. And I cannot tell you what it is like. It is much much more than anything I have ever experienced."

"Does it ever hurt?"

"No, it has never hurt me."

Aaron gazed at his feet. "Is it why you're so happy?"

"I am happy because I am loved. Yes, making love is part of why I am happy, but it is not the only reason I am happy. If Rain had not nearly forced it upon me, I would have been content to stay celibate."

"But you feel passion again, and desire and love…"

"Yes I do. I feel them through my lovers and because of my lovers."

As he answered Aaron, Tobias suddenly realized what Aaron was trying to say. Aaron wanted to know how Tobias felt his passion! Now Tobias saw the longing in Aaron's eyes, the jealousy and hopeless need, and ached to reach out. This was the Aaron Dorian had fallen in love with. It was peaking out from behind the soft, green eyes, trying to find a way to the surface, and it thought that Tobias had the keys to its freedom. Acting on impulse, he moved to the bed, sitting next to Aaron, and placed his hand upon Aaron's cheek.

"Aaron…" he whispered and kissed the black-haired vampire tenderly.

Aaron responded, kissing Tobias back and trembling.

"Shhhh. It's all right," Tobias cajoled as Aaron rested his head against his shoulder.

"I never realized how much of an empty shell I had become until you came back and had the passion again. It reminded me of everything I had lost."

"It's all right. I understand."

"I wanted to know what it was, then maybe I could feel it too. Maybe I would be able to feel joy and love again."

"Yes, yes," Tobias agreed, holding Aaron close.

"You are so happy. I was so jealous; I wanted to feel love so badly. And now Sky…"

"Sky? What about Sky?" Tobias asked, stroking Aaron's hair.

"I…I think I love him. But I don't know. It's been so long since I've felt these emotions, I don't know what they mean anymore. And besides, Dorian wants him too."

Small twinge of disappointment but mixed also with relief. He already had two lovers; he didn't need or want a third. Besides, Aaron needed a different kind of lover. He was a virgin in these matters, he needed a patient and understanding partner.

"I understand," Tobias murmured lovingly. "And don't worry about Dorian. Worry about what you are feeling for Sky."

He felt Aaron nod and gave him a pat on the shoulder. "Do you want to join the others, or do you want to stay here and let me hold you for a while?"

Aaron sighed. "Stay here and hold me. Even though it's been more than two weeks since you came back, sometimes I still think you're a figment of my imagination."

Tobias chuckled and nestled his chin into the top of Aaron's head.

Some hours later, in Tobias' bedroom, Sky paced nervously, spanning the breadth of the room like a caged panther, his hands clenched into fists. Rain sat quietly in the chair next to the bed, watching him, and occasionally casting a glance at the two vampires lying asleep on the mattress. Although the bedroom had no windows, she knew that sunrise had long since passed. Sky made a snorting sound, commanding her attention once again.

"I just don't understand it, Bina," he moaned, his face full of confusion.

'You are falling in love, and fighting it every step of the way,' she thought to herself.

"Last night when you sent me after him, he ran right into me and I had to stop him...and then I had my arms around him, and he relaxed, and put his head on my shoulder. And it made me feel...made me feel..."

"Good?" she offered innocently.

He looked at her quizzically, his eyes dilated, his teeth chewing nervously on his bottom lip. "Guess so...I remember feeling that way when I was...when I was..."

Rain's eyes opened a little wider. He was thinking of Waylan. Would he say the man's name? She had never heard him speak of Waylan. She knew of the older man from walking Sky's mind and witnessing his memories. He had taken a young, confused Sky under his wing when Sky was still mortal. But in all the years she had known him, she had never heard him talk about his first and only lover.

Sky sighed heavily. "I don't know. I don't know what I feel anymore. I want to go away. I do not want to be here any more."

'Damn! Quick, think fast...' she thought frantically. "You would hurt him terribly if you left without saying good-bye, and Dorian too."

His brow creased as he took in her words. "That's true, and I don't want to hurt him. He doesn't...deserve to be hurt."

He didn't hear Rain's exhale of relief.

"Do you think Aaron loves me?"

"I think he might."

Sky looked down at his hands. "You really think so?"

"Yes, I do."

"What am I to do, Bina?"

"You want me to make these decisions for you, but I cannot. You have to follow your own heart," she answered gently.

Inwardly, Rain's heart was fluttering nervously. Sky was entering the transitionary period where he would either make strong strides towards healing, or regress backward. It was a delicate time. Of all the ecomancers, Rain knew Sky was the most unstable, and in this, he could go either way. He was struggling with his feelings and memories, trying to sort things out, but he was hitting up against the barriers in his mind and they were confusing him.

"What do you want to do, right now, at this very moment?" she asked. "Don't think, just answer."

"I want do be with Aaron," he blurted, then became uncertain again, putting a hand to his head. "But I can't...I want to go away...Oh, I don't know what I want anymore..." He went to her, knelt at her feet and put his head in her lap. "Help me, Bina."

She curled herself over him, putting her arms around him and resting the side of her face against his back. "It's all right," she soothed.

It always came to this. The reminder that Sky, in many ways, was still broken. Within his own secure world, he was stable; but outside of it, he would fall to pieces, unable to assimilate or adapt. Why Aiya had chosen this flawed creature to be Her avatar, none of them knew. Had it been another, he probably would have been destroyed. Another question was why She had chosen Rain to be his mentor. Rain had been barely a hundred and twenty years old when Aiya handed her the unconscious body of Sky, and she had been ill prepared to handle such a wounded and tattered soul, but Aiya had decided she was to be the one. Sky had been part of her life ever since. Sometimes she thought Aiya had given her Sky in order to keep her from running to Tobias. There had been days where the vampire had been her primary focus, especially after her time with him in the Germany, and she often wondered if Sky was meant to be a diversion. Goddess knew that Sky had been quite a handful in those first few decades, while she tried to heal some of the damage done to him and piece together some of his broken mind. But she had to admit, he was much better than he used to be. Rain knew, however, that she had long since done all that she could for him. It was up to him to finish what she had started. He had been in this limbo, somewhere between sanity and madness, for over a century. And now, Sky was struggling with emotions he had little to no experience with, and he was once again clinging to Rain, leaning on her to protect and guide him until he was able to do it himself. She recognized the delicacy of her situation, and tried to decide how best to react.

"It will all work out, I promise you," she assured. "Just follow your heart. If it leads you to Aaron, then that is where you should be."

Sky did not answer. Instead Rain felt his body grow soft and alter shape until a large German Shepherd was in Sky's place, its head on her lap. The dog whined lowly and licked her hand, before backing out of her embrace and going to the bedroom door. It looked back at her, its tail wagging and barked once. Rain sighed and shook her head, standing and moving to the door to open it, and let the dog out.

Nine

"Sky is falling in love with Aaron," Rain stated cautiously.

The gentle blue eyes of her immortal lover met hers and blinked curiously as their owner took her into his tender embrace. "That is a good thing, is it not?"

They were alone in their bedroom, one of the few times since Etienne had arrived that he had left them alone. His sensitivity amazed her sometimes, how he knew that she wanted to be alone with Tobias and had graciously made himself scarce. Tobias was not complaining, but then, talking was not particularly on his mind as he bent his lips to her neck.

Beloved, please...this is important.

Tobias stopped, pouting, but only slightly. The pout disappeared when he saw her serious, grave face.

"Why does it bother you so?"

Rain looked away. "You...you do not know Sky's story. This is a very delicate time for him. If he accepts the love, it may do him a great deal of good, but if he becomes frightened and rejects it..."

"I understand. You are afraid he will go mad again, like you told me he used to do."

"Yes..." She looked away, her face pensive. "There is so much hope there, and yet so much room for disaster. You do not know what befell him; or why and how he was given to me, his mind broken into pieces..."

"Then tell me this story. I have wanted to know for a long time why you are so bound to each other," Tobias pressed, holding her hands.

Her gray eyes met his blue ones, soft and loving, and she smiled slightly. "Very well, I..."

The door to the bedroom flew open and Aaron, with all the demons of hell burning in his green eyes, burst into the room. Rain gave a cry of alarm as he fixed his gaze upon her and came rushing at her, his face a mask of terror.

"Help me!" Aaron cried, taking her by the arms as he dropped to his knees.

"Aaron? Aaron, what is it? What ails you?" Tobias demanded, grabbing on to Rain lest the black-haired vampire try to spirit her away.

"You can reach him, can't you? You can find him and tell him I'm sorry!" Aaron babbled to Rain, his eyes brimming with tears.

By now, Dorian and Etienne were peering in the doorway, wondering what was going on. Rain attempted to steady Aaron and make some sense out of what he was saying.

"Who? Reach who?"

"Sky!" Aaron answered, and it was almost a wail, pain filled and pitiful in its high pitched keen.

"What about Sky? What's happened?" Dorian asked, entering the room.

"He's gone," Aaron moaned, the tears starting to roll down his cheeks. "I drove him mad."

"You did no such thing, Aaron, I can assure you," Rain countered, shaking him a little to get his attention. "Now, tell me, what happened!"

"I...We...We were in the park...We stopped in a private little grove of trees and sat down, talking. He was telling me about how he felt for me and I was telling him about how I felt about him."

They were all listening carefully, and when Aaron stopped, they anxiously waited for him to continue.

"Go on, Aaron. What happened then?" Tobias asked.

Aaron looked up at Tobias, trembling slightly. "We started kissing. Then I bit him and he seemed to like it. His blood…it was so sweet…"

"I know the taste," Tobias reminded.

Aaron nodded and went on. "Things got a little out of hand. We were kissing and stroking each other and I let him have a taste of me, and we shared blood. It was incredible. I started moaning and asked him if he'd make love to me like you and Rain make love. He said yes, he could, and he began undressing me. He started talking about how he'd have to be really gentle because I was a virgin and it would be my first time, and about how everyone should have a good first time, and have a patient, tender lover to guide them and show them what feels good. Then, he started talking about his first time and how it was for him. So I asked him who his first lover was…"

Rain gasped, her eyes opening wide. She already knew what Aaron was going to say and dreaded hearing it. Aaron paused in his story telling to cast her a nervous glance.

"He said a name…Waylan…and then went mad."

"How do you mean, Aaron?" Dorian questioned, as Rain hung her head.

Aaron turned his head to see Dorian. "He went berserk. He started screaming. Something about fire and people coming to kill them. I tried to calm him, but I only made him worse. He attacked me, threw me against a tree. I was dazed and when I regained my senses he was gone." He returned his attention to Rain. "You have to find him. You have to tell him I'm sorry…"

Rain looked him directly in the eye. "Aaron, listen to me. This is not your fault. You didn't do anything wrong. If it is anyone's fault, it's mine because I should have warned you beforehand. I was afraid that something like this would happen."

"What did happen?" Aaron asked, a heart-broken edge to his voice.

"It's his memories. He's remembering his past and he can't handle it." She disengaged herself from his and Tobias' grip and stood.

"I have to find him and bring him back, before we lose him altogether. I will be back as soon as I can. I will tell you Sky's story when I return, and all will be explained."

With that, she morphed herself into a hawk, her silk sari falling to the floor in an empty heap as she sailed from the room and out the deck doors.

Once free of the house and high above the eyes of mortals, Rain transformed herself again, this time into a spirit bird, an elemental hawk that could fly across time and space. The world blurred around her as she crossed the threshold between the physical realm and the spirit realm, and she called with all her will through the vast emptiness, calling with Sky's ancient, human name into the void. The endless mist around her stirred and she felt the vibrations of her call echoing through the dimness, to be answered by a faint cry.

SKY! Sky, I am here! I have come for you!

No no...go away. You bring us pain! came the faint answer, shrill, a voice like that of a wounded animal.

Rain called out again, seeking to keep him talking, to strengthen the mental link until she could see him. *You are wrong. I am the healer of your wounds. I am the one to pluck the thorn from your paw.*

Bina? the trembling, timid mindvoice answered, full of torment and sorrow.

Yes, I am here.

No. Go away. We do not want to be found!

You will get lost and will not be able to find your way.

We will find our way. We will not get lost, came her answer.

He was fluctuating between sanity and madness, teetering on the edge, in danger of shifting over and never returning. She had to find him, she had to find him and bring him back. If she did not, she would lose him forever. She had one hope, one thing she was almost certain would bring him back to her.

Sky! Listen to me! Would you leave me? You are supposed to protect me! Ja'oi will come after me now! He will take me!

Ja'oi? Rogue? Killer of lovers and of all things loved?

Yes! He will kill me too, because I will have no one to protect me now that you are gone. He will win!

NO! No, He will not win!

Then come back! Come back to me and protect me from Him!

Coming...

Tell me where you are!

I do not know where I am! I am...I am lost. I cannot see you, Bina!

She searched for him with her spirit eyes, fancying for a moment that she could see him in the fog, a muted glow just below her own glowing wings.

I am here. I am coming for you.

Pain! Bina! It hurts! Make it stop! Bina! Help me!

Sky, where are you!

I can't stop remembering! Bina!

A mental scream pierced her mind, wave upon wave of heartwrenching agony, and she could feel him falling. Panic raced through her and she thought she saw movement, a bird plummeting through the haze. Fixing on it in desperate hope, she folded in her wings and dove.

• • •

The clock had just struck the lonely hour of three when Dorian came to offer a comforting hand. They were waiting, the four of them, in the living room, the fire burning low in the hearth, trying not to hear the dust fall.

"It will be all right, Aaron," Dorian consoled, trying to be supportive.

This latest turn of events wrenched at him. He was slightly happy, hoping that Sky would not come back, and that Aaron would be completely his once again. Then he looked at the heartbroken expression on Aaron's face, and immediately felt guilty. The emotions were still new: this learning to love again, and now Aaron's pain was plainly visible. It was a look that resembled the blank-eyed grief that Dorian had seen on his own face after his child Elizabeth had been murdered. Dorian grew angry. Every time

Aaron started to open up, something happened to make him withdraw again. It infuriated him because he wanted Aaron's passion back too.

"I know," Aaron answered, his voice flat.

"It will work out, Aaron. Rain will find him and bring him back," he added gently.

He sat beside his love and placed an arm around his shoulder. Quietly, Aaron rested his head in the crook of his arm, and let out a long sigh. Then Tobias sat up very straight, listening and scenting the air.

"What is it?" Aaron asked.

"They have returned," Tobias answered, his voice barely a whisper.

Just as Tobias was speaking, a gentle wind came blowing through the open deck doors, and Rain, naked and exhausted, appeared on the landing, the unconscious body of Sky in her arms. They stood up in unison as she entered the room.

"You can put him on my bed," Aaron hastily offered, rushing ahead of her to lead the way.

She followed him, the other vampires in her wake, to the bedroom and placed Sky on the large bed as Aaron held back the blankets. Tobias came up behind her and wrapped her sari around her body while Aaron tucked the bedclothes around Sky's shoulders. The male ecomancer did not stir or rise at Aaron's touch; he remained silent and still, his white hair falling over his face in a haphazard cascade of silken ice.

"Come, we must talk," Rain said in a hollow voice.

She moved to lead the way back to the living room but Aaron seemed reluctant to leave Sky's side.

"He will not wake for some time, Aaron. It is safe to leave him be," she assured, and reached for his arm to gently pull him away.

In the den she sat on the floor by the fireplace, nestled against Tobias and wedged between him and Etienne. Dorian made the fire glow brighter, warming her back and spreading its soft light throughout the room.

"Will he be all right?" Aaron asked.

Rain nodded wearily. "Yes, I think so."

"What happened here tonight?" Dorian questioned.

"You saw Sky's true nature. Forgive me, I failed to warn you."

"What do you mean?" Aaron pressed.

"Sky is not, by any means, sane. He gives the semblance of sanity, the illusion of stability, but do not be fooled. He is unstable and prone to bouts of madness. He controls it only with the now, with his bestial nature. Through the now, he holds onto the threads of his mind."

"The now?" Dorian inquired.

"Yes, the now of animal thought. An animal has no sense of the passage of time. Of course it knows the changing of the seasons and breeding times, but it has no real concept of past and future. It deals in the present, giving no thought to anything beyond the needs of the moment. This is called 'the now.' This is the way Sky prefers to be."

Dorian furrowed his brow in confusion. "Why?"

Rain looked away. "Because in the now, his past remains blocked, and he does not remember how he became one of us," she admitted, then continued, trying to explain. "You see, Sky shares a very special distinction among us, with only one other of our kind being able to claim the same distinction. Sky was chosen directly by the Mother."

"What does that mean? Chosen by the Mother?" Aaron questioned.

"It means he was taken directly by the goddess Herself. Chosen by Aiya," Tobias replied before Rain could answer, his voice full of self-realization. "But the only other who was chosen that way is..."

"Is Aerth. Yes," Rain finished.

"I don't understand," Aaron said.

Rain thought for a moment. "Normally, before one of us is made we are chosen by another ecomancer. That ecomancer becomes a mentor and a teacher to that person. Usually the chosen has some powers already, but most are dormant. The awakening of the powers is a gradual process that culminates when the chosen goes into the ground. It is a very slow and careful evolution from mortal to immortal. For instance, I was chosen by

Aerth. She is the one who taught me and helped me to learn control over my powers. I was four years in preparation before I became what I am now."

Aaron nodded. "I think I understand. It was not this way for Sky?"

Rain shook her head. "No. Sky came into his powers suddenly, abruptly. He lost control of them. We thought we were going to have to destroy him, but Aiya took him into Herself before we could."

Aaron raised an eyebrow. "Why? What happened to him?"

Rain sighed. "There was a peasant couple living in Germany during the 1600's. They had a farm outside a little settlement not far from Cologne. It was a time when those accused of witchcraft were routinely tortured and burned alive. To this couple was born a son destined to be one of us. The child was born with some of his gifts open, one of which was the ability to communicate with animals. He shared his gifts, as naive children are wont to do, with his parents. They...reacted badly."

She paused, letting her words settle upon them before continuing. Already she could see Dorian and Tobias drawing conclusions for themselves about what was to come. "They tried to beat it out of him, then tried exorcism, and any other means of ousting the 'demon' from him. He was all but outcast from the village and his fellows, spending more and more time alone and with the animals he had come to cherish. His gifts continued to develop on their own. He used the natural cunning and ability of the area predators to bring food to his parents in the harsh winters. They refused his gifts, saying the meat was tainted. When he was sixteen, he found a friend in the form of an older man. Waylan was a blacksmith, a kindhearted man who loved animals as much as the boy did, and they struck an unusual friendship."

"Waylan! That was the name Sky uttered before he went mad," Aaron exclaimed.

"Yes. Waylan was Sky's first lover, but I am getting to that."

"A homosexual boy in those times...if he was ever found out..." Dorian murmured, his eyes growing wider by the moment.

Rain met his eyes and nodded gravely. "Over the course of the next few months, the boy discovered that he had sexual desire for other men. It just so happened that Waylan was also so inclined, and they became lovers. It lasted through the winter, one of the few happy times in the boy's life, but come Spring, they were discovered. It was the last straw.

"The villagers rose against them, hunting them down as they tried to escape. Waylan was killed before the boy's very eyes, and the boy himself was captured, tried for witchcraft and heresy, found guilty and ordered executed. On the day of his execution, a mob came to the place where he was being held and demanded that he be released to them. His guards gave him over without protest. He had been tortured horribly, his nails had been ripped out and his hands and feet crushed. The townsfolk forced him to walk to his own death, flaying him with whips and scoring his flesh on the way to the pyre. He called the farm animals to his aid, and they answered, but were beaten back or killed by the angry people. He felt them all die. The pious townsfolk, his own parents included, strapped him to a wooden stake, piling wood high around his naked, bleeding form, and lit the fire.

"Desperate, pushed beyond all sanity, the boy reached into himself to use his gift as he had never used it before. He was hoping to call the forest animals to his aid, the predators, animals too big for the townspeople to fight off, but he touched a much more deadly power instead. He touched the weather magic. The force that answered was too much for his untrained mind to control, and he brought lightning down that set the entire town ablaze. We heard his mindscream even in the Sanctuary and felt the Power being wielded. We arrived on the scene in time to see the ground open up and Aiya take him directly into Herself. When he rose, he was...as he is now."

She paused, catching her breath. The vampires were silent, stunned. Aaron was trembling and held tightly to Dorian's hand.

"No wonder he's unstable," Tobias commented.

Rain agreed. "When he rose, Aiya gave him to me. I do not know why She chose me to be his caretaker, Goddess knows I was young and inexperienced, but...who am I to question the decisions of Aiya? I did as She asked of me. His mind was in pieces. I was the one who put him back

together. I am the closest thing he has to a mentor. Of all of us, I am the
only one he regularly sees and stays with. I am the only one who has come
even close to understanding him. He is unique among us. He is a loner,
preferring non-humans as his companions, disappearing for long periods of
time into the now. He has little love for human mortals, indeed he is the
only one of us who has ever used his powers to purposely kill. Sky is an
enigma to most of us."

"But not to you," Dorian commented.

"No, not to me. I have walked the broken pathways of his mind. I have
seen the terrors that lie behind his eyes. I understand that he will be
centuries in healing, and that what he needs most is to be loved. Which is
why I had such hopes for this union between Aaron and Sky. Never, since
Aiya handed him to me and he opened his sapphire eyes for the first time,
has he ever come this close to taking a lover. I saw the potential for it to do
great good to both of them. I was reluctant to interfere, and as a result, you
were ill advised as to Sky's mental state. For that, I am sorry."

Aaron thought for a moment. "There is no need to apologize. I understand why you stayed silent. I guess now, the question is: where do we go
from here? What can I do to help him?"

"Love him. It's all you can do. The rest is up to him," came Rain's simple reply.

Her head drooped as she felt her weariness, and Tobias stroked her hair
lovingly. Then, gathering her up in his capable arms, he carried her to
their bedroom and laid her gently on the bed. As she curled under the
blankets, both Etienne and Tobias settled in on either side of her, Tobias
pressing her to his chest while Etienne buried his face in her long hair.

I love you, came Tobias' mindvoice.

Love you, too, she answered, snuggling close.

In the meantime, Aaron had gone to his own room and was hovering
over Sky's still body. He was reluctant to touch Sky, but yet he did not want
to leave his side. Instead, he opted for a chair pulled close to the edge of the
bed, and sat in it, his legs curled up to his chest, staying there until the sun

rose and set, dozing in the chair. He broke his vigil only long enough to stalk and take a victim after sundown, and then, only when Rain had agreed to look after Sky while he was gone. Once back, he remained motionless and silent, listening for any change in the slow beating of Sky's heart, or the soft rhythm of his breath.

Finally, Aaron heard a marked pitch in the ecomancer's heartbeat and saw him draw a deeper breath. Sitting on the edge of his chair, he craned his neck to see Sky's face as the cascade of white moved. Two sapphires were revealed by the rising eyelids, a color of blue no human eyes ever possessed, and the dilated pupils seemed to take on merely a darker shade of the same color; Aaron held his breath.

"Sky?"

He heard the ecomancer exhale, almost sigh.

"No. Don't try to talk," Aaron said, putting up a hand.

He was suddenly very nervous and uncertain as to what to do next. Standing abruptly, he paced a little.

"Rain…she brought you back after…what happened. You've been unconscious ever since," he stammered, becoming more nervous and starting to feel the guilt again. He took a step towards the bed. "I wanted to say I'm sorry for hurting you…"

Sky made another sound, a small snort, and it seemed that he would try to rise. Aaron rushed at the bed, his arms out.

"No!" he blurted, his eyes wide. "Don't try to move. Please? I promise…I won't touch you. I'm sorry. I am sorry I hurt you. I did hurt you, and I can't forgive myself for that. I never wanted to hurt you. I only…" Tears rose to the corners of his eyes as he felt the strength of the emotions welling within him. "I love you."

Sky was motionless, watching him with those brilliant blue eyes, his face expressionless and impassive. Aaron stood beside the bed, feeling exposed and dejected, and unable to withstand the scrutiny of those eyes.

"Have you fed yet?" came a ragged voice from the mattress.

Aaron blinked at Sky, stunned. "Y…yes."

"Then come keep me warm. I'm so cold."

Aaron was stunned again, and he looked down at himself with uncertainty, running his hands over his dirty clothes. "I'm...I'm all dirty..."

"Don't care," Sky replied, his voice weak and weary. "Take them off, if you like."

Aaron almost blushed, but he managed a small smile. It was returned, and the sapphires peeking out from underneath the stray tendrils of white hair sparkled at him. Self-consciously he felt his clothes, then began pulling the sweater over his head. It fell to the floor as he worked his way out of his black jeans and shoes, leaving only his socks and undergarments left. Frowning, he peeled off the socks.

"These are all dirty too...I don't tend to watch where I walk."

Aaron saw Sky smile at him again and shift further to the side of the bed a little, making room for Aaron to come share the mattress with him.

"Should I leave the underpants on?" the vampire asked timidly.

"Only if you want to," came the soft, wry reply.

Aaron raised his eyebrows, then, in a moment of daring, he took off the underwear and slipped quickly into bed, covering himself with the blankets and shimmying across until he bumped into Sky.

"Goddess! You *are* cold," Aaron breathed as Sky's skin came into contact with his own.

"Mmm-hmm," Sky murmured, tucking his head under Aaron's chin as the vampire wrapped arms around him. He curled next to Aaron, wedging his arms between his and Aaron's chests, his head nestled in the soft spot of Aaron's throat, and closed his eyes. "Keep away my bad dreams," he whispered, feeling the arms around him tighten, and a hand stroke his hair.

"I'll try."

Sky smiled to himself and cuddled closer, listening to Aaron's steady heartbeat thrumming against his ear as he fell back to sleep.

Aaron felt Sky's body relax and knew the ecomancer had fallen asleep again. He didn't care. Sky was pressed against him in much the same way that Victoria had once done when they shared a bed, and he hadn't felt so needed and wanted since Victoria had left him. Love filled him and his heart nearly burst with it. He nuzzled Sky's snowy hair, murmuring soft words, and vowed to keep Sky warm all night, even if it meant having to kill again if his heat wore off before the dawn.

Standing silently in the doorway of Aaron's bedroom, Dorian saw two figures snuggled under the covers. Peeking out from underneath the satin and lace were parts of two heads. The only way he knew it was two heads was the difference in hair color. One swirled ebony black, while the other gleamed luminescent white, like diamonds on snow. The white head was securely tucked under the other's chin, with the most he could see of the face being a nose winking out from beneath the mop of hair.

Bittersweet sadness filled him as he watched Aaron holding Sky so close. Aaron had never done such a thing with him. Even if he had wanted to, would Dorian have allowed it? Not before all of this had happened, not when he was still the Prodigal Son, and love was on *his* terms only. Before, such a mutually needful embrace would have been unthinkable, an admission of weakness, and the Great Dorian was the epitome of strength. He would never have reduced himself to pressing his face into Aaron's chest, hearing the steady beat of the young vampire's almost human heart, clinging to him with almost mortal need. Never. The very idea of showing such a display of vulnerability would have egged him to fury. But now, after all that had happened, the thought of sinking himself into Aaron's tender embrace filled him with longing. Oh, how could he have been so stubborn and vain! And now it was too late. Aaron's heart belonged to another, once again going to someone who would not seek to possess him, as Dorian always had, but to merely love him for himself.

Dorian sighed, the tears welling in his eyes, and made a vow to himself. 'I will leave this alone. I will do it for Aaron and Sky, and, yes, for myself, in hopes that Aaron will still have love for me. If I try to break this bond, all I will do is destroy the thing I want and love most. No. I've had enough of hurting Aaron and the others I care about. This time, I promise to let things be. If I ever want him to come back to me, I must let Aaron go.' It was the hardest decision he had ever made, but he knew it was necessary. Going to the bed, he lovingly tucked the blankets up around Aaron's shoulders, careful not to wake him.

"I love you, Aaron. Be happy, and in doing so, make me happy," he whispered.

Aaron did not awaken; Dorian did not expect him to. He slowly backed out of the room, and closed the door behind him. Several hours later, Rain peered in to see Aaron and Sky still nestled together. Smiling to herself, she stepped into the room and ran her hand over the soft coverlet. Then she reached down and picked up the pile of soiled clothes. There was mud on the clothing, and it released a light shower of fine dust when disturbed. The dust rose into her face and she sneezed softly.

"Hmm?" came a muffled voice from beneath the covers.

Quickly, she went to the bed and put a restraining hand on Aaron's shoulder as he turned his head to see who was in his room.

"Shhhh. Go back to sleep."

"Mmm? What time is it?" he whispered, trying not to wake Sky.

"It's late, almost five."

Aaron frowned. "I should not have fallen asleep…I promised to keep Sky warm, now all my heat is nearly gone and it is almost dawn." He moved to rise from the bed, but Rain stopped him.

"No. Stay with him."

"I must feed if I want to be warm…"

She offered her wrist. "Then take my blood."

Aaron was shocked. "I could not…"

"Yes you can," she insisted. "I cannot give Sky what he needs, but you can. He needs you right now. He is unstable enough as it is, but if he wakes while you are gone…"

The vampire needed no further explanations. Gingerly, he took her arm in his hand as she sat on the bed, twisting her torso across his side as he raised her wrist to his mouth. His bite was tentative and uncertain, but his thirst soon took over, and he drank from her hungrily. She let him take as much as he wanted, regenerating what she was losing even as he swallowed it, until he was in danger of glutting himself.

"If you do not stop, Aaron, you will get sick," Tobias' voice said sternly.

The voice brought Aaron back to his senses, and he came out of his pleasure-filled haze to look at Tobias, gasping, his lips stained red with Rain's blood.

"Thank you."

Tobias gave him a wry smile. "I know how hard it is to stop. You are so used to it ending on its own."

"Yes," Aaron agreed.

Tobias came to the edge of the bed and took Rain's hand as she stood and pressed next to him, his arm around her shoulders. Aaron watched as they went through their little ritual of touch and counter touch, all silent, small messages of affection and love. Tobias fingered the ornament in her hair as she traced the edge of his ring, all of it quite unconscious, but no less meaningful. Aaron sighed and cast a wistful glance at the white-haired ecomancer curled next to him. Sky had not stirred, and remained cuddled against Aaron's newly warmed body. Aaron lowered his gaze sadly.

"It's almost dawn," he said unhappily. "I don't know if I should stay."

"You used to share a bed with Victoria all the time, Aaron. This is no different," Tobias reminded.

Rain reached out and placed her hand on his shoulder. "Stay with him, Aaron. Stay with him. Be for him, what I could not. Love him."

The look on her face said it all, and he nodded once, gravely, gathering Sky to himself again as Rain tucked the blankets around his shoulders. He stole another glance as Rain and Tobias left the room, and saw her face again as she moved to close the bedroom door. Her expression was one of sublime sorrow and bittersweet joy. Like any teacher, or mentor, or mother, she was finding that sometimes the hardest part of raising a fledgling to fly, was letting go.

Ten

"It itches," Sky bemoaned, wriggling uncomfortably, even before Aaron got the shirt buttoned.

"All right, when we go out tonight, we'll get you some silk. That won't itch, I promise," Aaron assured.

Aaron was attempting to get Sky into clothing. He'd been trying for the past three nights to get him to wear at least something substantial enough for the ecomancer to show himself in public. In four nights they would be leaving for Scotland and Aaron wanted Sky to be presentable. He had managed to get Sky into a pair of tight-fitting, soft, white trousers. They had to be soft, brushed cotton or knit, and fit snugly, so that they felt like a second skin. Sky had refused to wear any undergarments, and shoes were definitely a lost cause, but Aaron was determined to get Sky into a shirt. Unfortunately, he had chosen one if his white polyester shirts, and Sky was finding the material less than satisfactory.

"Are you sure?" Sky asked, squirming again.

"Yes, I'm sure. Now stay still."

There was a muffled giggle from the doorway, and they looked to see Rain peeking her head into the room. Sky did his best to look pitiful, but it only made her giggle more.

Look what he is doing to me, Bina! Sky complained.

It's your own fault. You know that clothes make the vampire.

I know. I know. But it doesn't make it any easier.

Sky hung his head and wrinkled his nose in distaste as Aaron finished buttoning up the shirt.

"You two are mind talking to each other again," Aaron stated.

"Always. It comes natural for us," Sky replied.

"I wish I could do it as well as you do."

"You will in time. I can help...Agh!" Sky yelped in alarm and jerked away as Aaron buttoned the topmost button on the shirt collar.

In a sudden panic, the ecomancer ripped the shirt down the front, panting, his eyes wide with haunted fear. Aaron was shocked speechless, and Rain stepped in to intervene. She placed a steadying hand upon Sky and one on Aaron, calming and reassuring both of them.

"Nothing that makes him feel confined, Aaron. Nothing that makes him feel confined," she reminded gently.

Aaron's face went two shades paler than it already was, and his jaw dropped as he realized what he had just done.

"Forgive me!" he said, genuinely anguished, and went to take Sky into his arms.

"It's okay," Sky whispered, holding Aaron as tightly as Aaron held him.

"No it's not," Aaron contradicted angrily, yanking the rest of the ripped shirt from Sky's body and throwing the pieces to the floor. "I'm asking you to change for me, and that's wrong." He looked at Sky, his face pained. "I'm sorry. Forgive me. I'll never do it again."

Sky was silent, a small, sweet smile on his lips, then he whispered tenderly. "I will wear a shirt for you. But let me choose which one it will be."

Aaron was humbled by Sky's quiet statement and wordlessly agreed, motioning for Sky to choose a garment from Aaron's closet or chest of drawers. As Sky sifted carefully through the shirts, Rain sidled up to Aaron and gave him a warm smile.

"Amazing the effect you are having on him," she said fondly. "Already you have managed to get him to do things I have never been able to. The last time I tried to get him to wear clothes, the most I could get him into was a loincloth. You're civilizing him, you know. You're taming his wild heart."

Aaron returned her smile. "I should hope never to do that. I love his wild heart."

There was the sound of someone clearing his throat and they found Dorian standing in the doorway, holding a bundle of white cloth. He seemed nervous, almost shy as his green eyes fixed on Sky, and he offered the cloth.

"I hope you don't mind...I overheard, and I thought this might do."

Sky accepted the bundle, unfurling it to reveal a loose silk shirt with a deep cut V-neck and billowy sleeves.

"It may be a bit big, I'm a bit wider at the shoulders than you, but it's loose and has a V-neck, so it won't constrict your throat in any way. And it's brushed silk, so it's very soft and smooth," the English vampire explained.

Sky smiled and rubbed his cheek with the silk, feeling its softness. "Yes. This is perfect. Thank you, Dorian."

Still smiling, Sky attempted to put the shirt on. Dorian helped him lift it over his head and pull it into place, then stepped back to let Aaron do the rest.

You're being awfully solicitous this evening, Rain mused to Dorian.

Dorian cast her a wry glance. *Aren't I always?*

No.

The vampire sighed, watching Aaron fuss with the shirt as Sky made faces at him.

You want Sky too, she observed.

Yes. Actually, I want both of them, but it's a lost cause. If I even hint at something like that, Aaron will shut down on me, and if I come between them Aaron will never forgive me. Even now, if I take Sky away from Aaron's attentions for even a moment, Aaron gets upset. I've never seen him this possessive about anything.

Rain nodded. She had noticed that herself. *He's scared, Dorian. He loves Sky. He's afraid Sky will go mad again, plus he is dealing with emotions that have been dormant for so long. He's raw...sensitive...*

I know. I know. And truth be told I love him more than anything. If he wants Sky for himself, I'll back off...for now.

Rain realized what an effort it was for Dorian to make that admission, and her respect for him grew ten-fold. She only hoped that Aaron would realize what his ex-lover was doing, and give it proper acknowledgment.

The shirt was a bit on the baggy side and rather long, but it showed off Sky's well muscled chest beautifully, the V-neck coming down just far enough to give the viewer a tantalizing peek. Aaron began tucking the excess silk into Sky's trousers, smoothing out the lines to avoid unsightly creases and wrinkles, and tried to use the front shirttails as pseudo-under-wear to hide the distinct outlines of Sky's unmentionables. As he pushed the material down to Sky's crotch, he brushed against Sky's organ and was surprised to feel it flush with heat and react to his touch. With a small gasp, he met Sky's sapphire eyes.

"Careful," Sky murmured, his lips curled into a sweet, secret smile.

Aaron stood transfixed, staring into Sky's eyes, and suddenly became aware that the ecomancer was still reacting to him even though he had removed his hand. The blue eyes held him in thrall as they bored into his very soul, and he could smell the scent of musk rising from Sky's body, mixed with the unique perfume of male sexual arousal. It made his heart flutter in his chest like a trapped bird, both excited and frightened.

"Perhaps we shouldn't go out tonight after all," Aaron breathed.

"Perhaps we shouldn't," Sky answered, his voice low and husky.

Rain tapped Dorian on the arm and touched his mind.

Come. Let's leave them to their privacy.

And if I want to watch? came the sly reply.

Not this time. Not the first time. If it even goes that far tonight. Sky intends to be very careful with Aaron. You'll get your chance to watch another time, but for now, let's leave them alone.

All right, but you owe me one.

I've no doubt of that. Maybe I'll sic Etienne on you, then you can experience it first hand.

Dorian snorted derisively. *I'd like to see him try.*

You'd like it.

That remains to be seen.

Rain gave him a knowing smile as she gave him a small push out of the room and shut the door behind her.

• • •

Back in Aaron's bedchamber, the vampire was still staring into Sky's eyes, held as if prisoner by the steady, almost predatory gaze. Licking his lips, he stepped closer, lifting his hands to place his fingertips lightly on Sky's chest, and bent his mouth close to Sky's face, closing his eyes. The thin lips touched his, and he could feel Sky's hot breath upon his skin as the mouth opened and pressed to his. Aaron responded, almost too eagerly, dropping his jaw and giving in to the kiss. He sighed and pressed closer to Sky's warmth, slipping his hands into the V-neck of the shirt to feel the hot skin beneath. Sky continued to kiss him, working mouth against mouth, the tension building until, abruptly, he broke it off.

"We should not do this," Sky choked, gasping for breath. "You aren't ready."

"I am ready," Aaron insisted, stymied. "I told you before that I was ready; that I wanted you."

"That was before all the walls came down. No, you don't know what you are getting yourself into," the ecomancer argued, backing away.

Aaron fumed. "Yes I do. Don't make these choices for me."

"It took me months to get into Waylan's bed. What makes you think you are ready to get into mine after only a few days?" he snapped irritably.

"It hasn't been a few days. I've been entertaining the idea ever since I walked in on Tobias, Etienne and Rain," Aaron countered, equally irritable. "Besides, I am not an eighteen year old boy who doesn't know the first thing about sex at all, let alone gay sex. I am a grown man. I was grown when Victoria made me. I am no stranger to sensual pleasures, and I know what I want."

"Do you? Are you so certain?"

"Yes."

Sky crossed his arms, waiting. "So, tell me. What is it that you want?"

Humiliation burned in Aaron's cheeks, but he knew this was a test, and he refused to fail it. "I want you. I want to love you the way Tobias loves Rain, and I want to be loved, both emotionally and physically, by you. I want you to make me feel the pleasure that had Tobias screaming in that old house."

Sky looked away and sat on the bed, his hands in his lap and his head bowed. "And if it is like it is with humans? Different for each one? If it is not the same for you as it is for Tobias? Then what? Will you still want me?"

Aaron bit back his angry reply as he suddenly realized why Sky was hesitating. Sky was afraid that he would not be able to please him! He was afraid that Aaron would be unhappy with him and then decide to leave! Aaron's heart melted and he went to Sky, sitting next to him on the edge of the bed, and pressing his head against Sky's.

"I love you," he whispered fervently.

"Are you certain?" Sky asked.

"Yes."

Sky rested his head on Aaron's shoulder.

"Do you love me?" Aaron questioned.

"Yes."

"Do you want me?"

"Yes…but…"

"Yes, but what?"

Sky looked at him. "But I've never taken a virgin before."

"Then it will be a first for both of us," he consoled, then whispered urgently, "Let me be your first, and I will let you be mine."

"You really aren't afraid, are you. Not in the least," Sky breathed, a touch of awe in his voice. "I was a nervous wreck."

"I would be a nervous wreck too, if I were a boy at risk of being found out that I was homosexual. But I'm not, and there is no danger here.

There is only love and trust. I love you, Sky, and I trust you." He took Sky's face in his hands and kissed him. "Make love to me."

The ecomancer still paused, but his body gave him away, the bulge in the crotch of the tight trousers growing and stretching the white material. Aaron reached down and stroked the warm mound, caressing it lovingly, almost reverently. Sky groaned and breathed through clenched teeth.

"You are positive that this is what you want?"

"Yes," Aaron answered without hesitation, continuing to run his hand along the bulge that was now elongating, fascinated by the transformation.

Sky placed his hand into the small of Aaron's back and ushered him to stand. Aaron obeyed, and Sky circled behind him, pressing his body against his side. The long, sensitive fingers caressed his cheek and Sky's lips, soft as rose petals kissed the lobe of his ear. He shuddered.

"So beautiful..." Sky's voice whispered huskily. "So virginal...I love you."

He let out a small cry of surprise as Sky swept him up into his arms, and draped him gently onto the center of the bed. He lay on his back, waiting, until Sky straddled his hips, his hands balancing on either side of Aaron's shoulders, and bent down to kiss him.

"Now. The first lesson. No matter what happens, you must not bite me. You must wait until I tell you it's okay to bite. You will want to bite desperately, but you must not. If you bite, it will ruin everything. Understand?" Sky whispered, pulling back.

Aaron looked into Sky's blue eyes, his heart pounding and his mouth suddenly dry. Licking his lips, he nodded. "Yes."

Sky grinned at him and bent to kiss him again. His white hair came cascading into Aaron's face, and the vampire hastily swiped it away as he lifted his mouth to Sky's lips. Breaking off the kiss, Sky sat back on his knees and opened his arms out about half way as he looked intently down at Aaron. Aaron took the hint and began pulling the shirttails out of the white trousers, working the material up Sky's torso and over his head. Sky bent down as Aaron pulled the shirt off, bringing his breast within reach of Aaron's face and, before he could move away, Aaron had taken it into his mouth and was licking and sucking at the nipple. Sky gasped at the sudden pleasure and tried to sit up, but Aaron's hands grabbed his sides and held him firmly where he was, forcing him to stay and have his breasts attended to.

Aaron worked the nipple in his mouth eagerly, nipping and licking until it was erect and hard. Then he switched to the other breast, ignoring Sky's moan, and began giving it the same treatment as he had the other. Sky stiffened and let out a choked cry, his hands gripping Aaron's shoulders tightly, as Aaron ardently laved the nipple with his tongue. The flavor of the ecomancer's skin sparked his blood lust, and he began to suck more insistently on the nipple. Sky's hands entwined themselves in his black hair as his hips lowered. Aaron raised up to meet Sky's pelvis as the ecomancer rubbed the now hard bulge against him.

"Oh, Aaron..."

Aaron released Sky's breast, trembling with blood lust and met Sky's misty gaze. "Do I make you desire me?" he asked, his voice thick.

"You do more than that," Sky replied, his voice breathless. "However I would desire you even more if you were out of those clothes."

Aaron grinned and let Sky go as the ecomancer began to peel off his clothes piece by piece. As he unbuttoned Aaron's shirt, Aaron reached up to hook the waistband of the white trousers Sky wore and lowered them down, revealing Sky's fully erect organ. He gasped, knowing that sometime soon, the entire length of it was going to be inside of him. Sky smiled down at him, then took his hand and placed it upon the organ, allowing him to feel its size and fullness. Aaron touched it with both hands, exploring it with the wonder of a small child while Sky crooned and sighed with pleasure. After a few moments of gentle fondling, Sky guided Aaron's hands away and returned to undressing his vampire lover. When they were both naked, Sky straddled Aaron again, grinning, and bent down to kiss him tenderly. He still had the broad smile on his face when he pulled back.

"Now..." he breathed. "Try that again."

Aaron smiled and placed both hands on Sky's sides as he bent his mouth to Sky's breast. He drew the right nipple into his mouth as Sky's pelvis came down to rub against his own. The organ was hot and throbbing as it slid against his cool skin, making all the hair on his body rise, and he ran his hand along Sky's back, feeling the well proportioned roundness of his buttocks. The blood lust crested but he fought it, and soon he began to feel a heat and tingling that spread throughout his body. He moaned. Then he felt a different sensation, the feeling of something thin and flexible pressing persistently at the muscles of his virgin anal opening. Eyes fluttering open in confusion, he realized that Sky was gently pushing a finger into him. The feeling was odd at first, then pleasurable as his anal ring allowed the first digit of the finger to enter. Closing his eyes again, he relaxed and gave himself over to Sky's tender ministrations.

An hour later, Aaron found himself on his side, pleasure coursing through every part of him, as Sky worked three well-lubricated fingers into his anus. Time had lost all meaning, and the only thing that mattered was the sweet invasion of his body. Ecstasy, combined with the reawakening of his body to sexual pleasure, had him reeling, and he groaned as Sky spread his buttocks apart to add another finger, gripping the sheets, squeezing his eyes shut and crying out.

"When? When will you take me?" he asked, gasping. "Will it be even better than this?"

"Yes. It will be much better than this. Much better," Sky's voice answered, soft and loving.

"How can it be better than this? Do it. Do it, I want to feel how it can be better."

"Not yet, not yet. I don't want to hurt you. I won't mount you until I'm sure you are ready."

"You can't hurt me, Sky."

Lips pressed to his cheek. "I'm not taking any chances. Let me do this my way. Besides, aren't you enjoying this?"

"Enjoying it? Can you keep doing it for a few years?"

Sky laughed softly and shifted positions, spooning his body behind Aaron's as he worked his fingers through the anal ring. Aaron shuddered and moaned as they slid in and out, opening him that much further. He continued to moan as all four fingers thrust lazily into him, slowly, methodically, moving to a rhythm set by instinct millions of years ago. Finally, some long minutes later, Aaron felt Sky shift positions again as the fingers left his body, and he felt the hot organ press against the coolness of his backside. Abruptly, he came out of his reverie.

"No! Want you face to face," he said, craning his head to see Sky.

Sky kissed him sweetly. "Shhhhh. First time is best on the side. Penetration won't be too deep or too shallow. Face to face and ram style are for deep thrusting, perhaps too deep for a virgin. I promise, the second time will be in any position you want. Now, drink while I do this," he explained, and offered Aaron his wrist.

"No."

"It's all right now. You can. You're already hard…"

Aaron shook his head. "No. I don't want blood lust to interfere with what you are going to do. I want to feel you when you mount me."

"Oh, don't worry about that, dearling. You'll feel me. Believe me, you'll feel me."

Sky wedged his knee between Aaron's legs and lifted the top most leg up, as his hand reached down to take the leg and pull it to rest atop his thigh. Shifting his pelvis forward to fit snugly against Aaron's rump, he carefully positioned his heavily lubricated organ at the entrance to Aaron's anal ring. Wrapping an arm around Aaron's hip and applying gentle pressure down, he arched his back and pushed upward, easing the tip of his erection through the sphincter muscle. The ring was still loose and well lubricated from the fingering it had just received, and it offered little resistance as Sky pressed forward, into Aaron.

Aaron let out a tiny cry as Sky mounted him, feeling the organ enter him in stages. First going only so far, then pulling back, then reentering and pulling back again, and continuing until at last, Sky thrust forward and buried his full length inside him. Aaron couldn't move or even breathe as Sky moved his arm to wrap around his trembling chest.

"Does it hurt you? Does it hurt you at all?" the ecomancer asked.

Aaron's eyes were shut tightly closed, and beads of sweat clung to his forehead.

"Aaron?"

Aaron groaned.

Sky became concerned and began to pull out, but was suddenly stopped by Aaron grabbing his hip.

"Not yet. Please?"

"Does it hurt?" Sky asked again.

"No. It's wonderful. Do that… thrusting? Like you did with your fingers."

Sky smiled and leaned his head over to kiss Aaron as he began to thrust slowly. Aaron responded eagerly, moaning and inciting Sky to increase his pace. The vampire's sounds of pleasure were intoxicating; it had been so long since Sky had indulged himself in sensual pleasures. More often than not, his sexual release came in the form of some animal during mating season: functional and brief, and rarely emotionally gratifying. It had been more than two centuries since he had actually had intercourse with another sentient being, and even then, it had been merely sex. It hadn't been anything like this. He thrust forward and Aaron suddenly let out a gasping cry.

"Oh! Yes, do that again!"

Sky obliged, thrusting again in the same manner and position. Again, Aaron tensed and cried out with pleasure. He tried it a third time, with the same results. Aaron was nearly dizzy with delight, and Sky smiled to himself. He had stumbled upon Aaron's sensitive spot, the place on his rectal wall that, when touched in the right way, sent a shock of pleasure through to his prostate, and the prostate then responded with a wave of pleasure of its own. Shifting to strike at a better angle, Sky began to steadily ride Aaron, continually bumping his spot with every thrust, driving him mad with pleasure. Aaron seized Sky's wrist and bit down, adding blood lust to the pleasures he was already feeling. He bucked and strained, tears rolling down his cheeks from the intensity of the feelings. Sky thrust harder, and Aaron timed his sucking with Sky's pace.

Aaron's leg came loose from Sky's thigh and slid to the mattress. It started a forward momentum from Sky's thrusting hips that resulted in Aaron rolling to his stomach. Aaron held on to Sky's wrist, both with his mouth and with his hand as he came to rest on his belly. Sky rolled with him, pulled by the arm that was locked to Aaron's lips, and soon found himself lying atop Aaron in a face down position. Before he could decide what to do, Aaron moaned loudly and spread his legs, arching his pelvis up and forcing the organ inside him to delve even deeper. The new depth made Aaron shake with ecstasy. Sky could feel Aaron's need building and obliged him in the new position, balancing himself on his knees and rocking Aaron against the mattress. Aaron responded with more loud groans and lifted his hips up, offering his body to Sky for even more attentions. Sky increased his pace again, thrusting hard and fast, much harder and faster than he had originally intended to go, but Aaron was wordlessly telling him that he wanted the faster ride.

After a few minutes of the quicker pace, Sky felt Aaron's anal muscles contract and knew that the vampire was close to reaching climax. He fully intended to pull out and switch positions to face-to-face before Aaron reached his pinnacle, but the next thrust brought the second wave, followed quickly by a third, indicating that Aaron was much closer than Sky had thought. Somehow he had miscalculated his vampire lover's sensitivity, and misjudged when he would be ready to climax. Aaron was moving with him now, urging him on with sounds and movement, practically begging for more. Sky tried to pull his wrist away so he could turn Aaron over, but it was too late. Aaron lifted up again, and this time, when Sky's organ pumped into him, his whole body shook violently. His mouth let out a strangled cry that was muffled by Sky's wrist as a powerful contraction clamped down on Sky's manhood, holding it inside him until the majority of the trembling stopped.

Sky was a little stunned that it had happened so fast. As he gathered his wits about him, he felt Aaron relax and release his wrist, allowing him to slide it out from under the vampire's chin. He was watching the two puncture wounds heal when he heard Aaron's satisfied sigh.

"You were right…" the vampire whispered dreamily. "It was much better."

Sky bent down to kiss Aaron's temple, lifting up his hips to carefully disengage himself. Aaron smiled and opened his eyes to look at Sky.

"Thank you," he murmured.

Sky returned the smile and settled down beside his lover. "You're welcome."

"Mmmm. I don't want to move now."

"Then don't."

"Want to clean off all the jelly…"

Sky patted Aaron's rump, making the vampire croon. "Allow me to do that. I have to clean up myself."

Sky reached over to the night table where he had placed a new box of tissues in case it would be needed for the very purpose that he was now reaching for it. He pulled out a wad of soft tissues and began wiping off his softening organ, and then wiped the lubricant from between Aaron's legs. As he spread Aaron's cheeks, he noticed that his anal opening was still loose and flushed a ruddy pink; a most arousing sight indeed, and he nearly responded to its silent invitation, but it was Aaron's careful voice that broke him from his amorous thoughts.

"You didn't climax, did you," the vampire stated flatly.

Sky finished his task and snuggled close to Aaron before answering. "No."

"Why not? Did I not please you?"

Sky laughed softly and kissed Aaron tenderly. "Yes, you pleased me."

"Then why?"

"I didn't need to, and frankly, you surprised me with how fast you came."

"Should I have tried to hold back? To wait for you?"

Sky smiled and nuzzled his lover affectionately. "No, Aaron. You should have done no such thing. With a little practice, we'll get more in tune with each other, but even then, I may not climax every time we make love."

"But…"

"A climax does not constitute the lovemaking, Aaron," Sky tried to explain. "A climax can be just sex, with no loving involved at all. Even though I did not climax tonight, you still gave me more loving than I have had in a very long time."

Aaron dejectedly pressed his face to Sky's chest, and Sky stroked his hair.

"Oh, Aaron. You've got it all wrong. You did please me. I just didn't need to climax. I spend a lot of time in animal form, it's the height of the mating season..."

"So you're telling me you didn't climax because you spend your days as an animal, mating?"

"Yes."

Aaron let out a heartbroken moan.

"I mean, no! I mean....Oh, Goddess, Aaron, stop it. You're confusing me, and you know how I get when I'm confused."

Aaron shivered and looked miserable. Sky was at a loss, until...

"Aaron...I love you. I don't have the words to explain how I feel or what we experienced tonight. All I can do is share my mind with you and let you see for yourself."

Sky placed his hands on either side of Aaron's head and touched his forehead with his own. He felt Aaron grip his arms as he opened his mind and swept Aaron into his memories. He heard Aaron gasp as he witnessed their joining from Sky's perspective, seeing the whole event through Sky's eyes, and feeling what Sky had felt. The whole experience was overwhelming for him and he lost consciousness, but not before Sky felt the rush of pure joy and unadulterated love that came from him in his last moments of awareness.

Sky was still battling confusion after Aaron fell asleep, so he went in search of Rain, and found her reading in the back library, alone. He had seen the others briefly when he glanced into the living room, and they all gave him curious, wry looks as he passed. They knew. He entered the library with a heavy heart and slumped down on the chair opposite Rain, his head in his hands. As always, she stopped what she was doing, folded her hands neatly in her lap and waited for him to speak.

"I just deflowered Aaron," he confessed.

"I know. How do you feel?" came her gentle answer.

"Cold."

"Then go back to bed and cuddle with your lover. I am certain if he wakes and finds himself alone, he will feel much colder."

Sky looked guilty. "You think I was wrong to leave him alone?"

"I think it would have been better if he had been awake when you left the bed."

"You're right. Waylan stayed with me for as long as he could after our first time. He was there when I woke up crying. He comforted me. He was the only one who ever really loved me," he remembered.

"In your previous life, I would agree."

"Oh yes, of course. In my previous life."

Sky grew quiet and pensive for long moments before speaking again.

"I made love to him...exactly the same way Waylan made love to me that first time. I did the same things, I used the same position, I even said the same words."

"And? Was it as fulfilling a first time for him as it was for you?"

"More so. He took the bit from me, had me going harder and faster than I had originally planned."

Rain laughed softly. "Found him to be a bit less timid than the wall-flower he seems to be, eh?"

Sky smiled. "Oh yes. He has the makings of a little harlot."

"Oh ho. Then you've got your work cut out for you. Tobias used to be in the harlot category. Still is actually, only now there's two of us to take care of him," Rain teased with a grin.

Sky flushed. "I should hope that he never gets as bad as Tobias used to be. I've heard the stories."

"Mmm-hmm," she replied, winking.

He smiled then hugged himself shyly. "Did I do the right thing, Bina?"

"In what respect?"

"In taking Aaron. In claiming him."

"Only you can answer that, priye."

He seemed unconvinced.

"Did you hurt him?" she asked.

"No."

"Did you force him?"

"No. He practically threw himself at me."

She smiled, having expected as much. Aaron could be aggressive when he wanted to, if given the right incentives.

"Did you thank him afterwards?"

Sky frowned and shook his head, his white hair catching sparks of light from the fire and throwing them off in rainbow bursts. "No. He thanked me."

"You should have thanked him. He gave you his virginity. It should not go unacknowledged."

"I know," he sighed, cowed under the gentle reprimand. "He didn't give me the chance to thank him. He got upset too quickly."

Rain's eyes widened. "Upset about what?"

"That I didn't climax. He thought he didn't please me."

"Did you explain to him why you didn't?"

"I tried. I finally gave up trying to tell him and just shared my mind with him. I think he understood."

She nodded. "He assumes that you will be like a mortal man and need to climax often. In time he will come to understand that it is not always a necessity."

"I'm hoping, yes."

"He will. I am sure of it. He just needs time, as do you," she assured, putting her hand upon his.

Sky agreed. "Yes, I am sure you are right."

"Go on back to him, little bird. I am sure he will be missing you before too long. He will miss your warmth. That is the one thing that I have discovered with both Tobias and Etienne, warmth is comfort for them. They are so cold most of the time, anything warm pleases them greatly."

Sky creased his brow in concern. "Do you think I can make him happy, Bina?"

"I think you already do, love. He trusted you enough to let you deflower him. That should say a lot about how he feels about you."

"You think so?"

She sighed and gave him a push. "Yes. Now go back to him. Don't make him regret his decision. Go cuddle with him and feel him press close to you. Hold him. Comfort him. Tell him he is beautiful. Love him, and watch him bloom for you."

He smiled and stood. "All right, Bina. I'll do as I'm told," he kidded wryly, and left the room.

Aaron was awake when he returned to the bed, and he immediately felt a pang of guilt. He slipped under the covers and snuggled close, smiling as Aaron responded by pressing his body against his own and wrapping an arm around his lover's side.

"How long have you been awake?" Sky asked, stroking Aaron's hair tenderly.

"Not long. A few minutes. Where did you go?"

"To have a little talk with Rain."

"Oh. I thought you may have gone to the latrine," he said, butting his head up under Sky's chin.

"Latrine?"

"Mmm-hmm. You know, modern day bathroom?"

"Why would I use one of them?"

Aaron lifted his head and blinked at Sky. "You mean, you don't?"

Sky gave him a wry look. "I'm not human, Aaron."

"But you eat food…"

"You drink blood. Do you need to use this…latrine?"

"No, but…"

Sky silenced him with a kiss and for several moments the question was moot.

"I love you," the ecomancer breathed happily when the kiss had ended. "You are just like me: innocent and worldly all at the same time. While I am in this form everything I eat is made into pure energy. There is no waste. When I take the form of an animal, then I become that animal and all its subsequent needs go along with it."

"I understand."

They smiled at each other, then Sky drew Aaron close.

"Rain told me warmth is comfort for you."

Aaron cuddled up. "It is. We cannot regulate our body temperatures…heat eases the chill."

"Yes, you are rather cold."

"The heat of my kill is wearing off. I am warm only after I've fed."

"Then you should feed."

Aaron pressed closer. "No. Would rather stay here and be with you."

"Why not do both?"

"How?…Oh. Oh no. No, I could not."

"Why not? You can't hurt me. Don't you like my taste?"

Aaron's green eyes met Sky's blue ones, turning predatory and intense. "I love your taste," he answered hungrily, his blood lust rising.

"Then drink from me."

"No. You are only for my pleasure…"

"This is only for pleasure. The pleasure of cuddling with two *warm* bodies. Now unless you want me to turn myself into something big and furry, I suggest you warm yourself up, little iceman."

Aaron chuckled and nuzzled Sky's throat. "Well, if you put it that way…"

His tongue slid out and licked Sky's soft skin, hunting out the artery he knew was there. Instinct and scent guided him to the jugular, and he found his mark, biting down and opening his mouth wide to catch the rush of blood that came gushing from the wounds. Aaron moaned as the sweet taste of Sky's blood filled his mouth, sliding down his throat and sending its heat to his limbs.

"Ahhhh, that's better," Sky whispered, feeling Aaron's body start to heat up.

The room was quiet, disturbed only by the soft, sucking sounds of the feeding vampire. Sky cradled his head and rocked him gently, feeling the double wave of pleasure that came from the bite and from Aaron. After several moments, he finally gave Aaron a pat on the rump.

"You'll get sick," he reminded.

Aaron made a small sound, and lifted his mouth away with a sigh. "You're right. Sorry. I'm still not used to having to stop on my own…" He looked at Sky, his eyes misty and soft. "Thank you."

Sky smiled and drew Aaron down to kiss him. "No. Thank *you*. For tonight. For letting me be your first."

Aaron played shy and coy, fingering Sky's nipple timidly. "It was…my pleasure."

Sky grinned and kissed him again. "I'm sure it was. Did I do all right by you? Was it what you wanted?"

Aaron gave him a sly, knowing look. "Well, it was my very first time…" he began innocently, already starting to let his hands wander down Sky's torso.

Sky raised his eyebrows and broke into a broad smile. "Yes…And?…"

"And I won't really know if it was what I wanted…until we do it again," he admitted, batting his eyelashes.

"Ooohh, I see. So the first time was just too much of a shock then," the ecomancer noted, already settling in next to Aaron and caressing his hip.

"Something like that," the vampire answered, running his fingers across the soft fuzz of Sky's pubic hair.

"Well, I can understand that. The first time is always a bit of a shock," he smoothed, his voice turning deep and husky.

"Yes…"

"I mean, with it being so new and all. All the new sensations, feelings, positions…It can be quite a traumatic experience."

"Yes, it can," Aaron agreed, letting one hand fondle Sky's breast while the other brushed against Sky's thigh.

"So, did I traumatize you? Are you in need of therapy? Some…mouth to mouth resuscitation?"

"Shut up and kiss me."

Sky giggled. "And here I thought you were this timid little wall flower."

"Surprise. Surprise."

"A pleasant one, I assure you. A most pleasant one," Sky breathed, lowering his mouth to Aaron's lips.

They kissed, arms entwining, and Sky rolled to cover Aaron with his body. Tentatively, Aaron pushed his tongue into Sky's mouth, and they French kissed passionately as Sky pulled the bottle of lubricant from the drawer of the night stand, and placed it within easy reach on the mattress.

Eleven

Dorian approached the castle with trepidation, remembering the last time he had come to this place. Ian's Keep was as ancient fortress built on a cliff overlooking a loch. Dorian had lived here with Ian and Tobias on and off again for almost two centuries. The castle itself did not have a name, but it was located on Clan MacKenzie ancestral lands. Although Ian did not often speak of his past, he knew that his maker was not a member of that Clan, but of an older, smaller one: the Clan Chisholm. Chisholm's lands were to the south of them, but Ian rarely went there. Something had happened in his maker's past to make him shun his Clan and live among MacKenzies, but Ian had never told them the story.

Ian had owned the castle for nearly six centuries, but lived in it only sporadically. Often in his years with his maker, they would pack up the castle and leave for decades at a time, returning when most of the locals had passed on and moving back in under the pretense of inheriting the structure and lands. In his two hundred and twenty years with his maker and brother, they had returned to the castle three times. They had not been living in the castle when he met and made Elizabeth, and her death had not occurred within its stone walls. If it had, he doubted that anything could have persuaded him to cross the ancient threshold.

As it was Aaron stayed beside him, sticking close, instinctively knowing how hard it was for him to be here again. Ian was waiting for them a few yards from the front of the castle, and he raised a hand in greeting as they crossed the open clearing that lead up to the castle's main gates. Dorian returned the greeting with a wave and a strained smile.

"Are you all right?" Aaron asked quietly.

"Yes," Dorian answered. "I'm fine, but thank you for asking, Aaron. How are you doing? You haven't been away from Sky for any significant amount time in a while."

Aaron smiled. "I'm fine. In spite of what you might think, Sky and I are not attached at the hips."

Dorian snorted, but his eyes danced with mirth. "Shall I do my best Aaron and Sky imitation?"

"No!" Aaron gasped, then laughed and gave Dorian a little shove.

"Oh Aaron, Aaron. I still love you."

Aaron grinned. "I love you too."

They had reached Ian and stopped in front of him.

"Hello again," Ian said.

"Hello," Dorian replied.

"Where are Tobias and Etienne?"

"They will be along in a minute. They were right behind us when Song appeared. They are saying goodnight to Rain. They are having their reckoning tonight," Aaron answered.

"Reckoning?" Ian asked.

"Yes, it's a meeting. Many of the ecomancers will be there tonight, convening and telling the others what they have been doing. That is where Rain, Song and Sky will be until tomorrow night," Dorian answered.

"Oh."

Just then Tobias and Etienne emerged from the forest, walking arm in arm to the house. The others watched as they crossed the grass and came to join them. Ian opened his arms and hugged his firstborn.

"My son," he whispered.

Tobias hugged him back. "Ian."

"How many are already here?" Etienne questioned.

"Of those we know, only Khristopher, John and Alexa have yet to arrive."

"Good," Tobias said. "All I will have to do is touch them and they will be brought back into the Circle."

Ian nodded. He knew Tobias was Aiya's ambassador. Having already been returned to the Circle by the Goddess, he was then able to bring others back into it. Any vampire he touched either mentally or physically would be rejoined to the Circle, and that vampire would then be able to bring others in as well. Ian did not tell Tobias that he had already touched most of the vampires in the castle. He knew that Tobias would want to make sure no one was overlooked.

"Then Victoria is…here?" Aaron asked tentatively.

"Yes. She is here, and waiting for you inside the house," Ian answered. "And there are quite a few new faces as well. We are about thirty-five in all, and the others tell me there are more on the way."

Dorian and Tobias fell silent, looking at the heavy oak door of the castle. Neither seemed to want to be the first to cross the threshold.

'We are at the point of no return,' Tobias thought to himself. 'I promised myself that I'd never come back here…'

"Well, are we going stand out here all night, or are we eventually going to go inside?" Ian inquired wryly, interrupting Tobias' thoughts.

Ian's two sons collected themselves and Dorian lightly grasped his elder brother's elbow.

"We are coming in now," he said guiding Tobias gently through the wide doorway with Aaron directly behind, following Ian into the vast, sprawling castle with its stone walls and old memories.

• • •

After the initial excitement of seeing familiar faces and trading tales, Aaron grew pensive and restless. Silently, he removed himself from the main meeting room and went wandering through the house. He remembered that Ian had kept a very impressive library, and after a few wrong turns, he finally found it. The library had two rooms: a room in which the books were stored away from direct sunlight, and a reading room with a large window that looked out over the loch. Wistfully, he found himself staring out over the dark water, wondering what Sky was doing, and if he was enjoying himself. Sky rarely spoke of the other ecomancers, Rain being the only one he would really talk about, and Aaron speculated that Sky was something of a black sheep among his own kind, very much like Aaron himself was among the vampires.

He sighed. It was a beautiful night. It was the kind of night he would have enjoyed spending with Sky. Perhaps Sky would have taken him high above the clouds, or maybe they would have walked to a secluded place in the forest and talked, maybe made love. They could have done any number of things, all of which Aaron would have found more pleasant than listening to the idle chatter of his own kind.

His thoughts were disturbed by the door opening and Tobias slipping in. The older vampire shut the heavy wooden door firmly behind him and leaned against it, his head bowed.

"Toby?" he ventured carefully.

The brown-haired vampire raised his head in surprise but relaxed when he saw who was in the room.

"Oh, it's just you Aaron."

"Are you all right?"

Tobias nodded, swallowing. "It is...very hard to be in this house again. There are so many memories. I needed to slip away for a few moments."

Aaron frowned and looked at him with sympathy. "I know what you mean. It's hard to see Victoria."

"Yes, and you are missing your love."

"Yes, very much."

The blue-eyed vampire came forward to look out of the window.

"Do you know where they are?" Aaron questioned coming to stand beside him.

"Yes. There is a grove of ancient trees with a small clearing in the center. They are there. There is a fire and a pillar of white stone in the middle."

"You have been there before?"

"No. It was an old pagan gathering place. I never ventured anywhere near there while I lived here. I see these things through Rain's eyes."

"Oh," Aaron said, and bowed his head. "Sky and I don't have much mindspeech. I'm not very strong in that respect. We meld when we make love, and he can share his mind with me, but it doesn't come easily."

"No. I did not think that it would. But the fact that you have Sky at all is somewhat of a small miracle."

Aaron blinked in confusion. "How so? Because of what happened to him?"

"Yes. It has them shocked, you know. The others. Rain said Song was quite surprised."

"She said I am his first since he..."

"You are. You are also the reason he has stayed in human form for more consecutive nights than he ever has since he learned to shape change. He must love you very much."

Aaron nodded. "I wish I was with him. I always worry. Our relationship is so new..."

Tobias placed his hand on Aaron's shoulder. "Have faith. He will be here tomorrow night. I do echo your sentiments though. I would rather be with Rain and Etienne than here as well."

Aaron sat down in a chair that faced the window and Tobias took the chair next to him, and they gazed out over the trees.

"I wonder what they are doing," Aaron mused.

"Rain told me the Reckoning is a time when all the ecomancers congregate to tell Song their tales. He records the histories."

"I would love to see his library. I can guess that he has thousands of books."

Tobias looked at Aaron with bemusement. "He has no library so to speak. All the histories are stored within the Memory Stones. Each Stone can hold a thousand years of history. When touched and asked what tale to tell, it will replay the story for the one who asked," he explained. "Of course, Song remembers most of it in his head naturally. He creates songs about the more exciting things."

Aaron grew pensive. "One night Sky took Dorian and I out to the heartstone and had us touch it. It was the first time I had ever touched a *living* stone. Dorian saw much more than I...he described seeing memories from the time of the dinosaurs. I saw bits and pieces of images, brief flashes of whatever memory I happened to touch."

"Stones have the longest memory of all. If you had stayed long enough, you would have seen images spanning the stone's entire lifetime. I wonder what stories these walls would tell," he commented, looking sadly around the library.

Aaron looked at the walls too, and made a small noise of agreement. Like all the rooms in the castle, the library was made of solid gray stone in hewn blocks with heavy wooden supports for the ceiling.

"I spent many years within the walls of this house." Tobias broke off and looked at his hands, then sighed and gazed out the window. "I wish Rain were here. I could use her counsel now."

"Why?"

"For some of the others. They are...skeptical and argumentative. Not that I expected them to be anything less where religion and gods are concerned, but still...Rain would do better to convince them than I."

"How do you think they will react to Song and the others?"

"I am not certain. I know that, of the vampires that were found, only those willing to believe came here."

The door opened again and Dorian slipped in, looking much the same way as Tobias had looked.

"You too, Ri-Ri?" Tobias asked gently.

Dorian gave a shuddering sigh and nodded. "In the past hour I have been forcefully reminded of every reason why I hate this house."

"I know exactly what you mean."

"Gods, Toby how did we ever live here?"

"Simple, we were so busy trying to maim and kill each other that we didn't notice what an oppressive place this was."

"Freezing too," Aaron added. "I don't know how you stand it."

Dorian looked up at the sound of Aaron's voice, as if hearing him for the first time.

"Oh, you're here too? What are you doing sulking here in the library?"

Aaron shrugged. "Same as you. I'm hiding from my past."

"I think I will go immerse myself back into the melee," Tobias said, bowing slightly to Dorian and Aaron. "If all of us are missing, someone is bound to come looking for us, and, forgive me for saying so Ri-Ri, but you look like you need the respite more than I. Besides, I am the Ambassador. It would not be good for me to neglect my duties. I'll see you later or tomorrow night."

With that, he walked out. Both Dorian and Aaron watched him go.

"Did you send him away?" Aaron asked, once the door had closed.

"Hmm? No. But I think he sensed that I wanted to be alone with you," Dorian answered, sitting down on the chair where Tobias had just been. "But you'd rather be with Sky, wouldn't you."

"Yes," Aaron replied simply, then saw Dorian's expression of sorrow. "You asked. Would you rather I have lied?"

"No...I would not have wanted to you lie."

Dorian struggled with his emotions. Vampires were, by nature, proud and jealous creatures, always seeking to seize dominance over each other. His first reaction was to lash out with anger, to hurt and wound Aaron so he would not know how much he was hurting himself, but he fought the urge and made the cruel words on his tongue die out. If there was one thing the centuries had taught him, it was that nothing in life was certain and that no one should be taken for granted. Love was meant to be expressed, and there was no time, not even for an immortal, for petty quarrels. Taking a deep breath, he spoke from his heart.

"I know you love him, and I would never begrudge you that love, but there was a time when I was good enough for you, when my voice and my presence were enough to make you happy. But it isn't that way anymore. I'm not enough for you anymore, and I am missing that," he said quietly.

"I know. You have been feeling left out."

"No. Not left out. More like I am wishing you still loved me like you used to."

Aaron's eyes turned soft with sympathy, and he reached across the chair to take Dorian's hand. "I *do* love you, Dorian."

Dorian met Aaron's eyes. "Do you? Do you still love me?"

"Yes."

Aaron stood up and motioned for Dorian to move over. "Here, make room for me and we'll share the chair."

Dorian regarded him with surprise, then did as Aaron asked and took Aaron into his arms when Aaron settled in beside him. They were a bit cramped, but it was wonderful to feel Aaron's body against his once again, and he was filled with simple joy as Aaron rested his head on his shoulder.

"I love you, Dorian."

"I love you too, Aaron."

"I know my relationship with Sky can't be easy for you…"

"It isn't, but I'm dealing with it," Dorian admitted.

"Thank you. Thank you for not being… how do they say in these times? A jealous pain in the ass?" He smiled, looking fondly at Dorian, his eyes sparkling with quiet humor, then gave his hand a light squeeze. "Give it time. I think that we may have room for another in our relationship once it settles, if that is what you want."

"I don't know what I want. It was easier when I was a selfish demon. Now that I have a so-called conscience, things are so much more compli-cated. As for my being a pain in the ass…well, Etienne says number one: if it hurts you're doing it wrong, and number two: anyone can do it. So…theoretically…" Dorian smoothed with a wry grin.

"Theoretically you *could* be something much more than a…" He paused, then broke into a mischievous grin. "…pain in my ass," he finished, nudging Dorian in the ribs playfully.

"Hey, *you* said it, you little harlot, *I* didn't," Dorian grinned, nudging back.

Aaron snickered, then leaned his face close to Dorian's and kissed him sweetly. Dorian was rather shocked at first, then gave into the kiss, sighing as he did so. They worked mouth against mouth, letting their tongues wrestle and explore each other, and Dorian let out a little moan as they began to pet each other ardently.

"I love you, Dorian," Aaron said again as he broke the kiss.

"Aaron…"

"I will always love you."

"I will always love you," Dorian repeated, breathless, his heart pounding.

Eyes closed, he let his head droop down to come to rest on Aaron's chest, reveling in the feel of him, the steady thrum of his heart. Suddenly, vulnerability and weakness seemed to be very paltry things in the face of such wonderful peace and tenderness.

"We'll just stay here and watch the stars," Aaron whispered lovingly, stroking the English vampire's raven tresses.

"Yes."

At that moment, Dorian could not imagine another place he would rather be.

Twelve

On the other side of the loch, in the grove of ancient trees, the ecomancers gathered where the bright fire burned. As Tobias had seen, there was a stone pillar near the fire, about four feet high, made of white marble with thin veins of green interspersed throughout it. About eight of the ecomancers were there when Rain and Sky arrived. Song had met them on the outskirts of the Circle and escorted them into the clearing.

Song's ecomancer partner, Leaves, watched as Song entered the circle. She wasn't certain if she should go to him or stay where she was. She was supposed to be Song's accomplice, but she was still unclear as to what that entailed. She had been sent to help Song when it was discovered that Ja'oi would not attack pairs of them, but she was the youngest of them all, having only been made that century, and her inexperience made her nervous.

You're doing fine, little sister, came a voice in her head.

Startled, she turned to see who it was, and her heart leapt in her chest. It was Wind, standing just as she remembered him, dressed in the ancestral clothing of his tribe. Embarrassed at having been surprised, she blushed and looked down at her lap, fingering her simple shift dress absently. Seeing Wind always brought back waves of memories, memories of how she became what she was, and why.

Leaves had been a Jewish girl living in Poland when Hitler rose to power; her family had been arrested by the Nazis and split apart. She was taken to the concentration camp at Treblinka, never to see any member of her family again. She was supposed to have died in the gas chambers, but Wind had come for her, in the form of a white dog. He appeared on the edge of the forest one morning when the guards took them out for exercise. She had met the dog's eyes and knew immediately that it was no ordinary animal. That night, as they lay huddled in their miserable masses, the girl knew something was about to happen. Her fingers tingled as they had been tingling lately, and she could feel energy pulsing through them.

As a child, she had discovered that she had some small control over the land, that if she concentrated hard enough and long enough, she could make her father's gardens grow. She had kept her talent a secret, afraid to believe it was true, but recently it had been growing and getting more powerful. In the camp, she had entertained ideas of willing the ground to open up, to make a tunnel that would take them to safety. As she waited, her heart pounding, she heard a scraping coming from a corner behind her. Crawling to it, she watched as the ground loosened and broke, opening up until the white dog came wriggling out of the hole that it had just dug under the wall of the compound. The dog licked her face eagerly and pulled on her tattered clothes as if telling her to follow, and began to dig more at the ground. She obeyed and soon attracted the attention of some other prisoners. She explained that the dog had made a tunnel under the wall and that they could all escape if they could make the hole big enough for them to crawl through. Some thought she was crazy, others were willing to give it a try, and soon there were six of them digging next to the dog. Then the girl raised her eyes and met the gaze of the dog, and was suddenly held by the dark, almost black eyes as a voice in her head rang clear:

If you call, the earth will obey you.

She had been shocked, but somehow she knew it was the dog that had spoken to her. *What should I ask?*

What do you want?

I want a tunnel that will take us far far away from here.

Then that is what you should ask.

How?

Ask, and it will obey.

So she had reached into herself as she had done with her father's plants and tried to envision a great passageway that lead far into the distance. A moment later there were excited sounds from the other prisoners. The ground was giving way and falling in huge clumps into an empty space. Soon there was a large hole, leading down into blackness. Someone took a tiny handmade lamp and went down to investigate. He came back a few minutes later to say that they had revealed a subterranean cavern beneath them and a passageway that led under the camp. There was light further up the tunnel; they had found a way out.

As the girl watched, dazed and amazed at what she had done, the others gathered up the prisoners and began ushering them into the tunnel. The dog sat down beside her as hopeful refugees scrambled together what few possessions they still had, and headed into the hole single file. She and the dog were the last to slide down the small incline, and the dog stood in front of her when she tried to follow the others. It gave her another hard stare, and she felt herself grow cold all over.

Now, make it close or the guards will follow.

Swallowing hard, she did as she was told, concentrating and envisioning the hole getting smaller and smaller until it no longer existed. When she opened her eyes to see her work, she saw the earth above her flowing like water, swirling until it met the opposite sides of the hole, sealing it shut. She watched for a few more moments to see if anything else would happen, then turned to look at the dog, but found it no longer there. In its place stood a naked man, an American Indian with long, braided black hair and the dark, almost black eyes the dog had possessed. Somehow she had not been terribly surprised to see him.

"Who are you?" she had said.

"I am Wind, and I have come for you," he had answered.

She looked at the cavern around her and now saw that there were two tunnels: one that the refugees had gone down, glowing warmly yellow, and another that led the other way, darker and glowing faintly green. She had been a little afraid of that tunnel.

"My people…" she began, taking a step for the yellow passageway.

"They have already forgotten you."

She had been angry at his simple words, but somehow she knew them to be true. To the people she had just saved, she no longer existed.

She stared for long moments looking at each tunnel and Wind had stayed silent, watching her, waiting for her to make the decision. Finally, tears in her eyes, she had turned and followed him down the green passage. Later she would learn that the yellow tunnel had led the starving, frightened refugees to the Holy Land: thousands of miles away from Poland and the Nazi regime.

The memory of how they arrived in Jerusalem had been erased, and replaced with a memory of them running from the Nazis and securing passage on a ship that had brought them to their new home. They praised Yahweh for bringing them safely to their destination, never to know that it was not their god who had answered their prayers, but an ancient goddess who had granted the last wish of a poor Jewish girl.

Leaves came out of her memories abruptly, as there was a bit of excitement in the circle. Fire came up to her hurriedly and placed a hand on her shoulder.

"Have you heard the news?" Fire asked.

"What news?"

"Sky has taken a lover."

"He has?"

Leaves did not know Sky very well, but she did know the stories about him. She had no idea what significance his taking a lover was, but it certainly had the others in a buzz; even Wind seemed to be brooding over this new bit of information.

"He has chosen from the vampires. His first since he was made. Song is making him tell him all about it, but he may make a Reckoning tonight and tell us."

"A Reckoning?"

"Yes," Fire confirmed exuberantly. "That will also be a first."

Leaves knew Sky had never made a Reckoning, although why he hadn't, she didn't really understand. It had something to do with his past, something the others did not like to discuss. She knew that he was different from the other ecomancers and that he had been chosen directly by Aiya Herself, but the exact reasons why and how it had happened, still remained a mystery to her.

The Reckoning was something each of them did at every formal meeting. At the beginning, one by one they would go to the Memory Stone, place a hand upon it and state who they were and who had chosen them. Once that was finished, they would then tell the others what they had been doing and what had been accomplished. It was all very simple. Sky should have done one centuries ago.

Song was listening with that intent, impassive look on his face that he always had when he was hearing a new tale, and it was making Sky uncomfortable. Rain could sense it as well, she had already moved closer to him and was allowing the edge of her sari to brush against his leg reassuringly.

"This should be shared with the others. You should make a Reckoning tonight and tell them," Song said quietly when he was finished.

Shivers ran up Sky's spine and he gritted his teeth. As always, Rain came to his defense.

"Do you think that is wise Song? You know the reasons behind Sky's silence," she said aloud, and mind sent to the historian, *And I will also not allow anyone or anything to interfere with this relationship. That includes our brethren, who are sometimes too nosy for their own good.*

"If Sky thinks he is ready, yes, I think it is wise. It's been three hundred years, Rain, and he has never touched the Memory Stone."

"Aiya has never told him that he must. She has not ordered him to make a Reckoning. He is Her chosen; who are we to question Her motives?" came Rain's rebuttal.

Sky knew she wasn't arguing for the sake of not questioning Aiya. He knew she was protecting him again, as she had always done. The Reckoning required he know who he had been in his previous life, something that would have sent him, screaming, into insanity only a few weeks ago, but now… now he had Aaron, and Aaron held him by his heart, keeping him sane and grounded.

Their long nights in bed together had not been seamless successions of sensual pleasures. They had talked for hours as they lay in each other's arms, sharing their lives and memories with each other. Aaron, merely by virtue of being loving and patient, was helping him to explore the uncharted areas of his mind to find what lay there, waiting to be rediscovered. Sometimes they would reawaken old nightmares, and he would cry and begin to shake, but always, Aaron was there, holding onto him, willing Sky to stay with him, to hold onto his clarity of thought. The moment would pass, he would calm, and Aaron would nuzzle him affectionately. They would kiss, Aaron soothing his lover's fears in the best way he knew how. It was helping him greatly, and he no longer feared his past. The Reckoning no longer seemed such a terrifying thing, but he still hesitated. Aaron did not know Sky's name. Rain knew it, although he had never told her. He had never told anyone. His name, like most of his past, had been buried deep inside him. He knew it now, and it no longer frightened him. He could make the Reckoning easily, but he did not want to, not before he had spoken to Aaron, not before he had told Aaron his name. Aaron deserved to be the first.

"Rain…" Sky began, commanding her attention. "It's all right."

She stopped and looked at him quizzically. He continued, speaking mostly to Song.

"I will make a Reckoning, but not tonight. There are things I would have my lover know first. Out of respect for him, I will refrain from telling others what he has not had the opportunity to know beforehand."

Song gave him a measured gaze and nodded. "As you wish."

With that Sky slowly walked away, retreating to the edge of the trees, away from the fire, even though he was naked and the night was cold.

Rain followed him as he sat down on the perimeter of the grove, and lowered herself to the grass beside him.

"You are missing Aaron," she stated calmly.

"Yes," he answered, bringing his knees up to his chest.

She placed her hand upon his shoulder and touched her head to his. He responded by pressing back with his head and sighing.

Bina…

She answered with his name: the name he had never told her, but that he had heard her use. There was a kind of intense intimacy associated with knowing an ecomancer's mortal name; it implied a bond that transcended everything; love, life, the Balance. He used her name freely, but she only used his on rare occasions. When she said it, it was like she was pulling the strings of his soul.

For three hundred years she had been his sole sentient companion, and he still remembered the day he had opened his eyes and saw her for the first time. Those early decades were hazy, littered with periods of nothingness and untamed rage. Rain had stood beside him when he exacted his vengeance upon the mortal world, pulling him away before he could do any permanent damage the Balance. Budding ecomancers had been destroyed for much lesser transgressions, but still Aiya willed that he live, and that Rain be his teacher. He had never understood why. An untrained ecomancer with his powers at full force was extremely dangerous, and time and time again he had proven that to be so. Even when all the others branded him a rogue and would have nothing to do with him, Rain stayed. She calmed his madness and dried his tears, and helped him through the long, arduous process of controlling his incredible powers. Then when the time came, she gave him willingly over to another who could help him finish what she had begun.

I love you, Bina, he told her suddenly.

I love you too, Sky, she answered without reservation.

I know it's been a long time since I've said it.

Only a couple of months, but I know you love me, even if you aren't saying it.

What a strange pair we make, he mused thoughtfully.

Always have.

Yes. And you are right, I am missing Aaron.

Do you want to go back to the house and be with him? I can tell the tale for both of us.

Sky made a small negative sound. *No. He is with his own kind tonight...* He laughed softly. *Strange. Not four months ago I was telling you Tobias was not our kind.*

Rain chuckled. *I know. Eating your words now?*

I guess I am.

Their focus was drawn to the center of the circle where Aerth now stood, her hand on the Memory Stone. She commanded their attention with her very presence, and Rain noticed that all of the others, except for Seed and Stone, had arrived while she and Sky were talking with Song. She presumed that Seed and Stone were with Placide in Rwanda. He must not yet be able to be left alone.

The oldest ecomancer was opening the meeting, beginning it with her Reckoning, and following it up with an ancient song. The avatars of Aiya did not sing much, nor were their songs praises to their goddess. Rather their hymns were accolades to Balance and life and the Great Web. One by one they joined in the song, their voices rising high over the trees, and the earth responded to them. The trees outstretched their limbs as the wind blew through the circle. Aerth stood with her arms out, her voice ringing clear above the wind as it swirled around her and the fire began glowing an unearthly white. As they sang, the power in the clearing grew until it exploded in a great burst, and the fire flared high into the sky, showering them with tiny sparkles of light, and in that rain of falling stars, they saw the goddess' face. The wind and burning embers raced around the circle, touching each of them in turn, until they were all faintly glowing.

"We are the Children of the Mother. We are Her Emissaries and Avatars. We uphold Her Laws, we support Her Balance, we keep Her Web. We meet here tonight to make our Reckoning, to lend our voices and tales to the historian. Who shall follow me?" Aerth said when the song and wind had quieted.

Song stood and entered the circle. Aerth gave way to him and stepped aside as he placed his hand upon the Memory Stone. "I am Song, Son of Aiya, Chosen by Aerth. I am the historian, the keeper of events and lives..."

Just then, there was a commotion in the forest and a woman, dressed in a plain black dress, came bolting into the circle to throw herself at Aerth's feet. She had moved too fast for a mortal, and in the light of the fire, they could see that the skin on her arms and hands was parchment white.

"She is a vampire," Rain breathed to Sky as they both rose to their feet. Instinctively, she looked for Tobias, and she could sense that Sky was doing the same for Aaron, but neither of their lovers were there.

The others were rising too, staring in shock at the weeping woman who had prostrated herself before Aerth. Aerth knelt down and stroked the woman's red hair.

"Rise. A goddess, I am not."

The vampire woman raised her head, revealing the tears that ran down her face. "I know you! I have seen your likeness in the temples. You are Diana."

As she said this, another vampire, this one a man, appeared on the edge of the circle, nearby Rain and Sky. He had blond hair, and an angled face, and his dark eyes were filled with fear. He was projecting his thoughts clearly. He was John, she was Alexa. He was afraid for Alexa and for himself, and his thoughts were turning dangerously violent. Rain knew she would have to act quickly if they were to avoid an unpleasant incident.

"Peace, John," she said, making him start and stare at her like a trapped deer. "No one will harm you here. Your kind are welcome in our circle."

He still regarded her with fear and she sent him a rush of calm reassurance, holding her hands open in a gesture of peace. Slowly, he calmed, the violence in his thoughts fading, but he was still confused and nervous. She waited patiently as he approached her.

"Is she Diana?" the vampire asked.

"No."

His eyes narrowed in sudden suspicion. "How did you know my name?"

"We are telepaths like yourself," Rain answered.

John blanched. He hadn't been guarding his thoughts; he had not thought it necessary. Apologetically, he moved to explain himself. "We heard voices and saw the light..."

"You were on your way to Ian's house," Rain stated.

"Yes. How did you know?"

Rain touched the dangle in her hair, drawing his attention to it. His eyes were already registering the color of the hair entwined in it, when she spoke again. "The vampire Tobias is my bonded."

"You are the avatar. The one who brought Tobias back from the dead," he breathed, a touch of awe in his voice.

"He wasn't dead, merely very close to death."

"Why has your companion thrown herself at Aerth's feet?" Sky inquired, breaking his curious silence.

John looked at him, his dark eyes traveling up and down Sky's naked body warily. "She believes that your friend is the Goddess Diana."

Rain turned her attention to Aerth and Alexa. Aerth had gotten the vampire to rise from her prostrated position, but she was still on her knees. Slowly, the others were gathering around them. Rain motioned to Sky and John. "Come."

Quietly, she made her way to the center of the circle where Aerth was calmly speaking to Alexa. As they were approaching, she saw Aerth place her hand upon Alexa's forehead and close her eyes. The others made way as she guided John to Aerth and waited for her to open her eyes.

"This is John. He is companion to the vampire Alexa," Rain said when Aerth looked at her.

"We did not mean to disturb your meeting. We were on our way to Ian's castle when Alexa saw your fire, and we came to investigate..."

The oldest ecomancer lifted her gaze to John and spoke gently, "You are welcome here."

Alexa was motionless with her head bowed as if in prayer, and John eyed her nervously. "What is wrong with her?"

"She is in need of healing. Her heart and soul are weary and worn," Aerth answered stroking Alexa's hair gently. "We can help her."

"You can help her?"

"Yes," she replied, nodding, and giving Alexa's red hair another few strokes. Then she turned to extend her arm to another ecomancer who was nearby. "Sun, my sister, you are adept in healing of this sort. Will you accept this task?"

Sun, radiant and practically glowing golden, stepped forward. "Yes, I will."

Aerth lifted Alexa's chin, and the vampire raised her head. "I give you my sister Sun. Go with her, and let your heart be eased and comforted."

Alexa stood and faced Sun.

"Be at ease, my friend. Your long journey is over," Sun soothed, reaching out to touch the woman vampire. "Come with me, and allow yourself to put aside your pain."

Sun put a comforting arm around her new charge and gently led her away. John became distressed as the others closed in around them, obscuring her from his view.

"What are you doing? Where are you taking her?" he demanded.

"Peace, brother. There is no need to be afraid. Sun knows what she is doing. By tomorrow night, Alexa will be whole again," Aerth told him firmly. "Come, join our circle and be part of us. Tomorrow you will herald our arrival at the castle above the loch."

Thirteen

Tobias surveyed the Great Room of the castle. It was a massive place with high ceilings and thick stone walls. Tapestries hung along the sides affording some measure of meager warmth against the cold that permeated the place. Nobles had once held court in this room, and banquets and parties had graced the solid, wooden floor. Now it was home to their own gathering of the Clan.

There were close to fifty of them now, all milling about. Of those, Tobias knew about twelve, Dorian, Aaron, Ian, Etienne, Barias and Victoria included. He did not see Khristopher or Leith, the vampire who had attacked him in Ecuador. He was profoundly relieved and happy to know that the vampire responsible for his brush with death had not chosen to show his face. Not that he was in any danger from the old vampire. Ian would turn anyone who threatened his sons into ashes before the attacker could draw another breath.

Looking around, he was surprised to see so many vampires of African and Indian descent. A good third of the vampires he did not know sported dark skin and hair, and some wore the clothing associated with their mortal race. All of them felt very old, much older than the European and American vampires that gathered in the room, and they kept to themselves in a corner, watching their brethren with both wary and curious eyes. He wondered about them, and thought about going over to introduce himself, he was the

Ambassador after all and they needed to be brought back into the Circle. Ian, however, stepped beside him before he could move toward them.

"Leave them be. They aren't quite comfortable here yet. I had a hard enough time convincing them to come. When they are ready to socialize, they will," his maker said. "Besides, I've already touched them for you."

"You know them?"

"Not all of them, but some. Arun and Inesh are from Delhi. I knew them before I made you. Usha is the woman with them," Ian explained, referring to a diminutive vampire with long black hair, standing beside two male Indian vampires. "I've never met her, but she's one of the oldest of our kind."

"Older than Barias?"

Ian nodded. "Yes. If there is anyone here who knows about Aurek, it's Usha. I'm very glad to see her. Inesh wasn't sure if he could convince her to come."

"I never knew there were so many from the East…"

"They're older and they keep to themselves, so you don't see or hear much of them. They stopped creating new fledglings about six centuries ago because of overpopulation and deforestation. The African covens have suffered greatly because of it. Remember that Ethiopia was once a forest."

Tobias indicated that he knew, then let his eye be drawn to a tall vampire with very short cropped, dark blond hair standing on the outskirts of the room, as if surveying over it.

"Who is that?"

"That is James. He was a British soldier stationed in India when he was brought over. Very militaristic, he likes to guard over things. He has a temper too, but it's a slow burn. Keep Etienne away from him."

"I will."

Tobias turned away and moved to join Etienne who was moderating a lively conversation between Aaron and Victoria. He frowned. He'd never been especially fond of Victoria, but she had made Aaron, and Aaron made Dorian happy. For that reason alone, he tolerated the French vampire's strong-willed and argumentative personality. She had completely cowed Aaron for years, and the young vampire was still partially under her thumb, as was evidenced by his haunted green eyes and somber expression. Seeing his maker again had to be difficult for the Amer-Asian, and he decided that perhaps he could effect a suitable rescue.

Eti? he sent.

Yeah? came his fledgling's flustered mindvoice.

Find Dorian. I'll help with this.

His child's relief was palpable. *Thank you.*

He watched Etienne as he disappeared into the crowd, then took a deep breath and plunged into the fray.

"Why should I believe anything that you say?" Victoria was saying angrily, her brown eyes blazing. "We are not the children of any god, we are their toys. This I have always known."

"Because I have seen Aiya. I have been in Her embrace," Tobias countered, moving smoothly between the woman and Aaron.

"Some claim to have seen the Virgin. Does this mean we should all bow down on our knees and subjugate ourselves?" she sneered.

"Aiya asks for no subjugation," Tobias replied coolly. "She asks only that we maintain the Balance."

"And what if I care nothing for this Balance. What if I choose not to serve this Balance?" Victoria snapped.

"Every time you kill, you serve Her," Aaron answered simply.

Victoria fumed at him and he sighed heavily. He did not want to be arguing. He and Victoria had been having the same fight since sundown, and neither was any closer to seeing the other's point of view. Damn the vampires and their stubborn pride. Aaron wanted to be away from them. He did not want to be in this room full of all the vampires he had ever known, and quite a few that he did not. He wanted to be with Sky. His heart was heavy with longing for him, and he had not realized how much he missed him until he had awakened in their subterranean room, cold, with no warm body pressed next to him. He and Dorian had risen and gone hunting together, but there was a tension between them. He had returned from their hunt to find Victoria waiting for him, ready to argue. Dorian had been dragged off by one of his older acquaintances, abandoning Aaron to his maker's wrath. He was moments from breaking when Tobias effortlessly interceded.

Tobias ground his teeth, preparing for the battle of wits and words that was to follow, but the truth was, he didn't care if Victoria believed in the ecomancers or not. Aaron had futilely tried to convince her of the ecomancers' authenticity, but the French vampire would have none of it. Tobias would have given up long ago, and just let the ecomancers themselves convince her when they arrived. But Aaron refused to quit, or rather, Victoria refused to let it die.

"How can you say these immortals are Avatars? They could be just very powerful beings with abilities we do not possess," Victoria pointed out.

"If I had not seen the goddess with my own eyes, I would believe the same thing. But I have seen things, Victoria…" Tobias explained.

"How can you trust what you see? Your eyes can easily deceive you!"

"Yes. But tell me, how can you explain Tobias? Tobias was dead, yet here he is, alive as I am. How can you discount what we have to say?" Aaron countered.

"Easily. These creatures that you have found have the ability to heal, just as we have the ability to kill. That does not make them Avatars," Victoria answered.

"But Victoria, if what Tobias and Aaron say is true, would we not be wise to listen?" Dorian broke-in, moving to stand beside his ex-lover, one comforting hand coming to rest on Aaron's shoulder.

Victoria turned a raging gaze to the English vampire. "Beware anything that comes in the name of religion. Religion has brought us nothing but pain!"

"We do not come to preach religion. We come to preach truth," Tobias corrected.

"And how many have come in the name of Truth? Do not use that argument on me, it won't work!"

Dorian spoke haltingly, his voice cutting through the melee. "It is true that I have no faith in God and the Devil, but I will tell you this: I have drunk from Tobias, I have seen through his eyes and felt his faith. Since he and Rain came into our lives, our spirits have been brightened."

"And I have found healing and love," Aaron added. "I do not care if Sky is an Avatar or not. Whatever he is, he has brought me great joy, and because of that, I will believe anything he tells me."

Victoria looked witheringly upon Aaron. "Of that I have no doubt."

"Look. It's almost nine," Dorian said. "They'll be here soon. We do not ask that you believe. We do not ask you to convert. We ask you to listen. It's important that you know the truth, for Ja'oi has deceived us all. Aurek is missing and we have to find him. There may be a war soon, and He may attack us overtly, using our greatest weaknesses against us."

"We already have protection spells upon us to hide us from Ja'oi's agents, but soon they may no longer be enough," Tobias continued. "We must be prepared. We must know what they know, so that we will be able to fight if we must."

"And the ecomancers can and have protected us themselves," Ian announced, adding his voice as he came to support his two sons. "Rain risked her life to protect us when Ja'oi's angels attacked Dorian's house in the Americas. She was badly drained and wounded, but she kept us safe."

Victoria sighed and put a hand to her head. This was all too much for her. It was giving her a headache.

"Very well. Out of respect for you, Ian, I will listen. But I do not promise anything," she conceded.

"That is all we ask," Dorian agreed.

Just then John appeared, literally. He materialized out of nothing and was standing there, rather dazed until he got his bearings.

"John!" Ian exclaimed as the others stared at the new vampire in shock.

"Yes," John answered, still a bit disoriented.

"How did you get here?" Aaron asked.

"They sent me. They wanted me to tell you that they are coming."

"Who is 'they'?" Victoria questioned.

"They…the ecomancers."

"John, where is Alexa?" Ian demanded.

John looked blankly at Ian, then said simply, "She is with them. They kept her. We were coming to the house last night, and she saw the fire. She threw herself at their feet. Sun took her."

"Sun? The sun took her? Is she dead?" Ian blurted.

"No, Ian. Sun is the name of an ecomancer," Tobias soothed gently, then pressed John, "Tell us what happened, John."

"Alexa saw the fire and wanted to investigate. She so rarely said or did anything that I obliged her. We found them, having a meeting. Alexa saw one of them, and, before I could stop her, went running into their midst. She threw herself at Aerth's feet, thinking she was the Goddess Diana…"

There was soft laughter in the room, and John stopped in mid-sentence.

"Go on…" Ian prodded.

"Aerth told me Alexa was wounded in mind and spirit, and that Sun would heal her. She gave Alexa to Sun and they walked away. I stayed and listened to their tales until dawn, then I went into the ground. When I rose, they were waiting for me."

"Was Alexa with them?" Etienne asked.

"Yes, but she is different…"

"How? What did they do to her?" Ian ordered.

"She has become an acolyte of the Earth Mother."

The whole room gasped in unison and looked at John with mute awe.

"Oh, I don't believe this!" Victoria seethed. "Someone comes with a tall tale and the rest of you are ready to follow like blind sheep to slaughter!"

Dorian fumed, his eyes smoldering with rage, but his outburst was cut short as a wind blew into the room, rustling their hair and the papers on the table, and they all felt a build-up of power, power that made their hands and fingers tingle.

"They're here," John announced.

The stone wall began to crackle and small pebbles broke free of it, plunking to the floor as it rumbled. With a protesting creak, the wall melted and swirled, opening up to reveal a gaping hole. Beyond the new doorway stood a group of people, in the forefront was a woman dressed in Grecian robes and a man dressed in midnight blue.

Aerth and Stars stepped into the room.

"I give you the Avatars of Aiya, the Earth Goddess," John said, his voice not his own.

They poured out of the hole in the wall, forming a small line just slightly behind Aerth and Stars. There were twelve in all, each more radiant than the next. Tobias strained to see his beloved and saw that she and Sky came last. She was more beautiful than he had ever seen her, her long, black hair combed smooth and reflecting shades of blue when the light hit it, and she had dressed in a black silk sari embroidered with strands of silver and tiny, sparkling stones. Their eyes met briefly, and she gave him a small smile, then turned her head to face in front of her. Tobias looked to see Aaron and found him staring at the figure standing next to Rain, an expression of unadulterated love and primal lust on his smooth face.

Sky was equally well prepared for this audience. He was dressed in white doeskin leather. The pants were painted on, leaving absolutely nothing to the imagination, while the shirt was loose, plunging at the neck but having cross-ties up the front that were left hanging, and sewn with silver beads and metal ornaments along the chest and neckline. He cast Aaron a knowing smile, his eyes twinkling with mirth. Tobias saw Aaron part his lips and run his tongue along the edge of his white teeth, desire burning out of control in his green eyes. Then draw breath and bite his lip when Sky had to turn away.

Alexa was in the midst of them, dressed in flowing white robes, her face a picture of sublime peace and tranquillity. Sun was beside her, her golden hair shining in the artificial light, and for a moment she looked like the sun as it blazed yellow all around her face. The vampires were utterly dumbstruck, even Victoria.

In the ensuing silence, Aerth spoke, "We thank you for welcoming us into your home."

One of the unknown vampires fell to his knees in supplication. Aerth looked at him with quiet grace. "Rise. Do not kneel before us. We are not gods. We are but messengers and healers. We are not deserving of your worship."

The vampire looked at her, his face full of abject awe, and Aerth continued. "Get up, Brother. We are no more or less than you."

He obeyed, and slowly rose to his feet, but he kept his head down and refused to look directly at them. Aerth turned her attention to Victoria.

"I am Aerth."

Victoria stammered for words. "I…"

Aerth cut her off, addressing the gathered crowd.

"We have come here tonight to speak with those of you who have gathered here. We bring both glad and poor tidings. Glad in that we are here to tell you of your true origins, and poor in that it should take such danger and crisis to bring us together. The world as we know it is changing. Aiya, our creator, will no longer stand idly by while Her children are destroyed by the Rogue God. As She rallies to defend them, sending us to act as Her agents, the fires of war begin to smolder and burn. Ja'oi does not take kindly to Her meddling in His plans, and seeks to thwart Her as She tries to save Her children. We have come to both protect and teach you. We also ask for your help in finding Aiya's son Aurek, who has been missing for many centuries. After this night, many of you will leave here, and go with some of my siblings. It is not safe for all of us to be in one place. It makes us a tempting target that is easy to attack. But for now, I would ask you to listen, for we have much to do, and very little time to plan."

The room erupted into voices, some concerned, some angry, some fearful. Questions came from every corner, a cacophony of preternatural voices. It was hard to filter out just one among the many who were speaking all at once. Ian grew impatient and gave off a display of his power by making a fire burst to life in the stone fireplace.

"Silence!" he commanded.

His will was promptly obeyed.

"What would you have us do?" the old vampire asked the ancient ecomancer.

Before she could answer however, there was a loud bang as the heavy wooden door of the castle slammed shut with force. The jolt shook them all into stunned silence and they waited in surprise as they heard the purposeful, confident strides of the newcomer walking towards the gathering room. Then the door to the room flew open with a crash and a new vampire entered. He was blond, and dressed from head to toe in fine black leather, complete with a long duster coat and pair of studded boots. He took off his sunglasses, shaking out his shoulder-length hair and grinned at them.

"I'm here! The party can start now!" he announced cheerfully.

He was met with stunned silence and he looked at all of the surprised faces staring back at him. His face fell and he gave a sheepish grin.

"Err... sorry I'm late?" he offered apologetically, the pointed to the door behind him. "My bike got stuck in customs and..."

They gave a collective sigh.

"Khristopher," Tobias said with a small smile.

Khristopher's grin widened. "In the flesh! Well...sort of."

"You've arrived just in time."

"Good, glad to know I didn't miss anything."

The blond vampire surveyed the huge room, taking in all the faces that were looking at him with interest. He whistled.

"Wow, Gramps, when you said family reunion, I didn't think you meant *family* reunion! Holy shit, I don't think I've seen this many blood-suckers since the reunion at Cambridge Law School."

Ian bristled. Khristopher was the son of his maker's youngest child, but Ian had cared for him in his youth and as a result the blond had taken to referring to him as his grandfather. He'd always hated the nickname and the impetuousness of the Swedish vampire.

"Khristopher, welcome," Ian began formally, using the Swedish pronunciation of the vampire's name.

"Thanks, Gramps," he replied, tossing his duster and gloves on a convenient table. "Err, who is everyone?"

"You'll be introduced later," Ian said, taking Khristopher's arm. "Right now we're busy."

"Busy?"

"Yes, busy. Aerth was just about to tell us what she would like us to do."

"Aerth?"

"Yes."

"Why do I feel like I've missed something important here?"

"Because you have. But that's normal for you," Etienne quipped with a smile, coming to stand next to the Swede. He and Khristopher were of like minds and got along well when they were together.

"Oh, yeah. Thanks for reminding me of that," Khristopher said good-naturedly.

"Anytime."

"Well, okay then. I can play catch-up." He waved a hand to the room. "Hi everybody. Err, you may proceed with whatever you were doing before I barged in here," he said with a deep bow.

Ian rolled his eyes and turned to Aerth who was smiling wryly. "Please continue."

"We would have you break into groups. We will move among you, joining with your groups, two of us for eight or so of you," Aerth replied.

The request was quickly fulfilled, and the room separated into groups of eight, and the ecomancers, in their preset pairs, segregated themselves among the groups. Once the groups and pairs of ecomancers were formed, the room became full of voices once again, but this time it was organized chaos and not the free-for-all melee it had been before. The ecomancers stayed and spoke until an hour before dawn, when, tired and hoarse, they bid the vampires good day. Sky joined Aaron for a brief kiss and cuddle before Aaron retired to their bedroom. Tobias and Etienne went off to share a few quiet moments with Rain. She was weary, and tired of talking, so they merely shared a couch in comfortable silence. A while later they headed to the room they shared together and prepared for bed.

Rain obscured the window of the bedroom while Tobias and Etienne snuggled under the covers. When she was finished her task, she looked at them and saw that they peering at her with glittering preternatural eyes. The 'come hither' look on Tobias' face was both irresistible and comic, and she smiled as she made her way to the bed. Climbing under the bedclothes, she pressed herself close to Tobias, who promptly wrapped both arms around her. Today Etienne had chosen to sleep behind Tobias, letting his maker be the one who secured the middle spot of their threesome. He had his arm around Tobias' waist, and both heads shared the same pillow.

"Are you going to go away after we go to sleep?" Tobias asked her.

"Yes. All of us are meeting in the forest this afternoon. We are going to decide who will be staying here and who will be leaving tomorrow night."

"You know that I am wherever you and Etienne are."

"And no doubt Aaron will be with us because he won't be separated from Sky. You should have seen him pining last night," Etienne noted.

Rain laughed softly. "I can imagine."

"Did you miss us?" Tobias questioned.

She smiled and kissed him. "Yes, I missed you."

"We were mooning last night: Aaron, Tobias, and I. We could have started a 'Vampire Lovers of Ecomancers' support group, and made a Twelve-Step program for dealing with the feelings of abandonment caused by being left behind," Etienne quipped.

A pillow was quickly tossed on his head and he snickered. "Hey! It's the truth!"

"Don't make me feel worse than I already do about leaving you poor, helpless souls alone for one evening," she jibed, but she was smiling.

"We're utterly lost without you, you know. I don't think Tobias knew what to do with his hands."

"Oh, don't turn it into a melodrama. You both survived," she chided.

"I contemplated suicide at least twice," Tobias deadpanned.

He was only joking, but her face told him that she had not found his comment funny.

"Don't say that. Don't ever say that, not even in jest," she breathed, her expression pained.

"I'm sorry," he said contritely. "You're right. It wasn't funny."

She sighed and nestled her head under his chin, her fingers reaching up to tangle in the ends of his brown hair. He held her close, acutely aware of her melancholy sadness.

"Liebchen?" he whispered.

"It's all right, Tobias," she answered, a note of exasperation in her voice.

He reacted by nuzzling her and burying his face in her hair. "Forgive me."

"There is nothing to forgive. I am just…remembering."

"The day I almost died?"

"Yes."

He did not know what to say, so he said nothing.

"Sometimes I think you forget what that did to me. Seeing you burn…" she murmured, shuddering. "It was my worst nightmare, ten-fold…"

"Shhhh, liebchen. I know. But you saved me, you did not let me die, and now we are together, so great good came of it."

Rain sobbed, her fingers closing over the collar of his shirt. "I never want to lose you. I love you. I would do anything for you, even die."

Tobias chose his words carefully. "You once said to me that you did not want me to die for you, that you wanted me to love you enough to live for you. I would ask the same of you. Love me enough to live for me."

"I will. For as long as I can," she answered cryptically.

She let her hand slide down Tobias' chest and abdomen until her fingers found Etienne's cool hand. The younger vampire wordlessly seized her hand in his own, squeezing tightly, letting the desperation of his grip say all the things he could not say.

"Sleep well, my beloveds. I will be here when you rise," she told them. "I love you."

We love you too, came their mindvoices in unison, before they fell asleep.

Rain stayed with them and slept for a few hours until Sky awakened her with a mental tap. She yawned and rousted herself from the bed, carefully slipping from Tobias' embrace.

"Is it time?" she asked sleepily.

Sky nodded. "Yes, they are waiting for us."

"What time is it?"

"Sometime after noon."

She yawned again and stood, stretching and cracking her back.

"Did you have a good nap?" he inquired.

"Yes. And you?"

"Yes."

"That's good." She smoothed her sari and ran her fingers through her hair. "Go on ahead of me. I'll be out in a minute."

Sky smiled and promptly disappeared. She joined him a few moments later and they went to find their brethren.

"How bad is it?" she asked as they joined the gathering.

They were in the clearing just on the edge of the forest, the castle looming like a lonely sentinel on top of the cliff.

"We have heard nothing," Wind informed.

"It bodes ill," Sea added.

"Yes, it does. We must seek to protect the vampires," Moon agreed.

"We have intentions of making the entire cliff a heartstone," Ice answered.

"Good idea. The heartstone Sky and I called in the Americas successfully fed the protection shields," Rain told them.

"We are concerned at Ja'oi's silence. Beware the quiet foe, for he is making plans against you," Sea said.

"Yes. So far, you, Rain, are the only one who has been overtly attacked. All the rest of us were mildly annoyed, but soon acquired partners. You were left unpartnered because Sky was on Indio," Sun commented.

Rain scowled inwardly. None of the others had been willing to take Sky on as a partner, so she had been left to herself until he returned from his errand. What would they have done if she had been unable to keep the

Seraphim at bay? Sky would have torn them to pieces if she had been seriously injured, and that would only have been after Aiya got finished with them. They knew it too. That was why none of them would answer her when she was calling from Washington. To have allowed their petty disapproval to interfere with her safety...

Peace, Rain, Aerth's voice said to her softly. *Yes, it is true what you are thinking. And yes, you have a right to be angry, but let it go. Aiya has already made Her displeasure known.*

Then why did you not come to me? You who chose me?

I would have, but I too, was on a mission for Aiya, and did not return before Sky. Believe me, if I had been here, you would have been partnered immediately. We were taken advantage of, and the others would not take Sky. Trust me, my friend. Aiya is well aware of what happened, and of the danger you were in, and She is not amused.

Neither was I, but it worked out for the best. I've never seen him so happy, she said, casting a glance at Sky.

That is true. It would seem that the Lost One may have finally found his way.

Yes.

"I think it is a good idea to make the cliff a heartstone, but it would also be prudent if the vampires were to disperse from here. Remember, Ja'oi's agents cannot find them," Stars said.

"But some should stay here as well to act as a gathering place and safe haven. Once we call the heartstone it should be secure," Rain announced.

"How many do you think will stay here?" Wind questioned.

"I should think Ian will stay. Tobias, Dorian, Aaron, Etienne, and Khristopher will probably stay with him. And perhaps Alexa, although I think it would be best if she stayed with Sun," Rain replied.

"Hmm, that is seven, possibly eight," Moon noted.

"Rain, you and Sky will most certainly stay. You can also continue your search for Aurek from here, although I doubt any of Ian's books will offer any useful information," Aerth decided. "And Song, I know you would prefer to remain here in case any progress is made on finding Aurek."

"Yes," Song agreed. "But Leaves should return to the Sanctuary. Her inexperience will work against her if Ja'oi attacks."

"That will leave you unpartnered. You are familiar with the pairs rule," Stars reminded.

"I will stay and be partner to Song," Ice piped in, glancing from Fire to Rain. "Fire can take Leaves and teach her battle skills."

Leaves cast a nervous glance at Fire. The red-haired ecomancer lived up to her namesake, and Leaves feared getting burned. But she knew Song was right, her inexperience would hinder them here. Fire, however, could teach her many things. Fire had been a hot-blooded fighter in her mortal life. The daughter of a Celtic warlord, she often used her infant powers of weather working to hamper the opposing army. Oh, how her father had mourned her when she was run through with a horseman's spear.

"Fire, are you willing?" Aerth asked.

"I am. Give her to me, and I will teach her what I know. When I am finished with her, Ja'oi's petty minions will tremble in fear at the sight of her," Fire answered.

"It is settled then. Rain, Sky, Song and Ice will stay to guard the vampires that remain here," Stars said. "The rest of us will spread out across the globe as we had before. Some vampires may come with us, while others may not. We will use what little information we garnered from the vampires to help us search for Aurek, but until we know what Ja'oi is going to do, the safety of the vampires takes precedence."

"Agreed," Aerth said, looking at Rain who nodded as well.

"We will take the Isles," Fire broke in. "They are closest to Highlands and can be reached easily should any trouble arise."

"Agreed," Stars concurred. "And the reverse is also true. Should you and Leaves experience difficulties, help will be nearby."

With that decided, they set to converting the cliff into a heartstone. The task was a monumental one and would take all of their combined strength to accomplish. Rather than calling a new stone, they had to transform the existing rock. The cliff was very old and had been dormant for a very long time, and it resisted the infusion of new life into it, rousing it from its slumber. Seven of them worked to tap the energy while three sought to direct it, and the remaining two weaved the protection spells that would eventually be linked to the stone. When they were finished, the cliff looked the same from the outside, but it pulsed with energy. The protection spells were attached to it and the entire Keep became shielded, and because the castle was built directly onto the cliff the shield was seamless and impenetrable. Not even an entire army of Ja'oi's minions would be able to breach it.

Their work complete, they retired, weak and drained, to the comfort of the old trees to rest. Ice strategically placed himself next to Rain. She glanced at him, knowing that he was trying to tell her that she had his full support and friendship. She and Ice had been lovers once. They had made a good pair until duty and troubles with Sky had forced them apart. He wasn't cold like his namesake; he was vibrant and warm. He and Fire suited each other very well, both as partners and as occasional lovers.

Permanent bondings among them were rare. More often than not, the pairing would end, usually because of duty, and the two would remain close and dear friends. There had been some exceptions, however. Aerth and Stars were the oldest pair, and Sea had been bonded to Air before he was killed, which explained her reluctance to enter into a new pairing. They had more success with other immortals outside of their immediate brethren. Song had been bonded to a dragon before she was killed. Considering he had yet to find and choose another lover, it proved that, at least in permanent relationships, the ecomancers were very picky.

Rain, on the other hand, had always known the name of the one she had chosen, and it was not Ice. Ice knew that and accepted it. He had never teased her or berated her for her love of Tobias. It was as if he knew how much the vampire truly meant to her. If Ice had ever known that she sometimes imagined him to be Tobias, he never gave any sign of it. He had always been such a tender and solicitous love. She looked at him and smiled.

He smiled back, brightening, and edged closer. His hand was right by hers, and she inched her fingers nearer until they touched. He lifted his palm and gingerly placed it on top of hers, squeezing lightly to offer comfort.

It was Sky, his white hair in disarray, who broke the quiet moment with his ragged voice. "I am hungry. I wish to propose a hunt."

Eleven sets of eyes regarded him with mild amusement and surprise.

"It has been a long time since so many of us have been together on the mortal world," Song answered.

"All the more reason to hunt. How long has it been since we surged as a pack and brought the quarry to bay?" Sky countered.

"What would we hunt?" Sun asked.

"Anything large enough to feed us all," Sky replied. "I am sure these forests harbor deer."

"I will hunt with you," Rain said.

"And I," added Ice. It was no surprise. He was trying to be supportive and he knew that if he hunted with Sky, she would look fondly upon him.

"I will go as well," Stars concurred.

Sky smiled. "Who else is with me?"

One by one, they agreed to join the hunt, until only Sea and Wind were left.

"We will stay and keep watch for trouble," Wind announced.

"As you wish," Rain told him as she began to unwrap her sari.

Wind nodded to her and took her silk from her as it fell free. He and Sea stood watch as the remaining ecomancers shape-shifted into wolves and went loping into the forest. After they were out of sight, a low, mournful howl echoed over the trees, answered by several others shortly thereafter. The hunt had begun.

Fourteen

Aaron drew a deep breath and slowly licked the blood from his lips, savoring the taste. The air in their bedroom was heavy with the scent of their lovemaking, the strong musky odor of Sky permeating the humid air around him. Sky lay next to him, his body still damp with sweat, his eyes closed, but he was far from asleep. Turning his head, his eyes locked onto the healing puncture wounds on Sky's throat, two tiny holes glowing faintly red against his lover's pale skin, and felt the thirst rise within him again. Rolling to his side, he covered the wounds with his mouth and sunk his teeth into them. He heard Sky's gasp of surprise as the hot blood bubbled into his mouth, hitting the roof of his palette before going down his throat. He moaned loudly as pleasure filled him and he wrapped his arms around Sky.

Drinking from Sky was like consuming pure light. The blood was hot and sweet, and flooded him with such exquisite ecstasy. It was a never-ending stream of pleasure that he could glut himself on every night, and there would still be more, and his lover would still be alive. He loved it. The room filled with the sound of his moans and the small sucking noises of his mouth on Sky's neck. As he drank, Sky rolled atop him, pinning him to the mattress for the second time that evening. Eagerly, he raised his legs as Sky's knees spread them, his lover's hips coming firmly into contact with his own as Sky mounted. He let out a little cry as the organ thrust into him, his body offering only the smallest of resistance, then a long groan of delight as Sky began to ride him.

Pleasure from the bite, pleasure from the joining. Aaron was bathed in it, and he moved with Sky, straining as hard as his lover, urging him on, begging for more. The pace was fast and hard, just the way Aaron wanted it. Amazing how Sky always knew what type of ride his lover wanted, whether slow and tender, or fast and rough, or a combination of the two. Aaron never had to tell Sky with words what would please him, somehow the ecomancer either knew or was able to read all the signals Aaron gave him, the little mews and sighs, the subtle shifting of his body weight when Sky reached the desired speed.

After several minutes of Sky's steady pumping, Aaron's body tensed. He sucked harder and raised his hips higher, forcing Sky to plunge even deeper into him. As the waves of pleasure began to build, he raked his sharp nails down Sky's back, and Sky responded by thrusting harder, pounding Aaron into the bed. He would have broken a mortal man's pelvis, but Aaron only writhed and pleaded for more. Aaron let out a strangled cry as he reached his pinnacle, the tidal wave of his climax crashing over him with its powerful force.

In the aftermath, Aaron released Sky's throat, licking away the droplets of blood that leaked from the wounds, and relaxed, letting his feet come to rest on the mattress. Sky still covered him, sweating, breathing heavily, and he playfully scratched his nails along Sky's back, feeling the gouges he had made earlier begin to heal and disappear. Shakily, Sky lifted himself up and attempted to disengage himself, but found his mouth quickly seized in a forceful kiss as two hands grabbed his sides and pulled him back down. His arms gave in and he fell back atop Aaron, his hips once again coming to rest between Aaron's legs and pushing his organ into Aaron's rectum. Aaron kissed him brutally, passionately, holding the kiss until Sky was forced to break it off so he could breathe.

"Goddess, *you're* in a mood tonight," the ecomancer gasped, a little more than amazed.

"Can't help it. My day was fraught with erotic dreams of you," Aaron answered, breathless, his hair tousled on the pillow and clinging to his forehead in damp ringlets.

"Oh? What brought that on?" he asked with a wry smile.

"Could be those white pants you've been wearing. Every time I see them, I just want to rip them off you."

"Would be a waste of good doeskin."

"I'd get you another pair…and rip them off too."

Sky chuckled and moved to get up. Once again, Aaron stopped him.

"I really should get up, dearling."

"Why bother? Just stay. I'm only going to want you again as soon as I catch my breath. Save yourself the trouble of having to reposition."

The ecomancer gave him an incredulous look. "Is this going to be one of those nights where we just stay in bed and do nothing but make love every hour?"

"Twice an hour," Aaron corrected. "My turn-around time is half an hour. We still have at least 7 hours left before dawn. That means we have enough time to make love at least fourteen more times."

Sky giggled at Aaron's brazenness. "Dearling, if we were to make love that many times between now and sunrise, your little hole would be very raw and very sore."

"Ooo. Hurt me."

Sky laughed out loud. "My! But you are the wanton harlot tonight! I was never such a hussy."

"You didn't have the world's greatest lover in your bed every night."

Sky shifted his weight, the position becoming uncomfortable. "Waylan wasn't all that bad a lover…I really do have to get up, love. This is no longer comfortable."

Aaron pouted, but allowed Sky to remove himself and come to rest beside him.

"Ach," Sky bemoaned as he settled on the mattress. "I have created a monster."

Aaron snickered and laid his head on Sky's chest lovingly. "Can't help it. I love you."

Sky tangled his fingers in his vampire lover's black hair. "I love you too, dearling, but I think we should save the all night lovemaking for when we are in a more private setting."

Aaron sighed. "I suppose you're right. Wouldn't want to frighten the natives now, would we."

Sky chuckled softly. "Think you'll survive?"

"Yes. I'll just be incorrigible for the next few nights."

"You're already are incorrigible," Sky teased.

"Yes, but I'll be even *more* incorrigible."

The deep rumble of Sky's laughter echoed in his ear and he snuggled close. Sky wrapped an arm around him, and they cuddled contentedly. Aaron was warm, having drank all the blood he needed to sustain him from Sky during their two bouts of lovemaking. There would be no need for him to go hunting later.

"There is something I want to talk to you about," Sky began hesitantly.

"Hmm? What is that?"

"At the meeting two nights ago I was asked to make a Reckoning. I've never done one..."

"What is a Reckoning? I thought it was some kind of meeting."

"Yes, the meeting is called a reckoning, but there is something else that occurs at the meeting which is also called a Reckoning. When an eco-mancer makes a Reckoning, he or she announces to the group who he or she is, and who they were chosen by..."

"But you were chosen by Aiya Herself..."

"Yes. The Reckoning requires you to know something of your past life. To know who you were, and how you became what you are now. This is something I was unable to face until only recently."

Aaron lifted his head to look down at Sky. His lover's face was thoughtful and far away, and there was an inexpressible sadness in his eyes, a sadness Aaron had never seen before.

"Rain has told me something of your past," he said carefully.

"I know. It was something I could not have done, but…because of you, I am now able to face my past. It no longer sends me into insanity, and I am no longer afraid of my name."

Sky rolled to his side and gently took Aaron's hand in his own, catching his green eyes in an intense stare. "Do you know what it means when an ecomancer tells you his mortal name?"

"What does it mean?" he asked in a breathless whisper.

"It's like you giving me your blood, or telling me your deepest, darkest secret. It's like giving me a piece of your soul."

Aaron was speechless, trembling, for he could feel the intimacy growing between them, an intimacy that transcended sex, or love, or the sharing of blood. He held his breath, waiting, afraid to speak lest he disturb the delicate mood that had settled upon them.

Sky lowered his gaze, refusing to meet Aaron's eyes, focusing instead on the delicate shape of his lover's fingers, and the long translucent fingernails, clear and hard as tinted glass. "I refused to make a Reckoning until I had spoken with you. Until I had told you things that I want you to know. It is right that you should be the first, because it is because of you that I can make a Reckoning at all."

Aaron remained silent, knowing that there was nothing he could say. Sky was opening up for him, about to lay bare a part of his innermost sanctum. Around them, the very room was registering the subtle change within the ecomancer, the energy patterns fluctuating and pulsing. Sky was about to speak. Aaron felt the hand around his squeeze tighter, and reflexively, he squeezed back.

"I was the only son of a German farmer. His only child in fact. The villagers would later say that I made Mother barren, because no woman could bear a normal child after birthing a demon. I could…talk to animals. I even saved my cousin Roald from a charging bull…made him stop and turn away. That was how they found out that I could…"

He paused, his face twisting with pain. Aaron held tight to his lover's hand.

"I'm here," he whispered tenderly.

Sky cast him a brief but fond glance and continued, "After that, everyone treated me differently. They said things about me behind my back, the children taunted me, the people made warding signs when they thought I wasn't looking…Mother and Father brought the priest over, he beat me and tried to drive the devil from me. Nothing worked. I was outcast. My parents lost their station in the community, and I learned the true meaning of loneliness."

He stopped for a moment, choosing his words, absently rubbing his thumb over Aaron's fingers, letting the touch comfort and strengthen him.

"The only man who ever cared about me was Waylan, the blacksmith. He treated me kindly, said I was gifted, not cursed. I helped him. I could make even the most nervous horses stand still. He liked having me around; he became a foster father to me. He was like rain in the desert. I drank him up, and fell in love with him. It was how I found out that I was not like the other boys my age."

He was struggling with the memories even more now, gripping Aaron's hand so tightly it was starting to hurt, but Aaron bore it, and when Sky looked at him, he gave only a sweet, understanding smile.

Tears rose in Sky's eyes as he went on. "I'm sure Rain told you what happened when the townsfolk found out about us. The animals warned us ahead of time that a mob was coming, but it was too late. We tried to get away, but they caught us. They beat Waylan to death as he tried to protect me. Me they took and…and…"

"Don't go there!" Aaron breathed fiercely, digging his nails into Sky's hand to keep Sky with him. "Don't go there. Don't even try to remember it. They beat you."

Sky nodded, quivering, the tears filling his eyes. "Yes."

"They tortured you."

"Yes."

"They burned you alive."

Sky clenched his eyes shut, the tears rolling down his cheeks. "Yes. And I...I called the animals, but they killed them!"

His blue eyes opened and focused on the ceiling. He was shaking violently now, and Aaron held firmly onto his arm with his free hand.

"They lit the fire. My own parents lit the fire! And I reached into myself to call the wild animals, and..." His face became a mask of torment and agony. "And fire came down from the sky. A great storm blew in from nowhere. A storm I had called. It poured hail and lightning down upon the town, it set the houses ablaze. The power channeled directly though me, burning me from the inside as the fire licked at my feet. I screamed and screamed..." Eyes widened in wonder as he saw it all over again: the vision of the earth opening up and the goddess coming to take him. "And then, I wasn't in pain anymore, and the most beautiful woman I had ever seen took me from the pyre and told me that everything was going to be all right. She told me to sleep, and I slipped into blackness. When I woke up, Rain was staring down at me."

Sky paused, breathing heavily, struggling with his memory and emotions. Aaron pinched him to give him something physical to focus on.

"Stay with me! Tell me more. That was how you became an ecomancer. Tell me what color your hair and eyes were before they were the color they are now."

"Brown," Sky blurted. "My eyes were brown. And my hair was dirty, scruffy blond. I didn't recognize myself at first when Rain first showed me a mirror."

"I can imagine."

The ecomancer rallied, beating down the surge of pain and terror. "After I was better, and Rain had taught me some control, I returned to my home village and slaughtered every person there. I ripped the hearts out of the people who killed Waylan, and left a trail of blood carnage in my wake. The townsfolk didn't recognize me. They fell on their knees, begging the Angel of Death for mercy. I spared no one, not even the infants in their cribs, and when no mortal was left alive, I burned the entire town to the ground. The whole damn thing became a giant funeral pyre, and I stood in the center of it all, laughing."

He stopped and looked at Aaron, expecting to see horror and accusations upon his lover's face, but found only love and tender patience. He decided to push even further, to tell it all. "But that was not the end of my revenge. Afterwards, I hunted the relatives of the townsfolk and murdered every last one."

Silence fell again as Sky raised his eyes timidly to meet Aaron's, afraid of what he would find there. "So now, I tell you. I am flawed. I have killed innocents. I have committed crimes that have been cause for budding ecomancers to be destroyed. I am damaged in ways I do not even understand. I tell you all of this, in faith and hope, and now that you know…Do you still want me?"

Aaron looked at him, his face softening with tenderness and unadulterated love. Gently he brushed his free hand through Sky's white hair and caressed his cheek.

"I have killed countless mortals. I have killed with no regard for gender or age. I have killed innocents and criminals. I will continue to kill because it is what I do. Now that you know this, do you still want me?" Aaron echoed.

"Yes," Sky answered desperately, without hesitation.

Aaron smiled, his lips quivering. "And I still want you."

Sky closed his eyes again as fresh tears made their way down his face, and he lowered his forehead to Aaron's chest, his voice raw with emotion.

"My name was Stephan."

Aaron drew breath, taking in the name, fighting back his own tears. "I am Aaron Lian-Chen Spencer."

Aaron wrapped his arms around Sky, holding him dear as his lover wept. They were both chaffed and flayed open, vulnerable and sensitive from what had just passed between them. Sky's arms slid around him, pressing them even closer together, and he could feel the hot tears rolling onto his cool skin. His fingers found Sky's hair and tangled in it. If there had been any barriers between them before, there were none now, and as the room echoed with Sky's muffled sobs, Aaron coveted him in a protective embrace. They were so close that they could have easily been mistaken for one person, sequestered under the bedcovers, and perhaps, for now, that was just the way it was supposed to be.

• • •

Rain was alone. Both Etienne and Tobias had gone to hunt and would probably be gone for quite some time. The vampires were steadily leaving in groups. Ian was overseeing their departures like the good host that he was. Her brethren were leaving as well. Now only Ian, Dorian, Aaron, Tobias, Etienne, and Khristopher remained. Song and Ice stayed behind as well. They were out in the wilds doing something, but she was not sure what. She was not concerned about them. She was, however, concerned about Sky.

Sky was inside with Aaron, baring his soul if her Empathy was any indicator, and she had no idea how many pieces of him would be left if things did not go well. Right now when she touched his mind he was at rest, but that was no indicator that all would be well when he awakened. She knew from experience that nothing was ever as it seemed with Sky.

Her worry for Sky, compiled with the general anxiety and danger of the situation with Ja'oi, left her melancholy and in search of solitude, something the Highlands offered in ample quantities. She found herself standing on the cliff overlooking the loch, oblivious to the wind that whipped at her hair and sari. There was a wild loneliness about this place and it called to her. She was preparing to shapeshift into a wolf and join the howl when a voice addressed her from behind.

"Sister."

It took her a moment to realize that she had been addressed in Hindi, a language she had not spoken in almost 400 years. She turned to face her addresser and found a diminutive Indian vampire standing there.

The vampire wore a homespun sari but had wrapped herself in a fur-lined great-cloak to ward of Scotland's cold. She seemed very lost and out of place.

"Yes?" she said in answer.

"I am Usha," the vampire answered, still in Hindi.

"I am Rain."

"I know. I was watching you last evening. You are Hindu, like me."

She nodded. "When I was mortal, yes."

They fell silent, and the wind filled the emptiness with its own voice. Rain saw Usha shiver.

"This place is horrible," Usha whispered. "It is desolate and peopled by barbarians."

"It has its own beauty in its emptiness."

Usha shook her head. "I am glad to be leaving."

"You are leaving tonight?"

"Yes. But I wished to speak to you before I left."

"Let us go inside. I see that the cold bothers you," she offered.

"Yes, that would be nice. Thank you."

Rain led the way back into the castle and they settled by the large hearth in the library. It was empty but for them and the fire.

"Why did you wish to speak to me?" Rain asked when they were warmer.

"You are looking for Aurek."

She struggled to hide her surprise. "You know him?"

"I know of him."

"Do you know where he is?"

"No," Usha replied then quickly continued, "He is not known to us as Aurek. He has many names, but mostly as Shardul, and his lover Raman who is beloved. Shardul and Raman were our grandparents' fathers."

Rain took a moment to digest the new information before speaking. "Do you know what became of Shardul and Raman?"

"We were told that Shardul wished to return to Kali but Shiva would not let him. Shiva was angry with Shardul because he hunted humans. He made the ground open up and demons swallowed him whole, and Raman, because he would not leave his beloved, went with him."

Usha paused. "Until tonight, I had thought this story a fable created by those who did not know the truth of our origins. But after hearing your old one speak last night, I came to think that there might be some truth in all of it and decided to tell you."

"Are any of your grandparents still alive? Ones who might know more?" Rain questioned, a cold fear building in her gut.

"No. Amar and I are the oldest that I know of. Indu created us three thousand years ago. I am sorry that I cannot tell you more."

Rain took Usha's hands in her own. "What you have told me is very helpful, and I thank you."

"I am glad that I was able to be of service to you."

Usha pulled her hands from Rain's grasp and turned to leave the room. "I must go now."

"Safe journeys and be careful. You know that now that the Circle has been restored, you can call on us for help at any time," Rain said.

"I know, and thank you. Good luck."

With that Usha walked out, leaving Rain to think about what she had been told. If Aurek changed his name, then that would be a plausible explanation as to why all trace of him disappeared. But the name change was not what bothered her the most. The story of Shiva and Kali, while no doubt influenced by the contemporary religion, might be steeped in truth. If that was so, then they might have a lead on what they needed to prove that Ja'oi had a hand in Aurek and Roshan's disappearance. Fear grew inside her and she felt her heart flutter. She had to share her information with the others right away.

Song? she mindcalled.

I am here.

I have news of Aurek.

Ice and I will come to you, as well as Seed, came the immediate reply.
Seed?
She...I'll explain when we get there. Where are you?
In the castle library.
We will join you there.

She debated calling Sky. As her partner, he should be included, but the last time she had checked on him, he was still asleep. She weighed the consequences of waking him against letting him sleep, and decided to let him choose for himself whether or not he wanted to join them.

Sky, she called gently, lightly tapping him with her mind.

She felt him rise hazily to consciousness. *Bina?*

Yes, it's me.

What's wrong?

The vampire Usha gave me some information about Aurek before she left. I have called Ice and Song; they are meeting me in the library. Would you like to be present?

There was a brief moment of silence then, *Yes. Aaron is coming too.*

As you wish.

We'll be there in a minute.

She had just broken off her link with Sky when the library door opened and Song entered. Ice was behind him, then Seed, and then a third man, one she did not know. He was very dark skinned, darker than Seed, and his hair was closely cropped to his head. His body was thin, lanky and tall, and he was dressed in a caftan of muted greens and browns. His face was narrow and his nose was small, but his eyes were wide and large, and they were a deep, vivid green. It was the eye color that gave him away. Like Sky's eyes, this man's eyes were a color no mortal could ever have. It would seem that Seed's Placide had crossed over.

As she took in the newcomer, Seed stepped forward.

"I give you my ward Tree."

"Tree," she repeated and bowed to him. "I welcome you, Tree; I am Rain."

Tree gave a nervous nod and small smile.

"I have brought him to you for safe keeping. Stone and I are returning to the Sanctuary, and we fear that it is not the safest of places," Seed informed.

Rain blinked. "What do you mean?"

"There is evidence that Ja'oi plans to move against Aiya," Song answered.

"Then we all must return..." Rain began.

"No, Rain. We have no real proof and to go back to the Sanctuary would let Ja'oi know we suspect his plans. Aiya seeks to trap him," Song explained. "Besides, if we returned, we would leave the vampires unprotected."

She bit her lip with worry, but said nothing.

"What news do you have of Aurek?" Ice asked.

"In a moment. We are waiting for Sky."

Just then Sky entered the room, dressed only in his doeskin trousers, followed by Aaron.

"What news?" Aaron questioned.

"Tree, this is my partner, Sky, and his lover Aaron. Aaron, Sky, this is Tree, Seed's ward," Rain introduced.

Sky and Aaron looked at Tree.

"Hello," Aaron greeted.

"Hi," Sky added.

Tree's eyes widened a bit and he looked over his shoulder at Seed.

"Vampir," Rain heard him whisper, then continue in a language she did not know. Seed answered him in kind, placing one hand on his shoulder in reassurance.

"Tell us what you learned," Sky said, ignoring Tree.

"Usha came to me this evening and told me that she knew of Aurek. Not as Aurek, but as Shardul."

"He changed his name," Song noted.

"Yes. And Roshan became known as Raman. They were the fathers of Usha's grandparents."

"Where are they now?" Ice asked.

"There is a legend about Shardul and Raman. It says that Shardul wanted to return to Kali but that Shiva would not let him. Shiva made the ground open up and demons swallow him and Raman as punishment for killing humans."

Song was quiet for a moment. "Ja'oi."

"Yes. If it is true then we may have proof that Ja'oi did something to Aurek and Roshan after Aerth was called away."

"He could not have killed them. Aiya would have felt Aurek's Passing," Seed insisted, turning away from Tree but leaving her hand on his shoulder.

"But He could be holding them prisoner," Ice informed.

"If that is the case, then it would explain how the Circle was broken," Song added.

"Then maybe we can use the Circle to find them," Sky said.

"Maybe…" Song agreed, thinking.

"Not if He is keeping them in the godlayers or between worlds," Ice cautioned.

"Perhaps not. Seed, take this information to Aiya when you return to the Sanctuary. I will tell Aerth what we learned today. There may be a way to track Aurek through the Circle," Song decided.

"Yes. I will tell Her. Maybe there is something She can do."

"We must be careful. If it we can prove He has done something with Aurek, then we must not let Him know we have proof until we are prepared to move against Him," Ice warned.

"Agreed. We must move with caution. We tell no one outside of Aerth and Aiya about this until we know more," Song decreed.

The others nodded.

"I must go. Stone is waiting for me," Seed announced.

"We will take good care of your ward," Rain assured.

Seed smiled at her, gave a little bow and left.

"What do we do now?" Rain asked Song.

"For now, we do nothing. I will contact Aerth and tell her what we have learned. The rest of us will remain here and wait until we are given further instructions. I have a feeling things will get much worse before we see the end of this," he answered.

The others remained silent. Song, who was Water before the deaths of Fire and Air, was one of the original four ecomancers created by Aiya. Although the ecomancer known as Song was only five thousand years old, the soul that inhabited his body was a great deal older. He had seen and done a great many things in his service of the goddess, and he was in a position to know what to expect from Ja'oi. His calm demeanor was a balm, but they suspected that his lack of concern only hid his true feelings.

Rain decided that she did not want to know how Song really felt. He and Aerth were the rocks. If they were frightened, what hope did any of them have?

Fifteen

Ur'al was unhappy. His God was unhappy so that made him unhappy. He had learned many millennia ago that things were only good when the god was pleased, and recently Ja'oi had been anything but pleased.

What news do you bring me, Ur'al? his god asked as he entered the sanctum of the temple.

"The Seraphim have been unsuccessful in forcing the heretics from the planet."

Ja'oi gave him an angry look, then sighed. *I did not think they would be able to.*

"Perhaps if we were to go…"

No. Only the Seraphim should go. To send any of the others would draw too much attention to us.

"But, my Lord, the Archangels can easily defeat these intruders…"

No! You must obey me. You and the others stay here until I need you. We must be patient, and wait for the right time to act. For now it is too early. Believe me, my faithful one, you will have your chance to serve me.

Ur'al bowed. "As you wish, my Lord."

Good.

Just then Lu'fahr, known to mortals as Lucifer or Satan, appeared in the temple and Ur'al growled when he saw him.

"You! What are you doing here? You defile the temple! You…"

ENOUGH! Ja'oi ordered and Ur'al cowered in fear. *He is here because I called him. We have matters to discuss.*

The angel left quickly, casting a hateful glance at Lu'fahr. Lu'fahr ignored him and faced his god.

"You called me, my Lord?"

Yes. I want to know how your special guests are doing.

Lu'fahr thought for a moment as to who Ja'oi meant. He had many special guests in Hell. Then he remembered the recent attacks on Aiya's avatars and knew which 'guests' Ja'oi was referring to.

"I have not killed them, as you ordered, my Lord."

Good. You must keep them alive a while longer. She will know if you kill the one.

"They have been kept safe, my Lord, as you instructed."

And I am sure you have been entertaining them.

Lu'fahr smiled wickedly. "Yes, my lord."

Ja'oi smiled back. *Good. But be warned that you may have to move them, just for a short while.*

"Why, my Lord?" Lu'fahr asked, confused.

Just in case someone comes looking for them.

"No one can breach the Gates without your or my knowledge."

No, but I want to be sure they are not discovered.

"They won't be. Although I do not understand why you fear the false goddess and Her minions."

Ja'oi looked at His fallen angel and gave him a tolerant smile. This one's faith had remained true throughout his punishment and exile.

I fear nothing. I am merely avoiding a confrontation. Once all of this is over, you will be able to kill both of them and not need to worry any longer. Until then, bide your time and keep them hidden.

Lu'fahr bowed. "As you wish my Lord."

Good. Now go and do as I command.

"I will, my Lord."

Ja'oi watched as the archangel left. He wasn't sure if Lu'fahr would do as He asked. The fallen angel was notorious for not following instructions, but He was relatively certain he would take at least some of it to heart. At least He hoped so. It would be problematic at best if the two were discovered before His plan to defeat Aiya was realized. He had already had to field questions from some of the Others who were concerned about Aiya's missing children. They had warned Him not to do anything rash or unwise, but little did they know that His plans were already in place. He was merely waiting for the right opportunity. Soon, most of Aiya's avatars would be out of Her Sanctuary, occupied with other tasks. He could then strike while She was at a disadvantage. He would be swift and catch all of them before they could run for help, then His victory would be assured. All He had to do was wait. The time would be right very soon.

Lu'fahr returned to Hell without delay. He always hated when Ja'oi called him back into the godlayer, but he knew the god did it to hurt him. Ja'oi, Lu'fahr had learned, was sadistic in His punishments, allowing him to revisit his former home before being forced back into exile in the World Between Worlds. It should have caused him pain, but that had dulled to a mere ache over the millennia. Ja'oi had not learned to vary the punishments in order to sustain the sting. And speaking of varying punishments...

A thought brought him to where he wanted to be: a forgotten corner of his realm peopled only by those he approved. Here was where he kept the political exiles, prisoners held there by Ja'oi's wishes that the god wanted kept hidden from the prying eyes of other gods and avatars. In this neglected hole in Hell two very special guests occupied space on the barren landscape. One he was forbidden to kill, the other he found more painful to the other to keep alive.

Aiya's vampire had shown remarkable resilience to pain, but had no taste to see his lover harmed. Lu'fahr had gleaned much enjoyment from devising new ways to torture the younger vampire, all for the purview of his maker. Forced to watch his child's pain over and over, the vampire could be reduced to wailing agony that would last years until the pain lost its shock and edge. Then Lu'fahr would be forced to think up a new punishment. The latest was a reenactment of the fateful tiger attack that had spurred the younger one's creation. Over and over the dark-haired vampire was attacked and gutted, all just out of the reach of his lover. He would die slowly, only to be revived again to have the process repeated.

He was arriving just as the lover was returning to life. He heard the intake of breath and the rattle of chains. Both vampires had been chained in some form or another since their abduction, usually just inches out of each other's reach. They had not been allowed to touch in almost three millennia, although sometimes he had teased them with the promise of it. He'd learned that vampires were very tactile creatures. He stopped to listen to the slow revival of the younger vampire and his maker's words. They spoke in a soft spidery language that had not been used on Earth for centuries, but their meaning was clear and heartfelt.

"You are with me again."

It was Aiya's child that spoke.

"Yes," his love answered.

"I am blessed. Every time, I fear he will take you from me for good. I fear that this time will be the last time."

"Then he would have nothing to torture you with," the child replied.

"Yes."

There was silence for a moment broken only by heavy breathing and the shifting of chains.

"Every time I see your wounds heal I know you are being given back to me. You are my most precious gift," he heard the firstborn whisper.

"Only you makes this situation bearable."

"The pain has lessened?"

"For the moment, until it comes again."

"I love you."

"And I you."

"It is the only thing that sustains us, and the only thing he cannot take away from us."

It was true, Lu'fahr acknowledged bitterly. In all the years of their confinement, their love and devotion to each other had not wavered. It had suffered periods of weakness in the earlier times, but it had never broken. Now, the two were united in their love and no amount of torture could shake it. The only option he had left to him was to kill one, but he had been forbidden to do so.

'Soon, though. I can kill them soon. Ja'oi promised me.'

"Give me your pain, my love," Aiya's child said.

"I would spare you it."

"No, pain shared is pain lessened. Give it to me and let me carry the burden for a while."

He heard the younger one sigh. "Only until it comes again."

He knew they were linking minds. That was another thing he had been unable to break. The blood that tied them together was too strong. He had been able to break the tie these two had with all of the others, but all of his attempts to break the tie between the firstborn and his first child had ended in failure. He was looking forward to finally killing them. Torture was growing tiresome because they simply accepted whatever he devised. No matter how sadistic or depraved his plans were, after the first few times a calm serenity would come over them. The firstborn carried Aiya's light within him, a light he knew he had no hope of extinguishing, and he shared it freely with his lover.

Gritting his teeth, he stalked away. There were other things he could be doing besides listening to his greatest failure. His god needed assistance and there were things he could do to further Ja'oi's cause. It would mean breaking some rules, but Ja'oi knew he never followed rules anyway. In fact, Ja'oi was probably anticipating that he would not obey. It would not do to disappoint his god. Plans began to form in his head. He knew some vampires had gathered in Scotland under the protection of Aiya's servants. He would not be able to breach the fortifications or attack outright, but perhaps he could affect a more covert maneuver. If he could manage to catch one...

Smiling to himself, he ran possible scenarios through his mind, leaving the lovers to their fate and sending the tiger to once again disembowel its helpless victim. In doing so, he did not hear the end of the conversation between the two.

"I think our time here is ending. I have felt...a stirring within me," Aurek whispered.

"As have I. How long do you think it has been that we have been here in this place?"

"A long time."

"Yes."

"But it will be over soon. I feel it. We will be gone from here soon, my love."

"I believe you."

They heard the growl and Roshan tensed.

"It's coming."

"Yes."

"I will try not to scream."

"Think of my love for you and know that your pain is mine."

"Yes. I love you always."

No more words were said as the tiger leaped out of the gloom.

Sixteen

"Ah. Just the person we were waiting for," Dorian smoothed as Rain entered the cozy den and settled on a couch next to Sky.

"Oh?" she asked with a wry smile on her lips.

"Yes. Aaron, Sky and I were having the most interesting conversation…" Dorian began.

"He's been watching 'I Dream of Jeannie' re-runs again," Aaron informed.

Dorian sniffed in Aaron's general direction and continued. "Well, yes, I have and we were discussing the philosophical ramifications of such a being existing…"

"He wants to know if genies exist and do you really get three wishes," Aaron finished, circumventing Dorian's elaborate explanation.

Rain laughed, and shook her head. "Dorian, you are impossible."

The English vampire grinned. "I never claimed to be anything but. Well? Do they exist or not?"

She smiled again and nodded. "Yes. They exist, but they are not Aiya's children. Anubis created them when He was still playing with Earth. He only made three or four, and I have no idea what happened to them. Why? Do you want to go hunting for magic lamps? Do you want three wishes?"

Dorian didn't answer, merely grinned and grinned, looking very much like a Cheshire cat, and a scheming one at that. She had to snicker.

"I've always been game for a good adventure," he finally said, his eyes dancing with mirth.

Rain laughed again. "You really are awful. Whatever would you wish for?"

"Yes, tell us, Dorian," Aaron broke-in, smiling. "What would your three wishes be?"

Dorian looked at the ceiling, thinking. "I would wish for the sun, to be able to go out in it, and not have to hide from it," he answered matter-of-factly.

"Oh I think any vampire would wish for that," Aaron said. "What else?"

"I think I would wish to be able to taste things. You know, eat small bits of food and drink. Not replace blood of course, but to be able to tolerate a sip of coffee or a piece of chocolate," he mused, crossing his leg and playing with the tassel on his boot.

"You wouldn't wish to be mortal again?" Sky asked teasingly.

Dorian scowled. "God no! I hated being mortal when I was mortal! Why on earth would I want to be that again?"

Sky laughed, his eyes bright. "Just asking! I don't know why you'd want to be mortal either."

"And what would your third wish be?" Aaron inquired.

Dorian grew serious and looked longingly at Aaron. He was quiet for several moments, raising his hand to lightly brush Aaron's pale cheek. "I would wish to have you forever in my life. To have your love and presence always with me through the centuries."

Aaron caught Dorian's hand as it passed over his face, and pressed his cheek into the palm, holding the hand tenderly. "I'd wish for that too."

Dorian's eyes cracked for a moment and it seemed that he would begin to cry, but as soon as the moist lines appeared along the rims of his eyes, he fought them back. Gently, but resolutely, he pulled his hand from Aaron's grasp, and regained his composure.

"So you see, not all my wishes would be frivolous fancies," he whispered softly.

Aaron reached out to touch Dorian's hand, uncertain if his ex-lover would tolerate the contact, and gingerly placed it upon Dorian's cool skin. "No, not frivolous at all."

Sky was watching the display of affection passing between Dorian and Aaron with calm self-assurance. He knew Aaron loved Dorian, and that Dorian loved Aaron more than anything. He trusted Aaron enough, and liked Dorian enough, not to become jealous when they touched each other or showed affection for each other. Dorian would leap at a chance to become part of their little arrangement, and Sky was not altogether against the idea. Aaron would take some time though. Dorian and Victoria had hurt him rather badly, and he was reluctant to trust the English rogue, but his relationship with Sky was making him bolder, more assertive, and he was willing to take more risks. Aaron knew that Sky would protect him if Dorian became his old domineering, temperamental self, and that gave him courage to try things he normally would not have attempted. Sky waited and watched with amusement as they played their little courtship games, then turned his attention to Rain. She was staring off into space, her face pensive and serious, and he frowned.

What is it? he queried.

Tree. He's out there again. She indicated the newest ecomancer out on the shore of the loch, just inside the protections but as far away from the castle as possible.

He doesn't like the vampires.

I know. That isn't good, she said, frowning.

He's just been made, Bina. Give him time. This world is new and frightening to him. Sky knew well how frightening the Change could be.

Perhaps I should speak with him.

Perhaps you should leave him alone, spend less time brooding and more time paying attention to your lovers. Etienne and Tobias are feeling very neglected, he admonished.

She sighed. *I know. It's…all of this. I am not handling it very well.*

Neither are they. They are putting brave faces on for you, Bina. You should go find them, be with them, let them draw comfort from you and you from them.

Aren't you the least bit afraid?

Sky looked at Aaron and she saw his face harden. *I will do whatever is necessary to protect him.*

I have no doubts that you will.

There is no need for you to hover, Bina. I am fine, but your lovers need you. They are in the old drawing room, he answered.

I know where they are.

Then go to them. I will be fine here with Aaron and Dorian.

You will call me if you have need of me?

Of course.

"Well, I will take my leave of you and go to find my lovers," she said aloud, standing up.

"The last time I saw them, they were in the drawing room with Khristopher," Dorian informed. "They should be half way to hysterics by now. Kristi's always good for a few laughs."

She had to smile at that. Etienne by himself was a handful, Etienne paired with Khristopher was impossible. But she really couldn't complain. The Swedish vampire was a source of joy and comic relief, something they all desperately needed, and she suspected he played the clown for just that reason. He always had a joke or a quick one-liner ready to bring a smile to someone's face. With Tobias' penchant for brooding, she was grateful for Khristopher's sharp wit.

"I can imagine."

"We'll see you later, Rain," Sky told her, smiling as he put his arm around Aaron.

"Yes."

And if you wish it, I will talk to Tree, he offered.

Yes, please.

Very well. I'll let you know what happens.

Thank you.

She bowed to them and then left to go in search of her lovers. She followed the threads of their minds through the twisting halls of the castle until she came to a large door. The room she entered had once been the

Lady's quarters where the wife of the Clan leader would live with her women, but it had been converted into a drawing room with paintings and tapestries on the walls. Scattered around the large room were couches and chairs and tables, arranged for gathering and the playing of board and card games. Sprawled lazily on one of the couches was Khristopher, his wide mouth turned up into a brilliant smile. Tobias was seated in a wingback chair adjacent to the couch while Eti was lying on the floor, gripping his sides as he tried to control his laughter. It would seem that Dorian was at least halfway correct. Etienne was in hysterics. Apparently she had come at just the right moment.

"Oh c'mon! Don't you think it's great that mortals and vampires alike will now be able to have sex in the back of a Chevette!" Khristopher enthused, acknowledging her entrance with a wink.

"Kristi, it's physically impossible to have sex in the back of a Chevette!" Etienne shot back from his place on the floor.

"Well, I don't know about that. If you push the seats all the way forward, and use the dashboard, and your partner is smaller than you…" Khristopher mused, touching one finger to his cheek, a wicked smile on his face.

"And a practiced contortionist…" Tobias added.

"Knowing you, Kristi, you and your chosen companion for the evening would be at a critical moment when one of you would kick the car into gear," Etienne teased, snorting with laughter.

"I can see having to explain that to the local police," Tobias said.

"They'd never believe I was having sex in the back of a Chevette," Khristopher remarked, pointing to his tall, robust body.

"That makes two of us," Tobias admitted.

Rain smiled and joined them.

"What is going on?" she asked.

"Oh the usual chaos, destruction and mayhem," Etienne answered, looking up at her, his mouth cracked into a grin.

"I see. Well, it would seem that there is at least one casualty of war," she remarked, looking down at his sprawled body on the rug.

"Yep."

Tobias stood to greet her properly, gifting her with a kiss. "Hello, liebchen."

"Mmm. Hello."

"Hey! What about me?" Etienne grumped.

Tobias smiled, a twinkle in his blue eyes, then knelt beside his fledgling and kissed him. "Hello, liebchen."

"Not you, her!"

"Oh, well, you didn't specify…"

"Pissant."

Rain laughed and lowered herself to the floor to kiss him.

"Oh boy, Eti you lucky dog. I've been trying for six hundred years to get a woman to go down on her knees for me!" Khristopher jibed.

"Watch it, this is my lover you're talking about. If I have to, I'll defend her honor," Etienne warned.

"Chivalry? Oh how quaint! Y'know, two monks got together one dreary day with nothing better to do except copy Liturgy and pray, and came up with this code to live by which no one ever took seriously except you and bunch of misguided knights," Khristopher answered.

"Hey, they had to do something to pass the time. They didn't have MTV back then," Etienne replied.

"Or Harleys," Khristopher agreed.

"They were truly deprived."

"Hell yes, you should have seen their bathrooms. Primitive, I tell you, positively primitive. And having to pee in those suits of armor? You know they had can openers long before they had cans!" Khristopher informed with mock-amazement.

Etienne lapsed back into hysterics.

"I always hated feeding on knights. It was so hard to bite through that thick outer layer, and the metal always got stuck in my teeth."

He made a dramatic gesture of picking out his front teeth with his fingernail.

"You didn't use the can opener?" Etienne joked.

"Hey the can opener had one purpose and one purpose only and I was *not* biting my victim *there!*"

"You're supposed to wait until after they've taken off the armor, Kristi. Even Ian taught me that!' Tobias needled.

Khristopher smacked his forehead. "Damn, now why didn't *I* think of that!"

Rain laughed and smiled, shaking her head. "And to think I came here seeking to offer comfort. You don't need it."

"Comfort for what?" Etienne asked.

She shrugged. "Just comfort. Sky sent me here because he said you needed my comforting."

Tobias put an arm around her. "We always need you."

"In whatever way we can get you!" Etienne added, sitting up and hugging her.

"Awww, ain't love grand?" Khristopher remarked sarcastically.

"Piss off Kristi," Etienne replied.

"Can't. Haven't had to piss in 700 years."

Etienne laughed again and Rain could feel it reverberating through her whole body. She couldn't help but laugh along, her spirits brightening.

Tucked in Etienne's arms, she suddenly realized what Sky had done.

'Sky, you sly one. Tobias and Etienne didn't need me. I needed them.'

She breathed in deeply, smelling the unique scent of her lovers and felt her world settle around her once again. Then she looked into Etienne's eyes and smiled.

"So, I gather you were telling Khristopher about sex," she said coyly.

"Really? How did you know?" the young vampire quipped with a grin.

"I didn't know. Just a lucky guess," she replied, still smiling. 'It was not me who did the comforting, and the one who was comforted was I.'

• • •

"So, what are you doing out here all by yourself?" Sky asked, coming up behind Tree as the new ecomancer stared out over the loch.

He'd promised Rain he would speak to the young ecomancer, and he decided that there was no better time than the present. He wasn't really looking forward to the conversation, but he felt that something needed to be done with Tree before he endangered all of them with his solitary wanderings.

Tree whirled at the sound of his voice, his green eyes wide with terror and flung up his arms to protect himself. He said something in a strange mix of French and Rwandan which Sky had no hope of understanding.

Speak so I can understand you. You will not be harmed. There is nothing to fear here, he sent forcefully, suddenly angry.

Tree blinked at him and he frowned. Had Seed not taught him Tongues or mindspeech?

Do you not understand me? he questioned.

I hear you, came the faltering reply.

Then answer. What are you doing out here by yourself? Where are Ice and Song? Don't you know the danger you are putting yourself in by being out here all alone?

I wanted to be alone. I do not know where Song and Ice are. And it is safer out here than in there!

Sky growled and Tree took a step back.

There is nothing inside the castle that can harm you. You are an immortal; you are a child of the goddess.

They are bloodsucking killers!

Yes, and Aiya made them so. They cannot harm you. Even if they were so inclined as to try to feed upon you, they could drink from you until they glutted themselves and you would be none the worse for wear.

If it were possible, Tree's eyes opened wider, and Sky's ire grew. He circled the young ecomancer, looking him up and down.

Didn't Seed teach you Tongues?

Tree paused then spoke aloud, "She...she did."

"Then speak in Tongues," he snapped. "The vampires are our brethren. Aiya made them to kill humans. Did Seed not teach you this?"

"She did," he stammered.

"Then you should know that they are bound to us by blood and by the Circle. They can do you no harm."

"The vampir come at night to kill the livestock and children. They curse the village and make the people fall dead with disease," Tree answered shakily.

The reply was so absurd it was almost funny. "What? What nonsense is this? Scary tales to make children behave? Be good or the big, bad vampire will come to snatch you as you sleep!"

On the last line he made to grab Tree, causing the young man to jump back with a cry of alarm.

"Did Seed teach you nothing?"

"Sky, what are you doing?" Song's voice interrupted.

Sky faced the ancient ecomancer, his teeth bared in his anger. "She spends the last four years training him, and he comes to us an ignorant child! Even I knew more when I was brought over!"

"What do you mean?"

"He fears the vampires! He still holds them as beasts that come at night to kill sheep and spread cholera!"

"Seed warned me about you," Tree said to Sky.

Sky glared at him. "I am sure she did. Believe everything she told you, little one. I will come when you are sleeping in the guise of a bat to *suck out your soul!*"

"Sky, that is enough!" Song commanded.

Sky cast Tree a look of utter disdain. "Do something with him, Song, before he gets himself killed. Seed would probably blame me for that."

Still fuming, he stalked off but was waylaid by Ice.

"What is happening?" the Japanese ecomancer asked.

"Tree," he ground out.

"What about him?"

"Rain asked me to speak with him about his fear of the vampires, and I found that Seed has taught him almost nothing."

Ice nodded. "Tree is Seed's first fosterling. I am not surprised that his training is incomplete. She has been very secretive about him from the beginning. She probably only brought him to us because she had no choice."

"She should not be allowed to foster another. She has done a poor job with this one," Sky snarled.

"Some would say the same thing about Rain with you," Ice pointed out.

Sky head snapped up and he bristled. "Rain did what she could with me. Don't blame her for my shortcomings."

Ice put up his hands. "Peace, Sky. I say no ill word about her. I know what she went through, but I was in the Sanctuary with her when she first received you. There were others who were not and they did not see what she accomplished. Seed was one of them."

"Seed should have made him shift into a vampire before she brought him here."

Ice nodded. "She should have, but she did not. All we can do is seek to further his education and help him. He has to be very confused right now, Sky."

"And I wasn't? I had no mentor, Ice. There was no long period of apprenticeship for me! One moment I was being burned alive by my family and neighbors, and the next I was in the Sanctuary with Rain. You ask me to have sympathy for one of us who spent years in apprenticeship and now finds the task of Master too hard!" Sky argued.

Ice sighed and held his tongue. "You are right. You had no mentor or apprenticeship. But we cannot sit in judgement of Tree. Seed probably brought him over as a means of protecting him. Perhaps she meant to foster him for a few more years and found herself with no other alternatives."

Sky conceded grudgingly. "Perhaps."

"Try to be patient and kind to him, Sky. He is afraid of you."

"That is something else Seed has done. He said she told him all about me."

Ice paused, his slanted eyes opening a fraction wider, then narrowing. "I see. That will not do. But I am sure Song will take care of it."

"What's done is done, Ice, and nothing can undo it."

"Well, I am sure your fit of temper did nothing to assuage his fears."

Sky gave Ice a sidelong glance. "I suppose not."

Ice gave him a small smile and placed a hand on his shoulder. "One day, you will foster another one of us and you will learn that it is not so easy a task."

"Me?" Sky blurted, allowing Ice to guide him back to the castle. "I think that is a scary thought."

"What is a scary thought?" Dorian asked as he approached them.

"Me fostering another one of us," Sky replied.

"Hmm, that is scary. I think any fosterling of yours would be very good at shapeshifting and fire starting."

"Dorian..." Ice admonished but Sky brushed him away with a little laugh.

"It's okay Ice, he's only teasing me."

"Don't I always?"

"Of course. Where is Aaron? What are you doing out here alone?"

"Aaron is in the library as usual, and I am going for a walk."

"A walk?" Ice repeated.

"He means he is heading out to feed," Sky explained.

"Oh."

"Don't be long Dorian. I feel safer if everyone stays within the shields. Or maybe you would prefer to feed on one of us instead of..." Sky said.

"Ah, thank you, but no, Sky. That is very generous of you, however I must regretfully decline," the vampire answered.

Ice nodded, seeing the unease in Dorian's eyes. "As you wish, but come back as soon as you can."

"I will. Good night, gentlemen."

"Good night, Dorian, and good hunting," Sky called as the vampire moved away.

Dorian waited until the ecomancers had resumed walking towards the castle before continuing on his path. Focusing with his vampire hearing, he half-heartedly listened in on their conversation about Sky's fostering skills or lack thereof. Once he heard them enter the building, he turned off the walkway and headed for the beckoning forest.

He hadn't really lied to Sky and Ice. It was Sky who assumed that he was going out to hunt and it had not served his purposes to correct the ecomancer. He crossed the open yard and entered the trees, moving silently and swiftly through the dense growth. He knew exactly where he was going. It was a place he had often gone to when he was in turmoil and in need of solitude. There was a grove of ancient pines, one of the last stands of them in Scotland, and it was in that grove that Dorian found comfort. In his younger years as a vampire, he had gone there after fights with Tobias and Ian to think and listen to the sounds of the night. There were nights when he swore he could hear the trees breathe. The grove had always called to him, and it was to it that he returned with his thoughts and heavy heart.

Once there, he looked up at the stars as he sat beneath the branches of the old pines, his vampire eyes seeing far more than a mortal's eyes would, and sighed wistfully. He was feeling very lonely and very unloved. After Rain had left the den to find Tobias and Etienne, the conversation had died off. Aaron had gone to the library and Sky had headed out to talk to Tree, leaving him alone with his thoughts and wounded feelings. His earlier admission of love, and Aaron's seeming acceptance of it, had only furthered his growing unhappiness. He'd been occupying himself for three nights, trying to keep himself busy so he would not think of how his lover had left him once again, and he had run out of suitable things to do. It was getting increasingly more difficult for him to keep his mind off his feelings.

Ever since Aaron kissed him that night in the library, his emotions had been in turmoil. He wanted so desperately to be included in Aaron's inner circle...if only on occasion. He loved Aaron, and now he was also in love with Sky. But Sky was Aaron's lover, and he accepted that, even though he was struggling. It was so hard for him to bite back his jealousy and natural possessive instincts, so hard to not be the center of Aaron's attentions. Didn't Aaron realize what Dorian was giving up, to be so accepting of his new lover? He could be the jealous, possessive bastard he really was. He could be incorrigible and spiteful and demand Aaron pay attention to him. But he was being none of those things. He was being nice, behaving himself. He just wished that they would still show him some affection, like Aaron had done in the library. Oh, how wonderful it had felt to hold Aaron in his arms and just watch the stars. Greater and more simple pleasures did not exist, and he was missing them sorely. He just wanted a little affection every now and then, to let him know that he was still loved. His needs were little, and so often ignored.

There was a rustling behind him, someone making sounds only an immortal could hear, and he turned his head to see Ian standing there. Ian always knew he could find his youngest son here. Old memories came back to him and he frowned, but he said nothing to his maker. There had been a time when he and Ian had been closer than lovers, when Ian's word was law and he would have done anything for the older vampire's approval. But those times were long over. Years of bitterness separated them now. This time together, however unwelcome and enforced, along with his own self-examinations, had gone a long way to healing the rift between them. He had hope of true reconciliation, the likes of which he was achieving with Tobias. Even though he no longer needed or lived with Ian, there was still love buried under all the hurt and anger, and it was oddly comforting to see him now. He gave a little smile and Ian smiled back, approaching him, sitting next to him on the grass.

"You are unhappy again," Ian stated matter-of-factly.

Dorian lowered his gaze. "Am I ever happy for very long?"

"No, but that was always your nature."

"That is true, but you always supported my rebellions."

"Yes. So what is it this time? Why do you seek out this lonely place away from your fellows?" he questioned, turning his face up to the sky.

"It is just my habit of never being satisfied with what I have, of always wanting something more, and trying to figure out a way to get it."

"You aren't going to do something stupid, are you? Like challenge an Archangel?"

Ian's face was serious and he laughed. "No. I have no intentions of challenging any deities or their servants."

He sighed with relief. "Good. I was afraid you would try to do something reckless."

"Not this time."

"That's good to hear," Ian agreed, smiling, then continued. "So tell me, what is it that is making you so unhappy?"

Dorian looked down at his hands. "It is Aaron. He has left me, and I am missing him."

"You've been enamoured with that young one for quite some time now," Ian noted.

"He is a perfect match for me."

Ian said nothing. Dorian knew Ian's viewpoints on long-term relationships among vampires.

"But Aaron is in love with Sky. They are...very close. I'm afraid I'm jealous," he continued.

"Because you still love Aaron and want him for yourself."

"No. I like Sky. I like Sky quite a lot. Too much, in fact. I wouldn't mind...sharing."

"Do they know how you feel?"

"Aaron does. I haven't had the chance to speak with Sky on the subject yet, but I will," he answered.

Ian looked at him, his eyes haunted and sad. "Speaking of Sky..."

Just as he spoke the name, Dorian felt a change in the air around them. His hair stood on end, and he suddenly became aware that they were being watched.

"Shhh!" he said, gripping Ian's arm.

Ian had not needed him to tell him to be quiet for he felt it too, and was now searching the clearing nervously, his eyes wary. There was a creaking, a breaking of branches, and then an ominous figure loomed from the trees. Dorian's eyes opened wide as the creature revealed itself. He saw its cloven hooves, its black wings, and terror seized him. He rose to his feet with Ian beside him.

"Oh goddess…" he breathed.

Ian grabbed his arm and began pulling him back. "Dorian…"

Vampires, a mindvoice spoke to them.

"Dorian, run," Ian hissed.

"No, I'm not leaving you."

"Don't worry about me! Run back to the castle."

The thing was coming closer, clearing the trees, and standing at least eight feet high, towering in the darkness. For a moment he was paralyzed with horror and he just stood there, staring, then Ian shoved him, hard.

"Run, damnit!"

Come to me…

The creaking of the earth giving way under the heavy weight of the beast snapped them out of their stupor and they bolted for the castle in unison.

Come to me. You cannot escape me. I am the darkness into which you were born.

Dorian let Ian run ahead, dropping back for a moment. He could hear the creature following behind them and knew that he needed to do something. Coming abruptly to a halt, he whirled to face his attacker.

"Who are you! What do you want?" he demanded, trying to ignore the smell of fear and death on the beast.

You know who I am, Dorian of Leeds.

Dorian's heart stopped in his chest. "No…" Then he rallied. "So Ja'oi has sent the big boys? Do you know what the consequences of this will be?"

Do you?

"Yes. Aiya will destroy you and Ja'oi. Both of you will be nothing but piles of ash by the time She gets through with you!"

You know nothing little fool. Now you are coming with me.
"Never!"

He pooled all his strength and sent out the biggest mind bolt he had ever thrown, praying it would be enough to unseat the Archangel long enough for him to get away. He was relatively certain that Ian had gotten enough of a head start to get safely back to the protection of the castle shields. The bolt hit the ground at Lu'fahr's feet, causing an explosion of earth and felling trees. He saw the devil's arms come up to protect his eyes and wasted no time.

Sending out a mental distress call, he tore for the loch, his feet not even touching the forest floor as he ran. Behind him, he heard Lu'fahr's roar of anger and pounding footsteps, hounding at his heels and gaining quickly. He began to weep, the tears being whisked away by the wind as he raced for safety. He wasn't fast enough, he wasn't going to make it…

He cleared the trees, and he could see the warm lights of the castle, but the clearing stretched out before him and Lu'fahr was right behind him.

Infidel!! I will catch you!

The voice in his head gave him the strength to run faster, and he screamed as he raced across the grass, his long hair flying behind him. He felt Lu'fahr make a grab at him, and he thought for certain he was lost. Then a streak of light came at him, and Song was there, his blue eyes on fire, his whole body glowing. Dorian passed him, feeling Lu'fahr's surprise and sudden fear. He did not look back. Ice met him as he crossed the perimeter of the protection shields, catching him as he collapsed, sobbing.

"It's all right. You're safe. You're safe now," the ecomancer soothed.

Dorian fell to his knees as Ian and the others came rushing to meet him. Aaron was there, pushing his way to the front to reach him. Rain and Sky came out of the house. They were poised to do battle, their hands and bodies glowing, their eyes filled with fear. Rain stopped to see him, but Sky went tearing out of the protections to join Song. His help, however, was not needed. Lu'fahr had already fled.

"What is it? What has happened?" Khristopher asked, frightened.

"Lu'fahr tried to take Dorian and Ian," Rain said gravely.

Aaron gasped and held Dorian tight, his green eyes terrified. They all looked to Sky and Song, who were now returning to the safety of the shields, silently begging for answers to their unasked questions. Song regarded them solemnly as Sky went to make certain Dorian was all right, and had one sentence for them all.

"It has begun."

Seventeen

Four nights later Rain woke up screaming. Tobias shook her desperately as she flailed at him in her agony. Etienne was forced to scramble out of the way of her flying fists, covering his ears to block out the sound of her screams, but it did little to block out the mental ones.

"Rain!" Tobias cried, his eyes dilated with fear as she came out of her dream, trembling violently. "What is it? What's happened?"

She seemed disoriented, her heart pounding wildly in her chest, at first not seeing him through her wide, terrified eyes. Then the door to their bedroom abruptly flung open and Sky was there, rushing to her and scrambling onto the bed. She raised up to embrace him, holding him tight, as they each sought to still the other's quivering. Aaron appeared in the doorway, half-dressed, and frightened.

"What is going on?" Etienne demanded of Aaron, the fear in the room rising exponentially as Rain began to sob.

"I don't know. Something has happened. Something terrible," came Aaron's reply. "Sky and I were cuddling when he suddenly went rigid, and his face twisted in pain. He wouldn't tell me what was wrong, instead he came running here."

Rain's screams had attracted the others, and soon many worried faces were peering into the room behind Aaron's shoulders. Dorian came forward and put a hand upon Aaron's back, his eyes haunted.

"Will someone tell us what is going on?" Ian demanded.

"We don't know…" Tobias began, but was cut off as Song and Ice parted the crowd and entered the bedroom.

"One of our kind has been attacked," Song informed.

Ice went to the bed and put his arms around both Sky and Rain, his head bowed as gasps came from the vampires.

"Who?" Ian asked, dreading to hear the name of Alexa's mentor.

"Moon," came Song's answer.

Ian winced. "He was Sun's partner. What has happened to…"

"Sun is all right, as far as I can tell. She and Alexa are coming here."

Rain looked at him, her eyes wet with tears. "Is he dead?"

Song shook his head. "No. I did not feel the Passing as I did when Fire and Air were murdered. Moon is badly wounded, but he will survive."

"But there is something else. Something equally as disturbing," Ice added. "We have been cut off from our fellows. It is as if a great net has entangled our thoughts and nothing can get through. The last message I received was from Fire, she and Leaves are on their way, then nothing."

"We have been blocked," Song affirmed.

"What do we do?" Khristopher asked.

"We stay here. This is where the others last knew we were," Song replied. "If they need to find us, we must stay put."

"But we are sitting ducks here!" Aaron cried.

"You forget that the entire cliff and Keep is a heartstone. It is the strongest and largest one we have ever made. Nothing is getting through the protection shields," the Nord reminded.

"If anything, our brethren are flocking here. This is a fortress, and a safe haven. I would begin to prepare for others to start arriving tonight," Ice said.

"I do not understand. Why are you not fleeing to the Sanctuary?" Tobias asked.

"Because that has been cut off too. It was the first thing that I tried. The gates have been closed. My only assumption is that something has happened that has caused Aiya to fortify and block off the entrances," Song informed gravely.

"But all of you are here except for Stone and Seed. That means the Sanctuary is undefended!" Tobias exclaimed.

"No. The Sanctuary is far from undefended. The dragons are there and they are a formidable army. As are the other creatures of mythos. Ja'oi has forgotten the sheer power of the High Magic. If He tries to take over the Sanctuary, He will be rudely reminded," Song assured.

"I will prepare as many rooms as I have," Ian broke in. "No doubt vampires will be coming too."

"Yes," Ice agreed.

Ian nodded and went to perform his task; Khristopher accompanied him.

"You should all feed," Song told the remaining vampires. "Go in a group and return quickly. I do not think it is safe for you to be out of the shields for long."

"We can extend them as well," Sky's voice broke in, speaking for the first time. "We can widen the set spell to include a good part of the front clearing…keep them further away from the castle."

"Agreed. That is very perceptive of you, Sky. Yes, I think that would be a good idea."

"Let's go do that. I don't want to be idle," Sky said, removing himself from Rain's embrace and rising from the bed.

"I understand," Song sympathized, watching as Sky came towards him and moved for the door. "Tree, you are with us," he added, addressing the youngest ecomancer as he fell into step behind Sky.

After Song, Tree and Sky left, Ice turned to Rain and she fell into his arms, still shaken. Tobias grimaced with jealousy, but swallowed it. In the background, the others were leaving, preparing to go hunting and separating into groups.

"How are you?" Ice asked her gently.

"I'll live," she replied, her voice dull.

"We should prepare to receive our brethren as well. They will need food and drink…"

Rain nodded. "I will bring gardens into the caverns under the castle."

"And I will call the water."

She pulled herself from Ice's arms and hugged Tobias, who was still on the bed. He held her close, stroking her hair.

"It will be all right," she whispered.

"I love you. I am frightened," he admitted.

"Don't worry. We are safe here. Ja'oi cannot harm us."

"I know, but I dread what lies ahead."

"We knew this was coming," Etienne said. "Ever since Lu'fahr tried to take Dorian and Ian, we've been expecting something to happen, and now it has."

"Yes. That is true," she agreed, gently leaving Tobias' arms and standing. "You two must feed. Ice and I have work to do. I will be in the lower chambers when you get back."

"Very well. We will look for you there," Tobias said.

She kissed him sweetly, then kissed Etienne, and followed Ice out of the room.

As Ice predicted, the ecomancers began to arrive shortly after midnight, along with some of the vampires who had traveled with them. Fire and Leaves were the first, but Sun and Alexa, carrying Moon, appeared an hour later. Moon's left arm had been torn off. By what, neither Sun nor Alexa would say, only that the arm had been "eaten." Moon himself was unconscious from shock and loss of blood. In time, his body would heal, but for now, he was vulnerable and weak. Sun had already healed him as much as she could. When he awoke, she would begin to undo the damage done to him mentally.

By dawn all but four of the ecomancers were there, and about a dozen more vampires, Victoria and Barias among them. Missing from the ecomancers were Aerth and Stars, and the two still in the Sanctuary, Seed and Stone.

While the vampires slept during the day, the avatars worried about their missing fellows and Moon, and prepared to protect their little safe haven. Nothing, however, happened. If anything, it was eerily quiet. The ecomancers found that, within the shelter of the shields, their mind speech was intact, but that outside the heartstone's protections, a wall came down between them. Something was most certainly amiss, and it had them all nervous and upset.

By sunset, they had retired to the inner sanctums of the cliff. Rain had carved out great caverns within its heart, caverns that pulsed with heart-stone energy. The ecomancers went there to replenish their energy and soothe their frazzled nerves. Ice had called both cold and hot water springs, and the hot water springs served as spas for sore muscles and weary minds. The ecomancers and several vampires: Tobias, Etienne, Aaron and Dorian included, were soaking in the steam pools when Barias came to interrupt them with his news.

"There is a strange light in the sky, and an odd movement of energy. I think you should come take a look at it," the ancient vampire said.

Concerned, they obeyed, rising from the heated water and dressing quickly. They gathered outside the castle, in the area of the clearing now protected by the shields, looking up at a yellow glow in the clouds. The glow was hazy and indistinct, but it seemed to be gathering the clouds to it, swirling them around it, and the wind was picking up.

"I've never seen the like," Song breathed.

"What do you think it is?" Ian asked.

"I don't know, but there might be a way to find out," the Nord answered.

Boldly, he stepped outside the shields, ignoring the cry of alarm Sun gave him, and stood, opening himself up and reaching out with his mind to probe the sky. The wind circled around him, blowing through his hair, and kicking up dead leaves around his feet until he crossed the boundary again.

"It feels of High Magic. An ancient Gate Spell of some sort. Not like any Gate Spell I have ever seen or felt, but it is getting larger and something is trying to come through," he informed.

"Is it friend or foe?" Wind asked.

"I cannot say, but we will know soon, for we are powerless to stop the Gate. The only one of us who has ever had experience working High Magic is Aerth," Song replied.

Blood Origins

"But you were bonded to a dragon, surely you know something of these spells," Leaves said.

"It is because of my bond to Shieera that I recognize the magic at all. Besides, this is ancient magic, much older than the kind Shieera used."

Rain stepped forward to the edge of the perimeter and bade Tobias to come with her.

"My love. Tell me what you see with your vampire eyes."

Tobias focused his vision on the glow. "I see nothing other than what you already see. A glow with no distinct edge."

"Keep watching, tell me if it changes at all," she said carefully.

"Rain? Do you have an idea?" Ice asked.

"Yes, I do, but I am lax to say…just yet."

There was a rumbling and a shift in power as flashes of light radiated from the glow like lightning. The wind was fierce now, making the tall trees' branches shake, and the tension was mounting.

"The glow has ripped!" Tobias announced. "There is something coming through! A great shape…"

"What is it?" Aaron demanded.

"I can't see, the clouds are in the way…"

They watched the sky, afraid to breathe, waiting for the shape to clear the clouds. Aaron clung to Dorian, his face a mask of terror. Victoria faced the glow, her eyes hard and challenging, while Etienne moved behind Tobias. Barias was pressed near to them, silently whispering something to himself as he looked up at the swirling clouds. Behind them were Ian, Khristopher, Alexa and the others that had come with the ecomancers. The glow was obscured briefly by something solid, and then it broke through the clouds.

"I can see it!" Tobias announced focusing on the great body that came though the layer of clouds.

The others waited anxiously, afraid to breathe until they knew what was barreling down at them from the sky.

"It's…It's a dragon!"

"What color?" Song asked.

"I...I can't tell. It's still too far away and the light masks its hide..."

Rain grabbed Tobias' arm as the dragon came closer, bobbing, its wings drooping. "There is something very wrong...The dragon is having a hard time flying."

"I can see it better now. It's white...no gray and it's wounded badly," Tobias said.

Fire thrust her way to the forefront, her eyes panicked. "Oh Goddess. It's Khirsha!"

A murmur of concern rumbled through the ecomancers as they watched the ancient silver dragon approach. As she got closer, they could see that she had large gaping wounds on her body and big tears in the membranes of both her wings.

"Both her wings are damaged! She's going to crash land!" Rain exclaimed.

Giving no regard to her safety, she ran out of the shields. She had meant to shapechange into a dragon to help Khirsha land, but it was too late. The ancient dragon was losing altitude swiftly, although desperately trying to slow her fall, and if she continued at her present speed, she would crash into the Keep. Sky came running up beside Rain.

"If we call the wind, maybe we can slow her down," he said.

"Yes," she replied and spread her arms.

Together, she and Sky wrapped the dragon in wind currents, catching what was left of her wings and creating a barrier of air. Khirsha was able to alter her course, but not enough to miss the trees. As they watched, horrified, the giant silver smashed into the first line of trees that bordered the clearing, ripping them down with her huge body as she skidded on her side for several dozen yards, and finally came to a halt not twenty feet from the castle walls.

The wind was dying down as the ecomancers ran to her, immediately setting to heal the massive rips in her sides. She lay still, her eyes closed, her mouth open, and her dragon tongue hanging out. She was alive and breathing heavily, but Rain recognized the scent of death upon the dragon's breath. In her huge front claws, she clutched a faintly glowing orb.

"Khirsha! What has happened?" she asked, kneeling down beside her friend.

"Oh Goddess," Fire sobbed. "Look what they've done to her wings!"

Khirsha's eye cracked open, and a hiss came from her throat. "I...brought you...key..."

The vampires were approaching slowly, led by Tobias. The ecomancers paid them no mind as they worked to stop the bleeding and repair the holes in Khirsha's hide.

"Key? Key to what Khirsha?" Rain questioned, leaning close to hear.

Khirsha sighed, and Rain could feel the dragon gathering her strength. When she spoke again, it was with force.

"Key to the door. He has locked them. With this, you can get in."

Rain guessed she meant the orb. "What door Khirsha, and who has locked them?"

"Ja'oi. In the Sanctuary. He has invaded..."

Cries of alarm rose from them, and they paused in their work.

"Oh Goddess..." Rain breathed, the tears rolling down her face.

"Not all is lost. Fighting is bitter, but He has yet to capture the Webs. We hold Him at bay, but...need help."

"Where is Aiya? What has happened to Seed and Stone?" Sun asked desperately.

"Aiya guards the Webs. Seed and Stone fight beside the dragons."

Khirsha was losing her strength again, her eye going out of focus and rolling into her head. She was fighting it, struggling to hold onto consciousness and life for a bit longer.

"Managed Gate spell. Old magic Ja'oi has forgotten...how to fight. To bring you the key. It will...open the door, so you can go..."

"Do you know what has become of Aerth and Stars?" Song inquired. "We are unable to communicate through mindspeech."

"Aerth and Stars escaped before…Ja'oi cast net…They…gathering forces among Aiya's allies. Ja'oi knows…not much time. Wants the Webs. Aiya fights Him but…Weary…need help."

"You have risked your life to bring us this key and this news. We will take it and crush Ja'oi's army," Ice said. "You have earned your rest. We will go, while Rain stays to tend you."

"That…will not be…necessary," Khirsha answered, her voice fading.

"What do you mean?" Leaves asked.

Rain already knew. Khirsha was dying. Her wounds were too great and her heart was failing her. No amount of healing could stop that now. She must have known before she cast the Gate, that it would be her last one, that she would not be coming back…

"Yes…Child…Ja'oi…cannot stop…my mind…speech. Yes…I am dying."

"No!" Fire cried, working ever more furiously on the wounds. Rain just looked at her, her eyes sad.

"Let me go…Tired…of being old. I serve…the Mother…one last time."

Her claws released the orb key and Rain grabbed it.

"Khirsha, how do we use this? We know nothing of High Magic," she admitted.

"Give to Song…it was…Shieera's."

"You can't die on me you old bat!" Fire wailed.

Khirsha managed a smile and a feeble, croaking laugh. "Time…for…the coat and boots…"

Rain placed a hand upon Khirsha's muzzle, her tears streaming down her face. "My friend, my dear friend. We will take your gift. We will defeat Ja'oi. Your sacrifice will not be in vain."

Khirsha managed to focus on her. "Always were…the heart. Always…the giver. Was why…Aiya chose you…for the…broken one."

Rain knew Khirsha meant Sky; that Sky was given to her because she had the biggest heart. Still weeping silently, she stroked the long neck.

"I will miss you."

"I go…in glory. The last dragonflight…was mine."

Khirsha's eye closed and she let out a heavy sigh, the breath escaping her, and with it, her life. They all felt her Passing, and stood still, all except for Fire, who was crying uncontrollably. Ice went to her and took her in his arms, as the other ecomancers formed a ring around the dragon's body, their faces solemn and drawn. Rain gave the orb key to Song.

"We will go, but we will see to Khirsha's body first," Song told them.

Tobias gently touched Rain's arm. "What will you do with the body?"

"We must destroy it, so that no trace of her is left for humans to find."

"Do you want part of the hide?" Ice asked Fire.

Fire shook her head, her face red and swollen from her crying, and stood away from the circle, hugging herself.

"What Ja'oi has done will not go unanswered. What Khirsha gave so we might go to fight, will not go unrecognized," Wind spoke, raising his arms.

"She was the oldest. The first of her kind. Created directly by Aiya Herself. She was a child of the oldest magic, and greatly loved. She will be sorely missed," Song added.

In concert with each other, the ecomancers called upon the earth magic. The wind answered their call and circled around them as Khirsha's body began to crumble and crack. As they worked, their eyes closed, the dragon disintegrated, the wind taking away bits of silver/gray dust as the body fell apart. In the middle of the task, a mournful wolf-like howl rose up from Sky, and the vampires looked at him to see the tears that leaked from his eyes.

Sky's howl was answered by Rain giving her own howl, and soon there was an entire chorus filling the clearing. The howl lasted as the wind carried away Khirsha's body, and died down when the last bit of dust was lifted up and dispersed over the land in a rain of shimmering particles. The oldest silver dragon was no more.

There was a heavy silence in the clearing as the wind quieted. In their grief, they had forgotten the vampires, and now turned to them.

"Our worst nightmare has come true. Ja'oi has invaded the Sanctuary," Wind informed. "Khirsha gave her life to bring us the means of opening the doorway to the Sanctuary, for we are unable to open gates into the temporal planes that gods use to house their souls."

"What will you do now?" Aaron asked respectfully.

"We will go to the aid of our goddess."

Ian stepped forward. "Is there anything we can do? I know that Dorian and I had some success in fighting off Ja'oi's Seraphim."

"The strongest of you may be of some service to us, but there is great risk. We would not ask you to join us, but if you decide to come, you will be welcomed," Wind answered.

"Then I will go with you," Ian said.

"I will join you as well," Barias broke-in, moving to stand next to Ian.

"And I go wherever Sun goes," Alexa's voice announced.

"Your help is much appreciated," Wind replied.

Sky went to Aaron, who grabbed his arms and clung to him, and stroked his lover's black hair. "You should stay here where it's safe."

"I know, but I do not want to live if you are killed. I'd rather go with you and risk death."

"I will not die, dearling, and I love you too much to let you take the risk. Stay here and be safe."

"If you don't come back to me..."

"I will come back, I promise you."

Tobias moved to speak with Rain, but she was not paying any attention to him. She was staring at the wreckage of trees on the edge of the clearing. Several of them had been smashed to the ground while others were ripped and scarred.

"My beloved, I..." he began, but stopped as she stepped away from him. "Where are you going?"

"To right a wrong."

He followed as she headed toward the fallen trees, but she turned and put her hand upon his arm. Her face was smooth, but her eyes told the story of her grief. "Stay near to the shields, my love. I'll be right here, and I won't take long."

What she was really trying to tell him was that she wished to be left alone for a little while, to deal with her sorrow in her own way. Recognizing this, Tobias nodded and let her go. He kissed her sweetly on the forehead, and returned to the group while she went on to the tree line. As he joined Etienne, placing a hand upon his child's shoulder, he felt Etienne step closer, seeking comfort.

"Where is she going?" he asked timidly.

"She is going to take care of the fallen trees," Tobias answered.

"Ah," Etienne said, nodding.

They turned their heads to see Rain walking among the downed pines. They had never seen her truly work her art, and they watched, transfixed as she made new trees sprout from the stumps of the smashed ones. A few moments later, voices next to them caught their attention, and they moved to listen to what was going on.

"When will you go?" Ian was saying.

"Soon. Not all of us will be going. One pair of us will stay and guard you," Song answered.

"Leaves, Moon, Tree and Rain will stay," Fire said. "I have already taught Leaves all I can for now, and I will not be denied vengeance for Khirsha's death. For this I will partner with Sky, for he is also no stranger to vengeance."

Fire gave Sky a measuring look, and he met her eyes steadily, saying nothing.

"Can you figure out how the key works?" Ice asked Song.

Song looked at the orb in his hand. "Shieera told me High Magic was mind magic. Many of the High Magic devices work by focusing thoughts through them. I would assume this one works the same way."

"So you just have to think about what you want it to do, and it will do it?" Sea questioned.

"Something like that. It isn't quite that simple, but I do think I can make it work. Khirsha would not have brought it to us if she did not believe one of us could use it."

"Give it a try," Fire said.

"Not yet. I want to have a plan ready for when we do go. We must be prepared for the worst," Song objected.

"I agree," Wind concurred. "We do not even know where the Gate will let us in. We may find ourselves intruding into a battle. We must go in prepared to come out fighting."

"No. Gates always disorient those going through them. Khirsha would have known this. I am certain it is set to let us into a safe area," Song countered, turning the orb over and over in his hands.

"And if it is not? Then what?" Wind challenged.

"We go in fighting," Sky answered coolly.

"Ah, you are ripe for battle, aren't you, little rogue?" Wind spat gruffly. "We have not forgotten the last time you met out retribution."

"I do not shun the kill," Sky replied. "I use my powers as I please. I have no love for Ja'oi or any of His minions. He has killed Khirsha and attacked the Sanctuary. For that I will have vengeance, as will Fire."

"We cannot speak of vengeance and anger," Sea's voice interrupted as the two glared at each other. "Our anger will make us hasty and easy to defeat. We must temper our fury and use it as a weapon against Ja'oi."

"Wise words, Sea," Song agreed. "And where is our other voice of temperance? Where is Rain?"

"She is by the tree-line, healing the damage done by Khirsha's fall," Tobias answered.

"What? You mean she is out of the shields?" Ice blurted.

Song looked to the forest and his eyes opened wide. All of them turned to see what he was staring at, and their hearts froze.

Rain had been forgotten when the conversation became heated. Now she was standing on the edge of the forest, her hands raised and her eyes closed as she made a tree grow from the remains of a fallen one, completely oblivious to the fact that Lu'fahr was right behind her.

The next series of events happened so quickly that they could have been a blur, except for the fact that each of them saw it in eerie slow motion. Tobias screamed a warning as he raced across the clearing. Rain heard him, coming out of her trance, and gave him a perplexed look, her brow furrowed as to why he was running at her at full speed. Then she looked behind her and saw what was there. Her hand came up to defend herself as she tried to put more distance between her and the devil, but Lu'fahr reached out and grabbed her by the throat. Tobias made a grab for Rain, who hung limply in Lu'fahr's grasp. Lu'fahr swung his arm, striking Tobias and sending him flying backwards, smashing him into a wall of trees with such force that his vampire body cracked the trunks of several of them before it came to rest in a broken heap some eight yards away.

Just as Tobias was reaching Rain and the devil, Sky transformed himself into a reptilian beast that was mostly speed and razor-sharp teeth, and went tearing across the grass. In his fearsome form, he barreled down upon Lu'fahr, and was met by a pack of hideous, dog-like creatures that were also mostly speed and teeth: no doubt the same type of creature that was responsible for Moon's missing arm. This theory was confirmed when Alexa started screaming hysterically. Sky attacked the beasts, tearing at them in a fury of teeth and claws. His offensive kept Lu'fahr's guards occupied while the other ecomancers rushed to Rain's aid.

Sky was ripping the creatures to shreds, swallowing huge chunks of them, even as they bit and ripped at him. Whirling, he snapped the neck of one and bit off its head, while his massive hindquarters crushed another. One jumped upon his back, tearing at his flesh. He screamed and reared up, snapping at it until he grabbed its leg and threw it down, trampling it. His injuries hurt him, but he kept attacking, slashing with his claws and rendering the beasts apart with his teeth. Within moments, all five of them lay in pieces on the grass.

Splattered with blood and breathing heavily, Sky shifted back into a man. He saw Ice and Leaves healing the broken, smashed body of Tobias, surrounded by Aaron, Etienne, Dorian and Ian. Alexa was hugging Sun desperately, her eyes blank with shock. Turning his head, he looked to see where Rain and Lu'fahr had been, but Song and the remaining ecomancers blocked his view, their eyes haunted and pained.

"Where is she?" Sky demanded, his face and hair stained red with blood.

They did not move or even speak to him, merely stared at him in sorrow and fear. Growling like an animal, he shoved through them, and stopped short when he broke free.

Rain lay motionless upon the grass, her eyes closed. She had not a mark upon her, but she did not move when he called her name. He fell to his knees, shaking her, crying, his panic rising.

"Why won't she answer me?" he screamed.

Song came forward and looked down at him, his face grave.

"Lu'fahr has taken her soul."

Eighteen

Tobias' cry of despair echoed off the trees. Lu'fahr had stolen Rain's soul. Her body remained, but it was an empty shell; she lay limp in her lover's arms, a life-size doll with pale skin and long, ebony black hair. He wept bitterly, his face in her dark hair, holding her close to his newly healed body. Etienne was beside him, weeping as well, but he brought little comfort.

Lu'fahr had spoken a warning before he disappeared. He had told them that Rain would be destroyed if they tried to interfere with the God Almighty. He had called them the Heretics, the Unbelievers, and told them they were doomed to fail. In truth, he left them with no choice. They had to help Aiya, even if Rain was sacrificed in the process, and there were no guarantees that he would not kill her anyway. They knew what they had to do, and they knew the price. All of them reluctantly accepted it; all except Sky.

Sky was standing motionless, facing Rain's new trees, his back to the Keep. He was naked, his doeskin clothing lying in tatters on the grass, and the night air bit at his skin, but he did not seem to notice. He had not spoken a single word or responded to anyone in any way since Song told him the news. They had left him, going to tend Alexa, who was still near hysteria, and to heal Tobias; and when Tobias started crying, he showed no sign of hearing the heartwrenching wail. Aaron came up to wrap a cloak around his shoulders, but he let it fall to the ground, and his lover finally gave up, sitting down next to him, waiting.

As he looked into his lover's eyes, Aaron saw that Sky's face was an unreadable mask, stoic and stony. The others said he was in shock, but Aaron could sense that something was building inside his lover. There was an invisible static shield forming around Sky's body, something that made Aaron's skin crawl, and he was deeply afraid. The remains of the Gate Spell were still dispersing, and the soft glow was fading in the sky. Aaron saw Sky raise his eyes and lock onto it with an intense stare.

The air around Sky became electrically charged, and he grimaced as an arc of power burst from him. Aaron did not see the power come from his lover, but he felt it and saw the effect it had. The remnants of the Gate flashed and pulsed. It got the attention of the other ecomancers, and they moved to see what was going on. Song approached worriedly.

"Sky? Sky, what are you doing?"

Sky did not answer. His eyes were still locked on the Gate, and there was another pull. The Gate flashed thin tendrils of lightning, and the clouds began to swirl around it again.

"Sky..." Song tried again, reaching out to touch Sky's shoulder.

Sparks and electric shocks struck Song, throwing him backwards as he let out a cry of pain and alarm. He sat up, stunned, rubbing his burned hand, staring at Sky in fear. Aaron looked at the Nord, then back at his lover, his heart pounding. Sky's face had changed. It was no longer blank; it was twisted with rage and concentration, his blue eyes burning with anger, and his jaw tight. The Gate sparked again, and now the wind was picking up, rustling the leaves of the trees.

Song scrambled to his feet and tried to touch Sky a second time, but the electric barrier met him even before he got within range. He let out another cry of pain and grew angry, attacking Sky with a bolt of power. The bolt struck the barrier, sparked, flashed blue light and fizzled out, and all the while, Sky continued to pull on the Gate.

"He's gone mad!" Sun said, taking Song by the arm.

"What in Aiya's name is he trying to do?" Ice exclaimed.

"He's trying to open the Gate," Wind answered.

"No. He's pulling the power from it, that's where the shield is coming from," Song corrected.

"How can he do that? We don't have that power!" Sun cried.

"I don't know," the Nord replied, looking as shocked as his brethren as Sky pulled on the power again.

A storm was building, a storm of tremendous proportions. The clouds were closing in, blocking out all the stars, and they could see the flashes of lightning within them as it approached. The wind was whipping through the trees, howling as it raced into the clearing, and Sky was at the center of its fury. It swirled around him, lifting and blowing his long hair, pelting him with debris as his body began to glow with an eerie yellow light. The others watched in shock, then rallied as the wind blasted them.

"We have to stop him! He'll tear the castle down!" Sun screamed over the cry of the storm, as the thunder cracked and lightning lit up the sky like fireworks.

Leaves made frantic motions to the vampires, pointing to the Keep. "Get inside! Get into the caverns! This storm will rip everything to pieces!"

Ian heard and understood, seeing with his own eyes the size and force of the gale-strength storm that was barreling down upon them. By all the gods, the sheer power of it would be enough to tear the whole cliff down. Would they even be safe inside? Leaves pointed again and repeated the warning, and this time Ian listened, ushering the vampires to the castle.

"Get inside! Go to the lower chambers! To the caverns! Go! Go!" the vampire ordered.

Hurrying, they flooded towards the castle and its underground caverns, Tobias carrying Rain's body to safety. All except Aaron, who still knelt, helpless at Sky's feet. Dorian turned back, into the wind, the dust and leaves striking him in the face.

"Aaron!" he cried, but Aaron did not move. He was staring up at Sky, his face a picture of agony and grief.

Dorian ran to Aaron as the ecomancers tried to break Sky's connection to the Gate. He fell to the grass beside Aaron as flashes of electricity burst out and encompassed Sky, protecting him from the attacks of his brethren.

"Aaron!" Dorian called again, crawling on his stomach to reach the black-haired vampire.

Aaron did not respond when Dorian touched him.

"Aaron! We have to get inside!"

The electric shield around Sky crackled and sparked again as the wind came blasting into the clearing. Dorian protected his face with his hand as branches and leaves came hurling at him. The debris struck Aaron, but he did not move or even acknowledge that he had been hit. Then a tree fell nearby and landed against two other trees with a great crash. Dorian panicked and grabbed Aaron, trying to pull him away, but it was like trying to move stone. Dorian, in spite of all his strength, could not budge his love. Aaron did not have such power, and that was when Dorian realized that it was Sky who was preventing him from moving Aaron.

"You'll kill him! Do you want that? Let him go!" Dorian screamed.

Another tree smashed down, and lightning crackled, hitting the top of the cliff. Sky was glowing even more now, and the cliff and castle began to glow too, forming a visible line of energy from the Gate to the top turret of the fortress. The ecomancers stepped back in horror, their faces full of terror and awe.

"He's linked the Gate to the heartstone!" Wind exclaimed as the power in the clearing tripled in the span of a heartbeat.

"By the Goddess, what is he doing?" Sea cried.

"I don't know, but we have no hope of stopping him now, short of killing him!" Song answered.

Dorian's panic grew, and he started to cry. "Please! Sky, let him go! You'll destroy him! Please, if you love him at all, don't do this!"

Sky showed no sign of hearing or understanding Dorian's plea. He was a statue, framed with yellow light, his white hair blowing around his face wildly, and his sapphire eyes reflecting nothing of the soul that lay behind them.

"Please! I love him too! Don't take him from me!" Dorian begged, wrapping his arms around Aaron to protect him from the brutal winds.

Sky did not physically react, but Aaron suddenly became much lighter and Dorian was able to pull him from Sky's immediate vicinity. As soon as Aaron was a few feet away, however, he came back to life violently, clawing at Dorian with his fingernails.

"No! Let me go!" Aaron begged.

"He's gone mad, Aaron!"

"They're going to kill him! NNNNOOOOOOOO!!"

Lightning hit the heartstone again, and the entire cliff flashed with a burning yellow light. The light formed a bolt of energy that lashed out and struck Sky in the back. The ecomancers were thrust away from Sky by the force of the pulse, tossed like toy soldiers on a child's battlefield. Picking themselves up, they pooled their strength to make one last attempt to stop their crazed brother. They attacked him in unison, using the elements and mind magic to breach his protections. Aaron screamed, tears streaming down his face, tearing and biting at Dorian to let him go, but Dorian held him firmly, even as his eyes were locked on the ecomancer who was now at the center of a ring of white fire. The power from the attacking ecomancers was wrenched from them forcefully, throwing them back once again, and their energy was added to the growing pool of magic. The flames around Sky grew higher, encompassing him to his chest, and his face transformed into a mask of rapture.

Suddenly Sky thrust out his arms, his entire body aflame with power as the energy began to wrap around him like a tempest. His eyes were closed, his back arched, and he was barely touching the ground. Then he pulled the power towards him, focusing it, directing it, and sent it flying at the new trees with full force. It surged from him in a great bolt, striking the trees, making the ground shake and groan as sparks and flames blew everywhere. Song cried a warning that was drowned out by the din of the resulting explosion as the space between two of the trees bent and warped, and there was a tremendous ripping that slashed through the temporal layers. A fissure of light appeared between the trees, widening and expanding until it encompassed the area between their trunks, opening a doorway into another temporal layer. Sky had created a Gate.

In the heavy silence that ensued, the Gate glowed with strange white-gray light, flickering but holding steady. Beyond it lay a broken landscape, filled with smoke and an eerie, burning light. Dorian stared at it in mute shock as the wind settled and the lightning faded. Looking around himself, he saw the clouds thinning and breaking apart as the power settled and dispersed, revealing sections of the nighttime sky in all its starlit glory.

Sky stood before the Gate, a ring of burnt grass around him where the white fire had been, and, as everyone stared in shock at what he had done, Aaron broke free of Dorian's numb grasp and ran to him.

"Sky!" he sobbed, throwing his arms around him.

Sky turned his head slowly, his eyes still glowing with the strange light, and looked at Aaron. The blue irises flickered and softened for a moment as he bent his mouth to kiss Aaron tenderly on the forehead.

"I love you. Don't wait for me," he whispered tenderly.

Aaron met his gaze, trembling. "What do you mean?"

"I'm going after Rain."

Aaron looked at the Gate fearfully, suddenly realizing where it led. Sky was gently removing himself from his arms, and he clutched his lover desperately.

"No!" he begged.

"I must. Now let me go."

Sky firmly pulled Aaron's arms away and stepped towards the Gate. Song came up, attempting to stop him, but Sky whirled his head around, his eyes glowing white and yellow, and stopped Song where he stood.

"Do not try to follow me. Go to the aid of Aiya."

He did not give Song a chance to answer as he walked ever closer to the doorway.

Aaron grabbed Dorian, his eyes pleading. "Go with him! Please!"

Dorian was stunned. "Aaron, I…"

"He needs help! And I'm not strong enough! Please! I'll do anything you want, but please go with him!"

Dorian stared at the Gate, seeing the eerie light of Hell, and his blood turned cold. Then he looked at Aaron's soulful, wide eyes.

"Please! I'll...I'll stay with you forever. I promise. I give you my word that I will never leave you...if you go with him."

Dorian's heart ached, and he hugged Aaron briefly. What he would give to be so loved. "All right. I will go, but not for the reasons that you think."

He gave Aaron a swift kiss and let him go, striding towards the Gate and crossing through a few seconds after Sky.

• • •

Song and Ice stared open mouthed as Sky walked through the Gate into Hell. A heartbeat later, they saw Dorian pass through after him, then the Gate flickered and slammed closed. The shift of power created a wave of backlash energy that sent shocks running back along the links to the heartstone. The heartstone shuddered and rumbled, but held solid, sparking off lightning bolts as the last of the power was released. The storm was all but gone, as was the yellow glow of the original Gate.

"By the Goddess, how did he do that?" Ice breathed.

"I don't know. Maybe his madness gives him power," Song replied, his voice hollow.

"We should check on the others. The heartstone may have collapsed some of the inner caverns in that last wave," Sea broke in.

"Agreed," Ice answered, and turned for the house.

Song spied Aaron kneeling on the grass, still staring at the place where the Gate had been. His face soft with sympathy, he went to the vampire and gently took his arm.

"It will be all right," he soothed to Aaron, who jolted and looked at him with wide, terrified eyes. "Come. Let me take you inside."

Aaron lowered his gaze and slowly rose to his feet, following Song into the house without a word.

The castle was remarkably undamaged. There were several broken windows, and many pictures and bookcases had fallen, but structurally, the dwelling was fine. Down in the lower chambers, they found the vampires huddled together in one of the caverns. Some rocks had broken free from the ceiling and walls, but no one was hurt and the damage was not serious. Against the far wall, Tobias was still clutching Rain's body, and Etienne was pressed near to them. Aaron timidly went to kneel beside Khristopher, who was holding Victoria, and accepted comfort from him as Khristopher put an arm around him.

"What has happened?" Etienne asked.

"Sky is gone, as is Dorian," Song answered.

"What? Where did they go?" Ian demanded from where he was sitting nearby Tobias.

"Sky called a Gate into Hell. He has gone to rescue Rain. Dorian went with him," came the tired reply.

"We do not have much time. Lu'fahr will know very soon that we are moving against Ja'oi, and he may attack us again," Fire informed. "We are going to use the Key Khirsha gave us. Those of you who would fight with us, say so now and come."

"I will go," Barias said.

"As will I," came Ian's voice.

"No Ian…" Etienne protested. "If Tobias loses you too…"

"I'll take the risk. I wish to see the Sanctuary, I wish to see the goddess."

"That is two. Who else?" Sea asked.

"Three," Alexa corrected.

Sea gave her a measuring glance. "Okay, three."

"Four," announced one of the African vampires.

"Five," said his partner.

In the end, a total of ten vampires agreed to go with the avatars. Those who remained behind watched from a safe distance as Song used the key

Khirsha had given them to open another Gate. This time there was no rogue storm or great pool of power. The orb shot out a beam of light that rippled then spread until it had created the desired doorway, and one by one, they passed through it. Sun was the last to enter. She turned back briefly to look at Leaves, Tree and Moon, who were staying behind, and waved lightly. Moon raised his hand in answer, and she smiled at him. Then she went through the Gate herself and it closed behind her.

The dragons were waiting for them when they came through the Gate. There were a least a dozen of them, mostly silvers and golds, gathered in the secluded ravine that the Gate opened into. Many of the vampires cried out in amazement when they realized they could see the sun, and fell to their knees, their hands out to hold the light. Sun moved among them, reassuring and settling them as the dragons turned to the ecomancers.

"We knew you were coming," one of the golds said, a large male and the oldest.

Song shook off his disorientation. "You felt the Gate."

The dragon nodded. "We have been waiting since the Elder left."

Sun stepped forward. "What are the chances of Ja'oi's minions having felt it?"

"None. We dampened the fields when we first began to feel the Gate," a female silver replied. "Besides, none of Ja'oi's minions know anything of High Magic."

"How is the Elder?" a third asked, this one a young gold.

The ecomancers bowed their heads. "Khirsha is dead. She did not survive the Gating," Song answered sadly.

The oldest gold closed his eyes in grief. "We suspected as much: that her injuries were too great. She led the raid upon the taken citadel to retrieve the Key. She was badly wounded in the battle."

"We tried to stop her," another gold, a female, said. "But it was too late. She cast the spell and was gone."

"Khirsha's heart was great. Her death will not go unavenged," Fire announced.

"No," the oldest agreed. "And word of her Passing will fuel our fight. She sacrificed herself to bring us your much needed help."

"Yes. And we have come to help, and we have brought more of Aiya's children, the vampires. They have come to lend us their aid," Sea told them.

The oldest gold looked down at the vampires appraisingly as Barias stepped forward.

"You are the leader?" the dragon asked.

"I am Barias. I am the oldest here," Barias answered.

"I am Koshe. The golds are my hatchlings."

"And I am Khaheera, leader of this little band of silvers," an older female silver said.

"What Magics do you possess?" Koshe asked.

"Magics?" Barias repeated.

"They have mind magic, Koshe. These are the most powerful of the vampires," Song spoke for them.

"Excellent. Mind magic will help us greatly," Koshe enthused. "We can pair them with us and with the unicorns."

"We could also use an ecomancer to help heal the wounded," Khaheera added.

"I will do that," Sun offered.

"Where are Seed and Stone?" Song asked.

"They are guarding the Heart. Ja'oi has sent his strongest against them. They are holding, but they need help," Koshe replied.

Just then another gold dragon came sweeping into the ravine, its claws raking on the rocks as it hurried over the ridge.

"Avatars! We need help, now!" the newcomer cried.

"Dharma, what is it?" Khaheera asked, frightened.

"Ja'oi's Seraphim have attacked the Library," came the answer.

Song's face twisted into a mask of rage.

"Come, we must go now! They have yet to breach the protections, but..." Dharma was saying, but Song was already moving.

"Wait!" Ian shouted. "I'm coming with you!"

The old vampire leaped onto the dragon's back as Dharma took to the air, following Song's streaking silhouette. The others watched them go.

"I will go to help Seed and Stone. I want a good battle to mete out my revenge for Khirsha's death," Fire informed.

"If it is a fight you are looking for, you will fare better helping to recapture the citadel," Koshe corrected.

"Very well. I'll go there."

"I will go with you," Ice said.

"Then Wind and I will go to help Seed and Stone," Sea spoke.

"Agreed. Go!" Ice affirmed.

Without further discussion, Sea and Wind vanished.

"I will go to heal the wounded. Alexa can assist me," Sun reminded.

"As you wish. You will find them by the steam pools. The area is somewhat safe from Ja'oi's army," Khaheera said.

"That leaves the rest of us and the vampires," Fire commented. "Lead us, Koshe."

"You will need these," one of the silvers said as she and two of her companions dropped an assortment of weapons into a pile by their feet.

"Very well. Those vampires who are coming with us choose a weapon and a dragon, and mount. Old one who calls himself Barias, you are with me. Climb on. We are leaving now," Koshe ordered.

Barias did not need to be told a second time. Immediately he grabbed a large spear from the pile of weapons and scaled the large wing. He had just enough time to get a good hold on the dragon's neck before they were airborne. He looked down from Koshe's back, watching as the landscape grew smaller and smaller. Next to him, Fire sat astride Khaheera, showing all the true colors of her Celtic heritage. She had her legs curled as high as they could go without losing grip on the dragon's hide, masking her silhouette from below because she did not want Ja'oi's minions to know she was there until it was too late. In her hand was a spear, exactly like the one he carried, and slung across her back was a hardwood bow and a quiver of arrows. These weapons could not be used against the Seraphim or other angels because Ja'oi had cast protection spells over them, but they could be used on Ja'oi's hellish war dogs.

The legion of dragons, some carrying vampires and ecomancers, flew across the ocean, heading towards the island that held the citadel. The island was small, surrounded by many miles of deep ocean and jagged, deadly barrier reefs. The only truly safe way to reach the citadel was by air or by magic. Ja'oi's army had captured the citadel in the beginning of their invasion, effectively cutting the dragons off from many of their most powerful magical weapons. Khirsha had sustained most of her damage when she had infiltrated the citadel to steal the Orb Key. After her successful raid upon the fortress, Ja'oi had reinforced the ranks guarding it, and the dragons had not been able to breach them since. But Koshe had told them that the attacking army had become complacent, satisfied with its repeated victories in keeping the dragons from reclaiming the citadel. And now the dragons were angry. The oldest silver had been killed, and their rage gave them new strength. They paired vampires with the strongest of them, hoping to combine minds in the heat of battle, and give them the extra edge they needed.

Twilight was falling and the sky was turning the color of Sky's eyes, dotted with stars. Barias smiled. 'Yes, let us attack them at night, when vampire eyes see best.' The wind whipped through his dark hair and he stole another glance at Fire. Her face was set in an expression akin to stone, her hand gripping the spear and holding it high, her long burnished red hair flying behind her. Yes, true warrior this one, and tempered by her want for revenge. Three dragons over was Ice, mounted upon another silver. The dragon's hide blended nicely with Ice's silver and midnight blue clothes. He had bound his long hair tightly in a braid, keeping it out of his face, and he carried his spear close to his body. His haunted expression betrayed his uncertainty.

Out of the blackness of the nighttime waters, Barias' eyes spotted the island and the citadel looming ahead of them. It was a waxing gibbous moon, reflecting its silver light on the water and across the dragon's wings. The ecomancers called a wind so the dragons could glide, adding silence to their stealthy approach. Barias held his breath as the towers of the citadel took shape against the night sky; they were nearly there. It seemed almost too soon; he barely had time to poise his spear and prepare as Fire gave a battle cry, and the dragons dived.

The element of surprise was theirs as they attacked, scattering the Seraphim on guard like frightened rabbits, but their advantage quickly disappeared when the dragons saw that the Seraphim had taken the magic objects and placed them outside the protection of the citadel. The fortress was built to withstand dragon-fire, but the objects were not. Many of them were Gate Keys like the one Khirsha had stolen, and, if they were ignited, would rip huge holes in the temporal layers. Realizing this, Khaheera sounded the warning and they dispersed their offensive, pulling back to regroup and formulate a new plan. Below, the Seraphim were taking to the air and hurling spears at the dragons, forcing them higher into the sky, into thinner layers where Ja'oi's minions could not go.

Fire was incensed, robbed of battle, her eyes ablaze with rage. Barias could feel her fury and hear her bitter thoughts.

I will call a tidal wave to flood the citadel and an earthquake to sink the entire island. The sea dragons will retrieve the magic objects from the bottom of the ocean.

Are you mad? Ice cried. *If you sink that island there is no telling what will happen!*

Ice is correct. What if the sea dragons do not find all of them? No, it is too dangerous, Khaheera agreed.

WELL, WHAT WOULD YOU HAVE ME DO? JUST SIT HERE? she railed.

Fire, please, listen to reason. Revenge is not the only reason we are here, Ice pleaded. *We cannot go into this with anger. It will be our defeat.*

I will not stand idly by and do nothing! Fire seethed and leaped from Khaheera's back.

Fire! Ice called.

She did not answer him. He saw her dive back towards the citadel and cursed. *FIRE!*

Her rage will be the downfall of us all, Khaheera warned.

I have to go after her, Ice said.

We will all go. We will use what weapons we still have available to us: our minds and our strength, the silver added.

Koshe's mind touched his gently. *Now it is time to prove your mind magic, Barias, my friend. Join with me and we will use our combined minds to fight the Rogue's slaves.*

Yes. Dorian told us he could fight the ones that attacked them with his mind.

Then that is what we will do.

Koshe opened his mind and Barias made the links that would join them. The awesome power of the dragon enveloped him, and for a moment he was afraid he would lose himself entirely in the meld, then the sheer wonder of what he saw banished his fears away. As he slipped into the joining, the dragon's lifetime swept by him, the centuries upon centuries of knowledge and experience. This was a true immortal, born immortal, not made by drinking tainted blood, and he was several thousand years older than the vampire who rode him. Incredible to see through the dragon's eyes, to see the world and time through the eyes of one who knew from birth that he was going to live forever.

He was adrift, floating within the vast expanse of Koshe's mind when he heard the dragon's voice call him back to the task at hand. *Now, my friend, gather your power. The time is nearly upon us.*

Barias did as the dragon asked, and they projected their attack as they dived towards the island. They sent their combined power in a great bolt that struck the front lines of Ja'oi's minions. The Seraphim fell back, gripping their heads in pain, and Barias smiled to himself, imagining the shock of hearing a sonic boom from inside one's head.

That went well, Koshe sent as they veered upward, climbing out of the way of the Seraphim's spears, and prepared for another dive.

The next will be even better if we group with another pair and catch them between our crossfire, the vampire suggested.

Soft mental laughter from the dragon. *You fight well. You are no stranger to battle.*

The statement made Barias think of Ice, and he looked for the white-haired ecomancer. He spied Ice working in concert with Fire. He was casting a protection shield around them both, while she viciously attacked. His barrier was preventing the Seraphim from harming them as Fire did her best to do the most damage. The image reminded Barias of a television show he had seen; Star Wars? No, that wasn't it. Space Rangers? No, not that either. Starman, Star Journeys... Star Trek! Of course, that was it. Star Trek. Etienne liked it. He had hooked Barias on it; so much, in fact, that he now regularly watched the modern version of the television program. Ice's shield brought to mind a particular episode and he mindtouched Koshe once again.

Koshe, can your kind cast illusions?

Yes, why do you ask? the dragon responded.

Can you make it seem as though the other ecomancers are attacking as well? The better to mislead the Seraphim's defense?

You infer a bluff? A fool's image?

Exactly! What better to deceive foolish creatures? Barias thought back with a smirk.

Koshe chuckled. *I like you, vampire. I will pass your suggestion on to the others.*

Within a few moments, Barias noted that the Seraphim were redirecting their spears along the water instead of into the air, thus making more openings for the dragons to attack. Looking out over the ocean, he saw, with a thrill of excitement, that the dragons were projecting illusions of more attackers rising from the sea. The ruse was working to draw the Seraphim's attention away from the real threat. But the new tactic was successful for only a short time. The Seraphim quickly discovered that these "new" enemies were merely phantoms, and returned to attacking the dragons. It had worked long enough, however, for some dragons to retrieve a few of the more volatile magic objects, thus creating some areas where dragon-fire could be used. They were forced to retreat again as the Seraphim came after them with spears.

Koshe cried out in pain and lurched as a spear pierced the sensitive membrane of his left wing,. Barias twisted his body to reach behind him and grab the shaft to pull the metal head out of the dragon's flesh. Blood poured from the wound, covering Barias' hands and filling his nostrils with the scent. 'Oh, what would it be like to drink dragon blood?' He raised his hand to lick the blood from his palm, but stopped as he abruptly remembered Koshe.

Are you badly wounded?

No. I can still fly, though tight maneuvering will be difficult, the dragon replied, using his magic to staunch the wound. *Others were not so lucky.*

Barias looked to see many of their force flying for the distant continent, spears jutting from various places on their bodies. The close fighting had made them easy targets, and many spears had hit their mark. None were so badly wounded as to be near death, but the fight was over for them.

I doubt your ruse would work a second time, my friend. Although we gained some ground with it. We are once again relegated to high strikes and mind magic. I do not think it will be enough to win us this battle, Koshe admitted.

What of Ice and Fire?

The last I saw of them, they were still fighting, but I fear that there are simply too many for them to defeat.

Then it is lost?

Koshe sighed. *If we retreat now, we can regroup and attack again on another night.*

No, all is not lost; not yet. Look! Khaheera answered reading Koshe's thoughts.

She was referring to the Gate opening up in the sky above them.

Another illusion? Barias questioned.

No. That is real, my friend, and it feels of strange magic, Koshe replied.

Barias raised his eyes to the Gate and saw it rip open. From the other side, a host of creatures came flying through. 'Creatures' was the only word he could use to aptly describe the entities that now entered their sky. They were translucent, shimmering beings with amorphous shapes. They flashed with inner light, glowing almost, and they rained down upon the Seraphim with purpose. Behind them came a man, a man with black hair and black eyes.

Stars. It is Stars! Koshe announced, his mind voice full of joy.

Stars? Barias queried.

Yes, he and Aerth escaped the net when Ja'oi cast it. He's brought help. The Allies have arrived!

Stars swept past them and the unharmed dragons dove with him, adding their might to the new attack. Koshe turned and headed down, going into a steep dive that had Barias plastered to his long neck for fear of being swept off. He folded his dragon wings, and combined his mind with his vampire rider. They hit the ranks of the Seraphim immediately after Stars' and the Allies' attack, watching with smug pleasure as the enemy buckled in towards the citadel.

But the tower would offer no refuge to the Seraphim as the attacks came from all sides, unrelenting, and, in the end, surrender was the only option they had left. Stars and the avatars of the god Bhanai had turned the tide of war against them. After hours of bitter fighting, they admitted their defeat, and the children of Aiya once again controlled the citadel.

Nineteen

She remembered falling into darkness and when she came to, she was in a strange place, where the landscape was desolate and the wind howled. She looked at her hands. They were fully formed and they moved at her mind's command: the fingers wiggled, she could feel touch, but there was something...something...

The memory came back to her suddenly. Khirsha dying, her warning, the dead trees, Tobias screaming, Sky shifting to a velociraptor...and Lu'fahr grabbing her. Lu'fahr! Lu'fahr had seized her; Lu'fahr had ripped her from her body. This was her soul.

Soft laughter, bitter and contemptuous, met her realization, and she looked up to see the Archangel sitting on a throne near to her.

"You are quick to realize your predicament," Lu'fahr said.

"What have you done?" Rain accused angrily, taking in her surroundings. She was naked and on the ground at the throne's base.

Lu'fahr shifted in his seat. "Bought some insurance as they would say in this century."

Her lips pursed. "You are holding me as hostage."

"In a manner of speaking, yes."

"You are a fool. This will not stop my brethren from going to help Aiya. And in doing so, you have broken the Law."

Lu'fahr laughed again. "Law? There is no higher law than my Lord's! Thou shalt have no other gods before me!"

Rain grew angry and she clenched her jaw. "The Law which states that no avatar of Aiya may be attacked unprovoked! Did your precious god tell you nothing? Did He not warn you of what would happen if you did this? Did He not tell you the story of Fire and Air?"

The Archangel did not answer her, merely regarded her with thinly veiled amusement. She stood and faced him defiantly. "You have attacked an avatar of Aiya, the Earth Mother, Keeper of the Balance and the Webs of Life. For this, you and all of Ja'oi's creations could be destroyed. This is the Law. Should Aiya seek retribution, you will pay with your very existence."

Uncertainty flashed briefly across Lu'fahr's face, but he said nothing. Rain squared her shoulders and stared him down, her eyes blazing with rage. It was a facade to hide her growing fear. Without her body, she was helpless, at his mercy. Her only hope was that he did not know that, that she could bluff him into releasing her.

"Now let me go."

"No," the Archangel answered.

"You do not honestly think they will leave me here."

Lu'fahr smiled menacingly. "Oh, but they already have. You see, my dear, I told your demon siblings that I would kill you if they tried to interfere with the God Almighty."

Terror gripped her, but she did not show it on her face. Instead, she managed a mirthless laugh. "Killing me would only seal your fate."

"My fate is already sealed. But if I help my god in defeating this false one, perhaps He will release me from it."

A frantic thought struck her. Lu'fahr's greatest weakness was his fractured devotion to Ja'oi. His questioning had gotten him cast out of Heaven, and into this horrible, desolate place. If she could shake his faith even more, if she could play on his own doubts… perhaps… She had to try.

"False one? False one? If Aiya is false, why does Ja'oi take such pains to defeat Her? Why does He not just cast Her down like He did with you?"

Lu'fahr's brow furrowed as if a thought had struck him. She continued, letting hope build inside of her.

"If Aiya is false, why does your god fear Her so?"

"My god fears no one! He is…merely prolonging the game for Her benefit," the Archangel snapped.

"If He is not afraid, then why am I here? Why have you taken me from my body and brought me to this place? Why did He tell you to do this?"

"He did not. I did it of my own accord, to help my god."

She brought the argument back to the original question, hounding him with it. "If Aiya is false, why would He need your help at all?"

Lu'fahr shifted again, uncomfortable. "He does not need my help. I thought merely to aid Him, to make His conquest easier for Him."

"Why? If Aiya is false, then I and my brethren must be false also and would pose no threat to your god. If that is so, then you have accomplished nothing."

"Stop twisting my words, demon!" he seethed, his eyes flashing rage.

Rain recoiled inwardly, but maintained her outward calm composure. She was making progress, all she had to do was keep pushing.

"I am merely stating the obvious, Lu'fahr. Your argument is flawed and you know it."

"No, it is not flawed. I am correct."

"If that is so, then why am I here? If I am no threat to your god, why have you done this? Why are you so afraid of us?"

Lu'fahr gripped the arms of the throne tightly, struggling for control. "No! I fear none of your kind!"

"Oh, but you do! You feared me enough to rip me from my body. Your god feared me enough to send His Seraphim against me! Look at the truth, Lu'fahr!"

"There is only one Truth!"

He had said it with conviction, but Rain saw the doubt in his eyes. Ruthlessly, desperately, she reached for that doubt, hoping to twist it to her advantage.

"Yes! And it is that there is no One True Way! There are thousands of ways, thousands of Truths, thousands of gods! Each defines His own way, His own Truth!"

"No…" the Archangel breathed, squeezing his eyes shut.

She was merciless. "Yes. You know I speak the truth, and that is why you fear me! You fear me because I am proof that there exists more than one god. I am proof that Ja'oi has deceived you."

"No. You lie! My god would never deceive me!"

His resolve was crumbling under her attack, and she grew bolder, more self-assured.

"He has. You know He has. Every time you look at me, you know He has lied to you! I am the avatar of another god! Your Almighty God is not alone in His rule. He is one of thousands, millions! You know this every time you look into my eyes!"

It was too much, and she knew it the moment she said it. Lu'fahr's face twisted upon itself in unchecked hatred and fury. Uncoiling from the throne like a striking snake, he came at her. She was powerless to stop him.

"No! You speak *LIES!* I will hear them no longer, heretic! Deceiver! False one!"

She was thrown back, thrust down and across the hard, rough ground. The surface ripped her skin, leaving streaks of blood on the blackened sand. She screamed.

"You will suffer as no other has ever suffered for your lies," she heard Lu'fahr's voice tell her coldly.

Scraping of taloned feet on the earth as the demon dogs were set upon her. And then the pain began. Agony the likes of which she had never endured before. She screamed until she no longer had a voice, forever hearing Lu'fahr's self-indulgent laughter. The pain suffused into everything, encompassing her every coherent thought, until she knew, with frightening clarity, that if someone did not come to save her soon, death would be her only salvation.

• • •

The Gate closed behind Dorian, and he had to fight to hold back the rush of panic that flooded through him. They were trapped in Hell. Sky was just ahead, surveying the broken landscape as the relentless wind blew through his hair, and he joined him. The wailing cries of the Damned could be heard above the howls of the wind, bringing with them the stench of fire and blood.

"Where are we?" he said.

Sky started at the sound of Dorian's voice and gave him an odd look. "What are you doing here?"

"I came to help you," Dorian replied.

The ecomancer returned his gaze to the emptiness, staring at the rocky crags that hissed smoke and steam.

"You were the one who was pleading for Aaron," Sky said suddenly.

"Yes."

"I heard you. You're right. I probably would have killed him. The force of that bolt would have shunted right into him..." He lowered his head. "Thank you."

Dorian looked down at the scratches and bite wounds on his arms. "I love him."

"I know. So do I."

For a moment, Sky touched Dorian's palm, letting the contact say all the things he could not. Healing power flooded into him and he watched the wounds on his arms heal. Then he broke away and motioned to the task ahead.

"Which way?"

Sky shrugged. "I'm not sure. Ahead. I think all directions will take us to the same place."

"All roads lead to Hell, eh?" Dorian joked slightly.

Sky managed a smile, then grew serious. "We don't have much time. We need to find Rain before *he* finds us."

Dorian nodded gravely. "Agreed."

They began to walk forward, keeping an eye out for any wandering souls that might see them.

"Do you think Lu...Lu'fahr felt the Gate?" Dorian asked.

"No. It was High Magic. Ja'oi's minions have no working knowledge of it."

"How are we going to get out of here? Will you make another Gate?"

Sky shook his head. "No. Technically I did the impossible. My kind is not supposed to be able to create Gates into these layers. I'm not even sure exactly how I did it, and I used an existing Gate. I don't think I could repeat it if I tried."

Dorian stopped, shocked. "Then how are we going to get out of here?"

"There is a Gate up the main stairs in the center of Hell."

"That is crazy! We will have to go into the lion's den to get there!" Dorian exclaimed.

"I know." He began to walk away. "C'mon, we're wasting time. We have to find Rain before Lu'fahr discovers that the others have gone to help fight."

"If they did go…"

Sky snorted. "Oh they went all right. They were willing to sacrifice Rain for it."

"How do you propose to find her?"

"I know her name. I can call her by it. No matter what state she is in, she will answer me."

"What about the 'net' that is blocking your mindspeech?"

"Rain and I are bonded soul to soul. Even with Ja'oi's net, she will still respond if I pull on that bond. Besides, we're between worlds, the net probably won't have any affect here."

"Are you getting a sense of her?"

"Not yet, but give me a moment."

Sky paused and closed his eyes, sending out a call with his heart and mind. *Bina…*

Her name was all he could manage; it would be the only thing that got through to her. He held his breath, listening with his entire being for that faint answering cry. Long moments later, it came, weak and broken, but it was enough.

Ste...phan...

Sky quickly homed in on the source of the call, letting the bonds of his soul tell him which way to go.

Urgently, he grabbed Dorian's arm. "I have her. This way. Quickly!"

They ran, crossing over the terrain like two souls flying until Sky took firm hold of Dorian's waist. "Hold on to me tightly. I am going to teleport us."

The vampire gripped Sky's shoulder and closed his eyes as he felt a rush of disorientation. When he opened them, he and Sky were still in Hell, but the landscape was different. They had materialized near a hillside and a road littered with rocks and dead trees. Up on the top of the hill was a large crowd of souls who were taunting and moaning at three others hung on crucifixes. The souls on crucifixes were hung low, nailed by their feet and wrists like Christ had been. Dorian swallowed hard at the sight and shuddered at the chorus of voices rising above the moans of the crucified.

"Repent! Repent! Disbeliveers!" one cloaked soul cried.

"The Almighty is your God and Father! Accept Him, repent your sins and you will be forgiven!" another croaked.

Cautiously, they made their way up the hill as Sky surveyed the souls hung on the crosses. It was a nearly complete replica of the Crucifixion, with one larger cross flanked by two smaller ones. From the two side crosses hung pale, male figures, one with long brown hair and the other with short black hair. The one with brown hair was much taller than his counterpart, but Sky could not see his face through the curtain of hair. The smaller victim turned his head to look at them and Sky felt Dorian tense.

They are vampires! Dorian announced in disbelief.

"By the Goddess," Sky breathed, forgetting to send.

Do you think...?

It must be. Aurek and Roshan! Then that means the center figure must be...

Sky's eyes fell upon the central cross. It had a particularly large crowd around it. Taking Dorian's arm again, he edged closer to see the naked figure that hung limply from it. The crowd was throwing stones and vegetables at the figure, crying and moaning more loudly than the souls around the other two crosses.

"Repent! Heretic! Servant of another god!"

"Heretic! You belong here! Fornicator with the Dead!"

"Repent! Repent!"

"The Almighty is the only One! His is the only true path! Accept Him, Disbeliever!"

The crowd's words caught Sky's attention, and he strained to see the bloody and mottled figure. It was a woman, bleeding badly from her wounds, her face and body slashed and bruised beyond all recognition. She was hanging low on the cross, her wrists and arms covered in blood from the nails that ripped her flesh. Whatever hair she might have possessed had been shorn off, and her eyes were swollen shut. Narrowing his eyes in suspicion, Sky began to move slowly forward.

Bina? he called tentatively.

And the battered figure on the cross answered faintly, *Stephan.*

The sound of the name echoing in his head drove him into a killing frenzy. Screaming with rage, he ripped his way through the crowd. Dorian was at his heels, helping him throw souls out of his way like rag dolls until they reached the center cross. Tearing it down with force, he yanked the nails out of Rain's limbs as Dorian prevented the wailing, howling souls from stopping him.

Bina! I'm here. You're safe now. I won't let them hurt you any more, Sky told her, taking her into his arms.

Her mind voice was very faint, but he felt her relief. * Stephan. Aurek and Roshan...*

He knew immediately what she meant and called to Dorian.

"Dorian, the other crosses!"

Dorian obeyed, tearing down the nearest cross and releasing its captive. The figure moaned and turned brown eyes upon him.

Who are you? the vampire asked weakly.

A friend. We are here to help you, Dorian answered.

Get Roshan...

Right away.

Dorian turned for the other cross, noting as he did so that Sky had erected a shield to prevent the howling souls from getting to them. Somehow he knew the shield would not hold for long so he wasted no time in getting Roshan down from his cross. As he placed the battered, Indian vampire on the hard ground, a shadow fell across them and he looked up to see Aurek standing there. His legs were shaking but he was on his feet, then he fell to his knees and reached for his lover, speaking in a soft language. Roshan turned his head and his black eyes fluttered open as Aurek touched him. Aurek made a choked sound and placed one hand on the round cheek, tears beginning to flow down his face.

"Sudayita..." he breathed.

Look, this is all very touching, but if you hadn't noticed we need to get out of here! Dorian snapped. *Can you stand? I can carry one of you if one can stand.*

I can stand, and I will carry him, Aurek answered, struggling to his feet.

You? You can't carry him! You can barely support your own weight!

I will carry him! Aurek insisted.

Look, we don't have time to argue about this!

"Are we ready? I can't hold this up much longer!" Sky warned.

Give him to me, Aurek commanded holding out his arms.

Dorian hesitated a moment longer before complying. He lifted Roshan up as he rose to his own feet and gently placed him in Aurek's arms.

You really are a stubborn...

"Heretics! Disbeliveers! We will get you! You will never escape!" the souls were screaming outside the shield.

"Repent! Repent! Repent!!"

"We have to go NOW," Sky ordered.

"Can't we invoke out of phase?" Dorian asked breathlessly.

"No, I can't carry all of you at the same time!"

"But at this rate, we're never going to make it! Lu'fahr is sure to know that we are here, and we still have to get to the stairs!" Dorian cried.

Sky shoved Rain into Dorian's arms. "Here! Take her!"

Dorian fumbled to catch her as Sky practically threw her at him. "Why? Where are you going?"

"Nowhere! I can't hold her and shapeshift at the same time! Run ahead, I'll be right behind you!"

The crowd was right at their heels as Dorian broke away from Sky. Amazingly, Aurek was right beside him, keeping pace even though it looked as if he were about to keel over at any moment.

How can you... he asked.

Roshan is giving me all of his strength. It is enough to keep me going.

The simple statement was beyond him and he stopped asking questions as they ran, hoping that Sky would choose a shape that would get them out of Hell. Behind them, he heard a great commotion and glanced back to see a silver dragon in the place of the ecomancer. The dragon was smaller than the ancient one that had died, but no less formidable. Dorian paused in his running to watch as the dragon took to the air in a great leap and sailed over his head, its shadow crossing over his face. It landed with a ground shaking thump in front of them.

With a grace that did not fit the beast's huge size, the dragon pivoted, swinging its flank to face them, and using its massive tail to literally sweep the crowd of souls away. Then the dragon's eyes locked upon his and presented him with a lowered wing.

"Get on!" the dragon commanded.

Dorian did not question. Holding Rain with one arm, he scaled the dragon's wing and threw his leg across its back. Aurek was right behind him, grabbing onto his waist. They weren't even fully settled when the dragon beat its huge, leathery wings and sailed upward.

Dorian looked down at the atrocities below as they crossed over Hell. Visions of souls in all manner of unspeakable tortures and the horrible cries of the condemned imprinted themselves on his memory. They flew over valleys and chasms, over vents spewing hot red liquid and a stench that burned his nose and throat. They struggled against the howling wind, and Dorian shut his eyes to block out the sights and tried to cut off the sound, clinging to Rain with one hand and the dragon's neck with the other. Behind him he could feel Aurek doing much the same: holding onto Roshan with one hand, and gripping Dorian's waist with the other.

"We're almost there!" Dorian heard the dragon say, and he cracked open his eyes to see the black spires of the Gates of Hell looming before them.

Hope rose high in him; he could see the way out. Then there was a great lurch and they began to fall.

"What's happening?" Dorian screamed as they plummeted towards the ground.

The vampire looked down at the dragon's side and saw the shaft of an enormous spear jutting out of the scaled hide, blood gushing from the wound.

"Save yourselves…" the dragon gasped. "Dorian…get them out of here."

"How? We're all falling with you!"

Before Sky could answer, Dorian felt the hand around his waist tighten and heard Aurek begin to utter something in a strange language.

"He's casting a levitation spell," Sky managed. "Hold tightly to him Dorian! Don't let go!"

Horrified, yet afraid that if they crashed all five of them would be at Lu'fahr's mercy, Dorian did as he was asked and grabbed onto Aurek with his free hand as they were lifted from the wounded dragon's back. Floating above the ground, they watched, helpless, as the dragon smashed into the hard soil, a huge cloud of dust billowing upward from the impact. A pack of the demon dogs of the type Sky had killed before was racing to the body. Then Aurek's strength failed him and they began to fall.

Aurek! What… Dorian cried, as they dropped to the ground.

Can't hold it any longer, came the answer.

Aurek was able to slow their fall, but not prevent it and they landed in a heap near Sky.

Aurek… Dorian prodded, getting to his feet and lifting Rain.

The oldest vampire did not move. Underneath him lay Roshan, who was also not moving.

Aurek, please, we have to… he pleaded.

Go. Go get help. I have no more strength.

Dorian was torn. A few hundred feet away was the Gate and freedom, but the others would surely be killed if he did not help them. Gritting his teeth, he made his choice. Racing towards the Gate, he leaped up the stairs as several of the damned souls came at him, their mouths open in silent screams. Holding Rain in both arms, he ran up the remaining stairs and threw her body through the doorway with all his strength.

"Go! Get out of here! Go back to Tobias!" he cried as her body turned to light energy the moment it crossed the threshold.

Dorian knew he was at the exit and there was a chance that his thoughts might cross over. With all his might he mindcalled to Tobias. *TOBIAS! CALL HER! SHE IS FREE! CALL HER TO YOU!!*

Rain, now a ball of flickering light, pulsed once very brightly then zoomed off into nothing.

Twenty

After the ecomancers and most of the vampires were gone, Tobias carried Rain's limp body to their bedroom. Etienne followed close at his heels, but he paid his fledgling no mind as he laid her on the bed and arranged her in a position of peaceful repose. Sitting on the edge of the bed, still ignoring Etienne, he took a brush and began to smooth her black tresses.

"I'm sure Sky and Dorian will find her," Etienne said, his voice betraying his uncertainty. "They have to…"

"I should have been the one to go with Sky…" Tobias' hollow voice answered, speaking for the first time in over an hour. "She is my beloved. Dorian should not be risking his life for her. It is I who should be taking the risk."

Etienne reached over to take the brush from Tobias's fingers. "I know. But Sky loves Rain too. He is her partner and he's been with her for over three centuries. He'll find her and he'll bring her back."

"If that is the case, then why did he need Dorian to go with him?" his maker replied, his breath catching on a sob.

Etienne sat behind his maker and wrapped arms around him. "I don't know. I didn't see what happened."

Tobias' hands came up to hold his child's arms tightly around him. "Eti, what are we going to do?"

Etienne took a deep breath, trying to get his thoughts together. "The first thing we should do is get you fed. You lost a great deal of blood; you need to replace it."

Tobias shook his head. "I can't leave her."

"I'll watch over her while you are gone."

"No." It was spoken with finality. "I left her before. I let her out of the shields…"

"It's not your fault."

"If I had not let her out of my sight…If I had only been faster or stronger…" Tobias argued, holding back another sob.

"There was nothing you could do. Toby, it's not your fault."

"I won't leave her again!" Tobias insisted.

"Alright then. I'll bring you a victim. What do you want? Human? Animal? Male? Female? Or does it not matter so long as it's warm and has a beating heart?"

"It does not matter."

Etienne pulled away slowly and moved to stand, but a hand snaked out with lightning speed and grabbed his wrist. He gasped at the strength of the grip and looked into Tobias' blue eyes.

"You'll be careful?"

He nodded, swallowing hard. "I'll take Khristi with me. We'll go and be back before you can miss us."

Tobias shook his head. "That is not possible. Go. Be swift and be careful. Come safely back to me. I could not bear…"

Etienne kissed his lover, cutting him off. "I will. I promise."

Before he could change his mind, Etienne slipped quickly out the door. After he left, Tobias looked at Rain, then slowly crawled into the bed. He did not even bother to change out of his ripped and bloodied clothing as he settled in beside her and put an arm around her. In truth he was weaker than even Etienne realized. While the avatars of Aiya were well versed in the healing arts, nothing could replace the restorative powers of blood.

Waiting there in the darkness, he tried not to cry, but failed. Rain lay still beside him, her body cold. She had never been cold like this: motionless, seemingly dead. If it had not been for her immortal status, her body would have begun to decompose. With her eyes closed, she almost looked to be sleeping, except that he had never seen her sleep so still. He wrapped himself around her right side as he cried, his arm across her chest, his hand clutching the dangle she wore in her hair. His weeping drained him even further and he fell into an uneasy sleep until the sound of the door opening awakened him.

"Etienne?" he asked when the silence went on too long.

"No," Aaron's voice answered, thick with tears. "They're not back yet."

He lifted up to see the young vampire, his eyes picking him out clearly in the dark. The poor fledgling looked horrible, his long hair raggedly braided, half of it flying loose around his head, his clothes torn and filthy. What in Aiya's name had happened to him? He watched as Aaron came close, moving cautiously, until he was beside the bed. Then he reached out with trembling hands and touched Rain's cold face. Tobias heard him make a choked sound and saw the tears start anew.

"Aaron..." he whispered, placing one hand on the young one's shoulder.

"I'm going to lose them both," Aaron whispered hoarsely.

The words were spoken with more raw emotion than either of them could handle and they simultaneously burst into tears. Tobias sat up and seized Aaron in a crushing grip.

I'm so frightened, Aaron admitted.

So am I.

Holding onto each other in desperation, they vented their grief until they had completely spent themselves. Etienne and Khristopher found them half an hour later, collapsed in a tangled heap on the bed. Tobias awakened at the sound of their entry, and raised his head to look at them, but Aaron did not stir.

Without a word, Khristopher lifted Aaron up without waking him and carried him out of the room, leaving Etienne alone with his maker. That was when Tobias noticed that his fledgling had not brought a victim with him.

"I thought in retrospect that maybe you didn't want to kill tonight," Etienne replied to his unspoken question. "Or that, if you did want to kill, you'd want it to be violent and I didn't think that would be appreciated. So I fed enough for both of us."

He managed a small smile. Etienne knew him well, and he watched with glittering eyes as his love came to him.

Eti laid down on his maker's other side, placing his maker between himself and Rain, and offered his neck. He shuddered when he felt Tobias' cool fingers brush over his throat.

"Did you make them suffer?" he heard Tobias ask.

"No. I didn't want to waste the time. We found a little gathering of Satanists. Crashed their Black Rites." He laughed without mirth. "They thought we were Hell's minions answering their summons."

"And you found these mortals?"

He shook his head. "No. Khristi did. Sometimes I forget that he can be ruthless. He only plays the part of the clown for our benefit, Toby. Under that smile, he's one of the most vicious vampires I know. It's been years since I hunted with him, but..." He shuddered. "He found those kids. He killed four of them himself, Toby."

Tobias nodded. "Khristopher is dangerous to those who hurt the ones he cares for. I know of one or two individuals who were unfortunate enough to fall under his angry gaze."

He agreed, then returned his attention to his lover. "How are you?"

Tobias' face fell and he felt the tears start to rise again. "I am...not well."

Etienne swallowed. "Me either."

He arched his neck, offering. "Drink. I know it won't ease the grief, but it will help with your weakness, and if we are ...attacked again we'll need your strength."

Tobias nuzzled his throat and he sighed. Blood sharing among vampires could be an intensely pleasurable and intimate act, but Etienne knew that tonight was not for pleasure. He quivered as he felt Tobias' fangs pierce his skin. At first his maker drank gently, then the need and thirst took over and he fed more urgently.

He let Tobias feed, feed voraciously, before giving in to his own blood lust. Then he bent his head down and latched on to Tobias' throat, completing the circuit of blood. The bloodsharing opened their minds, and Tobias' pain and grief flooded through him.

My fault... he heard Tobias sob.

No. No, there was nothing you could have done.

I let her go! It was a mental wail.

What happened wasn't your fault. Did you know he was out there? Did you feel him?

No.

Then how can you claim responsibility? He was coming for one of us. We knew that. Rain was just the one he caught, he tried.

He took her and left me alone! Alone...always alone!

NO! I am here! I am here and I love you.

Not enough. It will destroy us.

Only if we let it. Tobias, my beloved, I died for you. I love you.

Rain...

*Is our bonded. **Our** bonded, not just yours. I love her just as much as you do. If she is lost, then we must comfort each other,* Etienne insisted.

I do not want to live without her!

She wanted you to live for her! Do you think she would want you to follow her in death?

No, Tobias admitted.

Then don't give up. She isn't dead. Not yet. We can't give up hope.

No...Etienne, forgive me.

I do. I have.

I'm so frightened.

I know. So am I.

Tobias ceased his feeding and gently removed his fangs from Etienne's flesh, resting his head upon Etienne's shoulder, ignoring the moist, blood-soaked shirt under his cheek. Etienne stroked his hair comfortingly and crooned under his breath.

"It'll be all right. We still have each other," he whispered.

"I know," Tobias answered.

"They'll find her and they'll bring her back."

"And if they don't?" he heard Tobias ask in an oddly small voice.

"Then we will pave the way to Ja'oi's churches with blood."

His answer seemed to satisfy Tobias and they separated. Tobias lay back down, curling himself close to Rain's body and Etienne spooned himself behind him.

Sleep, he told his maker. *Sleep and dream.*

The night passed and cycled into a new one. Tobias refused to leave Rain's side, not even to hunt. The blood he had taken from Etienne had gone a long way to helping him regain his strength, but he needed more if he was to return to full power. Etienne tried to coax him from the room, but he would not be separated from her. They had heard no word from either Sky or the ecomancers who had gone into the Sanctuary so there was no way of telling who would be the victor in this battle. Tobias was afraid to leave Rain alone; afraid that if he left, her body would be taken and he would lose her forever. It was an irrational fear, he knew. There were three ecomancers and half a dozen powerful vampires in the castle. The chances of Rain being taken from within the fortified walls were slim, but he knew his feelings had little to do with rationality. He was still drowning in guilt, convinced that if he had not let Rain leave the protection of the shields she would never have been taken.

Khristopher came and went, as did Victoria. Aaron stayed with them for some hours, drawing comfort from him and Etienne. The young one was holding up remarkably well, all things considered; but then, Aaron always was stronger than he looked. Sometime after midnight, Khristopher took

Aaron and Etienne hunting. Tobias could see the need to maim and kill in the Swedish vampire's eyes, and he felt pity for the hapless mortals who would cross Khristi's path. Etienne was not far from the mark when he said Khristopher was ruthless. Right now the Swede was feeling rather power-less, but trying to hide his pain under his façade of joviality. Killing allowed him to vent his anger and grief. Tobias wished he dared that luxury. The pleasure of a hunt and violent kill might have helped alleviate some of his own impotent rage, but he would not leave Rain's side. They pleaded and cajoled for him to come, but he refused. Finally, they'd left without him, but not without a few angry words and accusations. In truth, the fight had felt good and he wished they had not gone so quickly.

Etienne returned from the hunt flushed with blood. He was full of power and tingling with the rush of the kills he had made. Khristi had led Aaron and him to another gathering of youths, and the three of them had loosed their rage and pain on those poor unfortunates. Now coming back, Khristi had taken him aside on his way to Tobias, his pale blue eyes blaz-ing, and spoken to him of his maker.

"Toby will self-destruct if he does not let his anger out. I can feel him stewing. He is itching for a fight."

Etienne's eyes widened a little. "You think?"

Khristi nodded. "Oh yes. Put him in a ring with Mike Tyson and we'll see who loses body parts."

In spite of himself, he had to laugh at that comment. "I see."

"Want me to do it? I can if you want. I know all of his buttons, and a little bloodletting might be what we both need."

Etienne shook his head, pushing down the shudders as he remembered the relish with which Khristi killed. "No. I'll do it. I know a few of his but-tons as well."

Khristopher grinned. "Want me to tell you a few more?"

He smiled and shook his head. "No. I think I can manage. Just don't be alarmed if you hear things crashing."

"I won't."

He nodded at the Swede and continued his way to the bedroom he
shared with Tobias…'and Rain,' he reminded himself. When he entered,
Tobias was pacing like a caged animal and he knew Khristopher had been
right. Setting his shoulders, he met the blue eyes calmly and decided on
the best course of action. He began the dance with an attack.

"You look like Death warmed over."

Tobias ceased his pacing for a moment and glared at him. "I *am* Death."

"Oh really? Seems to me that you've been neglecting your duties as of
late. Has Death taken a holiday?" he snapped back.

"No," Tobias growled, baring his teeth.

'Good, very good. He is spoiling for a fight. Well, if it's a fight he wants…'

"So Death has relegated himself to skulking in old castles, then?"

"I am *not* skulking!"

"Of course not. I have never seen you skulk. Not even once. Except
maybe that time with Andrea…"

"You leave her out of this!" came the immediate command.

'Bingo.'

"Why? She's dead. You killed her, remember?"

Tobias' hands clenched into tight fists. "I had no choice!"

"We all have choices!"

"It was her last wish!"

Etienne laughed mockingly. "As if! I begged you to kill me for years
before you finally did it. She only had to ask once!"

"She didn't want the blood!"

Tobias' eyes were blazing and Etienne knew it wouldn't take much more.

"You loved her more than me!"

Tobias blanched. "Never!"

"You gave her what she wanted. You always gave her whatever she
wanted! She never had to beg you for anything!"

"She never asked for more than I could give!"

The words hurt and he curled his lip back, letting Tobias see his fangs.
"And I always did, is that it?"

As if he realized that his verbal barb had cut his lover to the quick, Tobias backpedaled. "No, beloved. You never asked too much of me. I'm sorry. I didn't mean that," he apologized, his anger fading.

Etienne frowned. He hadn't wanted to quell Tobias' anger. He had meant to goad the older vampire into a further rage.

'Damn. Time to switch tactics. Time to get physical,' he thought to himself.

"Like Hell you didn't! You always mean what you say! I had to practically kill myself before you brought me over. But there is one good thing that came from your waiting so long. I'm as strong as you, if you've forgotten. If you don't go out to feed, I am going to make you. I will carry you out of here, and you won't be able to do a damn thing about it," Etienne threatened. "Wouldn't that be a sight for Ian to see? His firstborn slung over my shoulder like a sack of potatoes!"

That brought a mirthless laugh from Tobias, and the sound of his bitter chuckle echoed off the stone walls. He turned his back, refusing to look at Etienne.

"I will not let you wallow in self-pity any longer," Etienne said, moving near to him. "Come on then. Get moving. We're going into town. We'll find you a nice juicy morsel…"

Tobias felt Etienne touch him, and he used his mind to forcefully thrust his fledgling away. He heard Etienne curse, and then the sound of cracking wood and the thud of a body hitting the wall. He smiled viciously to himself and crawled back into bed, lying down next to Rain.

"That was not funny! You are behaving like a brat and I will not tolerate it," Etienne fumed, picking himself up off the floor.

Tobias heard Etienne advancing upon him and prepared another bolt, but then he felt Etienne's power envelop him and prevent him from attacking as his fledgling grabbed him. He found himself being yanked by his feet and pulled from the bed. Crashing to the floor, he looked up to see Etienne standing over him, a vision of rage and tempered pain.

"Come on. Get out of those clothes! They stink!" Etienne ordered, taking him by the arms and pulling him up. "You'll never be able to stalk a victim in those. They'll smell you a mile away."

Tobias thrust him back, making him stumble. He landed with a thud on the stone floor.

"Is that the best you can do?" Etienne taunted. "It's no wonder Lu'fahr was able to take Rain!"

That elicited a snarl from Tobias, and he saw the rage begin to creep into his maker's eyes again. He scrambled to his feet, keeping himself just out of Tobias' reach.

'Just a little more…'

"C'mon! Show me what you've got!"

Tobias advanced on him and he danced out of the way, ducking as a vase on the dresser shattered. He paused, half expecting the game to be interrupted by a well-meaning, but ill timed intruder, but instead he felt Khristopher's mind touch his.

All is well? he heard the Swede ask.

Yes, just taking your advice, he answered.

I will make sure you are not bothered. Throw a few punches for me; he's being an asshole.

He laughed at that, grinning ferally. "Khristi says you're being an ass-hole. I agree! I should beat you bloody for it!"

Tobias lunged, but Etienne leaped out of reach before the strong hands could grab him. The chair to the vanity exploded, sending splinters flying everywhere.

"Oo! I hope you intend to pay for that! Ian won't like you ruining his antiques!"

"I don't give a shit about the antiques!" Tobias bellowed, letting himself feel the anger within him.

"No, you don't," he answered, ducking again as Tobias made another grab for him. "You don't give a shit about anything! You only care about yourself! You didn't stay here because you wanted to protect Rain; you only stayed behind because you're afraid! Some protector you are! I'd do a better job of protecting her than you!"

He made a move towards Rain's motionless body, seeing the red glare in Tobias' eyes, knowing he was going in for the kill. Tobias was very very close to a complete breakdown. He was surprised the elder vampire had held onto his temper for this long.

"Don't you touch her," Tobias warned, murder in his voice.

"Why not? Are you going to stop me?"

He moved for her again, but he never got the chance. A blur of torn clothes and brown hair was upon him, smashing him into the wall. Tobias slashed at him with a fury, his eyes red with rage, and he refused to fight back. Long nails gashed his throat and the blood came gushing out in a red stream. The smell and sight of it triggered Tobias' self-preservation instincts, letting the hunger and blood lust take over. Etienne saw the raw thirst in his maker's eyes and knew he had succeeded. He let out a satisfied laugh as Tobias' teeth drove into his neck.

Twenty-One

Aiya sat silently within the Heart, connected to the Webs, feeling and seeing through them, knowing that soon it would all come to an end. Above Her, She could hear the sounds of battle and felt the reverberations of Power through the Webs. The Webs told Her that Khirsha's last flight had been successful, and now Her avatars were among the rest of Her children who now fought Ja'oi's invasion. Vampires too, had come, She could feel their unique energy signatures, and they were now pairing with the dragons. They also brought the news of Khirsha's death with them, and it was inciting the dragons to fight all the more viciously. She held back Her tears for the Passing of one of Her oldest children. Khirsha gave her life to turn the tide of war in her goddess' favor, an act worthy of her noble species. Yes, Her dragons were one of Her greatest achievements, even if the design had been copied by some of the Others and used to create a more sinister breed.

The Webs flared and pulsed with power: Indio, Shoshon, Vi, Kvist…all the worlds of Her greatest Allies were glowing with energy. She smiled. Aerth and Stars had also been successful. Her Allies were sending Her a sign: 'Be patient. Help is on the way.' She glanced up at the roof of the cavern, seeing beyond it to the rogue god who thought His victory was inevitable. He was oblivious to the danger He had placed Himself in, or of the tide of Power that was pooling against Him. His pride had always been His greatest flaw, and now it would prove to be His demise. The traps were being laid and set, all She had to do was wait. The fly would most certainly be coming to the spider.

Aiya's reverie was broken by a faint mindvoice. It was just an echo, a stray call bouncing off the temporal layers reserved for the gods. The sender was a vampire: the rascal, Dorian. His cry was for another: Tobias, beloved and bonded of Her child Rain. It was a plea, a command, sent in desperation: *Tobias! Call her! She is free! Call her!*

Confused, She sent out a query along the link, and was immediately answered by a flood of images. Ja'oi's minion Lu'fahr had stolen Rain. Her child Sky and the vampire Dorian had gone into Hell to save her. They had found her, and also Aurek and Roshan. Lu'fahr had been holding them in Hell all this time, making them suffer unspeakable tortures. Dorian and Sky had found and released them, but they, along with Sky and Dorian, were still in Hell, fighting Lu'fahr, and Sky was badly wounded, too weak to shapeshift back into his true form.

All of this came as a surprise, for She had known none of this. The Webs had not informed Her of this heinous crime: they could not have, for Earth's Web was far too damaged. Rage welled within Her, encompassing all the anger She had felt before, but She forced Herself to calm down. Rain's soul was free, drifting in the spirit layers. It would be her instinct to return to the Void and not to her own body, unless she had a guide to show her the way back to her physical form. Aiya could hear Tobias calling, but She knew it would not be enough of a link to guide Rain back. Aiya knew what would call Rain back to her body, and She had the means to tell Tobias. There was an odd hole in the temporal layer, a hole that sparked with Sky's energy patterns. It was strange, but She did not have time to ponder what had happened. She could use the hole to breach the spell Ja'oi had cast. Desperate not to lose Her most gentle child, She gave Tobias the key he needed to bring Rain back to him. She heard him call the name into the emptiness and felt Rain's soul answer. Her child was quickly heading back to her lover and safety, and She was comforted. If all went well it would be over very soon. Leaning back into the Webs, She settled in to wait.

• • •

"How did you know?" Tobias asked after he had taken his fill, and the blood lust had run its course.

He was lying in Etienne's arms, sprawled on the floor where they both had fallen. Their clothes were ripped to shreds, and blood was splattered on the floor amid the debris of broken furniture.

"Know what?" Etienne answered tenderly.

"What I needed. That I needed to let the rage out."

Etienne sighed. "I just knew how I was feeling. Killing felt good. It helped me deal with all of this. I knew you had to be feeling at least as badly as I was, but you were denying yourself the hunt. I figured if I could provoke you into a rage, then maybe you'd let some of it out rather than keeping all the anger inside."

Tobias was quiet for a moment. "When did you get to be so much smarter than me?"

Etienne laughed. "It's only temporary, I promise. I would never rob you of your position as sage."

Tobias snorted. "Sage indeed."

"I love you."

"I love you too, Eti. So much."

"We'll get through this. I promise."

"I believe you."

No more words were needed as they rested in each other's arms. Then Etienne tenderly ushered his maker to rise.

"We should get out of these clothes. They're ruined."

"Yes. I agree."

They stood and Etienne began peeling the soiled clothing from his maker's body. He was still rather gaunt and pale, but he looked a great deal better. He was halfway through undressing his lover, when Tobias went rigid, his whole body trembling.

"What is it?"

"Dorian…" Tobias breathed, then abruptly turned to the bed. "Rain is free! I have to call her!"

Opening his mind, Tobias called with all his heart, concentrating so hard he punctured his own palms with his nails, but there was no response from Rain at all. He was calling and calling, but still Rain did not react. He was shaking her, and Etienne was beside him, doing the same, one hand upon his maker and one upon his lover.

"Rain! Come back to us, please! We're here! We need you. We love you!" he heard his fledgling implore.

Rain did not move, and Tobias raged, his heart breaking in despair. He reached into himself, pooling his mental power in order to reach Rain through the bond they shared. He gathered the power up into his hands and prepared to direct it into Rain. Then the voice of Aiya, the Earth Mother, rang in his head.

Bina. Her name is Bina.

Frantic, Tobias seized the name and called with it, sending it out with all the force he had left, mind screaming it across time and space.

BINA!!

The bond between them vibrated, then sang, and he could feel her coming back to him, almost see her soul: a radiant ball of light, come streaking at him from the Nether planes. Then the body beside him flooded with warmth and drew a shuddering, sobbing breath. He cried out with joy as Rain's eyes fluttered open to look at him. Consumed with rapture, his tears flowing unchecked down his face, he took her into his arms and kissed her as Etienne stroked their hair and murmured endearments. Her hand reached up to lightly touch his shoulder, and he pulled back so he could see her face, his cheeks stained from his crying.

"You look terrible," she whispered, her voice barely audible.

Tobias laughed at her soft words, the tears falling ever more profusely down his face, as Etienne did the same. Moments later, the other vampires were pouring into the room, led by Aaron. They were full of questions and excited joy, their voices yammering at him from all angles. Tobias didn't hear them, he was too full of emotion to listen. He pressed his lips to

Rain's forehead and closed his eyes, too consumed with relief and love to care if anyone saw him crying.

"Moon and Leaves Felt you come back," Khristopher said to her.

"Sky and Dorian? Where are they?" Aaron asked urgently, pushing to the fore, his green eyes wide with hope and fear.

Rain put a hand to her head. "I...I don't know. I saw them...They were..." A faint look of surprise crossed her face. "I don't know. I can't remember."

"They went into Hell to free you! Surely you must remember something," Aaron pressed.

"I..." She paused, trying to remember.

In a great flood, the memory of her time in Hell rushed over her and she was seized with panic and pain. A wrenching cry escaped her lips as her eyes dilated with fear, and Tobias gripped her tightly, shaking her back to sanity.

"Beloved!"

"They fell! They fell from the sky...Lu'fahr has them! And he has Aurek and Roshan," she stammered, then burst into hysterical tears.

Tobias locked eyes upon Aaron, raw anger on his face. "Get out of here," he snapped.

Aaron backed away, stunned and frightened, his own tears rising. "I'm sorry..."

Etienne went to him and put a reassuring hand on his shoulder. "It's okay. He doesn't mean it. You know he doesn't."

Aaron sought the comfort of Etienne's arms, trembling, as Tobias attempted to quiet Rain. The black-haired vampire looked at her pleadingly, ignoring the warning stare from Tobias.

"Were they...were they dead?"

"No...they were both alive when Dorian threw me through the doorway," she managed, ceasing her tears.

"What happened?"

"I don't know. I wasn't able to see. Where are the others?"

"Moon and Leaves are here with Tree, they are probably on their way now...actually, I am surprised they aren't here yet. They stayed behind when the rest of the ecomancers went to fight. Several of us went with them," Khristopher replied.

As if on cue, Leaves came rushing in, followed closely by Moon. "Ja'oi's net is down! Our mindspeech is restored!" Leaves announced excitedly.

"Ja'oi is on the retreat. The allies have come and He is trapped. It will be over soon," Moon added.

Rain smiled softly. "I am glad. Now all we need to make it perfect is Dorian and Sky safely back with Aurek and Roshan."

"Aiya is aware of what has happened, She is sending help. This I heard from Sun," Moon told her.

"That brings me great comfort, Moon," Rain answered, then looked at Tobias, her brow furrowing at the sight of him. "Now. If you all will excuse us. My bonded needs to feed."

Respectfully they exited the room, leaving Rain alone with Tobias. Etienne moved to leave too, but Rain called after him.

"No, Etienne. Stay. You belong here with us too. You are part of us."

Etienne looked to his maker, and saw the deep, blue eyes flicker with guilt and remorse.

"Yes, Etienne. Please. You do belong with us; you are part of us."

Etienne's heart melted and he went into Tobias' arms.

Rain's hands were on his blond hair, comforting. "We love you, Etienne."

He lifted his head from Tobias' shoulder and kissed her, then he kissed his maker.

"Goddess, you are still so cold. Feed, my beloved. Take from both of us. Drink. We love you," he said tenderly.

Tobias smiled and bent his mouth to Rain's neck. Then Etienne heard Rain's small gasp and Tobias' sigh of relief.

Twenty-Two

Ja'oi took the arrival of the ecomancers lightly, although their presence angered Him. The vile dragon must have succeeded in bringing the avatars the Key. He would have to destroy them all now. Not that He hadn't planned to do so anyway, but it made His conviction all the more solid. He was also concerned that, if the dragon had gotten through the net He had cast, then so had others. At least two of Aiya's avatars were unaccounted for. If any of them had managed to escape, they could have gotten to one, or more, of Aiya's allies. If that was the case, then His time was running short. If He was going to capture the Webs, He must do so as quickly as possible. His Archangels were still attempting to get past the two avatars that guarded the entrance to the Heart. Aiya lay within, hiding like a rat in Her hole, but She was aware of Him. She had cast protections over Her avatars and other children, preventing Him from killing them outright. As a result, He had been forced to resort to more time-consuming methods of warfare.

"My God," the Archangel Ga'bral said, approaching with humility.

Yes? He replied, coming out of His thoughts.

"The way to the Heart is clear."

You have defeated the two guardians? He asked, His excitement growing.

"Yes, my Lord, and the two that came to help. We have them as our prisoners."

Excellent! We can dispose of them later. For now, I will attend to our last obstacle.

Triumphantly, He strode to the hillside and the opening to the Heart. Mi'skal and Ur'al were there to greet Him as He approached, and they bowed deeply as He entered the passageway. The three Archangels were behind Him as they moved down into the tunnel. Those Yet to Be Born clustered around them, clawing at their robes and hair, alarming the Archangels who spun around and waved their hands.

"What are they, my Lord?" Ga'bral cried, swatting at an invisible attacker.

They are nothing to be concerned with. They cannot harm you, Ja'oi answered, an air of exasperation in His voice. 'And soon they will all be *my* children anyway.'

He forged ahead, eager to meet His greatest foe, and quickened His step when He saw the glow, leaving His Archangels several paces behind. How long had He waited for this moment? He was bursting with satisfied glee and pleasure. The Great Mother would be no more, and none would challenge Him again. Fearlessly, He crossed the threshold and entered the Cavern of Webs. Immediately, the entrance slammed closed behind Him, the stone folding in upon itself, and shut His Archangels out.

Ja'oi scowled and looked around at the endless Webs weaved throughout the cavern, searching for Aiya, His hands upon His hips.

And what do you hope to accomplish by doing that? He hissed angrily.

More than you think, came the answer.

Show yourself, or are you afraid of me?

I? Afraid of you? Thief, Deceiver, arrogant rogue god! Do not flatter yourself. I am here; you need only to look in the right place.

Ja'oi scowled again and scanned the Cavern suspiciously. *I do not choose to play your little game. Show yourself or I will begin tearing down your precious Webs!*

Laughter, soft and faintly mocking, echoed off the rock walls. *I think not, Betrayer.*

Suddenly the cavern grew brighter and Ja'oi looked up to see Aiya seated in the Web above Him. She was radiant and the Webs glowed with Her light as the strands connected to Her, running in and out of Her in one seamless entity. He grinned and laughed.

I have you now!

She smiled a knowing smile, the smile of one who finds someone's words endlessly amusing, and it made Him rage with anger. He prepared to blast Her out of Her gossamer throne when He heard a voice address Him with contempt.

"Ja'oi. Once again you underestimate the power of Aiya."

Startled, He looked to see an avatar standing just beneath Aiya's web. It was the oldest one, Aerth; the one who had been harrowing His humans almost since they were created. He sneered. Killing this one would bring Him great pleasure. He moved to advance upon her, to destroy her in front of Aiya's very eyes, when an odd thought struck Him. How did she get here? His Archangels had said the way was clear, the avatars defeated…

"No, not defeated. Told to feign surrender so as to lure you here," Aerth informed, her voice hard.

Realization struck Him and He felt a shiver of fear. This one had been one of the ecomancers unaccounted for; this one must have escaped His net, and if that was the case then…

Then she has returned with help, came a new mindvoice.

Ja'oi whirled in sudden terror and found Himself faced with the brothers Inhotek and Bhanai.

As always, your arrogance and lack of vision have been your defeat. This time, for good, Bhanai informed Him.

He had no time to react, to put up a shield to protect Himself as all three deities attacked Him with their power. The bolts hit Him at full force, smashing Him into the cavern wall, and for a moment His sight went black. When He came to, Inhotek and Bhanai had already entrapped Him in bindings. He screamed in rage.

Struggle all you like, rogue, Inhotek seethed. *You have been bound by the Oaths you have broken; no bindings are stronger.*

Aiya came down from Her Web and stood before Him as He strained at His confines. *You will release my avatars and call off your minions,* She ordered.

Never! I will prevail!

No, you will not, and we will destroy all of your avatars and your sanctuaries, as is our right, Bhanai informed.

As Bhanai said this, Ja'oi heard the cries of fear and desperate pleading of His Archangels trapped on the other side of the wall, and His heart seized.

No...

Then let my avatars go, and call off your minions! Aiya demanded.

Done! He agreed desperately, sending the commands as He did so.

Aiya nodded in satisfaction. *Good. Now lift your net so that I may send aid to my children trapped in your Lu'fahr's Hell.*

Defeated, humbled, Ja'oi consented, and within moments four unicorns were speeding their way through a temporal Gate.

• • •

Dorian watched Rain's soul fly away until the damned souls grabbed his hair and clawed at his face. Howling in pain and fury, he turned upon them, slashing and shoving. At the base of the stairs, he could see the crowd that surrounded Sky's dragon body, and began to fight his way down the stairs.

The dragon was alive, feebly trying to fight and protect the two vampires next to him. Both wings were broken, one haphazardly stretched across Aurek and Roshan, and gaping wounds spilled blood onto the hard, rough ground. Dozens of damned souls circled the dragon, stabbing it with spears. The beast roared in pain, gasping on its breath, then choked violently as a gout of flame and gas came bursting out of its jaws. The damned souls scattered as the dragon breathed fire and paralyzing gas, and Dorian pushed past them, stealing a spear as he went, ripping his way to the dragon's side.

Dorian impaled one demon dog on his spear and threw the body aside, whirling to plunge the blade into another as the pack attacked him. He leaped into the air as the creatures converged, forcing them to crash into each other, and skewered two more as he came down. In his peripheral vision, he saw one launch itself towards his face, and he knew he did not have enough time to turn around...The massive jaws of the dragon snapped, snatching the dog in mid-leap and crushing it in its sharp teeth. Dorian gave the dragon an appreciative nod.

"Thanks."

"It's hopeless. Get out of here while you still can. Give my love to Aaron," Sky gasped, wheezing.

"Oh no. Aaron will kill me if I leave this place without you! It's all of us or none! And I intend it to be the former!" Dorian answered, plunging the spear into another demon dog with relish.

Laughter echoed hollowly around them, and Dorian looked up to see Lu'fahr standing a few feet away. The demon dogs dispersed, circling like vultures on the periphery as the dragon lowered its head to the ground, breathing heavily.

"Vampire!" the devil said triumphantly.

He was in his true form, the form of an Archangel, his face beautiful, his white wings fluttering behind him. Dorian faced him with the point of the spear.

"If you want them, you will have to go through me," the vampire threatened.

"You would risk your life to aid this heretic and your brethren?"

"He is not a heretic. He is an avatar like you. You have attacked and tortured an avatar of Aiya the Earth Mother. You have held Her children in this place and tormented them without cause. Your actions will have grave consequences," Dorian answered bravely.

Lu'fahr laughed again. "From whom? This is my realm! I rule supreme here."

"Aiya will seek vengeance upon you for what you have done."

"What do I have to fear from a weak, false goddess?" the devil taunted. "But you amuse me. I will strike you a bargain. If you agree to serve me, I will spare these unbelievers' lives."

Dorian's eyes narrowed in rage, and he gripped the spear in his hands tighter. "I will never be your minion. I am a child of Aiya. My soul does not belong to you!"

Lu'fahr grimaced in fury, his hands clenching. "Then you shall die as well!"

The demon dogs rushed in again, worrying the dragon's hindquarters and the side he could not defend because the spear was still in it.

"Ha ha! My god may have forgotten how to fight your wretched kind! But *I* have not!" Lu'fahr announced, laughing.

Dorian swung at the demon dogs with his spear, fighting them off as best he could, and this time Sky was not helping him at all. It was hopeless as Sky had said; there being simply too many of them to destroy. He was quickly losing his strength, expending far too much energy on trying to keep the hounds at bay. Lu'fahr laughed and laughed as Dorian struggled valiantly. Then there was a shifting of the wind and a sound came with it. The sound of lightly chiming bells. Lu'fahr heard it too, and paused in his laughter, listening as the sound drew closer and closer.

Suddenly the Gate to Hell pulsed and four white beasts came soaring through the doorway, clattering down the stairs. Lu'fahr had no time to react; he was barely able to turn his head to face his foe, before a unicorn buried his horn deep within the Archangel's back. The pearlescent spire, stained with blood, came thrusting out of the devil's chest, while the other three attacked the demon dogs, using hooves and horns to trample and spear the abominations. Lu'fahr collapsed to the soil, clutching his chest as the unicorn pulled his horn out and lightly leaped over him. Coming up to Dorian and the dragon, he locked eyes upon the vampire.

We have been sent by Aiya to aid you.

Dorian stared and gestured to the dragon. "Sky and..."

We are aware. My sister Idra will give him the strength he needs to trans-form himself again, and Jeren will help Aurek and his mate.

Dorian watched as two of the unicorns went to Sky, Aurek and Roshan. The larger of the two nuzzled Aurek, rousing him and lowering himself to the ground so that Aurek could drag himself and his lover onto its back. The other unicorn touched the dragon's muzzle with her horn, and the reptile condensed in upon itself until all that was left was the beaten, battered body of Sky. Dorian went to him and put an arm around him, lifting him up, letting the ecomancer lean heavily upon him.

You may ride if you wish, the unicorn Idra told him.

"No," Dorian replied, shuffling as he and Sky staggered towards the Stairs.

"Heretics! You cannot escape the will of God! His wrath will destroy you!" Lu'fahr cried in defeat, holding his wound as it healed.

"Let's get out of here," Dorian said, climbing the first few steps as the unicorns guarded their retreat.

Agreed, one of the unicorns concurred, leaping ahead of them and heralding their way out of the Gate.

Arms around each other, splattered with blood and rife with wounds, Dorian and Sky limped through the doorway. There was a rushing sensation as they passed through the temporal layers to find themselves back in the clearing in front of the Keep. They paused, looking at the sight that awaited them as they were looked at as well, knowing with cruel reality what they must look like after such an ordeal.

On the perimeter of the clearing were four deities, each glowing with their own supernatural presence. With them were some of their Avatars, creatures made of light and shimmering iridescence, and nearest to the Keep was a glowing goddess, surrounded by the ecomancers, Rain among them. Tobias was beside her, and all the vampires were gathered in a tight group on Her other side. Dorian saw Aaron's eyes flash with relief and pain as he saw them emerge from the Netherworld both alive, but badly beaten. Lastly, in bindings that held Him firmly in check, the rogue God Ja'oi was held prisoner by the two other gods, and He looked at Dorian briefly, His eyes showing His hatred.

Dorian managed a small smile of triumph before they both collapsed. Seconds later healing hands were upon them, and soft soothing voices were in their minds. Dorian's eyes opened slightly to see Aerth and Stars lay hands upon Sky as Song laid hands upon him. The energy filled him with soothing warmth and strength, and he sighed with relief. When he opened his eyes again, the goddess was standing before him.

You are deserving of the gifts I give you. You stayed with my avatar even when you could have escaped, and you made certain Rain was set free. For this you have earned your rewards, Aiya told him.

I want no gifts, my lady. I want only peace and sleep, Dorian answered with humility.

And you shall have both in ample quantities.

Collapsed with exhaustion, Dorian did not move when strong hands lifted him up and carried him into the house. He was taken to Aaron and Sky's bedroom and placed gently upon the bed. He felt the mattress shift as Sky was laid next to him, and then shift again as Aaron crawled in beside them. Thank goddess for King-sized beds.

"Dorian, Dorian..." Aaron's voice drifted down to him, and he felt Aaron's hand stroke his hair. He was too tired and weak to answer.

"It'll be different from now on. I promise. I promise that things will be different between us."

Aaron's voice was pained, but relieved. He still did not answer, but turned his cheek into the young vampire's touch.

"I love you, Dorian."

"Love...you...too..." he managed faintly.

Flanked on both sides by the two he loved most, Dorian found the peace he wanted. He breathed deeply, smiling as Aaron's cool, fleshy lips kissed his cheek, and promptly fell asleep.

• • •

Rain was standing beside Aerth when she saw streams of light cut through the temporal layers. Two unicorns leaped out of a doorway that opened on the far side of the clearing. Staggering behind them, bloodied and bruised, were two figures. They were barely recognizable, except for Sky's mane of silver-white hair, and both collapsed shortly after two more unicorns bounded out of the Gate, one of which was carrying Aurek and Roshan. Rain watched as Aerth, Stars and Song rushed to their aid, healing their many wounds. She knew she should be one of those going to help, but she stood where she was. Tobias put an arm around her and she pressed close to him, suddenly feeling very small and afraid. Lu'fahr had done something to her, something she had yet to define, but she knew it was there, eating away at her. She tried not to think about it, tried to be happy and feel the joy that came from everyone. Smiling she watched as they carried Sky and Dorian into the house. Sky's tired, blue eyes met hers as they passed, and she gave him a private look.

Bina, he mindspoke.

Stephan, she answered. *Thank you for my life.*

No, Bina… he replied. *Thank you…for mine.*

She sent him a rush of love and received one from him in return, and she was comforted. Sky was safe, as were Dorian, Aurek and Roshan, and for now, that was all that mattered. Her attention was drawn back to her goddess who was now addressing the group.

It is over. My Avatars and children have been safely returned to me, and my Sanctuary restored. The Webs are safe and undamaged. I am content, Aiya announced.

The doorway to Hell shimmered, and Lu'fahr rushed out, his form twisted into the hideous black half-goat/half-man that he was cursed with on Earth. At first he stood, staring in shock at the gathering before him, and when he saw his Almighty God, defeated and held captive, his jaw dropped in utter amazement.

"My God!" he cried. "What has happened?"

Aiya approached him, Her eyes flashing anger and malice. *You attacked my Avatar unprovoked. You stole her soul and subjected her to your tortures. You struck down another of my Avatars who was trying to save her. You kept two of my children prisoner without my knowledge and tortured them for four millennia. For this I could seek retribution. For this I could have you destroyed,* She told him acidly as he shivered on his knees at Her feet. *But I will not, for most of what you are is not your fault. Know this. Your God's unchallenged reign here is over. He will now have a co-ruler, and He will answer to me. Things are going to change, little man, and you had best be prepared to accept them.*

The only response from Lu'fahr was a heartbroken moan.

Epilogue

Rain sat staring at the fire, her eyes soft and semi-blank. It had been five weeks since she, Etienne and Tobias had moved into this renovated estate on Orcas Island. While Tobias and Dorian had reconciled enough to live in the same state, he was not so naive as to think that they could live in the same city. He had bought an enormous art collection to decorate the house, and paintings of inestimable value now covered their walls. He kept moving them, and she swore he had switched them around at least four times in the past six days. She imagined that he was trying to find something that would make her cheerful again. It wasn't working.

Ever since the initial excitement of victory and reunion had faded, Rain had entered a state of melancholy sadness. There was not one single reason for her depression, merely it simply was and nothing Tobias, or any of them, did could break her from her quiet, gloomy manner. Some said she was in a state of shock, which she probably was: some kind of delayed reaction to all that had happened to her. Rain's torment and crucifixion had only been the end of the torture Lu'fahr had put her through, and there were some parts of it she had purposefully blocked out, lest she become hysterical again. They assured Tobias that she would be fine. She just needed a little time, and she would heal on her own if given the opportunity.

In truth, she wasn't certain if she would ever heal. Her emotions were in chaos and she had lost her ecomancer powers. Since she had returned to life, Rain had not performed a single act of healing or weather working, and not even her inherent talent with plants seemed to be present. It was as if her trauma had severed the ties she had with that part of herself, as if Lu'fahr had somehow cut her off from who and what she was, rendering her useless and depressed. Aerth assured her that they would return in time, that she was just hurting, and the pain was blocking her. Somehow she wasn't so confident.

Tobias came into the room to ask her the same thing he had asked her every day for a month. "Will you come out with me?"

She answered with the same answer she had given him every day for a month. "No, thank you."

"It is no good for you to stay inside all of the time," he said softly, his eyes betraying his hurt. "And Aaron, Dorian and Sky are meeting us."

"I know, but I really don't feel like going. Go on without me, my love."

Tobias shifted uncomfortably. "I'd really rather not..."

"Please, love. I just...I just want to be left alone."

He sighed and kissed her tenderly on the cheek. "All right, but I wish you would change your mind."

She gave him a small smile and a pat. "I'll be fine."

He nodded, his eyes downcast, and left the room. She looked after him, her eyes sad. She knew she wasn't being very kind to him, and making him afraid, but this broken thing inside her just made her want to do nothing. So she did nothing. After he was gone, Rain sat in the chair, watching as the fire burned low and the light patterns on the walls changed. Her thoughts drifted aimlessly, turning inevitably to her nightmares: the nightmares that constantly disturbed her sleep, the ones she would not share with even her lovers. The nightmares of her tortures in Hell. These terrible dreams invaded her every waking and sleeping thought, frightening her and her lovers. They interfered with every tender moment, with every happy time, tainting everything with their blackness and despair. They caused her to retreat even further into herself, cutting her off from the ones who loved her most. She could see it happening, but there seemed to be nothing that she could do, and that only furthered to make her even more unhappy. It was a vicious cycle from which she could see no escape.

Hours passed in unbroken silence, her thoughts turning ever more dismal until she heard a small sound behind her and turned her head to see what it was. Sky was there, and Aaron, Dorian, Etienne and Tobias were behind him. Dorian and Aaron had dressed him; she could see the influence of both reflected in his tight leggings and soft, emerald green shirt. It would seem that he was taking the whole threesome thing in stride. Silently, he stepped into the room.

"Hello, Rain."

"Hello, Sky," she answered.

"We were missing you, so we decided to come see how you were doing."

"I know. I'm fine, really. Just not very social," she replied, averting her eyes from his relentless stare.

"I've brought you something that needs taking care of and it needs your special touch," he said tenderly.

"What is it?"

He approached her, and for the first time she saw that he held in his hands a tiny bundle of cloth. She looked at him, uncomprehending, and he returned her gaze. His face was serene and calm, but there was a tenseness in the room, a breathless expectancy that hung in the heavy silence.

Without another word, he offered her the bundle of cloth. Rain looked questioningly at him, then raised her hand to accept it as he placed it gently in her left palm. She stared at the bundle for long moments before carefully peeling back the folded material to reveal its contents, and made a little sobbing sound as the cloth fell away. Anxiously, Tobias and Etienne looked over Sky's shoulders while Dorian and Aaron peered around the ecomancer's sides, as they strained to see the tiny object in her hand.

It was a bird. A tiny, nondescript, brown-feathered bird. It was dead, its head at an odd angle from a broken neck. A wave of confusion passed through the vampires at the sight of the dead bird and Rain's reaction to it. That the dead bird meant something to her was obvious, for she began to cry softly, and Sky came closer, stroking her cheek tenderly with the back of his left hand, his eyes sympathetic and warm. Then gracefully, he motioned to the bird and spoke, his voice full of gentle pleading.

"If I can look after the sparrow…"

And for the first time, they realized that it *was* a sparrow: a little brown sparrow that had broken its neck. Rain brushed her fingers across the feathers, the tears rolling silently down her cheeks, and nodded.

Raising her head, she looked at Sky, her eyes misty, and smiled softly. He repeated the words across time, the same words she had spoken to him over three centuries ago, when he was first learning how to use his powers. He had asked her why he should become a healer when he hated all of humanity, and she had brought him the body of a poisoned bird: a tiny sparrow. 'This bird,' she had said, 'its life is short and full of hardships, yet it sings. If you can look after the sparrow, then you will have done all you need to do.' And now, when she was bereft of her abilities, he had brought her the same gift and spoken the same words.

"If I can look after the sparrow," she repeated, more to herself than to anyone else.

Then she lifted her hand up, leveling the body of the bird with her face, and covered it with her other hand. Closing her eyes and reaching as far into herself as she could, she concentrated.

Unexpectedly, the power in the room lurched and shifted in a great heave, like the transfer of energy after a lightning strike or a great storm. It pooled around Rain, infusing her with electric energy. It was as if her soul had finally moved, as if a missing piece had now been supplied and now the connections had been remade, the circuit completed. The feeling of chaos that emanated from her settled and was replaced by a calm serenity. And something inside her healed at last. Her face suffused with ecstasy, and she smiled, shunting the power into the sparrow with joy and love.

Everyone in the room could feel the power coursing through Rain's small frame and, when she pulled her hand away from the sparrow, they were all holding their breath. Rain blew gently upon the bird, and the eyes of the vampires opened wide as the sparrow lifted its head. Shivering, the tiny creature righted itself in Rain's open palm and fluffed its feathers. It looked like a tiny puff of brown down, collected in her hand, except that the puff breathed and had two tightly closed eyes. Sky warbled a call, and the bird answered with a faint chirp, opening its black eyes. Then as they watched, the sparrow that had just been dead, spread its tiny wings and fluttered to Sky's waiting hand. Rain let her arm fall to her side, the bundle of cloth that had been the bird's shroud slipping soundlessly to the floor, and regarded the sparrow with a peaceful expression on her face.

Her eyes met Sky's and he offered his hand to her, wordlessly asking her to come with him. She smiled and lowered her gaze in humility. Tobias and Etienne looked at her with hopeful faces, silently willing her to rise. Quietly, she placed both hands firmly upon the arms of the chair and stood. Sky grinned happily, let the sparrow fly back to her, and she raised her hand to let it land. It settled into the cup of her palm, twittering.

"You should set it free," Sky told her.

"Yes," she agreed. "I should."

Sky smiled, and pulled aside the heavy drapes that covered the window. The bright afternoon sunlight came streaming in, falling on her face and hands, and she lifted the bird into the light as Sky pushed up the window. Going to the open pane, she released the bird, watching it flutter away until it was just a speck of darker color against the endless blue sky.

Tobias came up to her, looking out the window with her, and drawing her attention to magnificent views of their property. Sunlight reflected off the waters of the Sound, and on the tall trees that stood as sentinels against the wind.

"Will you come out with me?" Tobias asked lovingly.

She looked at him, marveling at how the sunlight touched his brown hair and set it ablaze with colors, and nodded. "Yes."

She offered her hand and he took it tenderly, guiding her to the wide patio doors that Sky now pushed open, and led her gently into the light of day.

About the Author

T.Isilwath is a native of Pennsylvania, and resides in Centre County where she lives with her husband and a conglomeration of pets. At the time of printing, the critter-count is eight cats, five ferrets, two horses and a dog.

Her second greatest love is her gelding, Smoke, whom she honors as her friend and companion. She thanks him for choosing to be part of her life.